VALERIOS

ROAD TO MASTERY

4

aethonbooks.com

ROAD TO MASTERY 4
©2024 Valerios

Aethon Books
www.aethonbooks.com

Print and eBook design and formatting by Josh Hayes. Artwork provided by Kaion Luong.

Published by Aethon Books LLC.

ALSO IN SERIES

Road to Mastery

Road to Mastery 2

Road to Mastery 3

Road to Mastery 4

Road to Mastery 5

Check out the entire series here! (Tap and scan)

CHAPTER ONE
A NEW BEGINNING
BY VALERIOS

JACK GLANCED BETWEEN HIS FRIENDS AND THE DOOR. THE WAIT WAS KILLING him.

"Would you look at that!" Gan Salin, the loyal canine, exclaimed. "The almighty King of Earth intimidated by a closed door!"

"You'd be crying if you were about to have children," Nauja the Barbarian cut in, jabbing his shoulder.

"But I'm a guy. I can't give birth."

A moment of puzzled silence followed before Edgar, the pacifist magician, changed the subject. "Do you think it will be a boy or a girl?"

"I bet on a boy," Captain Dordok—or rather, former captain—replied. He laughed. "Jack has so much man in him, there's no way he can make a girl!"

The birds were chirping. The new sun was shining, and a slight coldness permeated the atmosphere, along with a faint morning mist hanging from tree branches. Everyone was gathered in the middle of the Forest of the Strong. This was where Jack's System life had begun—and now, it was about to become the place where an entirely new life started.

Vivi's pregnancy was coming to an end. Jack's child would be born today.

For this day, everyone unrelated had been chased out of the Forest. The remaining people were Jack, Edgar, Gan Salin, Nauja, Dordok, Brock, and Harambe. The professor was also present, but she insisted on being there with the nurse to make sure Vivi was okay. The Sage, as a D-Grade healer, was also inside the room.

Jack hadn't felt such anxiety since his fight against the planetary overseer three months ago. He clenched his fists.

His first child was about to be born. Would he be a good father? Would everything be okay, or would something terrible happen within that room?

Brock must have sensed his worries, because he placed a hand on Jack's shoulders. "All good. Big Sis strong. Baby bro strong. No worry."

"Thanks, Brock," Jack replied, feeling a little relieved. Brock was right. Vivi was a strong cultivator, and the baby carried his blood. There was no way anything would happen...

He glanced at the door again.

In fact, the people present weren't the only ones who couldn't wait. Across the entire planet, billions of people were glued to their screens, waiting for the announcement. The king and queen of Earth were having a child—what could be more important than this?

But the fame didn't make the almighty, so-called King of Earth any less worried. His heart was shaking like a leaf. It was an instinct stemming from deep inside his soul, something he neither wanted nor could stop.

Well, perhaps he could use his Dao to suppress these feelings, but who would do that?

He was about to become a father.

Harambe approached. A big, lazy smile was on his face, and he slung an enormous arm around Jack's shoulders. He then mimed that he'd felt the same when his girl was about to give birth, but it would be okay. Being a father was great. Jack would love it.

Easy for you to say, big guy, Jack thought but didn't speak the words.

Since Alexander Petrovic wounded and humiliated Harambe, over three months had passed. The big brorilla's body had healed, but his heart had not. Or, rather, it had changed. Harambe had mellowed. He remained strong and working out intensely, but he'd lost some of his edge, some of the dominating strictness he used to possess.

Perhaps it wasn't the injury, but the fact his own son avenged him, simultaneously claiming the position of big bro. It was the natural way of life; the old gave way to the young. For Harambe, it was like a huge weight had been lifted off his shoulders. When he lost the position and responsibilities of being his pack's big bro, he was finally able to enjoy life.

He had transitioned from a strict father into a dotting grandfather—though Brock was only a year old and childless.

Jack had even spotted him feeding bananarms to various Bare Fist Brotherhood members.

As disheartening as this change sounded, Jack enjoyed it. It brought him pride. The only reason Harambe could relax was because there was no danger afoot. The Animal Kingdom was gone. The planet was far outside System space. Jack was so overwhelmingly strong that any threat would disappear the moment it reared its head.

Finally, Earth was safe.

Jack looked to the sky and took a deep breath. The Fist inside him pulsed. The air hugged him, and the Dao cried out in joy.

He'd protected his home, family, and friends—what better way to honor the Dao of the Fist?

It wasn't just Harambe. In the three months since the planet was moved outside System space, peace had finally returned. The Ice Peak was dismantled. Any remaining Animal Kingdom members had been captured and isolated, and they would be gradually given a chance to integrate into society. Earth had entered an era of endless prosperity, where cultivators used their gifts to advance the world instead of ruining it. Already, food was aplenty, and many of the world's problems had been resolved.

Under the rule of Jack and the Bare Fist Brotherhood, everything was as great as it could be.

Edgar had retired to the mountains and begun constructing a magical academy; a literal castle on a hill, filled with magical artifacts of his creation. Though he could no longer advance in cultivation after breaking his deal with the echidna devil, the power he already possessed was more than enough for mundane applications.

The professor had taken over the administration of the entire Earth on Jack's behalf, doing a stellar job.

Sparman had recovered from his various injuries. After the war was over, many artificers and engineers of Earth had pooled their forces to repair him, making him as good as new—though his sarcastic wits remained unaffected. He'd also accepted the job of teaching combat at Edgar's still-under-construction academy.

Gan Salin and Nauja had moved into two little houses on a hill near the Forest of the Strong, splitting their days between cultivating and resting. They wouldn't stay here forever—after all, Nauja had abandoned her tribe to experience the wider world. However, they decided to wait until Jack's child was born.

Vanderdecken was the star of the planet, the second most famous person after Jack himself, and Brother Tao had gone on to found many monasteries teaching martial mastery and Buddhism. How his faith remained unchanged after meeting the System, no one knew.

Though, perhaps there was a hint of truth to it. Jack still remembered Chuto, the jovial fat guy he met in Trial Planet, whose powers resembled very closely the Buddha of Earth.

In these three months, Jack himself had also settled down, enjoying life as he stabilized his cultivation. The Sage was right. To reach the peak D-Grade in such a short time, he had advanced way too fast. He needed to slow down before he could advance again—at ever greater speeds. Moreover, the weird world inside his Dao Tree—the one with the monstrous, snorting turtle—never opened its door again for him. He didn't know when it would happen, or how to force it open, but there was nothing he could do about it.

Therefore, he relaxed. He and Vivi hadn't married, but they did spend a lot of time together. They became a couple, not just because they would soon have a baby together, but also because they liked and respected each other.

The only one who kept cultivating at full speed was Brock. He spent most of these three months in the D-Grade dungeons of Earth, conquering them one by one.

There were ten D-Grade dungeons on Earth. After Jack cleared out the one in Antarctica, where he hid before his final battle against the overseer, nine remained. Brock had conquered five of them. He'd traveled to the peak of Mount Everest, to the depths of the Marianna Trench, inside active volcanoes, and even on the clouds themselves. The spirit of brohood followed him everywhere. He didn't just conquer dungeons, he assimilated many of their denizens into the bro army. Now, Earth wasn't just protected by Jack, Brock, Dordok, and the Sage—the only D-Grades on the planet—but also by literal armies of D-Grade creatures ranging from fire elementals to cloud giants.

It was a shame they'd run out of enemies.

The only unknown variable still in play was the sole C-Grade dungeon of Earth, which remained undiscovered. Jack had people searching everywhere, yet it remained unfound. Where it could be, he had no idea. On the bright side, even if he found it, there was nothing he could do about it yet. He was only at the peak of the D-Grade. Though he could fight weak C-Grades, he couldn't advance any more without breaking through, so conquering that dungeon was out of the question.

After traveling and fighting ceaselessly for three months, Brock had increased his cultivation to the middle D-Grade. For the first time, he was actually approaching Jack. The two had even sparred once, and the brorilla could take a few moves. Until Jack broke through, the more time that passed, the more Brock would approach him in strength.

How far he's come... Jack thought, looking over at Brock with pride. *We are finally real brothers now. Equals. Standing side-by-side. He's the only one that can keep up with me—I can't wait to adventure together.*

Thinking to that point, Jack opened his status screen. Looking at it was a habit now, a calming one. It helped take his mind off the coming baby.

ERROR: PLEASE REPORT TO THE NEAREST AUTHORITIES IMMEDIATELY OR FACE EXTERMINATION.

Name: Jack Rust
Species: Human, Earth-387
Faction: Bare Fist Brotherhood (D)
Grade: D
Class: Cosmic Fist (King)
Level: 249

Strength: 1775
Dexterity: 1780
Constitution: 1775
Mental: 200
Will: 200

Dao Skills: Meteor Punch IV, Iron Fist Style III, Space Walk III, Neutron Star Body II, Brutalizing Aura III
Daos: Dao Tree of the Fist, Dao Root of Indomitable Will (fused), Dao Root of Life (fused), Dao Root of Power (fused), Dao Root of Weakness (fused)

Titles: Planetary Frontrunner (10), Planetary Torch-bearer (1), Ninth Ring Conqueror, Planetary Overlord (1), Grade Defier

The System hadn't forgotten that something was wrong with him—the Life Drop—but at least it was kind enough to keep displaying his stats. Perhaps this was its way of maintaining contact so he could be caught later.

Fortunately, it seemed that the Sage was right. The System had no way to locate him outside System space. Otherwise, three months was ample time for the Hand of God agents to arrive; and the person who protected them before, the Head Envoy of the Black Hole Church—the mischievous-looking Heavenly Spoon Sovereign—was long gone.

Jack would need to leave soon, too. Though Earth was safe, the universe kept moving. He didn't want to spend the rest of his life here. He wanted to visit the Black Hole Church, cultivate amongst peers, face trials and challenges, and reach the apex of strength. A fist could rest, but it could never stop.

He would wait a bit, though. His child would be born first. He would spend a some time with it, and only then would he depart for the wider world yet again.

He didn't know which of the two he looked forward to the most.

The answer gave itself. The closed door swung open, and Jack froze completely as he watched Vivi step out, covered in a white towel. Half his mind focused on her long, dark legs and bright smile. The other half went to her arms, which were gently wrapped around a large ball of fabric.

The professor and the Sage followed behind Vivi, each sporting a wide smile, but nobody even glanced at them.

"Well, what is it?" Gan Salin asked, seeing that Jack was tongue-tied. "A boy or a girl?"

"Both!" Vivi replied, opening her arms a bit to reveal that she was holding onto two little forms, not one. Her smile widened. "It's twins!"

Jack looked at his newly born children, the continuators of his bloodline, and his heart was filled with love, overflowing with joy. He laughed out loud, a booming, manly sound. "My children are here!" he shouted. "Celebrate, everyone. Today is a day we must remember!"

CHAPTER TWO

THE CALM BEFORE THE STORM

IF SOMEONE CLAIMED THAT THE ANIMAL KINGDOM WAS UPSET ABOUT everything that transpired, it would be a gross understatement.

The Kingdom's upper echelon hadn't been busier in millennia. Every capable cultivator was recalled, every deacon was summoned. Hell was emptied. The Kingdom's capital was weakened. It was all hands on deck, because Jack Rust had raised a storm that could give even the Faction Master nightmares.

"I don't care what you have to do, project an image of power!" were his orders, and the Grand Elder did his utmost to obey.

Overnight, shipments of strong cultivators were distributed across the Animal Kingdom constellation. The Kingdom's various strongholds were reinforced, and their experts picked fights against smaller factions over any excuse, stomping them into the ground to prove their superiority.

This was the only way the Kingdom knew to project their power. And every other time, it had worked. But not this time. Jack set fire to the hearts of the oppressed cultivators. What the hell! He was just a single man! If he had the guts to defy the Animal Kingdom, so did they!

The Kingdom's forceful reminder had the opposite effect of what they expected. If they beat down one group, another rose to take its place. For every fire they put out, three new ones were lit! Rebellious undercurrents flowed all across the constellation, and though nothing big had happened yet, it was only a matter of time.

For now, the disgruntled cultivators resisted the only way they could. They took on the mantle of pirates, hiding in the vastness of space and striking from the shadows. Thousands of starships dyed themselves black and flew into the deep reaches of space, boarded by rebels with burning hearts.

From now on, this period of time would be known as the Great Pirate Era.

Running a constellation of thousands of planets was a tremendous undertaking. It didn't matter that the Kingdom was stronger than the entire rest of the constellation put together. A single wrong variable, a single misjudgement, and everything would come crashing down on their heads. Every dissatisfied force on the inside and every rival faction on the outside would pounce like starving beasts at the first sign of weakness, and Jack had given them exactly that—multiple times.

The Animal Kingdom constellation was crumbling, and the Kingdom's higher-ups knew it. They couldn't step down or take soft measures. Their only option was to double down on their tyranny and push even harder, hoping for the best.

"Capture Jack Rust!" another order came down from above. "Find him, no matter what you have to do. We must use him to extinguish the flames of revolution. For our pride and survival... we must kill him!"

Jack himself was oblivious to the effects his actions had on the entire galaxy—though he did hold some suspicions.

For now, he remained isolated and peaceful on Earth, in a pocket of the galaxy far away from System space. Due to their location, certain System functions didn't work, rendering them unable to communicate with the wider galaxy.

Most people didn't mind. The only ones who did were Ar'Tazul and Ar'Karvahul, the two djinn merchants who wanted to become rich by broadcasting Jack's battle against the planetary overseer across the galaxy. Though they'd succeeded, they had forgotten about this tiny detail. Now, their wealth had accumulated to tens of millions of credits, but they were completely unable to spend it.

"Dammit!" Tazul exclaimed, fuming from the ears. "This is unfair!"

"It was all for nothing, all of that for nothing!" Karvahul shouted back. "I wanted to buy a brothel!"

"But, can't you do that on Earth, cousin?"

"Oh, right."

A merchant's appetite for gold knew no limits!

As for Jack himself, he was untouched by anything. On top of a mountain near the Forest of the Strong, there was a small but comfortable mansion, enjoying both privacy and a great view. The living room was framed by a glass wall that overlooked the forest underneath, while a lit fireplace dominated the other side of the room. The flames danced gracefully, shedding a flickering light on the small couch before them, where a man and a woman sat together.

Jack passed his arm around Vivi's shoulders, holding both her and their two children. They were tiny; two little humans, barely a few months old, with wide eyes and tiny hands that liked to hug Vivi's fingers.

The boy was named Eric Eragorn Rust, after Jack's adopted father. The girl was named Ebele Eragorn Rust, honoring Vivi's African roots. Ebele meant kindness and mercy; the qualities that Jack and Vivi wished both their children would inherit.

"Isn't it weird that they're so small?" Jack asked in a soft voice, his attention lost in the flames.

"There is nothing weird about our children. They're lovely."

"They can be both," Jack replied. Vivi laughed, but she had to stop when Jack planted a kiss on her lips.

"I don't want them to be weird," she added in a hesitant voice. "I want them to be strong and unique. To be accepted."

"Hmm. I guess you're right. Their tiny size is so exceptional, so extraordinary. They are like little marbles."

She laughed again, and Jack joined her. It was already March. Another three months had passed since the children's birth. Jack and Vivi had grown even more used to each other's presence. They enjoyed it deeply. Both bore their own sets of scars, but especially because of that, they could understand each other.

Jack adored Vivi's love for her people, her wild side that led the battle from the front, her fiery speeches and caring actions. Vivi admired his strength and resolve, his unyielding attitude, his bravery and wisdom.

They were two peas in a pod.

But, as it always happened, life was more complicated than that.

"I would love to watch them grow," Jack said, looking at the twin babies.

"You will," Vivi reassured him. "Just... with breaks."

"It's not the same..." Jack sighed, his words holding sadness.

"I know you have to go," Vivi comforted him, grabbing his hands in hers. She didn't mind the scars they bore or the blood that had once adorned them. "I understand. They will, too. I will tell them tales of their father, of your bravery and achievements. Even if you cannot be here in person, I will make sure they think about you."

Jack sighed again, but he did not respond. He really would have loved to spend a few decades here, in peace and quiet, but it was impossible. He owed it to the Black Hole Church to join them. And, even if he didn't, his burning heart would never let him rest. Already, these six months were a stretch. His cultivation was mostly stabilized. The itch to fight grew stronger, to better himself again. To challenge the world. Every day, that itch claimed more of his thoughts, until he had to go.

"I will visit often," he promised.

"You should," Vivi replied, planting a kiss on his cheek. Jack smiled.

Then came a knock on the door. "Oh!" Vivi exclaimed, switching to a slightly more dignified posture. "Did they come on time? That's a first."

"Let me check," Jack replied with laughter, heading for the door. "Hello?"

"Who is it?" came a voice from the other side.

Jack's brain short-circuited. "Uh… It's Jack," he replied, then pressed his eyes shut in frustration as muffled laughter came from behind the door. "Damn you and your tricks, Salin!" he exclaimed.

The door swung open, revealing Gan Salin and Nauja, each of whom were laughing. From behind Jack, so was Vivi. "It's Jack," Salin said in a mocking tone, then laughed harder. "How did you fall for that, man?"

"Yeah, yeah, make fun of me all you want. I'll shut the door in your face next time."

"Ha! Sorry, sorry, I couldn't help myself. The mind goblins made me do it."

"Mind goblins?"

"Mind gobblin' deez nu—"

"Salin!" Nauja cut him off, rolling her eyes in exasperation. "Sorry, guys, the Earth culture has gotten to him."

Jack opened the door wider, stepping aside. Hanging out with these two was never boring. "Come on in."

"Thanks! We brought wine!"

And the days passed like that. For the first time since the System arrived, Jack wasn't in constant danger. No enemies came to assault his family, no disaster struck the planet, no clock was ticking. They were just floating in a vacuum, isolated in a corner of the galaxy, alone and at peace. Life was good.

Until one day, Jack was outside the front door, dressed in full cultivator attire. Vivi looked at him from inside, various feelings playing in her eyes. "Can't you wait a little more?"

"You know I can't. It's already been too long. The Sage is pressuring me, Brock ran out of dungeons, and my heart..." He smiled at her, the wild, witty, radiant smile that had first charmed her at the Integration Tournament. "My heart calls for me to go."

"I understand," she replied. "Just be careful, okay?"

"I'll try my best," he promised. "When I get to the Black Hole Church, no going after trouble. I will just mind my own business and get stronger at a comfortable pace."

She nodded, satisfied. Then, she pecked at his lips. "Have fun," she told him.

"Thanks."

Their gazes said everything their mouths did not. He was strong, but so was she. This was a family of cultivators. Risking their lives was a normal occurrence.

"Grow strong, little ones," Jack said, bowing down to kiss both babies on the forehead. Their eyes, wide with wonder, reached straight into his heart and tried to bind it. Still, he only smiled bittersweetly. If he was a man who stayed here forever, he would not be their father.

"See you, Vivi," he said, rising to his full height again. "Take care."

"You too," she replied.

Jack turned around, walked a few steps, then took to the air. As he did, his entire countenance changed. Things that had long slept awakened. His eyes hardened, his aura deepened, his robes fluttered. A heavy presence blanketed the surrounding lands, making every cultivator and spirit beast raise their heads.

The King had returned. Jack Rust, the Cosmic Fist, had awakened.

Jack didn't look back. He flew down the mountain to the Forest of the Strong and landed inside it. The Sage waited there, along with Brock. The professor was also present, though just to say goodbye.

"Welcome, my friend," the Sage said cheerfully. "Are you ready for exciting new adventures and a little bit of war?"

"I was born ready," Jack replied, clasping hands with Brock. "Sup, brother?"

"Hello, Big Bro," Brock replied. His hand felt strong to the touch. While Jack relaxed, Brock had never stopped training. He'd swept eight D-Grade dungeons clean. His strength now reached the late D-Grade, and his perfect foundation made him at least as strong as most peak D-Grades.

An odd building stood beside them, smack dab in the center of the forest clearing, right next to the Clear Pond that Jack had wrestled away from the rock bear so long ago. It resembled a large purple oven, like most other teleporters, except its aura shimmered with hints of black. It was also much larger than others.

"Jack," the professor said, approaching with steady steps. "Please be safe, okay? And send word often. Don't make me worry too much again."

"I will do my best," Jack replied, wrapping her into a tight hug. "I will miss you."

"So will I, Jack."

The professor then bid goodbye to Brock and the Sage. Jack looked to the distance. He'd visited Edgar a few days ago, and Gan Salin with Nauja had already left Earth to travel the galaxy. Dordok was cultivating, and Sparman was preparing to teach combat at Edgar's academy.

Everything had taken its path. There was nothing left to do. He couldn't leave the planet in a better state.

"We can go," he said. Both Brock and the Sage nodded, then moved inside the teleporter. Jack was the last to enter. "See you soon," he whispered to the wind, then waved goodbye to the professor, who had tears in her eyes.

Purple light flickered, then erupted as a flood. Space ruptured and sucked them in. The Earth disappeared, replaced by endless stars.

They were headed to the Black Hole Church, one of the strongest forces in the universe. A whole new chapter was beginning.

CHAPTER THREE

THE SEA BETWEEN GALAXIES

JACK, BROCK, AND THE SAGE SHUTTLED THROUGH SPACE, AS IF THEY WERE and weren't there, passing through entire stars without feeling anything. They were like ghosts.

"The interspace," the Sage explained unprompted, his yellow teeth shining. "The space between space. The deeper into it a teleporter can push us, the faster we move in relation to regular space."

"How deep are we now?" Jack asked.

"Normal teleporters go around five to seven layers deep. This one..." The Sage smiled with pride. "Up to fourteen!"

"...That doesn't sound like a lot."

"It's exponential. Your ten-mile range teleportation is one layer deep. A regular teleporter can pierce through five layers of space, and that is enough to get you ten light years away in a few minutes. See the difference?"

Jack sucked in a cold breath. He'd never considered it like that before. "Why do we need fourteen?" he asked. "Isn't it overkill?"

"You'll see."

The stars zoomed past them. Now that Jack paid closer attention, he could tell that the speed at which they crossed space was vastly superior to regular teleporters. Even the large teleporter that had once transported him and Brock to Trial Planet moved at a turtle's pace compared to this. Brock was looking around in silent approval, admiring the view.

Soon, however, they noticed something peculiar. The stars around them were thinning. Up ahead, endless darkness took up an increasingly large part of their horizon.

"Are we..." Jack began, but he didn't need to finish the question.

"Yes," the Sage replied.

They shot out of the galaxy.

Jack could see it clearly now. A beautiful expanse of stars, vaster than anything his mind could fabricate. Even a tiny part of this colossal place would require millions of years to cross with a normal starship.

But the stars... The stars were endless. They stretched and stretched. As Jack and Brock flew farther away from their home galaxy, millions and billions of stars filled their view, their different colors combining into a single, blue radiance. The galactic spire appeared, then another. After a few minutes, the entire galaxy was visible, a swirling mass of light.

And Jack was pulled away from it. Into the endless darkness, a void so large it defied comprehension. Even this massively gigantic galaxy was a mere drop of water in the ocean.

There were always taller mountains, always greater talents. That was a saying Jack had heard many times in the cultivation world, but only now did he truly grasp its truth. The world was so vast. His current strength was nothing, absolutely nothing. And suddenly, he had the feeling that, before such vastness, no matter how much strength he attained, he would never amount to anything more than a grain of sand.

The galaxy was growing smaller in their sights. They'd left it far behind now, and darkness was overtaking their vision. They were plunging into an abyss. Though the coldness of space couldn't reach them here, a shiver still trailed down his soul, a reminder of his own mortality.

At least he had the Dao. And, besides that... he had Brock.

A warm smile spread over his face as he turned to regard his little brother. "What do you think, Brock?"

Brock cupped his chin in thought, then nodded. "Very big. More big than my biceps."

"It is, yeah..." Jack shook his head. Various memories passed through his mind. He saw Brock as a tiny little brorilla, so small he could stand on Jack's shoulders. Back then, he used to growl and throw poop at any threats. Now, he was a late D-Grade immortal beast with the power to smash mountains and convert even gods to broism.

They were brothers now, standing on the same stage.

Jack then turned to the Sage, who was staring the other way. His gaze pierced into the world-ending darkness, the endless, empty sea between galaxies. Giant beasts the size of stars could be hiding here, and Jack would be none the wiser.

"Where exactly are we headed, Sage?" he asked.

The Sage looked back, and Jack caught a hint of warmth in his eyes before it disappeared. "This is the empty space between galaxies," he explained. "It is so large it defies comprehension. Galaxies are grains of sand in its ocean."

"I gathered that much, yeah."

"Our current destination is a black hole lost in this empty space, one that is not near any galaxy. A founder of the Church discovered it accidentally once, then used it as the faction's headquarters. Finding it without knowing its exact location is impossible—that's why we've been able to remain hidden for so long."

Jack whistled. "But what was your founder doing out here?"

"A-Grades can travel between galaxies. They often do, either to search for resources or just to retire in undiscovered places where nobody will ever find them. There are even some who, as they approach the end of their lifespan, fly out into the void and try to reach the ends of the universe."

"Did anyone ever manage it?"

"Nobody returned." The Sage shook his head. "But, don't dream too big. Even B-Grades can only dream of crossing this empty space. If they tried, it would take half their lifespan just to reach the nearest galaxy."

Every word the Sage said birthed more questions in Jack's mind. "How long do A-Grades live for?" was the one he chose to ask.

"Around a million years. B-Grades live up to a hundred thousand, C-Grades to ten thousand, and D-Grades to a thousand, as I'm sure you already know."

Jack shook his head again. A million years... The entirety of recorded human history was around ten thousand years. A-Grades could live a hundred times that much. To them, history was just a slightly longer meditation session.

"The only truly immortal beings," the Sage continued, "are the Old Gods... and the Immortals. The robots that destroyed the Ancients. That's where they got their name."

"So nobody can escape mortality."

"Not unless you become a God."

"Is that possible?"

"Of course not." The Sage laughed. "And if it was, it wouldn't be your prize to claim, my friend. Focus on reaching the C-Grade for now. There is a long road ahead of you."

Jack nodded, but his mind was elsewhere. Brock, who hadn't spoken much, had also heard the Sage's words, and he shared Jack's thoughts. Both felt their horizons broaden. They were leaving their galaxy and entering a greater stage. There were people here who could live for a million years, treat planets like toys, and freely travel between galaxies.

It really was a brand-new world. The Animal Kingdom suddenly seemed so tiny.

"Wait." Jack snapped to attention. "Did you say we're going into a black hole?"

"I said we're going to a black hole."

"Sage?"

"Yeah?"

"I have a bad feeling."

"Don't worry. It's all going to be okay."

Jack was not the least bit placated by the Sage's nonchalance. Right then, the Sage raised his head. "We're here. Prepare yourselves."

Jack looked ahead, into the endless, spotless darkness. "I don't see any—"

A terrifying force of gravity pulled at him. He instantly felt elongated. His body, which was hard enough to endure a falling mountain, cracked and creaked. Brock groaned. Jack endured the pain and forced his eyes open, catching glimpses of something ahead of them.

That something was as dark as its surroundings, but the galaxies behind it appeared warped, as if falling into a dark sphere. Terror gripped Jack's soul. This was a black hole. The most destructive object in the universe. And he was falling into it. Even time lost its meaning, stretching and contorting without rhyme or reason.

Was this a trap? Was all he thought before time and space instantaneously solidified. Jack reeled like he'd been slapped in the face. The transition was too abrupt. He barely kept his stomach in check, while Brock couldn't take it and puked on the spot. As soon as he did, his stomach fluids fell toward the ground at extreme speed.

There was a ground.

Jack looked around. They were no longer moving. There was rock beneath their feet, twelve white columns around them, and endless darkness over their heads. No, it wasn't just darkness. To Jack's surprise, he could see galaxies in this sky, so distant they hung like stars. And they were moving. The entire sky was slowly but steadily rotating, as if time were flowing so fast he could see the movement of stars in the night sky.

It was both mesmerizing and terrifying. Jack's mind created images of his children growing old and dying before he could return to Earth, and despair gripped his heart.

"Relax," a calming voice reached his ears; the Sage. "Time is still flowing properly. We're just spinning around the black hole."

Jack struggled to grasp this. Finally, he lowered his gaze, but he shouldn't have—what awaited was just surprise after surprise, shock after shock. A few feet away from him, outside the perimeter of the twelve white columns, a man was sitting cross-legged. His eyes were closed, his robes were dark, and his body was so thin he could be called emaciated.

Yet, the moment Jack laid eyes on this man, he was instantly assaulted by a deep and heavy pressure. This man exuded a sensation of absolute power, as if his breathing was the Dao itself, as if his body was space and his will was time.

Jack froze. A moment later, he regained himself and nodded deeply. "Elder," he said, as superior cultivators were customarily referred to.

The man did not reply, but the Sage nudged Jack. "That is just an Envoy, not an Elder," he whispered.

If the Envoy was insulted by the Sage's words, he did not react.

"What?" Jack muttered back.

"This is an Envoy. A B-Grade disciple of the Black Hole Church. The Elders are all in the A-Grade, and I'm confident your mind would break if you saw one in person."

Jack was reeling. This person's aura far outstripped anyone he'd ever met. This man could have been made of the Dao itself... and he wasn't even an Elder?

"Come on, get it together. You're making me look bad," the Sage said, and Jack habitually restrained himself.

"Sorry," he said. "I was just a bit shocked."

"Understandably. Don't worry, it happens to everyone the first time. Outside this place, everyone at the D-Grade and above restrains their aura, so not many people have felt the real presence of a B-Grade before."

"I can understand why..." Jack replied numbly.

"Yeah. If a B-Grade released their aura on a random planet, every F-Grade nearby would drop dead. Here, the weakest people are at the D-Grade, so nobody needs to hide their presence. It also makes the Cathedral feel homely, like taking your shoes off after a long day at work."

"The Cathedral?"

"This place. The Cathedral, that's what we call it. Because we are a Church."

Jack shook his head.

"Move to register," the cross-legged B-Grade said.

"Yes, Envoy," the Sage replied, then motioned sideways. "Shall we?"

Jack made to move. Once he did, however, he found it difficult. Much harder than usual, like he was carrying a mountain on his shoulders. He frowned, then his brows rose in realization. "Ah," he said. "The gravity. That's why Brock's puke fell so fast before."

The Sage winked. "Exactly. The gravity here is a thousand times stronger than on Earth—it's part of the reason why the weakest people around are D-Grades. It also makes for great training."

Jack did not even reply, just shook his head in shock. What monstrous place did I dive into? Then he felt his fighting spirit fully roused, and his lips formed a wild grin.

Perfect.

CHAPTER FOUR
THE CATHEDRAL

THE CAPITAL OF THE BLACK HOLE CHURCH WAS NAMED THE CATHEDRAL. IT was a flat piece of land spinning in orbit around a black hole in the space between galaxies, rendering it almost impossible to locate.

The upper part of this piece of land was where everyone lived. The bottom part housed a colossal magic formation crafted by the Church's A-Grade Elders. It was this formation that counteracted the black hole's gravitational pull, allowing the Cathedral to remain at a steady orbit. Naturally, the Cathedral orbited the black hole in such a way that its bottom part was always facing the hole and the upper part always facing toward the outside—much like the moon of Earth always showed its same side to humans.

There was very little light on the Cathedral, the temperature was far below freezing, and there was no atmosphere. The only ones who could survive here were D-Grades and above, who could sustain themselves indefinitely on ambient Dao. Another effect of the Cathedral's special location was vastly increased gravity, one thousand times stronger than on Earth. Due to that, even most D-Grades wouldn't be able to handle the pressure and would die soon after arriving.

All in all, this was one of the roughest, most hostile inhabited places in the universe. Only the strongest D-Grades—and above—could survive.

At present, Jack could endure the gravity. Brock was worse off. His back was hunched, his teeth were gritted, and sweat dripped down his forehead, splashing onto the ground below them like bullets.

"I can carry you," Jack offered with a bit of worry, but Brock shook his head.

"I can," he said. "For now."

"You'll get used to it," the Sage said, comforting them both. "The body is a fascinating mechanism. It will slowly adjust to this gravity, especially if you keep increasing your strength. Consider this a type of intense workout."

Workout?

Brock's eyes flashed. He gritted his teeth even harder to straighten his back, then set his jaw and started taking one painful step at a time. After all, one of his Dao Roots was the Dao of Muscles. This place forced him to workout 24-7. It was perfect!

Jack meanwhile advanced with some difficulty as well. Can I even fight here? he wondered. The increased gravity strained his body, but that wasn't all. He could sense that the Dao was thicker here, like honey. Galvanizing it would be far more difficult than normal. Additionally, space was tightly compacted, making teleportation harder. He'd essentially walked into a higher-level world.

The Sage spoke up, "The difficulty of locating this place is only one of the reasons the Church chose it. Another is the many benefits it offers. As you know, talented cultivators thrive in difficulty. Everything is harder to do here. It will be slow at first, but eventually, you will be forced to optimize the use of both your body and Dao. When you return to normalcy, you will be surprised at just how much you have improved."

Jack nodded. He wasn't afraid of pain or difficulty. He just wanted to get stronger. "Have you been here before, Sage?"

"I have heard things."

"Mhm."

As they walked, Jack raised his head to take a better look at this place. It seemed... dead. Similar to the surface of the moon. The ground was gray stone, while the terrain was mostly flat except for what seemed like thin, natural stone obelisks rising from the ground. Coupled with the constant rotation of the night sky, they gave this place an astral, otherworldly feeling, as if Jack had stepped on a completely alien landscape.

"How fast are we spinning?" he asked, watching the distant galaxies move across the sky with speed visible to the naked eye.

"We circle the black hole once every half hour, roughly. Given that we're traveling along its ergosphere, which is a pretty wide radius, I can say with certainty that we're moving very quickly."

Jack raised a brow.

"The black hole itself isn't spinning though," the Sage continued. "Earth astronomers would call it a Schwarzschild black hole. Cultivators are not obsessed with putting their name on things, but they use a more macabre term: a stillborn black hole."

"What?"

"I know, terrible."

Jack blinked a few times as he digested this information. Back on Earth, he had some rudimentary understanding of popular physics concepts, but nowhere near enough to know about the different types of black holes. He also didn't care very much.

"You seem to know a lot about this place," he commented. "I thought you had only 'heard some things' about it."

"Aha! But, you see, I'm also a Sage. Knowing stuff is my job."

Jack threw the Sage a deep glance but didn't press further. By now, they had moved beyond the teleporter and were headed toward what seemed like a village. The houses here were made of white stone, easily distinguishable in the dark gray background. The sky was black, the ground gray, the buildings white, and the landscape alien. There was a certain aesthetic here.

In the distance, a white obelisk was barely visible, with what seemed like rows of names engraved into it, but Jack couldn't get a good look from this distance.

As for the houses before him, he could clearly see they had the dimensions of normal village cabins. It was hard to imagine almighty C-Grades living so modestly.

"I guess it's time to explain how things work around here," the Sage said as they approached. Jack's ears perked up, and even Brock, who was struggling step after step, glanced over. The Sage coughed in his hand, then started speaking.

"The Black Hole Church is one of the foremost forces in the universe. Its only rival is the Hand of God. These two factions are at the late A-Grade, and they lord over the rest of the universe. Compared to them, the B-Grade factions you're used to dealing with are nothing but ants.

"Naturally, the Black Hole Church has extremely high standards for its disciples. Everyone at the D-Grade and below is only considered an assistant. To become a real disciple of the Church, the minimum cultivation required is at the C-Grade, but that is not all. Over ninety percent of C-Grades are unworthy. The Church invests in quality, not quantity, so we only accept the most talented, most outstanding cultivators of the C-Grade. These C-Grades are the Church's outer disciples. The inner disciples—also called Envoys—are all B-Grades. A-Grades are Elders."

Jack felt like the Sage had taken a sledgehammer and used it to smash his current understanding of the world into smithereens.

C-Grades were just barely worthy of being outer disciples? B-Grades, those peak existences, were only inner disciples?

What the hell!

Back in Jack's galaxy, C-Grades were renowned Elders of the B-Grade factions. They basically ran the entire galaxy. They could destroy continents with a single blow!

And B-Grades were even worse! They were existences so high and mighty that, besides the Head Envoy that appeared once, Jack hadn't met any of them. They were completely apex cultivators who could ignore the world to focus on their Dao. They were like gods. They could break planets!

Yet, to the Black Hole Church, B-Grades were only inner disciples...

Back in the Exploding Sun, the outer disciples were E-Grades, the inner disciples were D-Grades, and C-Grades were worthy of being Elders. This Black Hole Church was two entire Grades stronger!

What sort of concept was this?

"I can sense you are a bit confused," the Sage said. "It is understandable. Compared to our galaxy's standards of strength, what I am describing must seem extreme, but you have to remember that our galaxy is a relatively new addition to System space. Older galaxies have more resources, better cultivation methods, higher competition, and more time to develop. Besides our Milky Way, every other galaxy has at least one A-Grade faction, and the standards of strength are much higher. The Black Hole Church pulls its disciples from the cream of the crop of the universe's seventy-two galaxies, excluding ours. It is only natural that it possesses such extreme power."

By his side, Brock's eyes flashed with excitement.

Jack shook his head. This was too much to take in. He thought he was close to the top of the world, but as it turned out, he wasn't even qualified to be an outer disciple of the Black Hole Church...

"Wait," he exclaimed. "I'm still at the D-Grade. How will I become a disciple here?"

The Sage laughed. "Rules are made to be broken. While the Church generally accepts C-Grades as its outer disciples, you are sufficiently talented. An exception will be made for you."

"Oh."

Jack didn't know whether to laugh or cry. He had been the first person in galactic history to conquer Trial Planet. He'd formed a perfect foundation, had ingested the Life Drop, overcame heavenly tribulation, and then used his own strength to repeatedly humiliate a B-Grade faction. Eventually, he even defeated a middle C-Grade while only at the peak of the D-Grade himself. He had made history... and all that was barely enough to be accepted as an outer disciple.

It really put his place in the world into perspective.

"Come on, don't pull yourself down," the Sage said. "Being here is a huge honor. This is the highest stage possible, where you can compete against the greatest talents of the universe, and you were even invited here before you reached the C-Grade. In the entire history of the universe, that is not too shabby at all!"

"I guess you're right," Jack replied, scratching his chin. His heart was strong, after all. He looked over the village of white stone again, considering things. "I guess this is where outer disciples live?"

"Precisely. This is the fourth village of the Cathedral. There are another eleven, but I am highly confident your residence will be in this one."

"Oh? Then, how many outer disciples are there?"

"Around a thousand. Well, a thousand active ones," he added, noticing Jack's surprise. "We also have many allies across the universe. Our disciples are the distilled talent of the Church's forces."

Jack nodded. A thousand outer disciples... That wasn't too many. Even the Exploding Sun had twenty thousand D-Grades and a million E-Grades. The Church really did invest in quality.

On the other hand, this meant that the competition here would be much fiercer than usual. A thousand people out of the entire galaxy... Jack may have been an extreme talent, but so was everyone else!

It really made him excited.

"And?" he asked, eager to get into things. "How does this faction work? What do I need to know?"

"Just one thing." The Sage's face fell a little, becoming apprehensive. "The Black Hole Church is an extremely competitive place. If you had in mind free benefits, you can forget about it. Here, everything depends on your own ability."

Jack and Brock raised their brows at the same time. This sounded right up their alley.

"See that huge thing?" the Sage said, pointing in the distance. His finger led directly to the huge obelisk Jack had noticed, the one with rows of names on it. "That is the ranking obelisk. Here, every C-Grade disciple is ranked, and the benefits you get depend almost entirely on your ranking. If you fall too low, you get nothing, but if you're high up, you get so many opportunities that your jaw will drop!"

Jack stared at the obelisk again. Taking a better look, he could see that in the large row of names, each had a number next to it. The topmost line read "1, Min Ling," and the last read "997, Duke Belzon."

"How does that work?" he asked.

"I'll show you later. It's a magic formation. For now, shall we proceed to the Envoy's office? We need to register your arrival."

Jack's blood was already boiling. He cast another glance at the ranking obelisk, then turned back to the Sage. "There won't be any problems because of my Grade, right?"

"Not at all. Actually, they're waiting for you."

CHAPTER FIVE
A MISTAKE?

JACK, BROCK, AND THE SAGE WALKED THROUGH THE VILLAGE OF WHITE obsidian cabins. Each was small, barely large enough for two rooms, and they also seemed empty. The windows were shut, and no sound came from inside.

The moment Jack set foot into the village, he was instantly overtaken by a feeling of immense dread. In his Dao perception, every single cabin overflowed with power. The invisible energy around them thrummed and pulsed, getting torn apart as each cabin pulled large chunks of Dao inside it.

Each cabin held a powerhouse, an unusually strong C-Grade. The weakest people present had to be around the planetary overseer's level, and there were dozens of them. The combined pressure could easily force Jack to the ground. His only saving grace was that these monstrous auras did not work together, nor did they care about him. When the initial shock wore off, he understood that these people were just cultivating in silence.

Jack couldn't quench his burning heart. This was a true gathering of elites, and he was about to be a part of it.

"Bro," a voice came from behind him. Turning to look, Jack found Brock still standing, but on shaky legs and sweating bullets.

"Are you okay, Brock?"

"Must rest."

Jack nodded. With Brock's proud mindset, he wouldn't admit this if he wasn't about to pass out. "Let's sit over there for a while," he said, pointing to a random stone on the ground. They could also lean against the walls of a cabin, but that might insult the expert inside. That, or Jack could carry Brock, but the proud brorilla would hate it.

Brock's strength relied on his Dao, not so much his body. After all, he didn't have access to the System, so he didn't possess all the titles Jack did. Purely stat-wise, he had roughly half of Jack's stats.

"You can use your Dao to resist the pressure," the Sage spoke up, drawing surprised looks from Jack and Brock. He raised a brow. "Why are you both looking at me like that? Did you think that I, a Mental cultivator, was resisting it so far with my body alone? Gravity is just another Dao. Of course you can use your own to weaken it."

Jack and Brock glanced at each other. They hadn't considered that. When a cultivator developed their Dao Tree and reached the D-Grade, they were no longer affected by minor forces like the gravity of a regular planet. It wasn't that they consciously fought it off, more that such minor forces were repelled by their mere presence.

And when gravity increased a thousandfold, that naturally stopped being the case.

Jack experimented. He released a little bit of his aura so as not to disturb the cultivators in the cabins around them. As he focused on the surrounding space, he found it curved, like he was standing on a slope with strong currents pulling him downward. By assimilating the surrounding Dao into his own, as all D-Grades could do, the pull lessened significantly. Jack exclaimed in joy. Though he still felt suppressed, it was much less compared to before.

The strain on his Dao remained significant. Continuously

resisting gravity used up roughly thirty percent of his power, and that was just to decrease its pull by half.

Jack whistled. "This place is not joking around."

"Tell me about it," the Sage replied bitterly. "More than half my Dao is spent just surviving. Physical cultivators really have an advantage here."

Jack couldn't help a small smile. Every branch of cultivators had their own advantages, but when it came to resisting the physical world, Physical cultivators were naturally superior.

"Got it," Brock said. His forehead remained creased, but he now stood more easily. His legs were no longer shaking.

"Can you keep it up, Brock?" Jack asked.

"Yes."

Jack shrugged. Given his Dao, Brock had probably taught gravity that pulling on its bros wasn't cool.

The three of them continued through the village, finally running into the first other cultivators here. A man and a woman walked together, each seemingly unfettered by the extreme gravity. The man was sharp-eyed, dressed in white and carrying a dark blade on his hip.

The woman was certainly the most impressive of the two. She was stunningly beautiful. Her waist was slender, her face pristine and symmetrical, her body toned in all the right places. Jack didn't look any more out of respect for both of them, and also himself, but she was certainly one of the prettiest women he'd ever met.

"Hello," he said. "My name is Jack, and these are Brock and the Sage."

"Marcus William," replied the man, frowning in their direction. "You are weak. What are you doing here?"

"The Church invited me to become an outer disciple," he replied, suddenly disinclined to give them any more information.

"A peak D-Grade outer disciple?" the woman said, her expression showing clear disdain. "Has the Church become desperate? Or are you the son of a higher-up?"

"Jack here is an extreme talent," the Sage cut in, sensing Jack's bad mood. "He was invited on the basis of his achievements, as was I. And I would suggest watching your words. A disciple should not insult the hand feeding them. If an Envoy heard your disrespectful words, you would be punished severely."

"Hmph. I only speak the truth. If a faction lowers their standards, they are lowering themselves."

Brock raised his proud head. "The only low here is you," he replied. The woman's brows rose like half-moons, while the man frowned deeply. A hint of his aura seeped out. Jack felt an irresistible power enveloping him, like a cold knife pressed against his Adam's apple.

Strong! This man was vastly stronger than the planetary overseer or Jack himself. There was no way to use the System's inspection outside System space, so Jack couldn't determine the man's level, but he had to be at least a late C-Grade, maybe even a peak one! His aura alone felt like the overseer's fully-released Dao Domain.

This was an opponent he absolutely couldn't defeat right now. However, that didn't mean Jack would cower away. He stared at the man, as did Brock. If any of them feared death, they wouldn't have reached these heights.

Besides, there was no way the disciples of the Church were allowed to just slaughter each other over a tiny argument.

"If you plan to do something, do it," Jack said. "If not, stop wasting our time."

Seeing their reactions, the woman snorted, while the man laughed coldly. His aura was retracted, and they both kept walking, no longer shooting Jack another glance. "Good luck, kids," the man said. "Try not to die by standing too long."

Jack's gaze burned their backs until they turned a corner and disappeared. Brock shook his head. "Not cool," he said, while Jack turned to the Sage.

"Who were they?"

"I don't know them personally. The man must have been a high-ranker, but the woman felt much weaker. She can't be higher than an early C-Grade."

"Was that normal? Is that how people act here?"

This time, the Sage thought about it before replying. "At the C-Grade, everyone has already embraced their Dao, so every cultivator has their own personality. Some are kind and respectful; others are brash and barbaric. This couple must have been the latter kind. But, in any case, don't take it to heart. We are still weak, so it is natural we don't command the respect of others. In a few years, when you realize your potential and climb to a good rank, nobody will dare treat you like that."

Jack thought about it, then nodded. "Without power, we are nothing. With power, we are gods. The truth of the cultivation world."

"The truth of every world. Now, shall we?"

They continued on their journey, passing through the village without meeting anyone else, to a larger cabin with an open door. As they stepped inside, Jack noticed stacks of paper neatly organized on bookshelves across the walls, while a desk was situated at the far end of the room. Of course, neither the paper, nor the bookshelves, nor the desk were ordinary. They were made of special and extremely durable materials—otherwise, the extreme gravity would have pulverized them.

A woman sat behind the desk. Her dark hair was made into braids, but besides that, she seemed to be of a species between humans and lizards. Her skin was covered by dark green scales, her head connected directly to her torso without passing through a neck, her eyes had thin vertical slits, and her hands ended in sharp claws. The only reason Jack knew she was a woman was due to reading her aura.

Said aura, of course, towered to the heavens. This was another B-Grade. Working an office job.

What a day... Jack thought, already numb to this. "Greetings, Envoy," he said. "I am here to register as an outer disciple."

The lizard woman raised her gaze and took him in. A forked tongue slipped out of her mouth, then back inside. "Jack Rust," she said in a normal-sounding voice. "Peak D-Grade, Dao of the Fist, perfect foundation."

"You read all that in my aura?"

"I read it in your file," she said, raising a sheet of paper that contained his face and details. "We were expecting you. Welcome to the Black Hole Church."

"Uh... Thank you."

It was so weird speaking to a world-ending alien like she worked at the neighborhood public office. The best Jack could do was remain as respectful as possible—after all, she could end him with a single finger.

"Your residence is cabin 425. Your spiritual companion can live with you. As for your friend..."

She took a look at the Sage, who simply shrugged and said, "I'm not a disciple. Just a guest."

"Very well. I recognize you, too. You should already know your residence number."

"I do."

"Would it kill you to stop being mysterious for a moment?" Jack asked, to which the Sage laughed.

"She started it!"

Jack's face went pale. That was no way to speak around a B-Grade... but the lizard woman didn't seem to mind.

"As an outer disciple, you will receive one Dao stone per universal year. Additional benefits can be earned as you climb the ranking obelisk, with the first threshold being at the ranking of 950. New disciples start at the bottom, which is currently rank 997." She opened a drawer and fished a small crystal the size of Jack's thumb, then tossed it at him. "Do you have any questions?"

He had. Many of them. For example, he wanted to know what a Dao stone was and what other benefits were available. At the same timed, he didn't want to bug this B-Grade too much and risk getting wiped out of existence. In the end, he settled for asking, "If you can spare the time to answer, how does one achieve a higher ranking?"

"The Church possesses a formation called the Ceaseless Murder Globe. In there, you battle phantasmal enemies of increasing strength and gather points based on how many you can defeat. Your ranking is determined based on your number of points compared to everyone else. I would not recommend visiting the Globe yet, tough. Even the weakest enemies it contains are at the C-Grade. Your current cultivation is far from sufficient to fight for rankings. Focus on breaking through first."

"I see. Thank you for your advice."

"Is there anything else?"

"That's all from me. Thank you."

The lizard woman nodded. Seeing that neither the Sage nor Brock had anything to add, the three of them exited the cabin. "That was all?" Jack asked. "I'm an outer disciple now?"

"Indeed."

"And what's the deal with that Ultimate Slaughter Globe?"

"Ceaseless Murder. But you don't need to bother with it yet. As the Envoy said, just focus on breaking through for now. The extreme gravity condenses the Dao around here, making the Cathedral an optimal place for cultivation, and this Dao stone you received can rapidly increase your cultivation, pushing you against the boundary of the C-Grade. It shouldn't take you too long; and then, you can begin to enjoy the real benefits this place has to offer."

Jack considered it. Indeed, the Dao around here was thick and creamy, perfect for cultivation. There was complete silence too, and zero distractions, letting him focus purely on cultivating.

Moreover, he no longer had a time limit. He had no reason to look for trouble before he was ready. He could just take it easy, avoid making enemies, and slowly but surely develop his strength.

"Alright," he said. "Brock, wanna check out our cabin?"

"Yes," Brock replied with a smile. Since he couldn't level up, he didn't need to fight anyone to advance, just meditate; the thick Dao here was perfect for him too.

Unfortunately, even if some people try to stay away from trouble, trouble has a way of finding them.

Some time later, a group of outer disciples were relaxing on the roof of a white obsidian cabin, enjoying some spirit wine. Coincidentally, one of these people was the beautiful woman that Jack's group had run into before.

Suddenly, all of them turned their heads toward the ranking obelisk. The last few rows of names shook. Then, a new name appeared: Jack Rust!

However, Jack's name wasn't at the bottom of the obelisk, where it should be. It had appeared at the number 950! Whatever benefit was received at the ranking of 950, Jack had gotten it, and the cultivator just displaced to 951, lost it.

"What?" one of the disciples exclaimed. "Jack Rust? I haven't seen that name before. It must be a new disciple."

"But how did they start at ranking 950?" another person replied, furrowing their brows. "The Ceaseless Murder Globe hasn't activated recently. That Jack Rust has to have cheated, or there was some mistake."

There weren't many things to do at the Cathedral, and the outer disciples were all highly competitive. This group abandoned their wine and rushed to the office of the lizard woman for explanations.

"I don't know either," she replied, seeming clearly unhappy. "This order came just now from the Head Envoy himself. If you have a problem with it, go ask him!"

The Head Envoy was the man Jack had met right before Earth teleported; the mischievous-looking Heavenly Spoon Sovereign. Naturally, these outer disciples wouldn't dare question someone of such high status in the Church, but they remained frustrated. Some had been here for centuries. The ranking was of great importance to them.

If someone could climb the ranks through pure favoritism, what was the point of it all?

"Let's go check out this Jack Rust," they agreed. "If he was really strong, he would be placed at a higher rank. Who cheats to get to 950? He must be weak."

"His cabin number is 425," replied the lizard woman, who equally disliked favoritism. After all, she had spent several millennia as an outer disciple herself. "Knock yourselves out."

CHAPTER SIX
NOT STIRRING TROUBLE, BUT TROUBLE STIRRING ITSELF!

In a distant part of the Cathedral, a plainly-dressed woman sipped on a cup of tea. Across from her sat the Heavenly Spoon Sovereign, the Head Envoy of the Black Hole Church, one of the most feared and mysterious people in the universe.

Of course, this woman didn't lack status herself.

"Are you certain?" she asked, calmly sipping on her tea as if discussing the weather. "By directly raising that disciple to 950, you aren't helping him, only giving him trouble. Everyone hates cheaters."

The Heavenly Spoon Sovereign did not respond. He wore an amused smile, using a silver teaspoon to slowly stir his tea.

"Come on," she said with mockery. "Surely you can tell me some of your plans, oh Head Envoy?"

The sovereign laughed. "Fine, fine. The 950 ranking will give him access to the Heavy Pagoda. That should help him a lot with breaking through."

"But he doesn't need it. With his talent and foundation, he will reach the C-Grade regardless. A few more months are nothing. One hour at the pagoda is nowhere near worth the enemies he'll make."

"Ah, but there is another reason."

"Which is?"

Suddenly, the sovereign's mouth curved into a wide, cheshire grin. His aura flickered with bottomless hunger, like a starving tiger which broke out of its cage. Despite that, the woman was unaffected, not showing the tiniest hint of fear.

"That child is extraordinary," the sovereign said. "His qualifications are outstanding, and he has a Life Artifact. His potential is limitless. There is even a slim chance of him reaching the A-Grade in the future... but a slim chance is not enough. An extra Envoy changes nothing, while an extra Elder changes everything. Therefore, I will hammer him until he breaks. I will not let him slow down. He will either be torn apart by the wolves or learn to rule them."

The woman's eyes widened. "You want him to make enemies. What are you thinking? He's only a child. If the high-rankers capitalize on his weakness to bully him endlessly, what can he do? His Dao will crack. You are ruining him."

"You have not seen what I have," the sovereign replied. Back in the Milky Way galaxy, he had watched all of Jack's battle recordings. The achievements he witnessed, the guts... No matter how great the Church's talents, which of them had such a background? Jack Rust was on a completely different trajectory than everyone else, and the Heavenly Spoon Sovereign was a man who enjoyed grand spectacles. "I don't know if he can handle the pressure," he admitted. "But I want to find out. And, who knows? He just might create another miracle. Worst case, we have some fun watching."

Jack, Brock, and the Sage arrived at Jack's cabin. Number 425—coincidentally, the same number of residence he had at the Integration Tournament.

It was a simple house. There was only a bathroom and a main

room, which contained a bed, a small bookshelf, and a meditation mat. That's it. The Church was minimalist, apparently.

There was also a single window with heavy curtains, but those were mostly ornamental. If another cultivator wanted to peek, their perception could easily pierce the walls.

"Hey, check it out," Jack said, approaching the bookshelf. He took out the only book on its shelves. "The Black Hole Church's Rulebook. This will come in handy."

Brock was testing the bed and grimacing. Not only was there a single bed, instead of two of them, it was also stone-hard. Jack guessed it was the best they could do on a planet with a thousand times the gravity.

Cultivators after the D-Grade didn't really need to sleep, but it could help sometimes. They also didn't need to eat, which was why the cabin didn't contain food or a kitchen.

"You should check out the meditation mat," the Sage said.

As Jack took a look, he discovered that the mat was indeed special. It seemed to be an advanced version of the one he had during the Integration Tournament. Just by touching it with his fingers, a soothing feeling spread over his body, and his entire being was aligned, reaching an optimal state for cultivation.

"Nice mat," he said.

"Right?" The Sage smiled. "You should also read the rulebook soon. If you make any major blunders, you cannot claim ignorance of the rules. For now, let's go for a walk. I have someone you want to meet."

"You have someone that I want to meet?"

"Oh, absolutely. You just don't know it yet."

Just as they were about to exit the cabin, a commanding feminine voice rang out from outside.

"Jack Rust! Come out!"

Jack raised a brow. "Who is it?" he asked back.

"Come out and you will see!"

Jack frowned. That was not a polite tone. Although, he did recognize this voice. It was the beautiful woman he'd met on the way in, the one who was part of a couple.

Did they change their mind and want to fight? he wondered. Reaching the door with two steps, he pushed it open.

As he'd suspected, the one shouting was the woman he'd met before. There was no sign of the man from before. Three other cultivators were though, all of whom Jack saw for the first time.

One was an insect person, like a standing praying mantis. Another was made entirely of glass, like a sentient window panel with limbs, and the third was a small green humanoid flying on thin wings. Jack couldn't use the System to inspect them, as they were outside System space, but he could tell from their auras that they were all C-Grades—though not too strong.

Oddly, even though the woman was at the front and speaking, her cultivation was the weakest of the four.

"Can I help you?" Jack asked.

"Help us?" the woman replied, already gearing up to fight. "Of course you can. You can help us understand what's happening. When I met you before, I thought you were an annoying but upstanding cultivator. Now, I see you really are nothing but trash."

Jack's brows fell. He hadn't even said anything rude yet, and this woman was already attacking him. Calm down, Jack, calm down. No stirring trouble. This is probably just a misunderstanding.

Except, something in her words did not add up.

"What are you talking about?" he asked.

"Hmph. Tell me, Jack Rust, how does it feel to depend on others for unfair benefits? How does it feel to cheat your way up?"

"Excuse me?"

"You are still pretending? Very well, let me spell it out for you: Just who is your daddy for your ranking to start at 950?"

Jack's face hardened, both because of her crass verbal assault and his incomprehension. 950? He glanced at the ranking obelisk visible in the distance. When his eyes adjusted, they widened. 950!

My name really is at the 950 ranking! What?

Seeing his puzzled expression, she laughed coldly. “Why do you insist on lying? Nobody here is an idiot. You cannot trick us. You thought the Heavy Pagoda would be a big help in your breakthrough, so you pulled some strings to steal another disciple’s position. Good, very good. I can only wonder who your backer is, for you to dare be so open about your cheating.”

Cultivators cared a lot about face. Even though the Envoy told them that Jack’s ranking change was a direct order of the Head Envoy, this woman didn’t dare call him out by name. She even pretended not to know. Otherwise, if she really offended the Head Envoy, it wouldn’t matter who was in the right; he could just use his authority to punish her or even expel her from the Church!

But there was a limit to corruption. If the Head Envoy acted out of turn to raise Jack’s ranking, and then even used his own superior power to bully those questioning Jack, that would be too much. Other higher-ups would have to step in.

That was why this woman dared to insult Jack in his face but didn’t dare to mention the Head Envoy’s name.

Jack was still reeling. He was puzzled and confused, yet at the same time, he was getting angry. He didn’t intend to look for trouble. However, if trouble looked for him, he wasn’t a coward who turned away!

“First of all, mind your ugly tongue. Second, I really don’t know what happened with my ranking. I thought I was at 997 until just now. It must have been an honest mistake.”

“Don’t try that with me, Jack Rust. I checked with the Envoy; she told me clearly that this is no mistake, it was a direct order from someone above. Such blatant favoritism is rare. If you were a strong cultivator, I would understand, but you’re just a lowly D-Grade. You clearly don’t deserve that rank. Even just being an outer disciple and benefiting from the same resources we do is spitting in our faces.”

Jack was startled. There was no mistake? An order had come down from above? Who could have done that, and why? The only person Jack knew was the Head Envoy, Sovereign Heavenly Spoon, but he hadn't seemed like a person who would act like this.

Moreover, it sucked! It had to be that sovereign, there was no one else, but Jack hadn't asked for it! He didn't even know what the Heavy Pagoda was! All he wanted was to cultivate in peace, and now the sovereign forced enemies to his front door.

Fuck your mother! Why couldn't you ask first, Sovereign!

But it was too late. Jack would try to meet the sovereign later and ask him about it, or maybe the Sage could help. For now, the dice had been cast, and all Jack could do was stand his ground.

After all, even if he insisted that this had nothing to do with him, nobody would believe him.

"Are you doubting the higher-ups?" he asked, adopting a strict look. "If what you say is true, they gave me this ranking. Do you think you know better than them?"

The woman's face mellowed into a malicious grin. This is where she hoped the conversation would end up. "Oh, I wouldn't dare question the Envoys," she said smoothly. "The only thing I question is your integrity. If the Envoys say you deserve that ranking, I can only believe them, but I have to admit my curiosity. How could a peak D-Grade possess such strength? Your talent must be extraordinary, your cultivation extremely gifted. A little person like me can only marvel at your potential."

Her words sounded genuine, but they were actually laced with sarcasm. She was mocking him. On cue, the three people behind her started laughing, emphasizing her words. Even the window pane jittered, laughing through a Dao-projected voice.

Jack's face was ugly. He had been put into this situation, and now he had to deal with it. "Just get to the point."

The woman smiled sweetly. "I am very curious about your powers. Could you grace me with a little duel, senior? My ranking is at 970. If you can defeat me, that will put to rest all accusations against you, and also satisfy my curiosity. What do you say?"

On the outside, Jack was calm like a brick wall. On the inside, he wanted to curse.

If he refused the duel, everyone would accuse him of cheating. If he accepted and lost, that would be even worse! He would be completely humiliated, and they would still think he was cheating! As for winning, that would be difficult. Six months ago, he had given it his all to just barely defeat the planetary overseer. The weakest people present, like this woman, had to be around that level as well, if not higher. Even if he used the Life Drop, the result would be uncertain.

What choice did he have? He'd just been challenged to a duel. He couldn't chicken out!

"Fine," he said. "Let's duel."

"Excellent!" The woman pretended to be honored. "But, since we're dueling, let's make things more interesting by making a small bet. Since you just arrived, you must have received a Dao stone, yes? Let's bet that."

In her heart, the woman was smiling devilishly. She didn't just want to teach Jack a lesson, she also wanted to steal his Dao stone to further her own cultivation.

Jack didn't know the value of such an object, but if a C-Grade placed it as stakes, it had to be pretty high. Then again, he couldn't refuse without admitting that his strength was inferior.

"Fine!" he said, his voice lowering. "One Dao stone. Let's bet that."

"Excellent! Then, if senior would do me the honor, how about we move to the fields and duel right now?"

The villages and buildings of the Cathedral only took up a small piece of its landmass. Everything else was empty and summarily called the fields. Under the increased gravity and thicker Dao, it could easily contain a battle between C-Grades.

Jack wanted to sigh. But since he was already on the dance floor, he had to dance. A little humiliation and a Dao stone, whatever its value was, were prices he could handle. Besides, his defeat wasn't certain. This woman was one of the weakest disciples on the entire Cathedral, and his strength had also increased a little since fighting the overseer. Maybe he could take her.

As he had that thought, Jack's chest began to burn with fervor. He was about to join the fray. He was jumping into a deep pool filled with the greatest talents of the universe.

Just how did he stack up against them?

CHAPTER SEVEN

RUINING REPUTATIONS

GLOOMILY, JACK HEADED FOR THE EMPTY FIELDS OUTSIDE THE VILLAGE—A rugged, alien landscape filled with nothing but highly compressed stone. It was almost completely flat, save for natural stone obelisks that rose from ten to ninety feet in height, carved by the extreme gravity.

Even exiting the village wasn't easy. As a peak D-Grade, Jack could naturally fly, but doing so in this gravity would quickly tire him out. Thankfully, his opponent didn't fly either—they just walked.

Jack himself, though not particularly fond of the incoming battle, led the way. He was a cultivator of the fist. No matter what he did, he did it with all his heart.

"This should be good enough," his opponent, the stunningly beautiful woman, said after a while. They weren't too far out. Just a couple miles. For C-Grades, this was nothing.

Jack turned around and raised a brow. "Aren't we too close to the village?"

"You overestimate yourself. This place is nothing like the planets you're used to. If you can demonstrate even one percent of your strength, I will be surprised."

"Suit yourself."

The woman's friends stood some distance away, as did Brock and the Sage. The brorilla was excited as if about to watch a good show, while the Sage seemed to be concentrating on something.

"I never got your name," Jack said, cracking his knuckles.

"You never deserved it. But no matter. Ley Vice."

Jack couldn't care less about her; he just wanted to know the name of the first person he would defeat in the Black Hole Church. His fiery spirit was rousing. Already, his heart was filled with fighting spirit, and his fists itched to be buried in her face.

He hadn't fought seriously in six months. Only now did he realize that he'd missed this feeling.

As the two were poised to fight, the Sage's voice suddenly rang in Jack's brain.

"*Wait!*" he warned. "*I just ran some divination. This woman is no one important, but her husband is! He's the man we met before, Marcus William, and he's ranked 281 across the entire Cathedral! He's extremely powerful. He is also a petty character known for bullying others. If you offend him by attacking his wife, he will suppress you for your entire stay on the Cathedral. Your life will become ten times more difficult!*"

Jack frowned. "*What do you suggest?*"

"*Step down. Don't fight. A little humiliation now is nothing compared to the consequences of fighting her.*"

"Impossible," Jack refused. He was a warrior of the Fist. Backing down now, after he'd already agreed to fight, would create doubts in his heart that would weaken his connection to the Dao.

"*Please consider it, Jack. If you fight her and lose, that will be fine, but if you win... your cultivation path may be blocked!*"

Jack did not reply outright. *My cultivation path may be blocked...*

It made sense. He had no idea how things worked around here, but someone at the rank of 281 had to be extremely powerful. If Marcus William was a petty person, as the Sage said, and Jack challenged him by defeating his wife, then Marcus would use his entire strength and influence to suppress him. Jack was a nobody here—there would be a million ways to make his life difficult.

However, even thinking up to that point, Jack shook his head. This was exactly why he'd tried to avoid trouble... but, if he was forced to fight, he would give it his all. Since when was he afraid of making enemies?

"*When I challenged the Animal Kingdom, I was less than an ant in their eyes,*" he transmitted to the Sage. "*And when I resolved to fight the planetary overseer, I was only at the F-Grade. I am a warrior. If that Marcus fellow wants to suppress me, he can try. I will punch him down like I did everyone else. However, if you want me to surrender now, that is impossible. This is my path of the Fist.*"

The Sage mutedly shook his head. "*As you wish. I will stay by your side regardless.*"

"*Thank you. You are a good friend.*"

"Are you done?" the woman said, having noticed that Jack was mentally conversing with someone. "You can call more favors if you want, but you would only humiliate yourself further."

"That won't happen. If you want to humiliate me, you'll have to do it yourself."

She grinned. "With pleasure."

Her pale, slender arms spread out. An invisible veil passed over the land, and Jack felt a mysterious force infiltrate his mind. It wasn't malevolent. It was a principle of the Dao itself, a law as ironclad as gravity.

He tried to resist, but such was hopeless. Even when he unleashed his Dao Domain, the mysterious force clung to him unobstructed, as if the Fist and this woman's Dao existed in completely separate dimensions.

"There is no point," the woman replied with a laugh. "This is my Truth Domain. In here, you cannot lie. The only words you can speak are the truth."

"I didn't plan to lie," Jack replied. Suddenly, that mysterious force passed over his brain. He sensed that, if there was even the slightest hint of falsehood in his words, that force would clamp down on him with tremendous force. No—if he even considered lying, he would still suffer a backlash.

Was this a Will attack?

"You wouldn't lie?" the woman replied. "Let's test that, shall we?"

Jack didn't plan to fall into her pace. He reared his fist back and shot out a Meteor Punch. After comprehending the concept of the Supernova, his Meteor Punch had reached tier IV and advanced in power, becoming a skill that could threaten even C-Grades.

However, the Dao here was extremely solid. As Jack unleashed his Meteor Punch, the light and sound pulsed slightly, then refused his summons. They weren't sucked into the punch. The meteor that formed was small, similar to the size of his real fist, and its purple starry tail only extended a foot behind it.

It still flew forward, carrying at least some force, but its energy was rapidly extinguished. The meteor had to penetrate the thick Dao to advance. For every inch forward, a tremendous strain pushed on his energy reserves. There was no meaning to shooting out his punch from this distance and let it wink out.

It was incredible. This meteor could annihilate entire countries back on Earth. Here, it was just a flying punch. It was like his cultivation had reverted to the E-Grade.

Of course, if an E-Grade cultivator or even a normal D-Grade appeared on the Cathedral, they wouldn't even be able to walk, let alone attack.

Jack wasn't willing to just give up. The Life Drop surged inside him. His body grew a foot taller, while two extra arms jutted out from under his armpits. He roared and charged, shooting out another Meteor Punch that was as large as his entire torso.

Facing this attack, Ley Vice actually showed a shocked expression. She had been here for centuries and knew exactly how difficult it was to galvanize the ambient Dao. Such an attack was the equivalent of an early to middle C-Grade—how could a mere D-Grade possess such strength?

Regardless, she was an experienced cultivator. Her expression returned to normal, and she raised a finger, shouting, "He speaks no truth!"

The mysterious force constraining Jack intensified. The meteor he'd shot out weakened until it dissipated into thin air.

Ley Vice grinned. "If you wish to ignore my domain, Jack Rust, I fear you will find it difficult."

"Hmph!"

Jack snorted. Inwardly, he was frantically searching for a way out. This domain restricted him, he couldn't neutralize it with his own, and he couldn't even reach her with his attacks.

How was he supposed to fight?

"*You must make the Truth Domain acknowledge you!*" the Sage hurriedly informed him. "*If you ignore it, you will need overwhelming force to even touch her!*"

Jack frowned. "How?"

"*By being true!*"

"Do you find me attractive, Jack Rust?" the woman asked.

"What?"

"I said, do you find me attractive?"

Her smile was devilish, if stunning. Jack did not reply immediately. This was too peculiar. Until he knew what she was going for, replying would be unwise. He charged again, reaching her with heavy steps and swinging. His fists burst with energy, unleashing purple flames everywhere they passed, but Ley Vice was not a damsel in distress. Her own fighting skills were nothing to scoff at. She dodged Jack's attacks, opening more distance between them.

Additionally, the more time that passed, the more her domain strangled him. He realized the reason; by not answering, he was suppressing his truth.

But there was another reason he hadn't already done so. The truth... was not something he wished to say!

"I do," he finally replied. It was the truth; while this woman was an unpleasant character, her physical charms were hard to deny. If Jack claimed he wasn't the least bit attracted to her, it would have been a lie.

He just didn't want to give her the satisfaction.

The moment he spoke his answer, the mysterious presence scanned him again. Finding his answer true, it relaxed its hold, letting him use more of his power. At the same time, however, Jack noticed that his own Dao grew weaker!

The higher one's cultivation, the more aligned they needed to be with their Dao. Admitting that his opponent was attractive mid-battle was not the conduct of a warrior. His Dao grew distracted, and his ability to invoke it was weakened.

So, that's how it is!

Jack's eyes widened. He finally understood this woman's fighting style.

Her Truth Domain was a dead-end. If he answered her expertly-crafted questions and spoke the truth, his Dao would be weakened. If he didn't answer, or if he lied, he would be so suppressed he couldn't fight.

Moreover, she had no reason to stop asking targeted questions against his Dao heart. Eventually, he would either break his own Dao or be suppressed to the point of defeat.

In truth, his combat skills easily outstripped his opponent's. The only reason he couldn't touch her was because of her domain.

What a fearsome power... he thought, a shiver running down his spine. *There has to be a way out. There is no way her domain is unbeatable.*

"So you do find me attractive." Ley Vice smiled sweetly. "Then, tell me... What would you do if you had me on your bed?"

Jack's eyes flashed. She was trying to find questions that would expose the weaknesses in his heart, but she had already failed. Despite what she might think... Jack was no weakling!

"Tell you to get dressed and leave," he replied honestly. The woman's smile froze on her face; her friends, who had been laughing and cheering, froze as well. Only Brock, who knew what was and wasn't bro-like, gave Jack a thumbs-up.

Every power had a weakness. In Ley Vice's case, the suppression of her Truth Domain relied on asking the perfect questions to rattle her opponent's heart. She was an expert at that. Her presence here, as one of the most talented C-Grades in the universe, was not an accident.

However, for her battle plan to work, she needed her opponent's heart to be unsteady. If there were even the slightest of cracks, she could identify and exploit them. All in all, her power had many constraints, and couldn't be used in every scenario, but she was a master at making it work. One of the reasons she challenged Jack was because she thought he had cheated his way up, which naturally indicated some weakness in her heart. In her mind, Jack was an insecure, ambitious person, and those people could never resist a beautiful woman on their bed. Even if they could, they would still feel guilty desire, and that was precisely why she'd asked those questions.

Unfortunately for Ley Vice, Jack was not the person she thought he was. His heart was incomparably solid and wholeheartedly aligned with the Fist. He was her natural counter. If she knew, she would never have dared to challenge him!

As her smile froze, and as she tried to discover where she'd gone wrong so she could backtrack, Jack realized this was his opportunity.

Two can play this game, bitch.

"In fact," he added, "I recognize your beauty, but I greatly dislike your character and would never deign to touch you. Even if you strip yourself naked and fall to all fours before me, I will feel disgust. There is almost no price in the world that can make me lower myself to be with a person like you."

Ley Vice was completely frozen. The Sage was staring wide-eyed. Her friends were all gaping, unable to comprehend what they were hearing. Jack Rust, this weakling who cheated on the ranking obelisk, had really just uttered these words?

It was impossible. He had to be lying. There was no way his heart was that steady.

Yet no matter how long they waited, the Truth Domain did not act against him. It was undeniable proof that his words were completely and utterly true. He'd meant exactly what he said.

Brock laughed out loud.

Ley Vice struggled to form words. His speech had impaled her heart and scorched it open. Was that really the impression she gave others? Did she deserve that response? Questions bubbled up her throat, but she didn't want to further humiliate herself by asking them.

And just like that, what goes around comes around. As she suppressed the things she wanted to say, her own domain fell around her, suppressing her.

Before she had time to recover, Jack charged forth and smashed a Meteor Punch into her pretty face. Ley Vice went flying, then quickly met the ground due to the increased gravity. Her nose was broken, her mouth bleeding.

Seeing her like that, Jack felt no pity at all. When two cultivators fought each other, gender did not matter—he would punch everyone who deserved it!

"...I admit defeat," Ley Vice mumbled. With a frigid expression, she turned to her friends and said, "Someone give him a Dao stone. I do not have one on me. I will pay you back."

The insectoid person fished out a Dao stone from his robes and tossed it to Jack, who caught it out of the air. "Thanks. At least you keep your word."

"We're going," Ley said, standing up and walking away. She did not spare Jack a single glance. Her friends did, as they followed her without another word, heading back toward the village.

"Well, that was easier than expected," Jack said as his own friends approached him.

"It was a good match-up for you," the Sage replied. "Ley Vice is a Will cultivator focused on exploiting the weaknesses of others, and you unknowingly tricked her before the fight even began. Moreover, her power is not originally meant for battle, which is why she hasn't been able to climb the rankings despite staying here for a millennium."

"Well, she did give me a Dao stone, so I can't complain."

"Don't joke around, Jack. This is serious." The Sage's gaze intensified. "Do you realize what you did? I was just telling you that Marcus William is a powerful, petty bully, and you went and insulted his wife. He won't just suppress you—he will use everything he has to completely crush you."

Faced with the Sage's worried expression, Jack was calm. He glanced over at Brock, and the two of them nodded at each other. "He can try," Jack replied, pocketing the extra Dao stone. "I, Jack Rust, am not afraid of any bully."

CHAPTER EIGHT
THE BANE OF EXISTENCE

After Jack defeated Ley Vice in such an embarrassing manner, news had no reason to spread. None of the involved parties would benefit.

Except their battle had taken place very close to the village. That was done on purpose by Ley, as she had planned to humiliate Jack, but her own sadism turned to bite her in the ass.

There weren't many things to do on the Cathedral. When a battle happened, many meditating C-Grades spread out their perceptions to watch. As a result, the humiliation of Ley Vice had been witnessed by dozens of outer disciples, who transmitted the news to their friends. Before long, the entire Cathedral knew what happened.

News eventually reached Marcus William, the husband of Ley Vice. According to the Sage, this man was an infamous bully, a man who kept a grudge and enjoyed pressing his opponents into the ground. When he heard how Jack Rust had publicly humiliated his wife, claiming that he wouldn't touch her even if she begged him, flames of fury rose in his heart. He wanted to immediately go and teach that little D-Grade a lesson.

Unfortunately, he was at a crucial point of his cultivation, so he couldn't interrupt it midway. He needed a few more days. Until then...

Marcus sent a voice transmission. "Cranxiao? I have a job for you."

Jack was meditating in his cabin. On the Cathedral, even this simple act was different. The Dao was dense and rich, allowing him to easily absorb it. He could spend half the effort for twice the results. His will spread to his surroundings, assimilating the surrounding Dao into the Fist and pulling it inside him, where he used it to nourish his Dao Tree.

By now, the tree was fully formed. Its trunk rose nine feet tall, while a crown of intertwined branches and leaves covered its top. Thanks to the Life Drop buried right under it, as well as Jack's perfect foundation, the entire tree was vibrant with life, each leaf shining like amethyst. Even the little veins on them were clearly visible, pulsing with tiny streams of power.

Jack had already reached the peak D-Grade and fully formed his Dao Tree. The next step would be to make it bloom, creating tiny flowers on its branches. A step which sounded easy, though was as hard as grabbing the clouds.

The so-called Dao Blooming was a major breakthrough on the cultivation path. A large number of flowers had to bloom at the same time, which required a tremendous amount of Dao energy. The process needed to be completed in one fell swoop. If anything went wrong, the blooming would stop midway, and the cultivator would be stuck in a limbo between the D and C-Grades, forever unable to progress further.

For that reason, one should gather as much momentum as possible before breaking through, ensuring they had enough energy. That was a tall task. Even Jack, with his perfect foundation and vibrant Dao Tree, did not feel confident in accomplishing it. Even if he completely stuffed his tree with energy until it began to leak out, it still might not be enough. The Life Drop couldn't be used either, as its Dao belonged to Life, not the Fist.

Of course, the energy Jack already gathered could be enough—it was hard to judge—but he only had one shot. If he rushed into it unprepared, he deserved to remain stranded at the D-Grade for the rest of his life.

The excessive demand for Dao energy was the reason why cultivators didn't typically achieve this breakthrough by themselves. They would first accumulate as much energy as they could, then gather treasures with dense and easily-digestible Dao. Throughout their breakthrough, they would gradually use up all those treasures to replenish some of their lost energy.

Unfortunately, such treasures were prohibitively rare. There were almost none of them on Earth, and even if one looked at the Merchant Alliance, such things were impossible to buy with money.

After all, credits were only useful up to the E or early D-Grade. After that, everyone had so much money they just didn't care. If someone came across such a treasure, they would either use it themselves or trade it for items of equal value.

Therefore, breaking into the C-Grade without the support of a powerful faction was almost impossible. Finding pure Dao treasures was one of the reasons Jack had come to the Church.

Truthfully, he'd thought it would be difficult. He imagined he would have to perform missions and jobs for the Church to even have a chance at acquiring the necessary treasures.

Never did he expect to receive such a treasure as a welcoming gift. The Dao stones he'd so easily acquired were pure Dao treasures!

The Church is scarily rich... Jack thought with a shiver.

Dao stones were created by people at the C-Grade and above. Instead of cultivating normally, they would spend their efforts controlling the ambient Dao and painstakingly forcing it into special crystals until the Dao density inside them was extremely high. When those crystals reached saturation, a Dao stone would form. By using that Dao stone later, a cultivator could absorb the large quantity of Dao in a very short period of time and with little effort, making Dao stones ideal treasures for both cultivating and breaking through bottlenecks. D and C-Grades went crazy over them.

The Sage had also explained a few more things about these stones.

Due to their usefulness and ease of creation, Dao stones had become something like currency for high-grade cultivators. One could exchange Dao stones for all sorts of treasures.

Of course, for every advantage that Dao stones had, they came with an equal number of disadvantages. For one, creating them was highly inefficient. A middle C-Grade would need to spend an entire month to create a single Dao stone instead of spending that time cultivating. Then, if the same C-Grade used the stone they'd created, the benefits they would receive would be roughly equal to three days of cultivation. Ninety percent of the energy was wasted.

Generally, only people who reached a dead-end in their cultivation would spend their time creating Dao stones. Either that, or cultivators in urgent need of money.

Jack now had two stones—one that he got from the Church, and one generously donated by Ley Vice. He would also receive one stone per year as a low-ranked outer disciple. If he wanted to spend Dao stones to break through... he estimated he could use up to twenty before his Dao Tree was unable to absorb anymore. Twenty Dao stones would give him the best chance at succeeding.

Eighteen years, he thought, pursing his lips. *That's too long. There has to be a better way.*

He could offer his services to other cultivators in exchange for Dao stones, but it would be hard for him to earn enough that way. After all, a Dao stone was very precious.

Another way would be to borrow from people he knew or even strangers, offering to repay them after reaching the C-Grade—but

Jack didn't want to be indebted to strangers. It was a risk. One of them may come later and ask for something Jack wasn't willing to do, and refusing would mean denying his favor—a behavior that wasn't aligned with the Fist.

As for borrowing from his friends, he was also unwilling to do that. Even if someone did possess Dao stones—like the Sage, who was mysterious enough to hide ten of them in his underwear—they were highly valuable, and he wasn't sure when or how he could repay them.

The only person he considered asking was the Head Envoy, who was certainly rich enough to not care about twenty Dao stones. However, not only were the two of them acquaintances, the Head Envoy had questionably raised Jack through the ranking obelisk. Since Jack wasn't sure about that man's intentions, he didn't want to owe him a debt.

In a few words, there was no one he could borrow from.

If only I could earn them through bets, that would be the dream... he thought, sighing. The one he'd gotten from Ley Vice was a lucky break. All sorts of coincidences had to come together for that to happen. If he tried to consciously trick and rob other C-Grades of their stones, not only would it probably backfire, it was also dishonest.

Finally, creating his own Dao stones instead of cultivating was impossible, as he hadn't yet reached the C-Grade.

Therefore, his only good option was to check if the Black Hole Church had any sort of quest system, where he could complete missions for payment in Dao stones.

Jack opened his eyes. His Dao Tree was already fully grown—meditation had little meaning.

"Life moves in circles," he muttered. "I ruled a planet and broke a galaxy, then suddenly, I am poor again."

As he opened his eyes, so did Brock. The two were sitting cross-legged, facing each other. However, while Jack's meditation was mostly spent worrying over his finances, Brock was brimming with joy. He hadn't reached the peak D-Grade yet. He could nourish his Dao Tree by simply assimilating the surrounding Dao and pulling it inside himself, a process that was far more effective here than on Earth.

Since Jack couldn't cultivate, he'd even let Brock sit on the cabin's magical meditation mat.

"Bro!" Brock said. "This is so good!"

"Yes, Brock, I'm sure it's great," Jack replied, not even pretending to be happy. Money really was the bane of existence.

However, how could Brock not see through his brother's thoughts? He jumped up and placed a hand on Jack's shoulders. "No worry," he said with a reassuring smile. "All good. World gives solutions. Hakuna matata."

Jack opened his mouth to respond, then heard the last few words and chuckled. "Where did you even hear that?"

"Dog bro."

"Of course." Jack smiled. "Thanks, Brock. I can always count on you."

Brock gave Jack a generous thumbs-up, then returned to meditation. Jack stood and dusted himself off—though there was no dust on the Cathedral. "I'll look around a bit. See if I can find a way to earn money."

"Have fun, bro."

"Thanks."

Jack opened the door, coming face-to-face with the Sage and an extremely wide young man. He was a human, just looking like he'd eaten three boars for breakfast. His belly flaps jiggled as he walked, his forehead was drenched in sweat, and his Asian features were so deformed that his eyes were barely visible between his forehead and... upper lip?

Though this man looked slightly familiar, Jack couldn't place it.

"Um, hi," he said. "I'm Jack."

The Sage chuckled.

"Your mother is Jack!" replied the fat man, seeming profoundly pissed. "You don't need to introduce yourself to me. You know me. I'm Dorman Whistles!"

Jack blinked. The slim, athletic teenager had turned into this mountain of meat? "Yeah, of course I remember. You're looking great."

"Great? Ohhh, I'll beat you to a pulp!"

CHAPTER NINE
LIFE CHOICES

JACK STARED UNBLINKINGLY AT THE MOUNTAIN OF A MAN BEFORE HIM. HE was short, wide like a plasma tv, and his name was Dorman Whistles.

It had only been a year since Jack last saw Dorman. How could he have tripled in weight?

"At the risk of sounding insensitive... what happened?"

"Dorman had a little accident," the Sage tried to reply, but Dorman only harrumphed.

"I was set up! Some woman fed me a treasure that made me fat!"

"Dorman, like yourself, arrived here at the D-Grade," the Sage spoke again. "He cultivated using the dense Dao but got desperate to advance quickly. After using his extreme speed to steal a treasure... this happened."

"There are treasures that can make you fat?" Jack asked.

"Even junk food on Earth can make you fat. How could Dao treasures be weaker than cheeseburgers?"

"Hmph." Dorman snorted, recovering his composure—letting Jack see him in this condition must have been a mental blow. "She knew I would take that treasure. She left it exposed on purpose. Now, my body isn't aerodynamic at all, limiting my speed. My combat ability has gone down a lot."

Dorman cultivated the Dao of Speed. This heavy form did not suit him very much.

"Who is the 'she' you keep talking about?" Jack asked.

"A late C-Grade bitch who refuses to take me seriously."

"If you tried to steal from her and she only punished you by making you fat, I would say that's pretty lenient."

Dorman seemed hurt. "She made it too easy."

"Yeah, and I see it turned out just fine."

"Listen, motherfucker, I can still beat you up anytime you want!"

Jack smirked, letting the challenge pass. He had confidence that nobody under the C-Grade could beat him, and Dorman was only a late D-Grade. Moreover, Jack saw no reason to push Dorman down at this point.

"Anyway, I was about to take a walk. Wanna join me? We could visit this Heavy Pagoda and see what it's about."

"Sure," the Sage replied, falling into step next to Jack. Dorman reluctantly followed. As for Brock, he'd heard their exchange but didn't bother getting up—he just wanted to cultivate.

As they walked, Jack felt an awkward atmosphere settling in. He turned to Dorman.

"So. How long have you been, uh, well-fed?"

"A few months." Dorman crossed his arms, not forgetting his previous anger. "That bitch refuses to give me the antidote."

"Hmm. Well, at least now you know that stealing is bad."

"I will seriously destroy you."

"By sitting on me?"

Dorman's eyes widened. "YOU!" he exclaimed, but before he could reach out, Jack had already blinked away laughing. Dorman's cultivation was weaker than Jack's, he wasn't aerodynamic, and the Cathedral's gravity amplified his already great weight. Under these conditions, Jack's speed was greater than Dorman's—which was supposed to be his specialty.

Really, becoming fat had ruined his combat prowess.

Dorman's eyes fell as he realized this, and he became sad.

"Come on, relax," Jack said, slowly approaching again. "I'm sorry. I shouldn't have said that."

"It's okay... I'm just a little sensitive right now, that's all. Sorry for cursing at you before."

"Why don't you leave here?" Jack asked with a little pity in his eyes. "With your cultivation, both weight and aerodynamics would mean nothing on a regular planet. Your speed would be almost intact. It's only here, where gravity is extremely strong, that your combat power is decreased."

Jack thought his question was valid. Then Dorman's brows rose, and he looked at the Sage. "You haven't told him?"

"It didn't come up yet."

"What didn't come up?" Jack asked, suddenly worried.

The Sage coughed in his hand. "Do you remember how, the higher you climb on the ranking obelisk, the more benefits and privileges you earn?"

"Yeah?"

"Using the teleporters is one of those privileges. Before you reach the ranking of eight hundred... you cannot leave."

The news fell like thunder. Jack's eyes turned wide as saucers. "I can't leave!" he shouted. "Sage! What the hell is wrong with you? Why didn't you mention it earlier?"

"Because it doesn't change much."

"Doesn't change much? I have *children*, you idiot. I have a home. If I cannot leave this place until I reach a high ranking, will I never see them growing up!"

Jack was livid. For the current him, even a ranking of 950 was a stretch. There was no way to reach 800 before breaking through, and that alone could take a long time. Years, maybe.

Was he really trapped here?

"Sage, this isn't a joke. If you make my children grow up fatherless, I will make you pay for it."

Facing Jack's billowing anger, the Sage was calm. "I told you, it will be fine. With your potential, breaking through won't take too long. Then, reaching 800 will be a breeze."

"Oh yeah? And how exactly will I break through? Because last time I checked, I would need two decades to gather enough Dao stones."

"I'm sure you'll find a way."

Jack couldn't believe the words that came out of the Sage's mouth. This was a set-up! He was trapped!

"You'd better give me some Dao stones, Sage, or I swear I'll break your face."

"When have I ever led you wrong? Trust me. It will be fine. If not, I will take full responsibility and use my connections to help you break through."

Jack closed his eyes and took deep breaths. Only now was he slightly pacified, but only slightly. He hated getting played like that. It was almost a betrayal. In his mind, he remembered that the Sage was a mysterious, enigmatic figure whose real motives remained unknown.

Perhaps trusting him too much was a bad idea.

"Do you understand now?" Dorman said with a sad smile. "I'm trapped here, too. I cannot leave before I reach the C-Grade, but I cannot reach the C-Grade without leaving. I'm not a disciple, so I don't get free Dao stones, and I'm only a D-Grade, so I cannot produce my own. I have no means to acquire them. Perhaps I could indebt myself to others if I still had my combat power, but... as I am right now, there is nothing I can offer to C-Grades. None of them would take me seriously. I'm stuck."

"Were you also lured here with lies?" Jack asked. Dorman shook his head.

"I knew I couldn't leave. I still chose to come, because this was the best place to cultivate, and I thought I would find a way to either break through or escape. That is why I got desperate and tried to steal a treasure."

Jack shook his head. This was a lot to take in. He needed to break through as soon as possible. He needed Dao stones.

"Sage, you put me into this mess, so you better help me get out. Can your contacts get me some Dao stones? I will repay them after I reach the C-Grade."

"They can. However, try to find some way to earn them yourself first. Give it three years. If you have not managed to collect them by then, I promise I will help you."

"Three years?"

That wasn't as long as eighteen years, but it remained a long time. He'd planned to visit home often. What would Vivi say if he went missing for three years? What would his children think of their father?

"It's too much," he eventually said. "I do not appreciate your actions. Six months. That is the most I will endure. After that, you will give me enough stones to break through. Is that clear?"

The Sage tightened his lips. He was about to say something, then thought better about it. In the end, he sighed. "Fine. Six months. But, Jack... I know how this sounds, but please believe in me. I would never betray you or keep you away from your family. The reason I dared to never say anything is because you told me you planned to return at six months, and I knew I would be able to provide the stones to aid your breakthrough by then.

"As for why I chose to keep this a secret... In truth, this is forbidden knowledge. Many disciples have people who depend on them back home. If their enemies knew they couldn't return for a long period of time, they would certainly burn these disciples' homes and kill their families. For that reason, we do not disseminate this knowledge unless absolutely necessary. I didn't think it was so in your case, so I said nothing."

Jack frowned deeply. His mind went over the Sage's words. They made sense. If he saw this objectively, he might have made the same choice in the Sage's shoes. However, being on the other end was unpleasant.

He chose to maintain his friendship with the Sage, but would keep an eye out. This was a man that kept secrets.

"Fine. Six months it is. Until then, is there some way to get Dao stones? I know I'm only a D-Grade, but I'm strong. Does the Church have some sort of quest system, where I can perform missions for payment?"

"Sadly, no. The Cathedral has few people, so there is little automation. Any missions are directly assigned to the right candidates—and, even if you could get one, they are meant for people of far higher strength than you. Mostly Envoys. That's where their title comes from."

Jack grumbled.

"There are services to be offered, though," the Sage added. "The Cathedral is a lonely place sorely lacking personnel. Cooking, cleaning, taking care of others, all those jobs can be performed if you put away your cultivator's pride. Moreover, if you possess any utility outside combat, there will certainly be some demand for you."

"What kind of utility?"

"Anything, really. Magic formations, smithing, Dao theory."

"What's Dao theory?"

"You get paid to debate the Dao against someone trying to breakthrough. Not many people use such a service, but it can help if you're really stuck at a bottleneck."

"I work as a Dao debater occasionally. I get roughly a Dao stone per year," Dorman said with a grimace. The Sage hadn't promised to give him any stones, but Jack didn't pry—it was their business.

His mind turned back to money-making. Specifically, Dao debating. He hesitated. He could maybe do that on the basis of his perfect foundation, but a Dao stone per year was far less than he needed.

"Can't I duel people for money?" he asked.

"Most use their friends for that. Plus, you're not strong enough." Seeing Jack deep in thought, the Sage kept trying. "Come on, Jack, don't get down. Tell me, is there anything you're good at besides combat?"

"...I'm a biologist, I guess. I can tell people how ants evolved."

"Hmm. That doesn't sound too useful..." Suddenly, the Sage's face brightened. "Ah! Have you considered becoming a healer?"

"A healer?"

"Yes. You have knowledge about how the body works, which is one of the hardest parts, and you possess a Dao Root of Life. Those are the minimum requirements already."

"Huh. I don't think so. My path involves breaking people, not fixing them."

The Sage laughed. "That's not a problem. Of all the side practices, healing is the one that can most directly influence your combat strength, both offensively and defensively. Plus, with the Life Drop inside you, not learning how to use it properly would be a big waste. Not to mention it's the path to easy Dao stones."

That made Jack think. He actually never considered using his Life Dao like that.

Even back at the Integration Tournament, the elef scion used the Dao of Life to heal people. Most other healers he'd met did the same. He could already heal himself. Why not others?

"Such a weird concept," he mused. "How would I sell my services? Perhaps I could break people's noses and charge them to fix it?"

"That would be improper, but maybe you can help them after someone else breaks their nose."

"Like, my accomplice?"

"Like any random cultivator after a duel. I don't think it's such a bad idea. Many people need healing, and you even have the Life Drop inside you to supply extra Life Dao. With a little bit of studying, you could become a passable healer."

Jack considered it more seriously. "Is healing lucrative?"

"Plenty. There is always demand for healers, and not many people cultivate the right Daos to become one. If you're good, you could even earn dozens of stones a year! But, of course, that's not easy."

Jack cupped his chin. He'd spent most of his life studying before the System came. Now, he was leery of falling back into the rabbit hole, but did he even have a choice? He needed Dao stones, and earning as many as he could himself was better than getting them through the Sage.

After all, though he wanted to return to Earth, relying too much on others would affect his Dao heart.

The more he considered it, the more virtues he found in the idea. Learning to control the Life Drop better would directly increase his combat strength. If he became a healer, his self-regeneration would probably rise even further in effectiveness, making him almost immortal. He could also use the excess Life Dao provided by the Life Drop to assist his friends if they got too injured or use it on strangers and earn a pretty penny. With money, his cultivation would advance much faster, both now and later.

Not to mention his background in biology. Though, how would his Earthen knowledge mesh with a multi-species magical practice?

I can take a look, he promised himself. *Couldn't hurt. Punching will always come first, but I could use a little side hustle—as long as it doesn't take up too much of my time.*

Plus, I almost have a PhD, goddammit! It's about time I used it!

"Look, we have arrived," Dorman said, pointing at a building in the distance. "The Heavy Pagoda!"

CHAPTER TEN
HEAVY PAGODA

If someone took an ancient Chinese pagoda and placed it in a weird alien setting, that would pretty closely resemble the Black Hole Church's Heavy Pagoda.

It had seven floors. The roofs between them extended out of the building, like open umbrellas, while the walls were smooth and completely vertical. The entire pagoda was constructed in a dark material that Jack couldn't identify, making it almost invisible against the dark sky. However, the ring of light around the pagoda's base illuminated it just fine.

As they approached, Jack saw that this ring of light was actually thousands of tiny symbols, each completely incomprehensible. With a cursory glance, he couldn't find even two that were identical.

"Those are Dao glyphs," the Sage explained. "The basis of magic formations. The language of the Dao. They aren't letters, more like instructions, with each symbol representing an entire sentence. Kind of like the eastern ideograms, but significantly more complex."

Jack whistled. "What do they say?"

"That this elevator goes down."

"Excuse me?"

The Sage laughed. “I don’t know how to read them. However, I know they are part of a gravity-enhancing formation. The Heavy Pagoda takes advantage of its environment and uses magic to amplify the already great gravity by a number of times.”

“A number of times?” Jack shivered. Just normal gravity here was a thousand times stronger than Earth’s. “You mean it gets even stronger?”

“Oh yeah. The first floor has gravity twice as powerful as the rest of the Cathedral. After that, every higher floor doubles it again. The seventh floor contains gravity that is one hundred and twenty-eight times stronger than the regular gravity around here. Just the body weight of a normal cultivator would number in the millions of pounds in there. For Dorman, think billions.”

“Hey!”

“What’s the use of such a thing?” Jack asked.

“You’ve experienced the Cathedral’s high concentration of Dao, right? Thanks to the thousandfold gravity, the Dao here is much more concentrated than elsewhere, making cultivation more efficient. That increase is further amplified in the Heavy Pagoda. Moreover, there are special meditation mats in there that read the cultivator’s Dao and help filter out the irrelevant particles, further increasing the speed of your cultivation. With those two advantages combined, even the first floor of the pagoda offers a roughly fifty percent increase in cultivation speed. There are also other advantages...”

Jack’s eyes widened. “What about the final floor?”

“The final floor?” The Sage laughed again. “With your current strength, even the first floor is a stretch. As for the final floor, nobody goes there. Even the current number one outer disciple, Min Ling, can only cultivate at the sixth floor.”

Jack considered it. *Makes sense. If my body weighed ten million pounds, I would just become paste.*

“The pagoda also helps with breakthroughs. Unfortunately, I cannot enter,” Dorman added in a sad voice. “Even if I successfully became a disciple and reached the 950 ranking, my weight has over-doubled due to my current form."

A hint of pity entered Jack's heart—Dorman was an extremely talented cultivator who'd bitten off more than he could chew. Now, he was trapped here, unable to either progress or leave, and he was forced to just watch as his potential dried out.

Oh, what the hell? We come from the same planet.

"Hey, Dorman," he said. "If I manage to get more resources in the future, I will definitely save some Dao stones to help you break through as well."

Dorman's eyes shone. "You would do that for me?"

"Absolutely."

"Thank you, Jack. Your words mean a lot to me. I will engrave this kindness into my heart."

"You don't have to go that far. Just don't forget about your home planet."

Hearing that, Dorman lowered his gaze in shame. He'd heard about the war that occurred on Earth. In fact, he would have joined if he wasn't trapped here.

But what could he say? Getting trapped was his own fault, and at the end of the day, he wasn't there when his planet needed him. All he could do was swallow the shame.

Jack did not wish to press the issue further. "I'll go test out the pagoda," he said.

"Then, I'll return to my cabin," the Sage replied. "No sense in watching the walls. Drop by later to drink some tea."

"I'll wait for you," Dorman said, raising his head with bright eyes. "Cultivating here or elsewhere makes little difference. I'll accompany you after you exit."

Jack gave him a deep look. This Dorman...

Back on Earth, during the Integration Tournament, Dorman had been cold and arrogant. He refused to put anyone in his eyes, refused to consider others, and had only acknowledged Jack after the two of them tied in a spar. Even after they met again in Trial Planet, Dorman's attitude hadn't changed much.

Now, Jack could see that Dorman's arrogance had been beaten out of him. He'd arrived at the Cathedral, where every single person was an outstanding, otherworldly talent. Here, Dorman was only average, and he had faced failure repeatedly. He could neither progress nor leave. Moreover, he had been trapped in a form that severely constrained his battle prowess, driving him further down to the bottom of the barrel.

It must have been a cold wake-up call...

That arrogant young man had been tempered, finally losing his cold heart and becoming earnest. He could now see past his pride. Jack had done him a favor by promising to help him in the future, so Dorman would wait outside the Heavy Pagoda for however long it took.

He had matured.

Jack nodded slowly, acknowledging Dorman in his heart. When he promised to give him some Dao stones before, it was only on account of them being from the same planet. Now, he genuinely wanted to help.

"Good," he said. "I don't know how long I'll take. If you get bored or tired, feel free to leave."

Dorman raised a brow. "You know you only get one hour, right?"

"I do?"

"You're ranked 950. You can enter the pagoda, but only for one hour a month. The next increment is at ranking 900, where you get two hours a month."

"Oh."

Jack hadn't known that. One hour was very little time. It was clearly meant to let the low-ranked disciples get a taste of the pagoda's benefits, making them strive harder for higher ranks.

"See you in an hour," Jack said, then boldly strode toward the pagoda. Dorman plopped his ass down where he stood, closed his eyes, and entered meditation.

His discipline was good.

The Sage had already left, so Jack approached the pagoda alone. The outside was empty, and the only person present was an Envoy, who was apparently responsible for managing the pagoda.

"Hello," Jack greeted him. "I am Jack Rust, ranked 950. I would like to enter the Heavy Pagoda please."

The Envoy shot him a glance. She was an older-looking human, with gray hair caught in a tight bun and simple robes hanging from her shoulders. Despite her old age, her body seemed robust and powerful, and her gaze was naturally hard—like a gladiator granny.

"One hour," she said, then closed her eyes again.

"Thank you."

Jack approached the first floor.

Each floor had its own entrance, but there were no stairs. To enter the second floor, one had to jump there or fly. Of course, to a cultivator who could handle the second floor, reaching it was a trivial matter.

Jack only had one hour, but he could enter any floor he wished. Naturally, he chose the first. He approached the door—a massive, unadorned block of dark stone—and pushed it open. It was heavy. Far too heavy. He had to use part of his Dao to open it, and yet, as the block of stone swung open, it made no sound at all.

The inside of the pagoda was pitch-black and completely silent. It was like entering a nightmare. Jack took a step inside.

The moment he did, the sky crashed down on his shoulders. The already extreme gravity doubled. Jack gasped, finding it hard to stay on his feet. He rapidly rotated his Dao. Even standing here consumed a frightening amount of energy. He could spare it for some minutes, but after that, he would get tired. If he meditated for too long and passed his limits, he could become unable to walk out.

Perhaps the one hour limit wasn't to tease him, but to protect him.

Jack gritted his teeth and endured the exertion. He forced himself forward, every step a hurdle. His perception spread out, and to his surprise, he found it was limited to within three feet of his person. Anything beyond that vanished like a stone thrown to the sea.

This had to be an effect of the pagoda's formation. It was probably meant to give privacy to the meditating cultivators. After all, nobody liked being watched, especially in such a demanding environment.

However, Jack also noticed a thin stream of Dao energy under his feet. It was flowing inward, as if showing him the path. It made sense. If he had to spend ten minutes looking for an empty mat in the darkness while dodging cross-legged cultivators, the pagoda would be nothing more than a joke.

Jack followed the thin stream of Dao between his feet. Every step was hard, but he pushed through. The stream led him in a curved path, presumably avoiding other cultivators, before a meditation mat finally entered his perception range. He couldn't see it, but he perceived it as made of gold. As he sat down, it was freezing to the touch, though that also helped calm his mind.

Now, I guess I meditate...

Jack was stranded in darkness, enduring extreme gravity, and the natural coldness of space. His purple robes clung to his body, and his dark hair was plastered to the back of his neck, the roots of each hair pulling on his skin as if they wanted to jump out. Jack's Dao was constantly active, neutralizing a large portion of the gravity, but even what remained was hard for his body to endure.

He pulled up his status screen, specifically observing his main stats.

Strength: 1775
Dexterity: 1780
Constitution: 1775

His titles also gave him a combined 100% increased efficacy for all his stats. All things considered, his Physical substats were at an effective 3500 points, roughly, which was seven hundred times greater than the average pre-System human.

With the current gravity at two thousand times that of Earth, and also the fact that his body wasn't optimized for such conditions… no wonder his waist hurt.

Still, Jack closed his eyes and attempted to cultivate. A small part of his mind remained vigilant—if an enemy approached him in the darkness, or if the drain on his energy became too much, he would immediately wake up and be ready to react.

Besides that small part of his mind, the rest of him closed out the world. Everything washed away. Even the immense weight was only a faint echo in the distance. His Dao Tree pulsed with power, and the surrounding Dao became his to wield.

At the same time, the meditation mat under him activated as well, drawing at the Fist-related Dao particles and pushing away everything else.

Jack fell into the familiar practice of meditation.

Though his progress in the D-Grade was mostly made through killing others, he'd actually spent most of his time meditating. It had almost become second nature. His perception spread out gently like a thousand slender fingers, picking out the Fist-adjacent Dao particles and drawing them inside his pores. From there, they traveled to his chest, where his soul was located, and slipped in. Another part of Jack's perception then pushed them inside his Dao Tree, where they filled it with vitality.

Normally, as Jack had already reached the limits of the D-Grade, cultivating like this would not bring any benefits. No matter how much power he crammed into his Dao Tree, its total capacity could increase no further until he broke through. He was only doing this now to increase his familiarity with the Dao of the Fist. Any excess energy would just disperse.

However, to his surprise, the energy actually accumulated!

Jack's closed eyes flickered. He drew short breaths due to excitement. The increased density in here increased his rate of cultivation, which meant he would progress faster if he wasn't already at the limit. To top it off, the pagoda's formation actually had a secondary benefit. Somehow, the Dao was artificially packed together, slightly decreasing its volume by increasing its density. That allowed Jack to accumulate more of it inside his Dao Tree, effectively supercharging it. This excess energy would eventually disperse, of course, but it wasn't instant. He could maintain this state for a few minutes.

Inside the Heavy Pagoda, the total energy he could accumulate had risen!

Jack's heart was jumping in excitement. The reason he needed Dao stones, the main reason he couldn't break through right now, was the limited amount of energy he could fit in his Dao Tree. If the Heavy Pagoda allowed him to temporarily increase that limit, even by a little... it could decrease the number of Dao stones he needed.

It could speed up his breakthrough!

Just by the little bit he'd experienced already, Jack estimated that if he filled up his Dao Tree here, he would only need fifteen Dao stones to break through, not twenty. That could already save him months of effort.

And this was just the first floor of the pagoda. Higher up, the Dao density would be even greater. A crazy thought entered Jack's mind.

What if I entered a higher floor?

CHAPTER ELEVEN
DON CRANXIAO

WHILE JACK DISCOVERED THE WONDERS OF THE HEAVY PAGODA, DORMAN waited outside. As a non-disciple, his privileges were limited. Let alone entering the Heavy Pagoda, even existing in its vicinity was a stretch.

As Dorman cultivated, using the ambient Dao to nourish his Dao Tree, a rough voice reached him from behind.

"Look at that," it said. "The fat beggar!"

Dorman opened his eyes and turned around. A tall, barbaric-looking human stood there. His hairy chest was shirtless, revealing dense musculature, while long gray hair floated over his tanned shoulders. He had arms the width of tree trunks and thighs like barrels. Moreover, his handsome face was warped into a rough, aggressive scowl.

This wasn't a human though. His eyes were gray.

"Don Cranxiao," Dorman muttered calmly, remaining seated. "What do you want today?"

"Come on, beggar. Is that any way to speak to your daddy?"

Cranxiao's smile was wide and predatory. Seeing that Dorman wasn't going to fall for his provocations, his gaze sharpened. "I am not here for you today. I heard that a man called Jack Rust came to the pagoda, so I wanted to take a look."

At this, Dorman showed some reaction. His brows fell, and his gaze was tinged with worry. "What do you want with Jack?"

"You know him?" Cranxiao burst into roaring laughter. "Birds of a feather flock together! I guess beggars and weaklings really are the same thing!"

"I said, what do you want with him?"

"Don't try your luck. Be a good boy and tell me how long ago he went in. Otherwise, you won't escape a beating today."

Don Cranxiao was an outer disciple ranked 811th. He was at the three-fruit boundary—the upper limit of the early C-Grade. Like most disciples of the Black Hole Church, he could jump tiers to fight. His actual battle strength was approaching the late C-Grade.

However, as far as power or talent were concerned, Don Cranxiao was only ordinary. His greatest discerning feature on the Cathedral was his complete disregard for reputation.

Around the lower-ranked outer disciples, Cranxiao was known as a complete bully. He wasn't like Marcus William, who simply used a heavy hand to oppress his enemies. Cranxiao would go around and beat up others for no reason at all. Moreover, he only targeted people weaker than himself. He cultivated the Dao of Tyranny, so this incessant bullying was a form of cultivation for him.

Unfortunately, the Church wouldn't interfere in battles between the outer disciples. Everyone was on their own, and Cranxiao was allowed to rampage free.

Due to his conduct and zero consideration for face, Don Cranxiao had a peculiar place in the Cathedral. He worked as easy muscle. Whenever a cultivator wanted to suppress another but couldn't or didn't want to act personally, they could just hire Cranxiao. For one Dao stone, he would kick the shit out of anyone under the ranking of 850.

Currently, as Cranxiao came looking for Jack, it didn't take a genius to realize who hired him. Marcus William had heard about his wife's humiliation and wanted to take revenge.

Dorman took a deep breath and rose to his feet. Compared to the towering Don Cranxiao, he seemed tiny and wholly unfit to fight. Their cultivations were far apart, too. This was absolutely not a battle he could win.

"What's one more beating?" he asked with a smile, reaching for his daggers. "All I have left is my honor. You aren't getting a word out of me."

The large man was surprised. Then, his lips curved into a malicious grin.

Jack was peacefully cultivating in the Heavy Pagoda, admiring the mysteries of dense Dao and marveling at how it could help him break through faster. However, only thirty minutes after coming in, he was awoken from meditation by an urgent feeling.

His muscles were sore. His chest was tight. His Dao, which partly neutralized the extreme force of gravity, was strained and on the verge of running out.

I need to get out of here!

He shot up, almost stumbling from the effort. His legs were numb and refused to work properly. It took him three tries to take a step. With the weight of a mountain pressing onto his shoulders, he slowly took one step after the other, following the thin stream of Dao that guided him outward.

When he reached the unadorned block of black stone, he almost couldn't open it. After he did, when the first crack of light was revealed, he finally breathed a sigh of relief.

I must be careful, he reminded himself. *When cultivating in the pagoda, I must save the energy to leave.*

Finally, he made it out. The thousandfold gravity was suddenly as light as a feather, and Jack's Dao exclaimed in joy as it began to replenish itself. He still felt weak and exhausted—a good few hours of meditation would be great right now.

However, right as he thought that, he froze in his steps. Two daggers lay on the ground. Thirty feet away, a large, bare-chested, muscular man stood straight, using a single hand to hold Dorman in the air by the throat.

Dorman bled from the nose. His arms hung limply, twitching. His robes were torn, revealing all sorts of black and blue bruises. As for his left eye, it was swollen to the point where it looked completely unnatural.

That's when the large man spotted him. "There you are," he said, turning back to Dorman. "It wasn't so tough, was it?"

He then flicked his arm and tossed Dorman, where he crash-landed on the ground under the force of a thousand gravities. Finally, the man wiped his hands on his pants as if to clear away the filth.

Jack's complexion darkened.

"What's going on?" he asked, kneeling to check on Dorman. "Who are you?"

"I'm Don Cranxiao. Pleased to make your acquaintance, though you won't be." The large man gave Jack a wide, toothy grin. "I'm here to make your life hell."

"What exactly is your problem?"

"Careful," Dorman said from the ground, coughing up a bit of blood. "He's... hired."

Jack wasn't sure what was going on, but he could easily enough surmise a good guess. His only enemies here were Marcus William and Ley Vice—one of them had hired this big brutish guy to kick his ass.

But how was Dorman involved?

"An outer disciple, even one as weak as yourself, shouldn't touch beggars," Cranxiao said patronizingly. "To be honest, I will wash my hands after this."

"Who the hell is a beggar?" Jack barked out. "If you're here for me, why did you harm Dorman?"

"I was bored. But don't worry—he's used to it by now." Seeing Jack's incredulous stare, Cranxiao broke out into roaring laughter. "Oh, that's hilarious! He didn't tell you? That homeless beggar by your feet is my favorite punching bag!"

Firecrackers erupted inside Jack's chest. His exhaustion disappeared as righteous fury took over. "Is that true, Dorman?" he asked, but the young man did not respond. It didn't matter. The gritting of his teeth was answer enough.

Jack stood up slowly, a wind of Dao billowing around him. The void was colored purple. Stars shimmered into existence, forming constellations around his body, while green shadows flickered through his eyes. A piercing, bone-biting cold spread out, making Cranxiao's shorts flutter.

"Oh, you're angry?" he taunted Jack with a lazy smile. "What are you going to do? Tickle me?"

Suddenly, Cranxiao's own Dao erupted from his body like a burning, oppressive desert wind. A colossal force rammed into Jack's Dao Domain. It shattered. The purple stars winked out, and Jack's face went pale. It was as if he were tied naked to a plank and Cranxiao stood over him holding a steel, barbed club. The club came crashing down.

In the next moment, Jack's Dao roared out. The Dao Root of Indomitable Will flared, breaking the illusion, and Jack's Brutalizing Aura spread, countering the other man's skill.

Though he stumbled, he could still stand.

"Oh?" Cranxiao said with a hint of surprise. "You possess a skill similar to my Terrorizing Aura?"

"I will destroy you," Jack replied with conviction. This man disgusted him. If he didn't plant his fist in that ugly face, he wouldn't be a cultivator of the Fist. The question was, could he do it right now?

"Oh yeah? Give it a shot, see what you can achieve."

Jack was painfully aware of his own weakness. This man was far stronger than the planetary overseer he'd once barely defeated, while Jack was currently exhausted from enduring the Heavy Pagoda. Even putting the exhaustion aside, he wouldn't be the other man's match.

The Dao of the Fist was that of a warrior. Unstoppable, unfettered, laughing in the face of the enemy. Not suicidal.

Sapasun, the canine who'd once broken all of Jack's limbs, taught him that lesson. A warrior never loses their mind. They always strive for victory. That lesson was precisely why Jack was still alive, while Sapasun had died to a single slap in front of the entire galaxy.

However, stepping back now would just make him a coward!

"I challenge you to a duel," Jack declared solemnly. The Dao billowed around him, an ominous wind of death. "Right now, our cultivations are too far apart. Give me three months. In three months, we will meet on the fields, and we will do battle with our honor on the line."

Three months was the maximum he could stand. Anything more would be too long. Moreover, though the Sage had agreed to help him break through after six months, special circumstances called for special measures. Three would have to work.

If he did break through before the duel, he had absolute confidence in defeating Cranxiao. As for fighting right now... that would only be venting his own frustration. A true warrior was not controlled by their base emotions. A defeat now would harm him in the long run. A promised duel would keep his anger alive, forcing him to his limits for three months, at which point he would defeat Cranxiao and take revenge. Most importantly, promising a duel at a later point was the only way not to retreat right now.

"Three months? Fool!" Cranxiao laughed. "What do I care about three hours or three months? I will beat you up today, tomorrow, and the day after. I will show up at your house every week for a little lesson. Why would I wait?"

"If I lose in three months, I will give you twenty Dao stones," Jack declared. Cranxiao's eyes shone with avarice, but Jack wasn't done yet. "Moreover... in a battle between cultivators, it is hard to restrain one's strength. Accidents can happen. In our duel three months from now, we can agree that if one of us happens to kill the other, there will be no consequences. If such an accident occurs, the debt will be paid by the loser's friends."

Cranxiao's eyes widened further. His lips broke into a wide smile.

On the Cathedral, fighting others was tacitly allowed by the Envoys, but stealing was not. Cranxiao couldn't just take the Dao stones of weaker cultivators.

A gambling stake was entirely different. If Jack agreed to owe him twenty stones, then Cranxiao could certainly take that amount! Even if Jack didn't possess any at that point, Cranxiao would have the right to pick up Jack's yearly Dao stone for the next twenty years, or harass his friends for those stones, provided they agreed to it before the fight. To him, who had stayed here for two millennia already, twenty years was nothing!

As for the second part of Jack's promise... Cranxiao couldn't help but lick his lips. Though he beat up others, he couldn't kill them. Agreement on a life or death duel was naturally allowed. Killing a talented opponent would enhance his Dao of Tyranny by leaps and bounds!

But Don Cranxiao was not an idiot. For Jack to offer something like this, he must have had confidence in winning. Cranxiao racked his brains for traps but found none. Regardless of treasures, breaking through to the C-Grade was very difficult—otherwise, everyone would do it. Even assuming Jack was talented enough and could acquire enough treasures in three months to breakthrough, Cranxiao remained absolutely certain of victory.

As for the Life Drop, since Ley Vice and her friends hadn't recognized it before, Cranxiao didn't know about it. Even if he did, it would change little.

After Jack broke through, he would be a one-fruit C-Grade. Cranxiao was a three-fruit C-Grade, and he possessed enough battle power to match a normal six-fruit cultivator. Moreover, his heavily

Strength-oriented stats gave him an almost unfair advantage on the Cathedral, as he could resist the gravity better than others.

Under those circumstances, there was no way Cranxiao could lose!

"Good!" he exclaimed, hurrying to agree before Jack could change his mind. This was a pie that fell from the sky! "We have a deal! In three months, we will duel for twenty Dao stones, and any accidents will be forgiven. The esteemed Envoy over there can be our witness. Deal, Jack Rust, deal!"

The Envoy responsible for managing the Heavy Pagoda was just to the side. Hearing the agreement between the two parties, she could only shake her head in disappointment. "I witnessed," she said. In her heart, she didn't think Jack had any chance of winning. She could only lament that such a talent could be so stupid.

Like most newcomers, he doesn't understand that everyone here is talented... she thought, sighing inwardly. *Whatever. That is his path to take. If luck favors him, he will escape death and use that experience to temper himself. If not, he can only blame himself.*

"Good," Jack said darkly. "It is a deal. Don Cranxiao, we will meet in precisely three months from now. Until then, you cannot touch me!"

"Naturally. A deal is a deal. I wouldn't cheat," Cranxiao said, splitting his lips into a grin. "However, to ensure you don't forget about our promise, I might come by every month to play with my favorite punching bag. If you want to stop me... Hehe, don't blame me for fighting back."

"You wouldn't dare."

"Hah! I'm Don Cranxiao, kid—I do whatever I want!"

"If you touch Dorman, our duel is off."

"Oh, you would go back on your word so easily? Here's what we're gonna do. For the next three months, I won't touch you so you can cultivate at peace. But I will touch my punching bag, as well as anyone else I want. If that's not fine with you, just don't bother showing up in three months. If you want to challenge me at any time before that, feel free!"

Cranxiao laughed. As for Jack, his gaze bore deep into the other man's eyes, but there was nothing he could say. If he wanted to protect his friends, he couldn't rely on the enemy's conscience. He had to do it himself.

Said enemy was currently feeling proud of himself. He wasn't leaving anything to chance. By targeting Dorman, he could pressure Jack into a dead-end, either forcing him to step in and take a beating or doubt his own Dao. As for Jack bringing any backers to stop that from happening...

Idiot! I'm Don Cranxiao! Half the high-rankers hire me regularly—if you want to find a backer, let's see if you can find someone stronger than I am!

Of course, Cranxiao was aware of Jack's relation to the Head Envoy, but someone like that wouldn't meddle in lowly affairs unless they were prepared to soil their reputation.

Even though Don Cranxiao had a hundred percent certainty in victory no matter what, he still played dirty. Under his rough exterior, he could be a calculating man. He didn't gain the qualifications to join the Black Hole Church by accident!

Jack's face darkened further, but there was nothing he could say to protect Dorman. He would have to find a way later. Before he could reply, Don Cranxiao laughed and turned away, walking into the distance.

"Enjoy your life, Jack Rust!" he shouted as he left. "See you in a month!"

Jack kept staring at the other man's back.

What a sly maneuver... In one month, I absolutely cannot let Dorman get beat up again because of me. I have to find someone to protect him... or stop Cranxiao myself.

Which was impossible. Even Jack, who knew his talent was far above that of Don Cranxiao, didn't have confidence in defeating him within a month. Hell, he didn't have confidence in beating him within three months. He just refused to step back.

Jack sighed. *Did I dig my own grave?*

CHAPTER TWELVE
CEASELESS MURDER GLOBE

After Don Cranxiao left, Jack remained silent for a moment. Then, he squatted next to Dorman. "Are you alright?"

"Yeah," Dorman coughed out in response. If anything, he looked more sad than hurt. "Sorry. This is my fault."

"You did nothing wrong." Jack placed a hand on the young man's shoulder. "If anything, you stood up for me. I will remember that. I also want to apologize—before, I thought you'd stolen that treasure because of greed. I didn't understand what you've been going through."

"It's okay. I'm used to it."

Dorman's words weren't offensive, just plain true. He was a teenager when Earth got Integrated, a teenager with an incomplete understanding of the world. He strove forward and reached great strength, ending in the top four of the Integration Tournament. Even after he joined Sage and the Black Hole Church, he remained alone in his mind.

So now, when he repeatedly failed and was beaten down, he suffered alone as well.

Jack gave a sad smile. "Can you walk?"

"In a few moments. My regeneration will kick in soon."

"Good. When you're ready, I'll walk you to your cabin."

Dorman chuckled darkly. "I have no cabin."

"No?"

"I am only a guest of the Church. If I want to stay somewhere, I have to pay for it. I've been living in the fields for the last few months."

Jack's heart clenched. To a cultivator, staying in a cabin or outside made little difference. It was the mental consolation of four walls and a roof that was priceless. It represented safety and privacy.

Dorman really had it rough.

"You'll be staying with me and Brock from now on," Jack said.

"What? I—"

"It wasn't a question. You're staying with us. I know a cabin may be crowded for three people, but having at least some privacy is infinitely better than none at all."

"But it's your cabin! I haven't earned it. I can't accept it."

"You don't need to. As I said, it wasn't a question." Jack smiled brightly. "Now, up you go."

He supported Dorman by the shoulders and pushed him up. After a lot of heaving and panting, the now-fat man managed to stand.

"Thanks," he said. "Life is difficult when you're wide."

"Tell me about it," Jack replied, wiping his forehead. Raising a mountain of fat in thousandfold gravity was not for the faint of heart. He struggled to imagine how Dorman could even walk.

His mind cut directly to the scene of Don Cranxiao easily holding up Dorman with one hand. His gaze darkened.

"Can you walk?" Jack asked again. This time, Dorman nodded, and the two of them got started on the way back.

Throughout all of this, the buff-old-lady Envoy remained completely unmoved thirty feet to the side. She hadn't raised a finger.

"Do you have confidence?" Dorman asked. "Against Cranxiao, I mean. I know you aren't stupid. Since you offered a duel, you probably have a plan."

Jack nodded. "The Sage promised to help me break through in six months. If I can convince him to move it up to three, then I'm confident."

"You know, Cranxiao is a genius, too. Everyone here is. He's only an early C-Grade, but he can fight almost like a late one."

"I can fight like an early C-Grade right now. If I break through, I got him."

Dorman's eyes widened. "For real?"

"For real."

The rest of the walk was in silence. Both remained in their own thoughts, considering the various problems plaguing them. Eventually, they entered the village, and Jack's cabin became visible. He pushed the door open and ushered Dorman inside.

"Hey, Brock," he said, finding that the brorilla hadn't moved at all since they left. "You remember Dorman, right? He has no house, so he'll be staying with us—if you don't mind."

Brock opened his eyes. He took in Dorman's beat-up look which hadn't fully healed, along with the awkwardness of his posture. He noticed the hidden worries clouding Jack's face.

Brock nodded. "Hey, bro," he told Dorman, standing up to clasp his hand. "Welcome home."

Dorman tightened his lips.

"Thank you again, both of you," he said. "This means a lot to me. I... I promise I will pay you back."

"Focus on taking care of yourself for now," Jack replied. "You're safe here. When Cranxiao shows up in a month, I won't let him touch you."

Dorman opened and closed his mouth. Finally, he said, "What are you going to do?"

"I don't know yet. But I'll find a way."

He did have a few ideas. For starters, breaking through within a month was impossible, and so was increasing his strength without breaking through. The best he could achieve was a skill upgrade, but that was far from enough to bridge the enormous gap between himself and Don Cranxiao.

Therefore, his only way to protect Dorman was to make connections. As for how he would do that, he had to either impress people with his strength, befriend them by being awesome, or make them owe him a favor.

And the best way to earn favors was to help them when they needed it.

Jack's heart was set on the way of the Fist. His main goal would always be to punch people, which was why he originally hesitated at the idea of becoming a healer. However, when cultivation was of little benefit, studying could be a good use of his time.

On one hand, he might be able to earn a few Dao stones. The Cathedral lacked healers, so even if he wasn't good, there had to be something he could offer.

On the other hand, the more he thought about it, involving his Life Drop with healing would make it a huge gift that only kept on giving, granting him vast amounts of Life Dao. The four-armed battle form was only one of its applications. Now that he could reveal the Life Drop and openly study it, he had a feeling there were many more benefits to reap.

Plus, there was the mysterious world inside his Dao Tree, where that tremendous turtle annihilated Jack with a single snort. That world had to be hiding some secrets. And, as everyone knows, secrets equal power.

Therefore, Jack decided to study at least the basics of healing with the end goal of using it to amplify his punching power.

Before that, there was another thing he wanted to do. Ever since he'd arrived at the Cathedral, he'd been hearing that everyone here was talented. But how much? How did he compare to them? His battle against Ley Vice was hardly satisfactory. He wanted a real battle to get his blood flowing.

"I'll be back soon," Jack said, leaving the cabin.

"Have fun, bro."

He walked alone through the village, heading for a massive structure in the distance. It wasn't the ranking obelisk, but a thousand-foot-tall stone dome with no visible windows. Its only entrance was a human-sized door near its base.

As he approached, he noticed a small group of people gathered outside the entrance, discussing spiritedly.

"Hey," Jack said, heading for the group. He put on a smile. "I'm Jack. Nice to meet you."

The other three people stopped talking to look at him. One was human, another was a mosquito-like humanoid, and the third was, surprisingly, a female djinn—a small blue person. All three had cultivations at the early C-Grade.

"Hey," the djinn replied. "Are you a new disciple?"

"Yeah. Just arrived today."

"Mhm. And you came to challenge the Ceaseless Murder Globe?"

"Who wouldn't?"

That was the dome's name. It was the Ceaseless Murder Globe, the magic formation used to rank the Church's outer disciples. Jack didn't know how it worked, but if its name was anything to go by, you had to go in and murder stuff.

That was right up his alley.

The djinn looked at him with pity. "Entering at only the peak D-Grade is pointless. You'll just get injured and have to recuperate."

She didn't seem particularly warm to Jack—after all, she hadn't given him her name—but she at least offered him an honest warning. Jack inwardly sighed in relief. After meeting Ley Vice, Marcus William, and Don Cranxiao in quick succession, he'd begun suspecting that everyone here was an asshole. It was great to know that wasn't the case.

Every faction had good and bad apples, especially one as competitive as the Black Hole Church.

"Thank you for the warning," he replied. "My self-healing is pretty good, so it shouldn't be a problem. I just want to see where I stand."

The three cultivators exchanged glances. In their eyes, Jack was just an upstart who was used to being a genius in his home faction. Many people were arrogant when they arrived at the Cathedral, but with the exception of some truly monstrous talents, all of them were quickly humbled.

"Suit yourself," the mosquitoid said. Its voice was buzzing. "Just be careful. You can't die in the Globe, but you can be severely injured. If you can't take it anymore, just yell that you give up."

"I will. Thank you very much," Jack said, nodding at the three cultivators before heading for the Globe.

"Ah, wait a moment!" the djinn shouted behind him. "Our friend is inside. You have to wait your turn."

"Oh, okay."

Jack waited. The three cultivators didn't seem very willing to include him in their conversation, so he just awkwardly stood by the side. Well, to each their own, he thought and sat down cross-legged to meditate. While he couldn't increase his power any more before breaking through, he could ponder on the Dao of the Fist.

Three minutes later, the Globe rumbled. Its door slid upward, revealing a dark opening from which a human walked out. Though he was handsome, his hair was disheveled, his pink robes were torn in places, and he was panting.

"You're out!" the djinn woman exclaimed, rushing to greet him. "How did it go?"

The man smiled. "Wait and see."

All four of them turned toward the obelisk. Jack, following their gazes, looked over as well.

In that moment, the obelisk gave a low rumble. The names on its lower half turned fuzzy, some magic moving them. Before Jack's shocked eyes, one name rose by around forty places, stopping at the number 793. The name was Osmu Sosmu.

"You did it!" the djinn woman exclaimed. "Top eight hundred! This is amazing, Osmu! You can leave now!"

The handsome man revealed a bright smile. In truth, since he'd just broken into the middle C-Grade, reaching 793 was not particularly impressive. It was even toward the lower end.

However, that mattered little because he was finally in the top eight hundred. He could use the teleporters to return to his home galaxy and see his family!

The four cultivators celebrated, not paying much attention to Jack. He wasn't too bothered, either. The one who'd just exited the Globe was the strongest of the four, but he was only ranked 793rd. Cranxiao was 811th. Even if Jack befriended these people, they would never help him stop Cranxiao from bullying Dorman, as their relative strengths were too close. He needed to find someone ranked far higher than Cranxiao.

Still, Jack was a cordial man.

"Congratulations," he said, standing slowly. "I only just arrived, but I suspect that is an excellent result!"

Jack didn't know what the rankings signified yet. He had mistaken the other cultivators' excitement and assumed the handsome man had done great, when he actually hadn't. As a result, the man only gave him an odd glance before replying, "Thanks."

Jack didn't bother anymore. He approached the entrance of the Globe, where the managing Envoy told him the rules. Basically, the formation would stop either when he was about to die or when he yelled that he gave up. Until then, he had to kill as many opponents as he could.

"Can my ranking drop?" Jack asked. After all, he was currently ranked 950th, but reaching that level through the Globe sounded difficult.

"That cannot happen," the Envoy replied, giving him an odd look. "The only way for your ranking to drop is for others to surpass you."

"I see. Thank you."

Jack stepped inside the open door, which closed behind him.

As for the other four cultivators, after exchanging glances with each other, they didn't leave yet. They wanted to see how Jack would do. Mostly, they wanted to see his reaction when he exited, and possibly comfort him a bit to ensure he wasn't traumatized by this failure.

After all, unless it was someone ridiculously gifted, a peak D-Grade couldn't defeat even the first opponent inside the Globe.

CHAPTER THIRTEEN
FIGHTING SHADOWS

Jack stepped into the Ceaseless Murder Globe. Besides a giant lamp stuck to the roof, there was nothing. Only black stone as far as the eye could see.

The lamplight fell down like a curtain, illuminating the center of the Globe. Of course, any C or D-Grade cultivator could use their perception to see perfectly well in the darkness—this lamp was probably meant to accommodate the users of light or darkness-oriented Daos.

The Globe had air inside it, but it was silent. Completely silent. Jack walked to the center, his steps echoing like gongs. The feeling was almost reverent, as if he'd stumbled into the basement of a church where he absolutely shouldn't be. The heavy air was pregnant with danger.

The moment his feet touched the light, a ripple of energy spread over the Globe, and the magic formation activated. Jack only sensed the Dao gathering like a storm opposite him. It coalesced into a humanoid shape, a warrior wielding a longsword. The shape had no features—it was a ghost formed of the Dao. Its body a shadow.

Its cultivation was at the early C-Grade, and a weak one, too.

This ghost was close to the bottom of all C-Grades, but it remained a C-Grade.

Without saying anything, it charged. Its feet produced dull thuds on the stone—its sword left no shadow. It reached Jack in an instant and cleaved down.

Jack's face blossomed with a grin. This was it. This feeling of urgent threat, the surging blood, the heat in his chest, the ice in his brain. This was the battle he was made for.

He clenched his fist and smashed it forward. His middle knuckle met the sword blade, and a sharp pain traveled up his arm as if his bones were jittery. His knuckle bled, but it was fine. A moment later, the wound disappeared.

The sword was pushed back. Jack's grin widened.

The gap between D and C-Grade was wide. Bridging it to fight was almost impossible. The cultivators outside had been reasonable to assume that Jack, a peak D-Grade, couldn't defeat even the first and weakest opponent in the Ceaseless Murder Globe.

But they didn't know Jack. They didn't know about his perfect foundation and alignment with his Dao. They didn't know about his collection of high-level System titles. They didn't know about the disasters he'd survived and the skills he'd gained in the process.

Even without the Life Drop, Jack was close to the limit of what D-Grades could achieve. It was time to test that.

His figure flashed through the Globe. His steps blurred. His punches shot out like meteors. Explosions rumbled. Fist met blade over and over, sparks rising when neither gave way. Jack and the figure seemed equally matched. After twenty exchanges, Jack focused inward.

His Dao Domain burst out, a purple sea of stars. Fist-shaped meteors sailed through the void, circling Jack, while the stars fell close to his body and formed a constellation. His fists clenched harder—ready to pounce.

In his domain, Jack was king.

However, to his surprise, the ghost released a domain of its own.

A sharp, metallic gray covered the Globe, contesting against his purple. Every gust of wind and air vibration turned into a blade as even the air was sliced apart. The ghost's sword flared with sharp light.

Jack exclaimed in wonder. This ghost had a Dao of its own!

This is even more interesting!

Jack had planned to end this quickly so he could see what opponents lay ahead... but now, he just wanted to fight. If this shadow could use skills as well, it would be a worthy challenge.

His feet tread on stone, bringing him before the ghost. Their domains clashed and ground against each other, each pressing harder now that their sources were nearby. The gray domain released a shrill scream, like a sword grinding on stone. The purple one produced a series of booms like a hundred fists striking out at once.

As Jack approached the ghost, he held nothing back besides the Life Drop. Brutalizing Aura erupted from his body, piercing into the shadow's psyche. Just like a real cultivator, it responded—a hint of dread appeared in its heart, reducing its power and increasing Jack's.

At the same time, the domain's purple light focused around Jack's fist, pulsing with increased intensity. He reared it back. The purple light was drawn deeper inside the fist, spiking in intensity and explosiveness. It combusted into purple flames that were barely held at bay. Faint purple stars trailed behind the punch.

He shot it forward. The ghost, sensing the power of this attack, slashed out. Its blade blurred as if there were three swords coming at once. It had to be a skill.

Mid-swing, Jack used a small part of his Dao to punch through space itself. He wanted to teleport behind the shadow, but he failed. Space here was hard! If it was normally a curtain he could part, it was now a wall he had to drill through.

Seeing the triple sword approach, he roared out and poured even more power into teleporting. He almost failed when space finally cracked open. Jack was sucked inside just as the three swords slashed through his previous location. He reappeared behind the ghost, only now completing his swing.

To its credit, the ghost reacted in time, ducking to avoid his punch. However, that was easier said than done. Meteor Punch impacted the air right above its head, all that compressed power erupting at once. This strike contained momentum and terrible striking power, but it also included an explosion powered by the great compression of Jack's Dao.

As this explosion rang out, the air was blown away, and the ground rumbled. Even space shivered lightly. The shadow's head was caved in, and lacking any form of regeneration, it dissipated.

Jack had won.

Before he could breathe a sigh of relief, the ambient Dao gathered again. Two shadows appeared, one holding a warhammer and the other a long staff. They were still early C-Grades, but each of these shadows was noticeably stronger than the previous one.

Jack, still panting, rejoiced in the excitement rising up inside him. This Ceaseless Murder Globe... was much to his liking!

He summoned the Life Drop. Life energy rampaged inside his body. He grew a foot taller, and two extra arms sprouted from under his armpits. He became stronger, faster, more durable, and far more regenerative.

"Bring it on!" he shouted, charging forward.

From outside the Globe, there was no way to tell how the person inside was doing. The four cultivators still waited, but they were beginning to wonder.

"It's been half a minute already," the female djinn said. "How has he lasted against the first opponent this long?"

The strongest of the four, the human who reached the middle C-Grade, cupped his chin. "Since he was accepted as an outer disciple at the D-Grade, he must possess great talent. If his Dao is one related to speed, he can probably last a minute or so by just running around... which is pointless, obviously, but exiting too soon would be embarrassing."

"Hmm, yes. That must be why." The other three nodded in agreement.

"I just wish he won't overtax himself due to stubbornness," the djinn girl added, sighing. "It's better to leave early than to suffer great injuries."

The handsome man gave a sad smile. He had once been in Jack's position as well. "That's the way of the world. Geniuses have to be humbled. Instead of being stubborn and dying in a real battlefield... experiencing defeat against the first shadow is much better."

Meanwhile, Jack crashed into the two shadows. He roared. Purple light flared in his surroundings, then was drawn into his fist and unleashed as a terrifying explosion that shook the air. The two shadows pulled back, then attacked him from one side each. The hammer-wielder smashed down in a heavy overhead strike, while the wizard compressed space around Jack to prevent him from escaping.

Jack laughed. He never planned on dodging. His forte wasn't speed, but strength!

Brutalizing Aura billowed out. A hint of fear dug into the shadows' hearts, pulling out a miniscule amount of power and giving it to Jack. This skill was most effective against weaker opponents.

Still, Jack smashed a Meteor Punch upward. It clashed directly against the falling hammerhead. Cracking sounds echoed as half the bones in his arm were compressed, but his shoulder held. The hammer was pushed back, and so was Jack, gritting his teeth through the pain.

In the next moment, his regeneration fixed him up. His arm was good as new, but his opponent was unharmed as well.

Jack could try to fight them in a battle of attrition. However, he had no desire to do so. He hadn't come all the way here to act like a turtle against two shadows!

He roared. Power rolled out of his body in waves, amplifying his domain. The purple stars increased in brightness, resisting the hammer-wielder's oppressive air and the wizard's etherealness. Jack launched himself at the hammer shadow. His fist pulled back, readying another Meteor Punch. Before he arrived, he broke through space and appeared next to the wizard, striking down on him.

These shadows were smarter than the last. They were not caught by surprise. The wizard held his ground, conjuring a space-warping spike that could create a fist-sized hole through Jack's chest. At the same time, the hammer-wielder teleported beside him, smashing his hammer into Jack's ribs.

Jack needed to pull back his strike and defend. But he didn't. He was not afraid of pain!

Amidst crazed laugher, Jack's fist sailed on, crashing into the wizard's head and exploding it in shards of shadow.

At the same time, the space spike warped the right side of his ribs so hard they shattered. His flesh and muscles were warped as well, following the sudden curvature in space, and Jack felt like a chunk of his body was ripped clean off. The hammer struck his chest from the front, catapulting him backward and into a wall of the Globe. Jack felt like he'd been struck by a mountain. He fell to the ground and stayed there a moment, his vision fuzzy as the hammer-wielding shadow came to finish him off.

If the four cultivators outside could see him right now, their eyes would pop out from the shock. A peak D-Grade had endured the attacks of two early C-Grades at the same time—and lived!

Jack chuckled, spitting out some blood. The hellish pain was dying down, and his wounds were regenerating at a speed visible to the naked eye. Bones knit back together, muscle and sinew were mended, skin regrew. Before the shadow could approach, Jack was completely healthy again.

He rose to his feet, smiling with blood-stained teeth. "Nice try. But I'm still here."

Jack's greatest advantage was not strength, but durability! Neutron Star Body gave his body extreme density and resilience, enabling him to survive the two deadly attacks. Then, as long as he didn't die instantly, the Life Drop's overwhelming energy would rapidly heal his wounds. He could recover from even life-threatening injuries in the blink of an eye.

Actually, this regeneration was too abnormal. Perhaps exploring it further and becoming a healer was indeed a great idea.

Seeing him stand up, the hammer-wielding shadow paused as if in disbelief. Jack gave it the finger. "Come get me, asshole."

The shadow charged. So did Jack. Fueled by his previous pain, the entire purple domain was sucked into his fist, where it was tightly compressed. The hammer struck down. Jack teleported behind the shadow, which teleported behind him in turn. Jack then spent a large amount of energy to punch through space yet again, re-teleporting over the shadow's head and smashing his fist down.

The hammer had no time to turn. Fist impacted hard flesh and caved it in. A colossal shockwave erupted, flooding the Globe with purple flames, and the hammer-wielding shadow dissipated.

Jack landed on his feet, panting heavily. The Life Drop contained vast amounts of energy, but it could only be used for regeneration. Everything else, be it attacking, defending, teleporting, or using his various skills, was solely supported by his Dao Tree. Right now, after fighting in thousandfold gravity for so long, he was basically running on fumes. He couldn't even teleport anymore.

The Dao gathered again. This time, three shadows appeared—and, though they remained early C-Grades, their power was vastly superior to the wizard and hammer-wielder he'd just fought.

Jack shook his head. "This is enough," he said. The Globe rumbled, while the shadows bowed and disappeared.

"It's been two minutes..." the djinn girl said, looking at the Globe with confusion. "What's going on? Do you think he managed to defeat the first shadow?"

"Impossible," the mosquitoid cut her off. "The first shadow has the power of a one-fruit C-Grade. To defeat it while in the D-Grade is just too difficult."

"Hmm," the handsome human muttered. "It is difficult... but not impossible. The difference between the D and C-Grades is roughly equivalent to three fruits inside the C-Grade."

"Are you saying he can jump three tiers to fight?" the djinn girl asked, her brows rising. "Isn't that too much?"

"Heh... You guys have only been here for a short time, but I've seen some of the high-rankers duel. For some of them, let alone jumping three tiers, even four isn't a problem!"

"Are you serious!"

"Absolutely. We'll see when he comes out. If his ranking is any better than 990, it means he defeated the first shadow. In that case, he's a rare talent even in the Black Hole Church! We should hurry and befriend him before he soars through the ranks!"

In the Ceaseless Murder Globe, the rankings up to 990 were for those with auxiliary powers who had little to no battle strength. They couldn't even defeat the first shadow. As for those who could defeat the first shadow but not the pair that came after, they were also very few, and they took up the positions between 990 and 975.

"What if he defeats the hammer-wizard pair as well?" asked the djinn girl.

The handsome human only laughed. "Then he would rank better than 975... but that's impossible. Only extreme geniuses, like Lady Min Ling, could achieve such a feat at his cultivation. If that happens, I'll eat my robes!"

At that moment, the Globe's door slid open. Jack walked out, still panting and disheveled, but uninjured.

"See?" said the insectoid. "He is tired but has no wounds. I told you he was just running away."

"Hmm. Yeah, that must be the case. I guess I was thinking too deep into it," the handsome human said.

Jack did not pay them any attention. He turned to the Envoy who operated the Globe and said, "Thank you for the experience. Could you tell me how I did?"

The four cultivators gave him a strange look. "Just look at the obelisk," the djinn girl reminded him. "If you achieved anything, your name there will move."

"My name is already at a higher ranking than my result would indicate. Therefore, I believe it will not move."

"What?"

They looked at the obelisk again. They hadn't checked before, but since Jack had already given them his name, they easily spotted him: 950, Jack Rust!

"What!"

Before they could ask anything more, however, the Envoy spoke up. "I can tell you where your current result would place you," he said. "Let me check. It's at..."

The Envoy—a well-dressed human man—hesitated. His eyes widened in disbelief.

"Well?" Jack asked innocently. "How did I do?"

"Uh... Excuse me. If your ranking wasn't already higher than that, you would have placed at..." He gulped. "959..."

CHAPTER FOURTEEN
CREATING AWE

As soon as the Envoy finished his words, the other four cultivators gasped.

959? There has to be a mistake!

In the Endless Murder Globe, the people who couldn't even defeat the first shadow ranked between 997 and 990. They were a sad minority. After that, the people who defeated the first shadow but lost to the next pair were ranked between 989 and 975.

Of course, this was the absolute bottom of the barrel on the Cathedral. Only the weakest or most utility-oriented disciples would place in those rankings. For everyone else, the first three battles of the Globe were considered a warm-up.

If placed amongst the entire Cathedral, Jack's result could be considered abysmal. However, what was his cultivation? He was only a peak D-Grade! He shouldn't even have the qualifications to enter the Globe, let alone defeat anything inside.

Even the first shadow was an early C-Grade. It wasn't something a D-Grade should be able to handle. Defeating it was a stellar result on Jack's part... but then, he'd actually defeated the next two shadows as well.

This was almost unheard of!

The four cultivators gaped at Jack, forgetting how to speak, and even the Envoy responsible for the Globe hesitated. If he didn't know that the Globe's formation was perfect, he would have suspected it made a mistake.

Jack's cultivation may have been low, but he was at the top of the Cathedral talent-wise! Such a person had great chances of becoming an Envoy in the future.

I must befriend him, was the common thought of everyone involved.

"What an amazing result!" the handsome human from before, Osmu Sosmu, exclaimed. He approached Jack with a friendly smile. "Reaching such rank while at the D-Grade is a tremendous achievement! Perhaps only the top talents, like Lady Min Ling, could match it. Congratulations! Can I call you Jack?"

Hearing those words, Jack simply smiled awkwardly. He knew better than anyone that the only reason he defeated the two shadows was the Life Drop, an item that even the Hand of God would covet. Simply based on his own ability, he could only defeat the first shadow.

Which remained a universally stunning achievement for a peak D-Grade, but nothing as grand as being one of the Cathedral's top talents.

If anything, he was more surprised that his result wasn't too good. He had the Life Drop—how were others able to match him without it?

I really underestimated the size of the universe... he thought.

There was always a higher mountain, always a greater talent. Back in the neophyte Milky Way galaxy, Jack was the strongest D-Grade without even using the Life Drop. Here, even if he did use it, there were others who could compare.

It really made his blood boil. The road ahead was long, one he looked forward to walking.

Of course, a cultivator's lucky chances were also part of their strength. Everyone had those, and everyone walked their own path in life. Moreover, Jack was currently forgetting that he'd only been Integrated for a year and a half.

If the other people present knew that, they would probably froth at the mouth.

"Sure, call me Jack. Thank you for the kind words."

"Don't mention it! Us disciples of the Black Hole Church aren't many, we should stick together!"

The djinn girl also approached. "I didn't mention my name before. I'm Mer Kar'Portul, nice to officially meet you."

"Bezz Massp," said the mosquitoid.

"John Anthem," added the other human, the last of the four cultivators.

Jack smiled again. These people weren't too bad. "A pleasure to meet you. Unfortunately, I am pressed for time, so I have to go. Perhaps we'll meet again."

"Mhm. Perhaps, yes..."

Jack walked away, followed by their piercing stares. The handsome man, especially, was shocked. Had he, a middle C-Grade, just been brushed off by a peak D-Grade like he was *nothing*?

The Envoy hadn't said anything besides announcing Jack's score, but his eyes followed him as he walked away.

Jack was feeling much better. Not only had he discovered that he remained ahead of the power curve, even when placed in the wider universe, but he'd also found out about other monstrous talents.

That was great! He had something to aim for. His eyes roved over the ranking obelisk, rising higher and higher until they rested on a single name.

1, Min Ling... I'm coming for you!

However, testing his strength wasn't his only source of joy. His result in the Ceaseless Murder Globe stunned everyone. If he managed to impress a high-ranker, or at least someone near the seven-hundred mark, perhaps he could convince them to protect Dorman from Don Cranxiao. Owing favors wasn't the best approach, but it was far better than letting his friend be bullied—especially now that he'd acknowledged Dorman and taken him under his roof.

A high-ranker at his back would give Jack ample time to prepare. In three months, he would break through to the C-Grade, and Cranxiao would be nothing but a fly on his shoulder.

He also needed to contact the Sage about that, actually, but he didn't know where he lived. He could ask Dorman later. Plus, Jack had a feeling the Sage already knew.

Jack walked with renewed vigor. He was getting used to the thousandfold gravity, too, so it didn't bother him that much. His body had adjusted.

Next stop... the library!

Dorman had mentioned this before. The Cathedral had a small library offering a collection of basic books. They mostly pertained to side professions, like formations and basic Dao theory... or healing.

Since Jack decided to try his hand at healing, the faster he started, the better.

The twelve villages of the Cathedral were arranged in a ring shape. In their center was a small area containing the many formations, like the Heavy Pagoda, the ranking obelisk, and the Ceaseless Murder Globe. Some administrative buildings were also there, including the tiny cabin that housed the library.

Jack didn't feel like spending more time than necessary. He walked there, greeted the pale, B-Grade vampire that served as the librarian, then picked up a book on healing and took his leave. For disciples of his ranking, one book at a time was the limit, and he could only keep it for a month or unless requested by a higher-ranking disciple.

With the heavy tome under his arm, Jack crossed the plain terrain of the Cathedral to arrive back at his cabin. "Guys, I'm home," he said, opening the door. Brock remained exactly where he'd left him, on the cabin's meditation mat. Dorman was leaning his large body against a side wall and cultivating. The cabin was deathly silent.

On hindsight, perhaps I shouldn't have shouted.

Brock's eyes snapped open. From their hidden excitement, Jack could tell the brorilla's cultivation was going great.

"Hey, bro. This place great."

"Glad to hear that, Brock."

"What that?" Brock asked, pointing at the book.

"Basic healing. I decided to become a part-time doctor."

The brorilla nodded like this was the most natural thing in the world. "Have fun," he said, then closed his eyes and returned to cultivation.

With such zeal, Brock would go far.

Jack climbed on the hard bed, sat cross-legged, and opened the book. It was titled *An Introduction to Healing Using the Dao of Life*, by a person named Madam Zi.

As Jack started reading, he found that this book really was about the fundamentals. The first chapter detailed the basic principles behind healing and some commonalities between all species of the universe.

To Jack's surprise, he discovered that a healer really was like a doctor. It wasn't just about pouring life energy inside a person until they became better. You had to carefully control it, scanning their body to discover the problem and then guiding your energy to resolve it. Mistakes could be disastrous—even killing the patient wasn't difficult, especially if they possessed lower cultivation. One wrong move from the life energy and their lungs or heart could seize.

The Dao was like a massive sledgehammer that could shake the universe. If someone allowed it into their bodies, one tiny mistake could wreak havoc.

Of course, some things were easier to treat than others. Superficial injuries were the simplest. Deeper ones were more difficult, followed by regenerating limbs, repairing organs, and all the way to things that modern medicine hadn't yet achieved, like repairing brain damage and curing some otherwise terminal diseases.

Jack was awed by what he discovered, but decided to take things slow. First, he would learn to treat the easiest, lightest, most superficial wounds. It was a good start for a novice, and these were also the most common injuries people suffered.

He dove deeper into the text. While studying was initially awkward, he fell into the rhythm, his brain remembering the thousands of hours he'd spent like this on Earth. Surprisingly, it was much easier than he remembered. Boredom and exhaustion were old concepts—he felt that he could easily spend days just reading texts. Moreover, he now possessed a photographic memory and a comprehension speed that would put Earthen scholars to shame.

His 200 Mental was no joke.

Jack also discovered that this book was far more complex than the ones he was used to. The wealth of knowledge it contained was staggering, and the degree to which it was distilled was mind-numbing. The author jumped from one subject to the other like a prancing gazelle, assuming the reader was a mega genius who could understand everything at a glance.

To be fair, Jack was a mega genius at this point, but he still struggled. This book was written for cultivators, not pre-System humans—the reader was assumed to have several hundred points in Mental, and this was just for an introductory book, the kind that low-level novices would read.

The more Jack read, the more he struggled, but his knowledge increased at tremendous speed. He felt like the god of biologists. The theories he found inside, the treaties on the bodies of alien species, the observations, the connections... It simultaneously expanded his understanding of the world and created even more questions.

On Earth, a doctor needed to treat humans. Veterinarians treated animals, usually specializing in one species or family.

In the cultivation world, a good healer needed to understand not just the human body, but the body of every species and what made them tick. Jack needed to be able to treat species he'd never heard about before, getting their inner workings right at the first try. It was orders of magnitude more difficult than he expected.

But he was also far more capable than any Earth scholar could dream to be.

The hours flowed like water. Brock and Dorman were deep in meditation, while Jack restlessly read from his book, absorbing knowledge like a sponge. His previous study experience came in handy. When problems cropped up or he realized he had a misunderstanding, he tackled the issue scientifically and found a solution.

Like this, the thick, mystical, heavily compact tome was slowly absorbed by Jack. The pages turned one after the other.

CHAPTER FIFTEEN
JACK'S PATH OF HEALING

VIVI SAT CROSS-LEGGED IN THE MIDDLE OF A FIELD, EXPERIENCING THE morning sun. Her breaths were deep, her brows relaxed, her mind free to gallop as it pleased. She was currently meditating on flames, as the Flame Dao was most vibrant in the morning. In the afternoons, she cultivated the River Dao, and at nights she rested.

She was just one step away from the D-Grade, but that step could be as short or long as she made it. Some cultivators broke through within days. Others tried for decades and never succeeded. The sprouting of a Dao Tree was an intricate process that depended not just on reaching the max Level of the E-Grade, but also having a deep and consistent understanding of your Dao.

Vivi wasn't in a hurry. Though she had reached the threshold of breaking through, she chose not to attempt it yet. After all, reaching the D-Grade earlier would earn her little. It was better to invest a few months in increasing her chances of success as much as possible, as well as establishing a more solid foundation.

At the end of the day, Jack was her man. She refused to be stopped at a mere D-Grade.

Not to mention she had more to do in life than cultivate.

Even while meditating, Vivi never cut off the world completely. Right now, hearing that something fun was going on, she cracked an eye open.

A few feet away, two babies were sitting on a blanket laid out on the grass. A kind-looking man with a goatee sat with them, spreading his arms and conjuring all sorts of dancing lights. The children clapped and laughed, making cute baby sounds. Eric was chewing on his foot, while Ebele was watching the spectacle with her wide open eyes.

All sorts of shapes emerged from between Edgar's hands. There were dogs, cats, giraffes, and people. A small green dragon flew around Ebele's neck, while a tiny blue fairy drew Eric's attention. Forgetting about chewing his foot, the little boy tried to grab her, but she only flew away, luring him to chase. All these shapes were made of bright colors as if tiny stars.

At this point, the shape of a heart flew out of Edgar's palms, slowly reaching the center of the picnic blanket. Eric was busy chasing the fairy, but Ebele looked at the heart, then tried to grab it. Her chubby little fingers passed right through the conjured image. She was startled, and kept trying. Finally, enough was enough. Firmly closing her little hand around the heart—and catching nothing—she raised her fist and crawled closer to Vivi, extending her hand and opening it.

"Mom!" she cried out, smiling brightly.

Vivi, with one eye open, smiled. As soon as Ebele's hand opened, harmless flames formed the image of a heart inside it, which Vivi grabbed and exclaimed.

"Thank you! This is beautiful!"

If Ebele was surprised that she'd finally captured the heart, she did not show it. She giggled merrily, and Vivi patted her head. The little girl then crawled back to Edgar and his magics, while Eric was still busy chasing the mischievous fairy who kept pecking him with little kisses.

Vivi smiled, watching her children play. The sun was bright and pleasantly warm, the grass was cool, the food in their baskets delicious. Laughter kept ringing. Her children's happiness warmed Vivi's heart.

Cultivation... was not the most important thing in life.

Jack sat in a cold, dark, silent place where a thousand gravities pressed down on him. Taking a deep breath, he slid a dagger across his palm, cutting a line of dripping blood. Before long, the blood stopped flowing, and the wound slowly but surely closed.

"Three breaths," he muttered.

He cut his palm again. This time, he activated the power of the Life Drop, enhancing his natural regeneration. The wound closed almost instantly. Jack shook his head.

Reaching into his soul, he grabbed the Life Drop and pulled out a tiny thread of Life energy, a miniscule amount. He guided it through his body until it reached his outstretched hand, then held it there. He sliced his palm a third time and gently guided the life energy into the open wound, trying not to waste any on the pristine skin surrounding it. He even directed the energy with his mind, teaching it how to best help his body heal.

A faint green light emerged from his palm. The wound knit itself together and disappeared, leaving not even a scar. This time, it only needed two breaths.

Jack smiled widely. "Good!"

Cultivation was about two processes, expansion and consolidation—theory and practice. By alternating between these two, you could steadily progress down the right path. This principle also wasn't limited to cultivation. It worked on anything from chess to boxing to science. In Jack's pre-System experience, this was the best way to progress in most human endeavors.

Healing was no different. Before he began practicing, he had spent a week studying the basic introduction to healing. Any more than that would fill his mind with more knowledge than he could digest, and any less wouldn't give him proper foundations, so his practice would delve into random directions and be inefficient.

Of course, this delicate balance was different for all people and tasks. Jack took a week because he was a super mega genius by pre-System standards. For most people, it was better to start with small bites.

Finally, he had succeeded on his first attempt. He'd healed a wound! It was only the most minor, easiest one, and it was also on himself, and he also accelerated self-healing by only a small amount, but it was a first step down a long road!

Jack called it a warm-up. He was not nearly done.

Reaching inside his soul, he pulled another tiny thread out of the Life Drop. This time, he didn't just move it to his hand. The soul was close to the heart. Wrapping that thread of life in a tiny bit of his own Dao so it wouldn't dissipate, he deposited it in his bloodstream and let it flow naturally. This process was easier on him and also faster. The thread of life followed his blood as it ran along his body, slowly circling it.

His perception remained locked onto the thread, guiding it along the right route.

This was where Jack's study came into play. He had already memorized the entire structure of a human's blood network. Blood flowed out of the heart and would return to the heart, but it didn't pass through every point of the body in every circle. The blood network contained innumerable branches, where the massive bloodstream parted and followed different routes before eventually returning to the heart. His thread of life wouldn't get stuck no matter what path it followed, but if he wanted to get it to his hand specifically, he needed to guide it well.

Though he had memorized every branch in the blood network, this task was easier said than done. Blood could move up to three feet per second. It was fast, and his perception was limited. He had to make continuous split-second decisions. The first ones were easy, as he just had to choose between the major arteries, but as the thread got closer and closer to his hand, the bloodstream broke into a vast number of increasingly tiny tunnels. The difficulty shot up.

Jack kept his eyes closed, fully engrossed in his task. On the Cathedral, he had nothing else to do, nor was there anything to distract him. Even sound itself was absent. Time lost its meaning and endlessly stretched on. Jack kept trying, the thread of life passing through innumerable circles in his body. Every time he failed, he memorized the mistake so he wouldn't make it again.

Slowly, the structure of his blood vessels was clarified in his mind, every branch becoming intimate. With each cycle, the thread was getting closer and closer to his palm. Then, it got closer and closer to the center of his palm, where he was guiding it.

But it didn't arrive immediately. This place had the tiniest vessels and highest degree of difficulty. Sometimes, the thread would rush up and down his fingers before moving back to the heart. Other times, it would stop at the wrist. Frustratingly, it could even circle the wound without actually touching it. Finding the precise path was like threading a needle blindfolded.

Jack didn't mind. He would get it eventually. A few more tries was nothing.

Time flowed.

Of course, in a real scenario, finding the wound would be much easier. The wounds that healers were called for were much larger and on more vital places than a tiny slit in the palm. The more blood that escaped a wound, the more central the blood vessels underneath, so the easier it was to reach them.

However, Jack didn't aim for mediocrity. If he did something, he wanted to do it well. This was just practice to increase his mastery.

The thread of life finally reached the wound that Jack had purposely kept open, and then he saw it close at a rate visible to the naked eye. He smiled. Success!

He then aimed at his right heel. Another thread of life entered his bloodstream, and he gently guided it over, once again making a ton of mistakes and learning from them.

His first goal was being able to reliably guide a thread through his bloodstream to anywhere in his body with a ninety percent success rate—on the first try. After that, he would increase the volume of life energy and try to achieve the same result. He would even experiment with guiding multiple threads at once. According to the book, guiding energy through the bloodstream should become second nature, to the point where he could do it completely on instinct.

The reason for that was because different people had different internal structures. If Jack could do it on himself, it didn't mean he could do it on Dorman or the Sage. Moreover, a healer had to deal with more than just humans. The universe was filled with all sorts of species, each of which had a very distinct internal structure. A real healer should be able to work on even a species they hadn't seen before, and that could only be achieved through a mind-boggling amount of experience.

Moreover, there were species that did not possess blood vessels but entirely different systems of internal energy transfer. The same principles applied then, but it was another step of difficulty higher. An expert healer could even handle those cases without prior experience.

Jack didn't hope to achieve that degree anytime soon—or ever. Hopefully, the Life Drop's ridiculous amounts of energy would make up for his insufficiency in finesse.

As for skipping the bloodstream control altogether... That was impossible. While he could push the life energy directly through his own body if he wanted to, he couldn't do the same for others. Their Dao and body would resist greatly. Unless he intended to brute-force the issue, the only way was to insert his life energy through an opening in their body and then gently guide it to the injury, influencing the patient as little as possible. Otherwise, you could even do more harm than good.

The path of a healer was long, hard, and could definitely not be walked in a few months or years. It was impossible for Jack to achieve that level of success in time for his battle against Don Cranxiao.

Thankfully, there were other ways. Many novice healers followed the Hail Mary approach, where they poured life energy into the patient's body, let it run free, and hoped for the best. It was far less efficient than the real approach, but it could work, especially if he used the Life Drop to completely disregard efficiency.

He grinned.

Healing is a hard, delicate practice... but I can just punch my way through with overwhelming power!

That will be my path of healing!

CHAPTER SIXTEEN
CHEATING CAPITALISM

Jack sat on his bed, letting three threads of life circulate his body through his bloodstream. His breath was even and deep, his brows relaxed. His perception was focused inward, capturing every change in a thread's trajectory.

By now, he knew his body in and out, every nook and cranny and tiny blood vessel. He could draw his entire blood system on paper if he wanted to. It had been two weeks since he started training, and it was going splendidly. His almost-PhD was finally coming in handy.

Yet, it was far from enough. Moving energy through his own body was only the most elementary foundation. It didn't even have practical applications—if he wanted to heal himself, he could just move the energy through his flesh. This was just training for the much harder task of moving his energy through the bloodstream of other humans, which he hadn't even started on yet.

If just his own body took two weeks, the next step would take even more. He would never make it in time. Cranxiao would come to beat up Dorman in two weeks, and Jack needed to have something by then so he could convince high-rankers to help. Otherwise, he would need to use his battle results in the Ceaseless Murder Globe to beg for favors, which was best avoided.

Luckily, Jack was a smart man with smart ideas.

He did not have expertise in healing, but he did have an ocean of life energy.

Opening his eyes, he grinned. An empty Dao stone was in his hands. These things were easy to come by as they were basically worthless—their value came from the Dao inside them, not the stone itself.

Taking a deep breath, Jack activated the Life Drop. A flood of energy rushed into his body, filling him up to the brim. His bones creaked as they expanded, his skin shivered as it grew, and the further excess of energy gathered into two new arms that wanted to burst out of Jack's armpits.

Before that could happen, he passed a tight harness over the energy. He forced it with his will. The life energy resisted, too great to be controlled, but his Indomitable Will and Dao Tree bore down on it at the same time, forcing it to obey.

The two new arms did not appear. The excess energy was like a pulsing bomb in his chest.

Jack was sweating. One mistake now could end with his body exploding. Maintaining concentration, he guided the energy through his body, through his bones and blood and flesh, and into his arms. He pushed it down until it reached his hands, then forced it to surface through his palms. The skin bubbled like boiling water. A couple extra fingers sprouted. The sight was grotesque, so Jack averted his gaze and used his willpower to force the life energy out of his body and into the empty Dao stone he held.

As it met the surface of his skin, it resisted fiercely, unwilling to go. Jack almost lost his grip. With a final effort, he pushed a corner of the energy into the empty Dao stone, and it was like he'd opened the floodgates. The energy moved from high to low density. It dove into the Dao stone and filled it up completely, swirling inside like a thick green snake. It was so potent that it was even visible to the naked eye.

Jack's eyes widened. Success!

That was the idea. If Dao stones could hold ambient Dao, why not Life Dao as well? Now, as soon as someone absorbed the energy contained in this stone, it would flood their body and heal their wounds. While it couldn't create the same effects as Jack's four-armed battle form, and it would dissipate through the user's pores with over ninety percent of the efficacy wasted, there would be at least some healing!

In Jack's knowledge, there wasn't any device like this. Even if there was, it wasn't wide-spread or easily available. If you wanted healing, you needed a healer. It made sense, too—the amount of energy he'd poured into the Dao stone was gargantuan. For a normal C-Grade healer, it was equivalent to a month's work. Nobody in their right mind would use their energy like this.

Unless, of course, they had the Life Drop in their body.

Jack laughed out loud, even disturbing Brock and Dorman who were meditating nearby. "What's going on?" Dorman asked, jumping to his feet.

"You're friends with a genius, that's what," Jack replied, pushing out the Dao stone with a wide smile. "I present to you, the life stone! Quick and easy healing at the tips of your fingers. Buy one now and get another for free."

Brock raised a brow in amusement. "Bro?"

Jack laughed. "Don't worry. I have it all figured out. These babies will make us rich!"

Dorman and Brock exchanged a glance. "What exactly is that?" Dorman asked.

"I call it Jack's Life Stone, patent pending. Its use is simple: if you are wounded in battle and need healing, just take a life stone out of your pocket and absorb the energy within. It will flood your body, healing you, then harmlessly dissipate. You no longer need to depend on your team's healer. Doesn't it sound extremely sellable?"

Dorman hesitated. "I guess… But if it was so easy, wouldn't it exist already? I mean, you made this in a few seconds."

"I'm special." Jack didn't explain further. While his Life Drop was no longer a secret, it also wasn't the matter at hand.

"Okay… But are you sure it works?"

"Not really. That's why you'll help me test it."

Dorman's eyes widened. "You're kidding. Look at me! I'm wide like Mount Tai, and it's all because I ate a Life treasure! Come on, man!"

Jack blinked in surprise. He'd forgotten about that.

Will people get fat if they use my Life stone? he wondered. *Would Dorman explode?*

"Okay, change of plans. Brock, it's your lucky day."

The brorilla laughed, then caught the Life stone that Jack threw over.

"Careful!" Dorman exclaimed. "If you recklessly absorb that thing, you could turn fat like me!"

"Even if that happens, the energy still comes from me. I have confidence in forcefully dissipating it," Jack said. "Brock, I'm ninety percent certain, but I need someone to test it out. The choice is yours."

"I trust Big Bro," Brock said without the slightest hesitation. He held the Life stone with both hands, concentrated, and gently tugged on a bit of energy. He pulled out the barest trickle, intending to start slow.

The moment that happened, the entire green snake burst out. It swam through space as if looking for prey, then dug into Brock's body before he could respond. Brock's eyes widened. Green flashes traveled up and down his limbs. Green smoke escaped his pores and orifices. He resembled a living pot for a moment, and then the energy abruptly calmed down.

Everyone held still. "Are you okay?" Jack asked.

Brock thought about it, then nodded. Nothing seemed different. He patted his belly and said, "Full."

Dorman and Jack both heaved a huge sigh of relief. After that, however, Jack revealed a disappointed expression. The Life stone was nowhere near as efficient as he'd hoped.

Half the energy dissipated right as it entered Brock's body. Even after that, the vast majority rushed to exit through his pores like it refused to stay inside him.

Only a tiny portion of the energy was forced to circulate through Brock, as it just couldn't exit fast enough. It would be enough to heal minor wounds, but nothing serious.

With a few quick calculations, Jack estimated that the efficacy of his Life stone was only a sad two percent. This sort of thing would be almost useless to C-Grades. He couldn't trade it for Dao stones.

I can make it work, he consoled himself. *This was just a prototype. If I can condense the energy further, the efficacy should rise. Also, if Brock uses his own Dao to keep the life energy from exiting his body, a larger portion of it will have no choice but to be absorbed.*

Should I include an instruction manual with my Life stones?

Hmm. Also, if there is some material that stops life energy from passing, I could use it to cover the stone so the energy doesn't dissipate before entering the user's body.

The easiest idea to test was Brock's control over the energy exiting his body. Jack returned to meditation, resting himself until he could draw on the Life Drop's energy again—controlling such a huge amount of energy overtaxed his mental reserves, so he needed time to rest between creating Life stones.

An hour later, he repeated the process to create a second one. He even used the same empty Dao stone as before, since it was reusable.

Environmentally friendly. This goes a long way for patents!

After he'd created a nearly identical Life stone, he once again passed it to Brock. This time, he instructed Brock to slice his foot a bit before using it, so the energy had somewhere to go. He also had Brock use his own Dao to block his pores so it couldn't easily dissipate.

Brock obliged. The energy escaped the stone, half of it dissipating in the process as before, while Brock absorbed the remaining half. Green smoke still escaped his body from everywhere, but it was slightly less than before. The green flashes rampaged on him. The small wound on his foot closed instantly, and Brock's belly bulged out almost imperceptibly.

Finally, all of the energy was absorbed, and Brock burped.

"Success!" Jack shouted again. Just with Brock keeping the energy in, the efficacy had risen to a whopping five percent! It couldn't heal grievous wounds, but even shallow sword slashes should disappear. To someone who did not possess self-regeneration, this could be the difference between life and death.

The minor side effect was that the user could gain weight if their injuries weren't heavy enough. But, for saving one's life, this was a small price to pay. Besides, they just had to be careful.

"Please never give me one of those," Dorman said tearfully, but Jack was too busy making business plans.

Don Cranxiao would arrive in two weeks. Until then, Jack needed to either break through or hire someone to help him protect Dorman. With these Life stones, he could easily gather enough Dao stones!

Perhaps one Life stone wasn't worth a Dao stone, but even if the ratio was three or five to one, what did Jack care? He had infinite. The Life Drop was a bottomless ocean of energy. The two stones he'd created weren't even enough to scratch the surface.

Who would have expected that this priceless treasure would be relegated to a money-making scheme by Jack?

I beat capitalism in two weeks. Woohoo!

Ah, life is so easy when you're smart. With all the Dao stones I can gather, my strength will increase by leaps and bounds!

Giggling to himself, he set to creating more Life stones. The downtime was used to keep practicing the bloodstream guidance technique as described in the introductory healing manual.

Throughout the next day, Jack produced twenty Life stones. If a normal C-Grade healer wanted to achieve the same result, they would need a year and a half! As for the Life Drop, its energy had only fallen by an imperceptible trickle. He could easily create thousands of Life stones.

Jack was very proud of himself. This was easy.

Too easy.

The world around him zoomed out like he was falling backward into a well. He felt himself sinking. Suddenly, he was in an endlessly deep, dark space filled with piercing cold and green mist. A green sphere hovered in the distance. Most importantly, a large turtle floated right before Jack, its beady eyes shining with anger.

"Kid!" it shouted with enough force to rupture his eardrums. "What the hell do you think you're doing!"

CHAPTER SEVENTEEN
ENTERING THE LIFE DROP

The turtle's roar echoed through the green-tinged void, rumbling space itself. Jack flew backward, cupping his ears to protect them. His teeth were chattering.

When the sound died down, he could finally raise his head again. The large turtle stared him down, its beady eyes exuding menace.

Jack's Dao perception spread out.

Last time he was here, this turtle had only been a vague shape in the distance. He hadn't had time to take a good look. This time, things were different. He could clearly make out the interconnected plates on its shell, its sharp teeth, its shrunk neck about to whip at him.

This creature looked like a normal snapping turtle, except the size of an elephant.

And its aura was gigantic. Just probing it with his perception made Jack nauseous. It tussled and turned like a sun trapped in a tiny body, a bastion of inestimably deep power. The turtle's aura alone could be a living creature, so grand was its strength, and Jack was nothing but a leaf waiting to be blown in the storm.

His legs went to jelly. Luckily, he was floating in the void, so he didn't need them. He also wasn't afraid of death. Realizing this creature could do whatever it wanted with him, he raised his head, unafraid of staring it down.

A shadow of approval flickered within those beady eyes, then disappeared.

"I ask you again, kid," the turtle spoke, this time in a normal, somewhat old and grating voice instead of an apocalyptic one. "What the hell do you think you're doing? How did you consume so much energy so quickly?"

"I was using the power of the Life Drop to make Life stones," Jack replied. In the face of absolute power, he was calm. He could die, but he could not cower.

"What the hell is a Life stone?"

"A device of my creation, esteemed elder. I pour life energy into an empty Dao stone, then sell it to people who lack self-regeneration. If they're injured, they can absorb the energy in the stone to quickly heal themselves."

It was his tensest elevator pitch ever. Yet, the turtle only revealed a stunned look. "You are using the Supreme Blood to create low-level trinkets?"

"And sell them," Jack couldn't help adding. "I have found myself in need of resources."

The turtle remained stunned for a good half minute. Jack was beginning to wonder if it died on the spot when it finally reacted, erupting with a fierce shout. "How dare you!"

The shout rumbled across space harder than the previous one had. Jack tried to defend, but it was useless. His body shattered like glass. He opened his eyes in the real world, rising so fast that the top of his head crashed into Brock's jaw.

"Bro!" the brorilla shouted, cupping his chin. "You back!"

"I—"

Jack barely had time to glimpse his cabin, where he apparently lay on the floor, before a furious voice echoed in his ears. "Get back here!"

Once again, he fell backward inside a well, watching the world get farther and farther away until he was again floating in the green void, faced with a furious, incomparably powerful turtle. His body was intact.

"What the hell?" was all he managed to say before the turtle laid into a huge tantrum.

"Insolence, blasphemy!" it shouted, rocking the void. It took everything Jack had to prevent his body from shattering again. "How the hell did some punk like you pass the trial? I should break your soul and fly off into the void. Even inhabiting a random space monster would be better than wasting divine gifts on party tricks and road-side begging!"

"Esteemed elder, please, just stop shouting!"

Jack was about to go crazy. The turtle's tantrum was vibrating all of the Dao inside him, his very Dao Tree. It was like he'd smoked expired mushrooms.

Finally, the turtle stopped erupting, though remained pissed.

"Give me a good reason not to destroy you right now," it said. "Go on. You have one breath."

Jack's mind raced. The turtle had offered him a chance—he just had to find the right words.

"I was in dire need of resources," he explained. "I am striving to reach the top, and I thought I should use all means at my disposal. These Life stones may be party tricks to you, but they are essential to me. I didn't think the Life Drop would mind a tiny bit of missing life energy."

"Hmph! Whether it minds or doesn't mind, that's up to me to decide, not you."

"Naturally. I would have asked if I could, but I was unable to enter this world again after that one time."

"Of course you were unable! You're just a tiny mortal. If you want to come in here, you have to prove your worth first!"

"So, since I'm here, does that mean I proved it?" Jack regretted his words the moment he spoke them. Seeing that the turtle was about to fly into another round of apoplectic rage, he quickly raised his hands and said, "Please calm down, senior. I had no intention to offend you. I am just confused from flying between worlds like a kite on a windmill."

The turtle snorted. Its mood softened a bit. "You better be. In any case, no more Life stones or anything like that. Understood?"

Jack was about to agree. However, cultivators know to respect their instincts. Right now, his intuition told him that, as much as this turtle liked to make a fuss, it wouldn't actually act against him. He had room to negotiate.

Of course, it could end terribly, but he would never reach the top by skipping the opportunities that presented themselves. If he missed this chance, who knew when he'd get another?

"Senior, please show some generosity. I really am struggling out there. If I limit my consumption of energy, can't I make just a few Life stones a day?"

The turtle's eyes flashed. "You're treading on dangerous waters, kid. One wrong word and I'll eat you alive."

"I understand, but I would still like to speak. If I can't take risks, what right do I have to call myself a cultivator?"

The turtle's aggressiveness did not abate in the slightest, but it also didn't strike out at him. Sensing this tacit agreement, Jack made his case.

"This Life Drop, or the Supreme Blood, as you called it, has chosen me for a reason. I braved many hurdles and surpassed many obstacles to reach this point. I have already proven my worth, at least to a degree. I do not know what goals you and the Supreme Blood have, but I believe I am part of them. If you want to find someone else, it is possible, but it will also be a huge hassle for you, since the Ancient Trial I passed to acquire the Supreme Blood is many galaxies away. We've already cooperated this long. Thus, we should work together."

The turtle remained silent. Its anger persisted, a shimmering coal in the depths of its aura, but it also seemed willing to listen to Jack.

"I already know all those," it replied. "Don't try to school me. Just tell me what you want."

"A few Life stones a day. That's all."

"Using the Supreme Blood for such a mortal reason like *money* is an affront to everything we stand for. Why should I let you do it?"

"Because I am a mortal, esteemed elder, and I need Dao stones to cultivate. Moreover, there are enemies after my life. If I die before I reach the peak, that will also set you back."

"If you die, it just means you were too weak."

"But what if I am delayed? What if the problems of today harm my potential and we have to spend millennia just to reach the C-Grade? Wouldn't that be a great loss to you?"

The turtle snorted. "You guess correctly. Your rise to power is indeed aligned with my and the Supreme Blood's interests, but that doesn't mean we will help you more than necessary. That crude use of the Supreme Blood you have discovered is already a major boon to you. If you cannot reach the apex with that, then... Hmph! You may as well retire and lead a mortal life."

Jack's ears perked up. The turtle was referring to his four-armed form, but... "The crude use I have discovered? Are you implying there are more ways to use the Supreme Blood, esteemed elder?"

"Naturally. The Supreme Blood is a divine artifact. A mere battle form is nothing."

"Then—"

"If you want something, go earn it. Don't ask me for free advice. I am not your father, though I may as well be your daddy."

Jack was taken aback, and mustered himself to say, "I did find another way to use the Supreme Blood, esteemed elder... but you're stopping me. Since that's the case, how about you recommend another way to make up for the one you take away from me? Or do you plan to just take without giving?"

This tone was borderline disrespectful, but it seemed to be working so far.

The turtle snorted. "And here I thought you were just a muscle-head... but look at that wily tongue. You sure can speak, kid, even if all you say is bullshit. Fine. Whatever."

Jack's eyes shone. "Then..."

"I will give you a hint. Not because you deserve it, but because I like your gutsy attitude. Not many would have the courage to stand up to me, nor the composure to make it worth it." The turtle's beady eyes gazed deeply into Jack's own, finding just the right mixture of respect and bravery. "Life energy is the energy of the body. Instead of just letting it rampage like a gung-ho barbarian, you can try to control it and nourish yourself for long-term benefits. That is the foundational function of the Supreme Blood."

"I see!" Jack said.

So I can push the life energy into my body to nourish it... Wait a moment. Isn't that exactly what Dorman did?

"But wouldn't that just make me fat?" he asked.

"Only if you do it wrong," the turtle replied with a snort. "But don't look at me. If you can't figure even that out by yourself, you really don't have the qualifications to use the Supreme Blood."

"Alright. I will certainly figure it out. Thank you, esteemed elder, you have been a great help."

The turtle scoffed. "And stop with esteemed elder this and esteemed elder that. You may call me Venerable Saint Thousand Shell."

"Absolutely!" he replied, while inwardly thinking, What a mouthful... "Thank you for your guidance, Venerable Saint Thousand Shell. Since I'm here... what exactly are you? Where is here? Are we inside the Supreme Blood?"

"Of course we are inside the Supreme Blood. What are you, stupid? Nevermind, don't answer—I don't want to know. As for the rest of your questions... When the time comes for you to know, you will naturally know. For now, just assume I am the caretaker of the Supreme Blood."

"Okay."

Jack didn't mind. This turtle still felt way above his paygrade, though the benefits it could offer were sweet. If he could form a good relationship with it...

As if it saw through his thoughts, the turtle snorted yet again, rocking the void. "As for those Life stones you mentioned... While I find such a use of the Supreme Blood debasing, I understand that certain concessions must be made for your... mundane circumstances. You may create one Life stone per seven days. That would match the Supreme Blood's current regeneration rate. If you can use it well, even that tiny amount of energy would be invaluable to someone of your cultivation."

Jack's gaze brightened. This turtle wasn't so bad after all!

"Thank you, Venerable Saint Thousand Shell. You're awesome!"

"Of course I am, but that is not for you to judge. Now, if that is all..."

Jack smiled wryly. "Just one more thing. If, in the future, I need to contact you again to make sure I'm not misusing the Supreme Blood in another way... how could I reach out?"

The turtle stared at him. "How stupid can you be, kid? Did I not create a door on your Dao Tree? Do you not know how to use doors?"

"I tried opening it, but it won't budge..."

"Because it's locked, you idiot! If you want to see me, just knock! I'll hear you. But if you disturb me for unimportant reasons, I will take away your benefits. Am I clear?"

"Crystal clear, sir."

"I am not *sir*. I am Venerable Saint Thousand Shell."

"Absolutely, Venerable Saint Thousand Shell."

"Very well. Now begone—and try to get stronger quickly, or I might reconsider your status as the Supreme Blood's holder."

Jack looked around the vast, dark void glimmering with faint green mist. "So, uh... That door you mentioned, would you mind showing me?"

For the first time, the turtle grinned. It was almost terrifying on its face. "Oh, I'll show you alright," it replied, then snorted with power.

The shockwave was unstoppable. Once again, Jack's entire body shattered like glass, and he found himself gasping on the hard bed of his cabin on the Cathedral.

"Jack!"

"Big Bro!" Dorman and Brock exclaimed, sitting next to him.

"Are you okay? What happened?"

"Uh..." Jack thought back to the turtle, its nonsensical attitude, and the benefits he'd reaped. With a smile, he replied, "I actually don't have the slightest idea."

CHAPTER EIGHTEEN
BODY TEMPERING

As Jack sat on his bed, he was extremely satisfied. Who said you can't have your cake and eat it too?

The turtle with a mouthful of a name had limited Jack's creation of Life stones, but he still had the twenty he'd made the day before! With a little business acumen, he was confident in exchanging them for at least five Dao stones. Along with the Heavy Pagoda's Dao-compressing properties, he would need only ten more stones to break through to the C-Grade.

Moreover, the turtle had hinted at another way to use the Life Drop. Jack was shivering with anticipation to test it.

Use the life energy to temper my body...

Closing his eyes, he sank into meditation. Wisps of life energy wafted from the Life Drop, spreading across his body and harmlessly dissipating. Jack pulled at them. The wisps turned into a current, then a raging stream as heaps of life energy emerged to fill his body. Before it could reach the point of transforming him into the four-armed form, he stopped.

Now, he just had an excess of life energy coursing through his body. This energy was mild and obedient. It followed his instructions perfectly and wouldn't merge into his body by itself. Otherwise, this energy alone would have bloated him like Dorman.

How do I go about this?

The four-armed transformation was also a form of body enhancement. When using it, the life energy dove into his entire body, essentially supercharging it. However, it couldn't be called tempering or nourishing. The excess energy gave him temporary power, then dissipated. It never truly became a part of him.

After the turtle's hint, Jack began to realize that a deeper fusion was also possible.

Everything in the world was made of Dao. That included the human body. From his bones to his skin, it was all a collection of Life-related Dao particles which combined into a functioning whole. His molecules themselves were made of tinier Dao particles.

Was it possible to infuse his body, which was made of Life Dao, with extra energy?

Focusing on the excess life energy currently circulating through him, Jack used his will to grab a tiny piece. It squirmed against his control, but he held on tight. Then, he slowly pushed it deeper inside his body, not on a physical level, but on a conceptual one. He didn't fuse it into his flesh and bones, but into the very essence which made them up, the foundation of his being.

The life energy resisted as it pushed against the Dao of Jack's body. These two were made of the same tiny particles, but in different combinations. They refused to work together. It was like forcing two pieces of the same puzzle that weren't meant to match.

Jack stopped and pondered this problem. A moment later, he tried again.

Grabbing the same segment of life energy as before, he attacked it. His will pressed down so hard that the helpless Dao was ground into nothingness, eventually breaking into its fundamental components.

Now, it resembled pure, ambient Life Dao. It could no longer be used to create his four-armed form, losing any sense of will or cohesion. It wanted to dissipate, but Jack clamped down with his entire willpower and forced it not to. Or, rather, he tried. The feeling was like trying to hold water in a basket. It kept leaking.

Frowning in concentration, Jack hurried to use it. He grabbed this ambient Life Dao and forcefully pushed it into himself, to combine with the stable Dao that made up his body. It was difficult. His body itself resisted. It was a complex machine, he couldn't just throw screws at it and hope to make it bigger.

However, a few particles still managed to make it in. They were lodged inside him, unable to escape or be absorbed. Jack even felt a stabbing pain in his bones.

Did I mess up? he wondered. *Randomly sticking things in my body probably isn't a good idea.*

Before he had time to consider it properly, the energy started melting. He would have cried out in joy if this conceptual melting wasn't accompanied by very real, excruciating heat. It rapidly spread across his body. He was on fire. His flesh was boiling, and his nerves were revolting like his bones were molten iron.

Jack gasped. He gritted his teeth, trying his hardest not to shout. Before anything else, he felt stubbornness. He'd endured the Life Drop fusing with his soul and the divine tribulation burning him inside out. Compared to those, this tiny bit of pain was nothing.

A few seconds later, it was over. Jack panted, leaning his back against the wall as he struggled to recover.

"Bro?" Brock asked from his meditation mat, deeply confused.

"I'm fine," Jack replied weakly. "Just had a breakthrough."

Brock stared at him deeply, then nodded and returned to cultivation. Dorman hadn't reacted—he was probably meditating on his Dao and had cut off the world.

Jack shook his head to clear it. What happened?

Looking into his body, he saw that the life energy he'd forcefully absorbed was gone. Judging by the searing pain, it had fused into his body.

Ah. My reasoning was wrong. I'm not throwing screws at a machine—I'm throwing them at the mechanic.

The human body was far more than a machine. It possessed highly complex internal mechanisms, including energy management. Combined with the nature of the Dao, it had managed to absorb the energy that Jack had stuck into it, essentially metabolizing it.

However, it wasn't as simple as consuming food. The fusion occurred at a deeper level, where it equally affected everything from skin to bone. The body had absorbed the energy completely, spreading it across itself to make the process easier.

As a result, he wasn't bigger, just... tempered. Enhanced.

Hmm. Wait. Do I feel... marginally stronger?

It couldn't be.

Yet if it was true... He didn't dare consider the implications. With a decisive move, Jack willed his status screen open.

ERROR: PLEASE REPORT TO THE NEAREST AUTHORITIES IMMEDIATELY OR FACE EXTERMINATION.

Name: Jack Rust
Species: Human, Earth-387
Faction: Bare Fist Brotherhood (D)
Grade: D
Class: Cosmic Fist (King)
Level: 249

Strength: 1776
Dexterity: 1781
Constitution: 1776
Mental: 200
Will: 200

Dao Skills: Meteor Punch IV, Iron Fist Style III, Space Walk III, Brutalizing Aura III, Neutron Star Body II
Daos: Dao Tree of the Fist, Dao Root of Indomitable Will (fused), Dao Root of Life (fused), Dao Root of Power (fused), Dao Root of Weakness (fused)
Titles: Planetary Frontrunner (10), Planetary Torch-bearer (1), Ninth Ring Conqueror, Planetary Leader (1), Grade Defier

His jaw went slack. His eyes widened.

In the status screen, most things had remained the same. His Level, Class, Skills, and Titles were all unchanged.

However, his Physical substats had all increased by one.

This was new! It was tiny, but... tremendous!

Jack started laughing, his previous pain all but forgotten. Brock once again raised a brow, then didn't bother. As for Jack, he was incredibly excited. His mind ran amok with possibilities.

I can enhance my stats! I can do it directly, without needing the System or level-ups! Haha, haha! This is amazing!

He'd long known that, on level-ups, the System somehow pushed ambient Dao into his body to enhance it. Everyone knew that. However, doing the same yourself wasn't possible.

But Jack had just achieved it!

What does this mean? Can I become infinitely strong? Can my strength rise without level-ups or breakthroughs? Can I become doubly as powerful, or even three or four times? Is there a limit, or am I God?

For the second time in a few hours, Jack believed he'd cracked the system. Unlike the previous time, he now had grounds to think it was true.

This tempering process wasn't something anyone could do. Even if they could, they wouldn't. The energy consumption was tremendous. If Jack didn't have the Life Drop, he would need to spend at least a few days gathering the energy to increase his stats by one point—it just wasn't worth it. And that was assuming he cultivated some version of the Dao of Life, which he didn't. Moreover, even if he did, he would need to use some energy storage method like a Life stone, which would incur a severe energy loss. It wouldn't be days, but more like a month.

As for the Life Drop, it contained practically infinite energy at this point, and the turtle didn't mind him using that energy for body tempering.

This was a method unique to Jack!

One more System mystery solved, one more peak conquered, he thought, unable to stop smiling. *I wonder, how does this affect my combat strength?*

The higher one rose, the more they relied on their Dao. The body was just a medium. However, that didn't mean it was useless. Thanks to his titles, Jack already had higher stats than almost everyone at his level, and that showed in every battle. He could strike harder, move faster, and endure for longer. It was part of the reason why he could fight higher-level opponents than himself.

Moreover, the body was the foundation of everything. That was why the System enhanced it at every level. The sturdier the body, the more powerful the Dao it could support. If Jack's bodily stats doubled, it wouldn't bring a mere twofold increase in his battle strength—it might even rise by five or ten times!

Okay, maybe not ten, but it will still be a huge asset! He finally calmed himself down. *Thank you, Venerable Saint Thousand Shell. You really helped me a lot this time.*

There were still many things Jack didn't understand. Naturally, this power wouldn't come without limitations, or he could just hide in a cave for a hundred years and emerge as a universal overlord.

He would discover those limits as he went.

Many calculations ran through Jack's mind. *Absorbing that bit of energy took me a few minutes. Including rest time, that is half an hour per stat point. If I cultivate non-stop, I can gather forty-eight in a day, or around three hundred and fifty every week.*

Cranxiao will come to beat up Dorman in two weeks. If I focus on body tempering, I could get seven hundred stat points by then...

Seven hundred points. That's like, seventy levels in the D-Grade. It could greatly enhance my combat strength! If I could beat the middle C-Grade planetary overseer before, then after these two weeks, could I defeat someone at the late C-Grade?

Could I... defeat Cranxiao in two weeks? Without even breaking through?

If I did break through, just how overwhelming would my strength be?

He was already giddy with anticipation. This body tempering method had opened a new world for him. He'd felt unqualified since arriving at the Cathedral, like a big fish that finally entered the shark-filled sea... Now he suddenly had hope.

The sharks could go fuck themselves. He wouldn't just stay afloat. He would dive down and eat them whole.

The prerequisite was that he would suffer excruciating pain every half hour... but every good cultivator was a bit of a masochist. Jack was more excited than afraid.

Bring it on! He shouted inwardly, resolving to pause his healing studies so he could focus on body tempering for the next two weeks. Solving his problems himself was much better than depending on others. He would work every minute of every day, not sleeping or resting, and in two weeks...

Cranxiao wouldn't know what hit him.

CHAPTER NINETEEN
RECRUITING NEW BROS

Brock opened his eyes.

Cultivating here was very efficient. His Big Thought was nourished well. Soon, it would approach the next transformation.

For now, he needed to rest.

Working too hard is bad. Few hours break, then cultivate another month.

Making up his mind, he stood. Big Bro sat on his bed, occasionally gritting his teeth. Intense ripples spread from his body, like a hundred small brorillas were hammering at his bones, but Brock didn't want to intrude. When Big Bro wanted to share, he would share.

Fat Bro opened his eyes. "Hey. Going out?"

"Yes."

A moment of silence passed. Fat Bro asked, "Can I use the magical meditation mat while you're gone? I will give it back as soon as you return, I promise."

Brock did not completely approve of that request. Fat Bro was a guest, and asking to borrow Medium Bro privileges was questionable. However, if he had his hierarchies straight, it wouldn't be a problem.

"Okay," he replied.

"Thanks!"

Fat Bro rushed to sit on the bromat and close his eyes. As for Brock, he left their little stone home.

Heavy darkness covered the void over the Church Place, pressing down on his shoulders like an angry sky. The ground was gray and stony, with no signs of life, while there wasn't even any air to breathe.

Hardly the place for a scenic walk.

Therefore, Brock decided to do the second best thing, which was head over to the Kill Kill Ball and test his current power.

It fun, so it part of my break.

Covering himself in the ripples of his Big Thought to defend against gravity, he made his way. The Ball was visible in the distance—a sphere of gray next to the obelisk.

He arrived quickly. A small crowd was gathered outside the Ball—young-looking human men and a single woman. Brock approached confidently. "Sup, bros?" he said, drawing everyone's attention. "Can I try the Kill Kill Ball, please?"

They looked at him, then at each other. "Do you mean the Ceaseless Murder Globe?" one of them asked.

"Yes. I speak not too well."

At this point, one of the people there made an ugly face and said, "What idiot left their pet unsupervised?"

A few of the people laughed, while Brock frowned slightly. "Pet? Glass people no pets. Animal people no pets. Why you think I pet?"

Before the man could muster his words, Brock continued.

"You pet to your masters. Pet to stronger humans. But I, no pet. I free because I want to."

The cultivators looked at him in disbelief. One nudged the speaking cultivator's shoulder, saying, "The hell?" A few others nodded in acknowledgement, while the last two shook their heads.

"I will not argue with a monkey," said the speaking cultivator. "Go away. Shoo."

Brock ignored him. He turned to the few who had approved of his words and said, "Name is Brock. Nice to meet you."

"Likewise, Brock," replied a human girl with a blue ponytail—the only woman present. "You're an odd one."

"Thanks. Odd can be good or bad, but I believe I good."

"Yes, I believe so too."

His polite yet sturdy manner of speech had drawn the attention of the small crowd. There was a magnetism to his aura, a draw to his personality that made most of those present surround him with lazy smiles. The rude cultivator from before now found himself outshined.

This wasn't a Dao attack or anything of the sort—it was just solid conduct and social skills coupled with an unusual, disarming appearance. After all, Brock was still only shoulder-height and superficially resembling a monkey.

"Can I try, or can I not try?" Brock asked, motioning at the Globe.

Ponytail Sis shook her head with a rueful smile. "Sorry, big guy. Only disciples can enter the Globe. You aren't one, are you?"

"Not yet. But I strong."

"Oh? You think you could defeat the first opponent?"

"How strong?"

"One-fruit C-Grade."

Brock didn't know what this meant, but it made him hungry. "What fruit?" he asked.

The girl laughed.

"Fruits are the minor stages inside the C-Grade," another bro explained. "The more of them you've grown on your Dao Tree, the stronger you are. One is the start of the C-Grade, and nine is the end."

"Okay. Thanks."

"No problem."

The more Brock spoke, the more he drew in the crowd. The rude cultivator from before could no longer take it and said, "Hmph! What idiot doesn't even know about the fruits of the C-Grade?"

"The same idiot who can make you jealous."

Brock's response had come instantly. Moreover, none of the people here were naive; they could tell just how on-the-nose it was and realized that the rude cultivator had been entirely defeated. As his face grew red, many others laughed, clearly siding with Brock.

"Mind your words, monkey," the cultivator responded. "I could destroy you with a snort."

"Hmph! You are the one who started it, and now you complain?"

Surprisingly, it was Ponytail Sis that stood up for Brock. "Get the hell out of here, or you will have to face my snort, and you know how that will end."

The rude cultivator's eyes widened in rage, and he turned around with a sneer, walking away.

Brock could sense their auras, and he already knew that the rude cultivator was one of the weakest people present, while Ponytail Sis was one of the strongest. Otherwise, he would have handled this situation differently.

"Sorry about that," Ponytail Sis told Brock. "Some people are just assholes."

"No problem. But why you with him?"

"We aren't in the same group. It's just that there is a small event going on, which is why there are so many people here."

"Oh?"

"Lady Min Ling, the first-ranked outer disciple, is currently inside the Globe!"

"Oh!" Brock exclaimed. He understood who that woman was, though he didn't feel much adoration. He would never blindly admire a stranger. If she was a good bro, then he would consider it.

Of course, no matter how awesome she was, could she be any more awesome than Big Bro?

Brock looked around. Once again, he noticed that most of the people here were young-looking, male humans. His eyes flashed. "I see. You bros want mate Strong Lady Bro."

If a thunderclap had fallen, these people would be less stunned.

"Of course not," a man hurried to respond. "We just admire her greatly, that's all."

"Then why your cheeks red?"

"That's... They're always that color."

"Oh. You come from red-cheek species? Look, they're even more red now. You no lying, are you?"

"No," the man replied. He seemed very young, barely a teen, and his awkwardness was plain for all to see. Brock didn't want to make him feel bad. Slinging an arm over the youth's shoulders, he said, "Nothing bad about love. You no need be embarrassed. It natural and proper. If you like girl, you bring gifts to girl, usually bananarms, and then mate if she wants to."

The youth had become beet-red, obviously unable to appreciate Brock's wisdom, but the brorilla didn't take it to heart.

"It ok, little bro," he said. "You try. Then, you understand."

Immature people were rare in the Cathedral, but not entirely absent. The C-Grade was far easier to reach in the wider galaxy than in Jack's, so many people weren't nearly as experienced as Jack and Brock. The young wizards, especially, were often recluses not well versed in human relationships.

While everyone here was a powerful cultivator and a local overlord where they came from, there were people like the youth under Brock's arm who were somewhat juvenile.

Moreover, many cultivators came from cultures far more conservative than the hotpot that was the Cathedral.

Hearing Brock's words, Ponytail Sis chuckled. The men surrounding her displayed expressions that ranged from mild embarrassment to amusement over the youth's situation.

"Unfortunately, human relationships are more complex than you think," Ponytail Sis said. "We can admire people without wanting to sleep with them. Of course, if Min Ling wanted to find a suitor, normal outer disciples wouldn't stand a chance."

"Oh?" Brock asked, letting go of his new little bro. "Why not?"

"Because she can have anyone she wants! The greater, the better. Only the other top talents could barely qualify."

Brock considered it. "Sorry. If lady friend wants great man, only one qualifies. My Big Bro, Jack Rust."

Brock was pretty sure Big Bro wasn't interested in anyone besides Big Sis at the moment. However, since Ponytail Sis asked, he had to let her know about Big Bro's unsurpassed awesomeness.

The men around them didn't take it well. Their expressions darkened. While they were only here to watch Lady Min Ling in the way that people watch celebrities, not really hoping for anything, Brock's words were a bit provocative.

"And what exactly makes your big bro better than us?" asked one man.

"He very strong. Big heart, strong mind, good bro. Handsome, too."

"You're speaking nonsense," another guy said. "If he's so great, why doesn't he come here and show us?"

"Jack Rust, you said?" another asked, looking at the obelisk. "He's ranked 950. That's even lower than me. How can you say he's very strong?"

"Because soon, he rise like meteor."

"As if! That's what we all said when we arrived, and look at us now. Your 'big bro' will be humbled very abruptly and very soon."

"We see," Brock replied diplomatically, not taking any of their comments to heart. After all, he was the one who teased them first.

"We see my ass. If that Jack Rust is as awesome as you say, I will eat my shoe and call you daddy!"

"Big bro is fine."

The crowd would have kept arguing, but the door of the Ceaseless Murder Globe slid open. The words died in their throats, and all gazes swiveled at the Globe at the same time.

A woman stepped out. She looked composed, if panting. Through a cut on her leather armor, a bleeding wound was visible on her ribs. On her back was a red spear, at least nine feet long, with a stark black head.

As for the woman herself, she was slim, athletic, and with long, dark hair that cascaded behind her. Brock had no way to judge her beauty, as all humans looked the same to him, but her aura was towering, billowing like a storm, erupting like a volcano. He lost his breath, and the thousandfold gravity seemed to intensify as her gaze fell on him.

Or, rather, on Ponytail Sis next to him.

"Hey, Min," Ponytail Sis said, stepping out of the crowd. "How did it go?"

"Decently," the spearwoman replied, completely ignoring the rest of the people present. None of them spoke up, either.

"Good! Let's go, we must celebrate."

The spearwoman nodded, leading Ponytail Sis away as the men around Brock nodded respectfully.

Brock finally recovered his breath. That a big sis alright, he thought. Very strong.

"Man, she's so impressive," said one of the men after the two women had left. "Rank one... If I can even reach the single-digits, I'll be satisfied."

"Please. Even the double-digits would be enough for me," replied a less talented man.

"Big Bro will reach rank one," Brock said, drawing everyone's incredulous gazes yet again. However, maybe it was the lasting impression of Min Ling or the fact they were all in the same boat, but nobody looked at him with hostility anymore.

"You don't understand what it means to be rank one," said a man with a wry smile. "Your big bro is just one of us... but that's alright. Next time, bring him along so we can all discuss together. There aren't many things to do here."

"I will try. Thanks."

The men laughed. Some introduced themselves to Brock, while most departed. Eventually, everyone started walking home, and Brock was left alone with the Kill Kill Ball and the Envoy who managed it.

Since he couldn't enter, there was no point staying here any longer. He would need to find another interesting place to recruit more bros for his big bro.

CHAPTER TWENTY
ENTERING THE SECOND LEVEL

Jack sat in silence. Darkness enveloped him. A thousand gravities pushed him down. Burning pain filled every inch of his body, but he endured it.

The small amount of life energy was finally fused into his body. Without giving himself a moment to hesitate, he dragged another out of the Life Drop and started fusing it as well. The pain returned. The hours passed.

For the last two weeks, Jack's days had been almost completely filled with body tempering. Cultivators of his level didn't need to eat or sleep, but the mental burden of this process was too much. Every day, he practiced body tempering for twenty hours and slept four. As soon as he woke up, he started all over again.

If he wanted to defeat Don Cranxiao within a month, he couldn't afford to slack off.

By this point, Jack's mind was in a permanent haze. His entire body was sore and burned, his bones swollen, his muscles cramped. Yet, his willpower was a fierce inferno, boiling in the depths of his soul and pushing him to keep going. As torturous as this practice was, the sensation of strengthening himself was addictive. It reminded him of the early days, when he could advance at breakneck pace by killing a few handfuls of goblins.

After two weeks, his progress was nothing to scoff at.

As the new thread of life energy was completely fused into his body, Jack's eyes cracked open. He summoned his status screen.

Strength: 2305
Dexterity: 2310
Constitution: 2305
Mental: 200
Will: 200

He was overcome with feeling. Just two weeks ago, his Physical substats were all stranded around seventeen hundred and eighty. They had increased by five hundred and thirty in two weeks.

This sort of progress was extreme! In the D-Grade, the System gave ten stat points for every level up. His progress was the equivalent of fifty-three levels, and he hadn't leveled up once. He remained at 249, the peak of the D-Grade.

These new stat points were not awarded by the System. They were something he achieved himself. The status screen was just quantifying his strength so the System could have a better understanding of him. He suspected that, given his outlaw status, the System might not reward him with stat points even if he did level up in the future.

Which was something else he wondered about. Since he had been clearly outlawed, why did the System still support him, even with things as minor as showing him his status screen?

It made little sense. The best explanation he could come up with was that the System was not omnipotent—it operated around and was restricted by certain principles.

For example, Earth was currently outside System space. The cultivators there could still access their status screen and level up, but they could not use most System functions—including the Inspection, Faction Shop, and telepathy.

Jack could only guess that the System implanted a mini System core inside every cultivator, using it to monitor their strength and increase it as needed through level up stat points, skills, or Dao breakthroughs. That mini core kept operating when it had no contact with the wider System, but it could only perform a small number of functions. Basically, everything internal to the cultivator, and nothing external. It was like a smartphone not connected to the network.

For Jack, that had both positives and negatives. He could not be traced by the Hand of God, nor could the System harm him in any way. At the same time, the people of Earth had lost many useful functions, and new cultivators—like babies—could not be inducted into the System. Jack's children had no status screens yet.

But those were drawbacks he could live without. The System wasn't the only way of progress—it was just a method of facilitating advancement and streamlining the Dao. With proper guidance, cultivators could still grow strong, if a bit slower.

And, who knows? Jack had already discovered how the System enhanced the bodies of cultivators. If he could perfect his understanding and imitate that process on a wider scale, perhaps he could even form his own System!

Of course, that was too far into the future. For now, he could barely enhance his own body through the strength of the Life Drop, and that was good enough.

Within a mere two weeks, his strength had increased by leaps and bounds. Every aspect of his body had been strengthened by around thirty-five percent. Given that his titles still worked as normal, he had an effective Physical of almost five thousand!

To the current Jack, the thousandfold gravity of the Cathedral was just like a normal human's gravity on Earth. It added no extra strain whatsoever. He had already stopped using the Dao to resist it and relied on his body.

In pure stats, even middle C-Grades might not be able to match him right now. And this was just the beginning. The only downside was that his method of body tempering was becoming less and less efficient the more he rose, but that was okay—it remained a massive boost.

Despite the pain wracking his body, Jack was in a great mood. Finally standing up, loud cracks were released from everywhere across his body.

"Oh?" Dorman said, opening his eyes. "You finally decided to stretch your legs?"

"Kind of." Jack didn't hide his happiness. "My body tempering has proceeded smoothly. I am now far stronger than I used to, and since Cranxiao will be here in a few hours, I want to test something out."

Dorman nodded. "That's great."

Jack hadn't hidden his body tempering from his friends. He couldn't, anyway—the stormy Dao collisions in his body were easily detectable.

Brock was sitting on the cabin's meditation mat. He did not open his eyes, too engrossed in cultivation, but Jack's gaze was filled with approval as. He could sense the brorilla's power slowly but steadily climbing. By now, he shouldn't be too far from the peak of the D-Grade. Dorman was only slightly behind.

Not wanting to waste any time, Jack opened the door and exited. The Cathedral's bleak landscape was as empty and colorless as ever—yet, standing here so effortlessly was exuberating. Jack's steps had a spring to them.

Cranxiao had once declared that he would stop by every month to beat up Dorman. That was an underhanded method to sabotage Jack's cultivation, but how could poor Cranxiao expect Jack's monstrous advancement? It had only been one month out of their three-month agreement, yet Jack was ninety-percent certain he could win right now.

When Cranxiao arrived in a few hours, Jack would fight him on the spot. Anything less would have a negative effect on his Dao, limiting his current strength and future cultivation.

Before that, Jack wanted to test something out. His steps crossed the empty landscape and brought him to a building that resembled an ancient Chinese pagoda. It had seven levels, each multiplying the Cathedral's already overwhelming gravity by a factor of two.

Jack had visited the Heavy Pagoda a month ago and spent half an hour at the first level. That had already pushed him to his limit. However, as the 950th ranked disciple, he had another half hour to use.

Luckily, nobody had overtaken his ranking. Even if they had, Jack was confident in claiming a position far better than 950 if he visited the Ceaseless Murder Globe right now—it was just that he didn't want to reveal his strength before fighting Cranxiao.

The Envoy responsible for the Heavy Pagoda, a human woman who looked like a muscular old lady, opened her eyes as Jack approached. He didn't have a good impression of her; back when Cranxiao beat up Dorman right in front of her, she had done nothing.

"Hello," Jack said. "I am Jack Rust, ranked 950th. I would like to access the pagoda."

She nodded as her eyes closed again. "You have half an hour."

Without responding, Jack looked at the entrance to the first level. Then, he took a step—and soared!

The Envoy's eyes snapped open. A peak D-Grade could fly in the Cathedral? Even many C-Grades couldn't do that! Before she could overcome her surprise, she saw Jack ignoring the pagoda's first floor and heading directly for the second one.

"Wait!" she shouted. "Every level redoubles the gravity. If you enter the second one, you might die!"

"Thank you, but I have already decided," Jack replied, firmly setting foot on the second level's doorstep. The Envoy no longer spoke but kept her eyes on him. If he was overwhelmed by the second level, she would rescue him before his organs were ground to paste.

Yet, she watched slack-jawed as Jack pushed open the heavy stone sealing the second floor and walked inside, closing the door behind him. He hadn't collapsed.

The Envoy didn't remove her eyes from the door for a good ten seconds before finally shaking her head. A peak D-Grade that could fly in the Cathedral and survive the Heavy Pagoda's second level... that was abnormal.

Jack was *not* as composed as he looked. The pagoda's second level was a new world of pressure. If it was him from a month ago, he would have immediately collapsed. Right now, he could barely hold on. His teeth were chattering, and his legs were shaking. He couldn't take this pressure for more than a few minutes.

A faint gust of Dao guided him to the nearest empty meditation mat, but Jack ignored it. He stepped to the side of the entrance and immediately sat down cross-legged. Not only could he not reach the mat, as his legs would give out first, he also didn't need it. He wasn't here to cultivate. He was here to consolidate his body tempering.

Throughout the last month, life energy had been continuously fused into his body. That had the effect of increasing his strength and durability, but it was also not a perfect process. Jack's control was lacking. There were many dregs and residues, or even places in his body where the life energy had been unevenly distributed. That greatly affected his combat prowess. It imbalanced him, ruined the harmony of his body, and disturbed his control of the Dao.

However, Jack had noticed that the Cathedral's gravity had a beneficial effect to those imperfections. It constantly pressured his body downward, washing them away. If that wasn't the case, Jack would need to stop often and smooth out the life energy in his body, which would delay him.

Unfortunately, even the thousandfold gravity was not enough. Over a month of tempering, Jack's body had accumulated many imperfections that needed to be fixed. He could spend a few days to do it himself—or he could see if the pagoda's increased gravity could have a stronger effect.

Right now, he was enduring four times the Cathedral's gravity. His body weighed over three hundred tons. It felt like a giant was sitting on his shoulders, trying to make him one with the floor. Even his organs were in pain as the flesh around them barely held on.

Jack gritted his teeth and endured it. His Dao could reinforce him, but he only used it to protect his organs. He wanted to withstand the pressure with his body, grinding out the imperfections.

As he sat there, time lost its meaning, and the pain mounted. His bones were rubbing against each other. He sported internal lacerations that his regeneration quickly healed. It was like his body was trapped between two large grinding stones trying to turn him into dust.

Even his heart was barely beating. This gravity was the maximum he could endure.

Of course, if the other disciples currently at this level knew he was using only his body to endure the gravity, they would cry out in protest. They were mostly middle C-Grades, and even they had to constantly cycle their Dao!

Outside the pagoda, the Envoy was no longer cultivating. She was constantly checking the control screen of the pagoda's formation—as soon as that peak D-Grade fell unconscious, it would inform her so she could go in and rescue him.

She was certain that moment would come soon.

However, one minute turned to three, which turned to ten. The Envoy could only gaze at the screen with disbelief as an entire half hour passed. At that point, she suspected the formation had made a mistake. Perhaps that talented D-Grade was already dead.

If that was the case, she would be in deep trouble. The Church didn't care if their disciples got beat up, but if one of them died under her watch, they would never let the matter rest.

The Envoy decided this wasn't a risk she could take. She flew up and was about to open the second floor's door when it opened by itself. A human man walked out—he had dark hair and brown, piercing eyes. His purple robes clung to his body, while sweat matted his hair and forehead. However, while his appearance itself was nothing extraordinary, there was something to his aura that gave the Envoy pause—it was deeper. Heavier. Primal.

This was not the kind of aura a D-Grade should have.

As she stared at him, lost in confusion, the D-Grade spoke up, "Oh? You came to welcome me? That is very thoughtful, thank you."

The Envoy's face scrounged up. Someone like her would obviously never come to welcome a mere outer disciple, but what could she say? That she thought he'd be dead?

"Your monthly time allotment is used up," she responded drily. "Please return next month."

"Thank you for the reminder. I absolutely will."

The peak D-Grade floated to the ground and walked away. Though he seemed exhausted, he didn't have trouble walking. In fact, the Envoy suddenly realized there were no Dao fluctuations coming from that boy—he was resisting the Cathedral's gravity with just his body!

How? was all she could think as she watched him pace away. *His name was... Jack Rust? Wasn't that the Head Envoy's protege?*

I will remember that name. Next time, I should be more friendly. There is no reason to make enemies with someone who might become a future Envoy.

As for Jack, he really was exhausted, but his face beamed. Spending half an hour at the pagoda's second level had ground away most of the imperfections in his body. Now, he would rest a bit to recover his power, and when Cranxiao came... he would be in for a surprise!

CHAPTER TWENTY-ONE

THE DUEL ARRIVES

NEWS OF JACK'S DUEL WITH CRANXIAO HAD SPREAD. IT WAS UNKNOWN WHO started the rumors, but soon, most cultivators across the Cathedral were aware.

The high-rankers wouldn't care about such a thing. However, the low-rankers didn't only care, they were personally invested. Don Cranxiao had been at their throats for centuries. Though they were certain Jack would fail and die, they still had to come.

Today wasn't the day of the duel. It was the one-month mark, when Cranxiao promised he would arrive to bully Jack's friend. Jack had to do something about it, so this was an opening act to the duel.

Since the previous day, a crowd of cultivators had discreetly gathered around Jack's cabin. They sat in the nearby empty fields, alone or in small groups, sipping alcohol while they waited. Conversation came and went, but it wasn't very spirited. Everyone expected Jack to be suppressed, and the villain to win.

Jack sat cross-legged outside his door. His eyes were closed, his breaths deep. He wasn't cultivating, just keeping himself at the optimal state. The crowd of cultivators watching him from a distance couldn't help but feel that something was off. Why was Jack's aura so deep? And why did his body exude such thick fighting intent?

"He couldn't be planning to fight today, could he?" asked a human.

A nearby feshkur, hearing that, shook his head. "It's a smart move. Since he'll lose anyway, why wait another two months and experience all that stress? It's better to fight now. Besides, the greater the disparity in power, the higher the chances that Cranxiao will choose not to kill him."

"I don't know about that," another cultivator weighed in. "Cranxiao follows the Dao of Tyranny. If he can step on a weakling's head and smash it, that will help his cultivation."

"Hmm. I guess you're right. It's a shame... Such a talented man, and he will fall so unjustly. If only he was smarter."

"It's not about smartness. I heard he follows the Dao of the Fist. If he rolled over and let people bully him, how would he cultivate in the future?"

"That's the problem with stubborn Daos. They're strong when you're ahead, but following them to your death is very easy..."

As these people conversed, Jack had obviously noticed them. He didn't care. His full attention was on the battle that lay ahead. Though he had a ninety percent confidence in victory, defeat would mean his death. He had to give it his all.

Whispers spread through the crowd. Jack cracked open an eye, anticipating that Cranxiao had arrived, but he hadn't.

Instead, a man similar to Cranxiao had appeared on a nearby rooftop as if he was too proud to mix with the rest of the crowd. He had silver eyes and hair that fell below his shoulder, while his skin was coppery. His wide chest was bare, revealing intense musculature.

He was so similar to Cranxiao, they could have been brothers, though his face was clearly different. While Cranxiao looked like a man in his late twenties, this one seemed closer to his forties.

Although, they were both C-Grade cultivators, so they could be thousands of years old.

This man appeared like a ghost and waited on the rooftop, arms crossed. He couldn't care less if the cabin below him belonged to somebody. The moment he showed up, the crowd burst into hushed whispers.

"That's Baron Longform!"

"What's someone like him doing here?"

Jack glanced at the new arrival. His aura was deep and tyrannical. He seemed unbreakable, unbendable, like the absolute overlord of everyone present. His strength was far greater than the planetary overseer Jack had fought before or even the Warden, to the degree where they weren't even comparable.

Is this what a peak C-Grade feels like? he wondered.

Baron Longform looked over at Jack, and their gazes met. Jack felt like a mountain had crashed into him, like he was stared at by a wild animal. The killing intent in the other man's gaze was palpable—you had to either bow or die, there was no third option.

The man looked away, not caring in the slightest about Jack, though Jack kept staring.

Baron Longform... I know that name.

The more he stared at this man, the more certain he was that he'd seen him before. The silver hair, the bare chest, the tyrannical aura... All those were familiar. But from where?

Jack's gaze fell on Baron Longform's chest, where he sported a tattoo of three parallel lines, as if wounds from a bear's claws. Suddenly, Jack made the connection. His eyes widened.

This guy is alive!

Back when he'd reached the E-Grade and become the Fiend of the Iron Fist, this man had been the protagonist of Jack's Dao Vision. He was the bare-chested man who single-handedly annihilated a stronghold of immortals. Jack remembered him clearly now. He was a gedritch, a species similar to humans, from the Iron Fist Empire. He also possessed an aura skill that had been the inspiration for Jack's Brutalizing Aura.

He'd always assumed the people he saw in Dao Visions were long dead. That they were ancient cultivators from millions of years ago. What were the chances he would personally meet them in the boundless universe and infinite river of time?

Yet, here he was. Against all odds, Baron Longform was standing right across Jack.

As Jack stared, Longform caught his gaze again, frowning slightly. Jack finally averted his eyes, not saying anything. His face sported a wry smile.

Baron Longform inadvertently helped him in the past. Jack owed him a favor. However, he was so similar to Cranxiao that they were probably related, so Jack chose not to speak. He simply savored the taste of this coincidence.

Could the people from my other visions be alive as well, like the A-Grade vampire woman who manipulated space? Or even... the man who defeated a giant beast with one punch?

Excitement burned in Jack eyes. At that point, the Sage's voice reached him—the old man was naturally part of the crowd.

"*That's Baron Longform,*" he explained. "*Don Cranxiao's cousin, and also the third-ranked outer disciple. His strength is unfathomable. He is part of the reason why Cranxiao can do whatever he wants and no high-ranker ever comes to stop him.*"

"*I see. Thank you.*"

Even between people cultivating the same Dao, there were always differences. Don Cranxiao and Baron Longform shared the Dao of Tyranny, but Cranxiao was more like a bully—he progressed in his cultivation by ruthlessly dominating others. As for Longform, his aura was sharper and far more dangerous. He was not a mustache-twirling villain—he was a bona-fide tyrant.

The crowd quietened. A man stepped out from between two cabins, seeming relaxed and cheerful. His silver hair fluttered in the void, his bare chest stuck out, and his lips were smiling while his eyes were not.

Jack slowly rose to his feet.

"Hey there, kid," Cranxiao said. "Don't mind me, I'm just here for some light exercise. Have you seen the beggar?"

"There is no beggar here, only a friend. However, if you want to touch him, you must get through me first."

"Oho! And how exactly will you stop me?"

"Simple. I will kill you."

Jack's aura, which had been kept in check so far, erupted. It was deep and compact, like a giant fist slowly rolling forth, and it also contained a primal strength that wholly out of place coming from a D-Grade. While everyone present was a C-Grade, the weakest among them felt pressured, like they were stared at by a predator. Some even took a step back.

This aura washed over the crowd and cabins like the breath of a death god.

Facing it, Cranxiao narrowed his eyes. His smile dropped. "You can't be planning to fight me alone. Bring out your backers. Let's see if they're superior to mine."

The reason for Longform's presence became clear, but Jack didn't care.

"I have no backers. Today, I will break you with my own two fists."

The crowd recovered and burst into fierce whispers. Jack was planning to fight? And not just that, but he was purposefully *taunting* Cranxiao? Why would he do that?

Could he be planning to win?

That was the only explanation. Yet, as people realized it, they shook their heads. To them, Jack was naive. Cranxiao was a talented cultivator—though he was at the early C-Grade, his strength approached the late C-Grade. Meanwhile, Jack was only at the peak D-Grade. No matter how they saw it, winning was impossible.

On the nearby rooftop, Baron Longform's eyes narrowed. He

didn't for a second believe that Jack was an idiot. What could he be planning?

Cranxio roared with laughter. His aura rolled out, matching Jack's in the void and causing sparks to fly. "You have balls! I see what you're doing. You want to play it strong so that your Dao isn't too impacted when you lose. An admirable plan. Unfortunately, no matter what you do, the situation remains the same. We have agreed on a fight to the death with an Envoy as the witness. If you wish to fight me today instead of prolonging your life by two months, then I will be happy to kill you. I will smash your skull under my boot and make you one of the endless tributes to my Dao of Tyranny."

Jack's voice remained calm. "If you think you can do it, go ahead and try."

Cranxiao did not attack immediately. Though he had a rough exterior, no cultivator who reached this point was an idiot. The reason he'd said what he said was to ensure nobody would accuse him after the duel. He expected Jack to retort, to claim the duel to the death would be in two months and that this was just a brawl... but he actually accepted?

Could he really have a death wish? Or was he just stupid? At this point, unless his backer was someone like the first-ranked Min Ling or an Envoy willing to drop their honor, he would most certainly die!

Cranxiao thought and thought, finding no traps. He glanced at his cousin, who nodded. At that, an ugly, bloodthirsty grin blossomed on Cranxiao's face.

"Looks like you really went crazy," he said. "Fine. Let me take your life. And, as for all of you watching, pay attention! This is what happens when you mess with me. Next time, when Daddy Cranxiao pays you a visit, you should be good boys and girls and let me do whatever I want!"

His laughter boomed, an ugly, grating sound. The surrounding crowd had dark faces. Most had been on the receiving end of Cranxiao's fists before. Being bullied by him was like an initiation ritual in the Cathedral, a reminder that while they may have been overlords out there, they were nothing here. Even if they became strong enough to surpass him, they still couldn't touch him because of his cousin's support.

The combined hatred of everyone rose like a dark bonfire, but Cranxiao only laughed harder. Though they hated him, they could do nothing—that was his Dao of Tyranny!

"Here I come!" he shouted, charging.

The crowd watched helplessly. Their hearts were united in Jack's favor—if they could spend a hundred years of their life to make him win, they would. Unfortunately, such was impossible. Jack was just too weak. Cranxiao would win yet again, he would get everything he wanted, and there was nothing they could do about it.

Tyranny would prevail—like always.

Cranxiao smashed out a punch. Though it wasn't a serious attack, it still contained enough power to injure an early C-Grade. He wanted to chase Jack around and humiliate him a bit first.

Facing him, Jack remained calm. He did not try to dodge. His aura was a towering mountain, a raging river. He pulled back a fist, and the world sharpened to a point. A terrifying pressure enveloped Cranxiao. Jack's fist shot forth.

The crowd looked away, unwilling to see Jack's arm mutilated.

Two fists collided. The shockwave shattered the hard stone beneath their feet—and, in front of everyone's incredulous gazes, Cranxiao flew back like a ragdoll.

CHAPTER TWENTY-TWO
DEFYING TYRANNY

The clash was too unexpected. Jack's fist shot out, then Cranxiao flew back. Moreover, a cracking sound clearly came from his fist.

The crowd of cultivators, most of whom were dreadfully awaiting Jack's defeat, took a moment to process this.

"What?"

"Cranxiao... lost the exchange?"

Even Baron Longform revealed a stunned expression. Even the all-knowing Sage blinked once in surprise before saying, "Oh, I see. It was about time." Only Brock and Dorman, who knew of Jack's recent increases in strength, were smug.

Cranxiao flew back only ten feet before the thousandfold gravity took hold of him and smashed him into the ground, cratering the hard stone. Even he was stunned—a moment later, his features contorted, and he flew into a rage. The stone under him cracked further as he shot upright.

"How!" he roared.

Jack kept that calm smile on his face. He slowly retracted his fist. "By being stronger than you."

What sort of concept was this? A peak D-Grade with the battle power of a late C-Grade? It was unheard of!

Cranxiao realized he'd fucked up. He'd provoked someone he never should have. As for the crowd, they cheered! Their shouts reached into the void of space, filling it with enthusiasm.

They didn't know how this had happened. But they didn't care. In their eyes, Jack was a hero!

"Jack Rust!" they chanted. "Jack Rust!"

Cranxiao's face darkened. He'd fucked up... and it was too late to step back now. A massive warhammer appeared in his hands out of nowhere. It was nine feet long and possessed a solid hammerhead made of dark stone. Jack couldn't identify the material, but it was so heavy it almost sucked in his Dao perception.

Cranxiao was sweating. His hands were shaking. Wielding this weapon in thousandfold gravity was a massive strain, requiring a large portion of his Dao to support it.

However, he had correctly judged that against Jack, frontal power was the name of the game.

Cranxiao's eyes sharpened. His aura billowed out unrestrained. He was no longer fighting to dominate—he was fighting to kill.

Without a word, he charged. His hammer rose to the sky and crashed down.

Jack grinned. Life Drop, activate! A deluge of life energy filled his body, infiltrating every nook and cranny. His skin itched, his bones groaned. He grew a foot in height and two extra arms sprouted out below his armpits.

Jack's four-armed form was originally a battleform that increased his bodily power. It still was—but, when used on top of his already-enhanced body, even Jack didn't know the limits of his current power. He only felt a bottomless, limitless strength, as if he could punch the sky asunder and shatter the earth.

The moment he transformed, the knowledgeable people in the crowd were swept over with disbelief. They could recognize a Life Artifact—and it was actually in the hands of a D-Grade?

The hammer was still crashing down. Cranxiao's domain rolled out—an oppressive gray pushing against Jack, locking down the surrounding space and preventing his escape, forcing him to meet the hammer head-on.

Jack roared. Purple stars erupted, flying everywhere. They were instantly suppressed by Cranxiao's gray domain—Jack's Dao remained far weaker than the other man's, but it was enough to give him freedom of movement.

He could have dodged. Could have.

In that moment, as his body filled with endless vitality, he didn't want to. His fist sailed upward, a comet in a clear sky. His knuckle met the falling hammer. Space shook. The ground rumbled. The hammerhead was too hard to break, but its wielder was not.

Cranxiao may as well have struck a mountain. His hammer stopped mid-swing, then recoiled. The impact traveled down to his palms and tore apart their webbing. He barely managed to hold onto the hammer as he once again flew backward, his hands dripping blood.

"What!"

The crowd was shaken. This was sensational! If Jack had used some powerful skill to defend against Cranxiao's casual strike, that would be one thing. But now, Cranxiao had taken out his weapon, released his Dao Domain, and attacked with full force. And he had *still* been forced back!

What the hell was happening? How was this the power of a peak D-Grade?

Jack laughed out loud. His hand had shattered in that exchange, but it was already patched up. He shot forward. His Dao remained suppressed by Cranxiao's, barely enough to let him move freely, but that was all he needed.

He possessed excellent titles and over five hundred extra stat points from body tempering. He was already far superior in bodily power, and then he'd activated the four-armed battle form which enhanced him further.

At this point, he didn't even need his Dao. In the Cathedral, where the thousandfold gravity was supposed to be a major constraint for everyone, he was fighting as freely as if he were on Earth. His every punch carried tens of tons of strength.

With his body alone, he was an unstoppable warrior. How could Cranxiao match up?

Jack's assault was relentless. He fell on his opponent, shooting out punches faster than the other man could react. Every punch was a falling comet, every swing a death sentence. Cranxiao didn't even have time to feel shocked. He was forced on the defensive, desperately blocking as he retreated.

His Dao specialized in oppressing weaker opponents. He usually relied on overwhelming strength to win his battles. Facing someone with even more overwhelming strength, just what could he do?

He wasn't even fast!

Hammers weren't good in close-quarters defense. Jack's fist slipped through, striking Cranxiao's abdomen like a cannonball. Cranxiao was pushed back, spitting blood all the while. Though he did possess some self-regeneration, it wasn't enough to heal wounds in the blink of an eye.

Don Cranxiao was injured!

The crowd went crazy. They couldn't understand what they were seeing, but it was a dream come true. Their throats went hoarse from shouting, and their chanting echoed across the entire Cathedral.

"Jack Rust! Jack Rust! Jack Rust!"

Jack had been one of them until now. They saw themselves in his despair. Now, when he erupted with unprecedented strength and pushed back the tyrant, they believed in him wholeheartedly. In just a few seconds, Jack had become these people's hero!

Cranxiao crashed against a cabin wall. He could still fight. Before he even stood, as Jack approached, Cranxiao's eyes went bloodshot and he shouted, "Tyrannical Aura!"

A wave of terror spread outward. Jack's steps faltered. In that wave was an attack on his psyche, the certainty of death if he kept defying this overlord. Cranxiao's aura crashed down on his soul like a second hammer, suppressing him through fear.

But who was Jack? He'd fought for his life since the Integration. He had faced death dozens of times. Had challenged and defeated an entire B-Grade faction before millions of people. He had ruled a planet.

How could a mere bully stop him?

Jack roared. His own skill was unleashed—Brutalizing Aura! Cranxiao's terror was brought to a standstill by Jack's. The two auras clashed midair, grounding against each other, sparks flying in the void. It was like two bloodthirsty beasts fighting for dominance.

And Jack was not driven back at all!

His Dao may have been limited by his cultivation, but when it came to resolve, he was confident he would lose to no one.

Cranxiao's eyes widened. The crowd roared more cheers. On the rooftop, Baron Longform narrowed his eyes in suspicion—Jack's skill was too similar to his own aura. Was it a coincidence?

Jack reached Cranxiao again. Hammer and fists clashed. Jack's hands were broken, but Cranxiao was sent flying back, passing between two cabins to land in the empty fields beyond. The crowd hurried to make more space.

Jack walked out from between the cabins like a god of death.

"You wanted to harm me and my friends," he said. "You wanted to kill me. I hope you are prepared to pay the price."

Cranxiao shot upright with hatred in his eyes. His hair was dirty, blood stained his shorts, and his face was warped in pain. Still, most of his power remained.

"I am Don Cranxiao!" he bellowed crazily. "I have never been defeated by someone weaker than me. It will not happen today! Come at me, you ant! Let me show you the power of tyranny!"

His aura boiled over. More and more of his Dao was pulled out of his body, focused on the hammerhead which glowed with a dark gray light. Bloodthirstiness erupted, filling the void, and the crowd took a few more steps back.

Cranxiao was betting everything, including his very Dao, on this strike. If it failed, he would no longer be a tyrant. Which was precisely the gamble that amplified his power. He raised his hammer and charged forward.

"Overlord Hammer!"

Jack didn't underestimate Cranxiao's final attack. The purple stars around him spun faster. His Brutalizing Aura flared. He clenched his fist, and the world's light and sound were drawn inside, making it a single purple star in an endless night.

He shot it out. A starry trail followed. His entire hand exploded against the falling hammerhead.

"Meteor Punch!"

All sound was swallowed in the blast. A burning shockwave erupted. The crowd covered their eyes, the ground cratered and shattered, stones crossed the air.

A hammer flew high.

The high gravity cleared the dust instantly. When it did, Cranxiao was revealed on the ground. His hands bled profusely. His breath was shallow, and more blood streamed out from between his lips, while the right side of his chest was caved in. Jack's punch hadn't only stopped the hammer. It'd broken through to strike Cranxiao's body.

As for Jack, he stood straight. Blood was pooled under him, but his hand was already regenerating at a rapid pace. As the crowd watched with wide eyes, his four-armed form receded, revealing an exhausted but victorious man.

Jack Rust... had won!

The crowd erupted in cheers. They thought they were dreaming, but that didn't stop them. Brock nodded with pride, Dorman smiled brightly, and the Sage's eyes were sparkling.

As for Jack, who stood over his opponent, his gaze remained hard. He did not seem ready to walk away.

This was a duel to the death. They had agreed so in the presence of an Envoy, and Cranxiao had already announced this to everyone.

If Jack wanted to strike out and kill Cranxiao right now, nobody could accuse him.

That was exactly what he intended to do. His fist rose, purple light budding over it.

"Stop!" a voice cried out. Baron Longform's aura billowed from the rooftop on which he stood, his face carrying caution. He didn't want to offend someone as promising as Jack, but he couldn't let his cousin die. "Let him leave. This is over. He will never bother you again."

"Hmph!" Jack sneered. "If he won, would he let me live?"

Longform's brows fell. "You're going too far."

"So what? This is a duel to the death, with everyone here and an Envoy as witnesses. I have every right to kill him."

"That man is my relative. Your duel has concluded. If you further harm him, I guarantee that you will die a horrible death."

The crowd had gone silent. Jack may have won... but he couldn't possibly defy Baron Longform. Even if he couldn't do anything right now, defying him was a death wish.

Jack was well aware of that. This man was not an enemy he wanted to make. The sensible solution would be to let the matter go —he'd already won, anyway.

But how could he stop now? Don Cranxiao was a detestable bully, a man who harmed a lot of people. He absolutely deserved death. Moreover, if Jack let him live, who knew how Cranxiao would get revenge in the future? He might target Jack's friends or even Jack himself in a moment of weakness. It was certainly something a man like him would do.

And, besides all those... the Fist was not a Dao of thoughtless mercy. When defeating a blood enemy, there was only one conclusion.

Death!

Jack's fist abruptly struck down.

"Stop!" Longform shouted again, releasing his full aura and

dashing forward, but it was too late. Jack's knuckle exploded on Cranxiao's throat, cleanly severing his head from his body. A hateful, disbelieving look was plastered on that ugly face for eternity.

Longform landed beside Jack a moment too late. He stilled, his body exuding waves of tyrannical aura. Without looking at Jack, he said, "You have made the wrong enemy."

Then, his aura receded. It was withdrawn and hidden deep inside himself like he felt no fury or hatred at all. Passing his hand over Cranxiao's body and head, Longform made them both disappear, then calmly walked away without giving Jack another glance.

These acts terrified Jack more than if Longform had thrown a tantrum. This was not a hotheaded brute like Cranxiao—Longform was a calculating, cold-hearted, powerful tyrant. His calmness made him a hundred times more dangerous, to the point where Jack was seriously worried.

However, he had done the right thing. When the consequences came, he would just have to deal with them. And, since they were already enemies...

"Wait a moment," Jack said.

Longform paused. "Are you talking to me?"

"Cranxiao and I had bet twenty Dao stones on our duel. It was also agreed that if we perished, the debt would be paid by our friends and family. I couldn't possibly force you to comply... but you wouldn't abandon your cousin's honor, would you?"

Longform's aura was still, like a volcano about to erupt. As he turned around, his eyes were dark and cold, overflowing with killing intent. Jack feared he'd gone too far, when Baron Longform reached into his pocket and fished out a small sack, tossing it over to Jack with enough force to defy the thousandfold gravity. Jack caught it cleanly.

The crowd remained deathly silent. Longform continued on, disappearing behind a corner.

A moment passed. Then another. The entire crowd found their

voice again, and they cheered with enough intensity to shake the Cathedral. Their eyes were starry, their expressions bright—to these low-rankers, Jack Rust was one of them who erupted with potential, killed Don Cranxiao, and openly defied Baron Longform. He had done what none of them would dare or be able to do.

He was their hero!

CHAPTER TWENTY-THREE
REVISITING THE GLOBE

AFTER THE DUEL'S CONCLUSION, THE CROWD REMAINED.

Most were low-rankers. Cranxiao had been a mountain to them, a devil they couldn't escape. Now, that devil had been defeated and even killed by a man whose ranking was close to theirs. The nightmare was over, and the dream began.

How could they not be happy?

"He amazing!" a voice cried out from somewhere in the crowd. "He protected us! He our hero! Our Big Bro!"

Most didn't see who spoke, only heard the words, but it was enough. They were overcome with sentiment. Which of these people wasn't an overlord back home? They were used to lording over others, but from the moment they came here, their halo had been completely extinguished. They were forced to endure mediocrity and even suppression.

And someone had reversed that. To all these fallen geniuses, that person... could only be a hero!

The crowd's cheers rose to the sky as many approached Jack to congratulate him.

"That was amazing!"

"From the bottom of my heart, thank you!"

"I will remember this favor. If you ever visit the Sky Eye galaxy, look for me in the Sky Eye faction!"

"That was so sexy!"

Those last words had been spoken by a human girl of a rowdy disposition, whom Jack looked at oddly then ignored.

Regardless, the crowd's heartfelt sentiments touched him. "Thank you for your kind words, everyone. I did what I had to do."

A man approached. Jack faintly remembered him as Osmu Sosmu, a guy who had been present when Jack attempted the Ceaseless Murder Globe. "There is no need to be modest. You did a great thing! Don Cranxiao was a blight, but which one of us had the strength to kill him? Even if we did, who possessed the courage? Nobody! Only you! Being our big bro is fitting indeed!"

"Being what?" Jack glanced at Brock, who sported an innocent look and whistled to the side. "Well, thank you all. I appreciate your kind words. In any case, I would like to head to my cabin and recover now, if you don't mind."

"Oh, of course!"

The crowd quickly dispersed. A couple girls shot him coquettish looks, then pouted when he didn't respond. Before long, the gathered people were gone—many planning to celebrate in small groups—leaving Jack alone with Brock, Dorman, and the Sage.

"You did well," the Sage said. That one phrase of praise fell harder than every word spoken by everyone else combined.

"Thank you."

"Did you practice body tempering, by any chance?"

Jack raised a brow. "Maybe. Do you know anything about it?"

"I've heard of it. It's a troublesome, expensive, yet highly effective process. I assume your Life Drop played a part?"

"Yeah. I used its life energy to temper my body."

"Fascinating."

"Wait!" Dorman exclaimed. "You can do that? The treasure I ate contained a ton of life energy—how come it only made me fat?"

"You're lucky you didn't explode," Jack said. "When I get the hang of it, I can try helping you get rid of all that extra energy."

"Awesome!"

"Speaking of that, Sage... can you tell me what's the deal with my Life Drop? I've been using it openly, just as you said, but isn't it a bit too useful at this point? Should I be afraid?"

The Sage shook his head. "Well asked. The Life Drop, as you call it, is one of many Life Artifacts. Most are owned by B or A-Grade powerhouses. They are exceedingly rare, but each of them is different. Some can give their wielder extreme compatibility with the Dao of Life; others can greatly increase their lifespan or nourish their Dao Tree. Your artifact, thankfully, is not too useful; it only reinforces your physical body, be it through tempering or a relatively powerful battle form. That is great for someone of your cultivation, but useless for A-Grades. So, don't worry; your body-oriented Life Artifact will only be coveted by B-Grades—at most."

"Only by B-Grades? Sage! That's terrible!"

"Better than having Elders at your doorstep. You'll be fine. With the Head Envoy behind you, no B-Grade can touch you in the Cathedral. Of course, if they were to find you outside, things would be different... so you'd best be careful."

"Yeah, I guess I will be!"

Jack was shaken. A-Grades, B-Grades... Those invincible existences might be coming after him?

Was it a mistake to reveal his Life Drop?

I didn't have a choice. I couldn't have defeated the overseer without the Life Drop. And Don Cranxiao... I could have waited another month or two to fight him, but people would still notice my abnormally strong body.

Whatever. I did what I had to do. As for the consequences, I'll handle them as they come.

He shook his head. He'd said this phrase a number of times since arriving at the Cathedral—it was a good sign that he needed to get stronger quickly. Both to chase the peak of cultivation, to protect his people from any dangers, and to protect himself from anyone coming after him for the Life Drop.

The Life Drop was a gift and a curse. With it, he would either soar to the heavens, or plunge down to hell. The middle road no longer existed for him.

Exactly how I like it, he thought, eyes sharpening.

"I'll go rest a bit," he told his friends. "Tomorrow, I'll visit the Ceaseless Murder Globe. I've been practicing in solitude for too long. It's time I see what the Cathedral can offer me."

Defeating Don Cranxiao was a loud statement, but it wasn't the limit of his strength. If he wanted to ride the high road, he had to stand out as much as possible, secure every benefit he could get his hands on. Thanks to Baron Longform's kind donation, he already had enough Dao stones to break through, but he still needed some time to prepare.

While doing so, he would awe the entire Cathedral once again.

Jack retreated to his cabin and sat down cross-legged. His strength had risen too abruptly—the battle against Cranxiao made him aware of a few imperfections in his body and Dao control, which he needed to correct. As he sat in meditation, grinding out imperfections and practicing in his soul world, the hours passed.

Finally, his eyes opened. He was ready.

Seeing him stand up, Brock and Dorman followed. The three of them started the trek to the Ceaseless Murder Globe. Before they even arrived, Jack noticed a crowd gathered.

Hmm? Is some celebrity attempting the Globe?

His steps slowed, but as he approached, the crowd turned toward him.

"He's here!"

"Big Bro!"

They made way, greeting him with smiles and raised fists. Jack was speechless. "How did you guys know I'd be here?"

"How could we not know about our Big Bro?" they replied,

laughing. "You are the strongest D-Grade we've ever seen—we want to see how high you'll reach!"

Jack narrowed his eyes in thought. He then turned to Brock, who was still whistling sideways. "Brock," he said slowly. "Did you..."

"Bros must support bros," the brorilla replied firmly.

Jack sighed. "Fine. Let me have a crowd."

These weren't just the people who'd watched him duel. Those were only a few dozen, but now, Jack counted over a hundred people surrounding him.

Even when Lady Min Ling visited the Globe, there wasn't such a crowd. Which was natural. She was already number one, so all the crowd could do was see her go in and out. Her ranking wouldn't change. For Jack, however, it was different. His final ranking was a hot debate topic. In some ways, it was the spiciest question on the Cathedral right now.

Since he'd defeated Cranxiao, he would almost certainly rank over 811. But by how much? Some people said 800, others said 770. A few brave ones even guessed ranks as high as 730!

Even though Jack cleanly defeated Cranxiao who was ranked 811th, the Globe's difficulty rose steeply as one advanced. The ranks below 700 were mostly occupied by the Cathedral's mid C-Grades, who were also geniuses themselves. As much as the crowd supported him, nobody believed a D-Grade could reach *that* high.

As for Jack, he also had no idea how he would do.

Passing through the crowd, he recognized a few people. Osmu Sosmu, that once-arrogant man who'd turned into a fan, was present. So were his three friends that Jack had briefly met the last time he was here. As for Jack's enemies, naturally, none of them were present—who knew what plans they were preparing.

Jack wasn't the only one who knew people. As Brock accompanied him, he suddenly said, "Oh. Hello, Ponytail Sis."

Jack turned, finding a human girl with blue hair done in a ponytail. She laughed as she greeted them. At the same time Jack turned, so did Dorman, and his pudgy eyes widened like saucers.

"The bitch!" he shouted. "What the hell are you doing here? Fuck off!"

She frowned, hurt. "That's no way to talk to a friend."

"What friend? You made me fat!"

"You started it."

"You guys know each other?" Jack asked.

"Damn right we do! That's the bitch who fed me the fat treasure."

Her face radiated anger. "As if! You were the one who stole it, and you still have the guts to complain? If you want to know, I paid a high price for that treasure, and I trusted you!"

"Please! You clearly placed it where you wanted me to take it."

"I wanted to see if you were a decent person! Good thing I found out before I helped you break through. Hmph!"

Dorman was about to respond, but Jack raised a brow in warning. To him, the girl was clearly in the right here.

Dorman had once been a conceited, prideful individual. Now, humiliated before a crowd of peers, his pride was rearing its head, and he wanted to lash out and defend himself.

Except, he did not do that. To Jack's surprise, he actually lowered his head and said, "Sorry. I shouldn't have stolen from you. I was just desperate because my planet was at war for survival, and I was stuck here getting bullied by everyone."

His voice remained bitter. Clearly, forcing himself to speak at this point was difficult, but he still said the words, even if he only half-meant them. Jack could appreciate that.

The girl nodded, not saying anything to forgive him. She turned to Jack. "Sorry for that. I'm Esmeralda Polen, ranked 479th. Nice to meet you."

"Likewise. However, Dorman aside… How do you know Brock?" Brock had called her *Ponytail Sis*.

"Oh, we've met before," she replied with a wry smile, turning to Brock. "So, this is the big bro you mentioned, huh? Let's see—is he really is as awesome as you say?"

"Of course."

"Just so you know, I'll tell my friend what happens here."

"Yes."

Jack raised a brow. "Do I want to know, or..."

"No," Brock and Esmeralda replied at once, leaving him speechless.

"Okay..."

Deciding he didn't want anything to do with all these bro antics, Jack pushed through the rest of the crowd and reached the Globe's entrance. The door was open—nobody was inside.

"Can I go in?" he asked the Envoy responsible, a red-skinned creature with four fingers on each hand. It kind of resembled a frog.

"You may," the Envoy responded. "Would you like to make the Globe transparent? It costs one additional Dao stone."

"No, thank you," Jack replied. He had enemies now—showing them his strengths and weaknesses just to excite a random crowd was hardly worth it. Right afterward, though, he noticed another thing the Envoy had said. "Sorry—additional?"

"Every cultivator gets a free run when they first arrive. After that, using the Globe costs a Dao stone. The magic formation consumes a lot of energy."

Jack hadn't known that. Thankfully, he had recently acquired twenty Dao stones. With his heart aching, he took out one and passed it to the frog person.

"You may enter."

Jack spared a final glance for the crowd—over a hundred people, all excitedly staring at him and awaiting his results. They wanted to witness the start of a legend—and Jack was inclined to give it to them.

He raised a fist, and the crowd rumbled with cheers. Brock shouted the hardest.

Then, Jack walked inside the Globe, and the door fell shut behind him. All sound was cut off. He was alone in silent darkness save for the single light illuminating the center.

His fighting spirit was roused. The irrelevant thoughts went away. The first shadow opponent was formed, and Jack charged.

CHAPTER TWENTY-FOUR
GOING ALL-OUT

Jack's fists were burning. His heart swam with passion, his eyes wide open in extreme focus.

His punch shot forward. An effective strength closing in on five thousand carried it onto the shadow's sword, through it, and into its face. The shadow exploded in a thousand tiny stars.

Jack paused. His grin widened into a full-blown smile. Last time he was here, this first shadow had taken a lot of effort to defeat... but now, it took a single punch.

The feeling of progress was addictive.

As the shadow died down, two formed in its place. One wielded a mace and the other a staff—a warrior and a wizard. Last time, these two opponents had driven Jack close to the limit of his abilities.

He rushed forward before they were even done forming. His fists sailed forth. The mace-wielder blocked them, galvanizing its domain of metal, while the wizard teleported behind Jack and pelted him with fireballs. For a time, the Globe became carnage. Blue flames licked the walls, parted by gray metal. There was little chance to see anything—Jack was moving purely based on his Dao perception.

A fireball flew for his face. He could have teleported out of the way, but he wanted to save his energy. He punched it directly. The ball erupted in a shower of sparks, raising the temperature to hundreds of degrees, but it was nothing to Jack's tempered body. He didn't even use his Dao to defend—he poured it all into attacking.

As the mace-wielder fell on him, a meteor sprang into existence. The light and heat of the flames were sucked in. The shockwaves reverted, tamed by the mother of all explosions. The world went still—and then erupted. A star died on the shadow's mace. Metal shattered, the gray domain cracked, and the shadow was blasted against the back wall with enough force to ricochet. Before it could even land, Jack sieged on the wizard, dancing at the edge of his range.

Space warped before him. It turned into a spike that jutted forth. If a person's body was struck by that, they would explode and paint the Globe with their innards.

However, magic was only as strong as its wielder. While this shadow wizard was an early C-Grade, it was not particularly outstanding—far weaker than Don Cranxiao had been. Facing its attack, Jack didn't back down. His fist shot out, coated in purple. He reached inside the space spike and directly twisted it apart, destroying it with sheer power.

Lacerations appeared on Jack's skin as it was stretched, but they healed quickly. His other fist shot out as well, impacting the wizard's shielding spell, then its face, breaking both. The shadow dissipated into motes of light.

The Globe didn't give him time to rest. True to its name, it instantly summoned three more shadows, each stronger than the two he'd just defeated—these new shadows were at the three-fruit boundary, the top of the early C-Grade.

That had also been Don Cranxiao's level. Of course, Cranxiao had been a genius—these shadows were nothing.

Last time he was here, Jack had forfeited when these shadows appeared. This time, he hadn't even used his Life Drop yet.

With a grin, he did. Life flooded his body. His bones stretched and his body expanded, pulsing with endless strength. Two new arms grew below his armpits. Feeling the familiar rush of power, Jack faintly realized it felt slightly more subdued than usual, as if he could control it better. He didn't have time to consider implications, and filed it away for later.

The shadows charged him. He charged right back, his laughter echoing across the Globe walls.

One shadow held a large shield, projecting a sturdy domain that enveloped all three of them. The second shadow wore a triangular hat—as it pointed at him, explosions resounded, and space cracked. Gravity started dancing, while snow and fire appeared on either side of him. His body struggled to endure both extreme temperatures at once.

At the same time, the darkness grew deeper. Monsters crawled out, malformed and twisted. Some resembled humans missing an assortment of limbs, while others were beings formed of pure malice. A bloodthirsty air filled the Globe—Jack's blood went cold and his mind spun into panic. He was surrounded by cold-blooded killers.

His gaze sharpened again. It pierced through the monsters to reach a shadow whose bald head was carved with tattoos. Its malevolent air was even more intense than the monsters'—this was the creator of the illusions.

Other outer disciples might have hesitated here, struggling to rid themselves of their fear. However, Jack had experienced life and death multiple times. Back on Hell, it wasn't just once or twice that he'd been surrounded by real cold-blooded killers.

Compared to them, these monsters were laughable.

"Fuck off!" he shouted.

His fists pierced the air, shattering everything. The killers and monsters dissipated, but one of them remained. It was a wolf wrought in shadows, and as its jaws clamped down on his arm, Jack understood this one was real.

It twisted its fangs and tore off an arm. Pain blotted out Jack's consciousness, but he forced it down. Clenching his other three fists, he hammered the wolf's head, killing it. He then teleported to avoid the dual assault of fire and snow.

His arm regrew, fueled by the vast life energy inside him, but his breath caught to his throat. Even this initial stage of the Globe contained tricks. That bald shadow wasn't just a Will cultivator, but also a summoner—if not for his extraordinary regeneration, he would have lost right there and then.

He steeled his mind, taking care not to underestimate the shadows again.

More monsters crawled out of the darkness. Jack unleashed his Dao, burning them through sheer power. All of them disappeared—with the wolf gone, the shadow couldn't summon another real monster. At least, so it pretended.

One wizard manipulating the elements, one summoner affecting Jack's mind, and a warrior protecting them both. These three shadows formed a good battle squad.

But they were too weak.

Jack rushed into them. His domain erupted purple, vanquishing the shadows. Fire roared at him, but he pushed right through. His fist pulled back. It shot out. A meteor crashed into the warrior's shield and dented it, then another broke cleanly through.

As the warrior dispersed in motes of light, the other two shadows followed quickly after.

New shadows appeared.

Jack expected a slightly increased number of stronger shadows, maybe four or five. Instead, nine formed, each at the two-fruit boundary. Their individual power was weaker than the shadows he'd just defeated, though their combined might was naturally greater.

He didn't have time to be surprised. The moment these shadows appeared, they erupted into battle. Attacks besieged him on all sides. Jack could no longer save energy. His domain operated at full force, barely enduring the suppression of nine others. Weapons and magic broke against his fists, but there were always more. The attacks came without pause.

Jack was forced to teleport. He punched through space, appearing behind a wizard shadow and shattering its spine. Yet, as he teleported away, a new shadow formed in its place.

What!

More attacks rained on him. In the Globe's restricted space, he barely had room to dodge. He couldn't use his superior strength to bully the shadows. He was forced into a run, only occasionally striking out and killing an enemy.

Yet, no matter how many he killed, new ones formed in their place. The new ones were also stronger. As he killed more of them, their strength climbed from the two-fruit to the three-fruit boundary, until a shadow appeared whose power eclipsed all others.

A mid C-Grade. About as strong as the planetary overseer had been.

Jack finally understood where the Ceaseless Murder Globe got its name. The first three battles were a warm-up. After that, shadows spawned endlessly, gradually becoming stronger and stronger. It really was ceaseless murder—if he stopped moving for even a fraction of a second, he would lose.

This sort of battle was frantic and absurd. Even keeping track of what was happening proved difficult. It pushed one to the very limits of their ability, forcing them to erupt with their full potential or die trying. It was a unique situation that could push one beyond the brink.

Jack loved it.

He had never felt so alive. His Dao flowed freely, his body rapidly regenerated, his fists kept breaking bodies. The battle filled his mind, became all he knew and could think about. There were no erroneous thoughts, no considerations, no fear. Only stone-cold killing.

It was difficult to describe the ecstasy that flooded Jack's soul. He was simultaneously a God and an ant. He was everything and nothing—the ultimate warrior.

Shadows kept dying. A second mid C-Grade appeared, then a third. Against those mighty shadows, Jack could only avoid them to fight others.

His margins of error were thinning. Even with his newly tempered body, he was nearing his limit. The only reason he still persisted was the regeneration offered by the four-armed battle form, which repaired his constantly injured body. Otherwise, he would have lost long ago.

Finally, an even stronger shadow appeared. This one was at the five-fruit boundary, its strength approaching the late Don Cranxiao's. With this addition, the battle sped up. Finally, Jack was cornered. Attacks rained down on him endlessly, while the five-fruit shadow locked space to prevent him from escaping. He lasted for only two seconds before he was overwhelmed, his domain was broken, and his body suffered countless blows.

A spear teleported before his throat and came to a stop, its tip only an inch away from ending his life.

At that moment, all shadows froze. They retrieved their weapons and bowed at him, then slowly disappeared.

Jack had finally lost. He sucked in a breath of cold air, exhausted. After fighting intensely for what felt like hours—but was probably just a few minutes—his brain struggled to return to normal.

The silence was deafening. The stillness, dizzying.

Finally, Jack regained his bearings. His robes were torn and his hair disheveled. As the Life Drop's energy receded, it left behind a body of shallow wounds, the kind he couldn't spare the energy to regenerate.

"I look like shit," he muttered, his voice echoing. "Heh."

Slowly, he walked to the Globe's exit. The door rose by itself, revealing the void outside and the excited stares of over a hundred talented C-Grade cultivators. Even the Envoy stared at him with curiosity.

As they saw his strained form, those gazes turned into incredulity.

Generally speaking, most cultivators would lose or give up before they reached the stage of looking like that. After all, nobody wanted to be ridiculed by others.

But Jack didn't care. As he walked out of the Globe, with his tattered robes barely covering his body, he carried the air of a gladiator. His fighting spirit still hadn't died down completely—the weakest of those present unconsciously took a step back, then caught themselves.

Were they really afraid of a D-Grade?

Everyone was filled with rising wonder. They turned their gazes to the ranking obelisk, which would reveal Jack's result. Brock looked on with pride, Dorman with excitement, and the ponytail girl with curiosity. The rest of the crowd shared a mix of those feelings.

While the Globe's magic formation assessed Jack's performance, the crowd erupted into discussions yet again.

"I think he'll rank at 780," said a man.

"I say 750."

"730."

"720!" Osmu Sosmu said, not really believing it but wanting to create excitement. A few others berated him good-heartedly. After all, even some mid C-Grades couldn't pass the 750 mark.

Jack looked on silently.

Finally, the obelisk rumbled. Jack's name disappeared from its previous place of 950, and a large row of names was wiped away as they all moved a rank down. People looked up to find the new position of Jack's name.

And up. And up.

Finally, when the first person spotted the name, he gasped. Others shared his reaction, while a few stared at Jack like he was pranking them.

Yet, the truth was clear for all to see. His name and ranking were perfectly visible on the ranking obelisk.

Rank 675... Jack Rust!

CHAPTER TWENTY-FIVE
AWING THE WORLD YET AGAIN

Everyone was stunned. They forgot to react. It took a few moments for these C-Grade cultivators to believe what they were seeing, and then the entire crowd erupted as one.

Rank 675! What sort of concept was that?

D-Grades shouldn't even be able to enter the Globe. If they did, achieving a rank in the mid-nine hundreds was an excellent achievement. That's what everyone believed, that's what they were used to.

But now, Jack Rust had completely wiped his butt with their preconceptions and rose to 675, leaving most early C-Grades in the dust!

And these weren't normal C-Grades. The Cathedral only accepted the most talented, most promising cultivators in the universe. Everyone here was the star disciple of some B or A-Grade faction, people who could jump ranks to fight.

Jack was just too abnormal!

The upheaval persisted for several minutes. Everyone spoke between themselves, then looked at Jack like he was a monster. All the while, he simply stood there, absorbing the ambient Dao and recovering his strength.

That he possessed a body-enhancing Life Artifact was not a secret. By now, all the smart ones had figured it out. However, that didn't diminish his achievements at all.

Who here didn't have their own lucky secrets? Everyone did, but nobody could recreate Jack's feat. There were many Life Artifacts in the universe—if it was so easy, anyone could do it.

In the cultivation world, lucky chances were aplenty. Many people found one. However, grasping it required competence and courage. In the million years of Trial Planet's existence in the Milky Way galaxy, the Ancient Trial had been discovered by thousands of aspiring cultivators, but all of them had failed and died. It was only Jack who succeeded and reaped the benefits.

Even if an inferior cultivator could acquire the Life Drop, they couldn't endure the torturous pain of body tempering for weeks in a row. Even if they could, it would only increase their strength by a bit. The only reasons the effect was so pronounced on Jack were his solid foundation, his alignment with his Dao, battle experience, and great titles. Even without the Life Drop, he would still be formidable—this was just a tiger given wings.

Everyone staring at Jack understood these things. In their eyes, he was simply a monster. These galaxy-level geniuses didn't even have the qualifications to be jealous.

A few people shook their heads and left dejected, while others had eyes filled with excitement. If this overwhelming power belonged to someone else, they might not be so happy... but Jack was awesome! He was a hero! He had dared to kill Cranxiao and oppose Baron Longform. Even on his first day here, he insulted the wife of the 281st ranked Marcus William.

If he could rise meteorically and break through all those illustrious opponents, how amazing a sight would that be?

The gazes that fell on Jack were warm, excited. The Cathedral had been infused with life. This was the start of a legend.

"That's a real big bro," a voice said from somewhere in the

crowd, discreetly reaching the ears of everyone. It was like the spark that set aflame their inner thoughts.

Indeed! If proud people like them admired someone as their big bro, that person could only be Jack!

As for Jack himself, he had no idea about the bro army swiftly forming around him. He stayed here not to enjoy everyone's admiring gazes, but to recover some of his strength. As soon as he felt somewhat okay, he opened his eyes.

"Congratulations!" Dorman said as he approached. "That's extremely good!"

"Thank you," Jack replied calmly.

"Good job, bro."

"Thanks, Brock. I tried my best."

Jack wasn't too excited. He'd been aware of his own strength since before he fought Cranxiao. Plus, the Globe greatly favored cultivators with high endurance and regeneration—it played to his strengths, which was part of the reason why he achieved such a good ranking.

But, still, the hint of pride in his chest was hard to extinguish.

"That was really great!" Esmeralda said, approaching as well and ignoring Dorman's fiery stare. "I don't even know if Min could do this at the D-Grade."

Jack raised a brow. "Min?"

"Nevermind about that. You're as great as Brock told me. I'll be sure to pass this message along."

"To whom?" Jack asked, but the blue-ponytail girl had already walked away. He turned to the brorilla. "Brock?"

"No bother, big bro. You get strong. I handle the rest."

"Okay..."

"Excuse me," a voice interrupted them. To his surprise, Jack saw the Envoy himself approaching—a man with red skin and four fingers on each hand. The entire crowd quietened.

Envoys were on a completely different level than outer disciples, both in strength and in status.

"I would like to congratulate you on your stellar result," the Envoy said.

"Thank you, Envoy."

"Mm. Now that you have reached the ranking of 675, you have unlocked extra privileges. Your Heavy Pagoda time allotment has increased from one to eight hours per month. Additionally, you can use the teleporters to freely leave the Cathedral, and you can also access the Dao Chamber."

"Dao Chamber? What's that?"

The Envoy smiled. "The Dao Chamber contains resources that can enhance or deepen a cultivator's Dao. A-Grade Dao Visions are only the appetizers. With your ranking, you can use the Fallen Genius Mirror, an ancient artifact with wondrous effects on one's Dao."

"Oh!" Jack exclaimed. "That sounds great."

"It is. Would you like me to guide you over now?"

The surrounding cultivators had wide eyes. The hell? This Envoy was responsible for operating the Ceaseless Murder Globe. If he abandoned his post to show Jack around, would the Globe go out of order?

Many sighed in their hearts. Different people got different treatment. This Envoy saw Jack's potential and wanted to befriend him, even going to the extent of bending the rules to do so.

Since the crowd could understand this, so could Jack. Unfortunately, he had different plans. "I am honored, Envoy, but I must do something else first. I appreciate the offer."

"No problem at all." The Envoy gave an easy-going smile. "If you need anything in the future, come find me. My name is Borkuren Madiba."

"If anything comes up, I absolutely will."

Borkuren said nothing more. He nodded and returned to his post.

Dorman turned to Jack, a hint of envy in his gaze. "Are you going back to Earth?" he asked.

"Now that I've reached within the ranking of eight hundred, I can return whenever I want to... but I won't go immediately. Another thing comes first."

"And what is that?"

Jack grinned. "Break through to the C-Grade."

On a different part of the Cathedral, an Asian-looking young woman sat cross-legged on a hard bed. Her raven black hair cascaded over her shoulders, and the air she exuded was one of pride and arrogance backed by absolute confidence.

This was the number one outer disciple of the Black Hole Church—Min Ling!

"675?" she asked, raising a slender brow.

"Exactly!" Emeralda replied excitedly. "I saw it with my own eyes. A peak D-Grade reaching the six hundreds... He's a peak talent!"

"He's decent," Min replied calmly. She was by far the strongest C-Grade on the Cathedral. At Jack's cultivation, she probably couldn't have reached that rank... but it mattered little. The C-Grade was very long. From the first to the ninth fruit, one had to cross many chasms and tribulations.

No matter how talented a D-Grade was, there were high chances their path would be severed somewhere in the C-Grade.

"So, what do you think?" Esmeralda asked with a sly smile. "His brorilla already indicated that Jack Rust is interested. You are both extreme talents. On the Cathedral, who else is more suitable for you?"

Min Ling frowned. "I don't have time for those things. Even if I did, I wouldn't choose someone just because they're strong."

"He's decently handsome, too."

"That's not what I meant."

Esmeralda laughed, her peal gentle like crystal water. "Come on, Min. Don't be so stuck-up. Since he's expressing the interest to know you, why not have some tea? You never know what could happen."

"I said no."

"Fine... Be boring."

Min Ling sighed. "He's only a child, Esmeralda, not even at the C-Grade. We're worlds apart. Even if I was interested in finding someone, which I'm not, I would never look at someone like him."

"Oh yeah? And who would you look at? The Spacewind Sovereign?"

Min's face darkened with disgust. "That's enough, Es. If there's nothing else, can you let me cultivate in peace?"

"Suit yourself. Tea in three months?"

"Sure."

"Great! See you then!"

The Heavenly Spoon Sovereign stared at a chessboard. Opposite him, an old woman had a glowing smile on her face as she moved a piece. He sighed. "I lose again."

"But you're making progress! Don't worry, you're still too young. In twenty thousand years, I'm sure you'll be my match."

"I don't know. If I fill my mind with chess, where will I fit cultivation?"

The old woman laughed. "Correct, correct. Then you can just lose for eternity."

"Yeah, I guess I will."

The sovereign did not take her words to heart. Chess was a fun way to reset his mind after intense bouts of cultivation—despite its seeming simplicity, even B-Grades couldn't completely solve it.

"Did you hear?" the woman said, gathering up the chessboard as she prepared to leave. "That new protege of yours achieved a ranking of 675."

"Oh yeah? That's decent, I guess."

"Before reaching the C-Grade."

The sovereign looked up. Faint amusement played on his lips. "Would you look at that. Impressive. But wasn't there someone who did even better six millennia ago?"

The woman rolled her eyes. "Don't play with me, Head Envoy. You're just too good. Anyone even remotely similar is a great asset to the Church."

"Naturally. What can I say? My vision is just that good."

"So now you'll leave him alone?"

"Oh, on the contrary. The more pressure he can take, the more I'll push. Let's see how high he can reach."

She frowned. "You're too cruel."

"I've met that boy—he is the type who thrives in adversity. If I don't create some enemies for him, he might stall, and how will he reach the peak then?"

"By taking his time. That's bullshit and you know it."

"Taking his time? What time?" The Head Envoy laughed. "The Hand of God is moving on us everywhere. Two Elders clashed in the Serpent's Fang galaxy. Our leaders are pushing for war, and so are the Immortals. Don't tell me you can't see the signs. We need to push the disciples harder, both the inner and outer ones, to squeeze them dry of potential as soon as possible. Otherwise, I'm afraid the crusade will eat them whole."

The Head Envoy took out a silver teaspoon from inside his robes, inspecting its head. His voice turned serious.

"Heed my words, Morgana. Slow accumulation is over. Now, we rush—and if we don't, we die."

Jack sat alone in his cabin. Brock and Dorman had temporarily left. He'd locked the door and closed the curtains, discovering they possessed Dao limiting properties. Until he opened the cabin again, nobody could spy on him.

Jack was now cross-legged on the magical meditation mat. Twenty-two Dao stones were arranged in a circle around him—twenty came from his bet against Cranxiao, and the other two also came from the same bet. Apparently, the bag that Baron Longform tossed over contained two extra stones, but he was too angry to count them out and humiliate himself further.

Before now, Jack had spent an hour at the third level of the Heavy Pagoda, enduring eight thousand gravities to compress his Dao to the maximum. Then, he rushed back home before the compressed Dao could escape, using it and these Dao stones to break through. According to his calculations, he would only need thirteen, but he'd laid down all of them. He only had one shot at this breakthrough—not being greedy would be completely idiotic.

He took a deep breath. His perception sank into his soul, finding the Dao Tree bursting with energy. It was mostly focused on the branches and leaves, ready to bloom to life, barely held back by Jack's will.

He touched his hand on the Dao Tree and released the pent-up energy. The Dao Blooming began.

He was breaking through to the C-Grade.

CHAPTER TWENTY-SIX
BREAKING THROUGH

Jack's Dao Tree erupted. All its restrained energy was released at once. The Dao Roots below it roared, the Life Drop glowed brilliantly, and the entire Dao of the Fist heralded the arrival of a new lord.

Below the tree's base was Jack's Dao Seed surrounded by his four Dao Roots—these five each represented a finger, forming a multicolored fist. From index to pinky, they were silver, red, green, and black—Indomitable Will, Power, Life, and Weakness—the four Dao Roots he'd developed during the F and E-Grades. Covering them was the thumb, a strong purple color representing the Fist itself, Jack's core Dao.

These five Daos formed a fist which floated in the middle of Jack's soul world, aimed downward. Buried at the wrist of this hand was a green light—the Life Drop—and over it grew the Dao Tree.

This tree was nine feet tall. It pulsed with life, breathing the Dao of the Fist, its bark a bright wood with hints of purple. Branches stuck out from the upper part of the tree, extending in all directions. They were covered in leaves—a lively green color, each verdant and full of energy—creating a thick crown of foliage. Jack had nourished this tree well. Then there was the door embedded on its trunk, almost a pattern of the bark itself.

However, while this tree grew from the Dao of the Fist, it bore little resemblance to it. The tree was lively, but empty—a fountain of power yet unclaimed. This wasn't Jack's fault. It was the nature of the D-Grade.

In the F-Grade, a cultivator enhanced themselves and chose a Dao to follow.

In the E-Grade, they walked down the road of that Dao, deepening their comprehension and supplementing it with secondary concepts, creating a Dao best suited to themselves. To break through, they had to cement their foundation and Dao.

These two Grades were the foundational part of the Road to Mastery.

Starting from the D-Grade, that foundation was built upon. A cultivator walked hand-in-hand with their Dao, attuning themselves to it, filling it with power. The Dao Tree sprouted from the Dao Seed, and the main job of a cultivator in the D-Grade was to nourish it and make it grow.

Therefore, the D-Grade was not about intense Dao exploration. It was a long consolidation phase, where a cultivator digested everything they had created in the previous Grades and grew to their potential, so they could later use it as the basis to delve deeper into the world's Dao.

This was also the reason why, throughout the D-Grade, Jack had focused on leveling up rather than comprehending the Dao.

The Dao Blooming was the transformation that occurred between the D and C-Grades. By now, a cultivator's tree had reached its peak. It could grow no more. That peak was signified by the blooming of flowers, each serving as a conduit of the cultivator's Dao and enhancing their power by a small degree.

Of course, if a cultivator's Dao was weak or unstable, their tree could stop growing at any point, and they would remain stuck at that level forever. In the same vein, if they could not prove their

Dao's sufficiency before the universe, then their Dao Blooming would fail midway and never advance further.

Jack hoped his Dao was excellent. He had no indications otherwise. He hoped to bloom with dazzling radiance, then advance into the C-Grade and eventually condense nine fruits, each signifying a different manifestation of his Dao.

Except he could never be too sure. There were records of bright geniuses who fell at this step—people who radiated excellence across the entire universe, only for their halo to shatter as their Dao was deemed inferior.

Those were people who drew power from various sources, like treasures or artificial means. They could possess power at the early stages of cultivation, but the further one advanced, the more everything converged to the Dao. All external help was useless.

That was why, as Jack faced his Dao Tree that was about to bloom, he was overcome with doubt.

What if my Dao is weak? he asked himself. *What if the reason for my power is my titles, my luck, or the Life Drop? What if my Fist is not solid enough?*

What if my journey ends here?

It was hard to contain one's nerves when the universe was about to pass judgment. There was nobody here to share his burden. Strangely, even Copy Jack was absent—the mystical energies of the Dao Blooming had pushed him away as if the universe demanded Jack's complete attention.

The tree erupted with purple power. Fists flew out—each stronger than the last, shooting into the void like comets. A thick column of purple shot to heights untold. The energy of the tree was being rapidly spent, the eruption dying down.

In the real world, the Dao stones surrounding him lost their luster. A cloud of pure Dao rose from them, so intense that it formed into mist, unfettered by mundane things like gravity or cold. Jack breathed in deeply, sucking that energy into his body. Half the mist was gone at once. His entire being became bloated, but this was not

Life energy—it could not be assimilated into his body. All he could do was manically stuff it down his soul, forcing it into the Dao Tree even as most of it dissipated.

The eruption of purple energy intensified. A wind blew in Jack's soul world, so powerful that it pushed him back. The purple column flared, shooting into the void as if to pierce the heavens. Jack was already like an ant before it, a mere mortal before the might of the universe—but it was his universe, and his might.

The purple column was wasted energy. The tree did not know how to bloom. He had to force it.

All doubts faded. His mind became the Fist. The Dao roared. The void trembled.

With a shout, Jack raised his hands and gripped them into fists. A tremendous force surged out of every inch of this soul space, locking the erupting column in place. The energy sought to escape, but Jack refused to let it. This world was under his command. He controlled it.

With a second shout, Jack punched down. The rampant energy went wild. It crashed into the column, surrounding and suppressing it. The Fist resisted. It did not seek to be controlled. The sound was like drilling glass, the spectacle apocalyptic. Jack's soul world lost its colors, and the void collapsed as his willpower fought his own Dao. He was left floating in darkness, with only himself and his Dao remaining intact.

The tree's energy had stopped shooting up, now just hovering above. It needed to return inside.

For the third time, Jack pushed down. His head was about to crack. This was too difficult—but he would persist until he died. That was his path. That was the Dao of the Fist.

The Dao issued a piercing cry. His willpower clamped down, reversing the flow of energy and sinking it back into the Dao Tree. The tree shook, its bark flaking, almost unable to contain the energy within. It looked about to burst, and Jack's chest was swollen by the pressure.

Not enough!

He breathed in again. The remaining mist of the Dao stones was sucked in, enhancing the Dao in his soul world. The pressure shot up another level, threatening to explode him. The Dao madly yearned for release.

Jack's eyes were bloodshot. His every instinct told him to let go or he would die, but he only pressed down harder. His soul world shook. Cracks formed everywhere, revealing an even deeper darkness.

With the groan of splintering wood, a crack appeared on the bark, crossing over the Life Drop's door. The energy demanded to be released, but Jack refused to let it.

"Kill me if you must, but I will never yield!"

His shout echoed across the soul world, seeping into the cracks, intensifying the already catastrophic war. He was past the point of no return. If he let the Dao go now, he would never recover.

The Dao Tree shuddered. The energy needed to be vented, but it couldn't. The pressure kept mounting, until Jack's entire soul was only a hairline away from shattering.

And then, he crossed that line. His Dao Tree gave out. It finally realized Jack would never let go—and, at the precipice of death, it was forced to find another way.

Energy rushed to the branches, then to the leaves. One after another, tiny shapes appeared—purple flowers, each glowing like a meteor in the night. The tree had been on the verge of collapsing, and now, after the first few flowers, more formed. They came faster and faster. The branches filled with purple, petals falling and dancing in the wind. The excess energy was consumed, used to form these flowers, and the rest discovered that it could use these flowers to freely exit the tree, shooting out like jets of purple.

Jack's dark soul world became illuminated. The tree a purple sun as energy flew everywhere, circling around to re-enter the tree through its roots. More and more flowers formed, populating the branches, and contrasting the leaves. Jack could feel his Dao strengthening at a rapid rate, his control rising, his Dao repository deepening. Just these flowers were a tremendous benefit to his cultivation.

His entire body was wracked with leftover pain, as it had almost exploded, but Jack was used to it. Pain was a friend now—the sign of progress.

However, it was too late to be happy. The Dao Blooming had begun in earnest, but that was the easy part—any cultivator could do it with enough resources and strong willpower.

Now came the hard part.

The blooming would continue for some time, no longer needing his guidance. At this moment, however, Jack sensed a gargantuan existence lock onto him. It was like the world itself stared over. He felt tiny—smaller than a grain of sand before the ocean.

CHAPTER TWENTY-SEVEN
C-GRADE!

As the flowers bloomed, a tremendous power reached into Jack's soul, completely disregarding any and all defenses, and whisked him away.

Jack found himself in a space he'd only seen once before. He was surrounded by nothingness. A large fist floated in the distance—it was impossible to estimate how far away or how large it was. The moment he saw this fist, Jack's feet went cold, his mind staggered, his Dao escaping his control.

This was the Dao of the Fist itself.

The first time Jack arrived here was when he first comprehended the Dao Root of the Fist, back in the F-Grade. He hadn't understood the significance of what he faced. Now, he did. This was a foundational force of the universe, a power above any cultivator. He was face-to-face with an aspect of the Dao, the beginning and end of everything.

The world had noticed his breakthrough. Witnessed him finalize his own Dao and start expanding. However, the Fist could not be tamed so simply. He already earned the right to use it, but if he wanted to build on it and manifest it into fruits, he needed to pass much stricter tests.

The Fist looked inside Jack. He didn't have a say. The Dao itself rampaged through his body and mind, scouting everything. His very self was laid bare.

Together with the Dao, he watched himself grow.

He saw little Jack, barely a few years old, pick up his suitcase and hug a smiling professor. He saw a sturdy-looking man tussle his hair. Saw himself growing through school, into university, into his life as a researcher.

The Dao of the Fist did not care about those. It skipped everything to arrive at the Integration, then paid closer attention.

He saw himself using his fists to kill that first goblin. He was shouting and crying back then. He killed more goblins, tempering himself into a warrior. The bears fell, the brorillas were defeated. Jack entered the Ice Pond and comprehended the Dao Root of the Fist, that first block on which he built everything.

His entire journey sped before his mind's eye. He defeated the twin black wolves and met Brock. He killed a person for the first time —Hugo, the man who kidnapped his mother under the orders of a local warlord. He freed his town, Valville, then went to the Integration Tournament.

When the Dao saw him using flip-flops and the so-called Dao of Spanking, Jack was embarrassed. He defeated numerous opponents, including the scions. He advanced as quickly as he could, breaking into the E-Grade and decisively killing Rufus Emberheart after a bloody battle.

His resolve solidified: he would save Earth or die trying.

He escaped to the wider constellation, boarded the *Trampling Ram*, and escaped the Hounds, then entered Trial Planet. He passed ring after ring, overcoming all sorts of difficulties to surpass his limits. His strength grew rapidly. He reached the third ring and earned the Life Drop's approval.

The Dao paused here, as if to consider this scene more deeply, then carried on.

He gradually outpaced everyone, outsmarted the Lords, earned the top treasures, and battled the Final Guardian, becoming the first person in his galaxy to conquer the entire Trial Planet. He broke through to the D-Grade, surviving the tests of the Dao and the divine tribulation that Axelor, an Old God, had smote him with due to the existence of the Life Drop.

Jack then traveled to the Exploding Sun, trained, and entered Hell where he went on a long killing spree. He kept rising meteorically. He dared to make vastly stronger enemies than himself and never once gave up, even when his limbs were broken and his teeth were shattered. He challenged the entire Animal Kingdom and won, shocking the galaxy—then rushed back to Earth and saved his planet from the C-Grade planetary overseer.

He had children and watched them grow a bit.

Finally, he came to the Cathedral, where he discovered body tempering, securing his place as a universal genius and finally attempting to reach the C-Grade. His life's story ended here for now—and the Dao fell silent.

Jack realized that the Fist was not judging his Dao. It was judging him. Everything he had ever done, the person he was in conjunction with his Dao. The intensity of it left him naked. There was no way to cheat. He would either be worthy, or he wouldn't be.

In his heart, Jack knew the result with absolute certainty. As he watched his own life go by, pride had blossomed in his chest. Fulfillment. Throughout his many adventures, maybe he did not agree with every decision he ever made, but he was never disappointed with himself. He remained true, kind, and just.

Jack was proud of the man he had become. Knowing that his life was meaningful and fulfilling, he felt such warmth that he even forgot about the ongoing breakthrough, shedding a single tear of happiness.

Even if he failed now, he'd already succeeded—he would always stand with his head raised high.

The Dao had seen enough. The fist in the distance approached rapidly—or maybe it was Jack that was moving. He fell under tremendous pressure, like a planet was heading for his face, as the fist grew larger and larger in his sight. Suddenly, it was larger than existence, larger than the world. For a single moment, Jack became aware of the universe's vastness, and he almost crumbled in insanity.

Then, his soul sank into the Fist, and he was standing on a grass field.

This was not his soul world. He couldn't see the Dao Tree or the colorful void. All that existed was him, standing alone in an endless prairie.

"Show me," the universe whispered, speaking deep inside his soul. "Show me who you are."

Jack understood. He raised his head and clenched his fist, losing everything else. This was the realest version of Jack, the most fundamental part of himself. The Fist blossomed around him, a halo of radiance, and tiny stars appeared everywhere he looked. The world was dyed purple. He became a meteor and crashed down, shattering the grass field.

Or—he tried.

A second fist smashed into his, breaking his hand and forcing him back. Another Jack stood before him. This was not Copy Jack—it was a version of himself formed by the Dao of the Fist, an anvil on which to prove himself. The second Jack was expressionless, yet his Fist was so pure it was blinding. This was the absolute Fist, without Dao Roots or emotions.

Jack understood. He followed the Fist, but he was not the Fist. Then, who was he? What made him different?

What made him Jack Rust?

Jack clenched his own two fists and roared out. He sank

completely into battle. Fist met fist, and every time, he was pushed back. His version of the Dao was weaker, and of course it was—how could he match the Fist itself?

Yet, after every exchange, his body healed completely. The second Jack never pursued him. It simply stood there, waiting for him to prove something.

Jack didn't know how many times he was defeated. He didn't know how long they fought for. It felt like days. Again and again, he charged, only to be sent flying back.

How could his own Dao surpass the Fist?

The question faced him unendingly. He could not leave this place until he figured it out or gave up. But he would not give up.

He was Jack Rust.

In the outside world, days passed. Weeks. A month, then a second. Jack's cabin door remained firmly shut, obstructing any perception skill. Nobody knew what was going on.

The small bro army spent their days in the nearby fields, waiting for news. Dorman grew more anxious with every passing day. Breakthroughs were not harmless—if one was not careful, they could die. Maybe Jack was dead already, his corpse lying in the cabin, and they just couldn't see it.

Only Brock did not have the slightest fear, spending his days merrily cultivating and conversing with the newly formed bro army.

Jack faced the Fist again and again. It was similar to him in every way, except its Dao was purer. Naturally, he lost every time.

His mind was in a trance. In this state, he completely lost track of time, completely forgot everything that wasn't related to the Dao. Unknowingly, his entire state of being was nourished during these battles. His mind and body grew fiercer, his connection to the Dao grew much more intimate. It was like training with Copy Jack, only far more intense.

And as he got stronger, Fist Jack advanced at exactly the same rate.

How do I win? Jack kept asking himself, charging again and again. *How? How do I use the Fist to defeat the Fist?*

He wasn't an idiot. A hundred ideas had passed through his mind, but everything he tried failed. He could make no progress. Nothing worked.

Finally, the Fist grew impatient. The sky began to crumble. Strips of blue tumbled to the ground, revealing an endless darkness. Holes appeared in the grass, and the air lost its luster. The second Jack, the one formed of the Fist, grew older and older, slowly resembling a wrinkled, white-haired man. Yet, its strength never diminished. Jack was equally unable to win.

He had to find a way. If this world crumbled before he succeeded, he would have failed the breakthrough. His path of cultivation would be cut short.

What makes me different? he asked with rising panic. *What is my Dao? Is it not the Fist? Where is my mistake?*

Sometimes, the simplest things can be the hardest to see. As the world around him was reduced to nothing, and as the endless grass field turned into a tiny island of green in a sea of darkness, in one of infinite exchanges, Jack suddenly saw the truth.

Ah.

It was like a veil had been lifted. His world turned crystal clear, and his entire being was aligned. After he was sent flying back, he did not charge immediately—he smiled from the bottom of his heart. And, for the first time, the expressionless Fist Jack smiled back.

"Come," he said, pulling back his fist. "Show me."

Jack laughed. "Face me!" he roared, then charged once again. His own fist reared back, then shot out like a purple meteor. It was stunning in the darkness. Fist Jack's punch also shot out, a pure fist that was one with its surroundings.

Nothing had changed from all the previous exchanges. But it didn't matter. Nothing had to change. Jack finally realized the truth.

He didn't have to defeat Fist Jack. He couldn't. All he had to do was embrace his own Dao and follow it to the end. This wasn't a battle.

His fist stopped an inch before collision. All its energy blew past and dissipated. The other Jack's punch also stopped, the two fists aimed at each other an inch apart, one purple and the other white.

Jack smiled brightly. His fist moved slowly, tapping against the other in a fist-bump.

"I am me," he said. "I don't cultivate the Fist. I cultivate my Fist."

His Dao erupted, not in an attack, but in a display of its identity. It bared itself, revealing its strengths and weaknesses, the things that made Jack human.

The other Jack stared deep into his eyes—and nodded.

The final patch of grass dissipated. Jack fell into the void, one man and his fist, forever.

In Jack's soul world, the Dao Blooming was over. The flowers were finished forming. Suddenly, one of them grew, and grew, and grew, transforming from a flower into a plump, purple fruit shaped as a fist that hung proudly from the Dao Tree's branches.

The moment this fruit appeared, the entire soul world shook. The real world followed. The Dao cried out in joy and shone with a million colors, heralding the arrival of a new C-Grade.

And Jack escaped the void, his eyes sparking purple thunder, his body hiding the strength of a titan. A strong wind blew around him, disintegrating the empty Dao stones around him and slamming open the cabin's windows.

For the first time in a while, a blue screen appeared of its own volition.

Congratulations! D-Grade → C-Grade

Class Upgrade available. Please choose your new Class:

Seeing it, he couldn't contain a wild grin. The void sang about a new master of the Fist. The universe celebrated, the stars shone brighter.

A new day had come—and Jack Rust, the C-Grade cultivator, was here for it.

CHAPTER TWENTY-EIGHT
NEW CLASS!

AFTER BREAKING THROUGH, JACK FELT IMMENSE POWER POOLING WITHIN HIS body, almost begging him to stand up and release it. He remained seated, enjoying this feeling, an excited smile playing on his lips.

He couldn't wait to go out and show Brock—but first, he wanted to tidy up his blue screens.

Congratulations! D-Grade → C-Grade
Congratulations! You have developed the Dao Fruit of the Fist, embarking on the path of manifesting your Dao.
All stats +100
Free stat points per Level Up: 10 → 20

Level Up! You have reached Level 250.

Congratulations! The Bare Fist Brotherhood faction has reached the C-Grade. New functions unlocked in the faction screen.

Class Upgrade available. Please choose your new Class:

Leaving the Class aside for now, Jack focused on the other news. He had reached the C-Grade—that much he knew. He'd also gotten an extra hundred stat points per stat, which was less impactful than it used to be but still welcome.

Once upon a time, I was enduring the Ice Pond to get one stat point, and now a hundred barely draws my eye... The world changes when you look at it from above.

Jack sighed.

The level up stat bonuses had doubled, which was both good and bad. Good because he would become stronger, bad because it made his body tempering relatively less powerful.

As for the Bare Fist Brotherhood leveling up, it didn't matter yet. He was cut off from the main System—it wouldn't know about his breakthrough until he returned to Earth or System space.

Jack sank into his soul world again. It had changed. Purple flowers blossomed on the tree branches, each like a piece of the night sky. His Dao had undergone a qualitative change, not increasing much but now significantly more lively.

This change came from the Dao Fruit of the Fist. Jack approached it for a better look. It hung from his Dao Tree proudly, like a plump apple roughly the size of his hand. Its shape was that of a fist pointed downward, and it was purple in color, with a faint aura rising like the starry trail of a comet.

Gingerly, he reached out to touch it; it was surprisingly soft, as if one pinch could pop it and waste its juices. Jack hurriedly withdrew his hand, though he suspected this softness was only an illusion—how could Dao Fruits be fragile?

My very own Dao Fruit... he thought, a sweet feeling rising in his chest. *I have finally reached the C-Grade.*

Back in the F-Grade, Jack had once bought and used a Dao Fruit of the Fist to further his own Dao. That fruit looked very similar to this one, and even their names were the same. Could it be that the fruit he once ingested came from the Dao Tree of a dead C-Grade?

He shook his head. *Impossible. There are billions of F-Grades for every C-Grade. If a Dao Fruit was that rare, it wouldn't have been my turn to consume it. There must be some way to mass-produce resources like this...*

Regardless, this was *his* Dao Fruit. It felt... comfy.

One down, eight to go.

Unlike the D-Grade, the C-Grade was a period of qualitative improvement. Besides cultivating and deepening his Dao reserve, he would focus on improving his understanding of the Dao and developing more Dao Fruits.

Of course, for Jack, his strength would also rise by forging his body into a weapon.

He spared a glance for the door on his Dao Tree. A crack had run through it during the time when his tree almost exploded from containing too much energy. Now, that crack had healed, leaving behind a long scar that made the door seem damaged.

It probably wasn't. He considered checking, but the turtle had told him not to disturb it for no reason. Therefore, Jack left his soul world, returning to the real one.

System, he thought, *show me my new Class.*

Class Upgrade available. Please choose your new Class:

Fist of Slaughter (King)
Your fist is a weapon of mass destruction. Build a staircase of corpses and struggle for the top through a road of blood.
"One fist to slaughter billions."

This probably originated from Jack's killing spree on Hell. Back then, he'd chopped down immortals like vegetables, destroying the Animal Kingdom's disciples to further his own cultivation. It was natural for the System to offer him such a Class.

However, it didn't fit with Jack's character. He could slaughter his enemies, but he wasn't a cold-blooded killing machine, nor did he want to be. Tying his advancement to the death of others sounded ominous.

Heroic Fist (King)

Lead the world into a better future. Rise against oppression, become a hero, and devote your life to squashing injustice where it appears.

"You raise your fist. The people cheer."

This... did sound nice. Fundamentally, Jack was a good guy—he wanted to help the world and stand up for the weak. The only problem was, he didn't plan on doing so right now.

This Class would only be with him during the C-Grade. His current plan was to spend this time in the Black Hole Church or in other adventures. He didn't want to start running around the universe putting out random fires—he would help if he could, but his current priority was the advancement of his cultivation. If he put the cart before the horse and tried to help people now, someone would kill him and steal his Life Drop. Not to mention that entering System space, where most people resided, was currently too dangerous.

Helping people was good—but it would have to come after he cemented his place in the world.

Thinking to that point, Jack looked away from this Class and moved on.

Fist of the System (King)

You have received divine providence. Devote your life to the service of the ultimate being who favored you, becoming their fist in the cultivation world.

The Immortal System offers additional benefits for the wielders of this Class, including increased attribute points and a Dao Vision for every Dao Fruit.

"For the Immortals!"

Jack was startled. Was this... a recruitment offer disguised as a Class?

The System must have been confused here. Jack was already an enemy of the Immortals. Yet, it spoke of receiving divine providence... Had it mistaken the Life Drop's assistance as a gift of the Immortals?

The additional benefits were interesting, but picking it was impossible. Though, he did wonder what would happen.

Gladiator Titan (King)

You possess extreme physical strength and the temperament of a gladiator. Use your fist to awe the highest of crowds as you vanquish every enemy in your way—with style!

"A punch flies, and the crowd roars."

Jack didn't know what to say.

With style? What style? I'm a C-Grade cultivator, not a clown!

It was rare for the System to have a sense of humor. Then again, maybe that wasn't the case—maybe being breathtaking was actually part of the Class.

The name does sound cool. And the ranking is King, which is the highest. Being a gladiator doesn't sound bad either, but... Can't I have something else? Like, Fist of Absolute Power?

Unfortunately, there were no more classes to choose from. That was all.

The System was not a fan of generality. His E and D-Grade classes had been tyranny-themed and space-themed respectively. Now, he once again had to choose a direction.

On the bright side, classes weren't too important. He had neither become a tyrant nor a spaceship. Classes only affected his choice of skills and the Dao Visions he received. Plus, the higher he advanced, the more everything depended on himself instead of the System.

Classes were a small but steady influence drawing him toward their namesake.

Of course, the Fist of the System was a clear exception, reading more like a contract, but Jack had already decided not to pick that one.

That left him with Fist of Slaughter, Heroic Fist, and Gladiator Titan.

The Fist of Slaughter represented a grim path he was wary of following. His road wasn't one of slaughter, but of integrity and power. Killing was just a part of it.

He had a feeling that, if he chose to become a Fist of Slaughter, his future would be dark and edgy. He decisively chose against it. Besides, he didn't need this Class to kill people.

That left two: Heroic Fist and Gladiator Titan.

Both were decent, actually. Each came with pros and cons. The Heroic Fist was based on his heroic exploits on Earth, when he saved the planet by showing up at the last moment and defeating the planetary overseer. Gladiator Titan probably originated from his grand duel on Hell, where he challenged the entire Animal Kingdom and defeated them before the entire galaxy. He even forced them to let him go after he'd killed their disciples and insulted their Elders. This Class also included the body tempering he'd recently discovered.

However, he neither wanted to run around being a hero nor make all his battles public and attention-needy.

Jack cupped his chin, deep in thought. He had to choose one of the two. Neither were clearly superior than the other, and both represented him to some degree. Actually, now that he thought about it better, he wanted to follow both. He enjoyed being a hero and a gladiator.

But, he could only pick one.

At the end of the day, it probably didn't matter too much. He could be anything he wanted regardless of classes. As for choosing, he could just go with the one that seemed coolest or more immediately useful.

When he considered it like that, one Class stood out more than the other. His lips formed into a wry smile. He'd wanted to pick this

Class since he saw its name, he just wasn't sure about the potential benefits.

Finally, he locked in his decision.

System... make me a Gladiator Titan.

He really looked forward to the coming blue screens. Class changes were accompanied by the upgrade of previous skills and the creation of new ones. If he was lucky, his strength would experience another massive leap forward!

Congratulations! You are now a Gladiator Titan (King).

Congratulations! New Dao Skill unlocked: Titan Taunt I.
Titan Taunt I: Channel your inner punchability to draw the opponent's ire, forcing them to fight you. You simultaneously affect their mental state, making them prone to misjudgements, and rile up the crowd.

Jack's brows fell. *I made a mistake. System, I changed my mind. Make me a Heroic Fist. Please!*

Unfortunately, no response came. Jack was stuck with a Class that sounded cool but only gave him a useless-looking taunting skill.

I must keep an open mind, he thought. *It's the skill of a C-Grade Class. It can't be bad—perhaps, when I use it, I'll be overawed by its usefulness.*

Taking his mind away from that, Jack opened his status screen.

Name: Jack Rust
Species: Human, Earth-387
Faction: Bare Fist Brotherhood (C)
Grade: C
Class: Gladiator Titan (King)
Level: 250

Strength: 2405 (+)

Dexterity: 2410 (+)
Constitution: 2405 (+)
Mental: 300 (+)
Will: 300 (+)
Free Points: 20

Dao Skills: Meteor Punch IV, Iron Fist Style III, Space Walk III, Brutalizing Aura III, Neutron Star Body II, Titan Taunt I
Dao Foundation: Dao Tree of the Fist, Dao Root of Indomitable Will (fused), Dao Root of Life (fused), Dao Root of Power (fused), Dao Root of Weakness (fused)
Dao Fruits: Fist
Titles: Planetary Frontrunner (10), Planetary Torch-bearer (1), Ninth Ring Conqueror, Planetary Overlord (1), Grade Defier

It was a sight to behold. After breaking through to the C-Grade, he finally reached Level 250, and a new section for Dao Fruits had appeared. It was unfortunate that there wasn't a title for being the first cultivator of Earth to reach the C-Grade, but still...

How far I've come...

Jack allowed himself a moment of sentimentality, then turned toward the free stat points. His plan was to invest everything in Mental and Will. His body tempering would enhance all his Physical substats, so he didn't want his other stats falling too far behind. The fewer weaknesses he had, the better.

That was a solid plan and Jack was determined to see it through. Until he looked over his stats and decided to finally solve another issue that had been bugging him. His three Physical substats had been unequal for a long time. Moreover, since every stat point in Physical represented exactly three substat points, it was impossible to make them equal again by only investing points, no matter how many he had. It needed to be a conscious decision of where the points pooled.

He put four points into Physical, turning them into twelve substat points. Five of them went into Strength, and five into Constitution, equalizing the three stats, and the last two went nowhere. He kept them unspent to maintain symmetry.

Get fucked, random fives.

After that, he invested the other eighteen points equally between his Mental and Will stats and admired the final result.

Strength: 2410 (+)
Dexterity: 2410 (+)
Constitution: 2410 (+)
Mental: 308
Will: 308
Free sub-points: 2

Was it pretty? No. But it was far better than the damn imbalance he'd been forced to endure for over a year now.

The joy that filled Jack at this monumental achievement was only slightly less than that of breaking through to the C-Grade. It made up for only receiving a taunting skill, too.

I really should test that, he thought, standing up. *All my new powers, actually, but they can wait a bit. For now, I have to let everyone know I'm okay. Who knows how long it's been since I began my breakthrough?*

After that will come testing... Thing is, where will I find suitable opponents? It's not like someone will just deliver themselves to me. Probably.

CHAPTER TWENTY-NINE
CHALLENGED

THE NEW BRO ARMY WAS HANGING OUT AT THE FIELDS AROUND JACK'S CABIN. Some of them had brought drinks, others carried snacks, while a few more spent their time meditating.

To C-Grades, who could live for up to ten thousand years, a couple months was nothing. Jack's two-month breakthrough passed in a flash, just another party. The notable exception was Brock, who'd gotten a meditation mat from someone and spent his days cross-legged in the middle of his bros, cultivating.

On this day, Brock's eyes snapped open. He'd almost reached the peak D-Grade, but that wasn't the reason he woke up. He glanced at the shut cabin.

A few others noticed as well. "Did you feel that?" someone asked.

"Yeah," a woman responded. "The Dao shook a little."

"Why would that happen?"

"Could it be..." Everyone's gazes swiveled at the cabin. Its door remained shut, its windows blocked by perception-stopping curtains. Nothing had changed. Yet, as they stared over, they couldn't stop a feeling of dread from rising. It was like looking at an active volcano, the open maw of a beast. Unease and fear crept up their spines, but also an unexpected emotion—excitement.

This wasn't the excitement of their big bro breaking through. It stemmed from deep within their souls, from where they connected to the grand Dao of the universe.

"What the hell is that?" a man asked, grabbing his chest. "Why do I feel so—"

His words were lost. Without warning, the cabin door flew open, the curtains rose to the wind. A bang resounded as a large quantity of Dao burst out of the cabin, soaring to the void between galaxies. Waves of energy spread, inciting more and more energy to move. The fabric of existence shuddered for hundreds of miles around them. The darkness shone purple, and the Dao cried out in joy as if welcoming its messiah.

The crowd jumped upright, abandoning their food and drinks. Even Brock slowly stood, his eyes shining with expectant light.

"What the hell!" someone asked. "Is this really the result of breaking into the C-Grade?"

Their own breakthroughs had been far less spectacular.

Brock smiled proudly. "Yes. Big Bro has the respect of the universe."

As they were lost for words, a man stepped out of the cabin. Deep purple robes fell over his body, while he had short dark hair and brown eyes as piercing as arrows. He was like a god walking the earth. He radiated absolute power. The moment he appeared, the already-thousandfold gravity seemed to intensify as a heavy pressure landed on everyone present. The weakest people stumbled, then paled.

A man thought, *He's at the same cultivation as me, and I'm a genius, but he can pressure me with just his aura?*

Jack's piercing gaze turned to them, further intensifying the pressure before he realized what he was doing. All at once, that oppressive sense of absolute power disappeared like it was never there, and Jack's titanic presence gave way to a relaxed attitude.

"Hey, guys," he said. "What are you doing here? Did you sense my breakthrough and come to see?"

"We waited," Brock replied for everyone.

"Oh? Yeah, I guess that's okay. How long did it take me?"

"Two months."

"Two months!"

Jack's eyes widened. He'd sensed months passing as he battled the Fist Jack on the endless grassy field, but he'd assumed it was an illusion. Turns out, it was real. He'd just spent two months sitting cross-legged—he wasn't even numb.

"Wait," he said. "You've been waiting here for two months?"

"I cultivated," Brock replied, shrugging.

Another person—Osmu Sosmu—stepped forward to add, "We are C-Grades. Two months really isn't that long."

As for Dorman, he simply said, "I was homeless anyway, so I might as well wait here."

Jack was stunned. Two months weren't much to these C-Grades, but they were a long time for other people—infants, for example. His children must have grown a lot by now. In the blink of an eye, it had been three months since he last saw them. He ought to pay a visit.

He took another look at the small crowd, and warm feelings welled up inside him.

These people waited two months for me... Damn.

The Cathedral was a place that encouraged growth through competition. A lot of cultivators here were arrogant, ruthless, aggressive, or just plain assholes. However, there were also many who were pure of heart. Jack was one of them, as was Brock. And these thirty people, who'd abandoned their arrogance to support him, were also great.

Jack spoke up, "I will remember your kindness, everyone. Two months may not be a lot to you, but you still spent it for me, and I can sense that your souls are pure. I, Jack Rust, am ruthless to my enemies but good to my friends. Since you want to follow me, let's walk together."

The crowd cheered. Brock grinned widely. Dorman looked around in surprise, and Jack himself smiled warmly, admiring how, in all the darkness of the Cathedral, good people had a tendency to group together.

Or, maybe, they didn't. He glanced at Brock, realizing that the brorilla was not as simple as he appeared. Suddenly, his gaze flickered.

"Brock! Did you reach the peak D-Grade?"

"Almost," Brock responded.

"That's great! You've grown so much!"

Age-wise, Brock wasn't even two years old. If the surrounding people knew that a two-year-old had almost reached the C-Grade, they might tear out their own hair in disbelief.

In a way, Brock was even more impressive than Jack.

"What are you going to do now, big bro?" Osmu Sosmu asked.

"Take a trip to my home planet," Jack replied. "I won't stay long, but I need to see my family."

"Oh... So, no Globe run to demonstrate your strength?"

Jack laughed. "Everything will come in time, Osmu. I also want to test myself, but—"

His words were cut short. A terrifying aura swept over the crowd, making them pale. The weakest people stepped back, while the strongest frowned as they looked at the distance.

A new cultivator flew in. That was already a terrible sign—not many people could fly freely in the Cathedral. He wore pristine white robes, had clear eyes, and carried a slender sword. His gaze was sharp, like being pierced by a blade.

As this cultivator landed across Jack, his robes flapped, and his gait remained steady. It was as if he didn't even feel the gravity.

"You finally dared to exit seclusion," the newcomer said. "I've been waiting a long time to face you."

Jack stared at this man for a long time. Finally, he tilted his head and asked, "Do I know you?"

The swordsman's sharp brows furrowed. "Mind tricks are useless against me, but I'll humor you. Of course you know me. I am Marcus William! Three months ago, you insulted my wife's honor. I was in a critical point of my cultivation then, so I couldn't be interrupted, but now I have come to restore our honor."

"Oh. Yeah, right. I totally remember you."

Jack had a faint memory of this man. Along with Ley Vice, he was one of the first two people Jack had met on the Cathedral—a couple who'd snubbed him for being a D-Grade. Soon after, when the Head Envoy changed Jack's ranking to 950, the woman of that couple had challenged him to a duel and used her Dao of Truth to pressure him into admitting she was attractive, thereby weakening his Dao.

Jack admitted he wouldn't touch her with a nine-foot-pole and punched her in the face.

He'd almost forgotten about that, though come to think of it, the Sage had told him her husband was a high-ranked man known for being petty. It was him who originally set Don Cranxiao after Jack.

That man was precisely Marcus William.

Remembering all that, Jack's gaze hardened a little. "Now I remember you. You're the little shit that paid Cranxiao to bully me."

The surrounding crowd gasped. For better or for worse, Marcus William was ranked 281st. He was a six-fruit C-Grade. That was an entire five boundaries above Jack! Speaking to him like that was tantamount to suicide.

At this point, a woman walked into view from behind some cabins, her beautiful face marred by a cruel smile. She was Ley Vice, who'd come to enjoy the show.

Marcus laughed coldly. "Good, very good. Your mouth is as dirty as I was told. Do you dare to back up your claims?"

"Why wouldn't I dare? I've already kicked the ass of many assholes—you're just the next in line."

Marcus laughed again. His aura swept out, a sharp wind that could slice through everything. As soon as the crowd sensed that, they got goosebumps and had to utilize their own Dao to avoid being cut by the aura itself.

"Excellent, Jack Rust!" Marcus said. "I won't have people say I bullied you. A month from now, when you'll have stabilized your cultivation in the C-Grade, we will fight with our honor as stakes."

Jack raised a brow. "A month from now? Honor as stakes?"

"Do you not dare?"

Actually, Marcus wasn't feeling too well at the moment. The reason he'd been in seclusion for the past three months was to form his seventh Dao Fruit and break into the late C-Grade, but he'd failed. Part of that was due to Jack beating up Marcus's wife, an insult he couldn't stomach easily. Bitterness ate at him from the inside.

On the path of cultivation, if one's thoughts weren't smooth, progressing was near-impossible. That was especially so for swordsmen, whose modus operandi was to cut through all.

Marcus accepted that he needed to first wash away this shame and exited seclusion without breaking through. He'd then waited a week for Jack to finish his own breakthrough so he could come and challenge him.

In truth, Marcus wasn't completely certain he could win. If Jack could reach a ranking of 675 as a D-Grade, there was no telling how high his strength would rise as a C-Grade. He might even be stronger than Marcus himself.

Therefore, as silly as it sounded to be wary of someone five fruits below him, he still decided to be cautious. He rushed here as soon as Jack left seclusion to challenge him, and even gave him a month to prepare. That was already a bit disgraceful, but Marcus was forced to do it; he simply didn't think he could defeat Jack in another year or two. As for just one month, he had over ninety percent confidence. If he lost to a mere one-fruit C-Grade, he might as well abandon cultivation and go retire at his home planet.

Hearing this proposition, Jack scratched his head. "I don't know about one month."

Marcus frowned. "If you don't dare in one month, we can make it two. However, matters like this should be resolved as quickly as possible. Honor waits for no one!"

"That's not what I meant. I may not be here in a month, nor do I want to wait. Let's fight right now and be done with it."

Hearing that, Marcus couldn't believe his luck. Still, he had to act gracefully. "You want to fight me right now? As much as I want to humiliate you, you should think about this better. I am a six-fruit C-Grade. Even after a single month, defeating me will be difficult. Right now, when you've just broken through and your strength is unstable, our duel will just be a joke."

"Let me judge whether it is a joke or not," Jack replied with a lazy smile. "As for who will be humiliated... Don't count your eggs before they hatch. In any case, I don't need any preparation to deal with trash like you. Unless, of course, you want the extra month to re-attempt that breakthrough you failed. In that case, I will reluctantly accept to wait. I wouldn't want to win too easily."

Protected in the crowd's anonymity, a few people couldn't help but snicker. Marcus's gaze sharpened, and his face darkened into a scowl. "What nonsense is that? You're giving me no face at all. You're courting death, kid!"

"Respect is earned," Jack said, clenching his fists. A heavy oppressive aura rolled out, clashing against Marcus's, and creating sparks in the air. The sound was like two glass tables grinding against each other. "Make your move."

The crowd hurried to give them some distance. Almost none believed Jack could win, but they still expected him to last a few moves, and a battle between high-rankers was not something they wanted to be near.

Marcus's aura evolved. His Dao deepened and sharpened, becoming an unsheathed blade. He did not draw his sword. Instead, he crossed his arms behind his back, seeming imperious. "Since you are so confident, how about we add some extra stakes to our duel?"

Jack raised a brow. This guy just wanted to lose everything. "I'm listening."

CHAPTER THIRTY

CONCLUSION OF THE DUEL

"What is a duel without betting some Dao stones?" Marcus asked, his lips curving. "I'm thinking a small amount. Thirty?"

The surrounding people shot him disgusted looks. In their eyes, he was already going too far by challenging Jack from five tiers higher—adding a bet on top of that was just being shameless.

Marcus was aware of that, but he'd made his decision. In for a penny, in for a pound.

Jack cupped his chin. "I don't know... Isn't thirty... a little embarrassing?"

"Embarrassing? What do you mean?"

Marcus was prepared for this. He only said thirty so Jack would haggle it down to twenty or so.

"I would expect a high-ranker like yourself to be a little more generous," Jack replied. "Thirty is too boring. How about fifty?"

Marcus's eyes widened. "You want to bet fifty Dao stones against me?"

"Yeah. Why? Are you afraid?"

"Hmph! I'm only afraid of what people are going to say after this... But, if you insist, so be it. Fifty Dao stones."

Jack grinned. "You said it."

The crowd was only getting more and more stunned. Thirty Dao stones were already a large number to them... but fifty? That was just obscene! Even Marcus shouldn't have that many, let alone Jack. They thought this was the high-ranker bullying the low-ranker, but now it was actually Jack who increased the stakes?

Could it be that... he thought he could win?

In truth, Jack did feel some confidence. He had fought the three-fruit Cranxiao at peak D-Grade. If every fruit was a tier, and the gap between D and C-Grades alone was roughly three tiers, that meant Jack had leapt six tiers to battle, and it hadn't been too difficult either. His current gap with Marcus was only five tiers—in theory, he should be able to handle this.

While Marcus was undoubtedly extremely talented himself, it couldn't be too much. Otherwise, his ranking wouldn't only be 281.

Jack had an eighty percent confidence he would win. Let alone fifty, he would even bet a hundred Dao stones if he had to.

"Make your move," Jack said, clenching his fists again. "Unless you want to bore me into forfeiting."

"Hmph! Let's see if you can even make me draw my sword."

Speaking to here, Marcus did not reach for the handle of his weapon. He stretched out two fingers.

Jack raised a brow. "You're joking."

Marcus slashed out with his fingers. He looked a bit ridiculous—not only was he not using a blade, but he was also striking empty air, as he and Jack remained a hundred feet apart.

As Jack was about to mock him, the smile froze on his lips. Marcus's sword fingers appeared simple, but they contained a deep Dao of the Sword. The moment he slashed with them, a raging river of energy flew toward Jack, crossing the hundred feet in an instant. Each Dao particle vibrated at a unique frequency, combining into a sharp flow that could slice him to dust.

Jack punched out. His fist exploded against the mighty river, splitting it like a steady rock. The energy flew to his left and right, carving deep trenches in the ground.

"Good!" Marcus exclaimed. "Again!"

His fingers slashed out thrice, each attack no weaker than the first. They swept at Jack like the slaps of an angry god, but he fought back. His fists were few but strong, easily breaking the energy as it came. The Dao in their battlefield became chaotic, a combination of sharpness and brutality cratering the ground.

The crowd cheered. A battle between high-rankers was a very rare sight!

While both fighters specialized in melee combat, they were still fighting from a distance. To Jack, it was a form of practice. When he first arrived at the Cathedral, even a full-power Meteor Punch could only go a few feet before dispersing—now, he could easily shoot his punch a hundred feet away.

Plus, he was using this time to adapt to his new power. His Dao was lively, explosive, far more purposeful and aligned. It was the difference between a water bomb and a water jet—his might was simply incomparable to before.

A dozen strikes later, he'd had enough. He smashed a Meteor Punch into Marcus's attack. The world was sucked inside his punch, then exploded—the sword energies rushed back, forcing Marcus to wave his hand and easily split them around him.

"Well done!" Marcus shouted. "Again!"

"Draw your sword, dickhead!"

"You are not qualified!"

Jack snorted coldly. Marcus's strength would rise tremendously when he used his weapon, but Jack also hadn't activated the Life Drop—he didn't want to go all-out first. However, this was getting annoying. The energy inside him was madly yearning release, and he could barely wait. He needed to know how strong he was.

He was about to activate the Life Drop when a different thought entered his mind.

Wait a moment. Isn't this the perfect moment for...

His new Class came with a Dao Skill—Titan Taunt. Its description said nothing that its name didn't. It was a taunting skill. Therefore, this was a fitting moment to use it.

Jack willed the skill to activate, letting it suck a tiny bit of his energy. The mini System core inside him guided his mind, body, and Dao to execute Titan Taunt.

Jack felt his mouth open and heard his own voice say, "Your mother is a fat pig."

Marcus paused his attacks. "Excuse me?"

"No wonder your wife came to fight me first. You never 'draw your blade' for her either."

Hearing these, the crowd froze, then erupted into laughter. Even Ley Vice was stunned. Marcus lost his words, and as for Jack himself... He was actually the most surprised of all. He hadn't wanted to say these things. He just activated the skill and his mouth moved by itself!

Motherfucker! he thought, fighting hard the urge to clamp his own mouth. The skill of a mighty C-Grade Class... was elementary school-level curses?

I've been scammed!

Before Jack could recover himself, Marcus's face darkened to the extreme. "Good, very good. I thought you were a man of honor, but you are just a clown. Aren't you ashamed of yourself, Jack Rust?"

"Isn't your mother ashamed of you? Don't answer—I know she is. She told me yesterday."

Jack's mouth just kept running! He quickly cut the flow of energy to the skill, deactivating it, but the harm had been done. Marcus William glared like he wanted to eat Jack alive, while the crowd struggled to believe what was happening. A moment later, their cheers returned amplified.

Their big bro had a dirty mouth... but so what? This was a great show!

Jack was panicking. *It can't be. There is no way my skill does just this. Sure, it seems to be working, my opponent is enraged and the crowd is excited... but come on! This is just too embarrassing! I refuse to believe a C-Grade skill is only this!*

There has to be some mystical Dao aspect I haven't figured out yet.

Marcus's gaze was dark and stormy. He relaxed his two sword fingers, slowly reaching for his handle. "Since you want to die, let me fulfill your wish. Any last words?"

Jack was torn. Whatever. How much worse can it get? He reactivated the skill, hoping to get some insight on the mystical principles behind it.

His body moved by itself. His hand raised a finger, while his mouth said, "Yeah. Sit on this."

Jack wanted to die of shame. That's it. Never again. He deactivated the skill and lowered his hand, trying his hardest to keep his face straight. No matter how embarrassed he was, he wouldn't admit it mid-battle. He had to seem strong!

Marcus's face split into a feral grin. "So be it."

His sword left its sheath. There was only a sharp, ringing noise. Jack saw nothing, yet instinctively jumped aside—a crescent moon of energy swept through his previous location, slicing the air itself as it impacted a distant hill and cut it in two.

Marcus's sword slowly returned to a neutral position. Its blade was completely dark, a stark contrast to his clothes, while the hilt was white. From afar, it looked like a white flower on a pond of darkness—and the increase it offered to Marcus's battle power was wild.

Jack didn't dare delay. He activated the Life Drop, growing larger and stronger as two new arms sprouted out below his armpits. At the same time, his perception sharpened, and his reflexes quickened—those invisible slices wouldn't surprise him any longer.

The crowd cheered. More people had arrived by now, streaming in from the nearby village and beyond—news had quickly spread. This crowd grouped up far to the side of the duel, not wanting to be accidentally sliced in half by Marcus's energy attacks.

"Show me what you got!" Jack roared, raising his fists. The crowd cheered harder. Marcus dashed. His sword swept out, a movement so fast it was barely perceptible. Jack didn't dare block it. He leaned sideways, letting the energy blade fly past him, then charged in himself.

In the instant it took them to cross a hundred feet, Marcus had unleashed five attacks. They were simply incomparable to before. His sword fingers had released raging streams of sharpness, but only a small part of their energy had hit Jack—most of it dissipated into the void. Wielding his sword, Marcus was like an entirely different person. Every strike contained the same amount of energy as before, except concentrated to a ridiculous extent. There was almost no leakage, which was why they were invisible and near-imperceptible. If they were only slightly more concentrated, Jack couldn't detect them and would have no choice but to be cut.

When those tremendous streams of energy were reduced to a hair-thin line, their slicing power could be imagined.

The two fighters reached each other. Marcus slashed down. Jack bellowed as he planted a foot into the ground, throwing a powerful straight punch at the incoming sword. He galvanized his Dao, pushing it into his knuckles to enhance their durability.

Punch met blade. A ribbon of blood flew out—Jack's hand had been sliced to the wrist, revealing a gruesome spectacle. The audience gasped, but Jack was relentless. This was acceptable. He'd sacrificed a fist to block the strike—that left him three more. As they shot out, surrounding Marcus from all directions, the swordsman's eyes narrowed. Space parted around him like a curtain. He disappeared.

Jack disappeared as well. The two fighters blinked into existence to clash and disappeared again, swimming through space. Their forms blurred, their movements so fast they left afterimages. Every impact was a resounding explosion. Their battle shook the void, and the ground below their feet was half-sliced and half-cratered. Sword and fist energies washed over their surroundings, forcing the crowd to back off again.

Marcus had contained his Dao into his blade, no longer sending out energy slices to avoid harming the onlookers. As a result, his black blade had turned even darker, pulling in the gaze of anyone looking. Every strike was deadly.

Jack fought him equally. Every time they clashed, he either dodged the blade or met it with his knuckles. The shattered hand regenerated quickly. At the same time, his other three fists looked to strike Marcus, forcing him to fight in a bee-like manner.

Jack specialized in strength and durability, not speed. In truth, while their battle appeared chaotic to most onlookers, Marcus was moving and teleporting twice as much as Jack. Jack mostly remained in place, defending against Marcus's attacks and trying to catch him. His punches were destructive—if even one landed, the battle was over.

Actually, in this battle, the one pressured was Marcus. He was walking a fine line, using extreme skill to remain in the game. Jack couldn't help but admire him. He was certainly a bright swordsman, the master of a generation.

Due to the gap in their cultivations, Jack had to admit that his Dao was inferior. Marcus had more and stronger energy and was better at controlling it. However, Jack had an extremely powerful body that could make up for his Dao deficiency.

He was titanic.

The battle heated up. The crowd could only see flashes, Jack's and Marcus's bodies appearing at random spots and disappearing again. The space of their battlefield turned into a sieve, and the ground below was finely carved up.

After a thousand exchanges, no winner had appeared. Jack wasn't spending too much energy—most of it came in the form of regeneration, generously provided by the Life Drop. In contrast, Marcus was teleporting all over the place and dancing on the razor's edge.

Finally, Marcus realized he would be the one to reach exhaustion first. He gritted his teeth, reappearing to glare at Jack.

"You have skill!" he exclaimed. "However, I refuse to lose to someone five fruits below me! Receive my strongest attack—if you can block it, I will admit defeat!"

This was clearly taunting. Jack only sneered, not replying. He had the upper hand—he would block or dodge as he saw fit.

Marcus raised his blade. A colossal amount of energy was sucked in from its surroundings, like the sword was a bottomless whirlpool. The Dao in a radius of several miles was disturbed, flying over to enter Marcus's blade—its edge became even darker than before, like nothing could escape it, not even light.

The power of this coming strike was evident. Jack had no illusions of blocking it.

Finally, the blade reached saturation. Hints of darkness escaped it, like black ribbons tied to the sword, dancing wildly in the angry winds. Contrasted with Marcus's white clothes and loosely floating hair, he resembled an angry god.

"Taste my blade!" he roared, struggling to control his own move. "Certain Death!"

A gutsy name.

His sword came down. Jack stared at it until Marcus teleported, appearing behind him to complete his swing.

Black energy washed over the world. Marcus and Jack were shrouded in darkness that blocked even Dao perception, leaving the audience wondering what had happened. No further sounds came. No clashes, no energy shockwaves. In the darkness, one of the two fought no longer.

The darkness cleared. The audience craned their heads to look, making out two warriors with their bodies intertwined.

"Heavens!" Osmu Sosmu cried out. "Is he holding the blade!"

"No," Dorman replied in an incredulous voice. "He's pinching it."

The darkness dissipated fully. The scene that was revealed etched itself deep into the hearts of everyone watching, ensuring they would never forget it.

Marcus's sword was stopped mid-swing, only half a foot from his opponent's face. Jack's four hands held it in place. His fingers had grabbed the sword not by the edge, but by the flat part.

Relief played in Jack's eyes. In truth, this was a last-minute inspiration. It could have gone horribly... but, luckily, his estimations were correct.

Jack possessed extraordinary stats. His titles were far wealthier than Marcus's. He also had over five hundred extra points in Physical due to his previous tempering, and his body was further augmented by the four-armed battle form. Moreover, Marcus specialized in Dexterity, not Strength. Even including the extra levels he had over Jack, Jack's strength was far superior to Marcus's.

He could have never caught the blade if not for this being Marcus's all-out strike, which also made it more predictable and a little slower than his other attacks. At the same time, all the energy of this strike was condensed on the very edge of the blade, which made it the only truly dangerous spot.

All these factors had combined in Jack essentially catching Marcus's blade.

The swordsman looked like he'd lost his soul. His eyes were askance, and his jaw was trembling. He hadn't moved a muscle. To a swordsman, there was no greater shame than this.

Moreover, even if he did want to recover his sword, he couldn't. Jack was far too strong. Marcus was essentially disarmed.

"Had enough?" Jack rumbled, his gaze piercing into his opponent's.

Marcus clenched his jaw. He refused to let go of his sword, but no matter how unwilling he was, the result was clear. Fighting himself every step of the way, he opened his mouth and muttered, "I admit defeat..."

The crowd erupted in cheers.

CHAPTER THIRTY-ONE
HIDDEN REALM

As soon as Marcus's words rang out, the crowd erupted into chaotic cheers. The entire Cathedral shook from their voices.

"What a battle!" Osmu Sosmu shouted, waving his fist in the air. "Go Jack!"

"Go Jack!" others echoed. Compared to this, Jack's previous duel against Don Cranxiao was nothing.

Jack let go of Marcus's sword, ever mindful of a surprise attack. But it wasn't coming. Marcus sighed deeply, sheathing his sword and walking away.

"You owe me fifty stones," Jack reminded him.

"I don't have them. Here's eighteen—you can pick up my monthly wage for the next seven months."

Marcus swiped his hand in the void, summoning a small bag out of nowhere. He tossed it over. Jack grabbed it, but his eyes remained on Marcus's hand. "How did you do that?" he asked.

"Do what?"

"Pull the bag out of space."

Marcus's eyes were colored with surprise, which soon turned to self-pity. He shook his head. "It's a space ring," he explained. "The Treasure Hall will give you one... Just ask."

Jack nodded. "Alright. Thanks."

Marcus didn't reply, ignoring the crowd as he left. His sword had been grabbed—this was a massive insult to any swordsman. He needed to meditate on what happened as soon as possible and try to clear his thoughts. If something went wrong and he lost faith in his blade, he might never be able to progress again.

But that was the price of competition: you could lose.

Jack watched Marcus William walk away, followed by a silent Ley Vice. He wasn't a senseless killer—Cranxiao had gotten what he deserved, but Marcus wasn't as bad. At least, not to the degree where Jack would murder him after surrendering.

Marcus's evil deeds came from a twisted exaggeration of "might makes right." And, well, Jack had insulted him pretty heavily in the past—sending Cranxiao after him wasn't completely unjustified.

With that, Jack put Marcus and Ley Vice away from his thoughts. The crowd of bros surged forward, almost rolling over him in congratulations. Their voices blurred together—Jack was overwhelmed in a positive way.

"Thank you, everyone," he replied, raising his hands. The four-armed form had receded by now, leaving him exhausted but in good health. Even his robes remained pristine, with only a few cuts at the hems. He'd met most of Marcus's attacks with his fists.

"That was awesome!" Osmu Sosmu exclaimed. "You caught the sword of someone ranked in the two hundreds! How strong are you now? Could you rank in the top one hundred!"

To these low-rankers, the top one hundred was a legendary realm. Everyone there was a master amongst masters. Even reaching nine-fruits didn't guarantee you'd be able to enter.

The only reason Osmu spoke so freely was that Jack already defied common sense, so defying it even further meant nothing.

Jack laughed. "Catching his sword was the result of many things.

I'm not that much stronger—if Marcus can rank at 281, I should be around 250 or so."

The crowd looked at each other. A one-fruit C-Grade ranking at 250... Were they dreaming?

In the past, some of them couldn't help but envy Jack's Life Artifact, which was a significant factor of his current strength. At this point, they had to admit that even with all the luck in the world, they could never match Jack's achievements. Many people had Life Artifacts in the past, and he was simply unprecedented.

"You really are worthy of being our big bro," Osmu Sosmu concluded, shaking his head.

Seeing everyone's dispirited gazes, Jack smiled at them. "Don't give up. As long as I am here, there will never be a second Don Cranxiao. We can band together as a fist and make sure we all have the opportunity to rise. Isn't that right, Brock?"

Brock raised his head. "Yes."

The crowd cheered again. These fallen geniuses were thoroughly convinced. They had forgotten their previous arrogance and genuinely acted as Jack's little bros.

"What now, big bro?" Osmu asked.

"I will visit my home planet. I won't stay long, but there are some things I need to do. As for all of you... Brock, will you join me?"

Brock shook his head.

"Are you sure? I know you want to cultivate, but seeing your family and friends is important as well."

"I know. But I too weak. If I return, I return with my power. I must deserve it."

Brock was currently registered as Jack's spiritual companion, not a disciple. He didn't need to reach the top eight hundred ranking to use the teleporter. However, that was the easy way. His bros were all suffering the Cathedral's constraints. If he didn't share their shackles, how could he call himself their second big bro?

"I become disciple too," Brock declared calmly. "When I reach good rank, I leave. Not before."

"Alright. I believe in you. Any help you need, I will provide."

Brock nodded. Between bros, there was no need to be modest. Gathering up the Dao stones he needed to break through would just be a waste of time and youthful potential. It was better to borrow from Jack and return them later.

Of course, while everyone here was a bro, not everyone could get this treatment. There just weren't enough Dao stones to go around. Brock was special.

Hearing Jack's assurance, Dorman's eyes blazed with fervor, though he said nothing. He was already receiving kindness—asking for more would just be ungrateful.

As for Jack's thoughts on that matter, he kept them tightly hidden. He cleared his throat. "Now, you will excuse me, everyone. I have a family to return to."

There were still many benefits to reap in the Cathedral. He needed to visit the Dao Chamber and test out the so-called Fallen Genius Mirror. He also wanted to see how high he could go in the Heavy Pagoda, as well as attempt the Ceaseless Murder Globe again to discover his current ranking and any new benefits he would unlock.

He wasn't in a hurry. He had the sense that, when he got started, he wouldn't want to stop. It was better to take a trip to Earth now, so he didn't have to interrupt himself later.

Plus, he missed his kids.

The bros dispersed. Dorman stayed in Jack's cabin to cultivate, while Jack and Brock walked to the nearest teleporter. It was the same one they'd arrived at. A ring of twelve white columns spearing up from the black stone ground, while a slim-looking Envoy sat cross-legged to the side.

The first time Jack saw this man, he'd been overwhelmed. He still was. He'd met a few Envoys so far, but this ascetic-looking man was leagues above the rest. His aura was like a sun condensed into a human body.

Perhaps guarding the teleporter was not as simple as Jack imagined.

As soon as he approached, the Envoy opened his eyes. A bright light flashed through them. “Destination?”

“Milky Way galaxy, Earth,” Jack replied, stepping into the teleporter. The Envoy nodded. There was no visible control panel, but Jack sensed the space around him squirm as the teleporter slowly hummed to life.

“See you soon, Brock,” he said. “I believe in you.”

“Have fun. When you return, I will be peak strong.”

Jack smiled. “Good.”

Space ruptured. Jack was sucked inside, instantly flung toward the distant Milky Way galaxy at a billion times the speed of light.

Brock nodded at the ascetic. “Thanks, senior bro,” he said, then walked away. It was time to make some waves.

The universe was gigantic beyond belief. The System only covered a tiny corner, but this corner remained large enough to accommodate the trillions of cultivators while also hiding all sorts of secrets.

In a distant galaxy at the edges of System space, a small starship shuttled through. It was red and covered in rust; it had existed for a very long time already. Inside it were three elderly cultivators—one man and two women.

However, they weren’t too strong. The man was at the middle D-Grade, and the women were even weaker, at the early D-Grade. They were approaching the end of their lives and had few descendants—therefore, they’d decided to leave System space and spend their remaining days as gods on an un-Integrated planet.

To that end, they had sold everything they owned and bought a space-warping starship.

The three of them were cruising through the fringes of the somewhat newly-Integrated Heaven Egg galaxy, where the System wasn’t expected to arrive for another ten thousand years. As they were morosely crossing the dark void, their eyes snapped open, and the starship came to a sudden halt.

One of the women opened her mouth. "Is that..."

A rainbow-colored light shone in the distance. It wasn't too far away. Their starship teleported once more, and they reached it.

A large, oval shape was revealed before them. It was two-dimensional, like a portal floating in space, and its surface was covered by swimming rainbow lights, preventing anyone from peeking through. Even Dao perception disappeared as it fell into the portal.

The three old people exited the starship, hovering before the oval with disbelief in their eyes. From here, they could feel the intense waves of Dao energy spreading out of the portal and into the universe.

"Heavens," the man whispered, and his eyes flashed with joy. "A hidden realm... We hit the jackpot!"

The women also revealed bright smiles. This was a massive wealth that fell into their laps.

The universe contained many secrets. Hidden realms were one of them. These people weren't clear on how such a place formed or what it contained, but they knew the major factions offered tremendous bounties for such discoveries. With that kind of wealth, they wouldn't need to leave System space—they could play gods at any low-level planet of their choosing!

"What if we entered the realm?" one of the women said, her eyes flashing. "Perhaps we could find a chance to reach the C-Grade!"

"Don't be blinded by greed," the man replied with a snort. "Given our age, progressing is almost impossible. Even if there was a great enough opportunity inside the realm, riches are always accompanied by danger—with our strength, we could never claim it."

"Then, what should we do?"

"Inform the factions, of course! The bounties they offer are extremely generous!"

The women looked at each other and nodded. “Which faction should we go to?” one asked.

The man smiled widely. “All of them!”

This man happened to have some connections—he wouldn’t only sell this information to the A-Grade faction of his galaxy, which would relay it to the Hand of God, but he would also sell it to the Black Hole Church.

What was better than one bounty? Two bounties!

As for what the large factions would do about the hidden realm... he naturally didn’t care. Those high-level struggles were far beyond his understanding.

“What are you waiting for? Let’s go!” he shouted, seeming five millennia younger. “The universe smiled at us today. If we are late and someone else reports this place first, that will really be a shame!”

CHAPTER THIRTY-TWO
VISITING HOME

"Jack!" Vivi was a blur as she rushed into Jack's arms, embracing him tightly. He laughed, easily enduring her tackle. "I missed you..."

"I missed you too," he replied. "I'm glad I came back."

"And you're so strong, too! Did you reach the C-Grade?"

He nodded. "Not just that. I discovered another way to use the Life Drop... but I'll tell you everything later."

The professor, who was also present and had already greeted Jack, was lost in thought. "Reaching the C-Grade is tremendous," she muttered. "Our member cap has been increased by ten times, and so many new functions were unlocked... I will need to review everything again!"

Though she said that, her eyes sparkled with enthusiasm. She looked forward to it.

"And how have you guys been doing?" Jack asked, gently placing his hands on top of the babies' heads. They were six months old now and had grown a bit since he last saw them. They had even started crawling!

Ebele, the girl of the twins, wore a pink cap and stared at him with wide, intelligent eyes. Eric wore a blue cap and was chewing on his foot, only remembering Jack when his hand touched the baby's head.

He laughed and picked them both up, admiring the life he'd created. Contrasted against the dark, lonely days of cultivation on the Cathedral, his family was a breath of fresh air, a reminder that there was more to this world than cultivation. However, this didn't affect his resolve in the slightest—it got even stronger. If he wasn't powerful, these babies wouldn't exist.

Of course, Jack had fully restrained his aura, resembling a common mortal. That didn't mean his perception was any less. Stretching it out, he could easily sense the entire Forest of the Strong and the area around it, even crossing several mountain peaks and reaching the nearby town. If he wanted to, he could read the license plate of every car in Valville.

At the same time, now that he'd left the Cathedral's thousand-fold gravity and suppression of energy, he felt like a god. That was no exaggeration. The space here was so fragile he could break it with a flick, the ground was soft, and the gravity so weak he was a thousand times stronger than on the Cathedral. All the Dao within his range of perception was his to wield. He could annihilate Valville with a thought. His every casual punch would carry the power of a high-magnitude nuclear bomb.

A long time ago, Nauja had told him that C-Grades held the power to crush continents. It seemed exaggerated then, but he fully accepted it now. With his late C-Grade power, demolishing the entire American continent would take less than an hour. He could destroy every continent on the planet in the time that corresponded to a normal person's workday.

Of course, that was only razing the surface of these continents. If he wanted to really destroy them, it would take much longer. As for cracking open the planet itself, that was simply impossible.

Though, maybe in a few Dao Fruits...

His thoughts snapped back from his near-omnipotence to gently cradling the babies in his arms. He smiled brightly at them, watching their little mouths hang. "Come on! Let's play with Daddy!"

A few hours later, Jack had taken his family and friends on a stroll through space. They were orbiting the Earth, watching its majesty from above and observing the wholly new astral field around them.

"Astronomers have gone crazy," the professor said, her eyes wide in wonder. "They're mapping out the terrain around us, but they still haven't figured out just where we are. Not a single star is recognizable. Your religious friends must have taken us halfway across the galaxy."

Jack laughed. "I don't know if I would call the Black Hole Church religious. When you know that your God exists, doesn't religion lose its point?"

"No. It's the exact opposite."

He considered it. "In any case, they have certainly transported us far away from System space. It only occupied one tenth of the galaxy to begin with. If I had to guess, it would take at least tens of thousands of years to reach us. By then, Earth will have grown enough to defend itself—and I will have the power to single-handedly rule the galaxy."

"Will you really?" the professor asked.

"I can already match the strongest C-Grades. As soon as I reach the B-Grade, I am confident that very few people in this galaxy will be my match—and B-Grades can live for a hundred thousand years, so I'll be around for—Eric, my boy, close your mouth. You're dripping."

He reached into his embrace and gently closed the mouth of Eric, who was completely lost in watching Earth spin below him. Of course, that wasn't a sign of low intelligence—it was perfectly normal behavior for a baby. On the other hand, Ebele was scanning the planet with wide eyes as if trying to see through its secrets.

Jack suspected his girl had a bright future ahead of her. His chest swelled with pride.

Of course, he was the one protecting everyone here from the void of space. With his powers, maintaining a bubble of air and pleasant temperature was child's play. He felt even more wizard-y than Edgar, who was also present, his eyes shut. The moment he'd seen Earth from above, his Dao of Magic had resonated with the majesty of this sight, and he'd gone into meditation. Harambe and Aya, Brock's parents, were also here and equally breath-taken.

Vivi sat by the side, enjoying the view. The only one not lost in wonder was Jack's mother, the professor.

"By the way," Jack told her, his voice turning slightly serious, "I have something for you."

"Oh? What is it?"

Letting the babies float in the protected void, Jack reached into his robes and removed a small sack. He passed it over. "These are ten Life stones and fifteen Dao stones. The Life stones are healing mechanisms. Anyone can use them, as long as they are under the D-Grade, any injuries on their body will be immediately and completely healed. Even immortals will enjoy great benefits. As for the Dao stones, they can be used for cultivation, breakthroughs, or operating high-level magic formations. Their effect is equally exaggerated. I leave these in your care—I don't know how long it will be before I return, so distribute them as you see fit."

He'd already given three Dao stones and three Life stones to Vivi—one of each for her and the babies.

The professor's eyes widened. "These are too precious! I can't possibly accept them."

"I won't miss them," Jack replied. "I have more at the Cathedral, and I suspect my rate of acquiring them will only speed up in the future."

"Still, the combined value of all these cannot be nothing! Why give it to us? We don't need such high-level resources. You can find much better uses for them."

"Their effect on my cultivation would be small. I want Earth to have them. Not only because you're close to me, but because I took control of the planet and moved it all the way out here. If I don't help Earth a little now, I won't be too good a ruler, will I?" He smiled. "I plan to raise Earth alongside me. I would like to see the Bare Fist Brotherhood teeming with D-Grades, rising to the level of a proper C-Grade faction in the future, or even higher. These Dao stones are just the beginning—as I grow stronger, I will bring more and better resources. Earth is my home—I want to watch it grow."

The professor's eyes moistened. Her son was saying such grand words, and they were absolutely true.

"Thank you, Jack," she replied, putting away the stones and hugging him. "I will handle them well, I promise."

Jack nodded.

Neither of them spoke out the obvious. Jack's life was exceedingly dangerous right now. If anything happened to him, Earth would be left defenseless and stranded in space. That was part of the reason why he gave out these stones now.

The days passed one at a time. Jack didn't plan to stay for a month, but it wouldn't be a week, either. Cultivation was a long road. Just his latest breakthrough had taken two months, and his meditation sessions were getting longer and longer. It wasn't strange for a C-Grade to meditate for months at a time. Therefore, he couldn't pop in constantly, as that would hinder his cultivation.

In other words, times like this were rare.

Jack enjoyed his days, accompanying Vivi and the babies. They toured the Earth together, seeing all sorts of landscapes and wonders. Under Jack's protection, even dangerous areas were accessible. They visited the inside of an active volcano, where Ebele and Eric got a lava lamp made from actual lava—very carefully made by Jack. It wouldn't break for a hundred years.

They also visited the dark ocean depths. Jack created a wide radius of light, and Eric swam alongside a giant squid while Ebele studied an anglerfish. They even entered the D-Grade dungeon at the depths of the Marianna Trench and met its boss, the kraken. Brock had visited the place in the past and almost cleaned it out, with only the kraken escaping—fighting at this depth wasn't easy.

All the while, Jack was filled with familial love. He never knew his heart could be so tender—the hands which recklessly killed his enemies were now gentle and soft. Vivi was always at his side, her lips rising as she saw her man playing with their children, and the budding love between the two grew even brighter.

After traveling for a week, they returned to their home and spent another week there, accompanied by family and friends. Dordok visited them often, as did Edgar and Sparman—though Gan Salin and Nauja had left the planet to explore the galaxy. As for Vlossana, the Saphira girl who fought Edgar in the final war, she remained unwilling to meet Jack.

Like this, two weeks had passed since Jack's return to Earth. His accumulated pain had been washed away by love—he felt ready to chase the peak of cultivation again, though he didn't want to leave.

But he knew he had to. Strength was the only way to protect his family—he refused to leave things to chance.

"I will miss you," Vivi said, hugging him tightly.

"So will I..." he whispered back. "Take care of the kids, okay?"

He then reached down to hug both of his children. Their little hands tried to grasp him—they didn't understand he was leaving, but they sensed his sadness and wanted to comfort him.

"I'll be back as soon as possible," he promised, patting their heads again. "I love you all."

Ebele opened her mouth. For a moment, Jack thought she would respond, but only baby noises came out.

His heart grew heavy. He wouldn't be present for his children's first words... but that was the price of cultivation. His love was present through the safety they enjoyed.

"Grow well," he said, hugging all three of them again. He then stepped toward the large teleporter—he'd already said his goodbyes to everyone else.

Vivi waved at him, holding back her tears. He waved back. Then, the teleporter flashed to life, and Jack tore through space at a billion times the speed of light. His organs shook like they wanted to jump out of his body, but he could easily handle this pressure.

He stared at the little blue dot that quickly disappeared. Then, he turned his gaze forward, into the darkness. His heart hardened again. This was his life, his battle. Piercing through the empty void. Becoming strong.

His chin was raised as he cruised through the cosmos, heading back to the cradle of strength that was called the Cathedral.

CHAPTER THIRTY-THREE
BROCKING

Brock strolled through the Cathedral. From the dark and lonely place it had been three months ago, it remained dark, only now he had his bros. Like always, brohood permeated the hearts of people, and the good ones stood out.

It made him proud of his Big Thought.

Now, it was time for Brock to share his bros' burdens. With solid steps, he approached the Kill Kill Ball and spoke to the Envoy in charge. "Hey."

The Envoy—the same red-skinned, frog-eyed, four-fingered fellow as before—cracked an eye open. "Can I help you?"

"I want to enter the Kill Kill Ball and become disciple."

The Envoy hesitated. "That is not how it works. Only disciples can enter the Globe."

"Then, how do I become disciple?"

"You need an Envoy's recommendation."

"Are you not an Envoy?"

The Envoy was conflicted. On one hand, he did want to foster good relations with Jack Rust. On the other, he wouldn't go as far as breaking the rules to let a monkey fumble around in the priceless Globe.

"Why do you want to enter the Globe?" he asked.

"Prove my strength."

"The very first opponent is an early C-Grade. While it is particularly weak, it is not an enemy you can defeat."

"I believe I can."

Facing Brock's resolve, the Envoy actually felt a bit helpless. He took a deeper look at Brock, having not yet done so because he assumed Brock was only Jack's spiritual companion with limited battle power.

The moment he peered deeper, he was surprised. Brock's foundation was solid, and the Dao that rolled off his body was neat and disciplined. It wasn't at the level where it could threaten a C-Grade, but there was an undercurrent, a mysterious property that the Envoy couldn't identify. It felt like a utility Dao, yet not quite.

Could the monkey have some strength? the Envoy asked himself. He would have discarded this notion if it was anyone else, but this particular monkey was connected to Jack Rust. How normal could it be?

Taking a step back, even if the monkey failed to defeat the first opponent, it shouldn't lose too abruptly. The Globe would protect it from major injuries. Then, when Jack returned, the Envoy letting the monkey enter could be considered as doing a favor to Jack.

As for the rules... Well, they never were a major issue.

"Do you have Dao stones?" he asked.

Brock shook his head.

"Hmm. Well, one stone is not much. How about this: I will provide the Dao stone needed to start the Globe. If you can defeat even the first opponent, then I will use my authority to directly register you as an outer disciple. However, if you lose, then Jack Rust will have to reimburse me for my stone. What do you think?"

"Sure." Brock didn't need to consider it. He wasn't certain he could win, but he had good chances. Even if he lost, one Dao stone was not much to Big Bro.

"Then, you may enter."

The Envoy took out a Dao stone and placed it in a groove of the control platform—a wooden screen on a marble altar. With a rumble, the door of the Globe slid upward, revealing a yawning void. Brock hefted his staff and walked in. The door slammed shut behind him, trapping him in darkness.

Suddenly, a pillar of light fell from the Globe's ceiling, landing in the center of the floor. The Dao swished. A humanoid form appeared in the column of light as if formed of shiny dust. It held a sword.

"Hello, dirty bro," Brock said, drawing the Staff of Stone from his back. In truth, the staff was beginning to fall behind. It could adjust its weight to accommodate the wielder's strength up to a thousand points, and Brock had almost reached that threshold—though he couldn't access the System or count his strength in points.

He would need to find a new weapon soon... For now, the loyal Staff of Stone was enough.

The dirty bro charged. Its sword cut toward Brock at a tricky angle—while it was the weakest of C-Grades, no C-Grade was really weak.

Brock didn't hold back. With one hand grasping the staff, he pushed out the other and opened it outward. An ethereal book manifested on his palm. It was black and golden-rimmed, with golden letters spelling out "Bro Code" on the cover. It flipped to a seemingly random page by itself, shining with golden splendor. That glow transmitted to the Staff of Stone, making it shine as well.

"You no real," Brock declared. "I real. I out-bro you!"

The book erupted golden, illuminating the Globe. Letters and runes were projected all over the walls, turning into a kaleidoscope of brohood. As the runes appeared everywhere, a holy aura filled the Globe, making the air heavy and sacred. The dirty bro's steps slowed—its sword faltered.

"Down!" Brock shouted, slamming the book shut and smashing out with his staff. Blade met staff. Metal met stone. An explosion resounded in the Globe, crashing shockwaves against the walls. Brock was flung back, while the dirty bro only needed to steady itself.

However, Brock was uninjured. He could fight. And, with the support of brohood, he would not lose!

He landed on his feet, golden light dancing around his body like ribbons. The radiance was blinding, the aura holy and majestic. The dirty bro shrank back a bit but still charged.

"Bros of the Church Place, lend me your power!" Brock shouted, raising his hands in the air.

Every single bro across the Cathedral felt a calling. They looked toward the Globe, sensing a trickle of their power leaving them. Some instinctively raised their hands. "What is going on?" they asked, rushing over. A feeling of urgency clouded their hearts—they were needed!

Thirty streams of energy penetrated the Globe's walls and rushed into Brock's body, increasing his brilliance to overwhelming levels. The Globe was filled with light. The dirty bro had to close its eyes, but Brock didn't. The light of brohood could never harm him, only illuminate him.

The dirty bro kept charging, its sword slashing out. Brock roared as he brought his staff down. "Break for me!"

The clash was ten times stronger than before. Brock's fur flew backward, as did his golden ribbons of brohood, but he remained in place. This time, it was the dirty bro that was flung away, crashing into the far wall. The wall was unharmed—the dirty bro was injured.

Brock laughed out loud. So what if this dirty bro was strong? With powerful enough little bros, he could never lose!

He rushed in, his entire being radiating light. The Staff of Stone came crashing down, carrying the weight of brohood. The ground sank. The dirty bro's grip loosened, and its sword went flying as the staff carried right through and into its head.

The dirty bro dispersed. Brock had won, but he was not finished.

With the power of brohood coursing through his body, he still had much to give.

"Come!" he shouted, watching two new dirty bros form in the center of the Globe. Right as they appeared, they were suppressed by the radiant aura. Brock charged them, his staff held high. "Fall for me!"

Outside the Globe, twenty-something people had gathered. Looking at each other, they realized they were all members of the newly formed bro squad.

"Were you also called here by a strange power?" Osmu Sosmu asked.

Everyone echoed in affirmation.

"What is going on?" Osmu continued, turning to the Envoy. "Excuse me, is Jack Rust inside the Globe again?"

"No," the Envoy replied expressionlessly. "It's his spiritual companion, Brock."

The eyes of the bros widened. They glanced at each other, then stared at the Globe. Their second big bro was fighting? Wasn't he at the peak D-Grade? What was the strange calling they'd all experienced?

And why were they feeling such intense excitement?

Without knowing it, their mouths opened to shout, "Go Brock!"

Inside the Globe, Brock couldn't hear them, but he sensed their support. The power he received intensified. He smashed out his staff, breaking through the magic bro's elemental prison, then mentally told space, "Come on, bro." Space parted to let him pass, and he teleported behind the mace bro, sticking the Bro Code in his face.

"Be out-bro'd!"

Bright golden light struck the mace bro's head like the world's strongest headlight. Its eyes were already closed, but this wasn't just a blinding attack, it contained Brock's will!

Brock wasn't just a Physical cultivator, but also a Will one!

The mace bro's mind was filled with heavenly chimes and buff brorillas dressed in white. These bro angels were enjoying a heartfelt night of drinking under the stars. As they appeared in his mind, they looked at him as if he was the intruder. They commanded him, "Stop. You are out-bro'd."

The mace bro tried to resist, but the righteous manliness of these brorillas was too much, and the mace bro itself was only a shadow of Dao. Its will was crushed. "I am out-bro'd," it muttered, then willingly dispersed itself.

Brock laughed, charging at the one remaining dirty bro. It was a two-fruit wizard, but how could it stand against Brock by itself? The brorilla teleported left and right, dodging elemental attacks and space spikes as he steadily grew closer. When he reached within thirty feet, he could no longer teleport as the wizard had locked down space. Therefore, he smashed through the space spikes the wizard sent his way and finally broke the dirty bro's head.

As the dirty bro dissipated, Brock was left panting. He wasn't too wounded, only sporting minor injuries, but his entire body trembled from exhaustion. His muscles were close to ripping. While he could augment himself by borrowing power from his little bros, the strain on his body and Dao was far too heavy.

As three new dirty bros appeared, Brock shook his head and put his staff away. The radiance covering his body receded. He cupped his hands at the three new bros and said, "Thanks, bros." He wasn't only referring to the present ones, but also the three he'd defeated.

The three dirty bros bowed at him and disappeared, while the entrance of the Ball slowly rose open. Brock took some time to gather his breath, then strolled out under the watchful gazes of his many bros.

"Big bro!" they exclaimed. "How was it?"

These low-rankers didn't know what to think. They'd never seen Brock fight. Like the Envoy, they assumed he was a background character with limited combat strength... but now, he had stayed in the Globe for enough time to have broken through the first opponent.

If he had really achieved that while at the peak D-Grade, his talent was superior to most of theirs!

"Sup, bros." Brock nodded at them, then asked the Envoy, "How did I do?"

The Envoy had an odd look, shaking his head. "See for yourself."

The ranking obelisk in the distance rumbled. The names at the lower end split apart, a new one appearing in their midst.

Rank 966... Brock!

Brock nodded like this was only natural. All his bros, however, opened their eyes and mouths wide.

They could accept being thoroughly surpassed by Jack. But now, they'd been soundly defeated by Jack's spiritual companion! Brock was only at the D-Grade—as soon as he reached the C-Grade, he would certainly achieve a ranking at the eight or seven hundreds, if not higher. Of the thirty bros, twenty-eight of them were below the ranking of eight hundred!

Osmu Sosmu shook. As one of the strongest bros, he was only ranked 793rd. At the end of the day, he could only shake his head and lament his own weakness.

"It's not just Jack," he muttered. "These guys... are both monsters!"

CHAPTER THIRTY-FOUR
DAO CHAMBER

Jack stepped onto the Cathedral with renewed resolve. His family time had reinforced his psyche, making him ready to face the world again.

As space stabilized around him, he found himself in the familiar teleporter—twelve white columns arranged in a ring spearing up from the dark ground of the Cathedral. The same ascetic old man guarded this place, looking like he hadn't moved a muscle. His aura remained unfathomable.

"Thank you," Jack said respectfully, to which the Envoy did not reply.

He walked deeper into the Cathedral, heading for the nearby village. The thousandfold gravity was a small shock, but it didn't stop Jack from having a spring in his step. There were so many things to do.

One at a time.

Naturally, he wanted to visit his cabin, but the teleporter was close to another building: the Treasure Hall.

When Jack defeated Marcus William, he'd asked him how

everyone seemed to conjure items out of thin air. Marcus had explained it was something called a "space ring," and that he could get one as well.

The Treasure Hall was a massive building. Its reinforced white walls reached a hundred feet into the air and stretched back for more than three hundred. It was the second largest building here after the Ceaseless Murder Globe.

Like most places in the Cathedral, the Treasure Hall was built with austerity. Its walls were unadorned, though its tiled roof resembled an ancient Greek temple. There were no windows, only a door thirty feet in height.

Jack pushed it open, finding himself in a small space that reeked of practicality. "Yes?" said a human Envoy sitting behind a desk—the only piece of furniture in the room. His eyes scanned Jack, then he frowned. "You do not have the ranking to request treasures."

Jack wasn't discouraged. "Hello. I was told I could get a space ring here—is that not the case?"

"Did you lose yours?"

"Kinda."

The Envoy fished into a crate by the side and took out a plain-looking metal ring. He tossed it over, and Jack caught it.

"There. Space ring. Enjoy."

"Uh... Thanks?"

The Envoy stared at Jack like he'd overstayed his welcome. Jack didn't care too much. "Excuse me," he asked again, "are these space rings... common?"

"In grade?"

"In rarity. Does everybody have one?"

The Envoy raised a brow. "Most C-Grades do. We offer them free of charge to any disciple who lost theirs or doesn't have one."

"I see... Thank you."

"No problem."

Jack resisted the urge to fiddle with his new toy and exited the

Treasure Hall, closing the door behind him. Then, he finally took a better look.

The spatial ring was made of plain metal. There were no carvings or insignias on it—if Jack didn't know better, he would have thought it just that, a piece of metal. However, as soon as he focused his Dao perception on it, his world widened.

The space ring contained its own little dimension. The space within was roughly nine by nine feet, enough to fit most things, and was stable. It wouldn't just collapse at random.

This was an extremely advanced application of the Dao of Space —Jack hadn't even known it was possible. Undoubtedly, this ring was a very precious item... and the Cathedral offered it free of charge.

Major factions sure had their benefits.

But why haven't I heard about these things? Jack asked himself. He'd interacted with various C-Grades in the past—Master Huali, the planetary overseer, the Warden, all the C-Grades who came to watch his grand duel on Hell. He would have noticed if any of them pulled things out of thin air.

My galaxy isn't connected with the wider universe yet. Maybe they don't have access to the market for space rings.

In any case, the important part was that Jack would no longer have to carry all sorts of items in his pockets. It could get quite ridiculous at times, not to mention inconvenient—he still remembered how, back in Trial Planet, he'd cut a hole in his pants to make a secret pocket.

He experimented a bit. Retrieving a Life stone from an inner pocket of his robes, he brought it close to the ring and waited. When nothing happened, he pushed the Life stone onto the ring until they touched. Still nothing.

That can't be right.

He tried a different approach. He used his perception to probe the ring, sensing the world inside, and then just sort of willed the Life stone to enter. To his surprise, it did. With a light whoosh, space around it distorted to pull the stone into the ring, where it then rested in a corner of the ring's dimension.

"Wow," he exclaimed breathlessly. He then willed the stone to exit—and it did! He didn't have to enter the dimension himself to search for it, just swipe his hand over the ring. It wasn't even necessary to locate the object. As long as he knew it was inside, he could use his will to instantly pull it out.

"The hell?" he muttered. "Can it read my mind?"

That wasn't too nice. Jack sat cross-legged against the wall of the Treasure Hall and sank his mind into the ring, inspecting it with great care. He made out faint inscriptions on its inner side. There were thousands of tiny symbols tightly clustered together. None were part of a language, as far as Jack knew, but the depth and direction of each line guided the Dao to flow in a certain pattern, achieving a result as impressive as the existence of an inner dimension. They formed a stable system that maintained a bubble of warped space regardless of the ring's surroundings.

And that wasn't even the end of it. If Jack wasn't wrong, there were even symbols that registered the items coming in and acted as connectors, allowing Jack's will to directly interact with them. In this way, any D-Grade cultivator and above could freely use the ring even without any attainments in the Dao of Space.

When Jack opened his eyes again, he was bewildered. The intricacy of such an object was beyond his imagination. He couldn't even begin to comprehend the principles behind it, let alone carve one himself. Even scrutinizing those myriad symbols was stretching his perception—they were too tiny.

And this thing was just casually tossed at him?

Maddening. The wealth of the Church was just unfathomable.

Then again, if most C-Grades in the universe have one, maybe they're not as valuable as I believe. Can they be mass-produced?

Thinking to here, Jack shook his head and stood up. Space rings were above his pay grade. For now, he would just enjoy the convenience. Passing all the items on his body into the ring—his credit card, his Cathedral identification token, and the bag containing ten Life stones—he was ready to embark toward his next destination.

But which one?

His cabin was always there, and he wanted to greet Brock, but he wasn't in a rush. The various common buildings of the Cathedral were all in the same area—if he wanted to visit the Ceaseless Murder Globe, the Heavy Pagoda, or the Dao Chamber, to which he'd recently gotten access, going now was the best choice.

He'd have to go to the Ceaseless Murder Globe soon to attain his new ranking and all the benefits that came with it. However, it could also wait. The Globe wouldn't go anywhere.

Dao Chamber it is, he decided, unwilling to suppress his curiosity. But... where is it?

He had no idea.

"Excuse me," Jack said again, his head peeking through the Treasure Hall's doors, "could you show me the way to the Dao Chamber?"

The Envoy inside looked annoyed. "That way."

"Thank you," Jack replied, closing the door again.

The Dao Chamber wasn't as close as he thought it would be. Twenty minutes of walking later, Jack arrived at a short but expansive building. Its door reached to the ceiling, barely nine feet off the ground, but the walls themselves stretched for a hundred feet in the distance.

The interior was mostly empty. Doors surrounded it on all sides, each painted a different color, while thin columns intermittently supported the low ceiling. An Envoy with a slimy body and eight tentacles sat at a desk in the middle of the large room, with its back against a column. There were also three cultivators meditating in random spots.

"Hello," Jack said in a low voice, careful not to disturb those meditating. "Is this the Dao Chamber?"

"It is," the octopus's voice reached his mind. It was sweet and tranquil—a woman's.

Jack felt like an idiot. He'd grown so used to echoing his voice through the void that he forgot he could communicate telepathically. "Great! I'm Jack Rust, ranked 675th. I'm new here. Could you explain what this Dao Chamber is about?"

The octopus' tentacles wiggled slightly. Finally, she replied, "*I can. The Dao Chamber is a place dedicated to enhancing the disciples' understanding into the Dao. We offer a variety of high-grade Dao Visions you can rent for one Dao stone per week. Moreover, each of the doors around us leads to a miniature dimension filled with the essence of a particular Dao. We have all the basic elements, along with Space, Time, Life, Death, and Mortality. Additionally, we possess some artifacts that can assist in furthering your own Dao. With your ranking, you can access the Fallen Genius Mirror.*"

Jack's eyes shone. The many doors surrounding this empty space were all differently colored, and each emanated a special aura: the red door felt like fire, the cyan door wind, the deep blue door emanated the aura of water, and so forth. He could also make out earth, lightning, wood, and metal. Finally, there were the five doors representing the other concepts the Envoy had mentioned.

Of those, the first four were easy to understand. But the last one...

"*What is Mortality?*" he asked.

"*Our Dao Chamber mostly contains physical Daos. They are the easiest to isolate and reproduce. However, many disciples pursue Daos related to emotions, thoughts, or mind states. To accommodate those as well, we have created the Dao Space of Mortality.*"

Jack nodded. His own Dao of the Fist was mostly related to the heart. It was about being free, unstoppable, laughing in the face of combat and death. While it technically belonged to the Dao of Life, it was more oriented to human nature.

To be precise, the Dao of the Fist belonged to the Dao of Life. His Dao of the Fist was both about Life and human nature. Of the Daos present, Mortality would probably suit him best.

"*Is it free to enter a room?*" Jack asked.

"*Each of these rooms can only accommodate one person at a time. Therefore, there is a price to rent them, and that price is determined by the amount of people interested in each room. That way, everyone gets their turn."*

"I see. And what do those prices look like?"

"Right now, they range from one to five Dao stones per day."

Jack grimaced. That was a steep price. "What about the Dao of Mortality?"

"It is one of our most sought-after rooms. Its price is at four Dao stones a day, and there is usually a waiting period of several days."

"What about the Dao of Life? Or the Dao of Space?" Jack asked. The Dao of Space was one he'd touched upon a little, using it to teleport and as the inspiration for some of his skills, while the Dao of Life was closely related to his Life Drop.

"Space is priced at three Dao stones per day. However, Life is our most expensive room—it goes for five stones a day."

Jack shook his head. He'd thought that finding fifteen or twenty stones to break through had been a lot, but that was just pocket change. High-ranking cultivators spent in spades.

Then again, there are a thousand outer disciples and only twelve rooms. High demand is only natural.

Jack didn't expect the Dao Chamber to be so expensive. Currently, he carried zero stones on him—he'd given everything he had to the professor. If he knew the prices would be so high, perhaps he would have kept some.

Then again, his monthly stipulation was three stones, and it would certainly rise once he visited the Globe and updated his ranking. Coupled with the thirty-two stones Marcus still owed him, he wasn't poor.

And let's not forget about Jack's Life Stones, the upcoming hot commodity of the Cathedral, he thought, his lips curving in a money-making grin.

If he came this far only to be defeated by capitalism, it would just be a joke!

The octopus Envoy must have suspected he had no stones. "The Fallen Genius Mirror, however, is free to use."

Jack's eyes shone. "Really? How come?"

"Most people only use it once or twice, so there is little demand. Moreover, it is an artifact that depends on the user's energy, so there are no operating costs. We do not wish to take advantage of our disciples; all our prices are at cost."

"Alright! Fallen Genius Mirror, you say... Let's test it out."

CHAPTER THIRTY-FIVE
FALLEN GENIUS MIRROR

THE OCTOPUS ENVOY LED JACK TO THE BACK OF THE DAO CHAMBER, TO ONE of two normal-looking steel doors. They didn't lead to Dao rooms, like most other doors here, just to a different part of the building. Her tentacle turned the knob, revealing a wide, short room.

"The Fallen Genius Mirror," she said, letting Jack through.

A large mirror covered the back wall. It was twelve feet wide and six feet tall, as if several people were meant to look at themselves here. Besides the two of them and the mirror, the room was empty.

"*What is it?*" Jack asked.

"*Better experienced than explained. Just know that this mirror is a precious artifact of the Cathedral. It is meant to show cultivators the breadth of the world, as well as help them find a path to success.*"

Jack approached the mirror, observing his crystal clear reflection. He could use a shave—and a hair-cut. "Do I just place my hand on it?"

"*Precisely. As soon as you touch the mirror, your mind will be presented with a variety of visions. The more stable your resolve and the greater your willpower, the more you will be able to benefit, and the sooner you will be done. Also, the first time using the mirror is the most effective, so I urge you to try your best."*

Jack nodded. When it came to resolve and willpower, he was confident he wouldn't lose to anyone.

"I will leave you now. Once I do, the door will lock, and it will only be able to open from the inside. Of course, please return as soon as you are done—more people may arrive to use the mirror."

"Understood. Thank you for the explanations, Envoy."

"The pleasure was all mine."

Dragging her slimy tentacles over the floor, the octopus Envoy slid out of the room and shut the door behind her. Jack was covered in darkness. It didn't matter—thanks to his Dao perception, vision was nearly obsolete.

Let's see what this is all about, he thought, stretching his hand forward. His palm reached a smooth, cool surface. The mirror was pleasant to the touch.

A tendril of consciousness extended from the mirror, seeking entry into Jack's mind. It felt invasive—had he messed up?

In the next moment, the mirror's insistence grew extreme. All of Jack's mental defenses were demolished. His mind was swarmed by visions, and his senses were cut off. He could neither feel nor move. He was completely alone.

He braced himself. When nothing bad happened for a few seconds, he finally relaxed.

This is why the door locks, he figured. *In this state, I'm defenseless.*

The world brightened again. Jack was floating through the air, a ghost with neither form nor power. Only his senses remained. He was an observer. The world around him felt completely real—from smell to sight, everything was in line, like in every Dao Vision he'd experienced.

He turned his gaze downward, finding that he floated over a desolate black swamp. In the skies below him, but still above the swamp, a youth faced down three opponents. This youth's dark hair floated wildly, his robes fluttering, and his gaze intense like it wanted to bore into the world. His aura was staggering—this was clearly a dragon amongst men, an elite of the world.

The three people opposite him seemed devilish. They were three women, all sharing a single eye—their remaining eye sockets were hollow, and their skin was dry and wrinkled as if about to tear.

All four of these people were early D-Grades.

The youth charged. He revealed a flaming sword that could burn the heavens. The witches cackled all at once, each drawing their own weapons. As the battle began, Jack found the two sides were equally matched—the youth was far stronger than each witch by herself, but the three of them battled in perfect unison, shoring up each other's weaknesses.

Half a minute after the battle started, the witches shrieked. "You're forcing us!" they shouted in one voice. The one holding the eye shattered it in her grip, releasing a large specter. The youth roared to the heavens, turning the flames of his swords from red to purple as he slashed down.

Specter and flames collided in a massive shockwave that uprooted several trees. Finally, the specter narrowly came out on top, piercing through the flames and the youth's chest. Blood spurted out. The proud youth fell from the heavens, smashing hard into the ground and being swiftly devoured by the specter.

A proud elite had just... fallen. It felt undeserved. Wrong.

Before Jack could consider this further, the scenery changed. He was now over an active volcano, watching a red-haired girl battle against a muscular old man. While both of them were D-Grades, her cultivation was far inferior—she was only an early D-Grade to his late D-Grade. The only reason she could fight him evenly was the volcano into which she'd lured him, using it to amplify her Fire Dao.

This girl was clearly another heaven-shaking elite. She fought well, expertly applying her Dao to break through her opponent's overwhelming force. She had all sorts of trump cards and genius maneuvers.

However, fighting this man remained a huge gamble on her part. After a long and fierce battle, she made a mistake. The old man teleported behind her, sticking his hand through her guts. Jack watched the girl's eyes widen in disbelief before all life left her body.

The scenery changed again.

From one to the next, Jack watched many battles. Some contained E-Grade cultivators, while others were between immortals. There were even the rare F and C-Grade fighters. What they all had in common was that at least one side of each conflict displayed a heroic youth—these people used their power to go against the odds and reach for opportunities beyond their level.

But they almost always lost. It was natural. They were defying all odds—it would be impressive if they did win.

Yet, somehow, Jack felt it wasn't right. These people were all extremely skilled. He expected them to prevail regardless, using the opportunities they secured to soar even higher into the cultivation world.

Were these the fallen geniuses of the mirror?

After a while, the pattern changed. Now, heroic youths occupied both sides of each conflict, ruthlessly tearing into each other. Every battle was to the death. Blood flew. Each of these people believed their destiny was greater than anyone else's, and in every battle, one side perished. Jack even saw some people win one battle only to lose in a later vision.

Across the visions, the amount of dead heroes was staggering. Their corpses could form mountains of bones, seas of blood. Each possessed had the potential to reach the heavens, and they all perished midway, dying on one of their steps to glory. Many times, the battles that killed them weren't even significant—they died to random opponents at random places, in what felt like minor encounters of their lives.

A deep sense of regret rose inside Jack. All these bright people, dead... How cruel was the world of cultivation.

Could I have been one of them? he wondered.

How many times had he come close to death? Innumerable. Ever since the Integration, at the Forest of the Strong, almost every encounter was life-threatening. His survival had been completely against the odds. Though he knew that, he'd never realized just how easy it would have been for things to go wrong.

Knowing was one thing, but seeing was another.

As Jack witnessed these geniuses fall, he imagined himself in their place. Maybe the black wolf of the Forest of the Strong didn't ignore him the first time they met. Maybe the rock bear had gotten the best of him. Maybe the goblin shaman had burned him to death, or maybe the very first goblin had gouged out his eyes before he could fight back. Maybe he'd frozen solid in the Ice Pond, his body a sculpture for future explorers to discover.

His exploits came with numerous benefits, but they were usually made against the odds. If all of those risks were added together, the chances of him surviving were negligible.

And it wasn't even that. Oftentimes, it wasn't his skill that saved him, but pure coincidence. When the Hounds of the Animal Kingdom found him on the *Trampling Ram*, the only reason he'd survived was because Gan Salin happened to be there and happened to have had a change of heart. If he hadn't luckily found the Life Drop in the third ring of Trial Planet, he would have never defeated the Final Guardian—he would have never broken through to the D-Grade as quickly, and he would have failed to defeat the overseer.

Jack didn't discount his own achievements. He'd almost always made the right calls, fought well, made good plans, and used his willpower to emerge victorious when the world was against him. He'd seized opportunities that others couldn't even fathom. He had worked extremely hard and defeated everyone in his way, becoming a fist shooting ever forward.

Even when it came to fallen geniuses, he wasn't a stranger. He'd felled many of them himself: Rufus Emberheart, Lord Longsword, Maximus Lonihor, the planetary overseer... All sorts of illustrious characters had been bested and often killed by him. Jack had emerged victorious through every clash so far, his destiny shooting into the heavens.

But, for every genius that triumphed, a million failed. Every genius Jack defeated had defeated numerous others, who had defeated numerous others. It was a mountain, a pyramid—and he was always a fine line away from turning into just another fallen genius, a pile of bones on another person's path. The people in these visions were all near his level of talent, but they fell left and right like random nobodies. It could have easily been him.

He stood on a huge mountain of corpses and coincidences.

Jack was chilled to the bone. Again, while he knew all these, it was only now that their tremendous weight landed. If he wanted to continue chasing the peak of cultivation, he would keep walking the same road. He would have to defy the odds and take all sorts of risks. The mountain beneath his feet would keep growing, and he could become part of it at any moment.

Over the course of his remaining cultivation path, the chances of him falling somewhere, anywhere, were sky-high. It was almost a certainty.

Do I want to go that way? he asked himself. He thought about Vivi and their children, the professor, and all his friends on Earth. He thought about Brock, treading the exact same path as himself.

To continue cultivating as he was, he would need to consign himself to death, which would affect all those people. Was he willing to do that? Or should he choose the safer road, cultivating peacefully until his potential eventually ran out?

No, he realized. I can't.

The Life Drop was in his soul. He was certain it couldn't be removed without killing him. If he fell behind the curve, the Church would never let him keep such a precious artifact—they would split him open to give it to someone more worthy.

He was already on the road of no return. He had to reach the peak or die trying.

However, even if he could turn back, he wouldn't. The Fist inside him was clear, and so was his own will. What was the problem with death? Even if he fell in a far-off land, buried in the dirt as just another fallen genius, never to see his friends and family again or enjoy life, that was fine. He would never stop advancing. A life without fighting, without purpose, was an empty life.

To him, it was a fate worse than death.

Jack was a Fist, and a Fist he would remain. Shooting ever forward.

Jack's mind hardened. His resolve, which had momentarily wavered, was reinforced. It didn't matter what the world threw at him. It didn't matter how difficult his path became. He would climb the mountain of corpses, endure any pain. He wasn't advancing for comfort or the privilege of being a strong cultivator. He was advancing because that's what gave his life meaning—it made him happier than anything before the Integration. He felt alive.

No matter what happened, he would never stop.

He was more aware of the mountain of bones beneath his feet now. His mind stirred. Thank you, he thought to all of the people who had fallen on his path. I am grateful. With your sacrifice... I, alone, will reach the peak of cultivation.

The mirror had kept showing Jack visions, but he'd long stopped watching. Finally, as his mind was set, the visions dispersed. The mirror released him from its grasp, and Jack opened his eyes in the real world, shining with the weight of realization.

A veil had been pulled off his eyes. His soul had matured, and he already had many new insights to work with. The resolve he'd just exhibited was relevant to his Dao of the Fist and how, through him, it manifested in the world—the crux of the C-Grade.

This mirror... is not simple, he thought, giving the mirror a final glance. It remained empty, showing only his reflection, but it had helped him a lot. His Dao was more stable than before—the weight of understanding had forged his soul and pulled it closer to reality.

Jack opened the single door, welcoming the Dao Chamber again.

The octopus Envoy glanced at him. “What happened?” she asked. “Did you change your mind? Are you not going to attempt the mirror?”

“I’m done,” he replied.

“*Already?*”

CHAPTER THIRTY-SIX
PLOWING THROUGH

Most people stayed in the mirror for hours. Some took entire days. The reason for that was their unfamiliarity with sudden death, as well as their lack of willpower that prevented them from seeing the truth.

Almost everyone on the Cathedral had risen through corpses, but not everyone realized it. When someone found success, it was easy to attribute it entirely to oneself, not taking into account their invisible advantages or all the things that could have gone wrong. It was difficult to acknowledge the great part of luck in any genius's rise.

However, to pursue the Dao was to pursue perfection. Such a blind spot would inevitably affect a cultivator. Therefore, the higher-ups of the Church created the Fallen Genius Mirror to absolve the C-Grade disciples of their delusions, preventing future problems.

Inside the mirror, images of long-dead geniuses would keep repeating—or being fabricated—until the user realized the point. The mirror would then release the cultivator. Generally speaking, the more talented a cultivator was, the stronger their delusions would be, and so the longer they would stay in the mirror.

But Jack had only been in the room for twenty minutes. It was ridiculous. The octopus Envoy even suspected he was lying and hadn't actually used the mirror—but the darkness in his eyes was hard to ignore.

Only twenty minutes... she thought, shivering. *He's so extremely talented... How can he be in touch with his mortality? How can he understand the woes of the weak? How can he embrace death and struggle so quickly?*

Just what has he been through!

"Is there a problem?" Jack asked, noticing her hesitation.

"No, no problem at all," she quickly responded. *"You were just faster than I expected. Thank you for using the Fallen Genius Mirror—I hope your gains were significant."*

Jack gave her a cool smile. That smile contained sadness and determination, like he'd seen through the world. "You could say that."

"Great! Is there anything else you would like to try in our Dao Chamber? If you have any questions, don't hesitate to ask!"

Envoys were on a completely different level than C-Grades. They lived in different worlds. Normally, they would be cold and distant when facing an outer disciple... but this octopus Envoy wasn't an idiot. She knew Jack was extraordinarily talented, and now she could also see that his maturity and experience was far above others of his cultivation level. He had already overcome the greatest weaknesses of geniuses. If there was no accident to befall him, she was ninety percent certain Jack would reach the B-Grade, and maybe he wouldn't even stop at the early B-Grade.

If she didn't take this chance to befriend him before he rose, her ten thousand years of life experience would have been in vain.

"Thank you, Envoy, but I think I'm done for now," Jack replied calmly.

"Alright. Take care. If you ever have questions about the Dao, feel free to look for me—my name is Ashly Sherry."

"I see. Thank you again."

With that, Jack left the Dao Chamber, leaving behind the octopus Envoy and the three meditating cultivators. Luckily, their conversation had been entirely telepathic. If those cultivators heard an Envoy reaching out to an outer disciple like that, who knows what they would think.

Jack did reap great benefits from the Fallen Genius Mirror. His already steely determination had taken another step forward, and his understanding of the road of cultivation had broadened. He now understood the significance of reaching the C-Grade. Nothing had changed on the surface, but the underlying truths were much clearer.

Fallen Genius Mirror... he thought, smirking as he walked. *What a fitting name.*

And now, what? I still have to visit the Globe, of course. I also want to meditate on the mirror's insights and stabilize my foundation in the Heavy Pagoda. I should also let Brock know I'm here and go to the disciple office to pick up my monthly wage of Dao stones—and the wage of Marcus William, which he owes me.

Let's start small. Brock, then Dao stones. Then, we'll see.

His steps took him across the Cathedral's bleak terrain, into the familiar fourth village. The paths were empty. Given the recent excitement of his bros, it was easy to forget that most of the Cathedral's occupants preferred to cultivate in their cabins.

Jack finally reached his cabin, knocked on the door, and entered. Dorman was meditating on the special mat, fat as ever. His eyes opened as Jack appeared—he wasn't too deep in meditation.

"Hey," he said. "You're back."

"I am. Where's Brock?"

"At his own cabin."

"His what?"

Dorman laughed. "Brock became an outer disciple right after you left. I don't know how he did it, but he actually surpassed me..." There was a hint of bitterness in his voice, but no resentment.

Jack's eyes shone with excitement. "Good! Excellent! Where is his cabin? I must congratulate him!"

"It's number 487, here in the same village."

"Alright. Are you coming?"

"I'll cultivate a bit more. I'm almost at the peak D-Grade now. And, Jack?" He hesitated a moment. "Thank you. For taking me in, getting rid of Cranxiao, and even letting me cultivate on your magical mat. I appreciate it. A lot."

Jack smiled brightly. "Don't mention it. Enjoy that mat, because I might be taking over soon. See you!"

"Yeah. See you."

Admiring the rare smile on Dorman's face, Jack closed the door and headed for cabin 487. It wasn't difficult—all cabins had a number over their door, and they were arranged in a logical manner. He arrived quickly and knocked.

"Yes?" a simple voice came from the inside.

"It's Jack."

"Big bro!"

The door swung open, revealing a brorilla flying at Jack. He gave Jack a manly hug, then patted him on the shoulder and said, "You back. How was home?"

Jack couldn't help laughing. "It was good, Brock. Everyone's doing well. And I heard you became a disciple? Good job!"

"Mm. I beat a dirty bro."

"Right... A dirty bro, yes. I totally understand."

"Don't stand at entrance. Come. We drink and talk—I have wine."

Jack followed Brock inside, finding a cabin as spartan as his but with a massive jug sitting in a corner. The two of them sat cross-legged on the floor, chatting and drinking—the wine had a strong fruity flavor, reminding Jack of the old times on Earth.

Jack described the situation on Earth, telling Brock all about his kids and the fun things they'd done together. He spoke about Edgar's progress in building the academy, the professor's exploits in bettering the planet, and how Brock's parents were doing great and missing him—he even said he'd taken them on a stroll through space.

Brock was overjoyed. "Parents are important bros," he admitted, then detailed his own experiences: how he'd made a friendly bet against the frog-like Envoy, won the first two battles of the Globe, and ended up becoming an outer disciple. He had his own cabin now, along with a monthly wage of one Dao stone. The bros were all excited for him and looked forward to his future progress—after all, Brock was only at the peak D-Grade.

"Your ranking is incredible," Jack admitted. "It's no worse than mine before I discovered body tempering."

Brock's sharp gaze perceived Jack's thoughts. "No fret. You experience more dangers than me. Naturally, you have more opportunities. I catch up in the future."

"I'm looking forward to that."

One man and one brorilla chatted for many hours, emptying Brock's jug. Of course, wine could never affect someone like Jack—he could expel the buzz with a thought.

My little brother has grown up and is even treating me to wine now... he thought, sentimentality rising through him. *He's not so little anymore, is he? Why does it feel like yesterday that he climbed on my shoulder and threw poop at strangers? Back then, he couldn't even talk; he spoke in mime.*

Once upon a time, Jack had more or less adopted baby Brock. Now, the two of them were equals, having crossed the universe together to enjoy wine at a landmass orbiting a black hole.

"What you do now, big bro?" Brock asked once the joy of their reunion died down.

"I'll stop by the registration office to pick up some Dao stones. Then, I think I'll visit the Globe to update my ranking, and finally go to the Heavy Pagoda to stabilize my foundation a bit. I didn't cultivate at all while on Earth."

"Sure. I'll come with."

"By the way, how close are you to breaking through?"

"My Big Thought is solid. I want some time to make sure all is okay, so... few weeks. Then, I only need stones."

"Excellent. When the time comes, I'll help you find them. Even if I don't have enough on me, it will be easy to borrow from someone given my current status."

"Good. I don't want delay your progress—you help me borrow, and I pay back."

"Spoken like a true gentleman!" Jack replied, laughing with a red face. Maybe it was the wine. Maybe it was happiness.

The two of them stayed a little longer, talking about various things, then it was time. They exited the cabin, and Jack dispersed the buzz of alcohol, while Brock pointed his finger at the empty sky and unleashed a golden ray of Dao. Suddenly, a large, golden "B" appeared overhead, accompanied by a loud bang that echoed across the Cathedral.

"What the hell was that?" Jack asked.

"I summon bros. You doing the Ball is big thing—they want be present."

Jack laughed as he shook his head. They walked to the Ceaseless Murder Globe, meeting many bros on the way. Apparently, anyone not intensely cultivating had rushed to join.

"Big bro! You're back!" Osmu Sosmu exclaimed, approaching Jack and clasping hands.

"I'm here, Osmu. Have you been well?"

"Of course! Ever since you killed Cranxiao, our days have been far more peaceful."

Jack nodded. At the same time, a light bulb went on inside his head. The Fallen Genius Mirror had taught him that no true genius could rise through a smooth path—could Cranxiao have been purposefully placed there by the Black Hole Church to stir the low-rankers' growth?

Huh.

It didn't change much. He would still kill Cranxiao if placed in the same position, but it was an interesting thought.

The entourage of bros kept growing. By the time Jack reached the Globe, over twenty people had appeared, all excitedly trying to predict Jack's new ranking. Most said a number between 280 and 270. Osmu Sosmu, ever the optimist, dared to say 260.

The higher the ranking, the larger the difference between each individual rank. Marcus William was ranked 281st, but anyone below the 250 or 200 mark could have easily defeated him. His battle against Jack had been close, so he couldn't be much stronger.

What these people didn't know, however, was that Jack's greatest strength lay in his resilience. He was much better suited for the Ceaseless Murder Globe than Marcus.

The same frog-like Envoy operated the Globe. He smiled and greeted Jack, congratulating him on Brock's success, then quickly opened the Globe for him. Jack had stopped by the registration office on the way, picking up his wage of three stones along with Marcus's seven. In total, he had ten Dao stones, so paying one to activate the Globe was easy.

"Good luck, big bro!" all the bros outside cheered. Jack raised his fist and walked inside, letting the entrance fall shut behind him.

He was alone now, and ready to fight. His blood was pumping.

The first shadow appeared. Though its cultivation level was the same as Jack's, their actual strengths were worlds apart—Jack only needed a casual punch to defeat it. The second and third battle were no different. Then came the nine shadows, each replaced by a stronger one as soon as it died. The ceaseless murder began.

Jack was a fist in water. Compared to last time, this battle was far easier. He destroyed these low-level opponents the moment they appeared.

The level of the shadows rose from two, to three, to four, then five fruits. Only now did it become slightly challenging. Jack activated the Life Drop, weaving between the many attacks and occasionally getting injured. Still, the shadows kept falling, and his energy expenditure wasn't too great.

Six-fruit shadows appeared, kicking up the difficulty. In the Globe's limited space—only three hundred feet across—dodging was easier said than done. Shockwaves were everywhere. Jack had to plow through them, expending more of his Dao to persevere. Thankfully, he could rely on his tempered and constantly-regenerating body, keeping the energy waste to a minimum.

The shadows died slower now. Reaching one and overpowering its defenses while dodging all the others was hard—the difficulty was rising exponentially.

Then a seven-fruit shadow appeared. It wasn't much weaker than Marcus William.

The shadows had strength similar to the average cultivator of their level, but as the fruits went up, the average cultivator who could reach that point grew more and more talented.

Don Cranxiao had been a three-fruit C-Grade whose actual fighting strength was somewhere between the five and six-fruits boundaries. Marcus was more talented than Cranxiao, but at the sixth fruit, his actual strength was only between the seventh and eighth.

If Marcus ever reached the nine-fruit boundary, he would be considered average for his level.

Jack kept fighting. It was an uphill struggle now. The shockwaves were so intense that his perception was hampered, making him unable to see the attacks until they were almost upon him. He was constantly teleporting, tearing through the distorted space to do so, pushing him more to the defensive than actually attacking. He managed to kill a few six-fruit shadows, but seven-fruit ones appeared in their place, further raising the difficulty.

Jack was constantly enduring injuries. If not for his extreme regeneration and tempered body, he wouldn't have lasted three seconds against this lineup.

When he was facing four seven-fruit shadows and five six-fruit ones, he was finally cornered. A barrage of attacks broke through his defenses, piercing his skin and stopping an inch before his heart. The shadows came to a halt. They bowed and disappeared, while Jack remained in a heightened battle state, all twitchy and tense.

He took half a minute to calm himself, then exited the Globe. The bros welcomed him with cheers. Jack smiled and waved at them, still panting, then turned to the Envoy.

"How did I do?"

CHAPTER THIRTY-SEVEN
SUMMONED

THE ENVOY DID NOT REPLY, EYES GLUED TO THE RANKING OBELISK. EVERYONE followed suit, including Jack—he had no idea where his current strength would rank.

When a cultivator's ranking changed, all names between their new and previous ranking would blur momentarily as they moved a step down. Usually, it was only a small part of the obelisk—maybe ten places, or fifty, even up to a hundred if one just had an important breakthrough.

Now, almost half the obelisk lit up. Between Jack's last ranking of 675 and his current one were more than four hundred names—four hundred geniuses, each with their own ambitions and dreams. All those names were dragged down a place, making room somewhere in the early two hundreds.

The spectators' eyes bulged. Even Osmu Sosmu had only dared guess a number around 260—if it was anywhere lower, Jack shouldn't have struggled so much against Marcus.

The truth was, Jack's power kit was far better suited for the Ceaseless Murder Globe than Marcus's.

Gradually, the obelisk dimmed. Before everyone's eyes, the new ranking was clear.

Rank 216... Jack Rust!

Uproar! People stared at Jack as if he were a monster. They struggled to believe their own eyes. Just two weeks ago, he'd barely defeated the cultivator ranked 281st. Those two ranks had an enormous difference between them. Had he lied that he was visiting his family and instead went to reap some unknown benefit that catapulted his strength?

Moreover, the rankings above 250 were almost solely occupied by high C-Grades. Even the Cathedral's six-fruit geniuses couldn't reach that high—how had Jack achieved it with just one Dao Fruit?

Was he a miracle maker?

Most of the bros present were at two fruits, and their ranking was only in the nine or eight hundreds. They had thought this a decent result, but now, they realized they weren't even comparable to Jack. He was a whole different beast.

These people had all grown up with the halo of a genius around them. Now, that had been abruptly and thoroughly shattered. Compared to Jack, they were nothing more than prancing clowns. It was impossible not to feel envy or bitterness—but the good bro is one who understands and hugs these emotions until they go away. They shook their heads, chuckled harshly, then moved on.

Trying to compare to Jack was like staring at the sun: pointless and idiotic. They completely accepted that he was an outlier and returned to competing with each other instead, taking him as a distant hero, a legend in the making.

In a way, Jack was the opposite of the Fallen Genius Mirror.

"Congratulations," the Envoy said, looking at Jack with new eyes. "Achieving rank 216 with your cultivation is extraordinary. Even in the Cathedral, the gathering grounds of genius, you are one of a kind. Your future accomplishments are inestimable."

"Thank you, Envoy," Jack replied calmly.

"You already know my name. Just call me Borkuren. Since we're going to be fellow Envoys in the future, there is no need for formalities." The Envoy laughed pleasantly as he said that. His words were mostly meant to befriend Jack, but Jack didn't mind. Borkuren gave him the feeling of a kind individual, not to mention he'd bent the rules to help Brock become an outer disciple.

"Alright, Borkuren. Thanks for letting me use the Globe."

"No problem. Now, let's jump to your benefits. You've climbed from 675 to 216. Your monthly wage has increased from three to nine Dao stones, and your Heavy Pagoda time allotment is now two days per month. In addition, if you ever find yourself in need of a specific item, like weapons or armor, you can request it from the Treasure Hall. You have a limit of one item at a time."

Jack's grin split his face. "I'll make good use of it."

"I expected nothing less," Borkuren replied. His red face and frog eyes looked a bit ridiculous, but his smile was bright.

Meanwhile, everyone else could only sigh at their own incompetence. Envoys enjoyed far higher status than outer disciples—let alone calling them by their first name, even speaking to one out of turn was considered disrespectful. All those customs melted like snow before absolute power. What could they say? Jack was absolutely worthy of special treatment.

"Thank you for your support, everyone, but I should head back now," Jack said, turning to the crowd.

"What?" Osmu exclaimed. "No wine celebration?"

Jack looked on helplessly. "I recently had some new insights into my Dao that I need to consider. Moreover, I only recently broke through to the C-Grade and my cultivation isn't stable yet—the sooner I go through with it, the better it will be."

The bros present were speechless. His cultivation wasn't stable yet? Was he implying that, if he meditated for a couple days, his ranking could rise even further?

Please, make it stop! was their shared thought, but nobody meant it. Watching the rise of a star was magnificent. They were drawn to it, eagerly anticipating to see how far Jack could go.

Perhaps, one day, he would even reach the number one ranking!

"Fine," Osmu replied, speaking for all the bros. "But we'll have a wine celebration eventually, yes? We can't not celebrate all those achievements of yours."

Jack laughed. "I promise. We'll have our celebration."

"Invite me too," Borkuren said from the side. "If I'm free at the time, I will join."

"Of course! The more, the merrier!"

Hearing this, the crowd had fires lit in their bellies. An opportunity to socialize with Jack Rust, an Envoy, and who knows who else... This party was one they absolutely had to attend!

From the moment he joined the Cathedral, Jack's abrupt rise through the ranking obelisk had granted him all sorts of privileges. It was all a bit chaotic at first. However, by now, he had explored most of them.

He was acquainted with the Ceaseless Murder Globe and the Heavy Pagoda—one was used for battle experience and the other for high-speed cultivation. He had gotten a space ring from Treasure Hall and experienced the Fallen Genius Mirror of the Dao Chamber. The only resource he hadn't tried yet were the Dao rooms of the Dao Chamber, but he temporarily put them aside. One's cultivation was always shaky after a breakthrough—first he would stabilize it, then he would revisit the Dao Chamber.

All those were resources that the average C-Grade couldn't even dream about. Back in the Milky Way galaxy, people like the Warden or the planetary overseer could only sit cross-legged and tough it out, painstakingly advancing one step at a time. If they wanted battle experience, they had to go out and find suitable opponents. If they wanted high-speed cultivation, they had to find or create a place overflowing with their Dao of choice. If they wanted to advance their Dao, they could only sit in meditation and ponder in their heads.

Compared to them, Jack could progress a hundred times faster. These were the benefits of joining a major faction.

Right now, Jack sat cross-legged inside the third floor of the Heavy Pagoda.

His new Dao Fruit was the focal point of his being. The power of the Dao surged from the environment into his soul world, into his Dao Roots, up his Dao Tree, and finally into the fruit, slowly but surely growing it to maturity. At the same time, any excess energy was released through the flowers of his tree, into the atmosphere of his soul world where it was reabsorbed by the roots and added to the cycle, ensuring that the Dao Fruit always received the maximum amount of energy.

The current Dao Tree formed a complete system.

The growing of the Dao Fruit was essential to cultivating in the C-Grade. Only when it was fully grown could a cultivator create the next fruit. Normally, even growing one fruit could take decades, but Jack had many outstanding factors.

His perfect foundation could absorb the ambient Dao at great speed, where it streamed up his vibrant Dao Tree. Thanks to his maturity and solid understanding of his Dao, the fruit he'd created had a thick and healthy stem, absorbing energy at a prodigious rate. At the same time, the large number of flowers he'd managed to grow during his Dao Blooming recycled the Dao at a rapid rate, accelerating the flow of energy and helping the Dao Fruit absorb it faster.

Additionally, his tempered body could withstand tremendous pressure, allowing him to cultivate at the Heavy Pagoda's third floor, where the energy density was eight thousand times higher than on Earth. The Dao here was viscous and thick like mercury—with great density came great efficiency, and he could flood his Dao Fruit at a speed that most one-fruit C-Grades would consider ungodly.

From the F to the C-Grade, every step so far had been taken to perfection, further accelerating Jack's progress.

He could spend two days at the Heavy Pagoda every month. After his recent breakthrough, he could endure the third level with reasonable comfort. He wasn't quite ready to challenge the fourth level yet, but he soon would be.

Jack opened his eyes. Purple lightning filled the world, spearing through all. A faint smile played on his lips.

Alright, he told himself. *I'm used to the process. After one day at the third floor, my cultivation is stable at the first fruit... I should go back and temper my body some more. Afterwards, I'll try to spend the remaining day of my monthly allotment at the fourth floor, if possible—cultivation will be much faster there.*

The fourth floor was usually reserved for particularly strong, high C-Grades. While he didn't hope to match the power of their Dao, he did have a much stronger body than them. Hopefully, he could use that to withstand the pressure and accelerate his cultivation even further.

As he stood to leave, however, a voice echoed across the Heavy Pagoda, penetrating its defensive layers to sink into his mind.

"All outer disciples of the Black Hole Church, report to the Cathedral Square immediately!"

Jack's mind shook from the intensity of the message. Whoever had sent it was extremely strong. He didn't know what was going on, but he rushed to exit the pagoda.

The message wasn't just meant for him. Rows of cultivators exited alongside him, many at the seven, eight, or nine-fruit boundaries. These were high-rankers he hadn't interacted with yet, but their rank granted them several days at the pagoda each month, so it was understandable that a lot of them were present.

When all of them were forced out of their cultivation, it was a sight to behold.

"What's going on, Envoy?" a nine-fruit C-Grade asked the Envoy responsible for managing the pagoda.

"Why are you asking me?" she replied sternly. "The orders were clear—rush to the Cathedral Square at once!"

Nobody rebuked her. As one, the high-rankers swarmed the air, while the low-rankers could only walk. Jack flew as well.

The Cathedral Square was a massive empty space in the middle of the Cathedral, close to the Envoys' quarters. As Jack arrived, cultivators streamed in from every direction. Hundreds of them piled into the square, with more arriving every moment. Jack was one of the first bros there. As more and more bros arrived, they gathered around him, forming a tightly-knit group. Even Brock rushed over, as did Dorman, who was not an outer disciple but wanted to see what the fuss was all about. Only the Sage was missing.

In another part of the square, Jack spotted Baron Longform. The third-ranked cultivator glanced over him then paid no attention as if Jack didn't exist.

As the cultivators gathered, more and more of them broke into heated discussions. A mass summon like this was rare. Had something happened? Were they going to war?

Suddenly, all discussions were sharply interrupted. Four figures appeared on a raised platform before the crowd.

One of them was a young-looking man with an aloof aura. Yet, as he rose to the platform, the weight of his cultivation pressed down on everyone present. He was like a god. This was the Heavenly Spoon Sovereign, the Head Envoy of the Black Hole Church. Besides the Elders, he was the greatest authority here. Everyone drew cold breaths upon seeing him.

The next two people were also Envoys, but their auras were deeper than most Envoys Jack had met so far. One was an old woman with kind eyes, and the second a dark-haired man who seemed to be in his thirties, with a sharp, fleeting, and oppressive aura.

The fourth person was much less impressive than the rest, almost being unnoticeable.

"The Sage?" Dorman exclaimed. "What is he doing there?"

Jack had the same question. He wasn't surprised to find that the Sage had also broken through to the one-fruit boundary, but what was he doing on the platform with the Envoys?

"Thank you for coming, everyone," the Head Envoy said as if they had a choice. His face was covered with a carefree grin. "We have great news!"

CHAPTER THIRTY-EIGHT
EXPEDITION

THE CATHEDRAL SQUARE WAS SO QUIET YOU COULD HEAR A PIN DROP. THE Head Envoy let his words hang. Then, as Jack was beginning to wonder if something was wrong, he continued.

"A hidden realm was recently discovered in the Heaven Egg galaxy. Additionally, our resident diviners"—he gestured at the Sage and the old woman Envoy—"estimate its rank to be in the upper B-Grade."

He paused again, letting everyone digest the meaning of his words. Jack had no idea what a hidden realm was. Most people, however, knew. Whispers spread like wildfire. Even the bros revealed expressions of wonder.

"What's that?" Jack asked Osmu Sosmu.

"You don't know?" Osmu replied. "Hidden realms are treasure troves! When a B-Grade or higher cultivator dies, sometimes their inner world will remain connected to our universe, letting cultivators go in and explore it. These worlds are exceedingly rare, and they are filled with all sorts of treasures! An inner world has a different Dao composition than the real one—all sorts of unique circumstances may appear."

Speaking up to here, Osmu's face passed from excitement to disappointment.

"But... a hidden realm has nothing to do with someone like me. The only ones to benefit will be the Envoys, and maybe some high-ranking C-Grades as well."

Jack frowned. If that was the case, why had the Head Envoy gathered everyone? To rub it in their faces?

Many people shared his suspicions. Some had eyes filled with doubt, and others with hope.

On the raised platform, the Heavenly Spoon Sovereign smiled. "An upper B-Grade realm is most useful for people at the low B-Grade or below—to cultivators of similar power as the realm's creator, anything inside is simply worthless. However, inner worlds can be vast. Lucky chances are aplenty, and while the best will be suitable for low B-Grades, there will be many lesser opportunities. For that reason, our exploration team will consist of elites ranging from the middle C-Grade to the low B-Grade. Once inside the realm, you can split up and explore the areas most suitable for each power group."

This was in line with what Osmu told him, but it still didn't explain why the Head Envoy had gathered everyone like this. Was it to celebrate?

Even as he heard about the realm's circumstances, however, Jack was intrigued. He was only at the first fruit, but his power was great—could he fight for a spot in the exploration team?

The hidden realm was full of opportunities. Even if there was some danger inside, he still wanted to enter—a cultivator who didn't adventure would end up weak.

"The expedition will be led by the Spacewind Sovereign, an outstanding individual in our ranks," the Head Envoy said, gesturing at the black-haired man next to him. He seemed valiant and mighty. "As for the leader of the C-Grades..." The Head Envoy smiled at the crowd. "Min Ling, please come up."

A woman flew over the crowd to land on the platform. Long dark hair covered her shoulders, while a dark spear with a red spearhead rested on her back. Her features were slim enough to be called Asian if she was on Earth, and while her body appeared gentle, there was a hidden power inside it that gave Jack pause.

He had seen her once before but hadn't been able to approximate her strength. Now, he could sense her towering aura, her tyrannical might. She could exterminate him with a flick of her spear—her power was vastly superior to that of Baron Longform, the third-ranked outer disciple.

But that was expected of the number one C-Grade. What gave Jack pause was that her cultivation was only at the seven-fruit boundary!

She dominated the entire Cathedral at two tiers below the other top rankers? he thought, eyes widening. *Holy shit! She's good!*

Jack himself could jump tiers to fight. Even against the other geniuses in the Cathedral, jumping four or five tiers was no problem. However, not only did the disparity between tiers increase the higher one went, the top rankers were also extreme geniuses themselves—especially the top hundred, the territory of the nine-fruit C-Grades.

In the Cathedral, C-Grades were generally required to leave once they reached a thousand years old—one tenth of their lifespan. At that point, their potential was considered mostly realized, so there was no reason for the Church to spend resources on them.

If one managed to become a nine-fruit C-Grade, that no longer applied. The nine-fruit C-Grade was only a step away from the B-Grade. Even if a cultivator's potential was mostly spent, there was always a chance they could take one or two extra steps in their lives. For that reason, the Cathedral continued investing on nine-fruit cultivators for as long as they'd like.

Everyone constantly cycled within the Cathedral, with a new batch of talents arriving every thousand years, but the nine-fruit cultivators remained. They were the outstanding talents who emerged from the last seven or eight disciple batches.

In other words, someone ranked two hundredth was number

two hundred of the current thousand disciples. Someone ranked ninetieth was actually ranked ninetieth amongst the last eight thousand disciples!

That was why the top hundred ranks were considered a different playing field. The strength discrepancy rose abruptly as one reached that rank. Moreover, even amongst those hundred nine-fruit disciples, there were vast differences. Someone like Baron Longform could absolutely wipe the floor with anyone ranked in the eighties. He was someone who could easily jump tiers to fight other outstanding geniuses of his level.

For Min Ling to rely on her seven-fruit cultivation to dominate every single other disciple... her talent was no less than Jack's. Who knew what lucky chances she had experienced to reach that level.

While Jack was marveling at the implications of Min Ling's cultivation, the Head Envoy kept speaking.

"In the hidden realm, there is a high chance that the B-Grades will enter the core areas, while the C-Grades will remain at the outer edges. If that happens, Min Ling will take over leading the C-Grades. With her exceptional talent and heaven-shaking battle ability, she has the highest chances of protecting everyone."

No one disagreed. It was hard to argue against absolute power. Min Ling herself stood on the platform with a calm look, like this was only natural.

The Spacewind Sovereign glanced at Min Ling with a smile. "I couldn't wish for a better assistant. Looks like I can relax and lead the sovereigns deep inside the realm—with you there, nobody can harm our outer disciples!"

Though his words were polite and pleasant, Min only gave him a sideways look and replied, "Thank you."

Jack was surprised. Was there some enmity between them? Were that the case, why was the Spacewind Sovereign speaking so relaxedly?

Could it be that Min Ling was arrogant? She didn't strike him as such a person, but you never knew.

If the Head Envoy was surprised, he did not show it.

"As for the rest of the expedition team," he said, "the ten Envoys participating will be decided internally. For the outer disciples, we will follow a distribution that can take maximum advantage of the hidden realm's resources. There will be ten nine-fruit C-Grades, ten eight-fruit C-Grades, five seven-fruit C-Grades, and five six-fruit C-Grades—or lower. All participants will be determined by their rank. At the discretion of myself, Spacewind, and Min Ling, exceptions can be made to accommodate for special powers not reflected by one's ranking. The expedition will take place in one year—that is also when the selection will be made, so I expect everyone to cultivate hard."

Determining participants by their rank made sense. For example, the five seven-fruit C-Grades participating would be those with the highest rank amongst seven-fruit C-Grades. In other words, if he wanted to participate, he had to become one of the five people with the best rank under the seven-fruit boundary.

Jack had absolute confidence in achieving that within the year. He was already close.

Just as everyone thought the announcement was over, the Head Envoy spoke again. "Normally, that should be all. However, this particular hidden realm's circumstances are different. That is... we won't be entering it alone. The Hand of God will join us."

The C-Grades fell into silence, then erupted in exclamations. They didn't even care about keeping their voices low. Even Min Ling, with her indifferent attitude, shot a stunned glance at the Head Envoy.

"Silence!" he commanded. A blanket of absolute power fell on the outer disciples. It was like the sky crashed down. Jack was completely unable to move—in his vision, the Head Envoy turned into a giant green-haired glutton thousands of feet tall, while the entire Cathedral Square was a spoon about to enter the glutton's mouth. A terrifying suction force fell on him. Even if he was a hundred times stronger, he would have no choice but to be sucked into that tooth-filled mouth.

The vision dispersed in the next moment, leaving Jack drenched in a cold sweat. So was everyone else. The whispers disappeared instantly, and every eye was glued to the Head Envoy, who once again resembled an aloof young man.

What the hell was that? Jack asked himself. *Are B-Grades that powerful!*

On the path of cultivation, every two Grades signified a major change. From the F to the E-Grade was considered a small gap, since the cultivator still relied on the Dao contained within their body. Breaking into the D-Grade was a greater change as the cultivator could now control the ambient Dao. The same process repeated afterward—from the D to the C-Grade was a small gap, and from C to B, where the cultivator formed their own inner world, was a larger gap.

For an extreme talent, leaping over the small Grade gaps to fight wasn't unreasonable, and why Jack and others could fight C-Grades while at the D-Grade themselves. The larger gaps were a different story entirely. That was why, in the Milky Way's million-year history, nobody had ever defeated the Final Guardian of Trial Planet.

This was Jack's first time experiencing the power of a B-Grade. Before the Head Envoy, he couldn't even move, let alone resist. It was maddening.

The universe was wide.

"As you know, the Black Hole Church and the Hand of God are enemies," the Head Envoy explained. "However, that doesn't mean we kill each other constantly. We are not in all-out war. There are often peaceful talks between the two factions, negotiations, or even exchanges regarding all sorts of matters. This hidden realm is the same. The two factions received the news at the same time, so we can only compromise: each faction will send in the same number of disciples, and everyone will get what they can. Of course, fighting inside the realm is expected. Each faction believes in their younger generation—do not disappoint me!"

Before the crowd of outer disciples could consider the implications, the Head Envoy continued.

"As this involves the dignity of the Black Hole Church, we will delegate a few extra resources to ensure our expedition is as formidable as possible. Min Ling, as the leader of the C-Grades, you are hereby awarded the Thunder Dao World—the crystalized inner world of a lightning-oriented A-Grade. While all resources inside it have been taken, we hope that the Dao principles it contains can help you develop an extra Dao Fruit in time for the expedition. This Thunder Dao World is lent to you by Elder Heavenstar, so you will have to return it before the expedition."

The Head Envoy opened his hand, revealing a purple glass bead. Its surface was covered with lightning, not letting anyone glimpse inside it, and the aura it emitted was absolutely heaven-shaking.

If the crowd hadn't already been suppressed, they would have erupted into whispers yet again. The crystallized inner world of an A-Grade! Even if its value wasn't obvious, the fact that an A-Grade Elder could only lend it, not gift it, spoke volumes.

Min Ling's indifferent attitude disappeared completely. "Thank you, Head Envoy," she said, respectfully receiving the Thunder Dao World. "Please pass my utmost gratitude to Elder Heavenstar. I deeply appreciate this favor."

Not many things could make the proud Min Ling speak like that, but this Thunder Dao World could.

The Head Envoy smiled. "Elder Heavenstar paused his own meditation on this world to lend it to you—I hope you can take full advantage of it. Now, please return."

Min Ling nodded deeply, then flew back into the crowd. Many people were jealous of her gift, especially those who cultivated lightning, but what could they say? If they possessed her talent, they would have received the Thunder Dao World as well.

At the end of the day, no matter what privileges Min Ling received, nobody could say anything. She absolutely deserved it.

As she left the stage, the Head Envoy's smile didn't drop—it only widened. "There is one last matter to discuss. Jack Rust, please come on stage."

CHAPTER THIRTY-NINE

PUBLIC ENEMY NUMBER ONE

"Huh?"

Every C-Grade below the platform glanced around, looking for Jack. They'd heard about him, of course, but he was far too young, far too weak. He was only a one-fruit C-Grade. This hidden realm should have nothing to do with him.

As for Jack himself, he was the most stunned of all. He thought he was a spectator. Why was his name called out all of a sudden!

"Jack Rust?" the Head Envoy repeated. "I can see you. Why are you not coming up?"

Jack finally recovered. "Sorry, Head Envoy. I was dazed for a second."

He rose through the air, passing over the crowd to reach the raised platform. The Heavenly Spoon Sovereign glanced over with interest. The old woman smiled at Jack, while the Spacewind Sovereign shot him a frigid glance.

Hmm? Have I offended him somehow? Jack thought but didn't pursue the issue.

Hundreds of C-Grade cultivators looked up at him. Each could easily be the ruler of their own planet, or even many planets. Some were stronger than him. A few, vastly so.

Yet he was worthy of standing on this stage.

Jack maintained a cool head as he respectfully greeted the Envoys.

"Your recent exploits have reached our ears," the Heavenly Spoon Sovereign—the Head Envoy—said with a smile. "Ranking 216th with a mere one-fruit cultivation. That hasn't happened in millennia. You are certainly poised for greatness. If nothing happens, we expect to receive you in the Envoy quarters within the next hundred years."

"I will try my best," Jack replied.

"Good. The Black Hole Church has always favored the powerful, but we favor the talented even more. Therefore, alongside Min Ling, we have prepared some benefits for you as well."

The Head Envoy closed his hand and reopened it. An object shimmered into existence. It was round and small, barely the size of a walnut, looking insignificant. When Jack's perception touched it, it was absorbed without a trace. He hurriedly pulled back. This common-looking orb not only contained an inner world, but also an intense gravitational pull. The only reason the Heavenly Spoon Sovereign could hold it so casually was his immense power.

"This is called a World Anchor. Do you know what it is?" the sovereign asked, looking tenderly at the orb.

"I do not," Jack admitted. Even in the crowd below, most people looked around in puzzlement. Besides a few exceptionally knowledgeable individuals, whose eyes shone with avarice, nobody had heard of a World Anchor before.

"I don't blame you," the sovereign said. "World Anchors are ridiculously rare. When a hidden realm reaches the end of its lifespan, it will naturally degrade into nothingness. However, if an A-Grade cultivator with extreme insights into the Dao of Space is present, they can capture the realm's essence into a separate dimension just before it dissipates. They then need to overcome a heavenly tribulation as the Dao of the universe demands to reclaim that world. Unless they are extremely powerful, it is possible that their foundation will be harmed in the process."

Jack's eyes were already wide. An A-Grade had to *personally* create this item, and it also had to coincide with the degradation of a hidden realm? They even had to endure a heavenly tribulation?

"Hidden realms are naturally rare," the Head Envoy continued. "Moreover, the A-Grade cultivator is vulnerable while sealing the realm's essence into an orb. It would be disastrous if their enemies caught wind of the situation. As a result, World Anchors are only produced when an A-Grade cultivator is aware of an undiscovered hidden realm nearing its end, or if they have more A-Grades protecting them. Even in the vast treasury of the Black Hole Church, the number of World Anchors can be counted on one hand. Their value is inestimable."

Jack was floored. "And, if I may... what does it do?"

"Ah, that's the good part." The Head Envoy broke into a playful grin. "A World Anchor is most effective when consumed by a C-Grade. It will fuse with your Dao Tree, greatly improving its stability and your cultivation speed. When you later reach the B-Grade and form your inner world, the World Anchor will greatly assist with your breakthrough. It will act as the center of your inner world, stabilizing it and allowing you to expand it much more than you otherwise could. You will be vastly superior to your peers, destined for greatness. Across the entire universe, there are few things as useful to a C-Grade as a World Anchor."

Jack's heart was racing. This World Anchor sounded absolutely tremendous. It could enhance his current strength, assist with the B-Grade breakthrough, and then further enhance his strength. Coupled with the Life Drop, he would be invincible at his level.

How could he not be tempted?

But something was wrong. The Head Envoy's gaze was almost... mocking? Playful? Expectant?

A light bulb went on inside Jack's head. He glanced at the crowd below, finding a thousand greedy gazes boring into him. The C-

Grades' eyes were veritably red, they were breathing heavily, and even the bros had started struggling.

Jack fully understood. His face paled. You fucked me over, Head Envoy!

When Min Ling received the Thunder Dao World, it hadn't been much of a problem. Her strength and talent were widely recognized, and the Thunder Dao World itself was only suitable for those cultivating the Dao of Lightning.

Jack's situation was completely different. The treasure he was offered could be of tremendous help to each and every person in the crowd. Moreover, it helped with the breakthrough to the B-Grade—the most daunting step of all.

From the C-Grade to the B-Grade, one had to completely shatter their Dao Tree and use it to form an inner world. It was an extremely challenging process, with a success rate that didn't even reach five percent. Moreover, in the event of failure, the only outcome was death.

There were many nine-fruit C-Grades in the Cathedral who could attempt to break through, but they didn't dare to. The risks were too high, and the price of failure too steep. No matter how much one wanted to chase the peak of cultivation, taking that step was difficult. After all, even if they didn't break through, they could live ten thousand years as kings and emperors of their planets. They could have anything they wanted in the entire world. Who would gamble it all away?

Unfortunately, those who reached the nine-fruit boundary were ambitious and determined individuals. They yearned for the B-Grade, but they still didn't dare to try. Some decided to stop cultivating and retire to enjoy life, while others spent their remaining years searching for opportunities that could even marginally increase their odds of success.

Waiting too long also wasn't an option. After one reached the middle point of their life, their chances of a successful breakthrough would only decrease. They had to make a decision when they were still young: would they gamble all their remaining years on the small chance of success, or give up and enjoy life?

To the nine-fruit cultivators of the Cathedral, the breakthrough to the B-Grade was a smiling devil that beckoned them, becoming their sole obsession and greatest fear. For the C-Grades who hadn't reached nine-fruits yet, it was a guillotine hanging over their heads, a dark promise they would have to face sooner or later.

Therefore, a treasure which could "greatly assist" with such a breakthrough was enough to turn any C-Grade mad with greed. They stared at Jack and the World Anchor like vultures. If the Envoys weren't present, a deadly melee would have already begun.

The only ones who weren't as tempted were Jack's closest friends, like Brock or Dorman, as well as Min Ling, who was confident she could break through anyway. Of course, even she longed for the world-enhancing properties of the World Anchor, but it wasn't to the point where she would disregard everything and throw her life away to claim it.

Realizing all these, Jack's excitement was doused in cold water. Shivers ran up and down his body. If this World Anchor came to his possession and he didn't absorb it immediately, he had no doubt someone would try to kill him for it.

His only saving grace was that the Cathedral's rules forbade robbing and killing. If someone did so, they would be executed by the Envoys, so there was no point in trying. But what if it was stolen discreetly? What if the Envoys themselves grew greedy and took it away from him?

An entire new slew of problems had been poured on Jack's head —and judging by the Head Envoy's smile, he had absolutely done it on purpose. Just like the time he directly moved Jack's name to the 950th ranking, he was deliberately creating enemies for Jack. Why?

Jack's anger threatened to rise, but he pushed it down. "Head Envoy, with all due respect, why do you treat me like this?"

His question sounded reasonable, but the intent was clear. The sovereign didn't seem to mind. He only casually replied, "I like helping talented cultivators."

Helping my ass! You're trying to get me killed! Jack wanted to retort, but he didn't. He hid his anger away for later and responded, "I see. Then, if someone absorbs the World Anchor, can it be extracted later?"

"Impossible. If you absorb the Anchor, it stays with you forever. Even if you die, it will disappear alongside your Dao."

At least this was something he didn't need to worry about. If he absorbed it, everything would be fine.

"And how long would it take to absorb?" he asked.

The Head Envoy smiled like a cat looking at a mouse. "Ah, you're a few steps ahead. The World Anchor isn't yours yet."

With a turn of his hand, the orb disappeared—probably into the space ring he wore.

Jack's brows rose. "It's not?"

"It is not. Just handing it to you would be no fun—the other outer disciples would certainly find fault with me, the Cathedral's cohesion would be harmed, and my pristine reputation would be soiled. No, I couldn't do something so partial. If you want this World Anchor, you have to earn it."

Jack resisted the urge to smack this guy in the face.

The Head Envoy turned toward the crowd. "This World Anchor was bestowed to the Cathedral by Elder Heavenstar. Jack Rust's talent was the deciding factor, but the Church has always distributed benefits fairly. Heed my words: To earn the World Anchor, Jack Rust must reach a ranking of one hundred on the ranking obelisk within a year, before the hidden realm expedition. If he does not achieve that, or if anything happens to him in the meantime, the World Anchor will be gifted to one of you according to your talent—we will hold a special selection when the time comes. Of course, since Min Ling has already received a gift from Elder Heavenstar, she will be excluded. Those are my wishes, as well as Elder Heavenstar's."

From the side, Jack was boiling. The more he listened to the Head Envoy's words, the more he wanted to punch him.

If anything happens to me? Fuck you!

Jack had never received a more direct, more impactful middle finger. The Head Envoy's words were precise. He'd clearly planned this all beforehand. He dangled the World Anchor before everyone, then directed their ill feelings onto Jack. If they could stop him from reaching the top hundred spots within a year, they would have a chance to receive the World Anchor. The sovereign even urged them to use underhanded means—he specifically mentioned that if anything happened to Jack, the World Anchor would go to someone else.

Moreover, he'd mentioned a vague trial of talent and excluded Min Ling. In such a situation, dozens of people from all cultivation levels would have a chance at winning the World Anchor.

With just a few words from the Head Envoy, Jack had become public enemy number one. If not for the Cathedral's strictly enforced rules, he would have been mobbed already. His enemies, like Baron Longform, were shooting him ugly smirks.

"With all due respect," Min Ling said, floating slightly over the crowd, "why am I excluded? I did not ask for the Thunder Dao World, and the World Anchor is far more precious."

Her protest was reasonable. The Head Envoy did not respond out loud, clearly having transmitted some thoughts to her, because she bowed and floated back down. Her face betrayed nothing.

"Of course," the Head Envoy added, "if Jack Rust wishes, he could give up all his rights to the World Anchor. Then, it would be directly awarded through a talent-based trial, and he would have nothing to do with it anymore. Would you like that, Jack?"

He faced Jack, giving him a clear stare, which Jack held. Then, he started laughing. His voice spread over the Cathedral Square, over all the gathered C-Grades who wanted to kill him, over the Envoys who put him in this position.

Fist meant power. His life and dream was chasing the peak of cultivation. If he was afraid of making enemies, he would have cultivated peacefully on Earth, not come to the dark and dangerous Cathedral.

Since when was Jack Rust afraid of danger?

"Well said, Head Envoy!" he responded. "My path will never change. Come hell or high water, I will never give up. No, I do not forfeit my rights to the World Anchor. I will fight for it. I will reach the top hundred rank no matter what obstacles appear in my way, and I will forge a perfect road for myself!"

"I thought so," the sovereign replied calmly. "Very well, everyone. You heard him. Things remain as I described and may the best cultivator win. As a special rule, assaulting others in any way will be forbidden for the next year. Violators will be executed."

Jack smiled while shaking his head. He was playing into the Head Envoy's hand a bit too much, but how could he say no? To reach the peak, he had to grasp every opportunity he was offered. After all, even with his current talent, reaching the A-Grade was nothing but a distant dream. He would never succeed if he didn't encounter more opportunities, more lucky chances, if he didn't make his path as perfect as possible.

The universe held quadrillions of cultivators. If even one of them reached the A-Grade every ten thousand years, that was already considered a lot. Compared to those mountains of talent, the thousand C-Grades of the Cathedral were really nothing much. How could Jack let them stop him?

The path of cultivation was unfathomably long, and he was determined to walk it all. He would look at the universe below his feet and admire it from the highest vantage point possible.

The numbers didn't matter. Jack's only rival was himself. And that was why he, out of everyone in the universe, would reach the peak of cultivation.

CHAPTER FORTY
JACK RUST AGAINST THE WORLD

THE HEAD ENVOY HAD PLANTED A BOMB IN EVERYONE'S HEART AND PAINTED a target on Jack's back, then he calmly strode away. The two other Envoys followed him, and the Sage promised to find Jack later before taking off.

Though the gathering was officially disbanded, the gathered cultivators did not disperse. Far too many things had happened. A hidden realm was discovered, Min Ling received a Thunder Dao World, and most importantly, Jack Rust had the chance to earn a World Anchor.

Many cultivators gave Jack burning stares. If he failed, they would have a slim chance of earning a World Anchor and eliminating the guillotine hanging over their heads. Everyone here was talented. Depending on the contents of the talent trial the Head Envoy suggested, winning was every bit within their grasp. Even if they failed, it was okay. If they could cause Jack to lose out on the World Anchor and a top ranker later got it, they would receive that top ranker's eternal gratitude.

Jack calmly floated to his bros, ignoring the storm of whispers around him. The battle had already started—everyone here was an enemy, and he would be damned if he gave them the satisfaction.

It was Jack Rust against the world.

"Listen to me," he said as he landed. All the bros stared at him; some were conflicted, others were fidgety, and a few seemed steadfast. Jack looked them all in the eyes as he spoke. "I am now public enemy number one. If you want to distance yourself from me, now is the time—I will not blame you. If you choose to stay, you will suffer pressure and humiliation, and your cultivation will be temporarily hindered. You might even experience danger. However, if you do remain by my side, we will be true brothers and sisters. When I rise in the future, I will not forget you. The choice is yours."

Speaking to this point, Jack crossed his arms and waited. Brock also said nothing, immediately stepping to Jack's side.

They remained in the middle of the crowd. All sorts of burning gazes landed on their location, as if they were surrounded and eyed by a pack of hyenas. The twenty-something bros felt their backs strain under the pressure. They emitted cold sweat.

The Cathedral was not a peaceful place. While it had rules, it also tacitly allowed bullying and pressuring others. It was meant to be a highly competitive environment where true geniuses could rise with everyone else acting as their foil. Now, the difficulty was cranked to the max for Jack. That would naturally include everyone around him. To remain by his side was to throw oneself into danger and gamble everything for questionable benefits. Not many could do that.

Even if all sorts of assault had been forbidden, there were many ways to bully people.

One by one, some bros slid into the crowd. They had joined for fun—they weren't really going to risk their lives for Jack, not to mention they were all on the weaker end of the Cathedral. Throughout the process, Jack and Brock remained silent, letting things play out.

Of the twenty-something bros, most left. When enough time had passed and the deed was done, only ten remained. That was already far more than Jack expected.

"You have helped me in the past, and we even come from the same planet," Dorman said, laughing. "If I abandoned you now, I would be the lowest of trash!"

"Once a bro, always a bro," Osmu Sosmu said, the handsome man who was ranked 793rd. His three friends—the djinn, the mosquitoid, and the other man—had disappeared.

Jack passed his gaze over the gathered people. They were weak and insignificant in the context of the Cathedral, yet they steadfastly remained by his side. He carved their names and faces into his heart.

"Well said, Osmu," he replied, warmth filling his chest. "You are true bros. Isn't that right, Brock?"

"Right," Brock replied simply. His eyes shone golden. "Fake bros—break!"

Every bro who abandoned Jack felt a sharp pain in their heart. It was grief. In that moment, they had lost something very important, though they didn't know what. A couple of them even considered going back, but it was too late now. They could only shake their heads—the decision had been made.

Jack wanted to say more things, but now wasn't the time. They were surrounded by a bunch of ruthless, greedy individuals. Thankfully, the Head Envoy had directly forbidden fighting, so they hadn't attacked him yet.

"Make way," he said. "We will pass."

The cultivators stared him down. They did not make way. Most were too weak to matter, but a few were ranked as high as Jack or even higher. Their eyes sparked with ideas; they weren't going to just let him leave like that.

Jack frowned. "Staring at me will change nothing. Make way or attack me if you dare."

Of course, only an idiot would blatantly break the rules of the Cathedral. But there were other ways.

"Funny you would say that," a deep voice came from the

crowd. A few people unwillingly parted to reveal a tall, tanned, muscular woman with red hair done in a ponytail. Her gaze was hardened, and on her back was a gray claymore. Unlike most cultivators, she did not wear robes, but brown shorts and an equally brown tank top. Jack thought she looked like a bloodthirsty army commander.

He took in the new arrival. Seven-fruit... Could be worse.

"What do you want?" he asked directly.

"I have long heard of your exploits," the woman replied. "A one-fruit C-Grade ranking higher than me... I would love to experience your Dao. What do you say? Are you up for a little spar?"

"And who are you?"

"Rank 220, Mabe Asphel," she replied. Her grin was savage. "But you can call me Mommy."

Some cultivators broke into laughter. Jack ignored them. As soon as their personal benefit was involved, all finesse went out of the window and they became nothing more than base animals, a part of the mob. It was impressive that people like that could reach the C-Grade.

However, he didn't have the mental resources to bother with them. This rough-looking woman had actually cornered him.

His ranking was 216th. Technically, her asking for a spar was not shameful. She had every right to challenge him. The problem was, Jack's ranking was a bit inflated. His regeneration helped him climb higher than he otherwise could—in a real duel, his strength was only around the 260th rank.

In other words, this woman was currently stronger than him. If they fought, it would be possible for her to "accidentally" kill him. She would be admonished and punished, of course, but not too seriously. Accidents could always happen when sparring with one's full strength.

Even if she didn't kill him, she could give him a grievous injury. The Life Drop was most useful for external wounds. If his heart was pierced, or if his leg was cut off, regenerating would consume a massive amount of time and energy. It would push back his cultivation by at least a couple weeks.

And that's without even mentioning the psychological effect of losing a duel. If he wanted to maximize his cultivation speed, he had to remain in tip-top mental form. Losing a close duel would be a blow.

Then again, so would be to shamefully decline.

This woman knew exactly what she was doing. He'd seen her conversing with Baron Longform while everyone was still gathering. The baron had seen his duel against Marcus William, where his fists kept getting sliced and regenerating. With the baron's experience, he could estimate the effect such a regeneration would have on his ranking and understand that this woman was the worst possible opponent for Jack.

"What's the matter?" Mabe asked. "Cat got your tongue?"

Jack did not respond. Mabe roared with laughter.

"Check it out, everyone! Jack Rust, the prodigy who blinded even the Envoys with his halo, is nothing but a tiny little coward!"

Some people followed her laughter, while others expected to see a show. The bros were all hesitating, not knowing what to do, while Brock remained calm and collected.

Jack chuckled. "It has nothing to do with bravery. I'm just lamenting how my fist would be wasted on trash like you."

"Oho?" Her gaze took on a dangerous tint. "Then why don't you try me, big boy?"

"I will. Of everyone here, you are the lowest of the low... but, unfortunately, I cannot refuse the challenge of someone lower in ranking than myself, or people will think I'm some sort of rubber ball they can push around."

"Well said!" the woman exclaimed, ignoring his insults. She was already growing excited.

"Just give me a bit of time to stabilize my foundation," Jack added, dousing her excitement. "I don't need too long. Six months should do. After all, I just broke through."

"Huh? Six months?" Her brows fell. "What are you talking about? Why would I wait six months for you?"

"I just broke through, and the Head Envoy's summons interrupted my meditation. As pitiful as you are, taking care of you would still require some energy, and my lingering insights would melt away. I will not delay my cultivation for a random tramp."

His repeated insults were finally getting to her. She snorted. "You speak a lot but do little. Your six months are clearly an excuse so you can increase your strength. If you don't dare to fight, just say it. Everyone here knows that only a coward would refuse a challenge from a lower-ranked cultivator. We can even bet if you want."

"Refuse a challenge? Hah!" Jack exclaimed, taking a step forward. "You say that I want to cultivate more and increase my strength before facing you, but what's the problem with that? If I have time to cultivate, so do you. Our current ranks are similar. Whether we fight now, in six months, or in six years, the gap between us shouldn't change much. Saying that is like admitting you're untalented. Moreover, six months is very, very little time. How could I break through before then?"

Mabe frowned. She believed Jack was spouting a ton of bullshit, but the truth was, she never thought he would actually agree to fight. She just wanted to humiliate him a bit. Thinking about it, six months really was a very short timespan. In the C-Grade, taking decades or even centuries between each fruit was normal, and taking a year was considered unbelievably fast. There was no way Jack could break through within six months. His strength couldn't grow so significantly.

Of course, Jack was undoubtably talented, and he also carried a body-enhancing Life Artifact. He would surely find some way to close the gap between them until then... but by how much? Mabe was ranked 220th, but in truth, she hadn't visited the Globe in a long time. Her current strength might even be able to break into the one hundreds.

Was it possible that Jack's strength would increase that much in a short six months?

Greed rooted in her mind. There were unknown variables, but victory would bring so many benefits. If she could seriously injure Jack, Baron had promised her a hundred Dao stones. If she could kill him, she would receive two hundred. Those would save her several years of cultivation.

"Fine," she agreed. "Six months from now, here, at the Cathedral Square. I will be waiting."

Many people groaned. Not only because they wanted to see a fight right now, but because they, too, wanted to challenge Jack. Now that he'd agreed to a duel in six months, challenging him before that would just be wasting saliva.

That didn't mean they wouldn't find other ways to hamper him.

"Good," Jack said, then raised his sight to the surrounding cultivators. "What exactly are you all waiting for?"

Reluctantly, the crowd parted. They let him pass. Jack, Brock, Dorman, and the rest of the bros passed, feeling as if they would be torn to pieces at any second.

But that didn't happen. They made it out of the square, then calmly headed toward village four, where most of them lived.

Jack looked back. His eyes were shining like stars. Deep inside, he enjoyed this situation. It was like Hell all over again—surrounded by enemies on all sides, only this time, he had the protection of rules, and a large number of resources propelling him forward. All those greedy cultivators would only serve as his steppingstones, punching bags on which to harden his fists.

Yes, they were all geniuses, but they were nothing compared to him. His path was inevitable.

"What will you do now, big bro?" Brock asked.

"Is there even a question?" Jack replied, his white teeth showing. "I'll do what I always do—get stronger!"

CHAPTER FORTY-ONE
RETURNING TO MORTALITY

JACK WAS INTO THE FIRE. HE NEEDED TO GET STRONGER QUICKLY, BUT WHAT he needed even more was a plan.

Back in his cabin, he sat on his bed and laid everything down.

I have a year to reach the top hundred ranks. Since my current strength is at the upper range of six-fruit cultivators, I will need to develop at least two more Dao Fruits. Alongside my body tempering, it should be enough to match the weakest nine-fruit C-Grades.

But I should work on my Dao as well. It will be vital throughout the C-Grade. Let alone enhancing my battle prowess, I need it to develop new fruits.

That makes three approaches: body tempering, cultivation, and Dao meditation.

Meditation will be most effective through the Dao Chamber. I have enough Dao stones to book it for a few days every month. Cultivation will be most effective in the Heavy Pagoda, where I can spend two days a month. The pagoda can also consolidate my body tempering, which can be done right here on my bed. At the same time, body tempering doesn't take too much mental energy, so I can maybe meditate a bit while doing it and consolidate my gains.

That's the plan. At the start of every month, I will spend all my Dao stones in the Dao Chamber. Every time I feel I've gotten enough insights, I will return here and practice body tempering while consolidating those insights, then return to the Dao Chamber. I will alternate between these two until I run out of Dao stones. Then, I will split the rest of my time between cultivation and body tempering. The final two days of the month will be spent at the Heavy Pagoda, at the highest level I can reach.

Good.

Jack opened his eyes. His two fists, which hadn't seen action in days, felt itchy. As for that large woman... He smirked. She's just a clown.

Of course, his plan was easier said than done. He was the eye of the storm now. People would undoubtedly find all sorts of ways to mess with him, but he'd take them as they came. At least his family was safe—the only way to find Earth was through the Black Hole Church, and Jack firmly believed the Envoys wouldn't go that far. As for Brock, Dorman, and the bros on the Cathedral, Jack's ability to protect them was limited. They would have to endure.

Sovereign Heavenly Spoon paced through a path of the Cathedral, accompanied by a kindly old woman.

"I didn't think you'd go that far," she said. "Pitting everyone against a one-fruit disciple... Don't you think you're being too harsh?"

"If he can't even handle this much, he doesn't deserve the World Anchor," the sovereign replied, his gaze exploring the distant stars as if they were a joke. "If he fails, I will apologize to the Elder, and that's that."

"That's that, he says." She chuckled. "If you weren't his disciple, Elder Heavenstar would cut off both your legs and feed them to space monsters."

"He can try."

"Jonas!"

The Head Envoy laughed. "Relax, Marissa. Even if Jack fails, the World Anchor will still go to Min Ling. It won't be a loss."

"But you said she'd be excluded from the talent trial."

"I lied. There won't be a talent trial. I'll just give it to her."

She raised a white brow. "That's a dangerous game you're playing. The outer disciples will be incensed."

"And what are they going to do about it? They're weak, and we already don't lack traitors." He waved a hand dismissively. "If needed, I'll give them some other resources to play with. It's no big deal."

"I beg to differ."

He shrugged. "Nothing matters before absolute power."

Marissa gave him a long glance, then sighed. "Do you think he will make it? Will Jack Rust reach the top one hundred in time?"

"I believe he has decent chances. Even if he doesn't make the top hundred, as long as he doesn't die, he will be able to enter the hidden realm. Then, everything will be up to destiny."

"Yes..." Silence dragged on. An hour later, Marissa said, "So, chess?"

"Chess. Let's go."

Jack stepped before the Dao Chamber. His gaze was hard—people had been glaring at him along the way, and while none had spoken out, it had not been pleasant. His mood was sour—a far cry from optimal for comprehending the Dao.

He took a deep breath, then another. He opened the door and entered the Dao Chamber.

A familiar scene stretched before his eyes. A low, wide space supported by columns, with colored doors littering the walls. A few people sat cross-legged between the columns, waiting for their turn, while an octopus-like Envoy stood behind a desk in the center of the room.

As Jack entered, the meditating people's eyes snapped open. Several sharp stares fell on him. He trudged forth regardless.

"*Welcome back,*" the octopus Envoy said. "*Will you try some of our chambers this time?*"

"*Yes,*" Jack replied. "*Three days at the Mortality Chamber, please.*"

After picking up his monthly wage, along with the wage of Marcus William that he was owed, Jack currently possessed sixteen Dao stones. One day at the Mortality Chamber cost four stones. The reason he only rented the place for three days was to keep some stones in hand.

"*The Mortality Chamber is currently occupied,*" the Envoy replied. "*I can put you down as the next in line, but you will need to wait for a few more hours. Is that okay?*"

"*Sure.*"

"*Excellent. That will be twelve Dao stones, please.*"

Jack swiped his hand over his space ring, withdrawing twelve Dao stones and handing them to the Envoy. She nodded. "If you need anything while waiting, please let me know."

"*Will do. Thank you, Envoy.*"

"*No problem.*"

He looked for an empty spot far away from everyone else and sat down. A few hours was nothing to a C-Grade cultivator—he would just meditate a bit.

Unfortunately, not everyone shared his thoughts.

"Hey, friend," another cultivator called out without standing. He was a weird chimera with the body of a human, the wings of a bat, and the head of a lion. His voice was deeply bass and struggling to sound friendly. "Which chamber are you waiting for? If it's the same as mine, I wouldn't mind giving you my spot. I know you're in a pinch."

Jack pursed his lips, not responding. The other cultivator waited a few moments, then frowned darkly and closed his eyes.

Jack wasn't an idiot. In this situation, nobody would give him freebies and place themselves against all other disciples for no reason. This cultivator just wanted to know Jack's room of preference so he could sell the information. After all, the prices of the Dao Chamber were determined by demand and supply. If a top ranker like Baron Longform learned that Jack liked the Mortality Chamber, it wouldn't be difficult to artificially drive up the price and make his life difficult.

Unfortunately, Jack could do nothing about this. His conversation with the octopus Envoy had occurred through telepathy, so it couldn't be overheard, but anyone could see him entering the Mortality Chamber when it was time. Withholding this information from the chimera cultivator did not bring any benefits—he only did so to fuck with the other guy.

Nobody else chatted him up. Jack spent the next few hours in meditation, thinking over his current Dao and adjusting himself to the peak mental state. Eventually, a human cultivator exited the Mortality Chamber, her face a mix of grief and thoughtfulness.

"It's your turn," the octopus Envoy reminded Jack, but he was already on his feet. With a few resolute steps, he reached the open door of the Mortality Chamber and closed it behind him.

Let's see... What exactly are these Dao Chambers? For their price, they better be good.

He was confused at first. The Mortality Chamber was an empty rectangular room, similar in size to his bedroom back on Earth. There were no windows or other doors. The only thing special about this room was that the walls seemed to undulate just below his perception, emitting an aura of endless years and vicissitudes.

The environment began to change. A light fog filled the room, impenetrable by Dao perception. When it receded, the walls were gone, and Jack was floating over a village of mortals.

He was like a ghost. His body was incorporeal, and most of his power was gone. Fields stretched out, dotted with rivers, thickets, and watermills. This place looked like the simplest village imaginable.

In the distance, the terrain changed. Different environments were in different directions. To the north was a sprawling metropolis. The south held a primitive warrior tribe surrounded by monsters, and the west a single farm. As for the east, it was just an endless jungle.

The Dao of Mortality...

Jack's eyes were already tender. All thoughts of cultivation left his mind, and he slowly descended to the village right below him.

It was the simplest medieval place. Nobody here was a cultivator. There were just a hundred families living ordinary lives. Some people were hunters, others were farmers, and a few were artisans. There were rich people, poor people, healthy people, sick people, powerful and weak people, children and their grandparents.

As Jack descended, nobody noticed his ghostly form. They went on with their lives. Jack, curious, found a random little girl and followed her. The girl returned home, carrying a basket of flowers, then proudly gave them to her mother. "Look! I got you flowers, like Daddy!"

The mother gave a strained smile. "Thank you, sweetie. Place them on the table please." This woman was bent over a table, looking over sheets of paper. Jack peeked over her shoulder. These were debt receipts. He also spotted a few letters of condolences—her husband had recently died to an illness.

Jack's heart grew heavy. This woman was buried in debt, supporting a household and a daughter by herself. If she didn't find someone to help her, the future would be grim.

He watched as the woman tiredly stood. She helped her daughter bathe in a barrel, then prepared a poor dinner from the few random vegetables she'd managed to gather—the soup was so thin it was almost water. The mother and daughter then sat at the table and tried to enjoy their meal while making lively conversation. The little girl, barely eight years old, couldn't see through her mother's emotions—but to Jack, it was clear the mother was trying to seem strong.

The girl ate most of the soup. The mother said she wasn't hungry. Later, she tucked her daughter into their shared bed and returned to the kitchen, where she silently cried herself to sleep.

Jack's heart was bleeding. A part of his mind told him these were only illusions, not real people, but so what? Even if these two weren't real, there were innumerable houses in the universe where the same situation was playing out.

To many people, life was full of pain. As Jack wondered why, his first response was because they lacked strength—if this family had managed to become rich in the past, they wouldn't be in this situation now.

That was far too callous though, far too dry. How could he face the ugly side of life and have these thoughts? That had been Jack's Dao speaking, but he was ashamed of himself. In turn, he couldn't help but wonder—if he suddenly took the place of this woman, could he follow his Dao to turn things around?

The Fist was about battle and glory, about freely charging forward. In this kind of situation, wasn't it useless?

No. It cannot be useless. It's just that my understanding is poor, my perspective is limited. My Dao of the Fist was developed according to my experiences, which never looked like this.

There were many kinds of hardships in life. Being chased down by enemies was one of them; being poor and helpless, driven against the wall, was another.

Jack didn't know how this woman would solve her problems, or how she could make things even a little bit better. He was as clueless as she was. All he could do was feel for her, sink deep into her situation, and share her despair.

The Mortality Chamber existed in time dilation. One month here was a day in the outside world. Jack spent a few days following this family, experiencing their rising despair. Eventually, he was suffering with them. The mother could earn very little money. Their debts kept growing, and sooner or later, they would burst.

Throughout the process, Jack could feel his fists soften. That wasn't a bad thing. He was just temporarily moving away from battle and into mortality, into the mundane. Deep inside his soul, at the heart of his Dao Tree, a soft transition was taking place. His Dao was shifting and evolving, transforming from a simple weapon into something deeper, wiser.

Eventually, people came to collect their debts. The mother's strong facade broke. She cried and begged for more time, while the daughter watched with wide, disbelieving eyes. Their house was taken, their possessions sifted through. The mother was sent to prison for some time, while the daughter was taken in by a rich old couple who felt pity at her situation. At least, they seemed kind.

Jack was doused in infinite sadness. He wanted to strike out and obliterate the people who separated this girl from her loving mother, but he was just a ghost. Any punch he threw just dissipated. This wasn't his battle; it was their reality.

Finally, Jack closed his eyes and took a deep, trembling breath. A seed was planted inside him—but, as to what it was, he wasn't clear yet. He would need to meditate on it later.

After the mother and daughter were separated, the world kept rolling. Everyone else went on with their lives. Jack chose not to observe the girl any longer and selected another part of the village. Everyone here was a mortal carrying their own fears, struggles, and dreams. A thousand facets of life were represented in this tiny village, more wisdom than a human mind could contain.

The weeks passed like water. With every day, Jack sank deeper into mortality, feeling his Dao undergo a transformation that made it more aware, more corporeal, more realized.

The Fist perfectly encompassed his life, but he was just one person. The world was vast—it contained much more than what he could experience. Compared to the endless lives in the universe, his Dao was tiny, a small part of humanity that was now slowly, step by step, growing outside him.

Jack's Dao was subtly ascending, approaching the true Dao of Life ever more.

CHAPTER FORTY-TWO
FIST OF MORTALITY

THREE MONTHS FLOWED BETWEEN JACK'S FINGERS. HE WAS IMMERSED IN the world of mortals, sharing their pains and sorrows, their joys and celebrations. He focused on the little things: a boy's rowdiness as he reached maturity, a girl's bashfulness, a father's silent pride, a mother's love.

The Mortality Chamber didn't contain a real world. It was a large-scale illusion meant to assist cultivators in their pursuit of the Dao. As a result, the density of feelings in this village was much higher than normal. Every house Jack visited contained something special. Emotions overflowed, and he sank deeper into them with every passing day.

Until, at some point, a gentle voice reached his ears.

"*Excuse me. Three days have passed. It is time to exit.*"

Jack's eyes snapped open. Still in his ghostly form, he sighed. With great reluctance, he extricated himself from the world of mortals and returned to the one of gods, where he belonged.

This illusion world wasn't meant to trap C-Grades. A low-grade cultivator might be stranded inside forever, but to Jack, just willing his awareness to surface was enough. His real eyes opened slowly, and he found himself standing upright in the same position he'd been three days ago.

Three mortal months... he thought with a sigh. *I really should visit home. But not now. The clock is ticking, and I'm at war...*

Such was the life of a cultivator. They could have family and friends, but they were destined to spend most of their lives alone. The Dao was their true companion.

"Thank you, Envoy," Jack said, exiting the Mortality Chamber. His eyes scanned the room—there were only two cultivators present, both of whom glanced at him before returning to meditation. Jack paid them no mind.

"*Would you like to reserve an appointment for next time?*" the octopus Envoy asked.

"*It's fine. Thank you.*"

"*No problem. Come back anytime!*"

Booking an appointment required paying in advance. Jack only had four Dao stones on his person, which was enough to book the Mortality Chamber for a single day. It was far from enough.

Besides, the future was hazy. He still needed to digest all the insights he'd gotten in these three days. Who knew how his Dao would react? Perhaps visiting the Mortality Chamber again would have reduced effectiveness, and it would be better to try another chamber.

He calmly exited the Dao Chamber, mind swimming in mortality. He wasn't too careful as he walked. A few people stared at him, but Jack ignored them completely. As if in a trance, his feet took him to his cabin, where he ignored Dorman and wordlessly sat on his bed.

His eyes closed. He sank in meditation.

Inside his soul, the many insights swam freely. The endless space around his Dao Tree was covered with visions of the mortals he'd observed in the Mortality Chamber, each laughing, crying, or struggling in their ordinary lives.

As a cultivator advanced, their bodies and minds were transformed, but their hearts remained human. They still possessed the emotions and weaknesses of mortals—they were just better at working with them. Understanding oneself was important, even to immortals, because it allowed them to realize their utmost potential and rise to their apex.

Copy Jack was also present in Jack's soul world. Ever since that time he'd been struck by the Life Drop, he'd grown cold and distant. Occasionally, he would erupt with a jovial and social mood, but most often he just liked to sit on his own, relaxing and enjoying the simple life he led inside Jack's soul. Right now, he gaped at the void, immersed in the memory fragments.

"Hey, Copy Jack," Jack said with a smile.

"Hey," Copy Jack replied, not glancing over. Jack shook his head, then once again sat cross-legged. His Dao Tree was at the front, and the memory fragments flowed around him.

When a mortal experienced important events, memories often lingered in their minds. What they needed to do was sit down and try to resolve them. Jack was experiencing the same thing, if a bit more directly.

His hands moved through the void. The memory fragments swirled around him, clashing with each other in sparks of emotion. Jack didn't hurry. He let the memories take their course as he slowly dove into each of them, experiencing them anew and comprehending them fully. These fragments were the distilled essence of his three months in mortality—they were not great in number or size.

As he absorbed their meaning, the fragments lost their luster. They turned colorless and empty, almost two-dimensional, then collapsed into their most vital essence. Pure emotions now circled Jack. Moving his hands, he beckoned them closer, weaving them together into a tapestry of mortality, where opposite extremes blended together like water of different rivers.

As he held the tapestry afloat, a fist shimmered into existence before him. It was purple and clean—his fist, a manifestation of his Dao. As it hovered there, it exuded a feeling of absolute power. Jack could feel that power was unorganized, disjointed from reality. It lacked purpose—to be precise, its purpose lacked depth.

Slowly, Jack morphed the tapestry of emotions into a thin sheet, then draped it over the fist. The two concepts collided, and his willpower pressed down and forced them to merge, until the fist was covered in shadows of laughter and tears, joys and sorrows.

Like forged metal, part of its aimless power had been transformed into a blade of emotions.

Jack admired his creation. Then, he gently pushed a palm forward, urging that fist to sink inside his Dao Tree, making it part of the whole. Something clicked inside him—the insights had been digested, and his Dao had grown. The process was complete.

His eyes opened in the real world. He felt physically and mentally drained—he could use a nap.

"Dorman?" he asked. "How long did I take?"

The meditating cultivator stirred. "Six days."

Jack nodded. Absorbing the insights had taken twice as long as getting them... That felt about right, for now. But it had still been nine days. In his one-year deadline to reach the top hundred, and in the six months it would take him to duel that large woman, nine days were not a negligible amount of time.

Although, his troubles were not without gain.

Congratulations! You have developed the Dao Skill, Fist of Mortality I.

Fist of Mortality I: One fist contains a thousand emotions. Through this skill, you can add a Will component to your attacks and attempt to confuse the opponent.

Jack gave a thin smile. It had been a while since the System spoke to him, much less acknowledge his efforts. In truth, after reaching his current level, the System was becoming less and less useful. Even this skill had been entirely developed by Jack. The System hadn't helped with forming it, nor could it help with using it. The results of his meditation were simply being stated.

Still, having his insights confirmed felt nice.

One more skill... he thought, looking at the ceiling. Is it enough?

Spending nine days to earn a Dao Skill was more than worth it. It wouldn't be too useful at the first tier, but it could enhance his battle prowess by a small degree. If he could achieve such results every nine days, he would be happy.

Unfortunately, that was impossible. The first time in each Dao Chamber would yield the best results. If he wanted to double his current comprehension of Mortality, he would need to spend ten or fifteen days in the Mortality Chamber, if not a month. That was just impossible. He could only slowly progress like everyone else.

But Jack didn't want to be like everyone else. He wanted to be better. He was still soaring through the ranks—if he wasted his momentum to focus on slow comprehension, it would just be ridiculous.

I should try a new Dao Chamber next time, he thought. *But which one?*

There weren't many compatible chambers for him. Life was one, as was Space. As for the rest, they mainly pertained to the elements, with which he'd never had any special contact. At this point, comprehending a new Dao from scratch just wasn't worth it.

Without a tremendous amount of Dao stones, he couldn't get significant benefits from the Dao Chamber within a year. At least, not significant enough to catapult his strength forward.

Likewise, his cultivation couldn't grow too quickly. Even if he could cultivate in the third or fourth floor of the Heavy Pagoda, where he could progress many times faster than other geniuses of his level, it just wasn't enough. Cultivation in the C-Grade happened over centuries. Wishing for meaningful advances within a year was empty talk. The only way would be for him to possess a great number of Dao stones, which could directly increase his cultivation as long as his Dao understanding could keep up.

As for his body tempering, while it was extremely useful, it was also constrained by time. The stronger his body was, the more difficult it would be to reach the next level. Within a year, he would at most be able to increase his bodily strength by another thirty or forty percent.

Combining the three approaches of cultivation, Dao meditation, and body tempering, Jack was confident he could achieve his deadlines. He would defeat the large woman in six months and reach the top hundred ranks within a year.

Jack yearned for the peak of cultivation. To reach it, he had to completely shatter every expectation and progress at speeds others found impossible. Meeting those deadlines was only the floor of his dreams. He hoped to rise even faster.

Moreover, the hidden realm expedition would contain some of the top nine-fruit C-Grades. If he reached the top hundred ranks, he couldn't contend with them—how could he hope to secure any important lucky chances?

No. He needed to advance even faster. He had to progress with unstoppable momentum, even if that made his foundation a bit shaky in the short-term. He could always stabilize it later.

And the only way to progress as quickly as he hoped were Dao stones.

Once again, Jack ran into the wall called wealth. If he just had infinite Dao stones, all his problems would be solved... Unfortunately, he didn't. The nine stones he received per month seemed like a fortune, but they were wholly inadequate to fully utilize the Dao Chamber, let alone using them to cultivate.

Luckily, Jack had a plan to make Dao stones. A ton of them. He hadn't become a healer for no reason, goddammit!

It was time to finally utilize "Jack's Life Stones."

CHAPTER FORTY-THREE
OPERATION LIFE STONES

"Absolutely not, kid."

"Come on, Venerable Saint Thousand Shell. One Life stone a week is nothing. Even if I made ten per day for a year, the Supreme Blood's energy would only decrease by a millionth."

"I said NO!"

In the vast, green-tinged space of the Life Drop, the large turtle huffed and puffed. It snorted, the shockwave once again striking Jack's body. Having tempered himself for some time, he wasn't destroyed, just heavily injured.

"Think about it," he said, enduring the pain as his body regenerated. "You and the Supreme Blood would benefit from me rising in power. It's a tremendous long-term benefit for a tiny short-term concession. How bad could it be?"

"Kid, you're getting on my nerves. I said one stone per week, so you will make one stone per week."

The elephant-sized snap jaw turtle glared at Jack, its neck shrunk back, ready to strike. Jack believed it was only a feint. The turtle had already invested too much into him. It wouldn't destroy everything just because Jack got a little disrespectful.

"Venerable Saint Thousand Shell, I completely understand. And, you know, think of it like this. I possess the utmost respect for you and the Supreme Blood. I would never ask for something like this if I wasn't convinced it's a good idea. I don't just want to help myself—we are a team, and I want to benefit us both."

"Save your sweet words, kid. I am not an idiot. You want to use the Supreme Blood's holy powers to create low-level trinkets and sell them. The answer is no."

Jack scratched his head. This turtle was a tough nut to crack... but, since it hadn't expelled him from this space yet, convincing it wasn't impossible.

He decided to change tactics.

"Is there any way I could reciprocate this to you or the Supreme Blood? Creating more Life stones would be of great help to me. How can I help you back?"

The turtle's face warped into an ugly scowl. "Help us back? Very easy. Just find a treasure with enough life energy to restore everything you're going to spend. Oh, but wait, if you could do that, you wouldn't need the Supreme Blood to create those Life stones, anyway. Whoops."

The turtle's words were bitter and laded with mockery. Jack didn't mind. He only saw this turtle as a somewhat senile old person—any bitterness it spat was doomed to be ignored.

In this case, Jack was even happy. The turtle's words had given him a direction to follow.

"Sounds great. I could do that," he replied.

The turtle shrunk back. "You could?"

"Of course. Life stones are precious, but they aren't everything. If you let me create as many as I want right now, I promise to repay all that energy within two years."

"Two years? Hah! As if the world is so easy! Do you really think I'm an idiot, kid? That I would let you benefit for free for two years based on a loose promise you once made?"

"No," Jack replied seriously. "The Supreme Blood has been with me for a long time now. You have certainly observed me. You know how I act. If I promise to repay you, then I absolutely will, even if I have to sell everything I own."

"And what if you don't?"

"Then you can destroy my body. You can withhold all further energy of the Life Drop or do as you wish."

"Hmm." The turtle extended its neck again, taking a closer look at Jack from only ten feet away. His stare remained steady. He could see in its eyes that it was moved. "I'll tell you what we'll do," the turtle said. "I will increase the limit from one stone per week to one stone per day. That is the lowest I'll go. In return, you will have to reimburse the Supreme Blood for every drop of energy you've used within two years—in double. Consider that interest."

"Double?" Jack's brows shot up. "You're scamming me!"

"Hmph! As if a venerable saint like myself would scam little humans. I said what I said, kid. If you don't think you can repay all the energy in double, then just go back. We have nothing more to discuss. And don't try to bargain—my patience is already spread thin."

Jack was angry. The Life Drop contained nearly infinite energy—the amount he was requesting was beyond negligible, yet the turtle wanted him to actually repay it not in full, but in double. This was just ridiculous. It was the greediest, skimpiest proposal he'd ever heard.

At the same time, he didn't want to negotiate further or the turtle really would expel him from this space. He needed those Life stones. As for finding a good enough Life treasure to repay it...

Sometimes, one has to believe in their future self.

"Deal!" he said, reaching out a hand. The turtle chuckled, ignoring it.

"Good," it replied. "If you fail to pay, then I will suck out every iota of life energy in your body until you are nothing but a desiccated corpse. That will be a fate worse than death. Now begone."

Debt was a dangerous game. To mortals, it could often destroy their lives—exactly what happened to the mother and daughter duo in the Mortality Chamber.

To Jack, that was a shallow way of looking at things. In truth, debt was a double-edged weapon. If one tried to bite off more than they could chew, or if they took a gamble that didn't pay off, they would suffer. At the same time, if used correctly, debt could greatly accelerate a person's ascent.

In this case, Jack was making a gamble, and he was confident in his chances. Those extra Life stones were very precious to him. With their help, he was certain that his progress would be massively accelerated. He would become stronger, which would allow him to grasp even more resources and become even stronger. If his foray into the hidden realm went well, securing life treasures with enough energy to pay off his debt to the turtle would be simple—he could afford to just buy them.

On the other hand, if the hidden realm didn't go well, he would probably die anyway. His debt would be meaningless.

At the end of the day, this was a decision that stemmed from Jack's utmost confidence in himself. It was no different than all other gambles he'd taken. If he could rise fast enough, everything would be fine. If not, he would plunge directly into hell.

The turtle's beady stare bore into him, so Jack quickly detonated his own body and exited the Life Drop space. He returned to the real world, somewhat stressed but hopeful.

Step one of the Life stone plan was complete. He had secured the ability to create thirty stones per month. If he could convert every two of them into a Dao stone, that was an extra fifteen Dao stones—enough to achieve his goals.

The next step was actually achieving that conversion. Jack's Life Stones would be a new addition to the Cathedral's market. While undoubtedly useful, it would take some time for them to catch on. Moreover, there would be a lot of resistance if people knew they came from Jack—nobody would want to give him Dao stones and help him make the one-year deadline.

Thankfully, he had an idea.

"Hohoho." The Sage chuckled. "We haven't seen each other in months—I didn't believe your first words would be a business proposal."

"There is no time to waste," Jack replied with a smile. He swiped his space ring—a sack of thirty Life stones appeared, each shimmering green. "If I try to sell these myself, people won't buy. If anyone else tries, they won't be able to explain how they came across them. Only you are mysterious enough to pull this off."

The Sage's eyes glinted with amusement, and his grin revealed two rows of yellow teeth. The two of them were currently in the Sage's living room, in a cabin larger than most with several rooms.

Jack still wasn't clear on the Sage's status. He was a one-fruit C-Grade but not an outer disciple. His name wasn't on the ranking obelisk. Moreover, he could live in a place like this while all outer disciples lived in tiny cabins, and he'd worked closely with the granny Envoy to divine the hidden realm's circumstances. Back in the Milky Way galaxy, he'd even seemed like friends with the Head Envoy.

All these were far too weird, but Jack had accepted it by now. He just went with the flow. As the Sage had told him a long time ago, his soul resonated with Enas—he could freely cultivate the Dao of Life and reach the B-Grade with no bottlenecks. It wasn't too strange for him to receive treatment on the level of an Envoy.

"I guess I could," the Sage replied with amusement.

"Thank you..." Jack said, heaving a huge sigh. "You would be doing me a huge favor. I can give you a part of the profits—"

The Sage laughed. "No need. These are produced by you, anyway—I'm just putting my name on them. Consider it a favor between friends. However, as for actually selling them, I'm afraid I cannot help. I, too, lead a busy life."

Jack's grin was wide. "That's not a problem. I have ways to handle the distribution. Using your name is more than enough."

"Then, I'm glad I could help."

Doing business with the Sage was refreshingly simple—if it was the turtle in his situation, it could have asked for half the profits. After shaking hands, Jack remained at the Sage's house for an hour, chatting over a pot of tea. Throughout the process, the Sage did not reveal the tiniest bit of extra information about himself.

Finally, Jack stood up.

"I have to go now, but it was great catching up. I'll see you around—and thanks again for your help."

"No problem. If you need me for anything else, let me know."

"I'll try not to," Jack replied with a laugh, and actually meant it. Ever since the Integration, he owed the Sage a large number of favors. It was making him a bit apprehensive.

Leaving the Sage's house—which was located on the outskirts of village four, far enough to be in its own space—Jack went straight to Brock's cabin.

"Sup, bro?" Brock asked with joy.

"Hey, Brock. Glad to see you're doing alright. I have something to ask of you and our bros."

Brock gave him a wide grin. "Speak. We help."

Jack's heart swam in warmth. He described the Life stone situation and what he needed, and Brock was quick to agree. After that, they spent a while ironing out the details. Brock promised to talk with the other bros and make it happen.

The plan was simple. Jack would produce thirty Life stones at the start of each month and hand them over to the bro squad. The bros would then work in shifts, spreading rumors about the Life stones' efficacy and selling them in any way they could. The Cathedral had no established marketplace, so selling them would depend on their skills. They would even go door-to-door if they had to.

Using the bros as salespeople would indirectly connect the Life stones to Jack, but it was the best they could do. Nobody else could be trusted. They just had to hope that labeling them "The Sage's Life Stones" would make the connection to Jack weak enough that people would buy.

It was a good thing he hadn't started selling them before, or this plan would never work.

As for the profits, they would all go to Jack. As much as he wanted to repay the bros, giving them one Dao stone a month off the profits would be too little to each of them and too much for him. He just promised to repay them in any way he could at a later time.

Once again, Jack found himself in a sort of debt, but nobody could advance without owing others.

With the details ironed out, Jack exited Brock's cabin, leaving behind the sack of thirty Life stones. Brock, in turn, went out to gather the bros and discuss how they would handle this. Jack believed in them.

As he returned to his own cabin to practice body tempering, he couldn't stop his grin from spreading. The Life stone plan was finally set to action—and he had a feeling it would do very, very well.

Not to mention how fun it would be.

CHAPTER FORTY-FOUR
REAPING THE BENEFITS

THE BRO SQUAD HAD TEN REMAINING MEMBERS. THE LEADER OF THOSE, besides Brock, was a handsome man named Osmu Sosmu, ranked 793rd on the ranking obelisk.

However, besides his loyalty and budding leadership qualities, Osmu possessed another trait: he came from a large merchant family.

As soon as the Life stones were mentioned, his eyes flashed. "Selling?" he said, thumping his chest. "Leave it to me. In the wide universe, there is nothing that I, Osmu Sosmu, cannot sell!"

"Good," Brock replied. "I trust you."

The Life stone business was quickly organized by Osmu Sosmu. A stall was set up next to the Dao Chamber—he reasoned that, since this was a place where cultivators spent a lot of Dao stones, spending a couple extra would be easier. The bros would take turns manning the stall and selling the Life stones to anyone interested. To C-Grade cultivators like themselves, a few days of work was nothing, let alone that they could cultivate between customers.

The stall was only part of the business. Osmu Sosmu and a few others took up the role of salespeople—they would go through the villages, door-to-door, and try to secure as many sales as they could while spreading the Life stones' reputation.

Osmu Sosmu, carrying a fashionable little sack, gently knocked on a door. He waited a bit. The Cathedral's outer disciples were often meditating, and interrupting their session was not always easy. If the occupant didn't reply, he wouldn't knock again, just move to another door.

The door swung open. A gruff, red-haired man with horns on his helmet stared at Osmu with confusion. "Can I help you?"

"Depends. Are you a healer?"

"No."

"Then how about I help you?" Osmu laughed, fishing a Life stone out of his sack. "This is a Life stone, the newest creation of the Sage."

The other cultivator was confused, but not suspicious. There were no scammers on the Cathedral. There hadn't been for millennia. "The Sage? Who's that?"

"Didn't you see a C-Grade on the raised platform when the Head Envoy announced the hidden realm? The diviner who helped Envoy Space Eye determine the realm's ranking?"

"Oh. There was a person like that, yes. He's called the Sage?"

"Apparently. Don't ask me why—he never tells. He's a pretty secretive guy, that Sage. All we know is that he's a one-fruit C-Grade diviner who enjoys special privileges on the Cathedral. He lives in his own little house, can you imagine that? It's like he's an Envoy."

The Viking frowned. "That little shit."

"Yes. Well, in any case, he's recently created a new life-saving device. It's this thing—a Life stone. One of these can regenerate a mid C-Grade's external injuries, giving them a second life if they're wounded while fighting or escaping. It's like having a healer at hand —and anyone can use it. No expertise necessary."

"A healer at hand, you say?" The Viking's eyes flickered. He wasn't an idiot—he understood by now that Osmu Sosmu was just a salesman. He also recognized him as one of the people who stood by Jack Rust at the Cathedral Square.

However, he chose not to mention those things, for the Life stone *was* tempting.

"How about I come in and discuss this further?" Osmu Sosmu asked.

"Please do," the Viking replied, opening his door wide.

Osmu smiled as he walked in. When it came to selling, he had a lifetime of experience and the teachings of several masters, but he didn't even need them yet. The easiest thing to sell was a good product.

To the average C-Grade, the Life stones really were worth it. They essentially sold themselves!

Meanwhile, another bro who looked like a glass pane with limbs approached the next house on her list. She raised her glass hand and knocked on the door twice, then waited. And waited.

Just as she was about to move on, the door opened a creak.

"Greetings!" said the bro, using the Dao to vibrate her glass body and produce a pleasantly shrill voice. "Can I—Ah!"

She stopped mid-speech, her body now vibrating to the tune of horror. The door had opened wider, and a beautiful woman stared back at her.

"What's this about?" she asked suspiciously. This woman was the number one outer disciple of the Cathedral—Min Ling!

How far the Life stone business had been budding, Jack had no idea. His only job was to get stronger, hence the need to outsource everything.

Even if he did know, he wouldn't have had the mental capacity to laugh at this point. He sat on his bed, painstakingly working on his body tempering. The sheets below him were already dotted with blood. Jack's body shook intermittently, his skin rupturing in different spots. His regeneration worked overtime to cover for the injuries, while new ones kept cropping up.

Body tempering was a simple, challenging process. It consisted of repeatedly drawing a tiny bit of energy from the Life Drop and forcefully fusing it into one's body. That was it. However, this fusion was immensely difficult.

The human body was a complete system formed of the Dao of Life. To cram more energy into it was unnatural. It went against his instincts. Every time Jack forced a fusion, his brain screamed that he was about to explode, and the pain was like driving iron pikes through his bones. The pain was real, but the feeling of incoming explosion was fake—just a reflex he had to suppress. Even if an accident did happen, it wouldn't kill him, just put him through even more harrowing pain.

That was the trouble of fusing one strand of life energy into the body, though in truth, one strand was nothing. This process was repeated every few minutes. As soon as Jack completed the fusion and escaped the pain, he would drag another strand out of the Life Drop and start again. Time passed. The strands added up, comprehensively tempering his body and raising all of his Physical stats.

And yet, Jack stoically endured the pain, single-mindedly forcing more life energy into his body.

The passage of time was hazy. At some point, he opened his eyes and nearly collapsed on his bed. He opened his mouth to puke out blood, then lay flat on his back with the lifeless eyes of a dead fish.

"Are you okay?" Dorman asked, his voice soft and concerned. "I didn't want to disturb you, but... your sheets..."

Jack closed his eyes. With great effort, he rolled over, finding that his bed was painted crimson. Blood dripped from the ends of the sheet, swiftly meeting the ground under the influence of the thousandfold gravity.

"I'm fine," he replied in a hoarse voice. "Just... tired."

"You don't sound fine," Dorman replied carefully. "Maybe you should... take it easy?"

"I'm fine," Jack repeated. Dorman didn't speak anymore, letting his friend recover.

The further one advanced on the path of body tempering, the more they approached their body's limits. He hadn't bled at the start—now, every fusion rocked him to his core, the life energy struggling to accommodate more of itself. Every fusion took longer and hurt more. Eventually, it would reach the degree where it was ineffective, but Jack wasn't there yet—and the pain, great as it was, amounted to nothing before his desire to get stronger.

That desire burned his soul and set his heart aflame. A little pain was a fine price to pay. It meant he was on the right path—if it was easy, everyone would do it.

"How long did my tempering take?" Jack asked, still gathering himself.

"Fifteen days," Dorman responded.

Fifteen... Coupled with the nine from before, it's been twenty-four days already. Almost a month. Have I gotten any stronger?

He willed open his status screen. His main goal was to inspect his stats and see how far they'd grown, but he also wanted to enjoy the visualization of his own strength. Even his willpower wasn't infinite—he needed something to hold onto.

Name: Jack Rust
Species: Human, Earth-387
Faction: Bare Fist Brotherhood (C)
Grade: C
Class: Gladiator Titan (King)
Level: 250

Strength: 2805 (+)
Dexterity: 2805 (+)
Constitution: 2805 (+)
Mental: 308
Will: 308
Free sub-points: 2

Dao Skills: Meteor Punch IV, Iron Fist Style III, Space Walk III, Brutalizing Aura III, Neutron Star Body II, Titan Taunt I, Fist of Mortality I
Dao Foundation: Dao Tree of the Fist, Dao Root of Indomitable Will (fused), Dao Root of Life (fused), Dao Root of Power (fused), Dao Root of Weakness (fused)
Dao Fruits: Fist
Titles: Planetary Frontrunner (10), Planetary Torch-bearer (1), Ninth Ring Conqueror, Planetary Overlord (1), Grade Defier

2805... he thought. *I got nearly four hundred points in two weeks. Last time I spent two weeks in body tempering, I got five hundred thirty. My progress was almost halved...*

He shook his head. Compared to cultivation, body tempering was far more difficult... but it worked.

As his powers returned, Jack realized his entire being was invigorated. Just clenching his fist could shatter a mountaintop. He had the reflexes and agility to dodge the rain, while his body was so dense he could endure even the hardest of strikes.

He grinned. This feeling made everything worth it.

"Alright!" he shouted, jumping to his feet. *It's only six days until the start of the next month. I should probably visit the Heavy Pagoda.*

The pagoda wasn't only good for cultivation, but also to consolidate his body tempering. Those innumerable fusions were not perfect—they left behind tiny wounds and imperfections. If he didn't iron them out, his body would be riddled with weak spots, and the best place to do so was the Heavy Pagoda, where the extreme gravity compacted even his powerful body near the point of collapse. All weak points could easily disappear.

Thanks to his current ranking, he could spend two days a month at the pagoda. He would use them all up now, then spend the remainder of the month cultivating in his cabin. At least, that was the plan.

"See you, Dorman," Jack said. Not waiting for a reply, he strolled onto the bleak terrain of the Cathedral. Dark stone lay beneath his feet and white buildings rose all around. He didn't even notice the thousandfold gravity at this point.

The cabins of the village gave way to desolation, then a pagoda with seven floors. It was manned by the same cultivator as before—a strong-looking older woman, though not the same one that accompanied the Head Envoy.

As Jack approached the Heavy Pagoda, he saw a small group resting and chatting beside its base. Normally, he would have ignored them. As he passed by, some of what the cultivators were saying caught his ear.

"...those Life stones are so good."

"Man, the Church is so stingy. Between cultivation, the Dao Chamber, and now these Life stones, where am I supposed to spend my three Dao stones?"

"Right, right. They should double our wages, otherwise, how do they expect us to advance quickly?"

One of the three cultivators, the one facing Jack's direction, spotted and recognized him. He stopped speaking, wearing a guarded look. His two friends hadn't noticed Jack, but he approached them.

"Hey there, random fellows," he said, stepping into their circle. "I heard you chatting about some Life stones. What's that about?"

The three cultivators eyed him carefully. They recognized him, of course, and had no intention of helping the public enemy of every other outer disciple. However, they were also a bit intimidated. Jack's talent rose to the heavens, and they were mere four-fruit immortals.

"You haven't heard about the Life stones?" one of them finally said. "What have you been doing for the past month?"

"Cultivating. Please enlighten me," he replied with a bright smile.

"Well..." a second cultivator couldn't help but say. "The Life stones are creations of the Sage—the dirty-looking diviner who gets special treatment. They're life-savers. Anyone can use them to just heal themselves—no need to look for expensive healers anymore while adventuring. Of course, they can't fix everything, but they do a pretty good job."

"Really?" Jack asked, pretending to be surprised. "They do sound useful. Perhaps I could use them myself. Do you have any idea where I could find them?"

"There's a stall by the Dao Chamber. They'll restock at the start of the month, but you may not be able to afford them... they go for one Dao stone apiece."

Jack froze. "Excuse me? How much?"

CHAPTER FORTY-FIVE
MIN LING'S RESOLVE

"One Dao stone apiece. What? You think that's too little?"

The three cultivators shot Jack odd glances, who did his best to contain his excitement. "Kind of," he replied. "I mean, such a life-saving treasure would certainly be worth more than a week's wage?"

"Hey, we can't all be like you and earn nine stones a month. Us middle-rankers have to settle for three or five. Plus, the Life stones have just appeared. Rumor has it the prices will grow soon, so we're in a hurry to buy."

Jack nodded. "I see. Well, nice chatting with you all, but I have a pagoda to tackle. See you around."

"Yeah, see you..." the cultivators replied, watching Jack pace toward the pagoda's managing Envoy. They glanced at each other.

"Which floor do you think he'll go to?" one of them whispered.

"The second," another replied without thinking.

The last cultivator shook his head and said, "I think he can reach the third."

"What? How? The third floor is usually for seven or eight-fruit disciples. Even if he can match a six-fruit in combat, there's no way he can match their pure volume of Dao."

As they were discussing, they saw Jack speak to the Envoy, then float upward. He rose over the first floor, then the second. "Is he really going for the third?" one of the cultivators exclaimed. "No way, right? He's just showing off."

Then, before their very eyes, Jack floated over the third floor and into the fourth! The three cultivators were speechless. Even the Envoy at the base of the pagoda did a double-take.

"No way..." the first cultivator muttered.

Jack pushed open the door and walked in, then closed it behind him. Half a minute passed. Then one. Jack hadn't exited, nor had the Envoy entered to rescue him. The only explanation was... he could handle the fourth level!

That was sixteen times the Cathedral's already extreme gravity!

"He's a monster..." one of the cultivators said, shaking his head. Right after, however, he remembered something else, and his eyes shone. He turned to find his friends returning the look.

The third-ranked outer disciple, Baron Longform, had a standing bounty on any information pertaining to Jack Rust. He offered between three and twenty Dao stones depending on the information's importance. As for Jack being able to enter the Heavy Pagoda's fourth level, that was certainly a scoop!

As one, the three cultivators rushed for village one, where Baron lived.

Jack could barely endure the fourth level. As soon as he stepped inside, a heavy pressure crashed down on him. He almost lost his footing—it felt like the entire sky had leaned on his shoulders.

But he could last here, at least for a bit.

Gritting his teeth, Jack closed the door and took a strained step to the side. Running out of strength, he didn't look for a meditation mat, choosing to sit down right where he was. The pressure became slightly more manageable, but it remained muscle-tearing.

The gravity of this floor was sixteen thousand times greater than Earth's. Jack weighed over a million tons. Even with his godlike Dao working hard to offset the pressure, and with his tempered body resisting far more than the average cultivator could, he was pushed to his limits.

One deep breath after another, he tried to adapt. His goal here wasn't to cultivate, but to use the extreme gravity to compact his body and get rid of all the leftover weaknesses of body tempering.

And boy, was it working. Jack could feel his cells grinding against each other, the weaker ones dying in droves. His regeneration worked in overdrive, producing more and stronger cells. Any gaps in his body's life energy were forcefully eliminated, distributing the energy uniformly in the same way a grinding stone flattened any mix.

Time passed one minute at a time. No matter how Jack gritted his teeth, the pressure refused to abate, but he could sense his body growing denser and more complete. His weaknesses were disappearing. The life energy fusions he'd accomplished were hammered flat.

After what felt like a year, but was only around twenty minutes, the process was complete. Jack's body settle down and became fully compact as if he were made of steel. With a heave of relief, he struggled to get up and exit this floor, going to the third one where he could cultivate more freely.

However, right as he managed to force himself upright, a blue screen appeared in his vision.

Congratulations! Neutron Star Body II → Neutron Star Body III
Neutron Star Body III: Neutron stars are made from the densest material in the universe. Your body inherits some of its properties, achieving extraordinary resilience and durability, increased weight and strength, as well as resistance to all elemental attacks. You also retain extreme regenerative properties.
By greatly increasing your body's density and achieving control

over life energy, you have gained the ability to manipulate your mass at will.

"Finally!" Jack exclaimed. This skill had been one of his greatest weapons in battle, but it hadn't increased in a very long time. Ever since he'd gotten it, before even leaving Trial Planet, it had remained at the second tier, stubbornly refusing to budge.

Being able to manipulate his mass—and therefore weight—came at the perfect time.

Increasing one's Physical stats was a mostly qualitative process of saturating oneself with the Dao of Life. The body's physical weight didn't increase much. After reaching a few thousand points, those little weight increases added up. Every C-Grade cultivator was heavier than a normal person—for Jack, whose Neutron Star Body also increased his weight, he was almost twice as heavy as before the Integration.

That created all sorts of problems and was especially prominent in the Cathedral and the Heavy Pagoda. In addition, he had long wondered about this: neutron stars should be extraordinarily dense, so how come the skill only made him twice as heavy?

Turns out, that density was just hidden behind the next tier.

The skill didn't mention the limits of his mass manipulation. While he yearned to test out its upper limit, the current circumstances demanded the opposite. Calling out to his skill, he observed the life energy as it worked on his body, Jack reduced his weight to the minimum.

It wasn't too much—it basically undid the skill's weight increase, reducing his current weight by around twenty percent. However, even that was a life-saver. The pressure of the pagoda's fourth level instantly decreased alongside his weight, letting him find his footing.

A smile bloomed on Jack's lips. While it wasn't comfortable, he could handle this pressure now. He didn't need to return to the third level—he could cultivate right here!

Just this fact would significantly increase his cultivation speed.

Thank you, System... Though, I guess I could have come up with this on my own.

The System did nothing but streamline the Dao. Everything it achieved, Jack could too. It just hadn't occurred to him that manipulating his mass was possible.

Testing the upper limit will come later. Now, it's cultivation time!

One step after the other, Jack walked deeper into the fourth level. A faint current of Dao led him to an unoccupied meditation mat, where he heavily sat down and closed his eyes.

The Dao here was rich beyond compare, and suffocating. Resisting the pressure, Jack opened his mind and soul to his environment. His Dao Tree breathed in and out. The Dao particles around him oscillated, then were sucked inside him. They didn't even look for his nostrils, just diving directly through his pores.

Jack's body was flooded with the power of the Dao. He revolved his own Dao of the Fist, causing the relevant particles to draw closer while repelling the others. The meditation mat below him assisted, magnifying his Dao.

Under the dual effects of drawing in the Dao and filtering out everything unrelated, a large quantity of Fist-adjacent particles flooded Jack's soul world, rushing to be sucked in by the Dao Tree's roots. A rich stream traveled up the trunk and sank into the Dao Fruit, pushing it toward maturity, while the rest was discharged through the many flowers and turned into mist that filled the soul world.

The entire system was operating to capacity. Thanks to the pagoda, these Dao particles were so densely clustered that large quantities could pass through the Dao Tree's thin roots.

Copy Jack laughed, watching the dancing mist around him. Jack himself couldn't help but grin. His cultivation was galloping forward. Just by cultivating in this floor of the pagoda for two days a month, he could form his second Dao Fruit before the one-year deadline! And, if he got his hands on Dao stones or other resources, perhaps it would be even quicker.

Most disciples of the Cathedral considered themselves lucky if they could grow one fruit every decade. If they found out Jack could grow it in a year and still wasn't satisfied, they might even faint on the spot.

"What nonsense is this?" Min Ling asked, holding a leaflet that proudly advertised 'The Sage's Life Stones.'

"It's the new hot thing!" Esmeralda replied, plopping into a chair beside her friend. She was the blue-haired girl Brock called Ponytail Sis. "It's a life-saving measure. You should buy a couple for the hidden realm—I know you have Dao stones to spare."

Min Ling hesitated. "Are they really useful for me?"

"You're strong, so maybe one Life stone wouldn't be enough. But you can always buy, like, a dozen."

"Hmm. I'll consider it. They seem a bit suspicious."

"Well, it's the Sage. You've heard about him, right? Everything he does is weird. I say you splurge a little bit. You've earned it, girl."

Min Ling gave her a sharp glance. "You know, I did hear some odd things about these Life stones."

"Oh?" Esmeralda replied, inspecting her nails. "Like what?"

"That their distribution is handled by Jack Rust's ragtag team of weaklings. And that the Sage is a friend of his."

"How preposterous! I had no idea."

"Es."

"What?"

"Don't lie to me. You know it's useless."

Esmeralda played coy for a minute, then laughed out loud. "Well, I think you're right. Most people have caught on by now, but the stones are just too good. Besides, even if it is Jack Rust hiding behind this, what do you care? It's not like his World Anchor will come to you if he fails."

"Perhaps," she replied with a small smile.

"Oh, I know what you're concerned about! You're interested in him."

Min Ling raised a brow. "I'm no—"

"Don't worry, I get it. He's the talk of the Cathedral, extremely talented, and with a cute monkey sidekick. He's handsome, too—did you see his upper robes getting torn off in that duel against Marcus William? I'm telling you, he had at least an eight-pack, and I would pay several Dao stones to be pressed into that manly chest of his."

"Now you're just being indecent."

"So what? It's just us. We can say whatever we like." She laughed again. "Come on, Min—don't tell me you've never thought about him, not even a little."

"Of course I haven't. We haven't even spoken once. My entire existence is devoted to cultivation, so why would I care about a man?"

"Well, Spacewind seems to think the opposite."

"Spacewind can go fuck himself." Min Ling's eyes became stormy, and she quickly suppressed her outburst. "Anyway... Your teasing aside, I might be interested in those Life stones. Even if they aren't too effective, having a few at hand couldn't hurt. Do you mind buying some for me the next time you visit their stall?"

"No problem. How many do you want?"

"As much as this can buy," Min said, handing over a little sack filled with Dao stones. Esmeralda's eyes widened, then she laughed.

"You got it, girl," she replied, pocketing the sack. "But aren't you worried about helping Jack Rust? Even if you don't care about his World Anchor, he might threaten your status as the top outer disciple."

"Status is nothing to me. I would gladly sacrifice it to have a rival," she said, sending her piercing gaze through the wall and into the void. "As for the World Anchor... I am not like those desperate weaklings that like to sabotage others. I would never drop so low. If he succeeds, he deserves it… and, if he doesn't, I will step on him fair and square like I have everyone else."

Esmeralda chuckled. "That kindness of yours will come back to bite you."

"If we lose our heart, what are we but animals?" Min Ling replied, her dark hair swishing as she turned. In that moment, her clear eyes and perfect face carried such beauty that even Esmeralda was momentarily dazed. "Whether it's Jack Rust, Jack Must, or Jack Lust, I don't care. My throne is right here. If anyone wants to take it, they're free to try."

CHAPTER FORTY-SIX
NOUVEAU RICHE

Every start of the month, the outer disciples of the Cathedral could go to the registration office and pick up their monthly stipulation of Dao stones. Usually, the cultivators streamed in, then casually walked out and headed to the various training grounds where they could spend them.

This time, the scenery was different. Some cultivators had waited there since the night before, forming a line before the door. More arrived every hour. As soon as the new day came, the registration office was swarmed with people looking to receive their stipulation only to dash away as fast as their legs could take them.

The resident Envoy had never seen such haste before.

After picking up their Dao stones, the place the cultivators rushed to was the Dao Chamber, but not to enter it. A small stall had been set up beside that wide and short building. This stall wouldn't be out of place if placed in a mortal market—there were just thirty fist-sized stones laid out on a thin blanket on top of a wooden bench. Over them, a sign proudly proclaimed, "Life Stones: Your Personal Healer!"

Manning the stall was Osmu Sosmu, the proud merchant and

third big bro of the bro squad, along with two other bros. Seeing a hundred cultivators rushing their way, he grinned. "Welcome, everyone, to this month's supply of Life stones!" he shouted, spreading his arms wide.

The Life stones weren't suitable for everyone on the Cathedral. Top rankers had powerful bodies flooded with their own Dao, so they would need multiple stones to feel a difference. Even to most high-rankers, the results wouldn't be too pronounced. As for the low-rankers, they didn't have many Dao stones to begin with, so they were wary of spending them on anything that wouldn't increase their cultivation.

The target audience of the Life stone business were the middle-rankers of the Cathedral, the people with four to six Dao Fruits. This category included hundreds of cultivators. Many of them wished to go out and adventure, or feared that the Sage would stop producing Life stones at some point. They mostly made up the crowd rushing for the stall at the start of this month.

Osmu Sosmu was familiar with these kinds of situations. Normally, he would have driven up the price to squeeze these customers dry, but the Cathedral's outer disciples were all intelligent people. A prudent approach was best. There was also Jack's delicate status and the fact that Life stones weren't truly established yet. The sight of people rushing the stall was helpful in validating the product in the customers' minds. Therefore, Osmu opted to double the price every month.

Now, it was one Dao stone apiece. Next month, it would be two, and it would keep increasing until the market reached a semblance of balance. Otherwise, if he tried doubling it again today, he feared that the customers would all turn around and leave.

The thirty Life stones flew off the shelves. Most people frowned when they saw the current price, which had doubled since last month, but a few chose to grit their teeth and buy. Everything was sold out on the first day.

"Pleasure doing business with you," Osmu Sosmu waved

goodbye to everyone as he picked up the stall and walked away. The smile on his face was inextinguishable. He arrived at his cabin, where he was visited by several bros. As everyone left, Osmu visited the Sage for some tea and to presumably deliver the profits. However, he didn't carry any Dao stones—the stall's earnings were secretly left with one of the bros who'd visited him before. That bro then waited a few hours before delivering the earnings to Brock, who in turn visited Jack's cabin.

Jack's eyes widened as he saw Brock proudly retrieve a large sack from his brand-new space ring. "All that?"

"All," Brock replied with a smile, emptying the sack on Jack's bed. Dozens of Dao stones rolled out. The nearby Dorman's mouth hung open, while even Jack struggled to believe his eyes.

"How many is that!"

"Forty-five!" Brock declared proudly—he could count up to a thousand now.

Jack had supplied Brock with thirty Life stones last month, and another thirty just the day before. The first batch had been sold at half a Dao stone per Life stone, while the second batch was sold at a ratio of one to one. Altogether, this amounted to forty-five Dao stones—a wealth that just seemed to fall from the sky.

Combined with Jack's nine stones for the month and Marcus's seven—whose wage was still taken by Jack—alongside the four he had remaining from last month, he now possessed a total of sixty-five Dao stones. He would get that amount every month, if not more. It was simply unimaginable wealth!

"Brock!" Jack exclaimed. "This is amazing! How... Just how did you achieve this?"

"Not me. Osmu. Third bro."

"Then thank Osmu for me. Tell him he's brilliant—he absolutely deserves it!" Jack was swimming in joy. He took in the Dao stones, quickly calculating in his mind. "Take back thirteen," he said. "Two for you, two for Osmu, and one for every other bro. There's one for Sage, too, as thanks for letting us use his name. I know it's far too little, but I truly am in dire need of Dao stones right now. I promise to thank everyone properly later."

"Thanks, bro. But I want to ask for more. I am close to making more Big Thought. Can I have stones?"

Jack did a double-take, then his face radiated joy. "You're going to break through?"

Brock nodded. "Big Thought is steady. Power is peak. I am ready."

"That's wonderful! Of course, of course; how many do you need?"

"Twenty," Brock replied. He was an outer disciple now, so he also had a small wage of Dao stones. He'd already absorbed one and calculated the needed amount.

"Very well. Twenty it is. Along with the eleven stones for everyone else, that's thirty-one."

Jack separated thirty-one stones from the pile and handed them over to Brock. It was a large amount, but he couldn't care less. His little brother was about to break through. If he was greedy at this time, then he really wouldn't deserve Brock.

The remaining thirty-four stones were more than enough, anyway.

"Thanks, big bro," Brock replied, fist-bumping Jack and receiving the stones in his space ring. "I make you proud."

"Always."

As the two were rejoicing, drunk in their brotherhood, Dorman was meditating on the cabin's meditation mat. His eyes were firmly shut, but his mind was in turmoil. Conflicting emotions warred inside him. He would reach the peak D-Grade soon, and he desperately needed Dao stones to break through. At the same time, Jack had already been kind to him—he couldn't possibly ask for more.

He didn't reveal any of these thoughts, but how could Jack not see them?

"Dorman," Jack said, making the younger man open his eyes. Jack smiled. "I haven't forgotten about you. When the time comes, I will naturally help you break through as well... but, before that, I want to help you restore your body to its optimal state. As soon as my control of life energy is precise enough, I am confident in removing the excess energy from your body."

Dorman's eyes widened like saucers. His heart cried out in joy, and emotions threatened to well up in his eyes.

"You don't have to..." Was all he managed to say, but Jack just laughed.

"We're friends. We're bros—and, moreover, we come from the same planet. Since helping you isn't too difficult, it would be a shame not to."

Dorman closed his eyes for a moment. When he reopened them, they were wide and clear. "Thank you. I will keep this favor in the depths of my heart. I will repay you."

"Just focus on yourself. You got this."

"You good bro," Brock added. "Bit stupid sometimes, but your heart is kind. I believe."

"Thanks, Brock," Dorman replied, touched.

Brock showed a toothy grin. "Call me bro."

The three of them spent some more time talking before Brock departed. Jack was left with thirty-four—an insane amount. Even Min Ling, the first-ranked outer disciple, didn't receive such a lofty monthly wage.

Jack was filthy rich.

Dao stones had two uses for the current him. One was renting out the various rooms of the Dao Chamber. The other was absorbing their Dao to directly speed up his cultivation.

Now that he had enough stones, he could finally do both.

Jack arrived at the Dao Chamber. The same octopus Envoy was behind the desk, while four cultivators meditated in various spots on the floor. One of them sat very close to the Envoy. As soon as Jack entered, that cultivator opened his eyes and immediately arrived at the desk.

"I would like to book the Mortality Chamber for ten days," he loudly declared.

Jack couldn't catch the Envoy's telepathic reply, but he did see her regretful gaze. "I'm sorry," she told him even as she spoke with the other cultivator. "This person is obstructing you, but I cannot do anything. The rules are clear."

Jack frowned. This cultivator was obviously acting against him on purpose. Since he'd visited the Mortality Chamber last time, his enemies had sent this guy to book out the chamber and slow down his cultivation.

Thankfully, Jack hadn't planned on entering the Mortality Chamber, but they didn't know that. Since they were against him, he could play them a bit.

"Hey," he said angrily. "What do you think you're doing?"

"What?" the other cultivator replied with an innocent look. "I'm just preparing to meditate on the Dao."

"You were clearly waiting for me. You jumped out to rent my Dao Chamber the moment I appeared."

"Hmph. The world doesn't revolve around you. I was only adjusting myself just now. This is the same chamber I always use, and you just happened to enter as I was about to stand up. If you have any proof of the opposite, bring it out!"

This was all a load of crap. The cultivator hadn't even bothered to hide the satisfaction in his eyes. Jack pretended to be angry.

"You sure can spout shit!" he said.

"You're still going on? What kind of idiot are you? I said I will rent this room, and I was here before you, so it's mine. If you want, you can wait ten days for your turn—assuming, of course, that the price remains where it is. If too many people ask for the same room, the price will go up, and poor upstarts like yourself will never be able to afford it."

"Oh yeah? Do you really think so?"

"So what if I do and so what if I don't? I just asked for ten days at four Dao stones each. If you have the ability, how about you offer more Dao stones than me and get the room first? How about that?"

"Fine!" Jack replied, pretending to fly off the handle. "I offer five stones for five days!"

"Then I offer six stones for ten days," the cultivator replied smoothly. It was like sixty Dao stones were nothing to him, so it stood to reason they weren't his to begin with. Someone had supplied him with Dao stones so he could bother Jack—and it wasn't difficult to guess who that was.

Still, the cultivator's telepathic message sealed the deal.

"*Give up, kid. Baron Longform will never let you use the Dao Chamber again—let's see you reaching the top hundred now.*"

His grin was savage, like looking at prey. Jack showed a face of indignation—though, inwardly, he was sneering at the other man's idiocy. You just wasted sixty Dao stones, asshole.

"Fine," he spat out in exasperation, then walked over to the octopus Envoy and spoke telepathically. "I would like the Space Chamber, please. For seven days."

If the Envoy saw through him, she betrayed nothing. "*Certainly. At three stones per day, that will be twenty-one stones, please. The chamber is unoccupied, so you can enter immediately.*"

Jack passed out the stones to her, sensing the other cultivator's gaze on his hands. Twenty-one stones were a multiple of three. However, there were many rooms costing three Dao stones, so the cultivator couldn't directly guess which room Jack requested. He would have to wait and see him enter.

"Well?" Jack asked. "Won't you go to your Mortality Chamber?"

"Oh, don't worry. My time has already started. I just had a sudden inspiration—I'll enter when I feel like it."

While most of Jack's anger was fake, and inwardly he was gloating, he really wanted to punch this guy in the face. It was clear that Baron Longform, possibly with the assistance of other top rankers, was determined to make his life difficult. If he hadn't come across sudden wealth, then he really would be unable to enter the Dao Chamber soon, which would severely impact his progress.

I will remember this, he promised, carving this enmity deep in his heart. Without another word, he walked to the Space Chamber and entered it. Next month, this chamber would surely be hotly contested—but Jack's pockets would keep getting deeper.

Baron Longform... he thought, seething on the inside. *Between you and me, let's see who has more money to waste!*

CHAPTER FORTY-SEVEN
SIX MONTHS

THE SPACE CHAMBER WAS UNLIKE ANYTHING JACK HAD EVER EXPERIENCED. As soon as he was sucked into its illusion, he found himself floating inside a small solar system. Or, maybe, it was him that was large.

His body was the size of the sun. Seven planets orbited that sun at random distances, along with a slew of other celestial bodies—meteors, comets, gasses, moons. Jack gaped. The sun was blinding, filling this space with light, and the colorful comet tails speared through the cosmos in resplendent beauty.

It was wonderful.

Edgar would love this... was Jack's first thought before he inspected the chamber more deeply. He quickly saw the point: with him being at this size, and with all other distractions cut away, the effect of curved space on this solar system was plain to see.

The entire cosmos was strung through by faint lines. They spread from one end to the other, and although they were straight, they also curved around the celestial bodies as if this entire place was a taut sheet draped over a gap. The lines were space, highlighting its curvature, letting Jack use his eyes to inspect them.

The sun, planets, and smaller bodies, all at his behest. Lines drawn over space itself. Jack used a finger to punch through space, finding it effortless, and discovered that even its inner void was covered in lines. They were a squiggly mess, of course, governed by unknown laws, but it didn't matter. He was finally able to interact with the mysterious space between space, the interspace.

Given enough time, the comprehensions he could gain here were endless!

Jack grinned with excitement and sat cross-legged. The entire solar system fell under his gaze. His Dao perception spread out, tracing every change. While he was acquainted with the basic principles of space from his time on Earth, knowing was one thing and seeing was another. Finally, he could interact with space as he liked, observe it in a vacuum, and witness the clearly visible truths that were usually hidden.

The Dao of Space was in plain sight. Meditating on it here would offer ten times the advantages with half the effort. Not to mention he already had an affinity to Space thanks to his previous Class, Cosmic Fist.

In the Cathedral, Dao understanding had been one of Jack's weaknesses... but now, he could begin to make up for it.

I love this place, he thought, then sank into meditation.

On the first month after the hidden realm announcement, Jack had spent twelve Dao stones.

On the second, he had thirty-four. Twenty-one went to renting the Space Chamber for a week, while the rest were cleanly absorbed by Jack to enhance his cultivation.

On the third month, Osmu Sosmu raised the price of Life stones to two Dao stones apiece, so Jack received sixty Dao stones. Along with his and Marcus's wage, they totaled to seventy-six.

Upon visiting the Dao Chamber, Baron Longform had sent his lackeys to book both the Mortality and Space chambers for ten days.

Thanks to prices going up, it cost him ninety Dao stones. He was certainly putting in the capital, and Jack only laughed and walked away. In truth, meditating in the Dao Chamber and body tempering were interoperable. There was no harm in waiting ten days to book the chamber of his choice. Therefore, he booked the Space Chamber in the middle of the month, content with letting Baron waste a bunch of his Dao stones.

On the fourth month, Baron Longform came up with even more stones. He had to be supported by other top rankers as well, because his lackeys showed up with no less than two hundred! Jack let them spend freely for the first fifteen days of the month, then directly offered seven stones per day and secured the Space Chamber for a week. His own income had increased as well—the Life stones now sold for three Dao stones a piece, netting him a total monthly income of a hundred Dao stones!

At this point, their war of resources had begun to escalate. The ripples were felt across the Cathedral—many disciples wanted to meditate on the Mortality and Space chambers, but they couldn't. Their prices had risen from four and three stones per day to eight and seven respectively. It was madness.

It was unknown whether Baron Longform and his accomplices had hidden stashes of Dao stones, or if they were asking for favors and borrowing from others. Either way, they were going all-out for the chance to earn the World Anchor. Entire fortunes were crumbling like sandcastles.

Yet all their efforts only amounted to a slight inconvenience for Jack. They hadn't accounted for his newfound wealth or the fact he could spend a lot of time tempering his body. If it was anyone else, the fastest path to advancement would be spending most of their time in the Dao Chamber. Therefore, from Baron Longform's perspective, what was occurring seemed like a victory—they had limited Jack to only using the Dao Chamber seven days a month, and they also forced him to spend over fifty Dao stones for it. They were taking away both his Dao Chamber time and cultivation resources.

In their eyes, they had him cornered, and so they gritted their teeth and kept spending wildly.

In truth, Jack was fine. He possessed more Dao stones than they could fathom. Seven days per month at the Dao Chamber was his optimal point. He also needed to spend roughly two weeks tempering his body, as well as a few days digesting his insights from the chamber. Finally, two days every month were spent at the Heavy Pagoda, where Jack absorbed Dao stones like candy. Under the combination of the stones and the pagoda's extremely dense Dao, his cultivation was advancing by leaps and bounds, steadily approaching maturity of the first fruit.

Jack's progress was close to optimal. All Baron and his accomplices were achieving was wasting their considerably deep pockets. The only real winner here was the Dao Chamber itself, which brought in massively increased profits. If this was all part of the Head Envoy's plan, Jack would have to tip his hat.

Moreover, due to this war of resources, the anti-Jack movement was beginning to lose ground with the other disciples. Most top rankers had already spent so much time at the Dao Chamber that they didn't mind staying away for a bit, but that wasn't true for the hundreds of mid-rankers. They were the ones who suffered from the Dao Chamber prices going up, as well as the permanent occupation of certain chambers.

At the same time, the bro squad discreetly but steadily advertised their brotherhood, forming a stark contrast against the top rankers' selfish behavior.

On the fifth month, the price of Life stones remained at three Dao stones apiece. It had stabilized, and the profits were more than enough for Jack. A hundred Dao stones entered his pockets every month. Then, fifty were spent at the Dao Chamber and another fifty were absorbed while cultivating in the Heavy Pagoda. He also saved a few for later.

As for Baron Longform's camp, even their coffers had begun to empty. They could no longer up the ante. Jack's Dao Chamber usage remained at seven days a month, which was plenty. He spent all of that time in the Space Chamber. Unlike the Mortality Chamber, space was practical and played to Jack's strengths. It could refine his teleportation, indirectly increasing his speed, and also contained many meteors on which he could meditate to increase his awareness of Meteor Punch.

While Meteor Punch itself didn't evolve, another skill did.

Congratulations! Dao Skill Space Walk III has been upgraded to Space Mastery II.

Space Mastery II: The power of space lies at your fingertips. This versatile skill allows you to incorporate the Dao of Space into your movements and attacks, as well as teleport quicker, farther, and with less preparation time.

The description was simple, but the skill itself was godly. It added a whole new weapon to Jack's repertoire. So far, he'd only been using space as a medium to teleport, but the more he meditated in the Space Chamber, the more uses he discovered. It was the fabric of reality, how could it be useless? How could it not be practical to the extreme?

The more time one spent at a Dao Chamber, the smaller their benefits would be. However, Jack had only just gotten started. His comprehension advanced by leaps and bounds, increasing his combat strength.

The Space Chamber was a gift that kept on giving.

As the sixth month came and went, the situation didn't change. Jack spent seven days at the Space Chamber and another three digesting his new insights. He spent nine days tempering his body, one painful fusion at a time, and then two days in the Heavy Pagoda's fourth level, where he cultivated using the dense Dao and the many Dao stones he had available.

Throughout these six months, his training regime had been absolutely luxurious. Even most top rankers couldn't afford seven days at the Dao Chamber each month, let alone using fifty Dao stones to cultivate. Thankfully, Jack kept his wealth carefully hidden, or anyone who heard might have suffered from apoplectic outrage.

At the end of the sixth month, Jack exited the Heavy Pagoda and calmly floated down. Everyone who saw him felt their vision tingling. It was like his mere physical body carried the aura of stars, as if he was a solid mountain in human form. Most people didn't know the cause of this aura and attributed it to Jack cultivating some weird Dao.

Thanks to his body tempering, Jack's body contained an immense, overbearing, tyrannical aura. If he let it loose, it would frighten everyone silly—so he kept it closely contained, revealing only the slightest hints of his power.

One week before the six-month duel, Jack sat alone in his cabin. He shut the door. Even Dorman had been temporarily pushed out, because breakthroughs warranted absolutely no distractions.

After six months of intense cultivation, Jack's first Dao Fruit had finally reached maturity. It had doubled in size since its creation, and the aura it contained was far more potent. However, it could no longer grow, making all the energy that filled Jack's soul world obsolete.

It was time to create a second fruit.

The minor breakthroughs inside the C-Grade—the development of new fruits—weren't difficult. As long as one's foundation was solid and they had enough energy, it was only a matter of deciding which Dao manifestation to use.

Although, being not difficult didn't mean all fruits were created equal.

Jack sat in meditation, considering his insights. The Dao of the Fist dominated his soul, the lenses through which he viewed the world. It was also his very first fruit. For every fruit after that, he would need to infuse another manifestation of his Dao.

Thankfully, he'd just spent five months meditating on the Dao of Space.

The ten Dao stones around him turned to dust, their energy easily sucked into his pores, yet it wasn't nearly enough. It sank into his body like a drop in an empty bucket.

Jack grinned. This was exactly what he expected.

When developing new fruits, the more energy one had, the larger the fruit they could create. Most cultivators gathered all the Dao stones they could, and were constrained by their bodily endurance and soul stability. In both of those respects, normal cultivators couldn't hold a candle to Jack.

Fifteen stones were enough for most cultivators. Jack had fifty.

All those crystals were spread in concentric circles around Jack. The second circle contained fifteen stones, while the third contained twenty-five. All of them disintegrated at once.

A vast amount of energy invaded Jack's body like galloping horses, wrecking his flesh and bones. Under such pressure, most C-Grade cultivators would have had their bodies broken and their organs melted. Jack could barely handle it.

Gritting his teeth, he drove all that energy into his soul, enduring the pain of the red hot flows searing his flesh. His soul world was about to burst—endless currents of energy flared through the void, drawn in by the Dao Tree's roots. The entire tree lit up like Christmas. Jack was floating in the soul world, enduring the pain of the tree almost exploding and his body breaking apart. He sealed the flowers, forcing the energy to remain contained inside the tree, slamming into the trunk's insides like raging dragons.

A normal cultivator would have long exploded, but Jack's Dao Tree had been enhanced by the Life Drop and was highly stable. Moreover, his Dao of the Fist was powerful, his foundation was perfect, and the hardness of his body carried over in his soul world, stabilizing it from the outside.

Even with all that, the strain remained extreme.

Jack's eyes were bloodshot. "Converge!" he shouted, his voice echoing across the entire world. The Dao stilled. Under the guidance of his will, it rammed towards an end of the branches, nearly blowing them up. All that energy dove into a single flower—that flower did not explode, but rather expanded, bloating until it transformed into a deep blue shape. Golden points dotted it like stars, while meteor tails streaked through its surface.

The new fruit sucked in energy like mad, growing at a painfully slow rate. Jack's hands were shaking as he drove more and more power into the fruit, until his Dao Tree, his soul world, and his entire body were devoid of energy. He felt empty. Finally, the energy ran out.

Jack slumped to the floor, falling into a deep slumber. Deep inside his soul, two fruits now hung from the tree branches, proud and carefree. One was purple and shaped as a fist, while the other was spherical, dark blue, and dotted like the starry night sky. This second fruit contained all of Jack's insights into the Dao of Space, enhancing them and representing how the fist interacted with space.

When Jack finally awoke, he felt rising excitement. Only six months after his last breakthrough, he was now a two-fruit C-Grade. Moreover, his fruit was larger than what most cultivators could achieve.

After completing his breakthrough, Jack spent a week stabilizing his foundation. Finally, his eyes opened, seeming like they contained endless stars. Six months had passed, his strength had risen by leaps and bounds, and he was itching to test his might against some of the brightest geniuses in the universe.

The time of his arranged duel had come. And Jack was determined to absolutely knock it out of the park.

CHAPTER FORTY-EIGHT
CHALLENGING EVERYONE

The Cathedral Square buzzed with excitement. People had started arriving since the early morning—from the low to the top rankers, nobody was willing to miss this spectacle. Moreover, since it had been announced six months in advance, everyone had made sure not to be in deep cultivation at this time.

As a result, of the Cathedral's thousand outer disciples, over eight hundred had arrived, and that was because the rest were outside the Cathedral. Almost every C-Grade on the Cathedral was right here!

The Cathedral Square, where the duel would play out, was expansive. It was a mile from end to end, leaving plenty of space for spectators. The top rankers were gathered in a corner, some clustered around Baron Longform and some around Min Ling—it seemed the top ranks were not as united as it once seemed.

Everyone else was gathered in their friend groups, waiting for the battle to start. One notable exception to the crowd were the bros—they were dressed in colorful garments salvaged from who knows where, held drums, gongs, and trumpets, and were led by a brorilla who wore nothing but red shorts.

This brorilla was Brock... and he had reached the C-Grade!

He wasn't a simple C-Grade, either. Soon after he broke through, he entered the Ceaseless Murder Globe and used his mere one-fruit cultivation to reach a ranking of 786. If not for Jack, this would have been the most impressive result in recent years.

As it was, Brock was overshadowed, but he didn't mind. Jack was his big bro. The glory of one was the glory of the other.

And, in any case, for this brother duo to be the two brightest rising stars was satisfying.

The crowd was busy making all sorts of guesses. Some thought Jack would win, while many didn't. It wasn't that they doubted his talent—given the suppression Jack had received in the past few months, most people just didn't see how he could progress.

A small stall stood on a corner of the square. It was covered in red fabrics and proudly proclaimed to be the "Betting Stall." Manning it was the smiling form of Osmu Sosmu. Normally, someone of his rank would never have the status to set up a betting stall, but selling all those Life stones had increased his reputation. Now, if he claimed he could pay people back their earnings, many were willing to trust him.

Such grand events didn't happen often at the Cathedral. Cultivators swarmed the stall, eager to bet a few Dao stones and participate in the excitement. Osmu Sosmu welcomed them all with smiles.

The entire Cathedral was wrapped in an electrified, excited air.

Suddenly, the void parted. A stately figure flew in, her fitting brown clothes striking alongside her short hair. A gray claymore was strapped to her hip. This was Mabe Asphel, Jack's opponent. As soon as she appeared, people noticed her towering aura and sharp gaze—while she hadn't developed a new Dao Fruit, her strength had clearly risen.

And it was no wonder. She had the support of Baron Longform and his herd of top rankers—she naturally advanced by leaps and bounds.

If she had another month or two, she might have broken through and reached the eight-fruit boundary.

Mabe landed on one side of the Cathedral Square and sat down cross-legged, adjusting her mental state to the peak. She was taking this seriously. With all the resources that had been poured into her and the rewards dangling before her, this was the greatest battle of her life.

As soon as she appeared, the audience caught glimpses of her sharp aura. Many glanced at each other, then rushed to the betting stall.

Osmu Sosmu smiled even wider. As one of the bros, he was aware of the massive amount of resources Jack had enjoyed in these past six months. With his talent, his current strength should be enough to win. Therefore, the more people who bet on Mabe, the more Dao stones Osmu would make.

Soon after, there was another disturbance. People looked over, expecting to see Jack. Instead, a dozen figures floated over the crowd, the barest trickle of their auras suffocating. Leading them was an aloof youth. Behind him came a kindly grandmother and a sharp-eyed young man, followed by another nine cultivators, including a frog-faced man and a woman who was part octopus.

As these twelve people flew in, they moved directly to the raised platform, then took out chairs from their space rings and sat down to enjoy the show.

The crowd drew cold gasps. Now they knew why none of the top rankers had dared climb the platform before: the Envoys had come to watch.

“Incredible,” a disciple muttered. “Since when do Envoys care about the struggles of us outer disciples?”

“I guess… they’re also bored?” another replied. “This is a grand event that concerns a future B-Grade. It isn’t weird that they’d come.”

After the B-Grades arrived, though they kept to themselves and didn’t interact with the C-Grades, the atmosphere grew even more electrified. The people present truly felt like they were about to witness something important. Even Mabe Asphel, who was meditating inside the square, could feel the pressure.

A dozen Envoys were watching her. If she could make a good impression, her future would be bright... but, if she made a fool of herself, she would need to find a stone to hide under.

More time passed. There was no specific time set for the duel, meaning Jack could arrive whenever he liked, but he'd still left everyone waiting for a solid two hours. No one complained. Two hours was the blink of an eye to them.

At some point, the Head Envoy raised his head and smiled. "He's here," he whispered.

The void grew heavier. The Dao deepened. Everyone turned toward the same direction at the same time as if beckoned by their instincts.

A lone man flew toward the square. He was dressed in purple, with short hair rising from his scalp and calm eyes that seemed to contain the universe. He moved neither slow nor fast, yet his movements resonated with the Dao itself. Numerous particles danced around his body, ignoring the Cathedral's thousandfold gravity. Everywhere he passed, the void became tinted purple, and his presence was so dense and solid that it felt like the center of the universe, as if he were an ancient titan of unfathomable power.

As everyone witnessed these phenomena, they were surprised. Even top rankers couldn't create such an impression—this was achieved through Jack's extreme body tempering.

He had even broken through and developed a new Dao Fruit!

Many rushed to the betting stall, discovering that Osmu Sosmu had already closed it.

Jack unhurriedly reached the center of the square and landed there, his presence dominating the space around him. Mabe Asphel rose to her feet—though Jack's aura was impressive, it did not necessarily reflect his strength. She maintained her confidence.

"You came," she said. "Brave of you."

"I couldn't kick your ass otherwise," Jack replied calmly.

The crowd was stunned, then erupted into uproar. In the wide universe, there were many people who possessed charming auras. Their every word carried peace and reason, and their rhetoric was able to reach even the most hateful of hearts. Jack was the exact opposite. The moment he opened his mouth, everyone wanted to beat him up.

Veins popped on Mabe's forehead. She had been hyping herself up while enduring tremendous pressure—she never expected the first words out of Jack's mouth to be so basefully insulting.

"Fine. If you want to die, let me be your guest!" she shouted, drawing her claymore. The tip cut through the void, leaving a gray line wherever it passed.

"One moment," Jack said, raising a hand. "I have some things to say first."

Then why didn't you say them before! Mabe thought, her brows spasming, but she remained silent.

"Thank you for coming to watch, everyone," Jack said. "Your presence honors me. Of course, for some of you, I'm surprised to see you here—like Baron Longform. After you wasted a thousand Dao stones to make my life difficult, I didn't think you'd want to personally experience my glory."

Jack's words were sharp and direct. His gaze pierced through a part of the spectators, clashing directly with the stare of Baron Longform, the third-ranked outer disciple. The gedritch—that was the name of Baron's species—narrowed his silver eyes. His face remained indifferent and proud, like a tyrant overlooking a dancing ant. He did not reply immediately; even he was taken aback by such directness.

Meanwhile, the rest of the crowd drew cold gasps. Jack was simply firing cannonballs from his mouth. The moment he appeared, his words were biting and venomous, giving absolutely no consideration for anyone's face.

I must never become his enemy, was the common thought of

everyone present. Against such a person, even if they won in the end, they would be so humiliated they could never recover!

"You speak like a low mortal," Baron Longform finally replied, his Dao-infused voice echoing across the square. "Your accusations are empty. I never bothered with you."

"Of course. I kill your cousin, but you don't bother with me. How... domineering of you," Jack mocked him. The crowd's eyes widened. "Well then, I must have been mistaken. I thought someone wasted hundreds of Dao stones to stop me from meditating in the Dao Chamber. But, who knows? Perhaps all those random cultivators were at a special point in their cultivation and needed to spend seven stones a day to constantly rent the Space and Mortality Chambers for half a year. Come to think of it, I really must have been mistaken. I'm sorry for accusing you—only a completely idiotic individual would go to such lengths to achieve jack shit, and there is no way you could be so pathetic."

The crowd held their breaths. Baron's words were only superficial—everyone knew he really had obstructed Jack every step of the way, spending a massive number of Dao stones to achieve it. Everyone also knew of Baron Longform's disposition—he was an overbearing, domineering, tyrannical individual who would repay every tiny insult a thousandfold.

Now, Jack had called that man idiotic and pathetic in his face. The enmity between these two had escalated way past the point of no return.

Moreover, Jack's words did hold a certain appeal. He reminded everyone that Baron Longform had spent a massive fortune on this—if he really hadn't managed to stop or at least slow down Jack's rise to power, then this really was blatant incompetence.

Facing all these insults, Baron Longform didn't reply. His face was frigid. His aura rose like tumultuous waves, crashing into the shore that was Jack's body again and again, striking him with the full might of an extreme nine-fruit C-Grade. Such an aura couldn't actually harm Jack, but it could make any other two-fruit C-Grade blanch and take a step back.

Jack didn't even change his expression, easily weathering the aura and further slapping Baron's face.

The crowd didn't feel like laughing anymore. This collision was just too brutal. It was like the stare down of two wild animals ready to tear each other apart.

"I am your opponent," Mabe said, giving Baron a way out. "Face me if you dare, Jack Rust!"

"You are my opponent?" Jack asked, a mocking smile on his face. "That's actually the issue I wanted to raise. I'm afraid you're just not worthy."

Her brows rose. "What bullshit are you spouting? You agreed on a duel with me! You cannot back away now!"

"That wasn't my intention," Jack replied calmly. "Since I promised, I will naturally beat you up. However, I'm afraid that such a short spectacle will make everyone think we've wasted their time. Therefore, I have a proposition: after our duel, let there be more. I know that many people in the audience want to fight me. As long as their ranking is below 150, and as long as they can bet fifty Dao stones against me, I will accept any and all comers!"

The crowd was stunned, then once again erupted. Even the bros were surprised by such a declaration.

Jack Rust was challenging the entire Cathedral? Anyone below the ranking of 150 could fight him, no matter how many people there were?

Heavens, what arrogance! He was only a two-fruit C-Grade!

Even the Envoys on the raised platform, who'd simply enjoyed the show so far, started whispering amongst themselves.

"Jack Rust!" Mabe Asphel yelled, her face red with anger. "I will not accept such humiliation!"

She was steaming in rage and indignation. This was supposed to be her fight, the most important battle of her life. She had trained hard and prepared herself for this. Even if she lost, she would have had the glory of facing Jack Rust before the entire Cathedral and even the Head Envoy.

Now, her moment of glory was stolen away, and she was relegated to the opening act. Her pride had been stomped into the ground. How could she not be furious?

"The only humiliation is your weakness," Jack replied. "If you have the power, then defeat me first. That will naturally void all other challenges."

Mabe opened her mouth to respond, but no words came. What could she say? Indeed, if she won, then Jack would be the one completely made a fool of. It was only if she lost, and lost decisively, that all this humiliation would fall on her head.

At the end, everything came down to power. She had to win.

"What an interesting proposition!" the Head Envoy said from the platform, his voice instantly captivating everyone. "I enjoy your daring. Very well. Your challenge is accepted, but a cultivator should never bite off more than they can chew! If you can defeat everyone, you won't even need to enter the Ceaseless Murder Globe, I'll give you the World Anchor right here and now! However, if you lose... you can forget about it!"

Jack's gaze remained resolute, carrying a hint of anger, while the crowd erupted in whispers. Even Baron Longform couldn't hide his smile. The Head Envoy's words were the same as decreasing Jack's time limit from one year to the present six months. It was simply squeezing water out of stone.

For all everyone knew, maybe Jack was just bluffing. Maybe he wanted to take this opportunity and cement his understandings through battle. For the Head Envoy to corner him like this was just too brutal!

Everyone expected Jack to protest. However, after a few moments went by, he proudly raised his head. "Fine. However, you are increasing the difficulty without increasing the stakes. You are simply taking advantage of me. How about this: If I lose, I can forget about the World Anchor. However, if I win, not only will I get the Anchor, you will even gift me a thousand Dao stones!"

The crowd couldn't believe their ears. Did Jack just try to barter with the Head Envoy? Did his arrogance know no limits?

The Head Envoy laughed. "I guess I have been pushing you a bit too hard. Who cares about Dao stones? If you win, I will let you use the Dao Chamber for free until the hidden realm expedition!"

It was hard for the excitement to rise any further. Even the bros had forgotten to bang on their drums and trumpets. As soon as the Head Envoy's voice fell, several people rushed through the crowd to reach the betting stall, where it stood to reason they could place their Dao stones to face Jack.

"Fifty Dao stones," said the first person to arrive—a man ranked 167th. The others cursed that they weren't first, but all they could do was rush faster.

To a high-ranker, fifty Dao stones were neither too much nor too little. Most had saved up this much over their many years. Moreover, Baron Longform had secretly contacted all his supporters ranked below 150, offering to cover their entrance fee and gift them with two hundred Dao stones if they could defeat Jack.

The rush was unprecedented. Over a dozen high-rankers fell on the betting stall, fighting to register before everyone else. Nobody thought Jack could win this massive battle, and the later one fought, the higher the chances that someone before them would defeat Jack and reap the rewards.

The betting stall finally shattered from the weight of all the Dao stones on it. Including the fifty stones from every high-ranker and all the bets from before, there were over a thousand Dao stones on its surface, forming a little mountain. How could wood handle that weight under the thousandfold gravity?

After some time, the high-rankers were done. Twenty-five had registered. There were more, but their power wasn't too great, and they didn't see any meaning to participating. There was no way Jack would stand after consecutively fighting twenty-six high-rankers. If he could achieve this, then his strength would already be approaching the domain of nine-fruit C-Grades!

Everything was said and done. If Jack could win, he would receive the World Anchor, free rein of the Dao Chamber, over a thousand Dao stones, and everyone's recognition. He would become a legend.

However, if he lost in the first match, then this would be the greatest joke in the Cathedral's history.

Mabe Asphel was still waiting, her face the color of ash. She really had been relegated to an opening act. Her moment of glory was completely and utterly ruined. She had never felt angrier in her life.

"Are you done!" she asked Jack.

"I guess so," Jack replied. His aura boiled over, upsetting the space around him. His eyes sharpened. Suddenly, Mabe felt the world's weight crash around her as if she was facing some ancient beast.

But it was too late. She could only do her best and hope to win, or at least not lose too badly.

"Then, take my blade!" she shouted, charging Jack.

CHAPTER FORTY-NINE

THE TITAN LAUGHS

MABE ASPHEL WAS DETERMINED TO RECLAIM HER HONOR. HER COPPERY SKIN was set on fire. Thin lines of blood emerged from her pores, wrapping around the claymore like silken death.

Her aura climbed to new heights, dying the world a thick crimson. Every low-ranker present felt their heart skip a beat.

"Die!" Mabe shouted, bringing her weapon down.

Jack simply stepped back. The claymore met the ground, creating a hundred-foot-long fissure, but the weapon itself was only part of her attack—it was the energy shockwave that was the most dangerous. Currents of blood streamed out, crashing into Jack from almost point-blank. The crimson world collapsed on his chest. His robes fluttered wildly, and the spectators couldn't believe their eyes—had he really forgotten about the energy shockwaves?

Yet, these shockwaves only broke against Jack's chest. They were merely fierce winds meeting a cliffside—completely harmless.

Jack met Mabe's eyes. He grinned. Power pumped into his arms, ready to strike.

Mabe was no amateur. Though surprised, she continued her attack, swiftly transitioning into a pommel strike. When Jack stepped away again, she swung around and cleaved at his head. The remaining blood threads on the claymore combusted, filling the blade with power. A new curtain of blood rose to the heavens, collapsing on Jack.

Out of her three-strike combination, this was the true killer move.

Facing this collapsing sky of blood, Jack remained calm. He did not form a fist—instead, he raised his hand. His speed skyrocketed to the point where Mabe could barely register it. His palm touched the side of the sword and gently pushed it aside, forcing it to veer off to his right.

The claymore struck the ground in an eruption of blood, and Jack weathered the shockwave like it was nothing. His robes fluttered—he was completely unharmed.

"What!" the audience exclaimed.

The weakest people present had no idea what happened. The stronger ones did, and they were shell-shocked. It was impossible to use a hand to deflect a cultivator's sword mid-swing. Your speed and dexterity would need to completely overwhelm your opponent's. And even then, you would have to instantly overpower them.

It was just not possible without a massive difference in strength.

The Head Envoy grinned. "Nice."

Out of everyone present, Mabe herself was the most shocked. She was no mortal, whose strength disappeared the moment their swing began. As her sword traveled, she remained in full control. In the instant when Jack pushed her sword away, she'd tried to resist, but it was futile—she'd been reduced to a child trying to resist an adult. The difference between their strengths was nothing short of extreme.

How is this possible? she screamed in her mind. *I'm a pure Physical cultivator! He... Just how strong is his body?*

She knew he practiced some form of body tempering. She'd expected to be outdone when it came to physical strength. But in this situation, she had used her body and Dao to deliver a strike at her maximum power... and Jack easily countered it through sheer physicality.

Whether it was speed or strength, she was outclassed.

Her sword remained stuck in the ground. There was no point pulling it out. Her eyes met Jack's, who shook his head. "Sorry," he said calmly, "but you are not my opponent."

His fist struck out. Mabe didn't even see it landing, but she felt her ribcage shatter, her entire body bending like a bow and flung backward at tremendous speed. She thought she was a goner.

Thankfully, a man appeared, catching her easily and neutralizing her momentum. He then let her drop like a sack of potatoes, not caring any longer. His hard silver eyes were glued to Jack, carrying great killing intent.

"What's the problem, Baron?" Jack asked him directly. "I told you—all those Dao stones you spent were wasted. I am right here. If you have any other lackeys under the ranking of 150, bring them out, and let me see the glory of your connections."

Baron Longform did not respond. The audience was frozen silent. Then, as one, they erupted, clamoring to the high heavens.

"What power is that?" someone asked. "Just his physical body is that powerful... Is he a space monster!"

Space monsters were the species known for their limited understanding of the Dao and extreme physical strength. They could use their formidable bodies to match someone at the C or even the B-Grade. In the spectators' eyes, Jack's current feat was no less impressive.

If just his body was so terrifying, what if he used his Dao?

"It's not that simple," the Head Envoy muttered, his eyes half-closed as he inspected Jack. "His body is superb, but his Dao is only that of a two-fruit C-Grade. It cannot increase his power by too much."

"Still, achieving such a body is nothing short of incredible. If it was easy, everyone would do it," the Space Eye Sovereign said, sitting next to him—she was the kindly old woman who served as the Cathedral's head diviner.

The Head Envoy chuckled. "Let's look at his Dao first before drawing any conclusions. This little girl was only ranked in the two hundreds—of the next twenty-five opponents, most are ranked significantly higher than her, and some are even hiding their strength. They will be able to bring out his full force."

Back in the crowd of C-Grades, Min Ling was carefully observing Jack.

"*Told you,*" Esmeralda said from the side, winking. "*Isn't he handsome?*"

Min rolled her eyes. "*I'm trying to perceive his hidden strength.*"

"*Sure. The strength between his—*"

"*Es. Stop. You're embarrassing me.*"

Esmeralda laughed. "*Sorry, sorry.*" Of course, they had only been transmitting their voices to each other, so nobody could overhear.

As for the bros... After a few moments of silence, Brock coughed. "One, two, three, four," he said, and the bros started beating on their drums and gongs and blowing their trumpets, raising hell on the Cathedral. Somehow, those sounds persisted through the lack of air. Two people unfurled a huge banner which spelled, "Go Big Bro or Go Home!" with dark letters on a purple background.

Esmeralda burst out laughing. Jack shook his head, somewhat embarrassed, but the sight made him happy. Having the support of your friends was always nice. "Who's next?" he asked.

"That would be me!" A petite woman stepped out of the crowd. She had blue skin, dark hair, pointy shoes, and a yellow turban over her head—she was a djinn. Jack found her cultivation to be an eight-fruit C-Grade—one fruit over the Mabe Asphel he'd just defeated.

"Sure," he said, nodding. "Come."

"Haha, don't mind if I do!"

She burst into battle. As she raised her blue arms, bubbles emerged. When they popped, their surface didn't shrink but instead widened, instantly encapsulating the whole world. Jack found himself floating in a multicolored void. Everything else, including the crowd and his opponent, had disappeared. All his senses were useless.

He snorted.

This place was clearly an illusion. The djinn had somehow obfuscated all his senses and even his Dao perception, cutting him off from the world. However, every illusion had a weakness.

His perception spread out, becoming one with the Dao of Space. After experiencing the Space Chamber for five months and developing a Space Dao Fruit, his compatibility with this Dao had risen tremendously. He wasn't a master, but he was good enough to use it against illusions.

An illusory world was a construct laid out around its victim. Forging fake sensations and hiding the Dao was easy, but perfectly masking spatial ripples was far more difficult. To achieve it, this djinn should have a space comprehension many times deeper than Jack's, and he did not believe that was the case.

As his Dao perception spread out, feeling for ripples in the fabric of space, he captured some. They weren't enough to reconstruct the real world outside of its illusions, but he only needed to sense the little body hurtling his way.

He turned and punched out in a seemingly random direction. A shriek entered his ears. The world of the illusion shattered, revealing a dagger-wielding djinn flying away. She quickly left the confines of the Cathedral Square, where someone caught her.

The entire battle hadn't taken more than two seconds.

"Next!" Jack shouted.

His next opponent was a lanky man with gray skin. He wasn't a feshkur, but something similar. His orange eyes flared with fire, and Jack felt an alien force invade his mind—like iron pliers grabbing his heart and twisting it. The pain was staggering. All resistance seemed futile.

Jack's Dao roared out. Wave after wave of the Fist broke out of his soul, flooding his body and colliding against the other man's attack. The two Daos tussled around like wild beasts fighting for their lives.

When it came to resisting Will attacks, the most important aspect wasn't the victim's Will attribute—that just had to be decent. The real deciding factor was the power of one's comprehensive Dao, as well as their willpower—and how could Jack lack willpower?

He resisted enough to maintain clarity. The world swam in colors and pain, but he could make out his surroundings. His fist flew out—the other man tried to defend by driving a spike of pain into Jack's mind, but Jack simply endured it. His fist smashed into the other cultivator's abdomen and sent him flying. The Will attack abated, and Jack easily suppressed it. The only lasting effect was a small but persistent headache.

The crowd roared. The bros banged on their instruments harder. They had witnessed everything clearly.

Three cultivators, three different specialties, three fists, three people sent flying. Each of these battles finished in a single move!

"Heavens! Does he have no weaknesses?" a cultivator shouted in the crowd, causing a dance of whispers to erupt.

As for Jack... Well, all he had to do was look at his status screen. How could he possibly lose?

Name: Jack Rust
Species: Human, Earth-387
Faction: Bare Fist Brotherhood (C)
Grade: C
Class: Gladiator Titan (King)
Level: 260

Strength: 3800 (+)
Dexterity: 3800 (+)
Constitution: 3800 (+)
Mental: 408
Will: 408

Free sub-points: 2

Dao Skills: Meteor Punch IV, Iron Fist Style III, Brutalizing Aura III, Neutron Star Body III, Space Mastery II, Titan Taunt I, Fist of Mortality I
Dao Roots: Indomitable Will, Life, Power, Weakness
Dao Fruits: Fist, Space
Titles: Planetary Frontrunner (10), Planetary Torchbearer (1), Ninth Ring Conqueror, Planetary Overlord (1), Grade Defier

The System had been streamlined a bit after his last breakthrough, clearly displaying his Dao Roots and Fruits.

In the C-Grade, the System awarded levels based on a cultivator growing their fruits. In raising his first fruit to maturity, Jack had gone from Level 250 to 259. Then, developing the second fruit pushed him to 260.

The first three fruits accounted for ten levels each, while the other six were twenty each. When a cultivator reached the peak of nine-fruits, they would be at Level 399—only one away from the B-Grade.

From rising ten levels in the C-Grade, Jack had gotten two hundred stat points, which he equally distributed between his Mental and Will attributes. Thanks to his Physical substats rising by body tempering, he was free to invest heavily in Mental and Will, shoring up his weaknesses. That was part of the reason why he so easily defeated the Mental and Will cultivators who fought him just now.

Of course, these two stats of his didn't even approach a real Mental or Will cultivator's, but defending against them was much easier than attacking, and the three stats were balanced anyway. Since he possessed far higher Mental and Will stats than other Physical cultivators, it was natural for him to have an advantage against Mental and Will cultivators.

As for his Physical stats... body tempering did not disappoint. Through his five months of grueling practice, he'd raised his stats from 2800 to 3800. That was an entire thousand! It was the equivalent of fifty levels in the C-Grade, or around three fruits. Combined with his previous tempering, along with his great titles and the Neutron Star Body skill, his actual physical prowess approached that of a nine-fruit C-Grade—how could the seven-fruit Mabe Asphel possibly hope to match him?

The progress of body tempering was still slowing down, but that only meant most of the benefits were already reaped. Jack was at his peak.

A physical body that surpassed most eight-fruit Physical cultivators.

A Mental stat that gave him an advantage against Mental cultivators, alongside a physical body that resisted magical attacks and the Dao of Space which countered illusions.

A willpower that had endured six months of silent torture in the form of body tempering.

At this point, Jack's weaknesses were already eliminated. He only had strong points and even stronger points. This was the only reason why he dared challenge everyone—just who could counter him?

The crowd cheered. The bros roared. The opponents kept coming.

CHAPTER FIFTY
GLADIATOR TITAN

THE FOURTH OPPONENT WAS A DEXTEROUS SWORDSMAN. THE FIFTH, A MAGE of the elements, and the sixth a wizard who used space as a weapon. All of them were easily dispatched by Jack, building up his momentum.

That didn't discourage the rest of his opponents. Everyone had their own strengths, and everyone wanted to compare against him—these battles weren't to the death, anyway.

The seventh opponent was an eight-fruit mace-wielder ranked in the hundred-sixties. Jack's physical superiority was no longer overwhelming. This was the first opponent who possessed the qualifications to seriously challenge him.

However, Jack was in a continuous fight. There were another eighteen people after this, some of whom would be even stronger than this mace-wielder. He couldn't afford to hold back and waste energy.

The Dao of Life billowed around him. Green ribbons flew into the void, conjuring up a storm. The sounds of beastly roars and deep gongs echoed through space. Jack's body grew taller, two extra arms appeared below his armpits, and his already towering aura climbed even higher, completely covering the Cathedral Square. For a moment, Jack was hidden in a rising column of green energy, only his intense eyes visible.

The energy dispersed, revealing a man with four arms and a titanic aura.

To the spectators, he seemed like a hundred-mile tall giant compressed to human size, as if his body contained endless strength. One finger could pierce a mountain, one roar could shatter space. His sheer physicality pressed down on everyone present like an uncaged beast staring right at them. After enduring so many shockwaves and now being stretched, his robes were barely hanging on.

This aura wasn't just an impression. It was the combination of Jack's Brutalizing Aura and extreme physicality. Even Titan Taunt, his seemingly useless skill, was activated, turning his aura into a proclamation of war against the world!

This pressure was real enough to push people down.

The weaker people lost their breath. The stronger frowned and revolved their Dao to resist the pressure. As for the mace-wielder facing Jack, he felt like a boat in an ocean storm, as if the waves of Jack's aura could capsize him at any moment. Thankfully, he was a hardened warrior. He roared, and his own aura rose to protect him, clashing against Jack's and barely enduring.

The mace-wielder jumped forward, bringing down his weapon like a smite of God. Jack raised a hand.

The mace smacked against Jack's palm. The spikes drew blood, but his arm remained outstretched. The mace came to an instant stop, and the other cultivator's palm ruptured as it endured the backlash.

However, the attack's shockwaves kept rolling. They washed over Jack, a storm of gray pulling at his hair and carving up the ground below him. His robes, which already teetered on the verge of collapse, were torn completely. Purple flew away, revealing an upper body as if sculpted of marble—perfect muscles covered every inch, not too tightly, just enough to be considered symmetrically beautiful. Abs were clearly delineated on his abdomen, his chest stuck out like hard pillows, and his arms seemed to contain infinite power. Coupled with his sharp and handsome face, Jack was a legend given form.

His other hand came around, smashing a Meteor Punch into the mace cultivator and sending him flying into the distance. "Next!" he roared, his voice a deeper bass.

Nobody moved. Jack's upper robes had flown away, his body was ripped and handsome, his strength was titanic, and his aura soared as he faced the entire Cathedral by himself. Such an image was simply stunning, deeply carving itself into the minds of everyone watching.

Esmeralda threw Min Ling a pointed glance, to which the other girl only scoffed. "What's the big deal?" she asked. "He's just an exhibitionist showing off." However, facing such a dashing sight, even she couldn't help but blush a little.

If Min Ling was slightly swayed, there was no need to speak about the rest of the Cathedral's women. Jack's strength and talent had already captivated them—now, as his naked upper body was revealed, a sculpture of the highest artisan, they simply felt their legs grow weak and their hearts flutter.

Jack Rust... was the man!

As for Jack himself, he didn't care about basking in everyone's sights. He hadn't even noticed. His own power was so great he was drunk in it, enjoying every moment. The four-armed battle form was originally meant to enhance his body. Now, after enduring so much tempering, the end result was simply too powerful. His current physical strength easily surpassed most nine-fruit C-Grades.

Packing so much strength into a human body was euphoric.

The next cultivator stepped up. In truth, after seeing him obliterate someone ranked in the hundred-sixties, most of his coming opponents felt like surrendering. They only persisted because Baron Longform secretly contacted them and demanded they step forth.

The eighth opponent, the ninth, the tenth, the eleventh. They were swept away. One punch was enough to defeat them all!

"Next!" Jack shouted again, his voice the death bell in the minds of his future opponents. Against Mental cultivators, Jack used his resilience to counter them. Even when he struggled, his extremely overpowered physical body could straightforwardly break through all illusions and magic. Against Will cultivators, his iron will rendered them useless. And there was no need to speak of Physical cultivators.

Of course, not all of Jack's opponents were weak. Some were in the hundred-fifties, including the person ranked exactly one hundred and fifty. Against a four-armed Jack, these people could last a few moves, sometimes inflicting minor injuries. They were all defeated, consuming some of his strength.

While his regeneration could last for a very long time, that did not include his stamina or Dao reserves.

The more Jack advanced, the fewer weak opponents he met—nobody would have registered to fight if someone much stronger was registered before them. By the twenty-first opponent, Jack was panting. By the twenty-fourth, he only had half his power left.

As the twenty-fifth opponent stepped out, a hard-faced woman holding a flute, a second person emerged from the crowd.

He was an old man wearing simple robes and with a wooden sword sheath strapped to his hip. His hair was sparse at the temples, but his eyes were sharper than blades. His cultivation was at the peak of eight-fruits.

"Jack Rust!" he shouted. "My name is Shi Mosh, ranked 117th. I do not meet your ranking requirements, but my heart insists I test my blade against you. For that, I am willing to part with five hundred Dao stones, my life savings. Are you willing?"

Jack looked straight into the old man's eyes. Someone of his age should have been kicked out of the Cathedral after not breaking through to the nine-fruit boundary, but there were always exceptions. In this case, this man was likely accepted due to his battle strength and soaring spirit. Just by glancing at him, Jack knew he was no lackey. He genuinely wanted to experience Jack's strength.

"How could I refuse a good battle?" he replied, laughing. "There is no need for extravagance. Fifty Dao stones would be enough—however, I will accept no further challenges after this."

It was no longer about the World Anchor or making a profit. Twenty-five consecutive battles had roused Jack's fighting spirit, awakening his primal self. All he desired now was to fight!

The old man wanted to experience Jack, but Jack also wanted to experience the strength of someone close to the top hundred ranks.

"Good!" the old man laughed. "Then, I shall wait for you!"

His name was added to the list of opponents. Jack faced the flute-wielding woman—she was the hardest opponent so far, alternating between illusions and Will attacks, using them to enhance each other. Jack defeated her, but not without cost—a splitting headache beat just behind his ears, taking away part of his concentration.

Finally, the last battle arrived. Shi Mo stepped into the square—the man ranked 117th.

"Thank you for accepting to fight me," he said, bowing at the waist.

"The pleasure is all mine," Jack replied. "Now, come. Let's battle!"

"Exactly what I wanted!"

Shi Mo drew a slim sword—a katana. At the same time, his upper robes expanded, then exploded in strips of fabric. This old man's body was smaller than Jack's, but his muscles were even more compact, even more packed together. He was simply a force of nature.

The audience cheered.

"Meet my blade!" Shi Mo shouted, exploding with a burst of speed that almost made him disappear. The thousandfold gravity was a breeze to him.

Jack felt shivers. He was extremely excited. He still hadn't discovered his limit, and this old man was the strongest opponent he'd ever faced.

He also disappeared. The two of them streaked across the square, leaving behind a series of afterimages. Clashes echoed. Metal struck skin. Blood erupted as Jack's fists were sliced apart then quickly regenerated.

The bros ramped up their drumming. The audience roared their cheers. Everyone stared carefully, and even the Envoys had leaned forward in their chairs.

"Jack Rust! Jack Rust!" the audience echoed, their roars splitting the Cathedral.

For a time, sparks filled the square, along with many afterimages. It was like three Jacks were fighting three old men. Only the strongest people present could follow their movements. Bangs were interspersed into the sounds of combat as Jack used Meteor Punches in succession. Space was split apart like thin curtains, further enhancing the speed of the two fighters.

Jack's physical prowess was far beyond a normal eight-fruit cultivator's, but the old man also specialized in physicality. His speed and strength were approaching Jack's, forcing him to constantly sacrifice his hands to survive. This battle style was similar to when Jack fought Marcus William, but at a far higher level.

Marcus, who was also in the crowd, could only sigh.

The old man possessed not only power and speed, but also experience. He combined simple moves into infinite variations. He remained unpredictable throughout the battle, occasionally erupting with tricks that Jack struggled to stand against.

Jack also had a trick, but he was saving it for the perfect moment.

Finally, at a completely random moment, the old man erupted with power, going all-out. There was no grandstanding, no preparation, no signs this would happen. He was far deadlier than the show-offish cultivators of the Cathedral—a true life or death warrior.

And who was Jack? He'd walked the razor's edge for a year. He had survived many life or death battles, often turning the tables to win. In those moments, a single mistake could have spelled his death—how could he be unfamiliar with real battle?

When the old man erupted with his full strength, Jack instantly followed. A blinking blade met a fist slower than the others, but far more powerful. Either Jack would blow away the old man, or he would be cut into two.

At the same time, another of Jack's four fists slithered. It used the properties of space to accelerate impossibly fast, reaching the old man before the other fist met the sword. Of course, for a fist to be this fast, it was necessarily weak—but it carried a hidden strike.

"Fist of Mortality!"

A thousand lifetimes burst into the old man's heart. He sank into visions of life and death, joy and sorrow, laughter and tears. He saw loved ones die and babies being born, the everyday person's struggle to survive. An entire world unraveled in an instant.

The old man guarded against the illusions, shielding his mind and using his Sword Dao to cut them away. However, that single instant had weakened his previous all-out attack—and, in a battle between masters, a single flaw could be fatal.

Jack's full-power Meteor Punch smashed against the old man's strongest strike. Purple met gray. Two auras expanded, covering the entire Cathedral Square in a flash, grinding against each other. A series of booms came from the epicenter, then everything folded back on itself as all sound and light were completely shattered, leaving the point of impact a wide sphere of nothingness.

The ringing of a blade resounded, covering all other sounds. The gray aura cleanly broke into two as the fist pierced through, reaching the old man's chest.

Shi Mo flew away with enough speed to sear the void. Blood left his mouth, and his innards were completely broken. He was only barely alive—but his grip on the sword remained as hard as ever.

A gentle power grabbed Shi Mo and stopped his flight, courtesy of the watching Envoys. And, as space repaired itself and light returned, everyone saw Jack Rust still standing at the center of the square, his body shaking, his panting ragged, his fists bloodied.

His aura, victorious.

Everyone erupted into cheers. Almost a thousand mouths opened to shout for the man who defeated everyone.

Jack Rust... had triumphed!

CHAPTER FIFTY-ONE

ABSORBING THE WORLD ANCHOR

THE SQUARE HAD GONE SILENT. THE CATHEDRAL HAD GONE SILENT. THAT entire patch of space had gone silent.

Jack Rust had challenged everyone ranked below 150 and won... and then he'd even defeated the 117th ranked Shi Mo!

Many people could have done the same, but Jack was only a two-fruit C-Grade! Just six or seven months ago, he'd struggled against Marcus William, who was ranked 281st. In the Cathedral, progress was counted with decades as the unit—such rapid advancement was simply unheard of.

How long had it been since a two-fruit C-Grade possessed such combat prowess? Perhaps even Sovereign Heavenly Spoon in his youth hadn't been so fierce!

"He is... interesting," Min Ling acknowledged, her sharp eyes focused on Jack.

On the raised platform, the Space Eye Sovereign leaned toward the Head Envoy. "You know, this is a bit too much. I'm beginning to suspect his Life Artifact is not as simple as we thought."

The Head Envoy—Sovereign Heavenly Spoon—only chuckled. "No matter how fierce, body enhancement is only useful up to the B-

Grade. Even then, it's vastly understated. Let him keep his lucky chance."

"I wasn't suggesting to take it away. I'm just saying, we should maybe start asking questions."

"But where's the fun in knowing? Is it not enough that he will shine for us in the hidden realm expedition and the banquet before? The Church has need for powerful C-Grades."

Space Eye's gaze was piercing, but the Head Envoy didn't budge. "As you wish," she said, pulling back. "You're in charge."

The Head Envoy nodded at her. Then, he rose, floating over the platform to face Jack and the crowd.

"This spectacle has ended in Jack Rust's complete and overwhelming victory!" he announced, his undertone bustling with excitement. "As the Head Envoy of the Black Hole Church, I congratulate your achievements, and I look forward to the excellence you will show in the future."

The crowd cheered in agreement.

"Now," the Head Envoy continued, reaching for his space ring. "As promised, the World Anchor is yours—you've earned it."

An orb of swimming colors appeared in his hand, then floated down to Jack. He reached out to grab it. As soon as the World Anchor made contact, Jack felt like he'd grabbed a falling star. His hand almost crashed into the ground, and he had to hurriedly pull it closer to his body to resist the weight.

So heavy! The Head Envoy was holding it casually because he's extremely strong!

It was hard to imagine that the Head Envoy's lanky body contained more strength than the ripped and beefy Jack Rust, but that's how cultivation worked. Not everything was visible to the naked eye.

Jack took the World Anchor into his space ring, relieving himself of the weight. He also felt the ring's inner dimension shake, as if about to shatter—it barely held.

How am I supposed to put that thing inside my body? he wondered. *I'll break!*

"I hope you'll put it to good use," the Head Envoy spoke from up above. "Additionally, as promised, you will enjoy free use of the Dao Chamber for the next six months. The only stipulation is that you need to book your stay beforehand so as not to obstruct the training of others, and I would also urge you not to hold onto the rooms for longer than necessary."

"Of course," Jack replied. "I will train hard, but I will also respect my fellow disciples. Thank you for this opportunity."

"You should thank yourself. The tests you passed were not easy."

Jack nodded deeply in gratitude.

Soon after, all the Envoys flew away.

"We're leaving," Baron Longform said sharply, not sparing Jack another glance. He and his followers flew away as well.

As they did, Jack's gaze remained on Baron. The two of them were irreconcilable enemies—Jack had killed the other's cousin, and now Baron had repeatedly tried to block Jack. Even if Jack once benefited from Baron Longform in the form of a Dao Vision, their enmity ran too deep. Sooner or later, they would need to battle, and one of the two would die.

I wonder what will happen in the hidden realm... Jack thought, then put the issue out of mind. For the next six months, he would keep training as hard as possible. Whatever happened in the hidden realm after that, his own strength was the only guarantee he could have.

A flood of people arrived to congratulate Jack. Leading them were the bros, who fell on him like excited children.

"You were awesome, big bro!"

"That was spectacular!"

"You are so handsome!"

That last comment was a little uncalled for, but it did remind Jack he remained shirtless. Oh, well.

"Thanks, guys. I couldn't have done it without you."

"Big bro," Brock said, approaching. "Good job. I proud."

"Hah. I'm sure your accomplishments will match mine soon," Jack replied, bumping fists with his brorilla.

Several other people congratulated him afterward. Most desired to befriend him, offering various gifts or inviting him to places, but Jack politely refused everything.

"Hey," said a blue-haired girl. Jack faintly remembered her as Esmeralda Polen, the one Dorman had tried to steal from. "That was a great fight!"

"Thank you," Jack replied.

"Hi, Ponytail Sis," Brock added. "Long time no see. What you doing here?"

"I couldn't miss such a spectacle, could I? My friend was here too, but she left already. Something about Jack being so powerful it inspired her to train. However..." She winked at Brock. "She was also impressed by Jack's performance. He really is as cool as you once claimed. The day when she takes this seriously is not too far away."

Brock nodded. "Naturally. Big Bro is the coolest."

Jack had no idea what they were talking about. He didn't even know what friend Esmeralda was referring to... Since Brock sounded like he had it under control, Jack saw no need to intervene.

The random cultivators congratulated Jack and walked away, leaving only the bros and Esmeralda, who seemed intent on sticking around. Jack invited everyone to the fields outside village four and treated them to some wine, finally relaxing a bit after six months of rigorous training.

Unfortunately, a bit of time was all he could spare. The duel was done, but the hidden realm still loomed in his future—and he had a premonition that, if his strength wasn't at the very limit, he would perish there.

After everyone relaxed and got a bit drunk, Jack left the gathering. He returned to his cabin, shut his door and windows, and sat cross-legged on his meditation mat. Utter silence filled the world. He was alone, hyping up himself for yet another fight.

After adjusting his mental state for a few minutes, he reached into his space ring and retrieved the World Anchor. It remained heavy—just holding it made his muscles bulge. Any other two-fruit C-Grade wouldn't even be able to lift it.

Jack held it to his eyes. A little ball of liquid was suspended in the center of this crystalline orb, pulsing slowly and shining with myriad colors. This was the essence of creation—the remnant core of an ancient powerhouse's inner world. This little bit of liquid contained all the rules needed to form a world, all the laws and concepts and Daos. It was not a world itself, but a core that would stabilize Jack's inner world in the future and help cleanse its impurities.

When he reached the B-Grade and formed his inner world, this core would be of immense assistance.

Even now, its value could not be understated.

Jack brought the World Anchor to his mouth. Taking a deep breath, he swallowed it, feeling it fall into the pit of his stomach like an iron anvil. Just this act of swallowing had injured his mouth, throat, and stomach. If a normal two-fruit C-Grade tried to absorb it, the World Anchor would probably fall right through them, killing them on the spot.

Of course, Jack had long ago asked about the dangers and method of absorbing it, so he knew he could handle it.

Inside his tempered body, the World Anchor remained as still as a stone. The walls of his stomach curved downward but contained it. Jack stilled his mind, enduring the pain.

The crystalline surface of the orb began to melt. It turned into pure Dao, which entered his body and nourished it, paving the way for the true World Anchor. The multicolored liquid remained by itself, suspended inside Jack's stomach, and it became clear that the source of the Anchor's immense weight was exactly this liquid.

Then, drop by drop, it began to disperse. It was absorbed into Jack, filling him completely, swarming his body with energy and his mind with visions of the infinite laws that held the universe together. Jack's heart skipped a beat—he submerged himself in these insights, unwilling to miss even a single one. Under the influence of the World Anchor, the purest and grandest Daos became clear, untainted by the many variables of the real world.

Jack sank into a trance. He lost track of time. The Anchor remained in his stomach, melting away over the course of several days. Jack's physical body was smoothened. The immense strain it had endured after so much tempering partly receded as the World Anchor changed his properties and transformed him into a being more compatible with the Dao of Life. It raised the ceiling of his body tempering.

At the same time, the visions hadn't stopped coming. Jack witnessed the endless void outside the universe, the endless nothingness where everything began. He saw a massive explosion that birthed a world, and spacetime expanding at speeds that vastly eclipsed the speed of light. In an instant, the newborn universe grew from a dot to the size of a solar system, then kept going.

He saw stars form. Galaxies. He witnessed the vast universe slowly cool down, allowing all sorts of phenomena to exist, and observed the endless cycle of existence. Even celestial bodies, though not alive, had their own life cycle. They formed out of dust, stabilized, expanded, then blew up and became dust again, joining massive depositories which would in time form new stars.

It was similar to how humans were born and died, always cycling, rising from dirt and falling to dirt.

Jack was one with the universe, experiencing the fundamental forces. Gravity was the interaction between matter and spacetime. Electricity was carried by the miniscule magnetic charge of infinitely tiny particles. Groups of particles were held together by vast amounts of energy, so dense it turned into matter, and even these particles were nothing but manifestations of even smaller particles vibrating in a specific way.

All these insights were far beyond the scope of Jack's current level, but they gave his Dao a foundation that other cultivators lacked. By gaining some insight into the fundamental properties of the universe, from which everything else was derived, he would always have a direction to walk toward. He could always validate his Dao against the core truths of the universe, avoiding many false insights and grasping things that others would find abstract.

His current Daos didn't progress much, but thanks to these visions, his future road would be much smoother. Just this benefit alone was tremendous.

Finally, the visions ended, and Jack found himself sitting on his meditation mat in the real world. It took him some time to adjust. When he did, he noticed that his stomach was empty—the World Anchor had already been completely absorbed by him, and it now hovered inside his soul world, a multicolored sheen covering his Dao Tree.

Just by probing it a little, he could sense that it slightly purified all of his Dao, pulling it closer to the source of all Daos. It hadn't changed in quantity, but its quality had risen. Not only did this World Anchor enhance his body and deepen his general understanding into the Dao, but it also increased his current strength.

Jack took a deep, excited breath. This treasure was possibly the greatest lucky chance he'd ever received, on a similar level as the Life Drop. It was also exactly what he needed.

His current achievements were in part due to the Life Drop. However, unless it had other uses he had yet to discover, its body-related benefits would taper off at the A-Grade. Even at the B-Grade they would be far more auxiliary than they currently were. At that point, he would need to depend on the robustness of his inner world and his comprehension of the Dao, which were exactly what the World Anchor focused on.

If the Life Drop was the foundation he needed to earn his place in the cultivation world, the World Anchor was a vehicle that could help him reach the end of the road. Of course, even the World Anchor could only assist him. In the end, everything would depend on himself.

And Jack was determined to succeed. As long as he didn't die, he had confidence that he would walk farther than anyone, look deeply into the Dao and step inside its heart. His own talent and determination were his greatest weapons, and he would utilize them to the fullest.

Jack's gaze sharpened. His aura rose, and an unstoppably dominant air erupted from his body, whipping the walls of his cabin and conjuring up a storm. His hair flew wildly. In that moment, Jack was not a human, not a man.

He was a cultivator of unstoppable will.

No matter what happens, with my own two feet... I will walk my Road to Mastery!

CHAPTER FIFTY-TWO
ANOTHER SIX MONTHS

THE TIME CHAMBER—THE DAO CHAMBER OF TIME—WAS THE MOST enigmatic place Jack had ever seen. He stood on a small grassland surrounded by countless flowers. These flowers were identical, but each grew at different speeds. Some were blooming and dying, only for their spores to bloom soon after. Some remained completely still, not even responding to the breeze as if frozen in time. Others followed even more confusing paths. They would bloom, then wilt, then reverse their aging, and bloom again, eternally suspended in a cycle that didn't let them die.

Time was warped in this place. It did not flow uniformly, but rather whimsically. Space was filled with currents of time, each moving at its own pace. Jack didn't know how these currents were created, but he could sense them sometimes crossing each other, drawing unexpected results. Other times, certain areas were stagnated of time, leading to a massive deceleration.

Of course, none of these time flows were particularly intense. They were only visible because this particular species of flower had a lifespan barely reaching two days. Even if Jack was stranded in one of the quickest currents, resisting it would be trivial.

Observing this grassland, Jack could make out a path to understanding Time. The first step was seeing through its nature. Then, one should use their Dao to create such currents of altered time flow, and finally he should be able to control the interactions of these currents to create complex results in an area of his choice.

These three steps would lead to a decent understanding of Time. As for what came after, he had no idea.

Even as he stood inside the grassland, Jack shook his head. He could tell that, ironically, comprehending these things would take time—time he didn't have. Even the simplest mysteries of the time currents were lost on him, as he felt no connection. It wasn't like the Dao of Space, which came to him instinctively, or the Dao of Life, which was somewhat aligned with the Fist.

Every cultivator was only compatible with certain Daos, depending on their character, worldview, and experiences. Trying to go wide was a terrible idea—it was better to be a master of one than a jack of none. Even when it came to one's secondary Daos, like Jack's Dao of Space, he needed to be careful and not invest too much. At the end of the day, his Dao followed the Fist, and anything else could only be auxiliary weapons.

After all, every Dao came from the same source. Their manifestations were wildly different from each other, but the higher one rose, the more each Dao resembled the others. By walking down the path of the Fist, Jack would naturally approach Life, Mortality, and other relevant Daos. By exploring the Dao of Space, he would naturally arrive at the Dao of Time, since the two were intertwined. Trying to study these other Daos individually was just a waste of time and effort.

For example, through his comprehension of Space, Jack could understand that time was just the concept of change. Its connecting point with space was through matter. Space was the foundation of matter, and time was nothing but the continuum on which matter existed.

Between these three—space, time, and matter—no two could

exist without the third. They formed a fundamental trifecta of the universe.

These were all a bit vague to the current Jack, but the point was, he should focus on Space to understand Time. That way, his comprehension of Time would advance faster than if he studied Time itself, and he would also get all sorts of other benefits.

To him, the Time Chamber was useless.

Jack exited the chamber, welcomed by a confused octopus Envoy. "*Done so quickly?*" she asked. "*Don't worry. Not all Daos are for everyone. It is best to expand little and focus on your strengths, forming a pyramid of understanding.*"

"*I understand. Thank you,*" Jack replied politely.

He'd already suspected Time would be fruitless.

After this, he also spent some time at the Life and Death Chambers, finding similar results. The two chambers contained a blooming world and a dying one respectively. Jack could sense they hid myriad insights, yet he was unable to grasp them. His own comprehensions of Life and Death would naturally sprout from the Fist—that was the lens through which he perceived them, therefore studying them individually was pointless. Even the Life Drop, which connected him to the Dao of Life, only did so indirectly—his high compatibility was best utilized through the Dao of the Fist.

Time, Life, and Death were out of the picture. The elements were even more pointless to attempt—he had no relation to any of them. The only Dao Chambers Jack could focus on were Mortality and Space; one helped with the comprehension of his own Dao, and the other directly increased his combat strength, though with declining efficiency, since he'd already spent a few months there.

The hidden realm expedition would come in six months. Therefore, Jack's priority was to increase his power as much as possible until then. Long-term benefits could wait.

Forming a six-month training plan was easy. The Dao Chamber, though he had free access now, wouldn't be too useful in the short-term. He decisively allocated little time to it, only a few days in total, and those were spent at the Mortality Chamber—Space was already offering diminishing returns.

Most of his effort was spent cultivating and body tempering—the two approaches that could increase his power the fastest.

Jack visited the Ceaseless Murder Globe and once again awed the Cathedral by securing a ranking of 98. He finally broke into the top hundred. This was a new legend!

But Jack was too busy to care about the praise. The only reason he increased his ranking was to secure more time at the Heavy Pagoda. He could now stay there for four days every month, double his previous limit, which was great news.

He also possessed a fortune of Dao stones. Just his twenty-five consecutive duels had earned him over a thousand. As for the betting stall's profits, those went entirely to the bros. After Jack finally revealed his connection with the Life stones, their price also rose to four Dao stones apiece, netting him a monthly profit of eighty stones, twenty of each were given to the bros as thanks for their assistance.

The bros profited wildly. Just by believing in Jack and putting in a few days of work, they had secured over a dozen Dao stones each—this was the equivalent of at least a year's wages.

Over the six months until the hidden realm, Jack gathered a total of one thousand five hundred Dao stones—and change. He was a tycoon. Moreover, since he no longer needed to hemorrhage on the Dao Chamber, he could freely spend all that wealth on his own cultivation.

For four days every month, he stayed at the Heavy Pagoda's fourth level and consumed Dao stones like candy. If others knew of this rate of consumption, they might have a heart attack and die on the spot.

The other twenty-six days of the month were spent on body tempering. Jack endured increasingly terrifying pain, fueled by his own desire to reach the top, to steadily stuff his body full of life energy.

Alternating these two practices without rest, Jack lost track of time. The months flowed like water.

Two months before the expedition, his breakneck cultivation bore fruit—literally. He broke through to the three-fruit realm. His third fruit was one of Life, incorporating his body tempering and the feeling of possessing a titanic body. With it, his combat prowess rose yet again, but he chose not to visit the Globe.

The hidden realm was in two months. Even if he earned an extra day per month at the Heavy Pagoda by increasing his rank, it wouldn't matter much—it was more important to keep his strength under wraps to guard against his enemies. After all, in the hidden realm, there was no guarantee that everyone from the Church would work together. Baron Longform would be there too, and Jack might come under attack at any point. It was better to hide his full abilities.

At almost the same time as Jack, Brock—who received a lot of Dao stones from his big bro—also broke through, developing his second Dao Fruit. After a few years of cultivation, the two of them were only one small boundary apart—ten levels. It really made Jack emotional.

For the two months after that, Jack kept cultivating like crazy, and his third Dao Fruit reached around forty percent maturity. He also had a few hundred Dao stones to spare. With a little more time, developing a fourth fruit wouldn't be difficult—though he needed to ensure his Dao understanding didn't lag behind.

One day, Jack opened his eyes. They shone like twin stars, shooting lightning into the world.

"My body is finally close to saturation..." he muttered, then cracked a smile. "Not bad."

Name: Jack Rust
Species: Human, Earth-387
Faction: Bare Fist Brotherhood (C)
Grade: C
Class: Gladiator Titan (King)

Level: 274

Strength: 4300 (+)
Dexterity: 4300 (+)
Constitution: 4300 (+)
Mental: 548
Will: 548
Free sub-points: 2

Dao Skills: Meteor Punch IV, Iron Fist Style III, Brutalizing Aura III, Neutron Star Body III, Space Mastery II, Titan Taunt I, Fist of Mortality I
Dao Roots: Indomitable Will, Life, Power, Weakness
Dao Fruits: Fist, Space, Life
Titles: Planetary Frontrunner (10), Planetary Torchbearer (1), Ninth Ring Conqueror, Planetary Overlord (1), Grade Defier

His Physical substats had grown by another five hundred. It was a significant increase, but the speed of body tempering had clearly gone down. During the last month, he only got forty points. It had finally reached the point of saturation. From now on, the bodily improvements would need to be made in step with his cultivation.

From growing his second fruit to maturity and then developing his third fruit to forty percent, he had gotten another fourteen levels, which translated to two hundred and eighty stat points. He had poured them all into Mental and Will, finally bringing them up to speed with the 8-1-1 distribution he followed. Now, unless some Mental or Will cultivator was far stronger than him, it could be said that Jack was their natural counter.

Future stat points would be poured into Physical, at least for a while. Jack was curious to see how his saturated body would affect the System's ability to enhance him further—but not curious enough to ruin his perfectly round numbers of 4300. Not yet, at least.

His cultivation had reached a plateau. It would be difficult to increase anything in the short-term, and even creating a fourth Dao Fruit would be difficult—if he wanted to maintain a solid foundation, he would need to work on his Dao understanding first.

When one reached such a plateau, the best thing to do was go out and adventure. Most cultivators would take all resources they could and explore the wide universe, observing the world and letting their Dao naturally develop. Through fighting others and experience life and death, they would naturally develop their Dao and discover the next steps on their path.

Expansion and consolidation. This rule applied from the start to the end of cultivation, from the humblest F-Grade to the godlike A-Grades.

Fortunately for Jack, he had no need to search for adventure. The hidden realm expedition was fifteen days away.

He wearily rose to his feet. His body was exhausted but also suffused with more power than he'd ever felt. If not for his iron will and determination, he might have already devolved to the point of thinking himself God.

Fifteen days... he thought, allowing himself a tired smile. *Since there is nothing important I can do until then, I might as well relax. I have to visit home. Vivi will be worried sick about me, and the children... I can't wait to see how much they've grown.*

A small break for my weary soul. And then, adventure!

CHAPTER FIFTY-THREE

ERIC AND EBELE

As Jack stepped out of the teleporter and onto green grass, he threw his head back and took a deep breath. After the Cathedral's dark, bleak, airless void, the forests of Earth were paradise.

It had already been a year since Jack's last visit. It felt shorter, for some reason—perhaps the constant training messed with his passage of time. Still, it made one think. Once upon a time, a year was the time from the Integration to when he defeated the planetary overseer. Now, it was just a long training session.

His children would have grown so much.

"What do you think, Brock?" Jack asked, turning to his best friend. "Will you come with me to see the kids?"

"Father and Mother first," Brock replied. "First old, then new."

Jack laughed. "Alright. You know where I live—see you soon!"

The two of them flew off in different directions. Their speed was leisurely, the equivalent of strolling through the air. Jack felt so light. So powerful. Space was fragile here, and all the natural forces were laughably weak. His perception covered a hundred miles. If he simply willed it, the entire sky within that range would come crashing down like a million little comets.

Any casual punch could easily level a state.

But, of course, Jack reined in his powers and aura. To anyone observing him, he seemed like a mortal. Only now did he understand the Sage's previous words, why all the high-level cultivators felt so relaxed on the Cathedral. Having to constantly restrain one's power was a similar feeling to wearing shoes: not bad, but it would feel amazing once you reached home and could take them off.

The trees passed by, swaying in the breeze, and the sun was bright. It was early autumn. The forest below was suffused with life, countless little creatures wandering around and struggling to survive. At this time of the year, food was aplenty, leading to fewer hunts and a more relaxed existence.

Jack's perception could capture everything in the forest below, and he shook his head. Animals lacked food in the winter and water in the summer. Really, they had it rough. The Dao of Mortality encapsulated them as well.

Trees gave way to hills. Jack ascended the nearby mountain, landing before a house that was elegant yet simple—wooden walls, a red-tiled roof, and a glass window overlooking the scenery. Emotions welled up inside him. He didn't need to knock—while his perception hadn't rudely intruded, he could easily sense the waves of energy radiating from this house, and their owner could sense him too.

The door swung open, revealing a dark-skinned woman in a blue dress. Her legs were long, her waist slender, and her eyes bright with kindness. Her aura surged—she was a D-Grade.

"Vivi," Jack muttered.

She smiled. "Welcome home," she said sweetly, then stepped aside. Two little forms were revealed behind her. The boy yelped and followed his mom, hiding behind her and peeking out his head, while the girl stood her ground, gazing at him with wide, bright eyes.

"This is Dad," Vivi said, emotion in her voice. She did not push them to move. Jack didn't either. He squatted down, bringing himself almost to eye level—they were tiny!—and smiling.

"Hey, kids," he said. "Ebele, Eric... I missed you."

Something in his voice reached them. They did not remember him, but they recognized that sound, that powerful warmth. Eric hesitantly walked out from behind Vivi and said, "Da?"

Ebele made the connection. Her face brightened, she shouted, "Papa!" and rushed into his arms. Jack laughed as he hugged her. Eric moved as well, emboldened by his sister, and fell onto Jack. Vivi watched this happen with a huge, sweet smile on her lips.

She wasn't tired from raising two children herself. However, watching her children rush into their father's embrace... That feeling was just something else.

As for Jack, the stress and exhaustion of the past year disappeared. All the pain he'd endured simply washed off him, leaving him fresh and full of love. He laughed out loud, rising to his feet with one child wrapped in each hand. They yelped but didn't cry.

"How brave you are!" he exclaimed, his own happiness transmitted through his aura. "I love you both! All three of you!"

"Will you eat with us?" Vivi asked. "We just finished making lunch, and we're looking forward to hearing about your adventures... Plus, I suspect you haven't eaten a proper meal since the last time you were here."

Jack felt like he'd been caught. He laughed again, unable to contain his joy, then gave Vivi a warm gaze. "Of course I'll eat. For the next two weeks... I'm all yours."

Lunch was heavenly. Jack really hadn't eaten a proper meal in a year —not only because he didn't need it, but also because very little food could survive on the Cathedral. He ravenously fell on the table, enjoying every taste.

Between bites, he narrated his experiences at the Cathedral. Not accurately, of course—the children were listening. He framed them as fairy tales, omitting the dangers and pain to focus on overcoming impossible odds to succeed.

Eric and Ebele listened with rapt attention, forgetting about food. Their little mouths hung open in wonder. Eric clenched his hands every time Jack spoke about danger, only to exhale in relief when everything was good. As for Ebele, her eyes shone throughout, blazing at his adventures.

Even though they were still toddlers and anything could change, some things were clear about their temperaments. Ebele was sharp and adventurous. Eric was more restrained, but that didn't make him any lesser than his sister—not everybody needed to be a warrior.

Fatherhood bloomed in Jack's chest. Every feature he discovered about his children was perfect, making him love them even more—although, in truth, they would have felt perfect no matter what.

As he detailed his adventures, Vivi was also listening. She could glean the things he hid away or softened. Her heart was clenched. Just by this fairy tale version of the last year, she could understand that Jack had been through a lot. His every day was a battle. However, she chose not to comment, because she could also tell he loved it.

And she loved him for it. Even if her heart shook and he made her worry.

"So many strong people..." she said in wonder. "And you said the strongest one is that woman named Min Ling, right? Is she pretty?"

This question would have stumped the common man, but Jack was no amateur. "She couldn't hold a candle to you, my love."

"Mhm. Right."

Vivi didn't necessarily believe him, but that was beside the point. Butterflies fluttered inside her stomach.

"Can we explore again?" Ebele asked, revealing both impressive communication skills and that she remembered last year's excursions with Jack.

"Of course!" Jack replied. "We can do whatever you like!"

"Yay!" both children cried out at once.

Vivi's raised brow gave Jack pause. "But only if your mother agrees," he added, making them turn their puppy eyes at Vivi. Under their pressure, she melted.

Jack and his family didn't step outside their house for the entire day. They played some games, Jack learned about their lives as well, and he generally tried to form beautiful memories with his children. He was painfully aware of how little time he would actually spend with them growing up—at times like this, his heart burned, and the sour taste of regret filled his mouth. But it was necessary. He was a cultivator. He had his path. As much as he loved his children, he couldn't betray himself—and them—to spend more time at home.

Enemies could appear at any moment. If he wasn't strong enough, they would suffer and die. He would never let that happen.

Night came, and Ebele with Eric went to sleep. Their room contained many toys and decorations, including a few Jack was familiar with. One was a picture of him from before the Integration—another was a lava lamp he'd personally forged for them inside an active volcano, and there was even a bowl filled with water from the deepest parts of the Marianna Trench.

The souvenirs from their shared adventures were proudly contained in the children's room. Jack never thought he'd feel so warm from such little things.

"Goodnight, Ebele. Goodnight, Eric," he said, planting a kiss on their foreheads and tucking them in. "I love you."

"We love you too, Daddy!" Ebele replied. Eric laughed and waved his arms around.

Jack and Vivi headed to their own room, where they undressed and lay together. "How do you feel?" Vivi asked, leaning against his chest.

"It's a new world," Jack admitted. "Increasing my cultivation makes me happy, but this... This makes me even happier in a completely different way. Ebele, Eric... you... staying here forever would be a blessed life."

"But not for you."

"But not for me." Jack sighed, then looked up at the ceiling. "I will be the best father I can, but above all else, I am a cultivator. Do you hate me for that?"

Vivi chuckled. "I knew it since the day I met you. That's why I slept with you." She rose from his chest to plant a kiss on his lips. "Your children are in good hands, Jack. Do what you have to do. Live your life. They will grow well, and they will love you for who you are."

Another wave of warmth filled his heart. People said that life couldn't be perfect... but, right now, it sure felt like it.

"Thank you," he replied, returning her kiss. One kiss led to many, and of increasing heat, until their two bodies were intertwined.

"I missed you," Vivi said with a hot breath.

"So did I..." Jack replied, sinking deep into her.

For the next two weeks, Jack remained with his family. They stayed at home, reveling in their love. They toured the world, exploring its wonders. They made memories. Jack was stuck to his children as if glued to them, and they loved every moment. Their carefree laughter echoed across the house, filling it with joy.

One day, Jack and Eric built a treehouse together—without using cultivator superpowers. The little boy was beyond excited. He rushed from side to side, happy to just be spending time with Jack and helping however he could. When they were done, Jack grabbed Eric and flew to the top. Eric cried out in joy. Then, Jack flew even higher, like a bird, using his aura to protect Eric from the sharp winds. Every peal of laughter was medicine to his soul—and the timid Eric believed in his father so fully that he never felt a shred of fear.

The two swam through the air for a while, their smiles unending.

Another day, Jack took Ebele to observe the clouds from above. Her eyes were wide in wonder, gazing at the infinite sea of white, then she yelped as they began free-falling, piercing through the white and toward the blue sea below.

Ebele was scared, but that only made her excited. She laughed through the wind, playing with it and admiring how her little limbs and hair flew upward. When they approached the surface of the ocean, Jack grabbed onto Ebele and swerved over it, cutting through the surface and raising waves. They then flew higher again, until the waves were nothing but lines on the vast blue. Ebele was having the time of her life.

"Again!" she shouted, and Jack had no choice but to keep going. Only an hour later, when Ebele was completely exhausted and almost fell asleep, did she let him leave. He hugged her tightly on the way back—not out of caution, but of love.

His children were different from each other, and he loved them equally. His heart couldn't grow any fuller. If anything ever happened to them...

He didn't want to think about that. He would grow so strong that he'd never have to.

Besides spending time with his family, Jack also met his other friends and relatives on Earth—his mother, Edgar, Harambe... Brock visited often, playing with the children and quickly becoming Uncle Brock. The children loved him. Somehow, his Dao of Brotherhood seeped through, making them see a wide world and learning to rely on each other.

While Jack and Brock were of different species, they regarded each other as brothers. He was also part of the family.

And so, two weeks passed, and there came a day when Jack would have to leave again.

"When will you return?" Vivi asked him at the front door. The children were inside—Jack had already bidden them goodbye.

"I don't know..." he admitted. "The Church hasn't scouted out the hidden realm. It could be long or short—I really have no idea."

Vivi nodded. Both knew the hidden realm would be an exceedingly dangerous place. Perhaps, Jack would never return... but they chose not to mention that.

"Be safe," Vivi said, tears sparkling in her eyes. She bit back everything else she wanted to tell him. "I love you."

"I love you too."

He planted a hot kiss on her lips, savoring this final moment of warmth before the storm. His heart felt weak—did he really have to leave this place and risk his life in an unknown land?

Soon, however, he suppressed the doubts. He was who he was. If he backed away now, he would never be able to live with himself.

"I'm going," he said. "Take care of the kids. Tell them I love them."

"They know," she replied with a smile, "but I'll tell them. Every day until you come back to us."

Jack looked deep into her eyes and nodded. Then, he flew away. Brock was already waiting for him at the teleporter. As he saw Jack arrive, he read all the emotions in his brother's heart. "A good bro makes hard decisions," he said softly, "and hard decisions make good bro. You best father I know. Believe."

Jack gave a tight smile. "Thanks, Brock. I needed that."

"No problem."

The two stepped into the teleporter, activated it, and set off for the Cathedral. The hidden realm expedition was upon them—the unknown and dangerous.

Jack was really looking forward to it.

CHAPTER FIFTY-FOUR
A-GRADE

THE CATHEDRAL WAS IN AN UPROAR.

Today, the hidden realm expedition was leaving. The participants had gathered in the Cathedral Square, while many other cultivators had come to watch.

For such an event, even an Elder might be mobilized—and, to these people, Elders were legends!

The Cathedral received a new generation of C-Grades every thousand years or so. However, A-Grade cultivators—the Elders—could live up to a million years. They could see a thousand batches of disciples come and go like an endless tide. Why would they bother?

Most Elders remained in permanent seclusion or were dealing with other affairs, meaning the C-Grade disciples almost never saw them. Even when it came to the most talented disciples, so what? They could be rank one, but that still meant little to an Elder. Hundreds of people would pass through that rank one position in their lifetime. Why would they care about any of them?

Therefore, opportunities to see an Elder were extremely rare.

Jack waited alongside Brock in the middle of the Cathedral

Square. Another twenty-eight people waited with them—ten nine-fruits, ten eight-fruits, five seven-fruits, and three six-fruits. Adding Jack and Brock, they were thirty in total.

Brock had nabbed one of the positions for six-fruit cultivators and below. This wasn't due to Jack—highly talented individuals were usually allowed to join even if their current strength was lacking, so Brock had been formally invited.

Of the other people, Jack was only familiar with a few. There was Min Ling, the number one outer disciple—who happened to be a seven-fruit cultivator. Baron Longform, who hadn't glanced in Jack's direction even once, and Shi Mo, the old eight-fruit swordsman who'd dueled Jack six months ago. Besides those, Jack recognized a couple faces but had no special impression.

There was one person he paid attention to, however. Min Ling was the number one disciple, and Baron Longform was number three. Then, who was number two?

It was easy to tell. Jack's gaze was drawn to a tall, burly man. While he possessed many human features, he clearly wasn't one. His fingers ended in sharp claws, two straight horns rose from the back of his head, and he possessed blue scales in place of skin. At the same time, his yellow eyes exuded a mix of primal threat and deep intelligence.

If Jack had to categorize him, he looked like a dragonman.

"Are you curious about Salazar?" a pleasant voice came from behind Jack. As he turned, he came face-to-face with a slim-featured, athletic woman clad in leather armor. A red spear with a black tip hung on her back, dark hair cascaded over her shoulders, while her wheat-colored skin radiated health and vigor.

Jack recognized her instantly. This was Min Ling, the number one disciple of the Cathedral and also the greatest talent of the last few thousand years.

"A bit," he replied. "I've never seen that species before."

"You wouldn't have. Salazar is a space monster."

"A space monster?"

"It happens," she explained. "When space monsters reach the C-Grade, they develop true intelligence. Some are even able to cultivate, though they follow a different path than us. Naturally, not all of them choose to be mindless killing machines. Some can reject their natural instincts and join the cultivation world, rising alongside us."

"Wow," Jack said. "The universe really is wide."

"Everything you can imagine exists," she replied with a smile that didn't reach her eyes. She then turned to the brorilla. "And you must be Brock."

"Yes."

"Pleased to make your acquaintance."

Brock nodded like it was natural.

"So are we," Jack responded. "Your talent is stunning."

"I could say the same thing about you. A two-fruit reaching the top hundred ranks is nothing short of incredible, and you've even developed another fruit since then. I wonder just how high your strength reaches..."

Jack only laughed. "Bold of you to speak to us," he said, changing the subject. "Aren't you afraid of angering Baron Longform?"

She took a moment to navigate his words. "There is no relation between myself and Longform. I can do whatever I want. And, in any case, his influence is not as far-reaching as you may think."

"Really? How so?"

"Well, he—"

Her next words were lost in the cheers of the crowd. A dozen forms descended from the sky, all wearing fluttering dark robes. The insignia of the Black Hole Church was clear: a black hole whose shape was accentuated by green lines, making it easily discernible despite the dark fabric.

These were the Envoys—the main force of the expedition.

Leading the twelve was a man who looked to be in his thirties, with dark hair and exceedingly sharp eyes. Before they even landed, Jack caught that man's gaze on him, and it gave him shivers. It wasn't the first time he got this impression—for some reason, this guy didn't like him, and Jack had no idea why.

"Tsk." Min Ling clicked her tongue. "Spacewind."

"Greetings, everyone," the man uttered, his steady voice overpowering the crowd. "I am Sovereign Spacewind. As you all know, I will be leading this expedition inside the hidden realm. It will be dangerous, but you have nothing to fear. I will protect all of you to the best of my ability."

The hostile air he'd shown before had disappeared. Now, his aura was deep and heroic, making the crowd cheer.

"Have I done anything to offend him?" Jack whispered, leaning closer to Min Ling.

"You still are... but he's just an asshole. If you stay out of his way, he won't go so far as to sell you out."

Jack nodded, understanding but not quite. *You still are? What is that supposed to mean?*

Of the eleven Envoys following Spacewind, Jack recognized the frog-like man who operated the Ceaseless Murder Globe and the octopus Envoy from the Dao Chamber. If he wasn't mistaken, their names were Borkuren Madiba and Ashly Sherry respectively. Both nodded at him, and he nodded back.

After the Envoys landed, the square quietened down. Min Ling moved away from Jack, and nobody else approached him, so he approached nobody either. After a while, Shi Mo stepped closer. "Greetings!" he said with a wide smile. "I never thanked you for last time. That was truly a splendid fight!"

Jack laughed. He could tell a fellow battle junky when he saw one. The three of them—including Brock—made some small talk. Time passed. An hour later, Jack was beginning to feel suspicious.

Everyone was here already. Why weren't they starting?

"I don't know either," Shi Mo replied, "but since we're waiting, there must be a reason."

Jack then saw this in another light. They weren't just waiting, this was an opportunity for all expedition members to get to know each other, and for those with great social skills to sharpen their blades.

Jack didn't think himself one of those people, but wasting this opportunity would be amateurish. Therefore, he led Brock to socialize. Shi Mo was happy to help—he introduced Jack and Brock to a few eight-fruit friends of his, then let them wander alone. Jack spoke to various people, acting the social butterfly while everyone else did the same. In this complicated dance, he was careful to avoid Baron Longform's people—this really was akin to dancing with your enemy and trying to step on each other's feet.

At this point, he and Baron Longform were public enemies. One had strength and connections, while the other wielded immeasurable potential—the degree of their influence was similar, therefore they devolved into a social battle for supporters.

Jack even chatted with Borkuren and Ashly, the two Envoys he was familiar with. Facing him, they did not display any of a B-Grade's arrogance. They chatted merrily, even cracking jokes, and this greatly increased Jack's prestige amongst the surrounding C-Grades.

Jack got to know a few people. More time passed. Finally, as he was speaking to a glass-pane cultivator, something changed.

It was subtle, yet clear. The quality of the void rose. Something new was added to the mix, birthing intense awe in Jack's heart. He turned around. At one end of the square, floating a few feet over the ground, were two individuals.

One was a kindly old man. His hair was white and his body slim, while he still exuded liveliness. He reminded Jack of some professors he'd met on Earth, the kind that remained excited about their subject even after decades of research. His robes were simple, practical, and colored a golden blue.

The other person had their entire body covered in a dark cloak. Pale, gaunt skin was visible under their hood, along with red eyes that made Jack's heart seize. If any mortal glanced at those eyes, they would die on the spot. Moreover, a scythe was on that person's back

—just looking at it filled Jack with fear, as if he was about to lose his soul.

This person was dressed exactly like a grim reaper.

The auras of these people were impossibly deep. As though staring into the depths of the ocean. Before them, Jack felt beyond helpless, nothing but a mortal before a god. There was only one group of people that could make him feel like this.

A-Grades. These people were Elders.

The square fell deathly silent. Whether consciously or unconsciously, everyone held their breath. Sovereign Spacewind was the first to break the silence, bowing at the waist for them.

"Elder Heavenstar. Elder Boatman," he said with utmost respect. "We are deeply honored by your presence."

"Greetings, Elders," everyone said at the same time, bowing, while Jack caught on halfway and mumbled, "—tings, Elders."

He was completely unaware of the decorum. With his heart racing, he also bowed his head, trying to glimpse at others and see what they were doing. Thankfully, the Elders themselves saved him.

Elder Boatman—the grim reaper lookalike—did not move or speak. He remained there, as sure as death. Elder Heavenstar, however, spoke lightly and carefreely.

"No need to stand on ceremony," he said. "Relax, everyone."

Jack rose slowly, making sure that everyone was rising alongside him. The last thing he wanted was to embarrass himself here.

Elder Heavenstar smiled, but Jack could tell he really didn't care about any of them. He was just trying to be polite. "If there is nothing more, let's get going."

Without waiting for a reply, the Elder raised his finger and summoned a massive starship above the square. It was several hundred feet from end to end. Jack had no idea how the Elder had summoned this thing, because it sure as hell couldn't fit into a space ring—not in Jack's space ring, anyway.

The Elders flew in first, entering from a door at the side, and Jack followed the rest of the cultivators as they headed inside. There was plenty of space and no staff. Everyone could easily get their own room.

Without any sort of ritual, the starship broke through space and disappeared. The Cathedral was flung far behind. Jack felt his excitement rising.

They were headed for the hidden realm.

CHAPTER FIFTY-FIVE
PRIDE AND HONOR

The hidden realm expedition shuttled through space. There were forty-four people in a giant starship, each with their own room.

The ship was powered by the Envoys, reaching unimaginable speeds. They were tearing through space like the waves of the sea. However, the ship remained slower than teleportation, and the Heaven Egg galaxy was far away—it would take them two weeks to arrive.

During that time, the Elders didn't step out of their rooms once. Most people spent their time cultivating, with perhaps small breaks to enjoy the view, and Jack with Brock were the same. The two of them huddled inside Jack's room, constantly getting stronger.

After all, they were headed to a battlefield.

Though that didn't mean they were oblivious to the scenery. The void outside the starship's windows was clustered with endless galaxies, shining like the stars of the night sky. Each of those bright dots housed billions of planets, potentially trillions of lives. The universe was vast beyond belief, and even A-Grades were nothing more than slightly larger ants compared to its majesty.

It was times like this that gave Jack perspective. The System had colonized a tiny part of the universe so far, a mere seventy-three galaxies. With the exception of the Milky Way, which was still young, each of those galaxies produced hundreds of B-Grades and one to perhaps several A-Grades.

If one day the cultivation world spread across the universe, to the hundreds of billions of galaxies, what would it look like? There would be infinite lives, trillions of A-Grades. At that point, being one of those trillion wouldn't really matter. Would all those people discover new Grades and realms above the A-Grade? Would there be A+, or S, or other classifications of power? Was there a limit? Would there be more Systems, each pursuing the peak in its way? Could humans one day reach the level of Old Gods, the rulers of the universe?

And what if those Old Gods had already colonized more corners of the universe besides the System's?

Jack didn't know. These seventy-three galaxies were the only ones containing cultivators. In a larger bubble around System space, the surrounding galaxies also contained life, originating from when the Ancients had spread their seed as far as they could. Yet all these remained nothing but a drop in the bucket.

It was terrifying to think of the cultivation world as a tiny island of light in an infinite dark sea. At the same time, it was heroic. Ambitious. They were just starting out; the universe was theirs to conquer, theirs to colonize. Perhaps in a trillion years, the entire universe would be lively, and the world would enter an era of unmatched prosperity that would echo across the eons.

By then, Jack would be nothing but dust. How nice would it be if he could contribute even a tiny bit to humanity's expansion?

"Thinking big?"

The question came so abruptly that Jack was startled. He hadn't noticed anyone approaching. He turned around, finding Envoy Spacewind standing behind him, staring with those sharp eyes of his.

"Envoy," Jack said respectfully.

"Spare me the ceremony. Just reply. Did the view inspire you to think big?"

Jack hesitated. He'd never spoken with Spacewind, but he'd sensed hostility from him a few times. Still, he couldn't just not respond. "It did. I find that the universe is vast, vaster than anyone can imagine. How can something that great not create great thoughts?"

"Great things create great thoughts... Well spoken," Spacewind replied, but his voice contained a hint of darkness. "However, I would advise you to be careful. Youth brings recklessness. It is best for one to understand where they can and cannot expand, which fruits are theirs to enjoy, and which belong to others. Those who reach beyond their means tend to suffer horrible fates."

Jack raised a brow. "I should... not think about other galaxies?"

"You should not think about Min Ling," Spacewind said directly. "She is an exceptional woman. I have to admit you are exceptional as well, but it doesn't matter. I am already courting her. If you continue your advances, then I will no longer chalk it up to ignorance and will take it as an insult."

Jack was stunned. This was what it was all about? Spacewind was being hostile because he thought Jack was hitting on Min Ling?

That was certainly not the case. He'd only spoken with her once, and there had been nothing weird about that interaction. He was even married; well, not quite, but he did regard Vivi as his life partner. He wouldn't randomly flirt with other women, even if they were beautiful and extremely talented.

He opened his mouth to explain these things to Spacewind... then stopped.

True, Spacewind had misunderstood. This situation could easily be resolved if Jack simply explained his side. However, regardless of misunderstandings or not, Spacewind's words had been far too imperious. He'd threatened Jack and spoken as he would to an ant. He'd also taken Min Ling as belonging to him even though that obviously wasn't the case. Jack recalled her cold reaction when

Spacewind appeared, and he easily understood she'd been rejecting his ceaseless advances.

Despite that, Spacewind had taken it upon himself to discourage all other admirers. That was the behavior of a narcissistic, selfish man. Moreover, a man that had chosen to pick a bone with Jack—even if their conflict was based on shaky ground.

All of a sudden, Jack didn't feel like patiently explaining himself to such a person, even if that person happened to be the leader of the expedition.

"I had no such intention," he replied coldly, "but with all due respect, even if I did, I do not believe it should be any of your concern."

"You are trying to court the woman I am courting. How is that not my concern?"

"And how is your courting going?"

Spacewind's gaze grew frigid. "This is not about success. If you aim for the same target as me, you are working against me, therefore you are my enemy. That is not something you want."

"I'm just not in the habit of cowering away," Jack replied calmly. "You cannot own people just because you saw them first. If you have some issue, bring it up with her. However, I will say this again, I had no intention of 'courting' anyone. And now, if you don't mind, I have some galaxies to look at."

Spacewind's eyes narrowed dangerously. "I am your superior. You do not get to dismiss me."

"With all due respect, sir, I can do whatever the fuck I want."

Jack left Spacewind standing alone, feeling the other man's gaze bore into his back all the while. Jack made it to his room and entered, heaving a tired sigh.

"What am I doing wrong, Brock?" he asked. "Why is it that everywhere I go, someone strong wants to beat me up?"

Brock, who was meditating, opened one eye. "Maybe you're just too cool."

"Yeah, that must be it."

Jack lay on his bed, once again sighing. At this point, creating powerful enemies was a routine. It would feel weird if there wasn't someone gunning for his back.

First Baron, then Spacewind... The hidden realm will sure be interesting.

Even if Jack often created enemies, he didn't do so thoughtlessly. His enmity with Spacewind wasn't particularly deep. At best, they had a stressed relationship. He didn't believe Spacewind would act against him on the battlefield against the Hand of God—after all, regardless of internal problems, everyone was unified against external enemies.

Moreover, even if Spacewind did harbor such intentions, they wouldn't be together inside the hidden realm. The B-Grades would explore the core areas, while the C-Grades would wander around the edges. Even if something did go wrong and Spacewind tried to act against him, Min Ling would definitely take Jack's side. She was the leader of the C-Grades and also exceptionally strong—there shouldn't be any problems.

After that, when they returned to the Cathedral, just one B-Grade enemy wasn't too much. He'd been through worse.

These had all been Jack's considerations as he refused to yield to Spacewind's intimidation, but they didn't negate the fact that he'd just created more problems for himself. He sighed again.

"What's the matter, bro?" Brock asked.

Jack explained the situation. At that point, Brock's mouth formed into an 'o'. He explained to Jack how he had joked about this with Esmeralda and the bros, which may have reached Spacewind and created some confusion.

"You did nothing wrong," Jack said when Brock was done. "You were just playing around and increasing my reputation. There was nothing weird about it. The only reason there are problems is because Spacewind is an asshole. Even if you didn't give him an excuse to act against me, he would have gone off sooner or later. The fault remains squarely on his shoulders."

Brock nodded.

"Any ideas?" Jack asked. "I don't mind the current situation but resolving it would also be good."

"I could throw some poop?"

It wasn't a real suggestion, and Jack laughed, a weight sliding off his shoulders. "Remember that time you threw poop at Rufus Emberheart? Those were the days."

"He was being an asshole," Brock added, nodding along with a big monkeyish grin. "I will give you poop in bag. Handy weapon. When asshole becomes big asshole, just throw."

"Please do," Jack replied, laughing again.

The two weeks passed easily. To cultivators of their level, their sense of time was greatly slowed down, meaning that two weeks were nothing but a cultivation session. Jack used up half his remaining Dao stones, also giving some to Brock, and advanced his third fruit to fifty percent maturity.

At some point, Jack sensed the starship moving oddly. It slowed and teleported in random directions, hiding their direction of origin. "We're here," he said.

He and Brock flew out of their room, followed by many other cultivators. Everyone headed for the front window.

An egg-shaped opening shimmered in the distance. It looked like a portal, its surface swimming with colors that nobody could see through. This was the hidden realm. Surprisingly, it wasn't too large—barely a thousand feet across.

"That's only the entrance," Shi Mo said from beside Jack. "The inside is a different dimension. It could be a thousand miles wide, a million miles, or maybe even larger! Nobody knows until we've entered."

"I see," Jack replied.

Close to the hidden realm opening was another starship, even larger than their own. It was simply gigantic. Multiple decks lined its interior, and its prow alone stretched for a mile outside the ship. Teleporting something that large must have cost an ungodly amount of energy.

The Black Hole Church's starship approached the other and stopped a hundred miles away. At this distance, Jack could make out a small crowd floating outside the other starship, but they weren't just standing there—they sat at tables and chairs that floated in the void, enjoying all sorts of drinks and delicacies.

Of those people, two seemed particularly mighty. They sat at the largest table all by themselves, and their auras were so powerful they pushed against Jack like powerful astral winds.

They were another two A-Grades. And Jack, who was a high and mighty C-Grade, suddenly felt like a big fish surrounded by sharks.

As Jack and the others waited inside the starship, Elders Heavenstar and Boatman appeared over their heads. "Follow us outside, everyone," Elder Heavenstar said, pulling out a chair from his space ring. "Let's celebrate a little."

CHAPTER FIFTY-SIX
BATTLE BANQUET

As soon as Jack flew out of the starship, a familiar blue screen unfurled in his vision.

You have returned to the New World. Welcome!

"Uh... Thanks?"

"Who you talking to?" Brock asked.

"The System. It seems we... re-entered."

That last word was spoken apprehensively. Jack was a fugitive. As far as he was concerned, being outside System space acted to his safety. Since he still hadn't found a way to deactivate or isolate the mini System core inside him—or even clearly discover it—who knew what capabilities System space offered to his enemies.

"It's fine," Shi Mo reassured him, floating beside them. "The Elders wouldn't bring us somewhere too dangerous. There shouldn't be a fallout. Besides, the Church has all sorts of ways to escape the System's surveillance even inside System space."

"Yeah," Jack replied with a sigh. "You're right. I just have bad memories."

"Don't worry. Our Elders are as high-value targets as can be. If they dare enter System space, so do we."

The Heaven Egg galaxy had long ago been integrated to System space, save for some remote corners. This place was one such corner, but given the hidden realm's significance, it wasn't weird for the Hand of God to expend some resources and expand System space to here.

Being in System space was a refreshing, almost nostalgic feeling. Jack had access to the System scanning again. The first thing he did was look at Brock.

Brorilla, Level 263 (King)
A gorilla variant from planet Green. Brorillas usually live with Gymonkeys and train them in the ways of working out. It is due to the Brorillas' unmatched pecks that Gymonkeys use poop to fight—they consider themselves too weak for anything else.
Brorillas are usually calm, measured animals. However, if anyone harms their little cousins or invades their territory, they go bananas.
This particular brorilla is a variant that visually resembles a gymonkey. Through cultivation, it has achieved a degree of power at the C-Grade, far surpassing the par for its species.
Extermination is advised.

Extermination is advised... Jack thought, his eyes shimmering with wrath. *I didn't miss you, System.*

He also inspected other people he was curious about. Min Ling was really a human, as was Shi Mo, while the second ranked, Salazar, was indeed a space monster.

Space Monster, Level 399
Experts speculate that, when large quantities of the Dao are left undisturbed for a long time, they can spontaneously coalesce into a

Space Monster. While this is a very rare occasion, the vastness of the void lends itself to the phenomenon. Space is filled with such monsters, especially outside System space.

However, due to the phenomenon's relative rarity and the requirement of a long-time undisturbed Dao, it has never been observed in controlled environments. The exact procedure of a Space Monster's birth has never been documented in the Immortal Archives.

Space Monsters are mostly mindless existences that seek only to feed on sources of the Dao, like natural treasures or cultivators. They grow larger and more intelligent in proportion to their strength. This specimen has developed to a very high level and attained complete sapience. Extermination is advised.

How cute the System was. To anything that wasn't a System cultivator, it advised instant extermination.

As for the Elders... Jack failed to scan them. It was like the System didn't register their presence.

This all happened very quickly. The Church group was still flying toward the Hand of God group, Elder Heavenstar holding a chair in the lead. Jack remained tense. Not only were these two opposing organizations, so anything could happen, but it was also his first time coming in contact with the high-level figures of the Hand of God. All previous interactions in the Milky Way galaxy were with people who didn't even qualify to be outer disciples.

The Hand's lineup was similar to the Church's. Thirty C-Grades and twelve B-Grades, accompanied by two A-Grade Elders. Their composition was even richer in humans than the Church's, while their two Elders were a blue-haired man and a silver-haired, silver-eyed woman who radiated extreme holiness.

Back in the Milky Way, Jack had been chased by a B-Grade member of the Hand of God, a woman called Eva Solvig who cultivated Purity. Despite that chase lasting many months, the two had never met—but, if they had, Jack would have noticed a striking resemblance to this silver-haired Elder before him. Were they related?

Whether by coincidence or not, that B-Grade was also in the crowd, her eyes glued to Jack. He, of course, did not recognize her.

"Blue hair weird," Brock said, squinting at the other Elder.

"That's Elder Ocean," Shi Mo said from the side. "It is said that every hair on his head contains an entire ocean!"

Jack took a better look. Indeed, that man's hair seemed weird. It was made up of thick hairs which moved by themselves, as if every hair possessed its own consciousness. Since they were much thicker than normal, his head couldn't possess more than a hundred hairs, but to say that each of them contained an ocean sounded exaggerated. That was fifteen times the entire water volume of Earth.

Well, approximately.

At that moment, Jack's stare was interrupted by Elder Ocean glancing in his direction. Jack felt like he was stranded deep inside the ocean, surrounded by endless water all around and gasping for breath.

The illusion disappeared in the next moment, but Jack was left sweating.

"Ocean! Purity!" Elder Heavenstar exclaimed, laughing. "I didn't expect the two of you to come. It's been a while!"

"The water whispered your arrival. How could I not accompany you?" Elder Ocean replied in an oddly normal voice. The two Hand of God Elders flew ahead, engaging the Church Elders in small talk that demonstrated peaceful intentions. Or, rather, it was better to say that Heavenstar and Ocean had small talk—Boatman and Purity simply stood there, their titanic auras anchored in the void.

"Don't be swayed by appearances," Shi Mo whispered, leaning closer to Jack. "Boatman and Purity are the real powerhouses here. They just don't like talking."

"Really?"

"Absolutely!"

Jack reevaluated his preconceptions of the Elders. It was his first time in the cultivation world that he saw the stronger party leaning back and letting others take the spotlight.

Of course, thinking of Heavenstar and Ocean as weak was a trap. Each of them could annihilate Jack with a thought.

"Your disciples are looking fine," Heavenstar said, passing his glance over the Hand of God expedition.

"They're adequate." Ocean shrugged. "I've heard your Church has a few good seedlings this time. I'm looking forward to their performance."

"Please. They couldn't hold a candle to yours."

As the Elders chatted merrily, the two expeditions were weighing each other. They didn't need to present fake peacefulness. Since they would soon clash, they were free to stare all they wanted. Sparks flew between the two groups. Many people found an opponent of similar strength and stared them down.

Jack and Brock stood out with their low cultivation, but nobody on the opposing team took them seriously. Talented but low-level cultivators like them were usually brought along to gain experience —they wouldn't actually participate in the battles inside the hidden realm.

Shi Mo leaned closer to Jack and Brock, introducing the important characters of the other side.

"That's Envoy Uruselam," he said, motioning at a calm, smiling man. His robes and hair were white, though he did not seem old, and he exuded a presence of immovable serenity. He did not at all resemble a warrior. Moreover, his white brows were so long that they fell to the sides of his chin, and his ears were so wide they could probably be used to swim.

"And that is Arkenstal," Shi Mo said, pointing at another man. He wore dark, wide robes that fluttered in the void, but his eyes belied a terrifying presence. Thanks to his insights, Jack could feel that spacetime was warped around that man, soft and ready to be molded by his will.

The stare-off continued for some time. Nobody seemed hasty to break the silence.

"Why they look but no attack?" Brock asked, annoyed that nobody was staring at him. "They are cowards, or we are too pretty."

His voice was just enough to reach the Church cultivators, making some smile wryly.

Finally, Elder Ocean said, "How about you join us in the banquet? The food is beginning to grow cold."

"Naturally!" Heavenstar replied. "How could we miss such an opportunity? Dying on an empty stomach wouldn't be fun at all. Everyone"—he turned to his expedition—"make yourself comfortable. Spacewind, make sure our tables are rich and full."

"Yes, Elder," Spacewind replied. The many Envoys reached inside their space rings and pulled out tables and chairs, setting them up across from the already existing furniture of the Hand of God. Spacewind retrieved all sorts of food and drinks and set them on the tables, whereupon the Church expedition members took their seat. Jack and Brock did so as well, positioned between Shi Mo and a seven-fruit cultivator Jack didn't know too well. Baron Longform was seated far away.

Jack had no idea what was going on. He expected to dive into the hidden realm. Wasn't this too peaceful?

The two groups had connected their tables, forming a large pi shape. Eighty-four people sat there, with two large starships and the hidden realm as their background. The two different organizations were clearly separated, their members not mingling; the tables of one were stitched with a green-shaded black hole, while the others displayed the Hand of God insignia—a palm with an open eye in the middle.

At the back of the pi was the Elders' table, large and filled with snacks. They were the only ones whose table was not connected to the rest.

Of course, all these tables weren't set on solid ground. They floated freely through the void, only held in place by the participants' supernatural powers.

As for the food and drinks, those were all extraordinary. Not much could survive the void of space, but this was taking it a step further. The two factions were competing over which could offer the most luxurious, most extravagant snacks, and each faction insisted on the other tasting their offerings.

Jack hadn't tasted anything yet, but the Hand of God was clearly winning on that front. Just sensing the auras of the different dishes was proof enough.

"What exactly is going on?" he asked Shi Mo. "Why are we celebrating now?"

"It's a custom," the old swordsman replied. "Every time there is a joint expedition anywhere, the two factions hold a banquet beforehand. It symbolizes their willingness to cooperate and not just exterminate each other inside."

"But I thought we were going to exterminate each other inside."

"Not necessarily. Hidden realms are full of resources, treasures with greater value than anything you've seen before. Compared to them, Dao stones are nothing but currency—the real treasures would never be so widely distributed. Hidden realms are the only opportunity for people like us to get those things, but... it's not that easy. Opportunities come with danger. Once inside, the two expedition teams will work together to explore and secure as many benefits as possible. After that, if the harvest is something small, we can divide it. Only when the benefits are too large will blood be spilled."

"I see..." Jack replied, deep in thought.

Shi Mo leaned back. "Of course, that mostly refers to the B-Grades. We will just split up and explore the periphery. If two people happen to meet out there and one of them dies... who would ever know? Killing others to steal their belongings is a very common practice. Keep an eye out."

Jack couldn't help but grin. Finally, this was something he was used to. "Have you been to a hidden realm before, Shi Mo?"

"I have, once. It was three thousand years ago... but it was not pleasant. My best friend died inside."

"I'm sorry to hear that."

"It's fine. Us cultivators should be used to death. It was a long time ago, anyway."

Before Jack could reply, a Hand of God six-fruit cultivator stood up and flew toward the open side of the pi formed by the banquet tables. It was the place where everyone could see him, including the Elders.

"Everyone," he said, "my name is Evrart Jin, and I would like to demonstrate my Dao to your entertainment."

"Haha!" A six-fruit man from the Church side flew out to meet him, laughing uproariously. "What a great idea! However, demonstrating by yourself would be too lonely. How about I, Kinfer Ain, accompany you?"

"Please, be my guest."

The two men flew one mile deeper into space. Of course, everyone present was a master, and their perception could easily capture everything at that distance. As soon as enough distance was between them, Jack felt excitement rise all around him as people turned to watch the show.

"What's going on now?" he asked.

Shi Mo had a wide grin. "You're going to love this. At banquets like this, it's customary for the weaker cultivators to spar against each other, demonstrating their power and earning fame for their faction."

"Really? We just go at it?"

"Mhm. It goes from the weakest to the strongest. First come the six-fruits, then the seven-fruits, then the eight-fruits. The nine-fruit and B-Grade cultivators will not fight in this case. They are the main force of each exhibition—nobody wants to demonstrate their hidden cards to the enemy."

Jack's eyes shone. "Can I participate as well?"

"Hah! It's not whether you can or not, with your strength, you absolutely have to participate. You are a great opportunity for the Church to display its superiority—though you shouldn't expose your full strength. In fact, if you don't step up, I suspect the Elders will be quite unhappy!"

Jack laughed. "Then, don't mind if I do!"

CHAPTER FIFTY-SEVEN
NEEDLESS CRUELTY

THE TWO CULTIVATORS STOPPED ONE MILE AWAY FROM THE BANQUET. THEY bowed at each other, then engaged in a brutal melee. One was a wizard and the other a swordsman—flames filled the void, apocalyptic blizzards crashed. A single blade swam through them like a sparrow, enduring the elements for a chance to strike. The battle was showy and intense, though it remained fought by six-fruits—in the expedition teams, this was the lowest level.

Eventually, the Hand of God wizard prevailed, freezing his opponent into an ice column before gently thawing him awake. The swordsman seemed unwilling, but there was nothing he could do. Biting back his bitterness, he said, "Thank you," and flew back to his seat.

The wizard laughed. He mustn't have spent too much strength because he loudly proclaimed, "Who's next!"

Jack looked toward the cultivators around him. According to Shi Mo, this went from weakest to strongest, so it wasn't his time yet. Below the nine-fruits, he was the strongest person present.

A green-skinned woman rose next. Even her hair was green, and Jack's inspection classified her as a dryad. She flew to the battle site a mile away and bowed lightly. "Please give me guidance," she said, then flashed into battle.

This spar remained low-level in Jack's eyes, though the green woman's battle style had him intrigued. She wielded the power of Life—yet, she was no Physical cultivator, but a wizard. Her Dao of Life was so vibrant and lively that it flooded the space around her, stretching out for miles. It formed tendrils which lashed at the Hand of God wizard. The tendrils swallowed the elements, taking them as nutrition. When the wizard summoned elementals, the tendrils directly flooded them with life energy, bloating their bodies until they exploded.

Finally, the wizard grew weary. The scales were tipped against him, and the tendrils lashed out to grab him. His entire body shone green. His own magic defended him, pushing back the rampant life energy, but they couldn't shut it out completely. New limbs speared out of his flesh, which then began to grow asymmetrically in various ways. He bent over as his back grew bubble-like tumors. His hair grew wildly until it covered his eyes. Sharp screams left his mouth as who-knows-what occurred inside his body.

"I admit defeat!" he managed to scream. The life invasion instantly withdrew, returning his body to normal but leaving his mind shaken. Without saying anything, he flew back to his seat and plopped down heavily.

Jack's gaze remained on those tendrils. He was intrigued. The Dao of Life can be used in such a way?

Perhaps he should look into it. After all, he possessed a veritable ocean of life energy, infinitely larger than what the dryad exhibited. If he could weaponize it, his power would rise yet again!

Jack was happy about this battle. The Hand of God, not so much. It was a bit too grotesque. Many cultivators had disgust in their eyes, but nobody spoke. Yet, at the great table of the Elders, someone did.

A woman whose entire body radiated untouchable holiness frowned. "What a disgusting power," she said directly.

That was Elder Purity, the greatest powerhouse present. Only Elder Boatman could match her.

Facing her words, the dryad was embarrassed, and the Black Hole Church cultivators were unhappy. She'd just publicly mocked one of them. Were the Elders going to say nothing?

At the Elders' table, Heavenstar shot a glance at Boatman, who was disinclined to bother. Therefore, the burden fell on Heavenstar himself, whose status was normally insufficient to argue with Purity.

"Life and death are the natural states of the world," he said. "For cultivators, power is the most important thing. Beauty can only come second."

Elder Ocean laughed. "Well spoken, Heavenstar. Only those with power can pursue beauty. For the weak, even freaks are prizes."

These words sounded nice on the surface, but they were actually vicious insults. In just three sentences, Ocean had called the Black Hole Church weak and its disciple a freak.

Heavenstar frowned. His kindly old man image dropped a little. "Who is weak and who is strong, let our disciples find out."

"Exactly my point!" Ocean replied, still laughing. He appeared extremely confident in their lineup. "Carry on, my disciples. Who here has a strong enough stomach to endure defeating that witch?"

"It would be my honor, Elder," a cultivator said, standing and flying over to the dryad. He was a broad-shouldered young man bursting with vitality. Jack even felt some hints of body tempering on him.

The dryad said nothing, directly attacking. Her tendrils covered the stars, swarming the youth from every direction. He laughed heroically. Space shattered under him, leading into a crazy dance of teleportation. He was everywhere and nowhere, dodging all tendrils. They couldn't even touch the hem of his robes.

At the C-Grade, most people possessed at least some control over space. The dryad couldn't lock it down everywhere to prevent him from moving, but she could stabilize her immediate surroundings—otherwise, he would teleport beside her and directly end the battle.

However, that wasn't enough. The young man appeared a mile away from her, then charged. The broadsword he held tore through the vines, and his Dao defended against the few that touched him. When he reached the dryad, he slapped the flat of his blade against her shoulder, sending her flying away.

The vines disappeared, the tension evaporated. The battle was over.

However, the tension between the Elders remained potent, and the youth was too smart to waste it. After slapping away the dryad, he frowned at his blade and wiped it against his sleeve, making a show of how dirty she was. That was provocation. It fanned the flames in the hearts of every Church cultivator, including the Elders.

Boatman, to their growing discomfort, remained completely unmoved. As for Heavenstar, he could only say so much by himself.

Nobody was laughing anymore. This was a battle concerning the honor of the two factions. And, even more, it concerned the confidence of each expedition team. This would have an impact inside the hidden realm.

A lightning cultivator stepped up for the Church. Her hair was wildly fluttering, and her eyes rained sparks. She tussled against the broad-shouldered young man for a minute before barely winning and regaining some honor for the Church. However, she was mostly spent. This was the third cultivator of the Church to fight, but the third cultivator of the Hand was only just stepping up, full of energy. In the battles so far, the Hand of God held a small but clear advantage.

Moreover, the remaining low-level cultivators for the Church were Brock and Jack. One was too weak to fight at this level, and the other had to save his strength for later. If Jack stood up now, he would easily persist until the eight-fruits of the Hand went up, and the battles could only rise in level. All the seven and eight-fruits of the Church would have lost their chance to compete.

"Oh, you actually sent out someone decent!" Elder Ocean

exclaimed, gazing at the lightning woman. "I expected Von to win a couple more times... In that case, Sassa, how about you step up?"

"Yes, master," a girl replied respectfully. She looked young and innocent, barely nineteen or twenty years old. Of course, her actual age was up to anyone's guess. Her youthful appearance just indicated that she'd reached the D-Grade very early in her life.

As she flew to the stage, everyone's gaze was on her. She had addressed Elder Ocean as master—was she his direct disciple? That was an extremely great position for a C-Grade! Her strength could be imagined.

Moreover... she was only at the five-fruit boundary.

In expeditions like these, it wasn't uncommon for low-level but promising cultivators to join along. That didn't mean they could jump multiple realms to fight—most of the time, they were just there for the experience. The Hand of God cultivators assumed Jack and Brock were such people, and the Church assumed this girl, Sassa, was one of those as well. Nobody took them seriously or expected them to fight. To everyone's eyes, they were just children dragged along.

Of course, the Church knew Jack was an exception.

If this girl now rose to the stage, and she was even specifically introduced by an Elder... could she possess extreme battle power?

"My name is Sassa. Please advise!" the girl said as she stood against the lightning woman. She was short and graceful, with dark hair done in a ponytail and fitting dark clothes covering her body. Her eyes sparked with a playful gaze, but for some reason, Jack felt uncomfortable as he observed them.

The lightning woman attacked. Space cracked all around them and thunder rumbled out, along with lightning bolts of extreme power. This wasn't the normal lightning of a storm, it was of far, far higher quality, and the power it contained was highly oppressive.

Since these were Dao Skills and guided by the woman, they couldn't actually move at the speed of the light, but they remained ungodly fast. They zapped at the girl near-instantly.

She dodged them.

Her body danced through the lightning, bending and curving with unnatural flexibility as if she had no bones. She laughed. "Is that all? I thought lightning was fast!"

She flew toward the lightning woman, dodging everything like a snake wading through grass. Just before she arrived, she slithered through space and reappeared behind the woman. Her hand shot out. Two fingers struck under the woman's ribs, directing an insidious shockwave into her body.

The lightning woman wasn't sent flying. Her eyes went blank, she spat out blood, and then fainted on the spot. Her lightning disappeared with her.

"Whoops," Sassa said, feigning surprise. "I thought she would be stronger... My bad!"

The Church cultivators seethed with anger. They didn't even wait for the Elders before shouting at the girl. She could say whatever she wanted, but this was clearly done on purpose. She had been heavy-handed and seriously injured someone. Depending on the degree of injuries, this could influence the lightning woman's fate in the hidden realm.

What a cruel move!

"What are you all blabbering about?" Elder Ocean thundered, his aura suppressing all the Church cultivators. "Sassa saw an opponent one fruit above her and didn't dare hold back. Isn't that common practice in the cultivation world? If your disciple was injured by the first move of a lower-level opponent, she can only blame her own weakness!"

The Church cultivators seethed, but what could they say? They couldn't argue against an Elder, and even if they could, their tongues were tied. Ocean's words were not incorrect. All that mattered was strength. Even though everyone knew this was done on purpose, refuting Ocean was difficult.

At the Elders' table, Boatman remained nonplussed, but Heavenstar's expression turned ugly. His aura spread out and shielded his cultivators from Ocean's pressure, then he said, "Accidents can happen in a spar. However, once is an accident, twice is on purpose. Don't let that happen again."

Ocean snorted. "I am not my disciples, Heavenstar. If an accident happens in a battle between opponents of similar strength, nobody can be blamed. Of course, we will be careful. Did you hear that, Sassa? If your opponents can't even take a casual strike, you should try not to injure them."

"Yes, master," Sassa replied obediently. Ocean's words were once again an insult aimed at the Black Hole Church, and they could only stomach it. Their disciples were being suppressed in battle. Unless that changed, anything they said would only be the excuses of the weak.

On stage, Sassa revealed an innocent look as she gazed at the Church side of the banquet. "Who's next?" she asked. Her eyes scanned over the seven-fruits and even the eight-fruits—her arrogance was off the charts!

Of course, she didn't even glance at Jack and Brock. In her eyes, they were barely even present. As for Jack, he also didn't stare too much, because he was afraid that his intentions would seep through. He yearned to go up and fight. However, doing so now would be improper. This girl's strength was at the seven-fruit boundary, so it was clearly the seven-fruits' turn.

The seven-fruits of the Church hesitated, glancing at each other. Nobody wanted to go up first. If they won, that would be fine. Though if they lost to someone two fruits below them, the humiliation would be hard to endure. After all, these weren't normal seven-fruits; they were the best elites the Cathedral had to offer. They were usually the ones jumping realms to fight, not the opposite.

"What are you waiting for?" Heavenstar shouted, his mood ruined. In hesitating to go up, they were making it seem as if they were afraid. "Step up!"

One seven-fruit bit the bullet. He flew to the space that served as the battle stage. He did not bow or show respect. He drew a spear from his space ring and directly charged. Every second of fighting this girl was a humiliation, he wanted to get it over with as soon as possible.

"Fierce!" Sassa exclaimed, her laughter cheerful. "Let's see what you can do!"

Suddenly, her eyes changed. The irises elongated, becoming slimmer and vertical. They now resembled the eyes of a snake. At the same time, her aura shot up.

"This girl is what's known as a prime genius," Shi Mo explained, leaning closer to Jack and Brock. "The two of you belong to that category too, as does Min Ling. It signifies people who can jump multiple ranks to fight other world-class elites. They don't appear often... Four of them being at the C-Grade at the same time is almost unheard of."

Jack nodded, his attention sqaurely on the battle.

The spear came down, and Sassa bent her body in a completely unnatural fashion, just like a snake. She then coiled around the spear shaft with extreme speed, reaching her opponent's hands.

This was an elite seven-fruit cultivator. He wasn't weak. With a shout, his aura flared, and his spear erupted with flames. Sassa chuckled as she disappeared, teleporting behind him—the man teleported as well. They exchanged a few moves, one spear fighting a snake as they danced around the void. However, no matter how he tried, he could not touch Sassa. Ten moves later, her hand swiped by his thigh. She used no weapon, only two fingers extended in the shape of snake fangs. As she passed by his leg, blood and flesh erupted, while the back half of his thigh disappeared.

The man's eyes widened. Sassa reappeared in the distance, covering her mouth as she laughed. At the same time, everyone saw her lick her blood-stained fingers. Coming from an innocent-looking young girl, that move was disturbing, but everyone was too shocked to say anything, and Elder Purity—who usually disliked anything ugly—naturally wouldn't speak against her own people.

The spear-wielder was unwilling. His face turned purple in anger as he clenched his spear, then fell still. That stillness continued for a suspiciously long amount of time. It was only then that an eight-fruit healer from the Church realized what was going on and rushed over.

Sassa's strike wasn't just bloody. It was also venomous.

After the healer treated the spear-wielder for a few seconds, he finally moved again, screaming out in pain. Whatever this poison had done to his body, it was not pleasant.

"Sorry!" Sassa exclaimed, the same look of innocence on her face. "I thought he was going to resist it."

The Church cultivators' eyes almost bulged out in anger. This Sassa seemed like a little girl, but she was actually a vicious snake. She was heavy-handed and injured others on purpose!

But what could they say? The man she fought had been two fruits higher than her. Any words to defend him would just paint him in an even more pathetic light than his current one.

Moreover, this was all part of Sassa's plan. She'd made one thing clear: anyone who stood against her would not escape lightly. She smiled coyly, then said, "Who's next?"

The seven-fruits stirred in their seats, none standing. They were not idiots. Whoever rose would be injured and humiliated. If that was the case, they might as well remain seated and suffer the humiliation. As for defeating her, none of the seven-fruits present had any hopes. Their battle powers weren't too far apart. If the spear-wielder had lost so casually, they would lose as well.

For a time, nobody moved. Elder Heavenstar didn't speak either.

It wasn't that the Church had nobody who could beat this girl. The eight-fruits could fight her equally, and the nine-fruits could easily defeat her. However, skipping all the seven-fruits to send up an eight-fruit would be a tacit admittance of defeat. No matter what happened later on, nothing would wash away this humiliation. At the same time, sending up a seven-fruit was hopeless. Even if Elder Heavenstar forced someone to go, they would just make a fool out of themselves.

As for Min Ling, even though she was a seven-fruit cultivator, she was far too strong. She was the Church's greatest C-Grade, and that was known to everyone. Sending her out to deal with a mere five-fruit girl would be even worse than sending out the eight-fruits.

And Jack was in a similar situation. Sending him out would imply that even their eight-fruits couldn't handle this girl.

"Hahaha!" Elder Ocean laughed. "What are your disciples doing, Heavenstar? Are they deaf?"

Heavenstar gritted his teeth. He was about to ask an eight-fruit cultivator to take the stage, but right as he opened his mouth, he paused. He sensed movement beside him. Elder Boatman, who had not moved an inch so far, finally spoke three words: "Jack Rust, go."

CHAPTER FIFTY-EIGHT

INSULTING AN ELDER

It was the bare minimum amount of words Boatman could say, as if his saliva was precious. His voice was hoarse and elderly, showing that he'd lived through the endless river of time, and even hearing it made one feel older.

As these words rang out, Jack grinned. He was part of the Church. The humiliation just now had been aimed at him as well, and it had taken everything he had to suppress himself and wait for his turn.

Hearing that he could fight, how could he not be elated?

The Hand of God people raised their brows as they saw him fly to the stage. They'd assumed he was just here for experience. Could he possess some battle power as well?

And, even if he did, could he really stand up to Sassa, whose power was similar to an elite eight-fruit cultivator?

"Looks like Boatman has gone senile," the Hand of God cultivators conversed telepathically—they would never dare say such words out loud.

But Purity would. "What is the meaning of this, Boatman?" Her voice came down like a divine decree. "Are you just trying to buy time for your faction? If so, I admire your decisiveness. Not many could sacrifice a promising young man to save some face."

Her words dripped with mockery, but Elder Boatman was completely unmoved. He didn't even bother to glance in her direction, as if she was nothing but an annoyance. This behavior alone was insulting. Purity frowned, then directly sent a sound transmission to Sassa: "Find a way to injure him, and I'll reward you."

"Okay!" she replied cheerfully. If an Elder rewarded someone, anything they casually handed out would be a great treasure. For that, provoking the Church a bit was nothing. Even if she overdid it, the two Elders had her back. At worst, she would be admonished.

She stared at Jack as he flew over, chuckling in her mind. *I'm sorry, little man... but you're about to be stepped on!*

Jack remained indifferent. He stopped three hundred feet away from Sassa, then said, "My name is Jack Rust. Please take it easy on me."

Sassa laughed. "I'll try my best!" she lied, then charged. Even if Elder Purity hadn't said anything, she would still injure Jack. Sending such a weakling to face her was clearly an insult, and she was a very proud individual.

She wanted to end this as soon as possible.

Her body appeared before Jack's almost instantly. Her hand shot out like a snake's fang. Yet, just in the nick of time, Jack drew back. Her fingers missed him. She tried again and again, but Jack always dodged at the last moment. Sassa twisted her body in snake-like ways, striking from tricky and unexpected angles, but none of her attacks landed.

She was shocked—even more, she was incensed. There was no way a three-fruit cultivator could match her. He must have been a speed-oriented expert at dodging, sent out specifically to mock her!

Her heart burned with anger. Her strikes accelerated, leaning harder into offense. She forewent defending. A dodging master couldn't possess the power to strike back. Yet, even a hundred exchanges later, she still hadn't managed to touch him.

"Coward!" she shouted. "Don't you even dare to show your Dao?"

Jack hadn't punched once. His Dao had not been made clear. Hearing her words, he only gazed at her as one would at an idiot. He teleported, appearing a mile away. "You do not possess the qualifications to meet my Dao," he said, extending a straight palm—his spanking prowess was about to be revealed. "However, I do have a secondary Dao. It is most suitable to deal with you—in fact, it is exactly what you need."

"I do not possess the qualifications!" Sassa did not understand the second part of his words, nor did she care. She was already fully incensed. Since when was she, a proud daughter of heaven, the direct disciple of an A-Grade Elder, mocked like this by someone of lower cultivation?

She had been at the peak of her glory just a moment ago, and now she was unable to touch him and was even mocked. Her previous achievement had evaporated. How was this happening?

"I'll fucking kill you!" she shouted. Her vertical irises sharpened. She shot forward faster than before, a blur through space, forgoing defense completely to ensure she struck him down. Even if she had to receive a minor wound in return, it was fine. She would make sure his injury was far heavier.

Space shattered. Sassa teleported a hundred times, until her afterimages were all around Jack, blocking visibility of the void. She appeared before him. One of her hands feinted a strike to the stomach. Right afterward, the other formed a fang-like shape and aimed directly for his eyes.

This strike was meant to directly blind him!

Facing this attack, Jack's gaze darkened. A hand clamped down on her wrist, abruptly stopping her. The world froze. Sassa's hand stopped just an inch away from Jack's eyes, her fingers poised to strike, and to her horror, she couldn't move at all. No matter how she struggled, Jack's hand was simply unmovable. She could neither advance nor retreat.

She was completely at his mercy.

At that moment, Sassa realized she'd made a mistake. Her heart grew cold. This man was not an expert in speed. He was an expert at everything physical, and she had completely underestimated him.

Her vertical irises disappeared, her face turning innocent. "You wouldn't hit a woman," she said.

Jack slapped her hard in the face. Teeth flew out. Her hair was disheveled. Her world shook. Her cheek tore up, and her eyes widened so much they almost popped out of their sockets.

Yet, despite the strength of this hit, Jack still held onto her wrist. She had not been allowed to fly away. "That was for your parents, who failed to make you a good person," he said. His hand returned, slapping her in a strong backhand. Her head rocked as if about to unscrew from her torso. Her vision was blurry. Even a snake, when slapped like this, could lose their awareness.

"That was for my fellow disciples, whom you injured needlessly," Jack said coldly.

Sassa barely registered his words. She couldn't believe what was happening. She, who had always been prouder than anyone... was being slapped around?

The weight of this humiliation, when contrasted against her tall pride, made Jack's slaps contain a mental attack as well. She could no longer understand the world.

"And this..." Jack said, winding up his palm to strike even harder, "is for trying to blind me."

"Stop!" a voice echoed.

Jack ignored it. His palm crashed down, striking Sassa even harder, simultaneously releasing her hand and sending her flying into the distance. A line of blood trailed behind her, interspersed with teeth floating in the void.

A figure appeared her path, grabbing her gently. Elder Ocean himself glanced down at his disciple. Half her teeth were missing, her face was bloodied all over, and her eyes were shaken.

Physical marks could be repaired. Even teeth could be regrown.

However, such humiliation would never wash away. Her heart and pride were injured, and even her future cultivation might be affected.

"Junior!" Elder Ocean roared, his eyes filling completely with blue. "You went too far!"

The wrath of an A-Grade was overwhelming. Space shattered completely, time slowed, and his aura crashed down on Jack like a towering mountain. He felt like a mortal facing a god, a starved beggar naked in a blizzard. Yet, Jack was not afraid. If he succumbed when he was right, what use was his fist? He might as well relinquish it and go be a farmer.

Jack raised his head. "I saw an opponent two fruits above me and didn't dare hold back," he said. "Isn't that common practice in the cultivation world? If your disciple was seriously injured by the first move of a lower-level opponent, she can only blame her own weakness!"

The entire banquet was shocked silent. These were the exact words Elder Ocean had used to justify Sassa's cruel attacks on other cultivators. Now, the situation had been reversed, and his words were tossed into his face. Moreover, his direct disciple had been manhandled right in front of him.

If Elder Ocean wasn't completely incensed after this, he was not a person.

His aura rose further, actually revealing killing intent. "I yelled at you to stop! Why did not you stop?"

"Why would I take orders from you? I'm not your disciple."

This scene played out in front of everyone. The Church cultivators could barely believe this. A C-Grade disciple had not only reclaimed their lost honor, but he also used his words to slap an Elder's face—*twice!* Such boldness was unheard of! It was almost too much.

As for the Hand of God cultivators, they were simultaneously furious and wanted to find a stone to hide under. Let alone them, even their Elder had been humiliated. Just how would they recover from this?

Jack's face became extremely punchable to all of them. They could barely restrain themselves from rushing in and beating him to a pulp.

In truth, that was a result of Jack's Titan Taunt skill. It didn't just work with words, it taunted others by making Jack so grating in their eyes that they really, *really* wanted to tear him to pieces.

However, at the Elders' table, Heavenstar was conflicted. Jack had acted well... but then he'd gone too far, way too far! He'd directly insulted an Elder. No matter how talented he was, there was a limit to how much Heavenstar could defend him. This involved more than the life of a disciple—it involved the delicate balance between their two factions.

"Good, good, very good," Elder Ocean said, his words seething with fury. "You think you are above the law, above propriety. Let me tell you this, in the cultivation world, power is all that matters. Since you have dared to insult and challenge me, let's see if you can take my attack!"

The killing intent of an A-Grade was fully released. It gained absolute dominance over the surrounding hundred miles. The disciples at the banquet, be they C or B-Grades, couldn't even move a finger.

As for Jack, it went without saying that his body was immobilized. There was absolutely nothing he could do to resist. His entire life was a joke before such power. As a torrent of blue water rushed for him, ready to turn him into a sieve and kill him instantly, he could only watch.

"Enough..." a tired voice echoed through the void. A black-robed figure appeared before Jack. The pressure covering him disappeared, and the black-robed figure didn't even draw a weapon—by raising a single finger, the water aiming for Jack rotted away and disappeared. "Let all return to nothingness," Elder Boatman said, directly dispersing all of Ocean's pressure.

Elder Ocean was clearly outclassed, but that didn't mean he would take this lying down. He chuckled hoarsely. "You would step forward to defend this disciple, Boatman? Is he really worth that much to you?"

"Perhaps," Elder Boatman replied.

"Hah! Then, how will you repay me? Even if he died a thousand times, that still wouldn't make up for the insults he hurled at my face. No, Boatman, this cannot be allowed. If you don't help me find justice here, then I swear that I will never drop this issue!"

Things had already escalated past a simple banquet or expedition. Ocean was directly threatening to pursue this matter. That could involve large-scale battles between the two factions. At the same time, Boatman had already declared his intentions. If he stepped back now, that would be the same as ridiculing himself before so many disciples.

Even Heavenstar was nervous. He did not possess the qualifications to advise Boatman, but he knew what should be done. Concessions had to be made from both sides. The question was, would Boatman offer something precious enough that Ocean would accept to drop this issue?

The insults he'd received were quite heavy. No Elder would tolerate being mocked by a disciple!

However, even Heavenstar did not expect Boatman's next words. "You will not drop this issue? So what? You are nothing but a fart to me. If I say that you do not get to touch this disciple, then you will not touch him."

CHAPTER FIFTY-NINE
ELDER BOATMAN

HEAVENSTAR ALMOST SWALLOWED HIS TONGUE IN SURPRISE. BOATMAN WAS just too domineering. Not only did he make zero concessions, he directly threatened Ocean. This was lunacy!

"Consider this well, Boatman!" he sent into the other Elder's mind but got no response.

Ocean's face was warped in anger and humiliation. "How nice! Like master, like disciple! I want to see just how long you'll support your claims!"

"For as long as I want," Boatman replied, still with the same calmness as before. "You think you are above the law, above propriety. Let me tell you this: in the cultivation world, power is all that matters. Since you dare to insult and challenge me, how about you take one of my attacks first?"

Elder Ocean wanted to explode. He had never been so humiliated in his life. These were the exact words he'd used against Jack before, and now Boatman had tossed them in his face. It was the second time in a few minutes this happened.

In this world, there was nothing more aggravating than having your own words used against you.

Moreover, he couldn't even retort! He was a mighty A-Grade, but compared to Boatman, he was nothing but trash. He really didn't think he could take a single attack.

All disciples, regardless of faction, were shocked. As for the Church cultivators, they burst with excitement. Just seeing an A-Grade cultivator was already extremely rare. Seeing two of them argue so overbearingly was just unheard of!

As for Heavenstar, he was already sweating bullets. In his opinion, Boatman was going way too far. This wasn't just slapping Ocean's face. He was directly dragging that face into the dirt and stomping it for fun.

He was leaving zero room for retreat!

Heavenstar glanced at Purity just in time to see her disappear. She reappeared beside Ocean and faintly ahead of him, her pressure rising to meet Boatman's. For a moment, every inch of space within sight was a battlefield. Half the world turned white, the other black. Their two powers mixed like fire and water—completely unreconcilable.

Many people assumed that life and death were opposites. That was not the case. Those two were part of the same cycle, each completing the other. The true opposite to life and death was a bleached, perfectly clean world where nothing could survive—which was precisely Purity's domain.

Elder Ocean re-ignited his aura as well. Heavenstar sighed and appeared beside Boatman, he too unleashing his pressure. The entire world became a battlefield between A-Grades. Everyone else was equally excited and horrified—if the Elders actually came to blows, every single disciple present would perish in the aftermath.

As for Jack, he stood right behind Boatman, enduring no pressure at all. He seemed relaxed, while his mind was tense. The only reason he'd acted so wildly before was that Boatman had telepathically promised to protect him.

Jack hadn't expected Elder Boatman to be so damn domineering.

The moment he'd appeared, he'd escalated wildly and shown zero consideration for anyone. He was just as bold as Jack.

Even now, when the balance was so delicate, Elder Boatman hadn't considered giving away Jack for even a moment. The auras of the Elders struggled, no side coming out on top.

"Why do you insist so much?" Purity asked. "He is just a disciple. If you let us have him, I can kill any of my own to make it up to you."

Her own disciples drew cold gasps, especially the stronger ones. She'd just directly sold them out!

"No," Boatman flat-out refused. His aura didn't feel particularly stronger than Purity's, he just didn't give a damn.

However, as their auras were still warring, Boatman's darkness gained a slight edge. One had to look very closely to see it, but all Elders naturally noticed it.

"Then, how do you want to resolve this?" Purity asked, taking a mental step back.

"Your disciple harmed mine. My disciple harmed yours. Let everything be resolved."

He was proposing to just forget about the entire ordeal. Purity frowned. She'd already taken a step back, yet Boatman remained so resolutely domineering. "My disciples insulted no Elder," she replied. "Injuries are nothing, but honor is important. There is no balance here."

Boatman chuckled, a hoarse, grating sound. "I am the old one, but it is your vision that is blurry. Did Ocean not suppress, threaten, and attack my disciple? Was that not an insult of my honor? Or do you think that my honor is worth less than his?"

"Ocean was only reacting. It was your disciple that instigated this. Moreover, he is not even your personal disciple. In such a direct matter, Ocean had no need to consult you before acting as he saw fit."

"He is not my personal disciple? Hehe, let's see." Boatman turned around, showing his back to Purity and facing Jack. "Jack Rust. Do you want to be my disciple?"

Jack never in a thousand years expected to be asked anything. Moreover, Elder Boatman, this unfathomably powerful figure, had just asked him to be his disciple. This was not just referring to being part of the same faction. It was an offer of forming a direct master-disciple relationship.

What could he even say? "Okay," he responded, short-circuiting a little, and Elder Boatman turned back to the other Elders.

"He is my disciple," he said. "Ocean directly acted against my personal disciple in my presence."

Purity was speechless. Everyone was, for that matter. This was all too sudden, too dangerous. One wrong move here could spark an all-out war between the factions, and Boatman was just being wildly unreasonable?

Finally, Purity said, "Even you cannot act like this, Boatman. He clearly just became your disciple. He was not before. Ocean did nothing wrong. Your argument is invalid."

"Not invalid, just lessened," Boatman replied. "Of course, attacking my almost-disciple is not the same as attacking my disciple. Our side insulted yours more heavily. However, I am stronger than Ocean, so my honor is worth more. Balance is achieved. The two insults cancel out. Unless you want to fight me here, you had best accept this and we can all return to our seats. Otherwise, not only will you fail to achieve any compensation, but it will be me pushing for Ocean to compensate my disciple."

Elder Boatman just didn't give a shit about anyone. In his words, the sharp insults of Jack against Ocean were the same as Ocean insulting Boatman by attacking someone who later became his disciple.

Even Jack thought this unreasonable.

However, the world revolved around strength. And, at the end of the day, it was the Hand of God side that started everything by having Sassa purposefully injure the Church cultivators.

The Elders remained at a tense impasse for some time. Everyone held their breath. Boatman was clearly a lunatic, so if the Hand of

God didn't relent now, things might really come down to a battle. That would easily kill every disciple present, and what an unjust death it would be.

The minutes flowed on, nobody giving ground. Finally, Purity said, "Your words are not reasonable, but they are not unreasonable, either. Since the truth is unclear, let us not pursue this issue further. Otherwise, if we really escalate a C-Grade's running mouth to this degree, we will become the laughingstock of the universe."

"Well said!" Heavenstar hurried to respond before Boatman could say anything further. "Our two major factions may not be allied, but we have a long history of working together for hidden realms such as this. Ruining such a grand event over a few errant words would really be unjust."

With that, the Elders slowly retrieved their auras, and space returned to a silent calmness. No disciple dared make a peep, and the Elders didn't say anything further either. They simply teleported back to their seats, picking up their plates and drinks as if nothing happened. Even Ocean seemed to have completely forgotten about the previous incident. If he was someone partial to his own emotions, he would have never survived until the A-Grade.

"Let the banquet continue," Elder Boatman said, reclining back in his chair and returning to his motionless state. "Jack Rust, show everyone the might of my disciple."

Jack was speechless. "Yes, master," he replied, then returned a mile away from the banquet tables—the place used as the battle stage.

Did I just become the disciple of an A-Grade? Moreover, a powerful A-Grade? He gulped. *And a somewhat insane one...*

"Would anyone like to spar?" he asked, looking at the Hand of God cultivators.

Nobody moved. Then, a seven-fruit cultivator shook off his numbness and rose to his feet. "Please advise me," he said. He flew to the battle site and faced off against Jack. His Dao was the Sword, which he wielded expertly against Jack's fists. However, at the end of the day, he was unable to resist. It only took Jack two moves to send him flying, and that's because he was being polite.

Jack's power had increased tremendously in the last six months. The greatest factor of that was the world-creation vision he'd experienced while absorbing the World Anchor—by observing energy in its elementary forms, he now had a much clearer understanding of how it all fit together, which guided his Dao comprehensions and made his progress in that regard far faster than it used to be.

As a result, these low-level geniuses couldn't hold a candle.

"Who's next?" he asked calmly.

A second seven-fruit C-Grade took the stage. He tussled against Jack for three moves, then was tossed away.

"Who's next?" Jack asked again, not even panting.

The Elder face-off was still fresh in everyone's minds, and no one had forgotten the previous situation. Sassa had repeatedly declared, "Who's next?" and challenged the Church cultivators. The seven-fruits didn't want to stand up and get humiliated, and the eight-fruit ones didn't know if it was their turn to go. That kind of suppression had felt very bitter. The Church cultivators had been grinding their teeth, while the Hand cultivators had been glowering.

Now, thanks to Jack's strength, the situation had been completely reversed.

An eight-fruit cultivator took up the gauntlet. Jack activated his Life Drop, causing his strength to rise precipitously. With this new addition, the eight-fruit cultivator only lasted four moves. Even the second eight-fruit cultivator, who also happened to be the strongest one, could only resist Jack for ten moves.

Before, everyone thought Jack had gotten lucky by becoming a disciple of Boatman. Only now did they understand that Boatman's offer wasn't forced or random. Jack really deserved it. He was a freak!

Even the title of prime genius wasn't enough to do him justice.

A three-fruit cultivator had completely wiped the floor with the Hand's most elite eight-fruit disciples. This was unheard of. And, most of all, everyone wondered: Could Jack even face the nine-fruit ones?

Just like in the Cathedral, the Hand of God also placed heavy emphasis on its nine-fruit cultivators. Moreover, these were the top ten nine-fruits of the Hand of God. If Jack could face any of them, it would be ridiculous.

In truth, even Jack didn't know if he could fight them. His last ranking was 98, but that was six months ago. He'd developed a new fruit since then, gained some levels, and also tempered his body. He estimated his current strength to be near the top ten of the Cathedral, maybe a bit worse. He could struggle against the weakest of these nine-fruit cultivators, but it would reveal his full strength, and that was something he wasn't comfortable doing.

Moreover, after everything that happened, he felt he'd already stood out enough.

"Thanks for your guidance," he said. "I am out of energy, so I will return now."

Nobody believed he was out of energy, and nobody refuted him either. Jack returned to his seat, and since no nine-fruit had taken the stage yet, the banquet continued with the eight-fruits fighting each other. The seven-fruits had lost their turn, but none were in the mood to fight anyway.

"Well done," Brock said after Jack sat down. "I am proud. Grandpa Dead is good bro too."

Jack laughed.

No more ill play ensued, and all the following fights were splendid. Shi Mo defeated one opponent and gained great honor, though he lost immediately after. Nobody earned a winning streak. Finally, a few nine-fruits fought as well, but only those at the bottom of the rankings. Nobody on the level of Baron Longform or Min Ling wanted to exhibit their strength. The purpose of this banquet fight was to let the weakest people show off a bit and entertain everyone.

As the banquet carried on, many eyes remained glued on Jack. He ignored them, focused on either his exceptionally tasty food and drinks or on making small talk with Brock and Shi Mo.

Min Ling was also a disciple of an Elder—Elder Heavenstar—but her master was weaker than Jack's. That lit a fire in her heart. She now saw him as a full-on rival. Noticing her fervent gaze on Jack, Spacewind frowned deeply and his eyes revealed even deeper bitterness.

As for Baron Longform, he revealed no change of expression despite everything that happened. His thoughts were known to him alone.

After six hours, the banquet was over. The tables and chairs were gathered, everyone revolved their Dao to remove the intoxication of alcohol. The egg-shaped portal in the distance was all the more inviting.

It was time to enter the hidden realm.

Before that, however, Elder Boatman approached Jack. "Come with me," he said, then the two of them disappeared.

CHAPTER SIXTY
BOATMAN'S INHERITANCE

ELDER BOATMAN TOOK JACK AND TELEPORTED A THOUSAND MILES AWAY IN an instant, easily escaping everyone's perception.

As soon as they came to a stop, the Elder's hand left Jack's shoulder, and he took a step back. "Greetings, master," Jack said respectfully.

"I am not your master yet," Boatman said in his hoarse, aged voice. Below his hood, red eyes shone dark. His elderly voice carried some energy now. "You were forced to accept before. Now, you can speak your truth. Do you really desire to learn under this old man?"

Jack hesitated for only a single instant. He considered how he didn't really know anything about Elder Boatman, barring his obvious relation to the Dao of Death and his unyielding attitude. But those were enough. He decided to accept.

In that instant of hesitation, however, Boatman spoke again.

"You are an outstanding cultivator," he said. "A prime genius, with a soul tempered in adversity and a body tempered in life. You have already become one with your Dao—as long as you don't fall, your achievements will be limitless. Any A-Grade would jump at the opportunity to take you as their disciple. As for me, while I am stronger than most, what you should consider is not your master's strength, but your compatibility."

Jack remained silent, letting the Elder speak.

"I cultivate the Dao of Death," Boatman continued. "Life and Death are two sides of the same coin. It is the cycle we cultivate, the balance. Through my tutelage, you can take your Dao of the Fist in a direction that approaches this duality, achieving union between your body—Life—and your intent—Death. I can sense both of their seeds inside you. This path of duality suits you most."

Thoughts warred inside Jack. This was possibly the most important conversation of his life. He didn't dare speak before thinking it through.

"My temperament, you have already witnessed," Boatman continued calmly. "However, if you do choose to become my disciple, know that it will not be easy. I will help you increase your powers in every way possible, but I will not help you survive. Your battles will be your own. Only by overcoming all obstacles through your own power will you possess the qualifications to strive for the peak. There will be no way out, no way back. You will rise to the heavens or fall into hell."

Jack took a trembling breath. Visions assaulted his mind, of a future where he fought his way across bloody battlefields, used his power to ruin the stars. Life and death were a duality he wielded, everything balanced within his fist. But his enemies were even stronger. And only by surpassing them could he survive.

Elder Boatman saw his struggle. "If you do not wish to become my disciple, I will not force you, nor will I hold this against you. I will even help you find a more suitable master. Heavenstar likes helping young cultivators, and his methods are softer—perhaps he could be a better fit."

Jack snapped out of it. He looked with renewed sight at this terrifying, black-robed, red-eyed man, this avatar of death, and he laughed. The sound was booming and true, coloring space with rampant life. Suddenly, Elder Boatman did not seem like death anymore—more like a strict and wise old man.

"There is no need," Jack replied. "Ever since I became a cultivator, I have lived my life on the razor's edge. I have struggled against powerful enemies and survived all sorts of impossible situations. I have made enemies all over and carved my own path into the heart of my galaxy. I have clawed for my current strength one fist at the time. This constant battle you speak of, this crucible, is where I already live. It is where I thrive. This resolve to reach the top or die trying, I already possess it. That is already my path. And as for life and death, that is the road I have been traveling since the very start, my body holding life and my path filled with death. You speak of the compatibility between us, what compatibility could be greater than this?" His eyes flared fiercely. "Elder Boatman, it would be my honor to become your disciple!"

Elder Boatman smiled—and despite his pale skin and red eyes, despite his unfathomable power and strict exterior, Jack recognized that smile as similar to his own. The two of them were peas in a pod. In truth, ever since Jack understood Boatman's temperament, he'd admired him and wanted to study under him.

"Good!" Boatman exclaimed, his voice heavy with approval. "No hesitating, just like a disciple of mine should. Very good. Jack Rust, let me formally accept you as my disciple. There is little time, but it is enough."

He stretched out a pale, boney finger. A dark light shone on a yellow nail—and instantly, that light beamed into Jack's forehead, drilling deep into his brain. Jack screamed. The pain was too sudden.

"What was that?" he exclaimed.

Elder Boatman grinned under his hood. "My inheritance! Have at it! A cultivator like you would never stay put for too long. An inheritance that can follow you around is the best way to teach you. I have transformed the core of my insights into a seed and planted it inside your brain. You can freely meditate on it. Such access should accelerate your progress, completely making up for any deficiencies in your Dao and letting you advance quickly without ruining your foundation. Of course, that is only raw knowledge. Whether you can turn it into true power, or whether you die in the hidden realm, that will depend entirely on you."

Jack gripped his head. It felt like someone had poked their finger deep inside his brain, leaving a wound. Only now was the hellish headache receding, but he'd heard Boatman's words clearly.

He was excited.

"Thank you, master," he said through gritted teeth. "I will study hard."

"As you should. Take this as well." Elder Boatman flicked his finger, tossing a beam of light at Jack. He grabbed it instinctively. It was a dark cube. Black smoke wafted off it in thin streams, carrying an aura of death so intense that a mortal would die on sight. On closer inspection, its surface was covered by extremely thin lines, blending into the darkness so perfectly he almost hadn't noticed them at first.

"What is this?" he asked.

"A material formed of pure death energy. After all, my Dao is my own interpretation—it is not necessarily suited to you. This cube will be your main study material for the Dao of Death. The experiences I inserted into your brain can only serve as practical exams and something to contrast against. When meditating, you should focus on using your Dao to perceive the mysteries of this death cube, then comparing it against my insights to refine your understanding. That will give you the best foundation of the Dao of Death. As for the Dao of Life, you are already on its path. You will naturally progress even if you don't do anything. When the two are of similar levels, you will be able to combine them, take them as the twin foundation of your Dao, and then pierce your fist into the sky. After that, the direction you will move in will be your choice."

Jack didn't understand all that, but he suspected it would become clearer after a while. "Thank you, master," he said, putting the death cube into his space ring.

"One more thing," Elder Boatman said. "That cube is a very precious item... You should not reveal it to anyone, or even A-Grades might covet it. Moreover, I have left a wisp of my aura with the cube. It cannot perceive anything, but I will be able to sense its location anywhere, regardless of distance, even in space rings or hidden realms. If you perish, I will make haste to the site of your death and destroy everything in my path to retrieve the cube. Otherwise, I will not use your location in any other way, nor will I disclose it to anyone."

Oh, wow, Jack thought. *Elder Boatman uses cookies.*

"That's fine," he replied. "Thank you. I will take good care of everything."

"I certainly hope so." Boatman returned to his calm ambience. "After you exit the hidden realm and have made some progress, come find me. I will help you take your cultivation to the next level."

"Thank you, master," Jack repeated, bowing his head.

"Mm." Boatman nodded imperceptibly. "Let us return."

Space warped around them. Before Jack knew it, they'd returned to the entrance of the hidden realm, where everyone was staring at them. Brock's gaze was filled with pride. Min Ling's, curiosity, and Baron Longform's, envy. As for the Hand of God cultivators, all of them were indifferent.

"Sorry for the delay, everyone," Jack said. "I am ready."

"Good," Spacewind replied. "Let's go. Elders, we respectfully bid you goodbye."

Boatman remained still. Heavenstar nodded lightly, while on the other side, the Hand of God people went through a similar ritual. All the B and C-Grades flew into the egg-shaped opening. Jack's world was covered in colors. Soon, he was floating in a multicolored space, surrounded by all the other cultivators. Excitement and tension were thick in the air—nobody knew whether they would emerge stronger from this hidden realm or die inside.

The transition lasted for some time. Jack felt a weird sensation, as if he wasn't gliding through space but rather... falling into it? His

Dao of Space was nowhere near advanced enough to decipher the sensation.

Through this strange transition, a subdued voice reached Jack's mind. "Kid, who the hell was that?"

"Mm?" Jack's brows rose. "Turtle!"

"It's Venerable Saint Thousand Shell, damn your pathetic memory. And you didn't answer. Who the hell was that!"

"You can speak to me?"

Jack hadn't seen the turtle since he convinced it to let him make more Life stones a year ago. He wasn't aware that it could reach him without him being inside the Life Drop space, nor did he know it could perceive the world around him.

Though it seemed pretty obvious in hindsight.

"Master Boatman. An A-Grade," he replied, not hiding anything. *"He took me in as his disciple."*

The turtle stayed silent for a moment. *"That was a High Demigod. A late A-Grade, in the System's language. I... did not expect you to meet such characters so early."*

There was regret in its voice. Almost guilt. "Did he sense the Life Drop?" Jack asked.

"I am not sure. I activated the Supreme Blood's defenses as quickly as I could... He should not have sensed us. At most, he felt something was off, but that shouldn't be enough for him to take his disciple apart."

"I don't think he would do that," Jack replied.

"He would if he knew. The Supreme Blood is not as simple as a Life Artifact."

"Wait, what?"

"That doesn't matter. Not yet. He let you go—that's the important thing. And he gave you significant benefits, too... That bundle of insights inside your mind is not simple to create, even for a demigod. He sacrificed a part of his own cultivation to give it to you. And that cube... He certainly thinks very highly of you."

"Sacrificed a part of his own cultivation!" Jack drew a sharp breath. Elder Boatman had mentioned he'd help Jack with all of his power... He'd believed it was just a figure of speech. Who knew Boatman would be so crazy as to go all-out for someone he just met?

In fact, it was even a bit suspicious. Could it be that Boatman discovered the Life Drop and this was all a masterplan with... some sort of goal in mind?

I'm thinking too much, Jack thought, shaking his head. *I'll be careful, but being paranoid will just mud my Dao.*

"*You should avoid people of such power in the future,*" the turtle spoke again. "*My own power is very far away from theirs. I can use the sanctity of your soul and the Supreme Blood's defenses to hide our presence, but even the blood is not omnipotent. If you spend enough time around that master, he might catch on.*"

"I'll be careful," Jack promised. On one hand, he was scared now —on the other, extremely excited. The Life Drop was more than a Life Artifact? Wasn't that great news for him?

Plus, if a late A-Grade used part of their cultivation to give him something, how precious would that be? How helpful? And that was without mentioning the death cube, which even A-Grades might covet.

He'd grown so strong, yet he wasn't even close to the end of the road. He couldn't wait to start exploring all these possibilities.

Suddenly, the colors around him were torn away. Jack and the others emerged into a new space, and a loud roar welcomed them. This place... was not what they expected.

CHAPTER SIXTY-ONE
ENTERING THE HIDDEN REALM

THE HIDDEN REALM WAS AN ENDLESS JUNGLE.

Jack and the others—eighty-four cultivators in total—floated roughly five miles over the ground. Their vision stretched for hundreds of miles, thousands. Yet, all they saw was the green of lush jungles interspersed with lakes and other water bodies. The sheer number of trees was incalculable.

And that wasn't all. No matter how far Jack looked, there was no curvature. This was not a planet but an incredibly vast, flat piece of land—or a planet of greater circumference than he could calculate.

"What is this place?" he muttered, looking in all directions. "Hidden realms are so... alive!"

Beside him, Shi Mo was breathless. "No they aren't. Hidden realms are barren places where even space and time are broken. I have no idea what's going on here..."

That was surprising. Jack looked around, finding that almost everyone sported looks of confusion. Shi Mo was right. This was not what they expected.

"Spacewind," Min Ling said, arriving next to the Church expedition leader. Her normal distaste for him was covered by professionalism. "Any idea what's going on?"

"This must have been the inner world of a Life cultivator. An extremely powerful one."

"I thought so as well, but it doesn't explain why it's still green. The formation of a hidden realm takes a long time. Any remnant energy should have run out long ago, so the world should be on the verge of collapsing. Even if it was a peak A-Grade, there is a limit to how much energy their inner world can hold."

"I see two possibilities," Monk Uruselam said. His long white brows fluttered in the wind, and his ears flapped like wings. "One is that the former owner of this world was a powerhouse far eclipsing our imaginations. They must have been a peak A-Grade who managed to form an almost perfect energy circulation system. They were on the verge of transforming their inner world into a real one, which is why it could sustain itself for such a long time."

Everyone listened, waiting for the second possibility he mentioned. This first one seemed too far-fetched. Throughout history, peak A-Grades were extremely rare; could they really be so lucky as to stumble upon such a world?

"The second possibility," Uruselam said, drawing out his words, "is that this ancient powerhouse possessed a bottomless source of life energy. That would explain this world's continued survival, and it would match with the life attribute we can sense in the air."

Life in the air? Jack wondered. He expanded his senses, and indeed—the Dao of this world was different than what he was used to. The power of life was more vibrant, while all other Daos were subdued. In fact, the Dao of Life was so dense and prevalent here that Jack realized he was suffocating. He stopped breathing or he might start hyperventilating.

"I favor the second possibility," Spacewind said, echoing everyone's thoughts. "Even throughout history, peak A-Grades have been utmost existences, leaders of the universe. If this was the inner world of such a powerhouse, our diviners would have known."

"I agree," Min Ling said. "It's impossible for this senior to have been a peak A-Grade. They must have possessed some extreme treasure with an endless supply of energy. That would make the most sense. However, for their inner world to be this large, they still must have reached the A-Grade."

"How can the diviners have been so wrong?" Arkenstal wondered out loud. "They said it was the world of a peak B-Grade... but this is clearly far from the truth. For our experts to make such a mistake is unheard of."

"Does it matter?" Spacewind asked, his gaze sharpening. "Whatever the case, we are here now. This can be considered good news as well. If our factions knew the true Grade of this place, it would have never been our turn to enter. The dangers will far eclipse what we expected, but the opportunities should be massive as well. If we can survive, we will emerge reborn."

Somber silence fell over their group. Everyone digested this situation. As for Jack, he suddenly realized something: the portal was no longer behind them. It never had been.

"What the hell?" he asked.

"Hidden realms have jumbled-up space," Shi Mo explained. "The points of entry and exit are not necessarily at the same place. They could be anywhere."

"We have to locate an exit in this large place?"

"Yes... but there are usually multiple, and usually gathered inside the core areas. The B-Grades will discover them and summon us once it's time to leave."

Jack was about to ask more, when the jungle below split apart. A flock of birds flew at them. No, these weren't birds—they were dragons!

Draconic Sharpwing, Level 145 (D-Grade)
A bird possessing dragon ancestry. Thought long extinct, this species inherits the characteristics of their ancestors to achieve much greater strength than ordinary sharpwings.

That was a lot of information. The System was active here—did it come with them, or had it infiltrated the hidden realm when the portal came into System space?

However, these draconic birds were not the pressing issue. The flock was merely of the D-Grade, they were not a threat to anyone present, but they were random critters.

Spacewind waved his sleeve, slicing the birds into ribbons. "Everything here is at the D-Grade and above," he said, his expression grim. "We're only at the periphery, too. Any local overlords should be at the C-Grade, and the monsters at the core area could be anywhere up to the peak B-Grade. This place... is dangerous."

Uruselam laughed. "Since when do cultivators fear a bit of danger?"

"Feel free to be careless." Spacewind's voice was serious and commanding. "Listen to me, everyone. We may be enemies outside this place, but here, we cannot afford infighting. I want everyone to work together. All opportunities will be split fairly between those who find them. Am I understood?"

The Church disciples nodded. Uruselam said, "Spacewind is wise. The Hand of God will act exactly like that. No infighting."

Everyone agreed, and thus an alliance was formed. Of course, it was at best frail. People might split lesser opportunities, but they would fight to the death for greater ones.

"Be careful as you explore," Spacewind added. "The outer areas should not have B-Grade monsters, but you never know. If you notice anything out of place, make a run for it and mark the position down for later. We will help you gather the most difficult resources on the way back."

As if to punctuate his words, a roar echoed through the air. It was bass and powerful, speaking of extreme strength. The world pulsed to its rhythm. The weakest people present shook, while those with faster reflexes used their Dao to cover their ears.

Jack felt the blood within his body shiver as if attempting to flow backward. Whatever released this roar was far, far more powerful than him. Possibly at the B-Grade.

The Envoys were not shaken, but their eyes gleamed with thought. This monster couldn't necessarily threaten them, but it was clearly far from the core area. Then, how dangerous would that area really be?

Since ancient times, hidden realms always came with risks. It wouldn't be the first time that an entire expedition was wiped.

"Shall we, Spacewind?" Uruselam asked, waving to where the life energy was densest—where the core of this hidden realm was located. That place would hold the greatest dangers and opportunities... Unfortunately, it was not somewhere Jack could go. With his current strength, dominating the outer areas would already be a challenge.

"We shall," Spacewind replied. "Min Ling, I leave the C-Grades to you. Make the Church proud. For Enas."

"For Enas," Min Ling replied.

Spacewind and Uruselam transformed into beams of light, diving deeper into the realm at speeds Jack could only dream of following. All other B-Grades rushed after them. Soon, they were gone, and the only people remaining were the sixty C-Grades, thirty from each faction.

"Alright, everyone," Min Ling said as she and Arkenstal took charge. "We will now split up and look for our lucky chances. With such thick life energy in the air, this place should be a treasury... Just remember to be careful. The dangers will be high, and lucky chances are seldom left unguarded. Only act if you have certainty of success."

"And no infighting," Arkenstal added. "This place will be difficult enough by itself. The last thing we need is cultivators stabbing each other in the back. Anyone found guilty of such behavior will be punished."

Everyone nodded. People were already looking left and right, wondering which direction held the most treasures. Seeing that, the leaders didn't hold them.

"Dismissed," they said, and everyone split up, flying away in groups of one to three people.

"I wish you luck," Shi Mo told Jack and Brock, preparing to fly off on his own. "The B-Grades carry communication devices. They will contact everyone when the exits are found and it's time to leave. Until then... do your best!"

"Good luck," Brock replied, and Shi Mo turned into a gust of wind and flew away.

Most people had already left, so Jack and Brock also chose a direction. They took off, the heavy winds pushing against their faces and making Jack's robes flap.

After a while, all other cultivators had been left far behind. Jack and Brock were alone, two bros flying over an endless jungle filled with danger and treasure.

What could possibly be better?

"How are you feeling, Brock?" Jack asked, giving his little brother a toothy grin.

"Never better," Brock replied. "Let's adventure!"

"Haha! Let's!"

They accelerated, heading even deeper. Their current direction was toward the center of this world—while the actual core area was too dangerous, they had the strength to explore just outside that. The closer to the center one went, the greater the danger would be, and the greater the opportunities.

Therefore, the sixty cultivators spread across the hidden realm, with the weaker ones remaining near the edges and the stronger ones closer to the center.

Jack and Brock flew for a while before making sure nobody was around them. No matter how the leaders prohibited infighting, only a fool would believe them.

Then, they flew closer to the ground, slowing so they could scan the jungle. However, their Dao perception was unneeded. It wasn't long until they discovered a large tree sticking out of the canopy.

Even from a distance, they could make out a gargantuan shape wrapped around this tree. It was a real dragon.

Jack and Brock couldn't contain their excitement. They were two bros adventuring together. They would have the time of their lives!

CHAPTER SIXTY-TWO
FIGHTING DRAGONS

Jack and Brock surveyed the situation from afar.

A tree larger than the rest stood out from the jungle. Its trunk rose a thousand feet into the air, and it was thick enough that even a dozen people together couldn't hug it. Its canopy was dense with leaves, each of which radiated life energy.

The real prize were its fruits. There were four, hanging close to the trunk. Each was perfectly round, containing enough energy that, by all means, they should have exploded long ago.

In nature, many things contained the power of the Dao. Even a simple apple contained life energy. As for heavenly treasures like these fruits, their energy was a trillion times greater than an apple's. Unfortunately, even though energy was abundant, most natural resources could not be consumed. Their energy was suited for them alone. Eating them would be the same thing as a mortal trying to eat rocks.

Those were not real treasures. At most, they were pretty to look at or could be used indirectly for minor benefits.

Some resources, however, contained a rare attribute: the energy they gathered was pure enough to resemble the ambient Dao and could be directly absorbed by cultivators. They were far more effective than Dao stones. When such resources were discovered, they were heavily sought-after, but their growth period was usually extremely long. Growing them was too difficult. The easiest way was to discover them in a hard-to-access location—for example, a hidden realm.

These were the so-called lucky chances that everyone was searching for. And these four fruits, as they proudly hung from the tree, were certainly such treasures. Despite being slightly life-oriented, Jack could sense the purity of their Dao blowing over him like a gentle breeze, opening his pores and begging him to absorb it.

"Here we are, Brock," he said. "This place really is filled with lucky chances. We only flew for half an hour and already ran into one."

"Hmm. Yes. But I think the dragon will not be happy."

There was a gargantuan brown dragon coiled around the tree. From afar, its scales looked like bark, while its great body must have been almost a mile long. Though asleep, a corrosive aura surrounded it, warning anyone against approaching.

They were currently far enough away that they could see the dragon but not reach it with their Dao perception. Naturally, it couldn't reach them either, so it was blissfully unaware.

"How could it be easy?" Jack said, shaking his head. "We can use these treasures to cultivate, but so can spiritual beasts. It's already lucky that we chanced upon the fruits as they are about to mature. This dragon must have kept watch for a long time, waiting for the fruits to reach their optimal state before consuming them. It didn't let anything else eat them; that's our luck."

"But it must be strong," Brock said. "Big bro of this area."

"I can take it. I'm not close enough to inspect it, but its aura isn't too powerful. And, even if it is, I am confident we can run away."

"Okay. Let's go."

"Yes."

They flew closer. The jungle was just below them now, their feet almost scraping the canopy. The tree loomed closer in their sights. Before long, they had approached close enough to scan the dragon.

??? Level ???
Unknown species. Compiling observations. Please wait.

Really damn useful, Jack thought, but it didn't matter. He had been outside System space for a long time now. He was used to estimating his opponent's power level through their aura—and his estimation told him this dragon was a late C-Grade.

Powerful, but not enough.

As Jack's perception reached the dragon, so did its own reach them. Its eyes opened. Dark green irises were revealed underneath, matching the bark-like skin. Was this a tree dragon?

It did not look happy.

"Hello, bro," Brock said, in case this creature could speak.

"Cultivators..." the dragon replied. Its voice was a deep bass, almost scratchy as if two branches were scraping each other inside its throat. Dark green fumes left its mouth every time it spoke, and sharp teeth were revealed. "My kin have sensed your arrival. You are destroying our jungle and killing us. Have you come to steal my fruits?"

"We are no thieves," Brock replied, then sighed deeply. "But... these are not your fruits. They belong to you because you strongest. Now, we strongest. That is the truth. Please, dragon bro, step aside."

The dragon stared deeply at them. Its eyes turned to Jack, who remained silent with a billowing aura. It could not see through his strength clearly, but it sensed he was weaker than it was. As for the speaking brorilla, it was even weaker.

The dragon's irises narrowed. Its huge maw opened wider, revealing the sharp teeth in full and a deep, dark throat. Dark green spit flew out—anything it touched sizzled and disappeared, corroded. "THIEVES!" it roared, its voice impacting them like a sonic wave. Leaves blew wildly, branches shook, small trees were uprooted. The dragon's roar echoed into the ground and air, reaching the ends of the world.

Jack expected this. He geared up for battle, summoning his Life Drop battle form. As two new arms grew under his armpits, the dragon showed no surprise.

"Since you dared to come," it growled, "you will never leave."

A torrent of dark green flew out of its mouth. Jack and Brock teleported away. An entire line of flora melted where the dragon's breath hit, creating an empty expanse. The dragon uncoiled its upper body. Two bark wings spread from its back, and its large form stood against the sky.

Jack snorted. "If you want to fight, we'll fight. Meteor Punch!"

The world darkened under his might. The ambient energy for several miles gathered around his fist, then exploded. The dragon took the fist head-on—its head was flung backward, but it endured. Sap bled out through a crater on its forehead.

While Jack was impressed, he refused to let up. Space shattered under him, his body flitting around the dragon and pelting it with attacks. Its defense was extraordinary, but so was Jack's endurance. Meanwhile, the dragon was madly clawing and biting, unable to touch him. He was like a wasp stinging it to death.

The dragon roared.

"Big bro!" Brock exclaimed. He stood farther away, as he didn't have the strength to participate in this battle, but how could it be so simple?

The jungle ground was covered with ferns. Neither Brock nor Jack had paid any special attention to them, but now, those plants were transforming. They pulled themselves out of the ground. The fern leaves were their wings, stones made up their fangs, and intertwined roots composed their bodies.

These were dragons.

Jack glanced at them.

Draconic Twig, Level 240 (D-Grade)

Roots taken draconic shape. These plant lifeforms like to cover vast areas, pretending to be harmless ferns. They do not attack others as they can sustain themselves through photosynthesis and absorbing nutrients from the soil. Their cultivation is passive and long. However, their minds are connected, and they all attack together if they sense danger.

Most Draconic Twigs are at the F and E-Grades. Through unknown means, this particular specimen has achieved far greater power. Due to their high numbers, caution is advised.

Jack drew a cold breath. In this place, even random plants were late D-Grade lifeforms. Just who could have such an inner world!

"Destroy them, my children!" the dragon roared, going all-out against Jack. It couldn't strike him, but it could keep him occupied while the twigs handled Brock.

Jack didn't mind. He clenched his four fists, shooting a barrage of Meteor Punches at the dragon as he chipped away its defenses. The bark scales were torn off, revealing wood-like skin underneath. Sap flowed from its wounds, and creaks followed its every movement.

Unfortunately for the twigs, Brock was also stronger than he looked. A book appeared in his one hand and a staff in the other. His entire body emitted golden radiance.

"We are stronger, but you refuse to yield," he declared solemnly. "That is un-bro-like. Shame!"

His voice smashed into the swarm of roots flying at him. They shook. Many fell from the sky, their minds consumed by illusions, while many more gave pained shrieks and started convulsing. The portion of twigs that were unaffected flew at Brock, their claws extended and their root jaws opened wide to crush him.

He drew back. His Staff of Stone became a dazzling gold as he smashed it down, felling the draconic twigs by the swathe. They swarmed him. He was too powerful. Jaws broke against his golden skin, and his staff sent dozens flying with each swing. In his other hand, the book shot out golden beams, paralyzing anything it hit.

Brock was a golden god in a sea of devils. He roared. His brorilla instincts surfaced. Twigs broke left and right, and though their numbers were endless, he did not seem the least bit tired. Even if they could eventually take him down, they would suffer extreme casualties.

Seeing this, the dragon showed hints of worry. "Children!" it roared, ignoring Jack and trying to fly Brock's way. As more and more of its body uncoiled from the trunk, Jack saw that it had no tail—the back end of its body was embedded into the tree, as if this entire dragon was a branch.

Only now did Jack realize that the dragon and the tree were the same creature. Magnificent. How the hell does that work?

There was no time to think. The dragon was headed for Brock. Jack punched space and teleported before the dragon, facing it like an ant against a giant. "Move!" the dragon roared, spitting a long breath of poison directly at him. There was no dodging this—if he did, the poison breath would fall onto Brock, who was too busy fighting to teleport.

Jack's gaze sharpened. His fists unclenched. His palms grabbed the air before him, and then, with a mighty roar, he pulled to the side.

The world twisted. The fabric of space itself had been pulled by Jack, stretched, so that what seemed like a straight line no longer was one. The poison breath changed its course, passing him and veering off to the side. He'd manipulated not the breath, but the space through which it flew.

This was Jack's Space Mastery!

The dragon came to a stop, its eyes widening. It had not expected such a usage of space. In truth, since its body was one with the tree, it couldn't fly too far away. It couldn't reach Brock. The only way to act against him was to shoot out poison breaths, but there was no meaning if Jack could just steer them away.

Behind Jack, Brock was still fighting off the draconic twigs. They broke with every hit of his staff. Though they didn't die immediately, as long as they jumped back into the fray and were hit a couple more times, they really would shatter.

And there was nothing the dragon could do about it.

"Enough!" it roared, its voice eclipsing the wind. "Stop! You win! Don't slaughter my children!"

The twigs froze, then retreated as quickly as they could. Brock was suddenly left alone, hovering like a victorious golden god. "Took you long enough," he said. "Sorry for harming your children. They attacked me first."

The dragon did not reply. Its body remained uncoiled and outstretched, its eyes exuding hatred. Yet, they also carried a hint of surprise.

"You stopped?" it asked in confusion. "Why?"

"Because you asked us to," Jack replied. "You gave up. Why would we kill you?"

"You are cultivators. You want my fruits. You want to kill me."

"I think you have the wrong idea about cultivators."

"Don't try to trick me," the dragon replied, its eyes wide in anger. "My kin is slaughtered by your people as we speak. Destruction is everywhere. You brought war and steel, killing us to steal our power!"

Jack frowned. "I am not them, nor can I control them. If other cultivators are killing your dragons across the jungle, that is regrettable, but neither can I stop them. As for me and Brock, we have no desire to kill anyone. We just want your fruits."

He glanced at the tree's base, where the tree and dragon merged as one. Since the two were the same creature, he could no longer claim that the dragon was in possession of the fruits because it was the strongest creature around. They really did belong to it. Suddenly, wanting to take them seemed a bit... unfair.

Brock stepped up. "We understand. We do not want to harm you. However, you are a tree, and these are your fruits. We want them. Let us have them, and we promise not to attack you anymore. We will also promise to plant the seeds in good location, so your tree children can grow big and safe."

The dragon gazed at them with deep suspicion. "You lie," it growled. "You will cut me down and use my body for alchemy. You will take my bark, my sap, my leaves, and my roots. You will tear me to pieces and destroy me, as the rest of your kind does."

"We will not do that," Brock replied calmly.

"Why should I believe you?"

"Because you have no choice."

That was the sad reality. The cultivation world was not a kind place. Everyone killed each other for treasures, and to abstain from that was to doom yourself to weakness. Jack and Brock were no saints. Even if the fruits belonged to the tree, they would still take them.

The dragon seethed in silent fury. Its gaze bore deep into theirs, as if trying to see their souls. After some time had passed, it finally agreed. "Fine. I will not fight you to the death. Take my fruits—but you must promise to leave the rest of me unharmed!"

"We promise," Jack and Brock replied.

The dragon drew back to the tree. Its claws rose toward the fruits, then pulled them out. It did not seem to feel any pain. Magical or not, trees were trees. The purpose of their fruits was to be consumed by others and have the seeds inside planted somewhere nice.

One dragon claw holding four fruits approached Jack and Brock, who took two each and placed them in their space rings. The claw drew back. Jack and Brock bowed lightly.

"Thank you," Jack said. "We will plant the seeds at a good place. We promise."

The tree dragon was clearly still on edge. "You really will not attack me?"

"Of course not," Brock replied. "Taking your fruits is one thing. Killing you and selling your body as materials is another. We are not monsters."

The dragon tree's eyes shimmered. "You... are not too detestable.

Better than the rest of you, anyway. Go. My fruits were my greatest treasures, but they will regrow. With them taken, no other hated cultivator will try to fight me. The rest of my body is not as precious."

"Thanks, tree dragon bro," Brock said, then looked to the ground, where the hundreds of draconic twigs still stared at him in apprehension. "Sorry for hitting you, little bros. Grow big and strong."

The two of them flew away. The dragon's gaze followed them for a long time. Then, it slowly closed its eyes and coiled back around the trunk, falling into the deep slumber that trees enjoyed.

The twigs dug back into the ground. They did not sleep yet. Their species formed a network covering a large part of the jungle, and their minds were all connected. Just like others had informed them of violent and destructive cultivators, these twigs also informed their kin about Jack and Brock, who were more reasonable than most.

CHAPTER SIXTY-THREE
INSPECTING THE DEATH CUBE

SPACEWIND CROSSED THE AIR. URUSELAM FLEW BESIDE HIM, WHILE THE other twenty-two B-Grades followed.

Their speed was tremendous. The jungle blurred below, and the clouds passed by and disappeared in seconds. There were many occasions when jungle creatures flew up to attack them, but they were all easily obliterated.

These twenty-four people each possessed the power to crack planets. They were not a procession that could be stopped.

After flying for many hours, Spacewind focused. "We're here."

A massive temple rose in the distance. Or, perhaps it was more accurate to call it a mountain. Its height reached ten miles into the sky, easily piercing the clouds, while its base stretched for dozens of miles all around. It was made of precisely cut stone, so that it really did resemble a temple, except gargantuan.

The closer the B-Grades approached, the more apparent the temple's size became. It really was a massive mountain that someone had carved into a temple. The effort poured into this was insane.

Then again, since this place used to be someone's inner world, many impossible things could happen.

The group stopped before the temple. They were mere bugs in the face of a massive tree—completely inconsequential. No matter how they looked, they were unable to see the its roof or sides. It simply took up their world.

Of course, as B-Grades, they possessed Dao perceptions that could cover the entire temple. Its shape was clear in their minds—a glided rooftop of valley-sized bricks, surrounded by miles of religious carvings. Some displayed gods, some demons, some mortals. In such lengthy engravings, all sorts of scenes could be found, but the general theme was about a massive dragon helping the world prosper. This dragon laughed with gods, killed devils, and was worshiped by mortals. Perhaps it was a god itself, but the drawing style indicated that was not the case.

"More dragons," Spacewind muttered, closing his eyes to better inspect the temple.

"Nature is beautiful," Uruselam said, cupping his hands. "We pay our deep respects, Elder Dragon. It is need that led us here, not desire. Please take no offense as we enter your temple to look for our survival. We will try to leave everything intact."

He bowed. Everyone followed, including Spacewind, though he snorted coldly on the inside.

He was familiar with Uruselam. This was a monk-looking individual who possessed no grace at all. No matter what he said now, he would rob this place clean and take away even the floor tiles if they were precious.

Places like this often contained hints of their creator's will. Speaking pretty words couldn't hurt.

The base of the temple was one with the ground, since it was originally a mountain, and its roof was covered in large bricks. Its sides and back were lined with gigantic columns, each multiple miles high and hundreds of feet in diameter. Behind those columns was a wall, indicating that one should not enter from there.

The only place not covered by that wall was the front of the temple, but it did not have a door. Rather, it was a wall of flat stone riddled with holes. In that sense, the entrance of the temple was more like a beehive than an actual entrance.

On closer inspection, there were ninety-nine circular holes, each ranging from a hundred feet to half a mile in diameter. The space inside was pitch-black, and, as the B-Grades tried to scan it with their Dao perception, a mysterious force stopped them.

"It's blocked," Uruselam said, furrowing his brows. His voice grew more earnest, dropping the monk facade a bit. "We should be careful. This is the inheritance of an A-Grade—any defenses still operating can easily destroy us all."

"Are you going to chicken out?" Spacewind asked.

"Of course not. Since we are here, we may as well experience this senior's methods."

Uruselam cupped his hands again, while Spacewind bravely gazed ahead. As his title indicated, he specialized in space and speed. If anything went wrong, he had the highest chances of surviving.

The B-Grade group approached the temple's entrance. They chose a hole that was three hundred feet in diameter—neither too large nor too small. They stopped a mile away.

"Let me test it," Uruselam said. Muttering some incoherent prayer, the phantasmal image of a golden buddha appeared behind him. This buddha extended its arm, which grew impossibly long, all the way until it reached the entrance of the hole. It tried to enter. A pale green barrier appeared out of thin air, blocking the hand's advance.

"There is an energy barrier," Uruselam said, "and it is not offensive."

"The same barrier covers all the holes," Spacewind added. He had been observing the entire temple just now, and he saw the same green light flicker everywhere. "There is no other way in. We have to get past this barrier."

"With the grace of the Immortals, we will succeed," Uruselam prayed again.

Spacewind gave him an odd look. "Since you possess their grace, how about you attack first?"

"This old monk already scouted the barrier. My friend Spacewind doesn't need to be modest—fell free to participate."

Spacewind cursed inwardly. They remained a mile away. By now, it had become clear that breaking this barrier was their only way forward, and there was no visible core or weakness to tamper with. They could only resort to brute-force.

He drew out a long sword, then casually swiped it out. A wave of black energy was emitted from the blade, shaped as a sword slash, which impacted against the distant barrier.

This was in no way Spacewind's all-out attack. It was just a light probing strike, but it still contained the power to slice through a normal mountain range. Yet, as this black slash rushed forth, the barrier only flickered slightly. The blade dissipated like a stone thrown into the sea, and the barrier shone for a brief moment before turning invisible again.

"No counterattack," Spacewind observed. "Its defensive properties are remarkable, but its regeneration is a bit too slow. If we all combine forces and constantly attack the barrier, we could overwhelm its regeneration and whittle it away. What do you think, Uruselam?"

The old monk thought for a second. "Brilliant observation. With everyone working together, I believe it should only take us a few days. There seems to be no danger, either."

"Good." Spacewind nodded.

Twenty-four B-Grades joining forces to slowly break apart a single barrier was not a noble sight. Yet, it was all they could do. This place was meant for A-Grades, or at least peak B-Grades. These twenty-four people were all at the early B-Grade. Just being able to enter was fortunate.

As things had turned out, Spacewind and Uruselam had no illusions of grasping this temple's core inheritances. They would be satisfied with any tiny opportunity they could get—at the level of this temple's creator, even the items they casually left around would be considered massive lucky chances to an early B-Grade.

The twenty-four of them organized into four teams of six. The teams would take turns attacking the barrier with their full power, changing every hour. At their level, nobody needed to sleep or even rest much. By constantly attacking, in just a few days, they would break the barrier and access the temple.

The potential treasures inside made even people like them salivate.

Deep inside a vibrant jungle, beneath a thousand-foot waterfall, was a tiny cave. It was only recently created. The stone walls were rough and sloppy, while no moss or insects had infiltrated it yet.

This cave was the temporary dwelling of two people: Jack and Brock.

After taking the four fruits of the tree dragon, they'd adventured for another three days. Nothing important occurred. They ran into a few lucky chances, but none comparable to the dragon fruits.

As for those fruits, Jack and Brock had long consumed them. The energy they contained was pure and massive. It had pushed Jack's third fruit closer to maturity, while Brock had just developed his own third fruit.

Right now, for a short period of time, the two of them were at the same boundary. Jack's happiness was hard to put into words.

But their goal here wasn't just to hunt lucky chances. They would remain in this hidden realm for an unknown amount of time—and Jack, who had recently received Elder Boatman's insights and death cube, had many things to meditate on.

The waterfall crashed down hard, spraying moisture into the air.

Inside the cave, Jack and Brock sat cross-legged on opposite ends, each sunk into their own meditation.

Brock was taking inspiration from the dense life energy in the atmosphere to tackle the Dao of Life.

Jack sat cross-legged, a small dark cube held between his hands. His fingers traced its surface, going from side to side, touching the edges. The cube was so black it sucked in the light, making it almost impossible to see clearly. However, Jack's perception could capture extremely shallow lines on its surface.

There were exactly 999 lines. Each formed a complete circuit, with no beginning or end. Some were short, and some were long. Some were straight, while others were curved or even tied into knots. These lines intersected into infinite shapes, forming patterns that were completely random and pointless, or at least seemed so.

Though Jack had this cube for three days, this was the first time he seriously inspected it. He was puzzled. Just what was this cube's secret?

His perception sank inside, reaching the cube's very core but finding only stone. There was nothing there. Even its surface was nothing but carved stone. Then, where did its aura of death come from?

What a riddle... he thought, his excitement rising. Cultivators pursued knowledge, therefore, they yearned for the unknown. Facing this cube that should contain nothing magical yet clearly emitted a powerful death aura, he was nothing but expectant.

Is it the material? he wondered. It did seem suspicious. Jack's perception was able to detect even the tiniest imperfections, the tiniest marks on the stone. Yet, in that sharp perception, this stone was completely natural. There was no sign that anyone had cut it into a cube or carved its surface. It was like this perfect cube had sprang into existence in its current state.

But that was impossible.

Or was it?

Even on Earth, all sorts of materials came with angles. Crystals, ore... It wouldn't be impossible for one of them to be shaped as a perfect cube, accurate to the atom. Extremely unlikely, sure, but not impossible. Then, if that material remained in a volatile area for a long time, it wouldn't be surprising for random marks to appear on its surface.

Of course, for those marks to be exactly 999 and have no ends, there had to be magic involved. Plus, even if the cube was placed at the bottom of the sea, there would always be one side touching the soil. How could all six of its sides be equally engraved?

On the other hand, if it was artificial, there would certainly be some evidence.

The origin of this cube was too mysterious. Even the material it was made of was a mystery to Jack. It felt like a particularly hard stone. As for its color, that was even more of a mystery; even the dark void of space wasn't that black. Back on Earth, he'd once visited his university's chemistry labs and witnessed vantablack, an artificial color that absorbed over ninety-nine percent of light. Even that vantablack was a sun before this thing.

Moreover, light was energy. Something that absorbed all light should be burning hot, but this stone was cool to the touch, even chilly.

Chilly like death.

Jack took a deep breath. He calmed his mind and closed his eyes, entering deeper meditation. His perception focused on the cube, observing every edge, every side, every line. He wanted to map those lines. He could sense that whatever secret this cube contained, the lines were the clue.

Everything else disappeared completely. The lines became his entire world, all 999 of them. Each was unique. They curved differently, had different depths and widths at various points, and they intersected with all others in a million ways.

Jack may have had an enhanced mind, but this was just too much.

He focused on one line chosen at random. It started around a corner of the cube, heading to the center of one side and then dipping back to its origin to form an oval shape. Simple. Easy. A great starting point.

His mind observed this line with the intensity of a C-Grade. Yet, it was a line. There wasn't much to observe.

He persisted. His perception dug deeper. He followed the line in a full cycle, then another. It started off shallow, then deepened gradually. It was narrow then wide, finally reaching its limit. It intersected with another line; this wasn't its first intersection so far, but there was something different about it. It was violent. Hard. Jagged. Like the two lines had clashed against each other. The other line continued, getting slightly deeper, but Jack's line seemed to lose its vigor. It grew shallow. Thin. It stopped advancing and dipped back, running parallel to its previous course to reach what Jack considered its starting point, the thinnest and shallowest it had been.

It made a full circle.

Jack paused. His forehead was wrinkled. There was something there. Did the line represent a life? It had grown stronger until it clashed against another line, lost, then weakened until it died and returned to its starting point?

What exactly was its meaning?

CHAPTER SIXTY-FOUR
NIHILITY

Something inside Jack stirred. Some nascent understanding raised its head, too weak to take shape but still present. His mind returned to the cube's lines almost by itself as if drawn to their mysteries.

He followed one line, then another. He branched out, letting his mind wander freely, not sticking to one line but changing at every intersection. He was no longer following, he was swimming. And as his mind curved around the cube, guided by all these lines, Jack felt as if he'd grasped onto a heavenly secret.

These lines he followed seemed random, but they were not. By sticking to them, his mind moved to a certain rhythm, as if tracing an invisible path that shouldn't be part of the world. As if he was interacting with something that wasn't there. These revolutions he carried out contained profound secrets, things he could just barely glimpse. Thoughts were born, spawning out of thin air. They were not his. Not exactly.

By tracing the lines of the cube, he made his brain follow very specific patterns which activated areas he was unaware of and formed novel connections. It felt like hacking his own brain. These connections made no sense, they were sounds and colors, striking chords inside Jack that made him melancholic. His emotions acted up. And suddenly, through all these puzzling emotions and sensations rose a deep, intimate understanding of death.

He didn't know how this was happening. He barely knew what was happening. Yet, through tracing these lines and trying to understand them, an awareness of Death gradually took shape in his mind.

Jack was stunned. His focus wavered for just a moment, and all the intricate meanings of the lines evaporated at once, becoming nothing but carvings on a stone.

"Life and Death are one," he whispered. "They are a cycle. One rises, one falls, and both connect to the same spot. They will always connect. Death is just the inevitable conclusion. What starts must finish. What rises must fall."

His eyes widened in realization. This was... Death?

Through meditating on this cube, Jack had directly comprehended the essence of Death. It was an infinitely small part, but it remained something that had been planted into his mind. Throughout his cultivation so far, everyone said that true understanding could only be achieved, not received.

Yet, this little dark cube had come dangerously close to directly carving its knowledge inside Jack's mind.

It was almost terrifying—and, at the same time, fantastical.

Just what is this thing? Jack asked himself. *How could anyone make this? Is it even possible?*

This item was extremely mystical. Jack didn't even know the right questions to ask, let alone the answers. Could Elder Boatman's achievements in the Dao of Death originate from this little cube?

Every high-level cultivator had their own lucky chances. The higher one went, the more world-shaking the lucky chances they'd discovered in their youths. This cube might have been the cause of Elder Boatman reaching the A-Grade... or it could have been something he created.

In any case, it was an extremely precious item. Only now did he understand why Elder Boatman had to leave a wisp of his aura with the cube, and why he would directly come to retrieve it the moment Jack died.

Jack's chest swelled with gratitude.

Thank you, master! he cried out inwardly. And it wasn't even the only gift he'd received.

The new insights he'd just gained were a bit too base. They were closest to the essence of Death, which made them hard to wield in battle. Jack had to view them through the lens of his own Dao and experiment until he discovered practical applications—and there was no guarantee his method would be optimal.

However, Elder Boatman had anticipated this, and directly given Jack his own insights. Jack was too excited to think anymore. He dove into his mind, reaching that ball of knowledge and sinking into it. His world fell away, becoming an endless river of darkness floating alongside the stars, filled with ghosts and ethereal bodies. Some were crying, others were laughing, and most seemed indifferent or even sleeping.

A man sat in the middle of that river, letting the dark waters wash over him. He had pale, wrinkled skin and red eyes. As his mouth opened and closed in an unknown incantation, Jack saw sharp fangs protrude from his lips.

Elder Boatman is a vampire?

But that wasn't important. Vampires were just one of the many species in the universe. Elder Boatman stood. His eyes locked onto a distant meteor passing over the river. He raised one finger, and the dark waters flowed around it, forming a little ball of death.

"Nihility," Boatman whispered. He flung the dark ball away, which reached the meteor in an instant. There was no explosion, no impact. Instead, the meteor dissipated. Endless years passed it by. Its form cracked and splintered, becoming a hail of stones which experienced their own death, turning into tiny particles that were no longer visible.

Boatman smiled. "Everything ends as it begins. What rises must fall. What is must cease to be. Let everything return to nothingness."

That was where the vision cut off. Jack was back in his own body in the cave, sweating. There had been no danger watching this illusion, but the dark river gave Jack a feeling of imminent death. If he visited there in person, he would die as soon as he touched the water, his soul just another ethereal remnant flowing along its waters.

There were more Dao Visions inside the ball of insights. However, Jack didn't watch them yet. This first one was enough. In it, Boatman had used the purest energy of death to make a meteor disappear. It was the basest, simplest application of death.

The perfect starting point.

Jack had an elementary awareness of death and a simple yet optimized application. All he needed to do was meditate on the cube and this Dao Vision alternatingly until, eventually, he could use the Dao of Death himself.

This was traveling a hundred miles with a single step. Having an A-Grade master truly made cultivation much simpler.

Jack sighed, then sank into meditation. There was no time to waste—he was impatient to learn. Time flowed. Jack and Brock meditated on their own things, one on death and one on life, forming a complete system. The inside of the cave turned half-black and half-white around their two bodies, like the shadow of a yin-yang diagram.

Neither noticed the phenomenon. They were too deep in meditation. Still, this was a happy accident, as the antithesis sharpened their respective Daos, making them clearer.

Eventually, Jack raised his hand. A tiny pebble flew into it. He stared at the pebble, deep in concentration, trying all sorts of things. Then something clicked inside his mind. His lips parted. "Nihility..." came a low whisper, and the pebble crumbled like a pile of dust blown by the wind.

Jack showed the slimmest smile.

Before he could truly rejoice, a massive roar echoed through the cave. The yin-yang diagram dissipated. Jack shot to his feet, and Brock's eyes snapped open, his cultivation interrupted.

"What happened?" he asked.

"I don't know," Jack replied. "I don't think that roar was aimed at us, but it came from nearby. Let's check it out."

Jack and Brock flew out of their cave and into the air. Vast blue skies met them, framed by an endless jungle that stretched as far as their eyes could reach.

"I don't see anything," Jack said. "What roared?"

A second roar followed. Out here, it was even more deafening than inside. The sky shook. The earth splintered. Massive trees toppled to the ground, while flocks of draconic birds took flight all across the jungle, escaping at their maximum speed.

"What the hell is going on?" Jack asked, his body sweating involuntarily. "Was that... a B-Grade?"

Such a great roar had swept over the world, and its origin was so far away, it wasn't even visible. It had probably echoed for thousands of miles. What creature could emit such power if not a B-Grade?

"It roars. It must be fighting," Brock said. He was conflicted, then his eyes steadied. "We should take a look."

Jack agreed. If such a creature was roaring, the most likely explanation was that the B-Grades were fighting it at the hidden realm's core area. The other possibility was that someone had stumbled into a hidden overlord of the periphery. In both cases, taking a look wouldn't hurt.

This realm had no curvature, giving a clear view of hundreds of miles in every direction, they should be completely safe. And, if this turned out to be a lucky chance they could participate in...

There was no need to think anymore. Jack and Brock turned into beams of light shooting into the distance. Endless jungle passed below them. As they approached the source of the massive roar, they could feel the energy density in the air rising. They were headed in the direction of the core area.

A few minutes later, a mountain entered their sight. It was

shaped as a wide pyramid, with smoke rising from its peak. The jungle stopped a dozen miles away from this mountain, giving way to a blackened, burnt expanse that harbored no life.

This was an active volcano.

Jack expected to see some massive dragon roaring in the air, but there was no such thing. The area was eerily empty—yet he could sense great energy fluctuations in the sky, as if a massive battle had recently taken place here.

Soon, they could make out an assortment of individuals standing in the sky fifty miles away from the volcano. They were a group of C-Grade Hand of God cultivators, including their leader, Arkenstal. However, he seemed hurt; blood oozed from under his ribs, one of his arms hung broken, his wizard robes were torn and charred, and an entire half of his body was scorched black. It was a miracle he was still alive.

Jack and Brock didn't get much closer. After all, these were Hand of God cultivators. Unsurprisingly, more people arrived. Everyone in the wider area had heard the massive roar, and they all rushed here to take a look. Of course, not all cultivators of the expedition were close enough, but Jack spotted Min Ling and Baron Longform. He and Brock joined their group as everyone gathered together.

Those who dared adventure this close to the core area were amongst the strongest individuals of the expedition. Besides himself, Brock, and Min Ling, Jack only saw a few eight-fruits. Most of the people present were nine-fruit cultivators.

Before long, a group of seventeen had gathered.

"What happened, Arkenstal?" Min Ling asked as everyone converged.

Arkenstal's angular face was cold. The more people who divided a lucky chance, the less each of them would get... but there was no helping it anymore. Not only had the roar summoned everyone, but even if it hadn't, he did not possess the strength to get this lucky chance by himself.

"There is a massive treasure trove inside that mountain," he said. "However, it is guarded by a B-Grade dragon."

Everyone was shaken, but they'd expected it. Arkenstal was not a normal nine-fruit—only a B-Grade creature could injure him so heavily.

"How powerful is it?" Min Ling asked.

"Not overwhelmingly so. It is only at the early B-Grade. I managed to escape with my life, so I'm confident we could take it if we all teamed up."

Min Ling considered it. As the leader of the Church C-Grades, she had to weigh her words very carefully. "It did not chase you. If it is reluctant to leave the volcano, there must be something it is afraid of having stolen."

"My thoughts exactly," Arkenstal replied. "This must be one of, if not the greatest lucky chance outside the core areas. I believe we should all work together to claim it, then divide it in accordance with everyone's contribution."

His words were also carefully chosen. Not to mention his great personal strength, but discovering this place could also be considered a contribution. He wanted the lion's share of the treasure.

As for his injuries, they would go away given a bit of time.

Everyone waited for Min Ling's response while she calculated their odds. If she judged that the danger was too high, then the Hand of God cultivators by themselves probably couldn't get the treasure, so they would be forced to give up—or take a massive risk.

However, no cultivator could reach this level without being prone to throwing their life away.

"Okay," Min Ling replied. "However, the benefits should be equally divided between our two factions. After that, each faction can assign them to its cultivators based on their contributions."

"Deal," Arkenstal quickly agreed. This was also reasonable. Since both factions needed the other to get the treasure, and equal split was fair. As for the contribution-based assignment later, it guaranteed the higher-level people would get more benefits—and encouraged everyone to actually help instead of pretending to assist while staying on the sidelines to avoid any danger.

Jack and Brock also liked this arrangement. They'd come here seeking lucky chances, and so far, the only decent thing they'd found were the tree dragon fruits. If Min Ling told the Church forces to withdraw, it would be unsatisfying.

The only problem here was that Jack's enemy, Baron Longform, was present. He would need to watch his back—and so would Baron.

CHAPTER SIXTY-FIVE

BRO TO BRO!

THE VOLCANO STOOD IN A BLACKENED LAND, SMOKING FROM ITS TOP. IN THE distance behind it, one could faintly make out a colossal temple—that was the realm's core area. They were very close.

Fifty miles away from the volcano, the C-Grade expedition members plotted their invasion.

"The volcano holds an early B-Grade dragon and several of its C-Grade children," Arkenstal explained. "I couldn't take a good look before, but the C-Grade children must be a dozen and all at the peak C-Grade."

"So strong!" someone exclaimed.

"Yes," Arkenstal replied without hesitation. "Whatever resource lies at the bottom of that volcano must be beyond extraordinary. Besides the dragon and its children, the area is filled with D-Grade Draconic Twigs. Their individual strength is nothing to worry about, but they could be dangerous if they swarm you."

Jack looked at the blackened area around the volcano. No plants grew there. The only exception were ferns that were actually draconic twigs—he and Brock had fought a few of those back at the tree dragon's lair.

These draconic twigs were thousands upon thousands, but contrasted with the lush jungle beside them, they really did make the area seem lifeless.

"Is that all?" Min Ling asked.

"As far as I could tell. However, there may be more protectors at the bottom of the volcano or around the treasure. We should take things one at a time."

"What if we distract the dragon while someone sneaks through to steal the treasure?"

"Impossible. The volcano is completely packed with draconic twigs. Not only will they swarm anyone who enters, they will also alert the dragon to the intruder—and, if someone gets trapped inside the volcano, they will not be able to survive the dragon's fire breath."

"Okay. Then, what is your plan?" Min Ling sked.

"We kill everything," Arkenstal said simply. "First, we roam the ten-mile area around the volcano and kill every draconic twig we find. Then, we assault the volcano itself, using area attacks to decimate the twigs packed inside. The two of us join forces to hold back the B-Grade dragon while everyone else kills its peak C-Grade children. Finally, everyone joins us, we slay the dragon, and search the volcano for any treasure."

Most people nodded. Min Ling, however, did not seem satisfied. "Is there any scout in our group?" she asked. "If we can map out the inside of the volcano, that would be best. Maybe we can teleport directly to the treasure, take it, then teleport out."

Their qualifications for coming here were decided by battle strength, not auxiliary skills. There were no scouts.

"I may can," came a voice from the group. Everyone looked to its origin—a young, shoulder-high brorilla barely at the three-fruit boundary.

"You?" Arkenstal snorted. "Dancing to distract them is not scouting. What could someone of your cultivation achieve?"

"I can control a dragon plant to scout the inside," Brock replied calmly, registering the insult and remembering it for later.

"Dragon plant?"

"A draconic twig," Jack explained.

Everyone glanced at each other. Min Ling stepped forth. "Brock and Jack are very capable. Since Brock says so, there is a chance he can do it. Let's let him try."

"Fine," Arkenstal replied, not seeming too convinced. "Do your thing, monkey."

Jack closed his eyes, reining in his temper. This was no time to act out. However, he would remember this man's tone.

Brock casually flew to the ground. He approached the edge of the blackened area and walked up to a draconic twig. As soon as he came within a hundred feet, two wooden eyes opened between its roots, staring at him.

"Hi," Brock said. "Can I speak?"

The draconic twig remained still. Brock took that as a yes. A golden book materialized in his hands, flipping to a certain page—a little dragon was displayed on it, petted by a kind brorilla. The page shone. The little dragon stirred. Its head rose from the page, then it unstuck its wings. It shivered, throwing off imaginary dust, and yelped in joy.

The little dragon was ready to fly.

The draconic twig was still watching, its thoughts unknown. Brock let the little golden dragon sit on his forearm for a bit, petting its little head and whispering something in its ear. The dragon nodded as if it understood. Its wings unfurled, and it flew to the draconic twig, entering its head as if it was only an illusion.

Jack, who was watching, raised his brows. He had no idea Brock could do this. In fact, there were many things he didn't know about Brock's current powers.

Brock closed his eyes, and so did the draconic twig, slowly, as if falling asleep. In the next moment, Brock and the draconic twig both appeared in a mental space that resembled a forest gym, with hand-made instruments lying around. This was the brorilla forest gym from back in the Forest of the Strong—Brock had chosen it as it was a place of nature.

"Hi," he said, more relaxed this time. "Welcome to brohood."

The twig shook its dragon head. It looked around with suspicion. "Where am I? Ah. I can talk!"

Though its voice was bass, its speaking manner was like that of a child. It leaped around excitedly, proud to develop speech.

"I know the feeling," Brock said. "You doing great."

"Who are you?" the twig asked, piercing him with its wooden eyes. "I will not trust you just because you helped me speak."

"That is fine. I do not want to harm you. I want to help."

"Help how?"

"The people with me are evil. They want to kill you all and then attack your friends inside the volcano. I can help you survive."

"What!" the twig exclaimed. "Kill us all?"

"Right."

"They can't! We'll bite them to pieces!"

"They can," Brock explained calmly. "They are very strong. Even the big dragon cannot stop them. Trust me."

The twig lost its vigor. Its wings drooped, its eyes grew dispirited, and it coiled around itself. "I know you... My kin has spoken about you and your friend. You are not like the others. You are good. I believe you. But... how will you help us?" it asked with sadness.

"I will tell you the truth. There is no way to stop us, all you can do is let us peacefully take the treasure at the bottom of the volcano."

Its eyes shook, then it lowered its head even further. "There is no treasure in the volcano."

"Isn't there something that can make dragons grow?"

"There is, but it is not a treasure. It is our mother."

"Your mother?" Brock was surprised. "Okay. Tell me about her."

"She is very pretty," the twig admitted. "Her crystals give life to all of us. Father eats them—that is why he is so big."

"Your father eats your mother's... crystals?"

“Mm.”

“Okay. Is your mother strong?”

“No... Father is strong. Mother is very weak... but pretty. Please don’t kill her,” the twig begged, its wide eyes pleading. In this space, it could sense that Brock was telling the truth.

Brock had lied to the cultivators. He wasn’t going to invade the twig’s mind. He was going to have an honest chat with it, bro to bro!

“I want to help you,” he said. “Tell me more.”

Getting an explanation out of the childlike draconic twig was difficult, but Brock managed it. Apparently, the father of these twigs was the B-Grade dragon that ruled this part of the hidden realm—hundreds of thousands of miles around them. Their mother was an entity that the twig couldn’t describe for the life of it. All Brock understood was that this mother was weak, not a dragon, and produced crystals filled with some kind of power that was very beneficial to dragons. The big dragon ate these crystals, which was how it had reached the B-Grade.

However, the relationship between those two entities was not harmonious. The twig called them Father and Mother, but Brock realized that the big dragon was the overlord, and the crystal-producing entity was just its slave.

“And why doesn’t your father eat your mother?” Brock asked. “If her crystals are so useful, surely the mother itself can make him even more powerful.”

“Mother is not that,” the twig replied in a low voice. “Mother can produce us and the crystals. Eating her would mean no crystals and no us. That would be bad.”

“Okay. I understand.”

A plan was beginning to form in Brock’s mind. “Do you like your father?”

“No. He eats us too sometimes. We fear him.”

“Okay. And are there any crystals right now?”

“There are!” the twig replied proudly. “Mother makes crystals every... very long time... so Father eats them slowly. There are eleven crystals now. And a half."

Brock nodded. "I know what to do, and you must help me."

"Save us, and I will!" the twig replied honestly.

"Good. Then, listen closely..."

Brock explained his plan. After making sure the twig understood, he then used their connection to speak to Jack, confirming the plan with him.

"I hope it all works out, bro," Brock said, petting the twig's head. They had become friends by now. The twig arced its back like a cat, letting him pet it.

In the outside world, everyone waited. They had seen Brock sink a golden dragonling into the twig's head, then both went still. It had been a few minutes already.

"Will it take long?" Arkenstal asked.

"I have no idea," Jack replied calmly. In his mind, however, he listened to Brock's message. His thoughts sharpened. He ran the calculations in his mind, then made a suggestion which Brock accepted. Without turning his head, he sent a telepathic message to someone else.

"*Hey. This is Jack. Don't change your expression—I have a proposition for you.*"

Brock spent ten minutes perfectly still and conversing with the draconic twig. Just as everyone began to grow impatient, he awoke, flying back to meet the others.

"Well?" Min Ling asked. "What happened?"

"Good news," Brock replied. "The plant dragons are not friends with the big dragon. If we do not attack them, they will not attack us."

"Even the ones inside the volcano?" Arkenstal asked.

"Yes... But, if we take the treasure, then they will attack."

"So we can attack the B-Grade and peak C-Grade dragons, kill them, and only then exterminate the twigs inside the volcano."

"Yes. However, the twigs are connected. If we harm one, all will attack us, so we have to absolutely avoid them until after the dragon. At that point, whether we kill them or not won't matter—they are too weak."

Jack admired Brock's coherent and grammatically correct speech. Everyone else nodded in affirmation. They suspected Brock might be hiding something, but they would never in a million years imagine that he was allied with the draconic twigs.

"Are you sure about what you said?" Arkenstal asked.

"Yes."

"Then, we should not exterminate the twigs in the surrounding area, or we will raise the ire of them all. This is good news indeed. If we are only facing the stronger dragons, I am ninety percent confident we can succeed with minimum casualties."

Everyone rejoiced. As for the weaker people present, who were likely to be those minimum casualties, they did not consider turning back—they were here precisely to risk their lives for treasure.

"There is no need to wait, or more people might show up," Min Ling said. "Let's storm the volcano as soon as Arkenstal's injuries are healed. What do you say?"

"I agree," he replied. A Hand of God healer had already tended to him while Brock spoke with the twig. "I need half an hour to return to my peak state. Everyone, adjust your minds. We attack soon."

Half an hour was nothing to these cultivators. Nobody new had showed up, and no movement had been observed on the volcano or the surrounding area. Arkenstal opened his eyes—they shone with deep awareness.

"Let's go," he said.

Seventeen powerful C-Grade cultivators flew out as one. Their might tore the clouds and shook the earth. They were not hiding their presence, but just as Brock had told them, no reaction came from the thousands of twigs below. They really didn't seem hostile.

That laid many of their worries to rest. Not everyone had believed Brock, but everyone believed the facts when they saw them.

The group stopped one mile away from the volcano. "DRAGON!" Arkenstal roared, fusing his Dao into his voice so that it echoed for hundreds of miles around. "COME OUT TO DIE!"

CHAPTER SIXTY-SIX

SINKING DEEP

Arkenstal's challenge was followed by silence. Then, the earth shook. The sky shuddered. Boulders tumbled down the volcano's sides, and droplets of magma spouted from its top.

The shaking built until it culminated into a roar so massive, so deafening, that the clouds were washed away and the earth splintered far below. For a moment, it felt like the world itself vibrated.

Then the roar cut off and a giant head emerged from the volcano.

Everyone, Jack included, drew cold breaths. This was most certainly a dragon, exactly as pictured in medieval stories. It possessed a serpentine body covered with crimson scales, two horns on its head, and eyes twisted with extreme, dark intelligence.

Red Dragon, Level ??? (B-Grade)

Dragons are the darlings of the Dao. They are creatures that can stand at the top of the universe. Their bodies are large, durable, and powerful, while the Dao itself is carved on their flesh and bones. They do not need to eat to survive, as they can absorb the power of the world. Despite that, they often dominate a large area around them, relishing in the mortal pleasures.

Red Dragons are born of the Dao of Fire. They possess extreme understandings since birth, and their insights will keep accumulating naturally as they grow up. They are highly resistant to all temperature changes, as well as spatial or time distortions, and their fire is one of the hottest states of matter known to the cultivation world.

Its head alone was the size of a hill. Its eyes were larger than Jack's body. Standing before it, everyone was like specks of dust. And its aura... It towered higher than the mountains, deeper than the ocean. It was an inextinguishable, endless vat of unadulterated power. The very air around the dragon was immolated by its wrath.

This dragon alone was far more dangerous than the volcano it occupied.

"You dare return?" it growled in its deep, malevolent voice. Dark steam escaped its nostrils and the ends of its lips. With every movement of its jaw, teeth the size of trees appeared, glinting in this world's sunlight.

"I do," Arkenstal replied, fearlessly pointing his sword at the dragon. "And I brought company."

"More coal to the fire." The dragon growled oddly, as if laughing from deep inside its belly. More of its body was dragged outside the volcano, revealing a torso the size of a mountain, wings that could hide the sky, legs that stood on the earth like divine columns, and claws that could tear apart the heavens.

But those were not enough to make the dragon a B-Grade existence. Its body was only part of its power. The fire that shimmered inside it was so hot, Jack could feel it from a mile away, as if staring at an open oven. The Fire Dao of the world was swiftly gathering at this location, rushing over from hundreds of miles away. The dragon's Dao understanding was in no way shallow.

All those together pushed this creature over the edge and let it take a solid step into the B-Grade.

The dragon rose out of the volcano completely, taking to the air.

Every flap of its wings sent strong gales over the land, climbing down the volcano slopes, traveling across the ground, and razing the jungle ten miles away. Those draconic twigs that were not well rooted were sent flying, their screams echoing through the air.

"Children!" the dragon roared. "Fight for me!"

The twigs did not respond. Out of the volcano, however, came another twelve dragons. They were as red as their father, though smaller. If the large dragon was a mountain, they were large hills.

The twelve smaller dragons roared as one, shaking the fabric of space.

Red Dragon, Level 399 (Elite)

Their System description was the same as their father's, though they were worlds apart in power. Still, even they were enough to stump the cultivators. Each was a peak C-Grade creature, and an Elite one, too. A normal peak C-Grade cultivator would lose easily.

However, these were not normal cultivators. They were the best of the best, dominating the gathering of genius that was the Cathedral. Those of the Hand of God were equally qualified. Every nine-fruit cultivator present was stronger than the small dragons, and there were eleven of them. There were also another six eight-fruit cultivators that could assist, and finally there was Jack, Brock, and Min Ling.

"For glory!" Min Ling shouted, grasping her spear and charging at the large dragon.

"For the Immortals!" Arkenstal cried out, taking his sword and joining her. The two leaders crossed space, near-instantly arriving before the dragon. The world shook from their clash. Space ruptured for miles around. The sky lost its color, lightning descended, and fire erupted with such intensity that it instantly shattered all other energies. Jack saw even space and time evaporate.

"YOU DARE CHALLENGE ME?" the dragon roared, leaping into combat against the two cultivators.

The clash in the high skies was the signal to start the battle. Eighteen cultivators and twelve dragons charged each other. There was havoc. The world shattered. All vegetation disappeared for a hundred miles around, leaving only the draconic twigs alive, and even they were flung away from the shockwave.

For a time, all sorts of Daos danced in the air. The world couldn't handle such an intense collision, instantly disintegrating below them. Space and time ran wild. The battlefield became chaos, completely filling the world.

Thankfully, they were many miles into the air, so the volcano itself could barely take the pressure.

Jack was lost. He and Brock remained side-by-side, warring against all enemies. With the distortion of spacetime, the world had become a blur. Energies were everywhere. They could barely tell friend from foe, and the chaos was so prevalent, they almost lost each other, let alone survey the state of the battle.

"Now!" Jack screamed in his mind. Brock rushed over, grabbing Jack's arm with enough strength to almost rip it out, and Jack used everything he had to teleport.

Their location changed wildly over the battlefield. With such an intense warping of space, they could not teleport where they wanted, only keep trying until they left the area. For a few moments, they were like ghosts flickering everywhere.

Suddenly, Jack felt something change. Space had solidified a tiny bit, so he used that opportunity to punch it with his full strength and forcefully straighten it. The world rang like a glass bell.

And then, stability. Jack and Brock appeared inside a large hole. Black stone surrounded them in all directions, and the sky was only visible through a circular opening far above. Currently, that sky was completely distorted by energy flows. The entire volcano was shaking, boulders falling everywhere.

They stood on a flat stone. Below and all around them, magma bubbled, rising in mighty waves due to the shockwaves raining from above. Brock raised his hand, forming a golden shield which blocked the magma.

"Bros!" he shouted. "Show me the path!"

Only now did Jack realize they were surrounded by draconic twigs. Across the miles of dark stone, every crevice was occupied by fern-like plants—draconic twigs in disguise. There had to be thousands of them, maybe tens of thousands. They were everywhere. If they attacked, even Jack would be hard-pressed to defend himself.

However, though the twigs had clearly detected their presence, they did not attack. One uprooted itself, raising a claw to point in a certain direction.

Jack and Brock were at the bottom of the volcano. All around them, various cave openings stood against the wall, some half-flooded by magma. It was one such opening the twig had indicated.

"Thanks!" Brock exclaimed. He and Jack dashed into the tunnel, forming shields around themselves to keep away the magma. They were chest-deep. The tunnel made odd twists and turns, and the magma level kept rising. It was also raging from the shockwaves outside. Waves crashed against Jack's face, threatening to burn him if he didn't protect himself with his Dao.

Even to people like him and Brock, swimming in magical magma was not easy. Their energy consumption was significant. Jack pulled Brock closer, changing tactics. His pure Dao shield fell, replaced by another. He warped their surroundings to create a bubble of space, isolating them from the surrounding space which contained the magma.

This wasn't easy, either. All Daos could interact with each other. The heat of the magma crashed against Jack's space bubble, trying to melt it, and Jack had to constantly supply it with energy.

At the end of the day, his comprehension was just not enough. This space bubble he'd created was a basic, imperfect variation. But it worked.

His energy expenditure was lessened. Brock was also safe beside him. The two of them swam through miles of underground tunnels, following twists and turns as they headed ever deeper. The magma covered all tunnels completely at this depth. They were diving through the openings that let it rise to the surface.

Finally, they reached a massive underground cavern. It was completely filled with magma, so visibility was non-existent. Even Jack's Dao perception could only reach a hundred feet out. They swam directly into the cave until all walls had left Jack's perception range. No matter how he searched, there was only lava.

He was struck by the realization that he was buried in miles of lava, deep underground, protected only by a space bubble which rapidly ate away at his energy.

Brock grabbed onto his shoulder. "Be strong, bro," he said, and Jack returned to his senses.

"Thanks," he muttered, accelerating.

In this large chamber of magma, they had no way of knowing which direction to take. Where was the twigs' "mother?"

This chamber was larger than they assumed. It took up a terrible amount of space—measured in cubic miles. Searching for something here with no visibility was pointless.

"Damn!" Jack exclaimed. He could last some time here, but not infinitely. If they took too long, they might need to retreat empty-handed. Moreover, the other cultivators would realize they were missing.

"I got this," Brock shouted. His aura erupted. A golden book appeared in his hand, flipping to a page that showed a brorilla and a human swimming through lava and rejoicing as they saw something that hid beyond the border of the page.

As soon as that image appeared, the golden aura of the book flared. It shot out like a sonar wave, bypassing Jack's space bubble and diving into the lava, spreading in all directions. Jack was stunned. Brock's closed eyes snapped open.

"There," he said, pointing in a direction. He then frowned. "Dragon bro mother is there... but this place is very deep. Very, very deep."

Jack directed his space bubble to fly over, crossing through endless lava. Eventually, his perception met a wall. And on it was something that seemed like a plant, yet was not.

This time, it wasn't just Jack who was stunned. Brock's jaw hung to his shoulders, and his brorilla eyes were wide in disbelief.

Here, buried under miles of lava, in temperatures that could evaporate anything but the hardest stone, was a single tree.

It wasn't too large, barely reaching Jack's height. Its roots dug into the wall of the cavern. Its trunk was made of gray wood, and its branches were transparent, as if made of jade, showcasing the delicate green veins inside.

That a tree could exist here was unthinkable. The System was also at a loss. All it displayed was question marks.

"Wow," Jack muttered breathlessly. Despite the danger and rush they were in, Jack deeply appreciated the beauty of the universe. Everything was possible. Such a magical world... Perhaps Edgar, with his Dao of Magic and Wonder, was right all along.

Jack shook himself awake. There was no time to think. They had to get the crystals and return to the surface before anyone discovered they were missing.

On the tree branches, hanging like fruits, were twelve crystals. One was half-eaten, exposing its green core. These crystals emitted unbelievable amounts of power. Their outer layer was made of pure Dao so dense it had crystallized. Using it to cultivate would be a hundred times better than using a Dao stone. Beneath that skin, the half-eaten fruit revealed a green core containing such a terrifying quantity of life energy that it made even Jack scared. Besides the Life Drop, these were by far the greatest life treasures he had ever experienced.

"Hurry!" Brock exclaimed. Jack was planning to. His space bubble collapsed, exposing their pure Dao shields to lava and shooting up their energy consumption. They reached the tree near-instantly. Jack grabbed for a fruit, and to his surprise, taking it away was as easy as plucking an apple.

Six fruits found their way into Jack's space ring. Five remained. The plan was simple: Jack, Brock, and their other partner would share these six fruits, while everyone else would get the remaining five. By leaving a few fruits on the tree, they would not raise any suspicions—provided they managed to return to the battle before it was over.

It was a risky plan, of course, but how could one advance without risk? And, as for stealing from the other cultivators... Jack couldn't give a single damn. Anybody else would also cheat if given the chance. Amongst cultivators, there was no justice, only strength.

The only one he cared about was Min Ling, but he'd make it up to her later.

Jack quickly reinstated the space bubble, hiding both himself and Brock inside. He took a final glance at the tree.

After half its fruits had been taken, the tree's aura had greatly declined. Jack had no doubt that everything on this tree, from its roots to its branches, was a treasure. However, the fruits were by far the greatest prize.

In the cultivation world, there were greedy people who would uproot this tree completely and take it with them. Such an action, however, would be extremely wasteful. Brock had promised to protect the "mother," and that was also in line with Jack's values. Always take the fruit—never the root. Like this, the tree would live, new fruits could grow in the future, and the cultivators who came next would have one more treasure to pursue. The cycle of life could continue.

Moreover, once the battle outside was over, Brock would claim he knew the treasure's position and lead them all here directly, so they had no need to kill the draconic twigs. Both they and the tree would be safe.

Jack and Brock bowed to the tree in deep gratitude. Facing such a marvel of nature, even they felt small.

Then, they shot back toward the cave entrance. There was no

time to waste. The winding tunnels so far had made their current location unclear, so the only way out was to retrace their steps.

Fortunately, Jack had an excellent memory, so he could track down the entrance of the cavern. Otherwise, they would be lost forever.

Magma floated by them. They reached the entrance, rushing at full speed, then came to a skidding halt.

Another space bubble blocked the cavern entrance. And inside it, with his hands crossed and a cold smile on his face, was Baron Longform.

CHAPTER SIXTY-SEVEN

DUEL IN THE SEA OF LAVA

SKILLS AND DAOS FLEW EVERYWHERE. THE WORLD WAS CHAOS. EVERYTHING was a wreck.

The red dragon roared as it covered the world in flames. Min Ling twirled her spear, absorbing them, while Arkenstal formed thousands of seals with his hands, sealing the flames in a separate spacetime.

Facing the B-Grade dragon, defense was all they could manage. Fortunately, they were no longer alone. A dozen cultivators flew around the dragon, striking it with their powers whenever they could. If the dragon tried to turn on them, Min Ling and Arkenstal took to the offense, forcing it to turn its attention back to them.

The dragon was already bleeding all over, but its vitality was overwhelming. It refused to fall. It refused to escape, either, as its mind was clouded by wrath, pride, and sorrow. All twelve of its children lay dead on the blackened ground below.

The battle had already flattened a hundred miles of jungle around them, but it remained white-hot.

"I WILL DESTROY YOU!" the dragon roared, wildly unleashing flames. The cultivators used everything they had to make some distance. A couple were already injured. Six more had died in the battle against the dragon children—it had turned out more difficult than they calculated.

The longer they delayed, the greater the chances of something going wrong. Everyone was trying their hardest to end this as soon as possible, fighting tooth and nail against the dragon.

Min Ling, however, wasn't really trying. She kept a good part of her strength in check, fighting in a very cautious manner. Arkenstal was forced to do the same—if any of the two grew exhausted while the other remained in top shape, it was possible that one faction would slaughter the other.

However, even with the two leaders holding back, the dragon was slowly but surely headed toward death.

I cannot delay any longer, Min Ling thought, grimly watching the dying dragon. *Jack Rust... You better make it back in time.*

Jack's space bubble came to a stop in the sea of magma. A hundred feet away was the entrance from which they'd entered, and from which they could reach the surface.

But it was blocked. A man stood before it, covered in his own space bubble, his arms crossed, and his lips raised into a cold smile.

"Baron Longform..." Jack muttered, his voice crossing the magma to reach him. "What are you doing here?"

"I could ask you the same thing," Baron replied lazily. "Abandoning the battle to steal the treasure... That is a heavy crime."

There was no point trying to deny this. Even if there was, time was precious. Every wasted second threatened the battle ending and Jack's plan being seen through. "What do you want?" he asked directly. "I'll give you a cut of the treasure. Half of my share."

"Even if you offered it all, I still wouldn't take it," Baron replied, breaking into a wide grin. "Have you forgotten, Jack Rust? You killed my cousin. You challenged my authority and humiliated me. You made me waste hundreds of Dao stones. The two of us are already enemies… The only thing I want is your death."

Jack's brows dropped. A tremendous sense of threat fell over him. "They will not believe you. If you fight me here until the battle ends, they will think you came for the treasure as well."

"I will surrender the treasure and let them inspect my space ring. They will believe me. With your monkey holding all the information, it will not be difficult to convince them of who the real thief was."

Jack gritted his teeth. This was terrible. If Baron wanted to hold them here, there was nothing they could do to escape. Let alone playing it innocent, even surviving until everyone arrived was questionable. Baron Longform was significantly stronger than Jack.

Is there no way out? His mind raced, coming up short. Teleporting far away was impossible. By observing the baron's space bubble, Jack could see that his own bubble was inferior. This reflected their understandings into space. If Baron Longform wanted to lock down space and prevent Jack from teleporting, he could do it.

Jack's eyes narrowed dangerously. His aura rose. "Must we fight?" he asked.

"We won't fight. I will murder you."

Baron Longform's aura erupted. The world was dyed gray. A spectral iron fist smashed into Jack's space bubble, shaking its integrity and almost making it collapse. This wasn't even a real attack, just a substantialization of Baron's aura.

"I have researched everything there is about you. I have compared your progress to other historical figures," Baron said. "Right now, your strength should be close to rank twenty of the Cathedral. Even if you're hiding something, you can reach top ten at most. As for me, I'm number three. I can easily destroy you."

Jack's mind shook. That was… accurate.

He took a deep breath. His mind flashed once more, making sure he missed nothing. At the end, he was forced to admit that Baron outmaneuvered him. He had bidden his time in the Cathedral, minimizing his threat level while preparing to ambush Jack. He had shown nothing, making Jack underestimate him, and waited for the perfect moment.

A single move led to check-mate.

Now, Jack and Brock were trapped. There was no way back, out, or forward. Diving deeper was also useless—even if this cavern was very, very deep, as Brock had said, the only exit was upward, and it was blocked. Since escape was impossible, the only thing Jack could do was fight—and hope for a miracle.

There is still a chance, he thought. *Min Ling is with us. If she arrives before Baron kills us, she can help... but I told her to delay the battle above for as long as possible. Shit.*

Baron moved. A hundred feet was nothing. He reached them instantly, smashing out a fist. A gray aura fell on Jack and Brock, suffocating them like an iron wire around the neck. At the same time, space around them solidified, becoming unbreakable.

Baron Longform's fist shuttled forth. Jack had no choice but to defend. He dissolved his space bubble, pouring everything into a punch of his own. "METEOR PUNCH!"

The magma around them vibrated. It bubbled, creating a large area of emptiness. Jack flew back, his fist broken. Two extra arms were already sprouting from his armpits, and his body was growing, but it would not be enough. Brock had flown away.

Baron gave chase. Facing him, everything was doomed to fail. All Jack could do was survive.

The gray aura returned. Jack felt fear rising in his soul, an awareness of his coming death, paralyzing him. He fought it off through sheer willpower, but the aura's effects persisted, limiting his power. His fist was shattered. The next one as well. Jack was sent flying backward, deeper into the ocean of lava, while Baron didn't let up for a single second. He used his full power—he wouldn't give Jack a single chance to survive.

Jack was forced to admit that Baron Longform was the most dangerous opponent he'd ever faced... but that didn't mean he would give up.

All hesitation melted inside him, giving rise to endless courage. His heart was on fire—his mind was frigid cold. The Dao flared, filling the lava. Jack released a roar. If he was going to die, he would die while going all-out.

He lifted every stop. Space pulsed as Jack's own aura of his own erupted from inside him, grinding against Baron's gray. This was Brutalizing Aura—and Baron's gray aura was the skill Jack had once seen in a Dao Vision, from which he'd been inspired to create Brutalizing Aura.

These two skills were similar.

For a moment, the lava was filled with grating sounds like saws grinding against each other. Currents were created. The locked-down space was disturbed. Jack's aura pushed against Baron's, momentarily achieving an equilibrium.

Then Baron pushed through. Jack's aura was limited to a foot outside his body, and his strength remained restrained by ten percent. At least, he could fight.

Baron had a cold, determined expression. He was always calculating. He wouldn't give Jack a single opening. His fists rained down, while Jack's rained up. Two storms collided. The lava exploded. Tons of stone fell around them, lost in the bottomless ocean. Jack was in perpetual retreat, and his regeneration could barely keep up with his swiftly-accumulating injuries. It took everything he had to stay alive.

"You can persist!" Baron noted. "Excellent! When I kill you, all your secrets will be mine!"

His attacks intensified. Jack had been flung around so much he had completely lost track of his position. All that remained was a frantic, ceaseless assault, pushing him to the brink every moment.

Am I going to die here? he thought. His mind looked for the turtle in the Life Drop, but it was unresponsive. He looked for the death cube and Boatman's insights in his mind, but they carried no hidden strength. Nothing could save him. He was alone.

At least Brock had escaped. Perhaps he could live. If he came back and was killed by a single stray attack of Baron, that would be so unfair...

Jack did not lose heart. Defense after defense, he persisted. When the bones in his hands shattered, he persisted. He would die before giving up.

Suddenly, a clarion cry cut through the lava. Jack's perception was limited to the space between himself and Baron—he had no idea what was going on. Baron Longform, however, did. He suddenly turned to the side, smashing out into the lava.

The world exploded—and from within it, small shapes appeared. They had ferns for wings and draconic faces. Their eyes were brown and their bodies made of wood.

They were draconic twigs.

"Attack!" a roar cut through the void as first a dozen, then a hundred, then hundreds of twigs broke through the lava to attack Baron. Their assault seemed never-ending. Baron Longform roared, expanding his gray aura and suppressing their power, but it proved ineffective. They fell on him, and he had to punch them away. It was like a warrior facing off against a crowd of angry geese.

"Big Bro! Attack!"

Jack was confused, but he did not hesitate. He rushed Baron Longform. The twigs were nothing but a distraction—without him there to assault the enemy, they were just dying for nothing.

Only as he rushed did his mind make the connection. Draconic twigs were plants, but also dragons. They must have been immune to the magma. Brock had disappeared not because he ran away, but because he'd rushed to bring this army of twig bros over to help Jack.

Jack's heart was filled with warmth. "Charge!" he shouted with all his strength, while Baron roared in reply. His fists were colored gray—he smashed away dozens of twigs with each strike, but they were resilient. One attack was not enough to kill them. They jumped right back into the fray, besieging him with their fangs and claws.

Brock was nowhere to be seen, remaining in the distance where he would be safe, but Jack was right there. His fists erupted with strength. He had four of them, while the baron only had two—that gave him an advantage in both defense and attack.

Longform rounded on him. His face was warped in fury, his eyes were cold, and his chest was puffed out, suffering only surface wounds from the twigs. "Begone!" he shouted, smashing them away with a sonic wave. Space formed a wide bubble around him, keeping the twigs at bay.

"Fist of Mortality!" Jack roared out, driving it into Baron. His mind shook for a second, losing focus on the bubble and allowing Jack's own space mastery to break it. The twigs rushed back inside, swarming Baron. He cried out in fury.

Baron clapped his hands together. An intense shockwave erupted, blowing back the twigs. Jack managed to sneak in a punch, sending him flying backward, but Baron withstood the injury. The phantom of a gray giant appeared behind him. Baron and the giant punched out at the same time—a massive shockwave rolled forth, creating a vacuum of lava behind it, and directly shattering the bodies of several twigs. Wood flew out, instantly immolated. Only splinters were left.

The rest of the twigs cried out in anger—and, from their bodies, the golden light of brohood emerged. Twelve twigs rushed at the weakened shockwave. The lights on them combined to form a shield and withstand the attack. The shockwave was dissolved. The twigs had prevailed.

These twigs were already connected. Each had some individuality, but they also shared one mind. Through that, Brock's brohood was enhanced, augmenting their power and letting them fight Baron. If not for that, they would have all become splinters already.

Brock was not mind-controlling the twigs. They'd joined the battle on their own initiative. Jack and Brock had risked themselves to save the twigs and their mother—and the twigs, already indoctrinated into the bro culture, would risk their lives in return.

CHAPTER SIXTY-EIGHT
FIGHTING BARON LONGFORM

The golden lights flickered after enduring Baron's attack, but then returned stronger. Jack shot forth. Flanked by a hundred twigs, his punch shot out, sucking in the surrounding lava to release it in a massive explosion. Baron Longform was still weakened from the large-scale attack he'd made. A hasty defense was all he had time to raise.

He was smashed and sent flying away, lost in the lava. He used the momentum to escape Jack's perception range. Jack remained on guard, focusing his perception on the space directly around him, capturing every minor change.

A tiny fluctuation.

Suddenly, Jack turned and punched the void. Space ripped apart right then, and Baron emerged, his own fist already shooting out.

Two fists collided—one purple and one gray. Space shattered. Both opponents were sent flying back—Baron was stronger, but part of his energy had gone to teleporting.

However, everybody had a weakness. Longform's powers of regeneration were not too pronounced. After enduring so many attacks from the twigs and Jack, he was injured, one hand hanging limply in the lava. A tiny space bubble still flickered around him, protecting him.

"I should have gotten the damn monkey," he said through gritted teeth.

"Too late," Jack said, panting but with his body in perfect condition. "You're dead."

He clenched his fist. Power rose all around him, forming a massive purple phantom of a fist that even sucked in the surrounding space.

Baron Longform broke into the laughter of desperation. "You think too highly of yourself!"

In Jack's perception, Baron's body exploded with power. His life was slipping away, his cultivation was slowly falling, but it was not without gain—all that energy, originating from the body of an extreme nine-fruit C-Grade, formed a large source of power behind the baron.

At the expense of his own life and cultivation, he had temporarily achieved power far greater than normal.

"A thousand years of my life and one fruit," Baron said. His silver hair fluttered wildly in the lava, his silver eyes glowed, and his bare chest exuded wild strength. "For the secrets on your body, it is worth it. Your Life Artifact will be mine. Your lucky chances will be mine. Your potential will be mine. *Everything will be mine!*"

Arkenstal's hands moved. A giant space spike appeared in the sky, falling over the dragon. It penetrated its skull. Hard bones splintered. The dragon roared one final time, then stopped moving forever.

Everyone remained on edge, panting. They were exhausted. Many were injured. Some were dead. Six cultivators had been lost in this battle—far more than Arkenstal expected.

"Shit!" he said breathlessly. "I thought this would be easier!"

Min Ling nodded, remaining silent. Arkenstal glanced at her.

Ever since the start, she had conserved way too much strength. Several people had died because of this, including cultivators from her faction.

Why?

Arkenstal's gaze flashed. With the chaotic attacks gone, space repaired itself, allowing his perception to cover everything. He quickly counted the bodies, both alive and dead. Three were missing: Baron Longform, Jack, and the brorilla. The other two aside, Baron was a precious combatant. His absence was why the battle had been so difficult!

But Arkenstal didn't care much about the losses. Even if it was people from his faction, one cultivator less meant one less person to share the treasure with. The real question was...

If those three weren't here, where were they?

"Min Ling!" he roared. "You want to steal the treasure!"

Everyone had realized the absence of those three at the same time as Arkenstal. They all glared at Min Ling, drawing their weapons—even those from the Black Hole Church.

"I don't know what is going on," she replied calmly. "I had nothing to do with this. Let's rush."

They didn't need to be told twice. Everyone passed through space, instantly arriving at the bottom of the volcano, which had already collapsed. As soon as they arrived, Arkenstal noticed something off. The draconic twigs here were far fewer than he had seen last time.

"That monkey..." he said, gritting his teeth. He easily connected the dots. "Find them!"

"There are Dao fluctuations deep underground," a man said. "They must be fighting something. The treasure's Final Guardian?"

"Great! Let's go!"

Arkenstal raised his hands, ready to tear space directly to the origin of the Dao fluctuations. Just as he began, however, he sensed something. His face paled.

"Careful!"

Jack was horrified. Baron Longform was already stronger than he was. If he sacrificed part of his life and cultivation to increase his power even further, that could only be terrible.

Baron's gray aura returned, completely different from before. It spread out to cover a mile. Every draconic twig cried out in pain, some folding over. Some hearts ceased beating. They were unable to approach.

Jack came under the suppression of this aura as well. His mind, his body, his soul, everything was suppressed. His power was limited to half of what it usually was. Primal fear clouded his mind, speaking of imminent, unavoidable death. At the same time, space locked down around him, much harder than it previously had.

Baron wasn't planning to defeat Jack. He was planning to kill him. The reason he'd sacrificed his own life and cultivation for extra power was to ensure that Jack could not escape.

And, indeed, he could not. Space was tight around him, pressing down from every direction. Let alone teleporting, even moving was difficult. He was trapped.

"Die!" Baron shouted, punching out. That enormous source of power flowed into his hand, erupting as a massive, gray shockwave. It took the shape of a fist. Everywhere it passed, space crumbled, lava was pushed away like air, and the Dao itself ceased to exist.

Behind the fist, Baron's body deflated, losing most of its strength. He'd bet everything on this one strike. The power of an absolutely all-out attack by such a character could be imagined.

Jack could already see his own death.

A flock of draconic twigs rushed for the gray fist. Their bodies flared with golden light, thirty-six of them combining to form three golden shields in a row. The fist rammed into them. All shields shattered. The twigs broke apart, their bodies instantly losing all life. They hadn't even had time to scream.

"Big Bro!"

A brorilla appeared in the path of the gray fist. His entire body was covered in soft golden light. He raised a book, flipping it to the page of a brorilla holding a shield, then his other hand smashed a golden staff into the fist, pouring everything he had into it.

The fist paused for just an instant before breaking through. Brock's Staff of Stone was snapped in two. He was sent flying far away, vomiting blood from the impact. His golden light weakened dangerously.

Thankfully, he knew he could not block this attack, so he'd kept his body out of the fist's direct trajectory. Otherwise, he would have died on the spot.

Brock and his twigs managed to weaken the fist by around two tenths of its original power. However, it remained extremely powerful, and there was nothing left to stand between it and Jack.

Facing this absolutely overwhelming attack, Jack didn't have false hopes. If he was struck, his body would shatter and he would die. No amount of tempering could save him. He could not escape, either.

All he could do was meet it head-on.

At that moment, Jack gathered every ounce of power in his body. His fist shone so brightly it was about to explode. Yet before the might of Baron's all-out attack, this power was nothing but a joke.

He dug deeper. He needed more power. He needed more power!

On the eve of death, Jack's mind erupted with potential. A spark was born, spreading over all his unrealized insights. The results of his past few months of meditation ignited, turning into smoke. Some was dark blue, and some was black—space and death.

Under the power of his despair, all that smoke crashed together, scrambling in the hopes that something, anything would be born.

Space and death combined—a hopeless union. These were two very different Daos. How could they result in anything?

Jack had come up with nothing. There was no breakthrough to be made. His insights just weren't enough. His current power was also not enough. The gray fist was approaching. He needed more power —but he didn't have any.

He roared, smashing out a Meteor Punch containing all of his power. Light and sound were sucked inside. It was the strongest strike he'd ever unleashed—and it paled in comparison to Baron's gray fist. He could not stop it, but he would do his best.

Even at the last moment, as he punched out, his mind never gave up. He kept scouring everything, looking for a path to survival. His entire life passed by his eyes. He saw himself on Earth, inside Trial Planet, at Hell, on the Cathedral.

His thoughts moved by themselves, surrendering to Jack's deepest instincts. A striking scene came to him—he was standing next to a starship, watching a distant star explode. In his desperate desire for power, his mind had retreated to the greatest power he'd ever seen displayed.

The memories of that event flooded back. He'd once spent months meditating on the supernova, but it was not meant for him —he had only achieved a small fusion into Meteor Punch.

But now, as he thought back to it, something was different. His horizons were wider. He knew so much more.

He understood space. He understood death. And suddenly, all those past realizations sprang to life, and Jack could finally see past the mysteries.

The supernova was the death of a star.

Space and death.

He recognized it now. All his insights into those two Daos, which he'd forcefully galvanized before, now ignited on their own. They went up in flames. Their smoke evaporated. A series of realizations sparked in Jack's mind, each leading to the next.

And, as all those insights combined with his old ones about the supernova, they combined together, forming a perfect whole.

Jack's eyes saw a whole new world.

The gray fist promised his death.

Jack completed his swing. Sound and light were dragged into his fist, but they never exited. His fist was a whirlpool, a bottomless pit of energy. The lava fell inside. Even time and space were sucked in. They formed a tiny core.

The concentration of energy was so intense, so potent, Jack had to release it or his entire body would explode. He roared in silence. His fist made contact with Baron's.

"SUPERNOVA!"

The world fell away. The entire cavern shattered. Tons of stone fell from the ceiling, while the nearby lava evaporated. The sea of lava and the ground shook for a hundred miles around them. A new sun had been born underground, destroying anything and everything around it.

A path of destruction was cut directly from the point of collision to the surface, breaking through everything in its path and shooting into the sky as a column of blinding light.

Jack's arm had disintegrated from the shoulder down. He was filled with pain and empty of energy, a lamp without oil. The entire front of his body had been charred black, a gruesome sight. In this state, even maintaining a shield against the lava was a struggle. He could only remain conscious thanks to the Life Drop.

Baron Longform was in a slightly better state. Even with Jack developing Supernova at the last moment, Baron had remained slightly stronger. His body was burnt. His skin was flaking. His fist had shattered, and his silver hair had evaporated.

However, he'd also burnt his life and cultivation to release this strike. Such a technique carried a terrible backlash. His entire body was in pain, almost paralyzed. He was in no condition to keep fighting.

Both combatants were out of the fight. As for Brock, he had been close to the impact, looking at it directly—half his fur had been seared from the heat, and his eyes only saw white. Coupled with his previous consumption of energy, he could barely maintain consciousness.

The draconic twigs were better off, since they were highly resistant to extreme temperatures, but they were scared out of their minds. Half of them had perished—the rest had run away as fast as their fern wings could carry them.

Jack struggled to remain conscious. He tried to raise his fist. Facing him, Baron Longform also tried to gather his remaining energy. Both were thinking the same thing. One of them had to die.

At that point, space split open between them. A dozen people walked out, easily parting the lava. "What the hell is going on!" Arkenstal roared.

CHAPTER SIXTY-NINE

THE DROWNING MAN'S DESPAIR

A DOZEN PEOPLE EMERGED FROM THE CRACK IN SPACE. ARKENSTAL LED THEM, closely followed by Min Ling. Both were lightly injured. Behind them came another ten cultivators, ranging anywhere from being perfectly safe to heavily wounded.

All of them were exhausted, too, having just been through a large battle. Jack, Baron, and Brock easily surpassed them in both exhaustion and injuries. They were barely in fighting condition.

Seeing the other cultivators appear, Jack knew things were terrible. There was a great chance he would die here. As he lay in the lava, he used his Dao to reach into his space ring and fish out a pill, which he immediately swallowed. A bit of strength returned to his body. It was filled with the uncomfortable heat of burning something precious.

Jack had bought this pill back in the Cathedral. If he was ever exhausted but still needed to fight, it could recover some of his strength at the price of weakening him for a period of time afterward. It was a desperate measure.

At the same time, the Life Drop's energy was seeping into his body, pushing his regeneration to unprecedented levels. His disintegrated right arm was slowly reforming, one tendril of flesh after another. Bones grew like fungi. The pain was so excruciating that even Jack could barely keep from screaming.

"What the hell is going on!" Arkenstal demanded to know, glaring at both Jack and Baron Longform.

"He wanted to steal," Baron said, blood leaking from the edges of his mouth. "I... stopped him."

"Are you telling me that *just him* brought you to such a state?"

This time, Baron didn't respond. Being unable to kill Jack here was his life's greatest shame.

Arkenstal then turned to Jack. "Do you have anything to say for yourself?" he asked coldly.

Jack pressed his eyes shut, struggling to subdue the pain. The space bubble protecting him flickered. Finally, he opened his mouth to speak laborious words, "It's not true. Baron chased me all the way here. He wanted to kill me. I only barely survived."

"Is that so? Are you saying he somehow pulled you out of the battle without anyone realizing it, and then you chose not to inform Min Ling and somehow managed to run all the way here? In this suspiciously large lava cavern positioned right below the volcano?"

Jack closed his eyes. "Yes."

"Do you think we are idiots, Jack Rust? You wanted to steal the treasure while we fought the dragon. It was your monkey who discovered the information—perhaps you hid some parts, like the treasure's precise location."

"That is not true," Jack replied resolutely. A small part of his strength had returned. Though even if he was at full power, wanting to escape from all these people would be near-impossible.

"Not true? Very well. How about you let us inspect your space ring first? And your monkey's, too. If we find no treasure, we can keep talking. However, if we do find something, I will kill you on the spot."

"Compose yourself, Arkenstal," Min Ling said, stepping up from beside him. "Jack belongs to my Black Hole Church. Even if he did try to steal something, punishing him is a duty that falls to us."

No matter what, Jack was a talented disciple of the Church as well as Elder Boatman's personal disciple. He had also informed her of his plan ahead of time, and she'd promised to help defend him if things turned ugly. She couldn't let him perish here.

Arkenstal was not surprised by her words. He faced her directly, gazing deep into her eyes. "You seem determined to protect him. Why is that? Is it simple devotion towards your Church, or is it something deeper? Because, Min Ling, I seem to recall some rumors about you and this Jack Rust. I also noticed that you delayed during the battle with the dragon, purposely letting more of our people die. At the time, I thought you were just being cowardly, but it is clear now. You were aware of Jack's attempts to steal the treasure. Maybe you even colluded with him, planning to split the spoils later. After all, how could he have the confidence to go against all of us without someone like you having his back?"

Min Ling's gaze turned frigid. Arkenstal had hit the nail in the head. "You are slandering me. What proof do you have? Bring it out or keep my name out of your mouth."

"Proof?" Arkenstal laughed. His robes flapped to the wind of his own voice, protected by the lava in a perfect space bubble. "I don't need proof. I am ninety percent sure you colluded with him, and that is enough for me. For us."

Min Ling's eyes flickered. She glanced around. Originally, the Church and Hand forces had been evenly matched, which was the only reason they dared to work together. Only now, Baron and Jack were out of commission. Baron, specifically, was a powerful combatant she relied on. Moreover, since her faction's battle prowess had been lacking in the dragon battle, most of the casualties had been from the Church.

Eight of the cultivators belonged to the Hand of God. Only four came from the Church. As for Jack, Brock, and Baron, they could no longer fight.

The two factions were enemies, and no matter how they spoke against infighting, Arkenstal had the greatest C-Grade of the Cathedral trapped underground and outnumbered. Killing her would be a great merit. Plus, they wouldn't need to split the treasure afterward.

It didn't matter if she really had colluded with Jack or not. Arkenstal was planning to kill them all here anyway.

Min Ling's heart went cold. Speaking was useless. A red, dark-tipped spear flew into her hands, erupting with pressure. The surrounding lava roiled and bubbled.

Everyone burst into motion at the same time. The Hand of God cultivators turned against the Church ones, who tried to escape. But it was useless. Arkenstal was a spacetime wizard. He raised his hands, trapping everyone in a spatial cage. The escaping cultivators ran into its side and bounced back, forced to defend against two people each. A woman was cut down on the spot.

Min Ling released a shout. Twin fire and lightning gathered around her spear, combining into a single golden light. She stabbed it forward, right at Arkenstal. He laughed. Two Hand cultivators flashed before him, working together to block her attack.

Min Ling was extremely powerful, but so was everyone else. The two cultivators weakened her attack enough that it simply broke against Arkenstal's chest, stopped by invisible space armor.

"It is useless," he said. "Die!"

His hands, which had been opened wide, clasped together. The spatial cage shrank. The three Church cultivators screamed as they were pushed into their enemies' weapons, murdered on the spot.

Jack, who was also in the cage, reached out and pulled Brock to his side. The brorilla was similarly exhausted, but he was also far weaker than everyone present. He needed protection or he would die instantly. Jack grabbed Brock, then frantically looked around, searching for a way out. His current strength was not enough to break through this cage. The only reason he was still alive was that no one had bothered to attack him.

Min Ling's hair rose in an invisible wind. Fire and lightning sparked around her body, pushing away the lava even as her strength rushed at the tip of her spear. She threw a final hateful glare at Arkenstal, then turned around and smashed into the spatial cage.

"Break!"

The world shattered. Lava recoiled for miles. Thunderfire shone on her spear, piercing straight into Arkenstal's space cage and twisting it until it shattered.

The two were of similar strength to begin with. Arkenstal's wide area cage couldn't resist Min Ling's focused attack.

As a hole appeared on the cage, Jack rushed over, carrying Brock. The Hand cultivators attacked. A sword slash came for Brock, forcing Jack to fly in the way. Defending would take too long—he withstood it with his back, a stream of blood flying out. The wound revealed white bone. If not for his tempered body, just that sword slash would have cleaved him in two.

Min Ling waved her spear, dissipating two more attacks. "Come!" she shouted. The lava came alive, pushing Jack's space bubble forward. He barely made it out of the space cage before its walls repaired themselves.

Min Ling grabbed Jack and Brock and pulled them along, using her lightning Dao to achieve extreme speed. They were a current rising through the lava, rushing for the surface. Jack was dizzy.

At the same time, as Arkenstal's attention was focused on their side, the other side of the cage burst open as well. Baron shot through, his entire body bloodied—he'd once again burned part of his cultivation for the strength to escape. Otherwise, he would have died there.

Of the original seven Church cultivators present, three had died. Baron was retreating deeper into the lava cavern, where he would have a tiny chance to escape his pursuers, while Min Ling was dragging Jack and Brock toward the surface.

Unfortunately, Arkenstal had used his control over space to completely lock it down. They could not teleport. Even if they could, he would catch up.

"After them!" Arkenstal shouted, drilling through space to achieve a speed even more extreme than Min Ling's. His followers entered the tunnel he carved through space, managing to keep up. Nobody went after Baron.

Jack saw everything. Baron was running away, injured within an inch of his life. Given his direction deeper into the lava, he would probably die even if nobody chased him.

Nine Hand of God cultivators flew after Jack's group, led by Arkenstal, who used the utility of space to both lock them down and increase his own speed. At the same time, Jack's strength was faltering. He'd suffered injury after injury and even sacrificed his arm. Just maintaining the space bubble took up his entire concentration, and he wouldn't be able to continue for long. They had to reach the surface.

Even then, the situation would remain hopeless. Min Ling possessed great speed, but Arkenstal's was even greater. He could easily catch up. The only reason Min Ling still persisted was that they were inside lava, where her Fire Dao gave her a small advantage.

Staying in the lava wouldn't work either. Jack would soon run out of strength. Brock, too. Min Ling couldn't spare the attention to shield them. The two of them would die, and she would be left alone, sprinting through endless red.

There was no way out.

Jack's gaze went cold. His heart was like a tundra. At this critical moment, he considered everything and came up with an idea that was extremely cruel to himself but also their only chance of survival.

"Can you break space?" he asked Min Ling.

"It's hard," she replied. By now, they had almost reached the entrance of this cavern, from where they could follow a series of tunnels to reach the surface.

"But can you?"

"I can. It's meaningless. I will use up my energy and they can just teleport after us."

"Do it. Break space. I'll teleport us."

She glanced at him. "Are you sure?"

His eyes were resolved. "I'm sure."

She chose to believe. Her spear struck out, clad in lightning fire. It pierced into the void. Cracks spread throughout the world, then shattered with the sound of breaking glass. Space was momentarily free.

Before Arkenstal could lock it down again, Jack punched through space, dragging all three of them along. Arkenstal laughed, preparing to follow them upward.

But Jack hadn't teleported to the surface. As their position stabilized, they remained inside the lava. They were even deeper than before. The Hand group was above them. They could no longer rise up, only dive into the bottomless cavern.

And right in front of Jack was Baron Longform. The baron's entire body was bloodied, while his eyes were lifeless. His aura was weak like a dying candle. He had been trying to escape, and as he saw Jack and the others appear, his eyes widened with disbelief. He tried to conjure a defense, but it was too late—Jack's punch tore through his guard, into his chest, and tore out his heart.

Baron was completely shocked. This had all happened in a single instant. Even until his heart was crushed inside Jack's hand, he still had no idea how or why he had died.

"No..." Was all he managed to mutter before his Dao collapsed and lava filled his body, burning him inside out.

Min Ling was also shocked. She'd never imagined that Jack would be so vicious—while running for his life and drowning in lava, not only had he not rushed to the surface, but he also used up part of his remaining energy to kill Baron Longform.

Just how great was the hatred between these two? How decisive was Jack?

In her heart, Min Ling felt confusion, but also a hint of admiration. She did not say anything. She pulled Jack and Brock, rushing deeper into the lava, into the bottomless cavern.

Her own Dao included Fire. Resisting the lava consumed very little energy. She could survive for a long time here, far longer than Arkenstal or any of his followers. In truth, diving deeper into the lava had been her best chance at survival, and the only reason she rushed to the surface was to protect Jack and Brock. If Jack chose to go deeper, she wouldn't refuse.

Such a large cavern had to have more exits or spots close to the surface. Perhaps they would find another way out. Or, perhaps, they would die.

CHAPTER SEVENTY

BURNED ALIVE

Jack's power was diminishing. His vision was blurry. The lava pressed down on him, both with heat and pressure, and keeping up the space bubble around himself and Brock was all he could do.

He was drowning inside a sea of lava.

In his situation, anyone would have chosen to rush to the surface and breathe freely. But not Jack. Going to the surface would only give him an insignificant chance of survival—the Hand of God would catch up and kill them. Not even Min Ling would survive.

Therefore, their best chance was to go down and hope for a miracle.

The drowning man had suppressed his panic and dove deeper. The bottom of this large cavern was a mystery. Brock had called it very, very deep—it should be many miles away and also have many tunnels that connected to other lava streams. There was no way such a great cavern was not connected to anything.

In those tunnels, the Hand of God would eventually stop chasing. They had to conserve enough energy to return as well, and they wouldn't dare chase the fire-attribute Min Ling forever. Once the chase stopped, perhaps Min Ling could find a way to reach the surface or directly teleport outside to a place where the Hand of God cultivators couldn't reach them.

However, the crux of this issue was that Jack and Brock had to persist long enough. Given that they were already very pressed, their chances were slim—it was the best they could do, so they had to grasp the opportunity with both hands.

In this situation, Jack had still chosen to spend some energy to kill Baron Longform. It was not an impulsive decision. Though Baron looked half-dead, Jack had a strong premonition that he would somehow survive if left alone. Then, given the hatred between them and Baron's character, he would just be a viper aiming at Jack's back. He would try to ambush him, attack his friends, and find any way possible to harm him.

Baron had already proven to be a cold and calculating individual. If Jack let him go now, who knows if he'd ever get another opportunity to kill him in the future.

Therefore, he'd endured the loss of energy to directly strike out and kill him. Even Baron himself hadn't expected this.

Such a great person, the genius of an era with extreme calculating skills, had died under Jack's hand, his body disappearing in an underground sea of lava in a hidden realm at the edge of the universe.

The three of them tore through the lava, heading ever deeper, the pressure rising. Along with the temperature. As time passed, Jack was more and more pressed to maintain the lava bubble.

"Can you see anything?" he weakly asked Min Ling.

"No," she replied. To the drowning man, that was a declaration of death.

The Hand of God cultivators maintained a steady distance. They could not get closer, but they refused to fall behind. Min Ling kept descending for half a minute, pulling Jack and Brock along. At their speed, that was enough to cross dozens of miles even through the lava, and the cavern still hadn't shown an end.

Finally, the pursuing cultivators slowed down, then stopped

chasing altogether. This was too deep for them. If they chased any farther and actually fought Min Ling, they might not have the strength to return.

Arkenstal watched them go with a gloating expression. Even if Min Ling herself escaped by finding another exit, he was almost completely certain that Jack and Brock would die. His achievements today were nothing short of spectacular.

"Let's go get the treasure," he told the rest of them, and they all swam back up.

Min Ling kept descending. There was no meaning to turning back. The other cultivators would certainly guard the entrance of the lava cavern.

Jack and Brock were nearing the end of the rope. At this depth, even teleporting outside was impossible.

Finding another exit was possible. However, doing so before Jack ran out of energy was highly unlikely. If they didn't find an exit, Min Ling could always rush back up and try to escape through the surface, but Jack and Brock would be long dead.

Actually, Min Ling could easily kill and rob them of everything if she wanted to. Yet, she did not. She kept pulling them along, deeper into the lava cavern.

"Why?" Jack asked.

"Because I promised," she replied calmly.

He gritted his teeth. "We're holding you back. If you spend your energy to drag us, you could run out."

"I'll be fine. This lava is my domain. If I do need to abandon you, rest assured that I will."

That shut him up. He could only let her pull them deeper. At this point, both the heat and pressure had climbed to incredible degrees. The lava was coalescing into clumps of heated stone through which they swam.

The cavern was shaped as a wide pipe digging deep into the ground. It was diagonal, at a forty-five degree angle. By now, they had moved dozens of miles underground and dozens away from the volcano.

"Can we try to teleport?" Jack asked.

"I cannot reach the surface from here," Min Ling replied. "Even if I could, Arkenstal would sense the spatial ripples and come after us. We have to keep going and hope this cavern connects to another place near the surface. Only from there could we teleport."

Jack nodded. Soon after, they finally reached the end of the cavern. It was a large wall of dark stone sporting various tunnels. At a glance, there were at least five, and that was in the few hundred feet radius of Jack's perception.

Min Ling's brows were furrowed. "Any idea?" she asked.

"None," Jack replied weakly.

Brock released a low growl. Golden light gathered in his hand. It formed a book on the verge of dissipating, and he barely managed to flip it to a certain page. Jack had seen this page before—it depicted a brorilla swimming through lava, smiling as he saw something beyond the edge of the cave.

Brock had used this page to locate the crystal tree. This time, his strength was barely enough to activate it, and he also had to scout a much larger distance. His eyes flared with resolve. He bit down on the tip of his tongue, spraying a mouthful of blood onto the book. It was cleanly absorbed. The page shone crimson golden.

"A bro chooses the right path..." Brock whispered, his voice barely audible. The page flared. A crimson-gold color spread outward, expanding past the range of Jack's perception. A moment later, Brock released a low moan. He used the spiritual connection between them to transfer a map of what he'd seen to Jack, then passed out.

Seeing his little brother in such a state, Jack's heart was stormy, but he suppressed it. He analyzed the image that Brock had sent him.

"Most tunnels lead to dead-ends," he said. "There is only one which Brock couldn't fully explore. There." He pointed to a tunnel that seemed smaller than the rest. "It extends in an almost straight line for at least a mile."

Min Ling charged into that tunnel. It was barely twenty feet wide. Jack felt extremely cramped, his perception stifled.

Though they rushed, they did not reach the end of the tunnel. After a dozen miles, it remained exactly the same, maintaining its direction and width. It was almost suspiciously uniform. If they ran into a dead end after coming this far, then this narrow, underground tunnel might become his grave.

It was a sobering thought.

"This could be man-made," Min Ling said, a hint of hope in her voice. "There might be a way out."

Jack gritted his teeth, not daring to hope.

The tunnel stretched on. A dozen miles, two dozen, three, four. It seemed endless. Jack's reserves had long ran dangerously low. If there really was an exit at the end of this tunnel and he just couldn't persist until they reached it, it would be the world's ugliest joke.

When they had traveled at least a hundred miles, Jack was finally reaching his limit. No amount of desperation could keep him going.

"I'm breaking," he whispered as loudly as he could.

Min Ling glanced at him with regret. "I am not good with space," she confessed. "My Fire Dao is barely enough to protect myself here. At most, I could shield one of you."

"Take Brock."

"Okay."

Jack pushed the brorilla onto her, and she hugged his body tightly, spreading her fire protection just a bit wider. This tiny exertion made her sweat.

Then something changed in the tunnel. Min Ling furrowed her brows. She could sense something up ahead, a faint flicker of energy blocking her path, but there was no way she would stop or turn back now. Let alone Jack, even she wasn't sure if she had the energy to reach the surface again.

Her spear appeared, and she used it to ram into the barrier without stopping. A pale green light appeared for a moment before shattering. All three of them passed through.

Min Ling was perplexed. This barrier contained some extremely powerful Daos, but it was weakened to the point where she could break it. Just what was going on?

She pressed forward. Despite passing the barrier, the only change in the tunnel was a slight incline upward.

Jack registered all this. Faint hope blossomed in his heart, but he could no longer persist. His space bubble flickered one last time, then dissipated. Dense lava surrounded his body. It was no longer the kind which coalesced into clumps, but it remained extremely potent. As it touched him, his clothes melted, all his hair evaporated, and his flesh was instantly charred black. Every inch of his skin was singed at the same time. The final bits of his energy went to a thin barrier keeping the lava from entering his orifices. The rest of him was completely exposed.

Jack had been through a lot of pain in his cultivation path. He had endured his limbs being broken, several hard beatings, his fists shattering often. He had practiced body tempering, survived when the Life Drop cracked his soul to enter, and had his entire body boil when he withstood the heavenly tribulation at Trial Planet.

Of all those kinds of pain, only the Life Drop tearing his soul apart could compare to the current one. Jack screamed. It felt like he was buried in hot oil. His tempered body could resist being instantly disintegrated, but it still melted over him, revealing his bones. An extreme current of life energy escaped the Life Drop, regenerating his skin just in time for it to melt again.

Jack was living through hell. Time stretched to infinity. All semblance of awareness left his mind, replaced only by endless, boundless, all-encompassing pain.

Even the Life Drop could not keep up with this degree of injury. His skin and organs melted faster than they could regrow. Jack remained alive only thanks to the Life Drop, until he was a blackened skeleton shuttling through the lava, barely clothed with molten flesh.

Min Ling dragged him with resolute finality. They shot out of the lava. Jack only felt his environment cool down and rock against his back before he passed out.

CHAPTER SEVENTY-ONE

CONSUMING THE FRUITS

Min Ling shot out of the lava and into a cave. Fluorescent moss covered the walls, illuminating it in an almost magical glow, while the lava lake in the middle added a sense of danger to the otherwise empty cave.

Min barely registered those. She emerged like a comet and almost crashed into the ceiling before catching herself. She then moved to the stone ground and gently deposited both Jack and Brock.

Brock remained unconscious. The fur on his back had been singed, offering him light burns, but he was okay. It was the greatest protection Min could have given him—though she had hugged him tightly to reduce their combined surface area, her own back had been burned as well.

As for Jack, he'd been forced to endure the lava with his body for around ten seconds. It was unimaginable how he was still alive. Min could clearly make out his skeleton covered in black, molten flesh which constantly squirmed, regrew, and reknit itself.

It was a miracle. Such regeneration, such survivability... It really tested her understanding of the world. Moreover, to survive in that state meant his mind hadn't given in. Even enduring the continuous immolation of his body, a part of him had persisted, refusing to lose consciousness—if he had, no amount of regeneration would have saved him. It was only after they escaped the lava that he fainted.

Min Ling remained silent. Her gaze was deep. The current Jack made for a very gruesome sight, but she could handle it. She had seen worse. Cultivators could awe the world with their powers, but the price was that their lives were filled with pain and loneliness. It was not a path meant for everyone.

In all that pain, most cultivators lost themselves, devolving to their base instincts to remain alive. But this man...

He'd risked his life to cut off an enemy's retreat, killing Baron Longform even when he didn't need to. Min didn't mind that. Her own relation with the baron had been strained, and between the two, Jack was far more valuable to the Church. If anything, his decisiveness was admirable. Most people would have let Baron escape and later lost their lives because of that.

After that, Jack didn't hesitate to dive deeper into the lava cavern. He suppressed his despair and accurately judged the only path to survival. When he was running out of power and Min Ling could only protect one person, Jack had instantly chosen Brock. He sacrificed himself for his spiritual companion...

Unconsciously, Min Ling shook her head. She was not in the habit of saving strangers, but this man—both of them—had earned her respect.

She had no idea where she was. It could be dangerous. But, even if they all perished here, dying alongside these two wasn't too bad.

Jack's eyes flickered open. His mind was filled with scorching red pain—magma trying to drill into his eyes and throat, to suffocate him even as it burned him alive. He screamed and jumped upright, only then realizing he was no longer dying.

How! he asked himself, still in shock.

"You are safe," came a woman's voice. Jack swiveled to see Min Ling resting on a nearby rock, her dark hair swiping its surface as her legs and spear were both relaxedly outstretched.

"What happened?" Jack asked. Realizing he was naked, he calmly removed a spare set of clothes from his space ring and put them on—a habit he'd had to repeat more often than he'd like lately.

"We made it through the lava. You were burned for a few seconds but somehow managed to survive..." She gave him a deep glance.

"I survived..." His eyes widened. "Brock!"

"He's right there. Look down."

Jack glanced at his feet, finding Brock sleeping soundly. He was even snoring. "Oh, thank God..." His voice almost broke.

Brock's body sported a few burnt hairs, but he was safe. Jack knew that was thanks to Min Ling. "Thank you," he said, turning to her. "We were strangers, but you risked your life to save us. I will never forget that favor."

"It wasn't much," she replied calmly. "My life was never in danger."

"It doesn't matter. You saved my little brother. If you ever need any help, let me know, and I will rush to your aid."

Facing such seriousness, her lips curved. "That's grand talk for someone who's only a three-fruit C-Grade."

"For now. In my defense, they're pretty good fruits."

"I'm sure they are." She jumped off her stone. "Mind waking up your... little brother? We have things to discuss."

Jack nudged Brock. He then nudged harder. Brock finally awoke, shooting to his feet and shouting, "Big Bro!" as he pulled Jack into a large hug that he refused to release for some time. Only then did he turn to Min Ling.

"Thank you, big sis," he said seriously. "You saved my big bro. I will remember this forever."

"You guys will make me puke..." she replied, shaking her head. "Whatever. You're welcome. Take a look around."

Jack complied. He saw a cave covered in green, fluorescent moss with a lava lake in the middle—that must be where they emerged from. The cave itself wasn't too large, while a passage on the other side led elsewhere.

The most striking thing was in the air. In the Dao. Every stone exuded an aura of endless years, as if this cave had existed since time immemorial. The air was heavy, almost sacred, and the Dao of Life that had been prevalent in the hidden realm was even more dominant here, nearly tinging the air green.

Jack felt like he'd intruded into a sacred ancient temple. It was a similar feeling to when he'd entered the Ancient ruins in Trial Planet.

"Where are we?" he asked, looking around in wonder. His perception was suppressed by the dense Dao. It could barely travel a hundred feet into the exit tunnel, finding nothing but stone.

"I have a suspicion," Min Ling replied. "When we entered the volcano, we could see a massive temple in the distance. That was the hidden realm's core area. I suspect the temple's creator drew lava from the underground repository we found, for some reason, and the long tunnel we followed led us directly inside the temple."

Jack took a moment to process this. His eyes widened. "We're in the core area?"

"It is possible... You may not remember it, but I broke through an energy barrier shortly before reaching this cave. That barrier held great Daos but was extremely weak. My guess is that it covered the entire temple, and it was only weak because the B-Grades had recently broken through it. If not for them, we would have been unable to cross, and you would have both died in the lava."

Jack maintained a solemn silence. This time, they had come far too close to death... Perhaps trying to grab the treasure under everyone's nose had been too greedy.

Or, perhaps, it wasn't the intention that was wrong, but the execution. Jack hadn't paid enough attention to Baron Longform. After that, everything spiraled out of control.

I cannot let my guard down...

His hands swiped over his space ring, retrieving a spherical object. It was composed of a green core of crystallized life energy, surrounded by pure Dao so dense it had gathered into a thick mass—like a normal fruit's edible, fleshy interior.

As soon as this item emerged from the space ring, waves of life spread out, covering the entire cave. Everyone's heartbeats quickened.

"What's that?" Min Ling asked.

"It's the treasure under the volcano," Jack explained, still observing the item. "The fruit of a crystal tree that thrived in lava. Have you ever heard of it?"

"Never," she replied. "I sense both life and Dao energy. No wonder the dragons grew so strong; the life energy enhanced their bodies, and the Dao energy enhanced their abilities."

Jack nodded. "I have six of these fruits. Since all three of us contributed, I say we divide them equally."

Min Ling had been part of the plan from the start. Her task had been to delay the battle outside and defend them verbally if need be. Of course, that task was less important than Jack and Brock's, but she'd saved them afterward. In Jack's opinion, the six fruits should be split equally.

Hopefully, Min Ling wouldn't use her strength to take everything.

"That's fine," she replied.

Jack passed two fruits to her and two to Brock. "If your assumptions are correct, we are at the core area of the hidden realm," he said. "This is not a place we should be able to survive in. Every threat here could instantly kill us. Therefore, I think we should absorb these fruits and increase our strength as much as possible before venturing outside the cave."

"Big bro wise," Brock said.

Min Ling thought about it. "I agree. Though we shouldn't delay too long. My strength is not too far away from the B-Grade—since I'm already here, I want to explore this place and see if I can find any lucky chances. Will you join me?"

"Of course," Jack replied. "That's fine. Let's absorb the fruits first, and then we can get going."

The cave wasn't large, but it was spacious enough. Each of the three retreated to a corner and focused on their fruits, slowly working out how to absorb them.

Jack gazed at one of his. Its flesh was full of ambient, purified Dao—like a Dao stone, but far richer. Absorbing it would greatly enhance his cultivation. As for the seed of the fruit, its life core, that wouldn't be as effective. It was milder than the Life Drop's energy, so he could absorb it faster and more efficiently, but his body had already reached a high degree of tempering. Any benefits in that regard would be minor.

Thinking to that point, Jack stood up again. "Hey, Min Ling," he said, walking over. "I have low cultivation and a strong body, while you have high cultivation and a—" She raised a brow, making him reconsider "—very decent physique. Wanna exchange? I get all the Dao flesh, you get all the life cores. I think that would increase our power the most in the short run."

She smirked. "Sure. But I'm close to a breakthrough, so I want to keep half a fruit's flesh."

"Then I'll keep half a core."

"That's fine."

They peeled their fruits, exchanged, and Jack returned to his corner. He started by absorbing the half of a life core. The energy flowed into his body, similar to the Life Drop's but milder. Its effect was also slightly different; it enhanced his body and even increased its saturation limit a little.

Apparently, this life energy was highly nourishing, but Jack didn't regret exchanging the rest of it. The Dao flesh was just too energy-rich. It was perfect for the current him.

Done with the life core, he proceeded to the main course. The Dao flesh hung between his arms like the most exquisite silk. His perception unraveled it, forming incorporeal strands of pure Dao power that he pulled inside his body. They entered the roots of his Dao Tree, washing over the trunk and sinking into his third fruit, which was rapidly approaching maturity.

Meditating in this underground cave, Jack lost track of time. Hours flowed like water. Shortly after he finished one piece of fruit flesh, his third Dao Fruit finally reached maturity. It was a healthy green, shaped as a fist and radiating life.

As soon as it fully matured, Jack took a deep breath. He then dove directly into forming his fourth fruit.

In the C-Grade, every Dao Fruit was a manifestation of the cultivator's Dao into the world. It was an aspect of the universe viewed through the lens of their individual Dao. For Jack, his three fruits so far were the Fist, Space, and Life.

Choosing which aspect to grow into a fruit was an important decision. To Jack, this fourth fruit was a no-brainer. He steadily dove into his soul, then exhaled deeply as if it was his final breath. The air that left his mouth was dark—and, as it landed on the leaves, it formed the outline of a pitch-black fruit.

It was Death.

After receiving the teachings of Elder Boatman and the death cube, Jack urgently needed a Dao Fruit of Death to complement his power in that direction.

The fruit of death was fist-shaped, as were all of them, but it radiated a dark aura that twisted the nearby leaves into dry, dead things. It seemed like a very dangerous thing to have inside one's soul, but Jack knew the truth. Life and Death were part of the same cycle. Death wasn't evil; it was just a natural state.

Under his firm grasp, it was harmless. If anything, it formed a clear contrast against his third fruit, the Life one, creating an interesting area on his Dao Tree where the leaves were constantly dying and growing anew.

There was wisdom in those leaves, but it was not wisdom Jack could currently grasp.

After developing his fourth fruit, he spent the remaining fruit flesh to push it as far along as possible. By the time he was done, the Death fruit was around forty percent mature.

Jack's eyes snapped open. In a short few hours—or was it days?—his power had grown significantly. He'd risen by a tier. If he fought Baron Longform again, he was confident in winning even without using Supernova.

Oh. I forgot to check that out, he realized. *System, do your thing, please.*

Name: Jack Rust
Species: Human, Earth-387
Faction: Bare Fist Brotherhood (C)
Grade: C
Class: Gladiator Titan (King)
Level: 288

Strength: 4400 (+)
Dexterity: 4400 (+)
Constitution: 4400 (+)
Mental: 688
Will: 688
Free sub-points: 2

Dao Skills: Meteor Punch IV, Iron Fist Style III, Brutalizing Aura III, Neutron Star Body III, Supernova III, Space Mastery II, Titan Taunt I, Fist of Mortality I
Dao Roots: Indomitable Will, Life, Power, Weakness
Dao Fruits: Fist, Space, Life, Death
Titles: Planetary Frontrunner (10), Planetary Torchbearer (1), Ninth Ring Conqueror, Planetary Overlord (1), Grade Defier

Supernova III: Some stars die in a massive explosion. You have mastered that process, imitating it with your fist. By drawing in

an enormous amount of energy, compressing it to the maximum, then releasing it at once, you can erupt with a punch that resembles one of the most violent events in the universe.

Supernova actually started from the third tier. That was odd.

Every other skill that started above the first had been an evolution of a previous skill. Moreover, these tiers represented proficiency with the skill, and Jack felt he had barely grasped the concept of Supernova.

The most likely explanation was that the threshold to acquiring this skill was too high, so the System had set it to the third tier for fairness sake.

Jack took that as an achievement.

His other stats were also coming along nicely. The life seed of the crystal fruit had pushed his Physical substats to a nice round 4400, while he'd invested all the level up points into Mental and Will. That would need to change soon—eliminating his weaknesses was nice, but maybe he was overdoing it at this point.

In the C-Grade, the first three fruits accounted for ten levels each, and the next six for twenty each. By reaching forty percent maturity in the fourth fruit, Jack had smoothly sailed to Level 288, a difference of thirteen levels and two hundred and sixty stat points since he entered the hidden realm.

Just three and a half pieces of fruit flesh had benefited him so much. If he had been able to acquire all eleven on that tree, would he have reached the fifth or even the sixth fruit?

High-level resources were maddening.

Of course, the difficulty of reaching maturity increased with every fruit. A treasure that could give him a whole fruit now would only give him a fraction by the time he reached the eighth or ninth. By then, he would need to find even more of these treasures... but that was fine. It was part of the charm.

CHAPTER SEVENTY-TWO
UNDERLEVELED

JACK STOOD UP, READY TO EXPLORE, AND FOUND THAT BROCK WITH MIN Ling were already waiting for him.

Brock hadn't managed to break through, but he had grown his third fruit to maturity. His body had grown stronger, as well. As for Min Ling...

"You made it!" Jack said, his eyes brightening. "Congratulations!"

"To you as well," she replied. Eight slightly different auras filled her body—the telltale sign of an eight-fruit cultivator.

Min Ling had been the undisputed strongest C-Grade of the Cathedral at only seven-fruits. Now, with her strength having taken a massive leap forward, who knew how powerful she'd become? Maybe she could even challenge the weakest B-Grades.

"Let's go," she said, bursting with barely contained excitement. Jack and Brock nodded, and the three of them finally stepped into the tunnel connecting their little cave to... something.

This tunnel would have felt out of place in any cave complex on Earth. It didn't seem so much hewn as naturally created. Yet, it was oddly uniform, maintaining a roughly circular shape with a diameter between nine and fifteen feet. It twisted at times, with a tendency to snake in random directions, making one feel as though they were following not a cave tunnel, but a gnarled tree root.

Green, fluorescent moss accompanied them throughout. It covered part of the walls, gently illuminating the tunnel, and seemed in tune with the heavy, sanctimonious Dao that filled this place.

They chose to move slowly. This wasn't only out of caution, but also due to a deep-seated respect for this place. It felt like they were in the presence of something ancient and majestic; rushing through would be almost blasphemous.

The tunnel they followed connected to a wider one at thirty feet in diameter, on average, with a faint breeze blowing through.

"We've already walked for miles," Jack observed. "This place must be huge."

"If it's the temple we saw before, it takes up many cubic miles," Min Ling replied. "And, if all these winding tunnels wrap around each other to fill it... The distance they can cover is practically infinite."

"Infinite is a brave word."

"Pretty big. There, happy?"

A bit of banter was all they had to break the monotony. Even that was kept at a whispering volume. The dense Dao limited their perceptions to only a few hundred feet away. That was barely enough to peek over the next bend in the tunnel. If anything lived here, it should have adapted to the pressure, so its perception would extend much farther. Chances were, it would spot them before they spotted it.

Not to mention that its cultivation would likely be at the B-Grade.

Jack and his group followed the faint breeze. They ran into other small tunnels like the one they'd followed to get here but stuck to the main one. Another change from before showed their tunnel becoming interspersed with what seemed like wood—brown surfaces glowing green, spearing through the ground and into the ceiling. They seemed natural and were even covered in bark. They were like colossal tree branches.

Min Ling used her spear to poke into one such wooden surface. It was impossibly hard, but under her power, the bark parted to reveal more wood underneath. Golden sap flowed out. Even smelling it made one's pores open, like it was some supreme treasure. Unfortunately, the sap lost its luster almost immediately upon exiting the wood, so it was unusable.

"What do you think is going on?" Jack asked.

"I am not sure... Those wooden things look like tree branches, but any tree that could grow this large is—"

The ground burst apart ahead of them and a large monster flew out, mandibles at the ready. There had been no indication. In the single instant they had before the monster snapped apart Jack's throat, their bodies erupted with power. Muscle memory took over. Jack clenched his fist, shooting out a Meteor Punch before his brain even understood what was happening.

The punch exploded on the monster's mandibles and dissipated against the tunnel walls, which didn't even crack. The monster slowed down but kept coming. Its mandibles snapped around Jack's neck, and he barely managed to lean back in time.

The monster geared up for another attack when red lightning struck it from the side, blasting it into the wall. A second spear strike followed, then a third, cracking the monster's carapace and breaking its legs. Only as Min Ling's spear tore into its head, killing it, did Jack manage to make out its form.

It had six legs, a large head, and two short but wickedly sharp mandibles sticking out of it. Its entire body was colored beige, while two antennas stuck out from the top of its head. That was where its similarities with an insect ended. Its entire body was covered in hard scales, forming something like a carapace, and its eyes had vertical irises. Between its mandibles, Jack could make out a serpent's mouth.

Draconic Termite, Level 249

Draconic Termites typically infest large wooden complexes. Their mandibles can tear through most materials, and their draconic ancestry gives them immunity to most kinds of elemental damage. This particular specimen is far stronger than most of its species. Extreme caution is advised.

"A termite?" Jack asked, gawking at the still monster that had almost killed him. "Chewing through rock? That's not right."

"Is that what you're concerned about?" Min Ling said, giving him a fierce glare.

"Bro!" Brock shouted, rushing to Jack's side. Throughout the battle, he'd barely had any time to react. "Sorry. Glad you're okay."

"It's fine, Brock. Don't worry."

Jack's eyes softened. In their previous lava adventure, Brock had suffered the greatest losses. His trusty Staff of Stone, which had followed him since Trial Planet, had been snapped in half by Baron Longform. He'd endured multiple attacks which left him injured, and then he'd overdrawn his powers to scout ahead until he passed out. He had even bitten the tip of his tongue to spray some blood onto his Bro Code. Jack didn't know the significance of that sacrifice, but even now, Brock looked anemic. His fur was sticking to his body and his aura was weaker than usual.

That blood he used up must have been precious. Recovering would take some time.

After all that, if Jack forced him to use his powers to save him again, then he wouldn't be much of a big brother.

"Stay on guard," Min Ling said, facing the front, spear at the ready. "No more talking. Let's go."

Though they had fought with their full strength just now, the walls hadn't even cracked. They were magically enhanced to withstand extreme impacts.

The three fell silent as they trekked onward. Everyone kept their perception stretched and their body on guard at all times. Like this, perhaps they could catch the slightest indication of an incoming attack.

Jack was absolutely certain that they were in grave danger. Even the periphery of this hidden realm contained B-Grade entities—the core area, if this really was it, should be overflowing with them. Just the most minor of enemies, a single ambushing termite, had nearly taken his life.

They were in over their heads... but, not all was lost. With danger came opportunity. In such a place, either they would die without a grave, or they would emerge reborn.

Jack hoped for the latter.

Time passed. No more monsters attacked, but the scenery began to change. Chambers appeared to the side of the tunnel. They were completely destroyed and ransacked, their walls showing all kinds of colors and their insides in ruins.

After investigating, a few things became clear. Each of these chambers held the remains of a powerful monster—stone guardians, clay soldiers, plant lifeforms... The commonality between all of them was that they possessed draconic features and had been dead for only a short period of time. Whatever killed them had done so within the last few hours. It could only be the B-Grades.

Besides these guardians, each chamber contained an empty altar. It wasn't hard to imagine that every altar once held some treasure, now taken by the B-Grades.

Jack, Min, and Brock put the rooms behind them, still on full alert. Finding the B-Grades and joining them would guarantee their safety, but it would also guarantee they wouldn't get any treasure. It wasn't necessarily the best case scenario.

On the other hand, if they didn't run into the B-Grades, escaping would be difficult. It was a large, three-dimensional maze. With all its winding and intersecting tunnels, locating the exit would be time-consuming. Running into the path of the B-Grades would more likely be a great coincidence.

As for following the destroyed chambers backward, that

wouldn't work. They only started appearing deep into the maze. Before that point, there was no way to backtrack on the B-Grades' route. Even if it was possible, the green barrier may have returned, and even if it hadn't... did they really want to exit?

The guardians of this temple, though destroyed, still emitted a formidable aura. They had all been B-Grade existences. If their little group separated from the path the B-Grades had followed and found unexplored treasure chambers, defeating the guardian was almost impossible. Their only chance of getting something was to follow the B-Grades from afar and carefully investigate every chamber they left behind in hopes they'd missed something.

At the end, even if they found nothing, following the B-Grades would lead them to the main treasure trove, where the B-Grades would probably have to fight some powerful guardian. As long as Jack and the others remained undiscovered, it wasn't impossible to fish for benefits in the chaos.

It was sad, but this was reality. In a dungeon where they were severely underleveled, Jack's only option was to act as a scavenger. Even the things that a B-Grade would consider garbage might be useful to him.

After walking for a while, the destroyed rooms became more recent. Wisps of auras and space disturbances remained in the air—they were catching up to the B-Grades.

At this point, Brock took the lead. Though still weakened by using his blood before, he could use his powers. He summoned the Bro Code and used the same scouting page as before to scan the way ahead, hoping to lock onto the B-Grades before they found him.

Since the B-Grades would naturally direct their attention forward, and since Brock's scouting covered a wider range than a normal cultivator's perception, he probably wouldn't get discovered.

Unfortunately, reality was often disappointing. Only half an hour after Brock took the lead, Min Ling tensed up. "I felt something. I think there was a Dao enchantment here. We stepped right into it."

"Should we run?" Jack asked.

Before she could reply, the world shook around them. "Who's there!" a voice rumbled through the corridor. "Come out slowly or prepare to die!"

Jack cursed in his mind. This was the voice of Uruselam, the Hand of God's B-Grade leader. They'd been caught.

B-Grades simply had superior methods.

CHAPTER SEVENTY-THREE
EXPLORING THE TEMPLE

Jack, Brock, and Min Ling glanced at each other. Brock shrugged.

After a few minutes, they emerged into a slightly larger cavern, empty if not for the twenty B-Grades staring them down. The pressure was palpable.

As soon as they appeared, Monk Uruselam chuckled, while Spacewind exclaimed, "What are you doing here?"

"We were trying to escape a dragon," Min Ling replied simply.

Jack took in the people present. Though twenty-four B-Grades had entered, only twenty remained. A casualty rate of one-sixth was no joke, especially since they hadn't reached the main part of the temple yet.

Spacewind's mind shook. He had gotten past his initial surprise and realized that Min Ling, the woman he desired, had shown up together with Jack Rust, whom he viewed as his opponent. The two had doubtlessly adventured together so far, giving Jack time to flirt and pursue her. Perhaps he'd even succeeded.

Spacewind's gaze grew frigid. He snorted coldly, then turned around. "You will follow us. Remain at the back. You will not fight, nor will you touch any treasures. Do you understand?"

"Yes, sir," Min Ling replied calmly.

Uruselam laughed kindly, cupping his hands before his chest. "It is unfortunate that you had to come here. Since that is the case, let us hope you stay safe. We will do our best to protect you."

There was nothing Uruselam would like more than to instantly kill them all. They were enemies. However, with Spacewind present, he didn't dare move on the Church's budding talents.

The rest of the B-Grades gave the new arrivals various looks. Some bore mockery—they enjoyed how these proud geniuses had bitten off more than they could chew and would now return empty-handed. After all, all of them had been inferior to Jack and Min Ling when at the C-Grade, so envy and bitterness gripped their hearts.

Only a few people showed looks of regret. By entering the core area, Jack and Min Ling were basically doomed to waste their time in the hidden realm. To geniuses like them, that was unfortunate.

The two Envoys that Jack was familiar with, Borkuren and Ashly, were part of this latter group.

"We're moving," Spacewind said coldly, stepping over the corpse of a fifteen-foot-tall dragon-faced humanoid—the former guardian of this cavern.

Everyone fell into formation. They didn't speak much. Jack, Brock, and Min Ling were positioned somewhere in the middle, where they would be protected.

Jack noticed that the front of their formation wasn't occupied by Spacewind or Uruselam, the strongest people present. Instead, other B-Grades had taken the lead, very carefully investigating the path ahead.

"*They're afraid of traps,*" Min Ling said telepathically. "*Since this is a high-level place, any trap might be deadly to the people in front, whether they're Spacewind or a weaker B-Grade. That's why those other cultivators are walking ahead—they're acting as meatshields.*"

Jack nodded. He had come to the same conclusion.

Thanks to the B-Grades' careful approach, nobody had a problem keeping up. However, that meant they were moving slowly, and the temple was a massive place. Tunnels snaked in all directions. There were many intersections. Every time they met one, Uruselam would use divination—after praying with his eyes closed for some time, he would point to the correct way forward.

Like this, they entered deeper into the mountain temple. Hours passed, and as they delved deeper, the scenery began to change. The earthen walls darkened, while the fluorescent green moss was replaced by blue and purple—the felling was like entering a mysterious, underground cave complex.

The difficulty also shot up.

Almost everyone here was a B-Grade. Their status was exalted across the universe. If any of these people came to the Milky Way galaxy, they would be one of the strongest cultivators there, being able to form their own B-Grade faction and rule over a constellation.

Yet in this temple, these people were nothing but foot soldiers.

Traps sprang unbridled. One time, a thin arrow was launched from the wall, penetrating the leading B-Grade's throat. Before anyone could react, that cultivator had melted into a puddle of goo. Everything had happened in a hundredth of a blink of an eye.

The rest of the cultivators present were shocked. Uruselam sighed, then cupped his hands and muttered something in prayer. "Regrettable, truly regrettable. A good life lost. You will be remembered," he said, waving his hand and pulling the puddle of goo into his space ring—the dead B-Grade had been from the Hand of God. "Benefactor Ren, would you do us the honor?"

The woman called Ren gulped. She looked around, but there was no escaping this. She took to the front. Then, as slowly as the others allowed her, she cautiously inched forward.

Entering such a high-level dungeon was both a fortune and a misfortune. If they survived, they would receive all sorts of wondrous treasures. However, a single step could lead to their deaths.

Throughout the exploration, the B-Grades took turns leading the group. They would change every hour or when someone died. Thankfully, while traps were common, deaths weren't.

Spacewind and Uruselam, as the leaders of their respective groups, were excluded from meatshield duty. That was reasonable. The two were the strongest people present. If either of them died, the other would instantly act and exterminate everyone from the dead leader's faction.

Cultivators were not kind people. They were vipers that would kill each other at the first opportunity. Even the kind-sounding Uruselam was no exception—he was only faking kindness, for his own reasons.

Jack, Brock, and Min Ling never took to the front. With their strength, they would die near-instantly, and as much as Spacewind disliked Jack, he couldn't justify murdering his faction's greatest talents.

They didn't meet only traps. Occasionally, monsters sprang from the walls, including groups of draconic termites and all sorts of draconic insects. They ran into patrolling guardians, who were humanoids made of stone with dragon-shaped heads. Each of these guardians was at the early B-Grade.

These fights were swift and usually without casualties on the cultivator side. They were almost twenty people strong—the guards, who came in groups of three to five, were not a match.

The strongest enemy they ran into was a massive millipede, wide enough to fit the tunnel. Thankfully, they'd heard its chittering from afar and prepared. Though it was at the middle B-Grade, the cultivators had worked together to defeat it without a single casualty. A few people had been injured, but nothing some medicine couldn't fix.

The weirdest thing, however, was that even when B-Grades battled, the tunnel walls did not break. Only a few cracks appeared, quickly healing themselves. This place was clearly enhanced with superior Daos to withstand extreme impacts.

In all these battles, Jack was carefully observing the power of B-Grades. They not only used the ambient Dao, as C-Grades did, they erupted with power from the inside, presumably from their inner world. That power was far more than what a human body could handle. Even under the suppression of this temple's heavy Dao, the B-Grades could make the walls shake for miles. Spacewind and Uruselam were especially fierce.

After his recent breakthrough, Jack was confident he was the strongest C-Grade of the Cathedral besides Min Ling. Yet, seeing these B-Grades fight, he admitted that he wasn't their match at all. Even the weakest could easily defeat him.

However, perhaps in a few more fruits...

Two days passed. Out of the twenty B-Grades, sixteen remained, and that was after they had taken every possible precaution while traveling. At this point, everyone was shaken. They had no idea how long they still had to go. If this exploration continued for a week, wouldn't they all die?

Moreover, nobody knew who the next victim would be. Despite their every precaution, some traps were just impossible to discover.

Cultivators liked to risk their lives for treasure, but that didn't mean they would commit suicide by temple. One third of their number had perished and they'd only found minor treasures. It was disheartening. Thoughts of retreat were already going through most people's minds, but nobody dared say it out aloud.

Throughout the exploration, Uruselam's directions had often led them to exit portals. They were oval doors embedded in the walls, made not of wood but of warped space. Stepping into one would deliver the cultivators directly outside the hidden realm. These portals emitted an aura which confused Uruselam's methods, leading them in circles and slowing down their progress.

Of course, nobody used the portals, but they amplified the thoughts of retreat in various people's minds.

At some point, Uruselam paused. "Wait..." Everyone froze mid-step.

"What is it?" Spacewind asked.

"I sense something up ahead. It should be..." He inhaled deeply as if trying to smell something. "It should be treasure."

The cultivators' eyes lit up. They advanced carefully, and only half an hour later, their tunnel opened into what seemed like an indoor forest. A cave thousands of feet tall appeared before them. It stretched on for miles, occupying a good part of the mountain's volume, and it was filled with lush greenery. Despite the lack of natural sunlight, all the plants were thriving; the life energy was at its densest here.

There was also a set of great double doors at the back of the cave, standing over a hundred feet tall.

As soon as the cultivators entered the cave, the intense fragrance of the Dao assaulted their nostrils, even infiltrating their bodies from their pores. Just this fragrance was highly beneficial. If an F-Grade mortal took a single breath here, they could level up a few times and extend their life by ten years.

"This must be the temple's medicine garden," Uruselam said. "After being left alone here for who knows how long, the spiritual plants must have grown to unimaginable heights... Our efforts were not for naught. This is a great harvest!"

Spiritual plants were plants that contained pure Dao energy. They could either be directly consumed by cultivators or made into pills. The tree dragon that Jack and Brock had found before was also a spiritual plant, though intelligent. The more docile plants were sometimes gathered by strong cultivators and planted in special medicine gardens, where they could be grown and regularly harvested for millennia. These gardens often served as the backbone of powerful factions.

The Black Hole Church had its own medicine gardens, as did all the B-Grade factions of Jack's home galaxy. It was just that they were so closely guarded he'd never had a chance to see them.

Most importantly, such places almost never had guardians or traps, as any strong disturbance could destroy many precious plants.

"Disperse, everyone," Spacewind said, already flying ahead. "Anything you find belongs to you!"

The B-Grades didn't need to be told twice. They spread out in all directions. Due to the ever-present Life Dao, using one's perception to discover spiritual plants was difficult. They had to search using their own eyes and hands, shuffling through the greenery to find them.

Still, nobody complained. The plants grown here would be very precious. Each one they found represented a small fortune!

Jack, Min Ling, and Brock also spread out to search. Spacewind hadn't told them to stay away, and they weren't idiots.

Jack dove into the greenery. His connection to the Dao of Life gave him a slight advantage, but it was nothing compared to the B-Grades' higher speed and sharper senses.

After searching for a while, he discovered a plant! It was a root buried almost entirely into the ground, resembling something between a potato and a carrot. Yet, despite its simple appearance, the wealth of pure Dao it contained was staggering. Just this simple root was as valuable as the two tree dragon fruits he'd consumed before.

As he dug it out, he was full of smiles.

"Oho, what a rare find! That is a Twisted Orange Root. Great job," a pleasant voice came from behind him. Jack turned to find Uruselam standing only a few feet away, his face covered by a kind smile. "Coincidentally, I happen to need such a root. How about giving it to me, benefactor Jack? I'll compensate you fairly."

A small sack appeared in his hands. With a quick scan, Jack saw it contained a hundred Dao stones. His face darkened. That was a ridiculously low price for this root. To B-Grades, a hundred Dao stones were nothing, but treasures weren't easy to find.

However, could he refuse?

Seeing him hesitate, Uruselam laughed good-heartedly and added, "Here, I'll throw in another ten stones. I wouldn't want to make you refuse. That would be rude, and it would put you in quite the tight spot!"

Though everything in his expression and words radiated kindness, they were actually malicious. He was just trying to bully Jack using his superior cultivation.

Jack didn't want to be taken advantage of like that. Uruselam wasn't even in the same faction. Spacewind would most likely protect him from any backlash.

Just as he was about to open his mouth and refuse, the wind whistled. Spacewind landed between them, glaring at Uruselam. "Why are you bullying my faction members?" he asked.

"Ohoho. I was simply making a trade offer. If benefactor Jack wants to refuse, he is free to do so."

"There is no need. I refuse for him."

Jack raised his brow. Spacewind sounded pretty nice right now, but there was no way it was that simple. The two of them were enemies. If Spacewind helped him now, there was certainly another reason.

It didn't take long for that reason to be revealed. Spacewind turned to Jack and said, "To a cultivator as weak as yourself, holding onto treasures could get you into trouble. Give me that root. I'll keep it for you until we exit."

Jack was speechless. What "keep until you exit?" Spacewind would certainly take the root for himself, and he hadn't even offered a token price like Uruselam. He'd just directly demanded the root!

Jack did not enjoy being bullied. "It's fine. I would rather keep it myself."

Spacewind's face darkened. "What did you say? Your survival is only due to my kindness. You messed up entering the temple, and we didn't even have you lead the way as you ought to. Your survival is already a great bargain, but you also want treasures? Dream on!"

Jack did not reply.

"Give me the root," Spacewind added coldly. "Otherwise I will use my authority to execute you on the spot as a traitor."

Jack snorted. "You are bullying me."

"Hand it over."

I will hand your mother, Jack wanted to reply, but he kept it in. He suspected that, if he kept pushing, Spacewind really would kill him on the spot, and there would be nothing he could do about it.

These were the woes of the weak. Before a powerful B-Grade, the current Jack could do nothing to resist... but that wouldn't be true forever. He would be sure to take revenge.

"Take it," he replied coldly, tossing the root over. Spacewind received it into his ring.

I will make sure you pay a hundredfold, Jack thought as he walked away. He no longer searched for spiritual plants and directly flew to an empty area at the back of the cave, near the double doors. There was no point in finding anything only for Spacewind to take it away again.

Min Ling and Brock awaited him in that empty area. They were empty-handed and dark-faced. Clearly, their experience had been similar to his. As the weakest people present, there was always someone who would wrestle away their benefits.

The three of them sat down and waited, cultivating in the meantime. An hour later, the B-Grades were done searching. They all gathered at the empty area. Nobody discussed what they'd found—their eyes turned to the set of large double doors at the end of the cave.

"Brace yourselves, everyone," Spacewind said. "This must be the main chamber. Who knows what awaits us."

He and Uruselam touched one side of the double doors each, and then they pushed together. The doors creaked open.

CHAPTER SEVENTY-FOUR
FIGHTING THE BOSS

A DEADLY SCENERY WAS REVEALED BEHIND THE DOUBLE DOORS.

The entire cavern was surrounded by light stone. Though it appeared brittle, just scouring it with one's perception was enough to indicate it was actually extremely durable, even more so than in the tunnels leading here. The cavern was roughly circular with a diameter of several miles, larger than the previous one, and it was mostly empty.

Three human-sized boxes stood on the ground in the middle of the cavern, though were more like cubical rock formations. They were made of a brown material, with various lines running over their edges and no visible way to open them. Of the three, one was larger and also exuded a much richer aura.

Beyond those was a large hole in the ground at the far side. Its lip was green, almost suffocating with life energy, and from where they stood, it was impossible to look into. The extreme life energy of the hole made a stark contrast against the death dragon slumbering in the middle of the cavern, whose eyes snapped open at the same time as the doors. It stood and roared, the sound washing away the world. If space wasn't extremely stable here, and if the rock surrounding this cavern wasn't magically enhanced, just this roar could have annihilated the entire temple and a hundred miles around it.

The dragon had dark scales and scalding red eyes. Its body only stretched for three hundred feet, but the sheer power it exuded was leagues beyond the red dragon of the volcano, to the degree where they were simply incomparable. Jack was almost blinded by its aura. Drowned. Every thought of resistance fled his mind as only one remained: death.

This creature was something he could not endure.

Black Dragon, Level ??? (B-Grade)
Dragons are the darlings of the Dao. They are creatures that can stand at the top of the universe. Their bodies are large, durable, and powerful, while the Dao itself is carved on their flesh and bones. They do not need to eat to survive, as they can absorb the power of the world. Despite that, they often dominate a large area around them, relishing in the mortal pleasures.
Black Dragons are born of the Dao of Death. They possess extreme understandings since birth, and their insights will keep accumulating naturally as they grow up. Their bodies are near-immutable, they are resistant to spatial or time distortions, and their mere presence can slowly deteriorate a planet.

That last statement was heavy. A dragon's mere presence could cause an entire planet to deteriorate. Who would believe something like that?

And yet, it was true. Jack felt it in his bones. The double doors had been isolating the dragon's aura, but now that it struck them in the face, it brought with it the stench of death. If a mortal stood here, they would dissolve into dust. Even Jack's powerful body shook, his dense cells working together to resist.

Most importantly, the dragon's aura eclipsed all of the B-Grades present.

Spacewind's expression was dignified. Even the always calm and collected Uruselam had turned solemn. "Late B-Grade," he muttered. "Benefactors... It is time to fight for our destiny."

Late B-Grade!

Jack drew in a cold breath. B-Grades were said to be able to crack planets, but actually, most of them couldn't do it. What was a planet? It was a ball thousands of miles in diameter, composed of innumerable ores. Compared to the hard materials near the core, the surface was nothing but clay. Meanwhile, humans were just a few feet tall.

For a human to destroy a planet, that was a monumental feat of power. Only the strongest B-Grades could achieve such a thing. None of the cultivators present possessed that power—but this dragon did. That was the strength of a late B-Grade.

Jack himself was an extremely mighty individual. He could shatter continents with his bare hands. Yet, his power was a far cry from the early B-Grades surrounding him. Even if his cultivation suddenly increased by five fruits and a major breakthrough to reach the early B-Grade, he still wouldn't have any confidence facing this dragon.

Between Jack and a monster at the late B-Grade, they could only be described as immeasurably far apart.

"Cultivators," the dragon said, its voice aged and hoarse. It somewhat resembled Elder Boatman's, only deeper and more draconic. "Since you came, don't think about leaving!"

A strong gust blew from behind them. Everyone was shoved inside the dragon's cavern with no opportunity to resist—this was clearly no normal wind. At the same time, the double doors slammed shut behind them, trapping them in here with the dragon. Jack guessed that even if they tried to open the doors again, it would be impossible. At best, it would take long enough that they'd have to fight the dragon first.

Jack didn't think the creator of this place cared about them escaping. This wind mechanism was clearly designed to protect the medicine garden in the previous cavern from the dragon's death aura. Yet, it had now forced them into a corner. They had to defeat this black dragon or die trying.

Jack had no idea if the B-Grades could do it. And the worst part was, he could do nothing to help. He was just too weak. Even if their side won, just the shockwaves of the battle might kill him.

The dragon's face warped into a cruel grin. Black smoke escaped the sides of its mouth. Its red eyes flared with bloodthirstiness.

Spacewind drew his sword. Facing this dragon, though his aura was inferior, he did not wish to be overshadowed.

"Go all-out," he commanded, his gaze grim. "Galvanize your inner world. Detonate it if you must. If we hold back in the slightest, we will all die here."

The bodies of sixteen B-Grades erupted with power. Among them, Spacewind and Uruselam were the brightest stars, their auras a good chunk superior to everyone else's. Yet, facing them, the dragon wasn't daunted in the slightest.

"Death is inevitable," it said. "And yours, even more so."

As battle was about to erupt, Jack, Brock, and Min Ling glanced at each other with panic. They were not planning to participate—not because they didn't want to help, but because they couldn't.

"Jack Rust!" Spacewind roared heroically. "Fight with us! I will protect you!"

Jack barely held his tongue. What a joke! If he tried to join in, even the slightest ripples of power would tear him apart. Spacewind couldn't protect him if he wanted to, but he certainly had no such plans. He was just trying to get Jack killed.

Jack, Brock, and Min Ling didn't need to speak. They came to an instant agreement. They rushed to the farthest corner of the cavern, where the shockwaves would be weakest, and huddled together closely. They made themselves as small as possible. Min Ling's slender body pressed into Jack's, but at this moment, he had no time to care about such things.

Just as they arrived at their corner, they turned around and saw the B-Grades collide with the dragon. The extremely stable space was torn apart like paper. Time grew erratic. Elements scattered everywhere, while all sorts of weapons clashed against scales.

It was Armageddon. Each of these beings could crush celestial bodies. With all of them fighting at the same time, even the escaping shockwaves were beyond horrifying. They crashed into the stones around the cavern, some absorbed into them and some reflected.

Thankfully, the walls held, or the entire hidden realm might have been at risk. However, that was terrible news for Jack and the others. Some of the power within the shockwaves was absorbed with every reflection, but a terrifying amount still spread across the cavern, building up with every clash. The situation instantly became explosive. Fighting in such a stormy terrain, the weakest B-Grades could barely hold on. Some were directly injured. Spacewind and Uruselam took the brunt of the dragon's attacks, but even they were on the verge of collapsing.

In the C-Grade, every three fruits corresponded to one tier of power—from the early to the middle, to the late C-Grade. At the B-Grade, the difference between each tier was even greater. Though these early B-Grades were all extreme characters, and though there were sixteen of them, they were at a disadvantage against a single late B-Grade dragon.

Jack and the others could not bother with the state of the battle. They were enduring their own life and death calamity. With all the shockwaves reflecting off the walls, the density of power in the cavern had climbed to unprecedented degrees. It was like they were trapped in a closed room where nuclear bombs constantly exploded.

Thankfully, the small corner they'd huddled into protected them from most of the fallout, but a few snaked through. Defending against them was an ordeal. Three Dao shields superimposed over each other, from the weakest to the strongest: a golden shield of brohood, a purple aura of the Fist, and a red-cyan domain of lightningfire.

Min Ling's shield was the outermost one, so she had to bear the brunt of the shockwaves. Her entire body rocked in tune with her

Dao shield. Her face paled, and she forcibly swallowed the blood she was about to puke.

"Let me help!" Jack growled.

Min Ling didn't respond, but holes appeared on her Dao shield. A few shockwaves slipped through, impacting Jack's shield instead. It warped and contorted, cracking like glass. His entire body shook. He barely stayed on his feet. He had already assumed his four-armed battle form, but it couldn't help in this case—the only thing it enhanced was his body, not his Dao.

Like this, Jack and Min Ling together could barely resist the shockwaves. Their Dao shields twisted but held. As for Brock, he was too weak to assist them directly. His golden shield was their last, desperate line of defense.

"Go, bros!" he shouted, manifesting a large golden trumpet that he blew to encourage them—like a football fan.

At this point, the reflected shockwaves had grown so strong that even the B-Grades could not endure them. They'd all come together inside a bubble of protection. That bubble originated from Uruselam, who had taken charge of their defense. It was unknown what principles operated this bubble, but when passing through it, the shockwaves were weakened, allowing the B-Grades inside to barely endure them. Otherwise, half of them would have perished already, and the rest wouldn't be able to take on the dragon.

The bubble itself was spectacular. It was a creamy white, with various runes swimming along its surface and the faint sound of hymns echoing in the surrounding space.

Maintaining the bubble was taking a massive toll on Uruselam, leaving him unable to attack. But that was fine. Spacewind was in charge of offense, leading every other B-Grade to combine their powers against the dragon. The world splintered. The power released was so tremendous that even through the magically enhanced cavern, the entire hidden realm was shaking in a massive earthquake. Ravines had opened everywhere, lakes were leaking, rivers were changing course. The entire realm had been thrown into uproar.

The black dragon's body was beyond durable—it could withstand this onslaught for some time. Its situation was even better than the cultivators'.

"Turn to ash!" it roared, opening its jaws wide and releasing a torrent of black foam. As soon as it touched Uruselam's defensive bubble, its surface was corroded. Uruselam paled and spat out blood. This blood flew to the destroyed part of the bubble, hastily repairing it, but a portion of the black foam had already seeped through. As it fell on a B-Grade's body, the man screamed—his body deteriorated as if enduring the passage of a million years, then turned desiccated and dissolved into dust. He'd died in less than a second with no ability to resist.

The rest of the B-Grades made as much distance from the body as possible. Five of them combined their powers to suppress the black foam, while the rest continued attacking the dragon.

The greatest price of this was not the dead B-Grade, but Uruselam's weakening. His face was pale, his raised arms were shaking, and the bubble he had conjured, while enduring, was flickering. "I cannot last much longer," he said through gritted teeth.

The dragon's red eyes revealed joy. Drawing a deep breath, it gathered its power and prepared to unleash another dark breath. If it struck the cultivators, Uruselam's bubble would shatter, and they would all die horrible deaths. The battle was going terribly.

At this moment, Spacewind's gaze went cold. He did not wish to die like this. Suddenly, his hand shot to the side. A large palm of wind grabbed a Church cultivator without any warning and flung her through the bubble, directly onto the black dragon!

Everyone was stunned. Even the black dragon paused for an instant, not expecting this.

"Detonate your inner world!" Spacewind roared. "Do it and I will protect your family on the outside. Otherwise, I will torture and murder them all!"

There was no time to think. The dragon's claw slashed down at the cultivator even as her body was assaulted by numerous shockwaves. Her defenses crumbled instantly. In this situation, she was deader than dead.

At her last moments, the cultivator's heart shook. Her face formed an ugly, pitiful smile, and then her entire body imploded. "Curse you, Spacewind!" her last words echoed alongside a massive explosion.

CHAPTER SEVENTY-FIVE
ENDURING

A B-Grade cultivator's inner world represented their entire life and soul. It was their everything. When such an inner world was detonated, the cultivator would instantly die, but the power unleashed would be far superior to their all-out attack.

Although this cultivator was nobody special compared to the rest, the moment she detonated, a tremendous explosion rocked the cavern. The shockwaves were momentarily deflected, and even Uruselam's bubble wavered. Thankfully, they had only endured a small portion of the impact—the full force was aimed at the dragon.

Facing such an attack, the dragon didn't have time to defend. A vast amount of energy assaulted its body, blasting it backward. It crashed into a wall, releasing a pained roar. One of its wings had been broken, while some of its scales bulged out due to broken bones on the inside.

"Cultivators!" it roared in fury. "I never thought you would be so ruthless! But even so, you cannot defeat me! I am inevitable! Unstoppable! I am death!"

The dragon pushed off the wall and launched itself at the cultivators' bubble, unleashing a barrage of attacks. Despite its wounds, its battle power hadn't dropped by much. It could still fight. The body of a dragon was no joke.

Meanwhile, the shockwaves of that explosion had ricocheted off the walls. Part of them struck Jack's corner. Min Ling's shield faltered, nearly shattering beneath this power—the previous shockwaves were already her limit. As for Jack, the part that seeped through to his shield nearly overwhelmed him. He wouldn't last much longer.

Neither of the two could take much more strain, and Brock didn't have the power to help. At this rate, just enduring the shockwaves was questionable, let alone the rest of the battle. If they didn't do something, they would soon meet their end.

Jack's gaze went frenzied. "Combine!" he shouted. His arm wrapped around Min Ling's waist, pulling her closer. At the same time, his Dao spread through her body, aggressively merging into hers and enhancing her power. Jack's shield dissipated, but Min Ling's shone with splendor, regaining its past power and forcibly withstanding the onslaught. A purple tinge appeared on its surface.

In the cultivation world, where backstabbings were commonplace, touching another's body was a taboo. Pouring one's Dao into another was also an extremely invasive maneuver, since it basically gave Jack a full awareness of Min Ling's body. All her hidden weaknesses were seen through, all her weak spots were laid bare, the path of her energy circulation was clear as day. If they ever were to fight, this knowledge would give him a massive advantage.

However, Jack had no choice but to act like this. Combining two different powers was easier said than done, and they could afford no risks right now. Directly pouring his power into her body and merging it with hers was the most direct approach, as well as the safest. It guaranteed the greatest chance of a successful fusion. Moreover, the greater the surface of contact, the faster he could pour power into her, so he had directly pulled her body onto his. To mature people like them, a little bodily contact was no big deal.

Thankfully, their Daos were somewhat compatible, so they had succeeded.

But this also came with a deep price for Jack. To fuse his power into hers, he was pouring his Dao into her body and then forcibly severing his connection to it, turning it into raw power. That allowed her to control it like her own energy, but at the same time, Jack felt like someone was hacking at his soul with a cleaver. A cultivator was deeply connected with their Dao. Forcibly severing it was extremely painful and also carried the danger of hidden injuries.

But what choice was there?

Min Ling did not hesitate. She guided both powers into her shield, achieving a fusion greater than the sum of its parts. She managed to barely resist the shockwaves. As soon as the explosion died down, they would be a little more comfortable.

Spacewind had been paying attention to the C-Grades in the corner. Jack and Min Ling had no weird thoughts about their bodily contact—they were just trying to survive. When those actions fell into Spacewind's eyes, however, his heart shimmered with actual killing intent.

But the battle was still not over. The pain and injuries had driven the black dragon insane. It attacked the cultivators without a care in the world.

The cultivators were suppressed. They could barely persist.

"Everyone!" Spacewind shouted. "Detonate your inner worlds! Otherwise, we will all die!"

The cultivators glanced at each other. Nobody was willing to commit suicide to help the others. At that time, Uruselam clenched his teeth and dropped his kindly act. "Those who hesitate, I will curse their bloodline. Even if we all perish here, that person's descendants will die horrible deaths!"

Everyone went cold. All sense of unity had shattered between them. They were each fighting for their own survival.

But that didn't mean Uruselam's threat could be ignored. Faith-oriented Daos were often associated with karma and curses.

Someone of his power could very probably carry out his threat and use a curse that affected not just them, but all their descendants as well.

At this time, without any warning, the dragon opened its mouth and spat out another torrent of black foam. Their attacks melted as they entered this foam. Once it struck the bubble, they would all die.

Spacewind did not wait for someone to take the initiative. He reached to the side and grabbed a cultivator, then directly tossed her at the black foam. To the side, Uruselam suppressed his injuries to do the exact same thing, conjuring a massive palm and throwing a cultivator outside the bubble. He was just as ruthless as Spacewind.

The cultivator Spacewind had chosen was Ashly Shelly, the octopus Envoy who helped Jack in the past.

The two cultivators had expected this would happen, but in this battle, they had no way to protect themselves. They had only been hoping they wouldn't be the ones to go. Sadly, luck was not on their side.

Right before they died, their smiles were bitter and self-deprecating. They refused to go like this... but what choice did they have?

The two of them made the same choice. Their bodies combusted into massive infernos, instantly turning the world into hell. The dragon's breath was washed away, and even the magically enhanced walls cracked against this impact.

The bubble almost shattered. As for the dragon, which faced the brunt of the explosions, it was once again blasted against the back wall. More of its body broke. Pained roars echoed, imbued with fury. It still intended to fight, but the cultivators wouldn't give it the chance.

Spacewind and Uruselam each grabbed another cultivator each, flinging them at the dragon. Both before and now, they had chosen the people most attached to their families or factions. The two cultivators disappeared into the storm of shockwaves, then another two massive explosions erupted. The world shook. The void had long disintegrated, turning the entire cavern into spaceless nihility.

Heart-wrenching roars echoed. Black blood filled the world, resisting even the shattered spacetime. Uruselam's bubble finally shattered, but it had endured most of the shockwaves.

"Attack!" Spacewind shouted, shooting into the fray, followed by every other cultivator. No more self-detonations erupted, but the shockwaves grew even more intense as they directly struck the dragon.

As for Jack's corner, their situation was as ugly as could be. They had barely endured one explosion before—now, four occurred at quick succession. The shockwaves reached unprecedented heights. Min Ling's shield held for a while, violently contorting—even with Jack's assistance, there was a limit to what she could endure.

Jack gritted his teeth, pulling her tighter and pouring every bit of his Dao into her. This caused internal injuries for both of them, but survival was the most important thing. The shield flared majestically, imbued by the totality of their powers, yet still it struggled. It endured the first and second shockwaves. The third bent it like a torn sheet. When the fourth arrived, the shield could take no more. It wasted over half of the shockwave's power but finally shattered, the backlash injuring Min Ling. She could no longer resist.

The shockwave burst through, striking Brock's golden Dao shield, their last line of defense. Though it was weakened, how could Brock compare to even a fraction of a B-Grade's self-detonation? The shield persisted for barely an instant before shattering, letting the shockwave attack them directly.

However, that instant Brock earned them had been critical. Min Ling and Brock were both suffering the backlashes of their Dao shattering. Jack knew that if the shockwave hit either of them, they would die.

In that moment, he growled. He grabbed Min Ling by the waist and tossed her behind him. He stepped forward. His fist shone purple, his entire body radiated green power as its life energy was cranked to the max, and he roared out with all his strength.

"SUPERNOVA!"

Min Ling was shaken. Just as her powers were ebbing and she thought she was about to die, she had been thrown backward by Jack. His robust body stepped in front of her, shielding her. The image was forever imprinted into her mind. Nobody could endure that shockwave, and he would *sacrifice* himself?

At that moment, her heart was in pain. They had traveled together for some time, shared life and death. She realized she cared about him—she didn't want him to die. Worry clouded her mind. Pain.

"Jack!" she screamed.

"Bro!" Brock roared.

Their voices were swallowed in the explosion. Min Ling saw the entire world pulled into Jack's fist, condensed to an impossible degree. It all erupted. His fist smashed into the shockwave, unleashing all that power at once even as the fist itself evaporated.

His upper robes disintegrated instantly, revealing a brave back that could shield the world.

A tremendous explosion filled the cavern. The shockwave was halted, kept away from Min Ling and Brock, but Jack himself bore the brunt of the explosion. Min Ling saw his offensive arm disintegrate. The other three arms were crossed before his face, but they all shattered. Bones flew out of his body. Strips of flesh flew through the air even as they burned. Jack's entire body was blasted into the wall over their heads with such power that it shook the cavern, and he was almost flattened as all his bones broke. His chest was a blackened cavity. His lungs were nowhere to be seen, and even his heart had melted. His mouth opened but made no sound.

Min Ling screamed.

CHAPTER SEVENTY-SIX

I'M GONNA DO IT EVEN HARDER!

JACK'S BODY HAD BEEN BROKEN BEYOND RECOGNITION. EVEN HIS FACE HAD been burned—if Min Ling didn't know it was him, she wouldn't be able to recognize him.

His embers of life were already disappearing. He was just a moment away from death.

In that moment, his body suddenly erupted with indescribably dense, unfathomably deep life energy. It was like a million lives bloomed in his chest. The world was colored green, and Min Ling could feel her own wounds regenerating just from being nearby.

Jack was bathed in power. His ruined body slowly returned from the precipice of destruction. His organs regrew, his bones squirmed together, and his blackened flesh tumbled to the floor as new, rosy skin took its place. Even his eyes, which had been burned to cinders, reconstructed themselves.

It wasn't the first time Min Ling saw such regenerative powers. The same had occurred after Jack was almost burned to death by the magma. The sight remained as gruesome as last time, but now, that feeling was overshadowed by incomparable relief.

He'd almost sacrificed himself to save her. When her shield had shattered, she'd been enduring the backlash and was completely defenseless. Jack could have tossed her into the shockwaves to consume some of their power and increase his own chances of survival. Instead, he pulled her behind him and stepped forward to take the blow.

Anyone would feel immense gratitude after being treated like that, and Min Ling was no exception. Her heart swam with relief as she saw him recover. If he really died, she had no idea how she would feel.

"Thank you," she whispered, tears of gratitude welling up in her eyes. The next instant, she suppressed them. She rose and stepped before Jack's body, facing the inside of the cavern.

Though she was incomparably weak right now, her powers all spent, she would rather die than let a single shockwave touch Jack.

A brorilla stepped up beside her. His eyes were hard, and his body shone with golden radiance. He was as hurt as she was, but he also rose to fight.

Thankfully, no more shockwaves came. The cavern was silent. Some of the previous power still reverberated against the walls, but it was nothing they couldn't handle, even in their current weakened state.

Space slowly restored itself. Min Ling saw endless cracks on the walls, but they all stood. As for the black dragon, its body was lying on the ground, broken beyond recognition. A headless corpse was grasped in its claws.

The dragon's tenacity had been unrivaled. Even after enduring all those explosions, it had still managed to kill one more cultivator before finally succumbing to death.

Of the sixteen B-Grades who entered this cavern, nine remained. They were all sitting or standing around the dragon, recovering their energy as quickly as they could. Especially Spacewind and Uruselam—if one of them was overly weakened, the other might launch a sneak attack.

Though it seemed that would not happen. Spacewind had

conserved enough of his energy, and so had Uruselam—his bubble hadn't shattered because he ran out of power, but because he dissolved it when his reserves ran low.

As Min Ling saw them, they also saw her. Spacewind opened an eye to glance coldly at her. "You survived," he said. At that point, his indifference was so striking against Jack's willingness to sacrifice himself that Min Ling felt disgusted. She did not even reply.

Instead, she turned to Uruselam and asked, "Is your healer still alive?"

The only B-Grade healer present was part of the Hand of God. He was also alive, since Uruselam had protected him. The monk nodded, and the healer stepped forth, approaching Jack's unconscious body.

Seeing that, Spacewind's gaze went even more frigid. Min Ling, the woman he desired, had not even replied to him. Her first reaction was to look for a healer to cure another man—a man to whom she had been plastered to a moment ago.

The flames of hatred in his heart burned more intensely, but he concealed them. He had already decided to kill Jack. Doing so now, in front of everyone, would be considered treason to his faction. However, to exit the hidden realm they would need to pass through an unstable space tunnel. At that time, Spacewind was certain he could arrange an accident for Jack, and even if someone saw through him, they would have no proof.

I hope you are still alive, he thought, staring at Jack's unconscious body. *I want to kill you myself. Then, we'll see if Min Ling still appreciates you.*

The healer inspected Jack, then frowned. "This man is perfectly healthy," he said, glancing at Min Ling. "Why did you call me?"

"Just making sure. Thank you," she replied calmly, and the healer walked away.

Only Min Ling and Brock knew what terrible state Jack had been in just moments ago. Recovering from that was nothing short of a miracle. If Min Ling still believed the Life Artifact in Jack's body was simple, she would be plain stupid.

But she did not say anything. She didn't even harbor evil intentions. Jack had saved her, and Min Ling was a woman who knew right from wrong. No matter how great a treasure he hid, if she were to betray him now, she might as well kill herself.

Jack's eyes opened. He blinked slowly. Cracked stone entered his sight, alongside a very concerned brorilla face.

"Oh!" Brock said. "Bro is awake. Big happy!"

"Hey, Brock. Like you can't imagine," Jack replied, his smile strained.

He hadn't expected to wake up. When he positioned himself before that massive shockwave, he'd thought that was the end of the line. It was a miracle.

But how? he wondered. *I'm pretty sure my organs all shattered. I should have died.*

It was only after a few seconds of blankness that a last memory reached his brain. Right before he passed out, a vast, verdant green filled his world. The purest life energy.

The Life Drop... Only then did he let himself relax, the back of his head resting calmly on the stone. It saved me...

"*No it didn't. I did,*" a voice spoke inside his mind. "*And I gotta say, kid, you're really making me work here!*"

"Hmm?" Jack's eyes shot open again. "Turtle?"

"*My name is not turtle, goddammit! I am Venerable Saint Thousand Shell!*"

"*You were the one who saved me?*" Jack asked. "*You really are kinder than you seem.*"

"*What's that supposed to mean!*"

Jack smiled. "Thank you."

"Hmph! You still owe me all that life energy, you little piece of shit. You don't get to die unless I say so!"

Jack's smile widened. The turtle's voice was as imperious as ever, but after everything that just happened, Jack couldn't bring himself to take it seriously. "In any case, I owe you one," he said.

"You owe me multiple! The Supreme Blood is meant to last you millennia, but you're spending all the energy like candy!"

Jack frowned. I'm spending energy like candy? His gaze turned inward, focusing on the Life Drop. It remained an ocean of energy—yet, it wasn't as unfathomable as it used to be. Though still enormous, Jack had the feeling that the ocean's volume had decreased by a bit. Maybe around one percent.

"Oh," was all he said.

Using the four-armed form or regenerating himself took up a lot of energy. Back when he was a D-Grade, the amount was nothing to speak of. However, as his body increased in power, the energy needed to regenerate it naturally increased as well. The strain he put on the Life Drop was no longer negligible. By the time he reached the B-Grade, perhaps the Life Drop would no longer be as useful.

"What's that, kid!" the turtle thundered. *"You are shielding your mind, but I know you are thinking something blasphemous! Go on, spit it out. See if I dare to disintegrate you!"*

"I, uh, was thinking of how incredibly skilled you are at using this energy," Jack replied with a wry smile.

"Then why are smiling like that?"

"My face muscles are still a bit twitchy."

"You're lying! I made sure to fix those! I didn't want that little girl to think you're ugly."

"It's not like that..." Jack replied, shaking his head.

The turtle harrumphed once—or was it laughing?—before its voice turned serious. *"In any case, listen well. This is the second time in a short while that I've had to actively galvanize the Supreme Blood to heal you. That's what it's made for, so I can't blame you, but you really need to stop trying to sacrifice yourself for others! Anyway, the Supreme Blood may be extraordinary, but my own power isn't endless. I'll have to fall into slumber for a while. Try not to die while I'm gone, okay?"*

"How long will that be?" Jack asked but got no response. The turtle had fallen asleep as soon as it said so. What an enviable superpower.

After asking a couple more times and becoming convinced that the turtle was already deeply asleep, Jack sighed.

The Life Drop's regenerative properties were meant to supplement his powers, not overshadow them. The two times he'd been healed—once now and once after swimming in lava—were already too much. Such intense regeneration would be unavailable for the near future, but Jack was fine with it.

And, besides, he didn't regret his former decisions. Perhaps he would have died without the turtle's assistance, but he would have done so to save Brock and Min Ling respectively. The former went without saying, and as for Min Ling, she had saved his life and Brock's life once. He owed it to her.

The turtle being asleep meant nothing. Even if he really was going to die, he would sacrifice himself all the same. Being alive was meaningless if it meant abandoning his path.

"How long are you going to sleep for?" a woman's voice reached his ears. "Get up already."

He opened one eye. Min Ling was bent over him, inspecting him with her brows creased. As she noticed he was awake, a hint of relief passed over her eyes, disappearing in the next instant.

"You're alive," Jack said, breaking into a wide smile. "I'm glad."

"Of course I am," she replied, turning away.

Jack slowly forced himself to stand. Though he was healed, everything still hurt. He'd overdrawn himself. It would be hard to fight at full power until he rested.

As soon as he was up, he surveyed his surroundings. The double doors had been reopened, allowing more light into the cavern. A black dragon corpse lay at one end of the cavern, ruined beyond recognition. Besides being dead, it also looked like it had been scavenged. Most of its scales were missing, while its belly had been torn open and several organs removed. Anything of value had been taken by the B-Grade cultivators.

Speaking of B-Grades, the nine remaining were all meditating, restoring themselves to their optimal state. Spacewind and Uruselam were still alive. Of the rest, three belonged to the Black Hole Church and four to the Hand of God. The balance of power remained.

The B-Grades of each faction had gathered in two separate corners, while Jack, Brock, and Min Ling were in yet another. As soon as Jack rose, the meditating Spacewind cracked open his eyes, coldly inspecting him before closing them again. To Jack's surprise, the enmity he felt in that gaze was even deeper than before.

How the hell did I upset him this time? he wondered, then put the issue to rest. All he could do was be careful.

"I believe it is time, fellow benefactors," a voice echoed through the cavern, originating from Uruselam. His white robes were pristine, while one of his long brows still hung below his chin. The other was cut off at the level of his nose.

At Uruselam's words, the cultivators of his faction rose, as did the Church ones. Only now did Jack notice the three cubes in the middle of the cavern. In fact, he had seen them once before the dragon attacked. The surprising part was that they remained intact after that battle. They didn't even have a scratch on them.

"Did they wait for me to inspect them?" Jack asked.

"Of course not, you idiot," Min Ling replied. "You just happened to wake up on time."

CHAPTER SEVENTY-SEVEN

HOLE OF CERTAIN DEATH

The B-Grades cautiously approached the cubes. There were three of them—two small ones the size of bathtubs, and a larger one that reached Jack's shoulders. Their size alone wasn't too impressive, and they were made of the same stone as the surrounding cavern.

Some things were different, though. For one, they were carved into perfect cubes. They were also unharmed by the massive battle that occurred around them. The most important thing, however, was that they were covered in hundreds of intersecting lines.

As soon as Jack saw cubes covered in lines, he instantly thought of his own death cube. These were different. The death cube seemed naturally formed, while these ones were clearly carved by someone—Jack could see imperfections on their lines as if drawn by a masterful yet imperfect sculptor. Moreover, some of these lines had an end and a beginning, not looping back into themselves—on the death cube, every line formed a perfect loop.

In other words, these cubes were both similar and different than the death cube. Jack would be damned if there wasn't a connection.

Of course, he didn't say anything. He let the B-Grades inspect them as they liked.

Nine B-Grades approached the cubes and scanned them with their perception. Some walked around, while others used various arcane skills to try and peek through their walls.

"There are treasures inside," Uruselam said. "I can sense a faint aura wafting through. The smaller cubes should contain identical things, two of a pair. The largest cube... has something else."

"The question is, how do we get through?" Spacewind added, rubbing his chin.

This wasn't a place meant for early B-Grades. They had only managed to enter the temple because the barrier had been weakened by endless years, and half of them had to self-detonate their inner worlds to best the guardian. The treasures in those cubes would no doubt be priceless, but let alone getting to them, these B-Grades weren't even able to identify them.

"Breaking through is impossible," Uruselam said. Unless he and Spacewind detonated their inner worlds at the same time, it was impossible to achieve greater power than during the cataclysmic battle before. "We have to solve the cubes."

"Do you think that's possible?" Spacewind asked.

"Who builds containers that cannot open?"

Jack had to admit this made sense. He had approached as well, accompanied by Min Ling and Brock, and all three of them were inspecting the cubes alongside everyone.

Jack had already suspected these cubes were similar to his death cube and was trying to draw connections between the two sets of lines and see if he could find something useful. Unfortunately, they were too dissimilar. He was progressing too slowly.

His focus must have stood out. Spacewind turned to him and raised a brow. "What are you looking at? Do you think you can find something that we cannot?"

"I can try," Jack replied, not willing to back down. When he had seen Spacewind throw his fellow cultivators into the fire to save himself, his opinion of the man had dropped to rock bottom.

Spacewind was about to say something, but it was Uruselam

who spoke first. “There is no harm in letting the C-Grades look. Even monkeys can solve riddles with enough luck.”

Jack raised a brow. Uruselam seemed like a kind monk, but he was actually the master of passive-aggressiveness. Hearing his words, Spacewind snorted and didn’t bother further, turning his full attention to the cubes.

Time was a loose concept for people as long-lived as cultivators. They stood before the cubes for many hours, staring at the lines and trying to make out their meaning. Some scanned the cubes extensively with their perception, while others resorted to simpler means and patted down the cubes in their entirety.

A man even tested the floor around the cubes, finding it as hard as the cubes themselves. Using force to break through was impossible. They had to find a certain way to open them—but how?

Twelve hours later, nobody had any idea.

“It’s not a problem,” Spacewind said. “We’ve fought hard for these treasures. Even if we have to spend months and years meditating on the lines, we’ll figure it out.”

Everyone nodded. To these B-Grades, who could live for a hundred thousand years, spending two or three of those to get a treasure wasn’t a problem. However, Jack’s entire cultivation journey so far had lasted only three years. He was unwilling to spend another three staring at walls.

More importantly… he felt he shouldn’t need that long. Like everyone, he had walked around the cubes a few times, and he’d finally discovered a few lines that were very similar to the death cube’s. By contrasting the two sets, he got the feeling he would arrive at a solution within a much shorter timeframe than years.

The problem was that, even if he did manage to solve the cubes, Spacewind would just take everything. Jack would get a tiny corner of the treasures at best. That wasn’t enough. Between sharing treasures with these cold-blooded killers or taking them for himself and his friends, the choice was obvious.

If he could solve the cubes first, how would he get the treasures under everyone's nose?

He had no answer to that.

Besides the cubes and the dragon corpse, the cavern was not completely empty. It had two exits. One was the towering double doors leading to the already-emptied medicine garden. The other was a large hole on the floor in the far side of the cavern. Just like the cube, this hole was completely unaffected by the previous battle.

Now that there was no dragon to draw everyone's attention, Jack could make out carvings on the wall behind the hole. It was a few simple words:

No treasure lies here.
To those who enter deeper... Death!

Carving words into these hard walls was already an impressive feat. Moreover, these simple words carried a heavy killing intent, making all those who saw them avert their eyes. If a mortal so much as looked at the words, their heart would seize on the spot.

Could it be the creator of this hidden realm? Jack wondered. *But why would he write such a thing? Did he expect people to wander in here after his death?*

In any case, these were just the words of a long-dead cultivator. Even if he had been the master of this place, that didn't mean people would do as he said.

Besides the threatening words, the hole had few special features—it was just a tunnel dug vertically into the ground. Nobody could tell where it led or how deep it was. Thick darkness gathered just a mile into it, dispersing all Dao perception. Moreover, an astonishing force of gravity covered the hole. Anyone who took even a step inside would not be able to fly out, and they would instead be sucked deep into its depths.

And, beyond all those, the hole was suffused with an extremely potent aura. It wasn't powerful per se—even Jack and Brock could easily withstand it. However, this aura's most terrifying aspect was not its quantity, but its quality. It carried a concept of endless years, a bottomless, all-encompassing Dao. It was like staring at the mouth of a god.

Before such profoundness, even the Daos of all B-Grades present were like the drawings of children: extremely crude.

Uruselam inspected the hole with his perception, then shook his head regretfully. "Alas, that is the pressure of an A-Grade existence. It is likely the temple has a second level... but we are too weak. Even this guardian nearly took our lives. Going any deeper is suicide—we should be content with the treasures of the three boxes, then return to our factions and have them send some peak B-Grades to explore the rest of this place."

Nobody believed the words on the stone. How could there not be priceless treasures inside that hole? Nobody was willing to stop after coming this far, but unfortunately, there was nothing they could do. Entering the hole would be throwing their lives away. They had no choice but to let stronger people take this opportunity.

Everyone turned away and left. There was no point in torturing themselves. Just staring at the hole made their hearts ache with desire.

As they walked away, Jack was the last. He spared the hole a final glance—in that extremely profound life energy, he felt a hint of a familiar aura. Whatever exuded this aura resonated faintly with his Life Drop. Perhaps it was another Life Artifact related to Enas, or maybe a guardian of similar origin to the turtle.

Unfortunately, even Jack could only shake his head. Being courageous was one thing, but being reckless was another. Just the faint resonance of the Life Drop was in no way a guarantee of success. If he entered that hole, chances were he would perish just like everyone else.

It was regretful, but some opportunities had to be let go.

Everyone abandoned the hole leading deeper and returned to the cubes. This was the opportunity they could grasp—and they would give it their all. Even if nobody could make sense of those mysterious lines, they would keep trying until they succeeded.

Spacewind and Uruselam gathered what remained of their party after speaking privately for a while.

"Listen up, everyone," Spacewind said. "We have come to an agreement. Until we resolve these cubes, we will stay in this place for as long as necessary. All treasures will be split fairly once we find them. However, until then, we have to ask that everyone remains inside this cavern. We cannot risk one of you notifying the factions of this place's real potential, or these treasures will no longer be ours. Anyone who goes even one step beyond the doors will be considered a traitor and jointly pursued by me and Uruselam."

As if to emphasize his point, Spacewind waved his sleeve, causing a strong wind to blow the double doors shut. The cavern was sunk in darkness. His meaning was clear—until they solved the cubes, those doors would not open, no matter how long it took.

Many people were disgruntled. Even if they did open the boxes, who told them that the treasures could be split nine-ways? Perhaps it was a single item in each box. If that was the case, most would get nothing. The only ones who were guaranteed to earn a reward were Spacewind and Uruselam.

Unfortunately, they were also the strongest people present, so they had the power to lock everyone inside. As for everyone else joining forces to demand they leave, that was just a joke. Spacewind and Uruselam were stronger than the other seven B-Grades combined, and they would not hesitate to kill them all if it meant getting the treasures.

The only reason they hadn't done so already was that even they wouldn't recklessly kill people of their own faction. Otherwise, nobody would have followed them here.

Therefore, everyone was dissatisfied, but they could only comply. A couple years was nothing to them, anyway. But those years mattered to Jack and Brock. Let alone the fact that they would be presumed dead and their families on Earth would miss them, wasting precious cultivation time on treasure that wouldn't even become theirs was far too much.

Min Ling was in the same boat. She was also in the prime of her youth. Wasting her years here was just too bad.

And the worst thing for Jack was that he soon might discover the solution to the cubes. Would he be forced to share it, knowing he wouldn't see even a corner of the treasures, or would he need to wait several years until everyone else got too bored to continue?

Was there really no other way?

CHAPTER SEVENTY-EIGHT
FISHING FOR BENEFITS

In the Black Dragon's cavern, everyone inspected the three cubes and meditated. The doors were closed. They would not open until the cubes did.

Like this, a month passed.

Meditating on some lines was not a quick process, but it also wasn't a hopeless one. The more abstract the subject, the more ways there were to see it. The B-Grades had not lost their vigor—if anything, the challenge had ignited their competitiveness, causing them to dive even deeper into their attempts at comprehension.

This was also true for the weaker B-Grades present. Though they didn't have much hope of actually earning anything inside the boxes, the lines themselves hid insights into the Dao. Meditating on them was a slow process of enlightenment, as if some wisdom was carving itself into the backs of their minds.

To B-Grades, this feeling was priceless. They had eventually realized that, let alone the treasures, even meditating on these lines was a lucky chance.

As for Min Ling and Brock, they too spent their time gazing at the lines. They held infinite complexity. There were 999 of them across the three cubes, each of irregular depth and width, and all of them intersected in a million different ways. Each tiny change was a clue, and all of those together would form an image.

Spacewind and Uruselam were right. Given time, they would indeed decode these cubes. It would take anywhere from half a year to three years.

However, that applied to most people. Jack was different.

He'd seen these lines before. He possessed the death cube—a cube also covered in 999 lines of irregular depth and width. Though the death cube depicted many differences, they were clearly similar.

Moreover, the death cube was much easier to comprehend. Its insights were richer and more condensed, each line forming a complete system. When he had meditated on it for a few days, it had been enough to gain a significant harvest. By using the death cube as the key to decoding the other three cubes, his progress was much faster than everybody else's.

After a week, though he wasn't halfway there, he had taken significant steps. He now understood that, while the death cube concerned death, these cubes of similar origin concerned life.

When contrasting the two side-by-side, many things became clear. The death cube's lines were all perfect loops with no end or beginning. That was because each line signified a life, and since the death cube spoke about death, each of those lives had already reached its end and returned to the starting point.

On the other hand, these three cubes represented the concept of life. Each of their lines represented a life, and unlike the death cube's, not all of them were over. Some were depicted at the prime of their youth, in the decline of old years, or in various other states. That was why these cubes had lines with beginnings and ends, while the death cube only contained perfect loops.

Of course, these three cubes were far inferior to the death cube in quality. The main reason for that was their imperfections—the lines of the three cubes were not perfectly carved, containing various tiny differences from the real thing. Perhaps a carving was one inch too shallow, or half an inch too wide, or slightly more angular than it should have been. On such a profound system, however, it was difficult to distinguish which of these were carving mistakes and which were intended as part of the cube.

These all originated from the fact that these cubes were not natural, like the death cube, but artificially carved. It was like someone possessed a genuine Life Cube and had tried to duplicate it. That was why they were so much larger than the death cube—to give the sculptor more space—and also why they contained imperfections—when carving such complicated lines, even an A-Grade engraver could make mistakes.

As it was, these mistakes greatly increased the difficulty, mostly because nobody had recognized they existed. Everyone else took the mistakes as part of the puzzle; they had no way of knowing better. Only Jack could contrast the two systems and find the minor inconsistencies.

These cubes, by themselves, were a great lucky chance. That was especially so for Jack. He cultivated life and death, but for death, he had the death cube and Elder Boatman's crystallized insights. His attainments in that Dao were currently low, but they would climb meteorically. As for Life, he had no such shortcuts. All he could rely on were his Life-related accumulated insights from practicing the Fist, but those would eventually be outpaced by his comprehensions of Death, and then his entire Dao system would be imbalanced.

He was in dire need of a way to comprehend Life... and these cubes were exactly that.

Gazing into the lines, Jack lost track of time. Everything else disappeared—the cultivators, the cavern, the treasures, everything turned to smoke. It was just him and the three cubes, which he restlessly studied. Every line was a story. He traced every change in depth, every widening and narrowing, every curve and intersection with others.

999 lives. None of them were ordinary. As Jack understood more and more things, he discovered that the lines were talking about

kings and gods, about devils, martyrs, heroes, and those who suffered most. Each life was extreme. The insights hidden inside them were far richer than in a regular person's.

In truth, the three cubes were all part of a whole. The two small ones held 250 lines each, and the larger one held 499, for a total of 999 lines—999 lives.

Jack sat cross-legged in front of each cube for a long amount of time. He entered a completely pure meditation state, where the entire world melted away. The only hints of movement came when he stood up and moved to a different side of the cube or to a different cube entirely.

Meditating on those lines was somewhat similar to experiencing the Dao Chamber of Mortality but incomparably more effective. Moreover, he observed them for far longer. During this time, his understanding of Life shot up. Without knowing it, his Fist of Mortality skill had risen from the first to the second tier, bordering on the third, and the Dao Fruit of Life in his soul was growing ever brighter like a green star.

One day, Jack finished observing the last line. His mind snapped into focus, returning to the dark cavern with the closed doors. Looking down, a faint layer of dust had gathered on his legs.

How long was I sitting for? he wondered.

Slowly, he stood, finding that the space around him was filled with other meditating cultivators. None of them had entered the depths he did—the imperfections of the carvings would create contradictions, constantly shaking them out of their spiritual focus and preventing them from achieving the same state of nirvana as Jack. Even Spacewind and Uruselam had faint creases in their brows.

Jack discovered Brock standing in a corner, reading from a golden book in his lap. As he approached, Jack saw that the book only held images, not letters—Brock had never learned to read.

"Hey," he said.

Brock looked up from his book. "Sup. Are you winning, bro?"

"I, uh... Kinda? Those carvings are complex, but I think I may have understood one line by now," Jack replied out loud. Through telepathy, however, he informed Brock of his real progress. He had fully comprehended the lines enough that he was confident he could unlock the cubes.

Brock nodded.

"How long was I meditating for?" Jack asked.

"Three months."

Three months... Jack shook his head. *Cultivation really is timeless. I wonder how my kids have grown. Perhaps I should go out and see them.*

He spoke into the brorilla's mind. "Are you ready to go?"

"*I was born ready, brother.*"

Jack smiled. "Alright."

He turned back to the cubes. He was confident he could unlock them. The problem was that, even if he did, all those B-Grades would just take the treasures and give him nothing. He wasn't willing to let that happen.

He needed a plan.

And, thankfully, Jack had a penchant for imaginative, unlikely, yet oddly successful plans.

But first, he needed to get Min Ling on board. They were friends now. He didn't want to share with all those cut-throat B-Grades, but he would with her and Brock.

One day later, Jack sat and gazed at the cubes alongside everyone else. They were meditating on them. He was trying to solve them.

Life and death... he thought, letting the connections happen in his mind. *Two parts of a whole. One without the other is incomplete. To solve the cubes, I must simulate the progression of all the incomplete lines until they form a perfect loop—until they die and return to their starting point. That is how I prove my comprehension. That is how I solve the riddle.*

He smiled. The Sage had once said that divination was part of the Dao of Life. Jack hadn't understood at the time, but now he did. By observing and understanding all these complete lines, he could infer the ends of the incomplete lines as well. He could predict their future.

Of course, he was still a novice. He couldn't do it too well. But after meditating on these cubes as well as the death cube, he felt a degree of confidence—and, even if his predictions weren't perfect, neither were the lines themselves. Whoever set this puzzle should have left a generous error margin.

Jack stared at one of the smaller cubes. It contained two hundred and fifty lines; of those, only twenty-five were incomplete. He extrapolated their future course, confirming his predictions over and over again until they were as good as he could make them. Then, he held the complete solution in his mind... and waited.

One hour passed. Then another. Jack was patient, like a hunter stalking his prey.

The other cultivators couldn't completely immerse themselves in these lines like he had. They would often stand up to stretch their legs or reset their thoughts. A few cultivators did, but Jack still waited. He let time pass.

Finally, five days after he'd locked onto the solution, Spacewind also moved. He dusted himself off and strolled to the large hole on the far side of the cavern. He often looked at it. Perhaps it stoked his greed.

As soon as Jack saw Spacewind rising, he knew the time was near. He waited until the other man was over the hole, gazing into its depths. Then, with a single flex of his mind, Jack constructed twenty-five perfect lines of Dao and plastered them at the end of the small cube's incomplete lines.

It happened too quickly for anyone to realize who did what. The entire cube shone like a green beacon. All the lines disappeared, and the stone of the cube melted away, revealing a green bean underneath.

Though this was just a tiny bean, it emitted intense amounts of power. Jack's mind was almost shaken. This was absolutely an extreme treasure! A treasure that would make even peak B-Grades froth with greed, let alone these early B-Grades!

Everything had happened too fast and without warning. Most cultivators remained stunned. Spacewind, who was in the distance, had just turned his head, his mouth wide open in shock.

Uruselam, however, was right next to the small cube. His face hardened. His eyes shone with avarice. He shouted out loud, unleashing a massive wind that blew everyone far away. His hand snaked forward.

The bean entered Uruselam's space ring. He then shot to his feet and flew toward the doors quickly enough to create multiple sonic booms. Spacewind was also flying over, but he was a bit too far away—the distance would be hard to cover. "Stop him!" he roared.

Two Church cultivators flew in Uruselam's path.

"Out of my way!" shouted the monk. A massive golden palm appeared, slapping the two cultivators at full power. Their defenses burst apart. Both of them spat blood and crashed into the walls, and Uruselam safely flew between them. With another shout, that golden palm slammed into the giant double doors, smashing them open so abruptly they were almost ripped from their hinges.

Uruselam flew out at maximum speed. Spacewind followed an instant later. By now, every other B-Grade had reacted as well, and they activated their movement skills to rush after their leaders as quickly as they could. Shouts and shockwaves came from afar—the medicine garden was torn apart, the entire mountain shook, and the B-Grades disappeared into the tunnels at multiple times the speed of sound.

Only three people were left behind: Jack, Brock, and Min Ling.

Everything had gone according to Jack's plan.

When the cube opened, nobody cared how or who achieved it. They only wanted the treasure. They were ready to erupt into a bloody battle, and thanks to Jack's calculations, Spacewind had been away. Thus, the strongest person present was clearly Uruselam, who easily took ahold of the treasure.

After that, he wasn't an idiot to stay there and wait for Spacewind to catch up. If that happened, they would be forced to split the treasure—if they fought instead, one would die, and the other would be so weakened that someone else might kill him afterward.

Therefore, Uruselam rapidly calculated everything and chose the only sensible option: flee to the nearest exit portal. He could directly leave the hidden realm, keep the bean, and then invite stronger people to compete for the rest of the treasures.

After all, just this bean was an extreme treasure. Taking it was far better than striving for the contents of the larger cube and probably dying in the process, not to mention the benefits he would receive from his faction if he notified them about all these.

Spacewind couldn't let that happen. As soon as Uruselam fled, he followed at high speed, using everything he had to catch up. If Uruselam exited the hidden realm, Spacewind would get absolutely nothing!

As for everyone else, staying here was meaningless. They could only follow their leaders and participate in the potential battle.

All those conditions resulted in the cavern emptying in the blink of an eye. The only ones remaining were Jack, Brock, and Min Ling—the three C-Grades. Nobody found that weird, either. Why would they want to rush into a B-Grade battle?

As everyone ran away, Brock and Min Ling converged to the remaining two cubes. Jack was already there, meditating on the second small cube with every ounce of concentration he possessed. Nobody disturbed him. Only a few seconds later, a Dao construct of lines fell on the second cube, smoothly melting it and revealing a second green bean.

"I'll keep this for now," Min Ling said, drawing it into her space ring. Brock didn't disagree, and Jack was already meditating on the largest cube.

They wouldn't take just one treasure. They would take everything!

But, they were also against the clock. Jack had calculated everything many times. He'd concluded that, after Uruselam took off, Spacewind would catch up before they reached the nearest exit portal. After all, space and wind both focused on speed. The B-Grades of both factions would engage in a brutal melee, and that would give Jack the time he needed to open both cubes, take the treasures, then rush to another exit portal and leave this place.

After all, they'd walked for a long time and arrived at multiple exit portals. To reach the nearest, the B-Grades would exit the medicine garden cavern and turn sharply to the right. However, Jack kept the three-dimensional map of this temple in his mind, and he knew that if he turned sharply to the left after exiting the medicine garden, he would also arrive at a portal. It would just be somewhat farther away than the right one.

The portals had confused Uruselam's divination as they explored the temple, making them work in circles. Those circles now worked in Jack's favor.

He was fairly certain this plan would work, but anything could go wrong in the process. Perhaps Uruselam would make it to the exit portal. Perhaps a B-Grade would catch on and return to the cavern.

So, they had to hurry. Jack had already simulated the opening of the cubes until they were muscle memory, which was why he was so quick, but he still needed a few seconds. The large cube, in particular, was the most challenging one. Constructing all those lines took enough time that Jack felt like he was suffocating—every second brought them closer to death.

He hastily completed the lines and sent them onto the cube. They latched and he looked on with bated breath. After all, he wasn't perfect. In this situation, he only had a sixty percent confidence in solving the cube on the first try.

The lines glowed, then a particular spot darkened. They all died down and disappeared.

Jack's heart reached his throat. He'd failed! However, that short darkening had shown him where he was wrong. He was confident there were no other mistakes. He could unlock it on the next try. But did he have the time?

"Go for it," Min Lin said quickly. "We should make it. We have to risk it!"

He nodded. The construct gathered in his mind, a mass of swirling lines undergoing a thousand variations every second. His eyes scanned the cube. This was his last chance. He had to get it right.

The lines smashed onto the cube with force. The entire thing shone—then, before their eyes, it melted. Jack cried out in relief. His hand shot into the cube before it even melted completely, grabbing a small wooden key, and shoving it into his space ring.

Then, without a word, the three of them shot away!

All the treasures had been taken. The exit portal was nearby. It was time to run!

CHAPTER SEVENTY-NINE
DESPERATE MEASURES

SPACEWIND SOARED THROUGH THE TUNNELS. HIS HAND SHOT OUT, SHAPED AS a claw, and directly tore apart Uruselam's space restraints. Space shattered, moving him miles ahead. The wind carried him through the crack like a second teleportation.

In this lineup, he was confident he was the fastest, so he would eventually close in. But would he make it in time?

Damn it all! he cried in his mind. *How did this happen? I only stepped away for a few seconds!*

It didn't take a genius to realize this wasn't a coincidence. Uruselam must have come up with the method to solve the cube and waited for Spacewind to step away. That was the only scenario that made sense.

A monk has an advantage when it comes to the Life Dao! Spacewind thought, gritting his teeth. *I should have fought him to the death. If he escapes, I get nothing!*

Thinking to that point, he accelerated, pushing his speed to the very limit. Space shattered again behind him, and the sonic booms pushed against him, shooting him forward.

Miles of tunnels disappeared in the blink of an eye.

Finally, a white-browed monk entered Spacewind's perception range. His white robes fluttered with no semblance of grace. He was running as quickly as he could, but there was no way he could match Spacewind.

"Break!" Spacewind shouted, slashing out with his sword. Space itself formed a blade that shot forward.

"May the Immortals protect me!"

Uruselam slammed his palm into the floor. A pale white wall rose behind him, sealing off the entire tunnel. Runes swam on its surface, and faint hymns resounded through the air. Behind his new wall, Uruselam resumed running.

How could such a hasty defense stand up to Spacewind? Space itself smashed into the wall, shaking it from end to end, and the wind forcefully tore it apart. At this critical juncture, Spacewind hadn't hesitated to invest some of his world essence in the attack. That was the essence of his inner world—it could enhance his power, but every B-Grade cultivator only had a finite amount of world essence, and it was very difficult to restore. If Spacewind failed here, he would have suffered a heavy loss.

"Stop right there!" he yelled, shooting through the tunnels. Uruselam could not escape this strike. He turned and smashed a palm into Spacewind's slash, enduring the heavy injury to use the momentum and shoot himself deeper into the tunnels.

Spacewind roared as he followed. Far behind them, the other B-Grades were covering ground as quickly as they could, each faction guarding against the other.

They had expected a bloodbath when they entered this realm. Now, it seemed that moment was not too far away.

Uruselam had approached a teleporter. Only a few more miles left to go. However, escaping Spacewind was no longer possible.

Wind rose to block the monk's path. Space turned into saws,

grinding into Uruselam's body and trying to tear him to pieces. Under this pressure that could instantly eradicate a mountain ridge, the monk shouted, "Diamond Body!"

A brilliant white glow appeared. As the saws of space ground against him, he barely resisted them. "Palm of Immortality!" Uruselam shouted again. His white brows were fluttering wildly, as were his robes, and he no longer resembled a serene monk but a crazed martial artist. He smashed a palm into space, shattering the saws. The energy of this palm carried on, striking the incoming space slash and causing both attacks to disintegrate.

"You cannot escape!" Spacewind roared out, flying at Uruselam like a shooting star.

"Genesis!" Uruselam madly shouted.

Two extreme forces collided. The tunnel washed away, the tempered stone barely withstanding the impact. Space crumbled for miles around them. Gravity lost its grip, and the flow of time turned chaotic. The two B-Grades clashed a dozen times in a thousandth of an instant.

"*Let's split it, Spacewind!*" Uruselam shouted telepathically mid-battle when he could no longer escape. "*If we fight here, we will both die!*"

"*You despicable little monk, as if I would believe you!*" Spacewind roared back. "*Fool me once, shame on you. Fool me twice, shame on me!*"

"*What? I never fooled you!*"

"*Do you think I am an idiot? You had the solution and waited for me to step away so you could take the treasure for yourself! We had a deal!*"

The two were embroiled in their fight, spitting their words mentally as that was all the focus that could be spread—this entire conversation happened near-instantly.

"*I did not solve the cube!*" *Uruselam cried out.* "*I don't know who did it!*"

"*As if I'd—*"

"*It is the truth!*" Uruselam struck out with a strong palm that sent them both flying backward. He wasn't an idiot. Now that he was no longer running for his life, he was beginning to realize that this was suspicious. Of everyone present, he had the highest attainments in the Dao of Life, and he wasn't even halfway to the solution. There shouldn't be anybody capable of solving it!

Moreover, the cube was solved right as Spacewind had walked away. That was no coincidence. Whoever did this had planned everything out. Perhaps even this entire chase was part of their plan.

And, as Uruselam's mind traveled in that direction, it suddenly occurred to him that whoever solved one cube could probably solve the others as well. They wanted the other treasures for themselves. That was the reason.

Uruselam felt sick. "We have been tricked, Spacewind! I did not solve the cube, I swear on the Immortals!"

His voice reverberated across the walls. Spacewind narrowed his eyes, ceasing his attacks. If Uruselam made such a heavy vow, he was probably telling the truth. In that case...

If Uruselam could think all those things, so could Spacewind. His eyes widened. "We've been tricked!" he shouted out loud. "Who? Who was it!"

"We must run back!" Uruselam said. There were no eternal enemies, only eternal benefits. These two people who had been killing each other just a moment ago were now allied.

Uruselam reached into his space ring and retrieved the magic bean, then directly broke it in two and tossed one half to Spacewind. Only like this could they trust each other.

"Someone must have seen those lines before and tried to trick us, but we are still the strongest people present," Uruselam spoke quickly. "We must run back. We can catch them in the act!"

"Whoever is missing is the traitor," Spacewind growled, his dark hair floating wildly. He knew that the rest of the B-Grades were following them—they had almost caught up by now. His aura swept out, covering them all, and then his brows rose. "Everyone is here. Then who—"

He froze. The answer came to him. "The C-Grades!"

"After them!" Uruselam roared, mad with fury. Getting tricked by a fellow B-Grade would be unfortunate, but it was something he could stomach. If he was tricked by a mere C-Grade, this would be the greatest embarrassment of his life.

The two of them shot out. Telepathic messages rang, and all other B-Grades were instantly in the know. All nine of them rushed back at their highest speed, but two people were fastest: Spacewind and Uruselam.

And, of the two, Spacewind was even faster! Hatred burned in his heart. Of the three C-Grades left behind, the monkey could be ignored. Then, if Min Ling was the one to trick them all, he could just barely accept it.

But if it was Jack Rust...

His eyes shimmered. The wind around him howled, chipping away at the enhanced walls. Space shrunk below his feet and the tunnels zoomed past.

Jack Rust had already made advances on the woman Spacewind desired. He had challenged him to his face. If he now managed to trick them all and escape with the treasures under everyone's nose, Spacewind would never be able to live with this insult. He had to catch them.

More world essence seeped out of his body. It was a heavy price, but he had no time to care for such things. He accelerated, turning into a dark star that charged far ahead of the other B-Grades. At this moment, Spacewind was using every single technique he knew to go even faster.

No matter what, he had to make it in time!

Jack grabbed the wooden key and stashed it into his space ring, instantly shooting out. Min Ling was close behind him, carrying Brock under her arm—she was the fastest and strongest present, so her speed while carrying Brock was similar to Jack's.

"Faster, faster!" Jack shouted. "We must make it!"

They shot through the open double doors, burning through the medicine garden like twin comets.

"We're almost there!" Min Ling cried out.

"Too late!" Brock shouted, snapping his eyes open. He had been scouting ahead all this time, watching for signs of the approaching B-Grades. "They're coming."

Jack and Min Ling skidded to an instant halt, their minds racing faster than their mouths could ever hope for. They looked at each other with horror. The B-Grades were coming...

"*Dammit!*" Min Ling said. "*We should have more time! How did they figure it out so quickly? Did Uruselam escape?*"

If only they had a few more seconds, they could have made it. However, the reason didn't matter, only the consequences.

It was too late to feign ignorance. The cubes were all solved. The treasures were in their grasp. If they kept running, the B-Grades would easily catch up and capture them, and then who knows how they'd get revenge.

This had all been a calculated risk... Sometimes, calculated risks didn't work out.

"*What do we do now?*" Min Ling asked.

"*We can surrender,*" Jack replied. "*Maybe then they'll—*"

"JACK RUST!" a voice echoed from the tunnels, riding the wind even faster than the B-Grades themselves. "I WILL TEAR YOU TO FUCKING PIECES!"

They glanced at each other. "*Well, there goes my surrender,*" Jack said. "*There is only one path we can take... but it is the most dangerous one. Brock and I must go. Will you follow us?*"

Min Ling didn't consider it at all. Her beautiful eyes met Jack's and she said, "*Spacewind will not let me off either. If I'm going to lose everything, I might as well risk it. Let's go.*"

The path they were referring to was the hole at the far end of the cube cavern. It exuded such a potent aura and such powerful gravity that nobody had dared enter it—any experienced dungeon delver saw it as almost certain death. Even if Jack felt something faintly resonating with the Life Drop from its depths, it remained extremely dangerous. Even he wouldn't willingly enter.

Yet, what choice did he have?

They were still skidding to a stop, their conversation having lasted a single telepathic instant. As one, they pushed against the ground and flew backward. The medicine garden around them, ruined by Spacewind's previous attacks, warned of their future should they be caught.

Two lines shot through the cavern, one red and one purple. A golden trail was left behind them both—that was Brock, who was currently setting up barriers to slow down Spacewind.

Right as they set foot between the huge double doors that separated the two caverns, a dark light shot out of the tunnels. It was a man clad in black with wildly floating hair. His gaze was furious—and, as it set on them, it promised nothing but a violent death.

"STOP!" he roared, charging at full speed.

"No, you stop!" Brock shouted back. They weren't idiots; they kept running.

Their distance from the hole was only a fraction of what Spacewind had to cover to catch them. However, he was far faster. They couldn't even compare to a normal low B-Grade in speed, let alone him.

"Go!" Jack shouted. He overdrew his powers, stomping on the ground while releasing miniature Meteor Punches from his feet. His shoes disintegrated, letting his bare feet crash against the stone, and the entire cavern reverberated from the impacts. Beside him, Min Ling changed her aura into cyan, that of lightning.

Both were spending their energy as quickly as possible to achieve the highest maximum speed. The hole was only half a mile ahead of them. They had to reach it, or they would die.

That distance was nothing to them, but it was even less to Spacewind. The gap was evaporating. He roared, flying so fast his body narrowed and elongated. He was an arrow flying behind them—impossible to outrun.

"Dammit!" Jack roared. He turned, shouted, and smashed out a punch into the void.

Light disappeared. So did sound, space, and even time. The entire world was sucked into his fist, forming the beginnings of a singularity, then exploded with enough force to illuminate the entire cavern.

"SUPERNOVA!"

Supersonic flames shot out in every direction. Part of the impact rushed at Spacewind, but he passed right through it. An attack of this level couldn't touch him.

But that wasn't Jack's goal to begin with. The explosion struck him hard, sending him flying forward at a speed vastly eclipsing his previous one. Min Ling and Brock were caught in the shockwave as well, following him as he headed directly for the hole. They were almost there.

At their current speed, they would barely have time to enter the hole before Spacewind caught up—but he didn't need to reach them to attack.

"If you won't stop, then die!" he roared. His sword slashed out. His body decelerated, and all that momentum was absorbed by his sword slash, which sliced forward at speeds Spacewind himself could never achieve. It reached them almost instantly. There was no way they could enter the hole in time. The attack would strike them.

An ugly smile adorned Spacewind's lips. He desired Min Ling, but if she was going to choose another man, she might as well die. He could find more women.

A terrible black sword slash fell on the three of them. Space constricted, limiting their movement. They could not teleport away, nor could they dodge. They had to face the attack head-on.

This was a strike made by an exceptional early B-Grade, someone at the top of that realm. The aura it carried was striking. Before it, they were small—insufficient.

In that critical moment, all three of them realized they had to block or die. They shouted out at the same time. All sorts of energies gathered around them, galvanized by their Daos.

Min Ling's spear was covered in lightningfire, a shower of red sparks so massive that it doubled her spear's length. She directly flung it out, aimed at the incoming sword slash.

Brock raised the Bro Code, which shone golden, and tore off a page. Instantly, his face paled, and blood trickled out of all his orifices, but he decisively crumpled up the page and burned it. Golden flames enveloped the space around them, forming into a massive golden brorilla that extended a palm to block the slash.

Jack punched out. Though one of his arms had already disintegrated from the last Supernova, he still had another three. This attack wasn't something he could control. Only the Life Drop's regenerative properties made it possible. Thankfully, as long as it was just his arms disintegrating, he could heal it without the turtle's active assistance.

The world was sucked inside his punch, then violently exploded.

All three of them used their all-out attacks, aiming directly at the sword slash.

"Judgment of the Fire God!"

"Big Bro Aegis!"

"Supernova!"

The world exploded. Spacetime shattered. Even the enhanced walls cracked, chips of stone flying everywhere.

Spacewind's slash was too overbearing. It met the tip of Min Ling's spear, pausing for only a second before shattering her strike and flinging the spear away. It then cut into the golden brorilla's palm, slicing right through it, his arm, and his body. The golden brorilla was cleaved in two, though the slash wasn't unharmed. It flickered, a good part of its energy spent.

Finally, a Supernova erupted on the slash point. It shook. The flames and shockwaves ground away at it, imbued with the Dao of the Fist which refused to yield.

As the slash broke through, it had been weakened to only a fraction of its original strength. Jack stepped forth to take it. It cut into his chest, but his enhanced body wasn't easy to penetrate. The slash carried on until it struck his ribcage, where it finally dissipated, leaving him with nothing but medium injuries.

Spacewind was askance. The other B-Grades, who had just entered the medicine garden, widened their eyes like saucers.

They blocked it!

Three C-Grades blocking one of Spacewind's attacks... Even if it wasn't made at full strength, and even if he spent part of his power to lock the space around them, it remained something they shouldn't be able to match.

Min Ling's attack in particular had approached the standard of a weak B-Grade.

Just what was going on!

There was no time to think. As the slash dissipated against Jack's chest, it shot him backward with incredible momentum, sweeping Min Ling and Brock alongside him. The three flew into the hole like missiles. Min Ling's spear, which she'd shot out before, was also pulled into the hole by the strong gravity.

"No!" Spacewind roared, arriving at its lip a moment later. He slashed out again, but the aura rising from the hole weakened his strike so much that it dissipated just a few hundred feet away. It never reached them.

Jack, Brock, and Min Ling disappeared inside the hole. As for Spacewind, he was left steaming in frustration but not daring to enter himself. Jack Rust had tricked him, taken the treasures and woman that belonged to him, and then even blocked his strike. At this moment, Spacewind was so filled with hatred and unwillingness that he thought his heart would blow up. He'd even spent some of his world essence to catch up, harming his own cultivation!

He had never felt so useless.

"FUCK!" he shouted with all the power in his lungs.

CHAPTER EIGHTY
ARCHON

As Spacewind's attack dissipated on the space above Jack, Brock, and Min Ling as they descended, they were relieved—which quickly turned into new worries as they gazed down. They were falling through seemingly infinite darkness. The walls were smooth, and there was no bottom in sight.

"This can't be good," Jack said.

"Big fall for big bro," Brock added like it was natural.

"Try to slow down!" Min Ling shouted. They galvanized their Dao, but it was useless. At best, they could decelerate a little. The gravity here wasn't only extreme—dozens of Earth gravities strong and rising—but it was also magical. It possessed its own Dao field, greatly limiting their ability to resist.

Even people like Spacewind or Uruselam couldn't fly upwards in this hole. As for Jack and the rest, they could only fall a tiny bit slower.

They braced themselves. Half a minute passed with them falling at blinding speed, yet they hadn't reached the bottom.

"I check," Brock said, releasing a bro pulse that ran down the shaft even faster than they could. "Okay. I have good news and bad news. What first?"

"The good news," Jack said at the same time that Min Ling said, "The bad news." They glared at each other.

"The good news is that bottom safe. No spikes. No monsters."

"Great," Min replied. "And the bad news?"

"Bottom not far away."

They crashed into hard rock. The air left Jack's lungs. The rock below was as magically enhanced as the rest—it didn't even budge.

Thankfully, Jack's body was highly tempered so it could resist the impact, but the others weren't so fortunate. They lay there, gasping for breath as they slowly recovered.

However, these injuries were unimportant. Jack forgot all about them as he stared at the view.

They lay inside a small cave at the edge of a large cavern. That cavern was several miles tall and several wide, its floor covered by a pool of glowing red lava. The most striking sight was a massive tree that stood in the center. Its roots dug deep into the lava, while its tallest branches stabbed high into the ceiling, stretching for who knows how long. The other branches were gnarled, carved to end in what resembled wooden dragon heads, and though they exuded an indescribably ancient aura, they also contained vigorous life force. As for the trunk, it was a mile wide and covered in bark that had naturally formed into engravings of dragons.

As soon as Jack laid eyes on this tree, he gaped. The aura it exuded, the timelessness, the strength... It was like staring at a dying God. He instantly knew this tree was the origin of the temple's sacred and heavy Dao, the very reason the temple had been built for. In fact, this tree could be the core of the entire hidden realm, its branches spreading for miles underground to become the pieces of wood that speared through the temple tunnels.

As Jack was lost, so were the rest. They could only gape, lost in the majesty. It was only some time later that Brock managed to say, "Wow."

"This tree..." Min Ling said, whispering unconsciously. "It's so old. So powerful. What could it be?"

Jack couldn't tell whether this tree had its own conscience. If it had, it was deeply asleep. Even so, this was not an existence they could afford to antagonize. Judging by its aura alone, it was probably at the A-Grade.

At least, this place looked devoid of danger.

A thought struck Jack. Besides their own, there was no other tunnel leading upward—none that he could see, anyway. There was no exit portal either. It was just them. The tree. A hole they couldn't climb. And a hermetically shut cave.

"Shit," he said.

The temperature was high, but nothing they couldn't withstand. A lava lake filled most of the cavern, surrounded by a thin strip of stone between it and the walls, while more stones surfaced from the lava, forming what seemed like a path between the tree and Jack's current position.

The three looked at each other, then advanced to the strip. They weren't too hurt—Min Ling had even found her spear, which had bounced off into the hole after helping block Spacewind's attack.

Soon, they reached the lip of the lava lake where the path of stones led to the tree in its center, almost inviting in its desolation. Yet how could things be so simple? The writing over the hole had promised certain death. There had to be danger.

"Let's walk around," Jack suggested.

The three followed the edge of the lake, circling the cavern. They lowered their speed to that of mortals, maintaining full vigilance. Nothing jumped at them. No monster rose from the lake. Not even the slightest wave splashed on the stone, evidence of magma so dense it was immovable.

The silence was deafening—pregnant with danger.

In that tension, they completed half a turn around the lake. That was when Jack felt something. It was an odd calling at the back of his mind, a faint ripple in his Dao perception.

Brock and Min Ling had also sensed it. "Over there," Min said, pointing at a crack on the wall. It wasn't particularly large—in fact, it could barely fit a grown man. It also looked man-made. Its edges were jagged and torn, covered by cracked stone, as if someone had taken a sword and madly dug here.

The three glanced at each other. "Let me," Jack said. "If anything happens, I can survive the longest."

"Lucky you," Min Ling replied, a faint smile on her lips.

Jack led the way. He grabbed one edge of the crack and pulled himself into it, tasting the smell of sulfur and death. The path went on. Jack followed a faint vertical decline, which came to a dead end only a hundred feet in.

Here, the crack didn't widen in the slightest. It looked as if whoever dug this place had stopped here, either due to exhaustion or death. The latter was probably true—the digger of this crack lay at the very end, a crumpled skeleton folded with no semblance of dignity. It barely fit between the walls. In its hands, a sword was aimed at itself, having penetrated the skeleton's belly.

This person had dug all the way here and committed suicide.

Jack was shocked. Generally speaking, cultivators possessed incredible mental fortitude. Killing themselves was very rare.

"What do you think happened here?" he muttered.

"Look," Min Ling said. The three of them were cramped inside this crack, but she managed to extend her arm and point at a broken-off sword tip on the ground. Looking closer, the sword with which this cultivator had ended his life also lacked a tip.

This all painted a gruesome picture. Whoever this person was, they had used their sword to dig a tunnel through the enhanced wall, but swords weren't meant for digging—the tip had broken off, and the cultivator, in despair, chose to end his own life.

Between Jack and Min Ling, Brock shook his head. "Sorry, bro... We were too late."

"What could have led this person to such a state?" Jack wondered aloud. His other question remained unsaid, but it was clear: would they suffer the same fate?

"Who even is he?" Min Ling asked, furrowing her brows. "We should be the first to discover the hidden realm. Yet, this person looks like they've been here for many years..."

"That's not necessarily true," Jack retorted. "There are no bugs in this place. His flesh has decomposed not because it was consumed, but because it melted by the extreme heat after it lost his Dao protection. This could have taken anywhere from a few days to a few months."

"Maybe, but this person killed themselves. Do you think a cultivator able to reach this point would despair so quickly? Who knows how long they spent here before something drove them to suicide?"

"Unless it was madness," Brock intoned heavily. "The mind is a delicate thing."

Jack gave Brock a surprised glance—he didn't expect such eloquent words. He then said, "Both possibilities are valid. In any case, this person wasn't part of our expedition, or we would have known. Let's keep searching."

In this dangerous place, advancing without proper care was as suicidal as this unknown cultivator jabbing a sword into their belly. They set their minds to acquiring as much information as possible before venturing into the lava lake.

It was easier than expected. Two seconds into searching, Jack discovered faint writing on the wall behind the skeleton's back. "I'm sorry, senior," he said, gently moving the body to the opposite wall. Words were revealed—carved roughly into the stone, as if whoever did it was using a broken sword tip. But the wall was hard. Most letters were barely recognizable. It took Jack and the rest a few minutes of staring to make out the entire text.

Like most writing in the universe, it wasn't English, but Jack found himself able to read it.

A thousand years of solitude. I can take no more! Blade, pierce my wall! Release me!

Curse you, Dragon Archon, for the hell you trapped me in! There is no key. The key is up there. How could I have known? HOW COULD I HAVE KNOWN?

There was no signature, no name. The text itself barely made sense, the ramblings of someone who'd already lost their mind. This was likely the unknown cultivator's death rattle.

Yet, the information it contained was important.

"Dragon Archon... Is that the creator of this place?" Jack wondered. He got no response. Turning back, he saw that Min Ling's face had gone pale as a sheet. "What?"

She took some time to form words. "Archon... Do you know what that title means?"

"No."

"It's transcendence. In this world, the strongest people are A-Grades. That is the highest known realm. However, at the very peak of the A-Grade lies transcendence. A legendary realm of existence, the absolute apex of cultivation, and the cultivators who reach it are titled Archons. Even Old Gods, if their strength had to be categorized, would be particularly strong Archons."

Jack's eyes widened. "What!"

"It is true," she replied, her chest fluttering. "My master once spoke of these things. It shouldn't be false."

Jack was stunned. A realm at the end of the A-Grade—transcendence?

"So Archons are peak A-Grades?" he asked.

"Not exactly. Archons are entities that have taken half a step beyond the A-Grade. Their power is greater than a peak A-Grade's, though they haven't really broken through to the next realm, if it exists."

"And you're saying that the Old Gods are such Archons? That the creator of this hidden realm was an Archon? Could it be an Old God!"

"There is no Old God who appears as a dragon." Min Ling shook her head. "If this place really was made by an Archon, it could only be a cultivator—unless this skeleton was mistaken, of course. But..." Her composure returned, overcoming the surprise of encountering the word *Archon*. "This can't be right. If this place really was the hidden realm of a deceased Archon, there is no way our diviners could get it so horribly wrong. Plus, there would be A-Grade existences serving as guardians, not B-Grade ones."

"Then..."

"I don't know. Let's just keep looking. The truth will come to light eventually."

Jack nodded, as did Brock.

"Look," the brorilla said, pointing back at the writing. "A thousand years... That is long. Poor skeleton bro. Why does he talk about key?"

Jack and Min Ling also returned their attention to the writing. In his final words, this unknown cultivator was raving about a key.

"There is no key. The key is up there. How could I have known?" Jack read, squinting at the letters. Then his mind flashed. He turned his hand and an item appeared.

This was the treasure of the largest cube. Before, he'd just grabbed it and fled—there was no time to inspect it. Now, however... It did resemble a key.

The back half of this item was like the handle of a key. A green dragon head adorned its rear end, while the entire item was made of aged wood. As for its front, it was not like a normal key, more like a complex seal—innumerable tiny lines covered a wooden square an inch wide, forming a shape vaguely like a roaring dragon head. Yet, its complexity was unfathomable. Replicating this seal would be impossible.

The key emitted no ripples, no aura. If it hadn't been the sole content of the central cube from before, Jack would have taken it for decoration.

"Could the key this cultivator missed... be this one?" he couldn't help but ask. His mind instantly reached a sad possibility. "I think I know what happened. This cultivator must have wandered the universe outside System space and stumbled upon this hidden realm. He entered, and being a weak B-Grade, rushed past the death dragon without defeating it to reach this place—or, perhaps, he failed to defeat the dragon and had to escape through the hole. He was then stuck here forever. This key must be needed to exit, but after entering this cavern, there was no way to fly back through the hole. The cultivator advanced too quickly, missed a single item, and that completely destroyed him."

Min Ling felt chills crawl down her spine. "What a horrifying fate. For a B-Grade to die like this is just awful."

"But fair," Brock replied heavily. "Dragon Big Bro wrote it on the wall: only death is here. If skeleton bro entered and died, he can only blame himself."

Those were harsh words, especially when spoken in front of the body. However, no one refuted Brock. The cultivation world was harsh. Death lurked behind every corner. This cultivator challenged the hidden realm by himself, desiring to reach the apex, and paid the ultimate price.

"What a cruel trap," Min Ling couldn't help saying.

Jack was silent. He bowed slightly to the skeleton, then received it inside his space ring alongside the broken sword. "We do not know your name, but this is no resting place. You suffered enough in life. Once we exit, I promise to find a good place to bury you."

"If we exit," Brock replied, ever the optimist.

Jack gave a sad smile. "Let's return to the lava lake. Let's see what this senior never did."

CHAPTER EIGHTY-ONE

INHERITANCE TRIAL

The lava lake welcomed them yet again. It was calm and silent—full of hidden danger.

Yet, after reading the skeleton's last message, they suspected it was safe.

Jack took the lead. He stepped on the first stone over the sea of lava. Each stone was barely large enough for a foot—one slip could end at a dip in condensed lava.

Of course, Jack could fly, but he didn't do so. He thought it disrespectful, and so followed the stone steps through the lava, experiencing its blazing heat which made even him sweat. Every root that stood out from the lava was like a dragon head staring him down.

Nothing jumped out. No monster rose with jaws wide open to swallow him. Jack smoothly crossed the lava lake and arrived before the massive tree. He was a speck of dust before it. His gaze became lost in endless leaves and verdant greenery. Though ancient, this tree was full of life.

Back under the volcano, Jack and Brock had discovered a tree that lived and thrived in an underground pool of lava. They did not know its name, but it was certainly a heavenly treasure, a medicinal plant of the highest quality.

This current tree was far, far superior. Whereas the previous tree lived in underground magma, this one was rooted in lava dozens of times hotter, like substantialized Fire Dao. Moreover, the previous tree had only been the size of a human, while this one rose for miles. Its branches possibly ran under the entire hidden realm.

Jack suspected this place was the very heart of the realm.

He took a deep breath. Reverence filled him. Then, he took the last few steps and arrived before the tree.

A small square indentation met his gaze. Its edges were straight, as if purposely cut, and innumerable tiny lines spread over its surface. Jack didn't need to look to know that the size of this square matched perfectly with the key in his hands.

"Insert the key," a voice rang inside his mind. It was not the voice of someone present, but a pre-recorded message that reached whoever approached the tree. Jack could only imagine that the dead cultivator had heard this message countless times, agonizing over his lack of a key. He must have received no other clues, no messages, no acknowledgement of his existence besides this impersonal requirement he could never fulfill.

Such a death was truly cruel. Who knows how many times the cultivator had shouted at the tree, receiving only silence as a response? How many times he must have attacked, only for his sword to be bounced back?

Thankfully, Jack had solved the cubes before diving into the hole. He raised the key and gently pressed it into the indentation, finding that it matched. All the innumerable tiny lines of the key and indentation combined. A perfect union was formed. The key shone green, and suddenly, Jack saw green lines flare to life. They started from the location of his key and spread outward, snaking across the tree. They resembled runes—like a divine tapestry that hugged this entire tree, this entire realm.

Before long, the tree was covered in these runes. They were faint, yet clearly present—and they spoke of secrets Jack was not the least bit privy to. This was not about Life or Death; it was something else.

Suddenly, the tree flared to life as if awakened. The cavern shook. Blazing green erupted from within the bark, and the leaves far above stood straight, filled with vigor.

"I am Archon Green Dragon," a voice calmly intoned. It echoed everywhere—the majesty inside it was so dense it gave Jack a sense of awe, as if staring at the endless starry heavens. "And this is my inheritance trial!"

Jack's mind was shaken. Suppressing the urge to bow, he looked back at his friends, who were busy gawking at the tree runes.

Inheritance trials were not an unknown concept—back in Trial Planet, the Space and Labyrinth Rings were filled with all sorts of inheritances left behind by ancient powerhouses. An inheritance was the sum of its creator's life, the path of cultivation they had carved into the universe—and they were always accompanied by a trial. Nobody wanted their inheritance grasped by weaklings. The ancient masters set harsh trials for their descendants, testing their talent to deem them worthy.

Across the universe, inheritances and trials were not uncommon at all. However, the inheritance of an Archon was a completely different matter.

This was a being at the very peak of the cultivation world. Throughout the years, how many Archons could there have been? Ten? Twenty? A hundred? Even the Old Gods were only strong Archons.

The inheritance of such a character was absolutely world-shaking, but that was not the first thing that came to Jack's mind.

The stronger the master, the better the inheritance. And the better the inheritance, the stricter the criteria with which a trial taker was judged. The trial of an Archon would be hundreds and thousands of times harder than a random B-Grade's. Only the very peak geniuses of the universe could hope to meet the exacting standards of such a powerhouse.

Was Jack such a person?

It wasn't that he underestimated himself. He was the most talented cultivator of the Cathedral, with potential that vastly outstripped his contemporaries. Yet, before an Archon, that was nothing.

Archons could live for a million years, maybe even more. Being the greatest genius of a generation meant nothing to them, because they had seen thousands of generations come and go, and their trial would be open to challengers for many more thousands.

Jack was very talented, sure. He'd worked hard and fought hard, securing all sorts of lucky chances. Amongst C-Grades, his current potential could be said to be one of the greatest in the universe. But wasn't that the case for all the peak geniuses of every generation?

Jack's true competition was not his contemporaries, but the greatest talents that had emerged over the last hundreds of thousands of years. In such a gathering, even Min Ling could only be considered average. As for Jack, he had no idea how he stacked up.

There was a saying in the universe: Three years to the D-Grade, ten to the C-Grade, a hundred to the B-Grade, and a thousand to the A-Grade. That was the minimum cultivation speed of a prime genius at every Grade. They were so far ahead of the power curve that their cultivation galloped forth at great speeds, rushing to the ends of their potential. When it began to slow down, that was when they knew they were approaching their limit.

Of course, being a prime genius at the C-Grade did not mean they would be a prime genius at the B-Grade as well. After all, the crowd they competed against would grow vastly more competent with every breakthrough. Everyone that reached the middle B-Grade had been a prime genius in their youth.

Jack was one of those prime geniuses, but in the entire universe, such a character would emerge every few centuries and live for hundreds of thousands of years. They weren't too rare. The only reason he hadn't met many of them was that they spent too little time at the low Grades, making it hard for two prime geniuses to coincide.

That all goes to say, the pool of candidates that an Archon's trial looked at was far more expansive than what Jack had seen in the Cathedral. Even if he was the greatest C-Grade in the current universe, that wasn't too great a title.

The only hint he had of his standing amongst prime geniuses of other generations was the Life Drop trial he had passed at Trial Planet. That was a trial for a relic of an Old God. It had to have high standards—a point proven by how Jack, who was above and beyond any other E-Grade at his level, had only barely survived.

And a drop of blood from an Archon was naturally inferior to another Archon's true inheritance. It was highly probable that the Life Drop trial was not even arranged by Enas, but by his followers.

The difficulty of this trial would be even higher. And that was why, as soon as Jack heard the words *inheritance trial*, he blanched.

Quickly, however, he recovered his composure. He had not failed yet—facing an opportunity to compare himself against the highest standards, his competitive spirit boiled over, his excitement rose.

Could he succeed? If he did... just how precious would the reward be? That was the inheritance of an Archon! A peak existence of the universe!

The green runes spread fully across the tree, then stopped. Their glow slowly receded to the point where they were barely visible. The tree remained in a vigorous state, and the energy density remained high.

The voice of Archon Green Dragon resounded again, regal and impartial, "I was born as a green dragon. My body follows the Dao of Life, but I reached transcendence through the path of Space and Time! That is my highest inheritance, and I refuse to see it wasted. From my true heir, I demand no less than perfection!

"Only those who understand Life can solve my Life Cube test and earn the key. Now, you must meditate on my spacetime runes and unravel the complexity of this cavern. Only then will you possess the qualifications to attempt the true trial and, should you succeed, refine the Dragonlife Realm Heart supporting this minor realm I have created!"

Hearing this, Jack was finally enlightened. No wonder the diviners misjudged the grade of this place. It wasn't a dead powerhouse's inner world, but a separate dimension that Archon Green Dragon once established.

What power was that! This green dragon had comprehended spacetime to such a degree that he sundered it apart, creating his own realm within the folds of the universe!

The spacetime inheritance of such a character would be nothing short of heaven-defying!

And that was only on the condition that Jack could claim it.

"There is no time limit for this trial," the ancient voice resounded again. "You may meditate on these runes until you succeed. If you fail, you will have to die here—your life is a small price to pay for the chance to acquire my legacy."

"Hey!" Brock shouted in the distance. "Not cool!"

The voice could either not hear him or completely ignored him. "No further assistance will be provided. This cavern will be completely sealed up until you succeed or die—nobody will be able to enter or exit unless their understandings in spacetime surpass mine. Moreover, to avoid the interference of other Archons, the entire realm will be sealed off as well. I wish you luck!"

With that, the voice echoed away, leaving Jack stunned. The entire realm is sealed... Could it be...

"Jack!" Min Ling shouted. "The entrance!"

He turned around just in time to see the hole they'd fallen through disappear. Only stone stood in its place as if there had never been a hole. Moreover, Jack felt heavy spacetime restraints cover the entire cavern. The stone hardened, and the already-locked space became completely impenetrable.

It was like the magic formation running this place had been in energy-saving mode before, and it was now fully activated.

Jack looked at Min Ling and Brock, then at the tree. "Guys... I think we're stuck."

The changes weren't limited to Jack's cavern. Outside, the B-Grades had been holding council, debating whether to enter the hole or not. Suddenly, the entire temple shook. They sensed the walls harden, and space was completely locked down around them. Even Spacewind was completely unable to affect it. Let alone teleporting, he couldn't even make it budge!

"What's happening?" everyone shouted, but it was too late. Before their very eyes, the hole leading deeper inside vanished, replaced by solid stone. They glanced at each other, then came to an instant agreement. They rushed through the corridors. Only seconds later, they arrived at the location of the nearest exit portal, only for their eyes to widen in horror.

"No..." Spacewind muttered. "This is impossible!"

Where an exit portal used to stand, there was now only stone. It wasn't hard to imagine that the rest of the portals had disappeared as well.

They were stuck.

On the outside world, the four A-Grades had been calmly meditating before the entrance of the hidden realm. They wouldn't let anyone enter or affect it. At once, their eyes snapped open. "The portal!" Heavenstar shouted.

The egg-shaped opening flickered. Then, it simply winked out of existence.

Boatman's eyes widened. "No!" he growled. He instantly arrived at the portal's previous location and jabbed his hand into spacetime, using his considerable understandings to keep the portal from collapsing.

However, how could Elder Boatman's spacetime Dao compare with Archon Green Dragon's? Not only was his cultivation boundary lower, but he also didn't focus on spacetime to begin with.

Heavenstar did. He arrived only an instant later and spread his perception over the location, investigating the tiniest abnormalities. Everyone waited expectantly for an explanation. Finally, Heavenstar opened his eyes, his expression tinged with disbelief.

"Well?" Purity asked. "What happened? Did the portal collapse?"

"That's not it..." Heavenstar said in a voice as if even he struggled to believe himself. "It did not collapse. It just... closed."

Boatman frowned dangerously. "Did someone interfere?"

To affect a portal so close to them without leaving a trace, one would need to be at least a late A-Grade focusing on spacetime. Possibly even stronger.

"I don't think that is the case." Heavenstar shook his head. He still sounded puzzled. "It's like... the portal no longer exists. Any connection it had to our universe has been cleanly severed. Reopening it is far beyond my powers. I dare to say that even if a spacetime Archon arrived here, they would still be unable to open it, because there is simply no connection between here and there anymore."

"What are you saying?" Ocean asked. "How can there be no connection? Are you implying the hidden realm is in another spacetime altogether?"

"I believe so," Heavenstar replied.

They all frowned. Hidden realms were normally adjacent to the universe, like a pimple sticking out of someone's skin. That was their nature. If this hidden realm was not such a case but was located in a separate spacetime, then it could not be the inner world of a dead expert as they expected. There were a few more alternatives, but they were all equally terrifying.

"What can we do?" Boatman asked.

"Nothing. The realm was cut off by its own inner workings. Whether it chooses to reappear or not is completely up to the realm. It could even reopen in a completely different location of our universe—though I estimate it will still be within the Heaven's Egg galaxy."

"So our disciples are trapped in there but there is nothing we can do about it."

"Correct. The only other way would be for someone in the hidden realm to shatter space and reconnect with our universe, but that is completely impossible for them. Even I might fail. So... We can only hope."

Boatman snorted. His gaze was dark and dangerous—not only was Jack in there, his most recent disciple, but also the incomparably precious death cube! Losing it would be terrible.

If he had known this would happen, then no matter how much he appreciated Jack, he would have never given him the cube.

But, not all was lost. The cube contained a wisp of Boatman's soul; he had a deep connection to it that could even penetrate spacetime to a degree, and even while being cut off from him like this, it could still persist for at least a year without extinguishing. If he found a peak A-Grade who specialized in spacetime... perhaps there was a chance.

Naturally, he wouldn't let anyone else know about this.

"If that is so, there is no point in staying here," Boatman said. "I'm leaving."

Space parted and he departed without waiting for an answer. As for Heavenstar, he quickly ran away as well—he wouldn't stay near Purity without Boatman for support. The two Hand of God Elders also left after some time—there was no meaning to Heavenstar lying about something so minor as a B-Grade hidden realm.

Boatman had rushed to find a peak A-Grade cultivator he had some relationship with and who also practiced spacetime. However, his attempt was doomed to fail. How could the dimension hidden by an Archon be so easy to discover? The only chance was if someone appeared who had considerably deeper understandings into space-time than Archon Green Dragon, but... that was a pipe dream. Even if the spacetime Old Gods personally arrived, they still might not be enough.

In other words, the green dragon hidden realm had been completely isolated. And the only one with the power to change things... was Jack.

CHAPTER EIGHTY-TWO
SPACEWIND'S TROUBLES

A BUBBLE BURST ON THE SURFACE OF THE LAVA LAKE, RELEASING HOT GASSES that rose to the cavern ceiling. After the cavern's formations were activated, even the lava was agitated—it had gone from completely still to slowly boiling, filling the air with harmful gasses. Jack, Brock, and Min Ling could easily resist them.

"Spacetime..." Min Ling said, furrowing her brows as she gazed at the tree's runes. "I have little connection to that Dao. I can barely teleport."

"Same," Brock added.

"You'll have to do it alone," she continued, looking at Jack. "Can you?"

"Honestly? I have no idea." His eyes ran over the massive tree and the runes crisscrossing its surface, illuminating it in a faint green light that contrasted the lava. "But I can try."

"There is no I can't, only I don't want to," Brock helpfully added.

"Thanks, Brock. I never realized the only thing standing between me and everything I have ever dreamed of was my secret desire to fail."

"No problem," the brorilla replied sagely, and both laughed.

Jack then looked back at the tree. "In any case... This will take some time. Make yourselves comfortable."

"Oh, I don't mind," Min Ling replied, sitting down cross-legged at the edge of the lava lake. "My Lightning Dao has surpassed my Fire one recently. This is a good opportunity to meditate on the lava."

Her hand reached into the lake, cupping a handful of lava. Molten metal leaked between her fingers—yet, miraculously, she remained unhurt. This wasn't even normal lava. It was magically enhanced to burn several times hotter.

"I mind a little," Brock said, "but nothing we can do. I needed to study anyway." He also sat down cross-legged, summoning his golden Bro Code to read from its pages. Jack snuck a peek from behind his shoulder—just as before, there was no text, only images formed of swirling golden lights that seemed to contain endless mysteries.

Some cultivation paths were different than others. Jack meditated on the world, so he first understood things and then they became part of his Dao. Brock had somehow conjured a book containing more insights than he currently understood, then meditated on that. Moreover, these insights were expressed as brorillas doing stuff.

Cultivation really was boundless.

As Brock and Min Ling settled down to meditate, so did Jack. He had a lot of things to consider. Expansion and consolidation. After the many battles of this hidden realm, he required some time in quiet meditation to digest all those insights. Moreover, he needed to study the death cube and the spacetime runes on the massive tree, as well as discover how to merge them with his fist.

The more he thought about it, the more things he had to meditate on. And, conveniently, he was placed in a sealed, perfectly safe chamber with no time limit. Wasn't this just perfect?

As for his family... they could only wait. Even if Jack tried to open this place as quickly as he could, it would still take a massive amount of time. Alternating his focus between different Daos would help refresh his mind, which would only be beneficial.

Therefore, Jack sat down to meditate. And time passed.

Jack, Brock, and Min Ling had a perfect grasp of what was happening, so they could be calm. The people outside, however, didn't.

At this point, the remaining nine B-Grades were convening again. Their voices were agitated—they had no idea what was going on.

"It has to be related to them," Spacewind spat hatefully. "The exits closed only minutes after they entered that hole. Moreover, the hole itself disappeared. There is no way they are unrelated!"

"I agree," Uruselam said, cupping his hands. "However, putting the blame on others will get us nowhere. Let us try to resolve this situation to the best of our ability."

"That is naturally what we'll do. Why do you even bother with that fake religious crap anymore? Are you telling me you wouldn't rip those C-Grades apart if they appeared in your face?"

Uruselam kept his hands cupped, bowing a little. "I ask for Benefactor Spacewind's forgiveness. This old monk is devoted to his worship."

Spacewind rolled his eyes.

"So, what should we do?" another B-Grade asked. "If the exits are closed, forcing them open with our strength is laughable. Should we just sit around and wait?"

"Absolutely not," Spacewind replied. "What if they never reopen? We should search around. Perhaps there are clues inside this temple —or even in the jungle outside."

"The temple is a dangerous place, Benefactor Spacewind, and we have explored less than half of it."

"Then what do you suggest? That we wait and hope?"

Uruselam remained silent.

"If we do explore the temple," another B-Grade rose to speak, "are the seven of us expected to take the front again?" This was a cultivator Jack had some relationship with—Borkuren Madiba, the frog-like Envoy who had managed the Ceaseless Murder Globe for a while. Currently, however, his muscles were tense, and his face was dark.

On the way here, every B-Grade besides Spacewind and Uruselam had been taking turns leading the group and face-checking any traps. A few of them had died. Now, with another half a temple to explore and only seven people to serve as meatshields, their unwillingness was expected.

"What other choice is there?" Spacewind retorted, releasing a bit of his aura. He was planning to bully all the other B-Grades into silence.

Borkuren kept his head up. "You are stronger than us. Your chances of surviving a trap are much higher. Since we led the way before, how about you shoulder some responsibility now?"

Spacewind had not expected to be challenged. His eyes sharpened, and his already ruinous temper was on the verge of erupting. "I am the leader here. Are you defying my orders?" he asked coldly.

"I just don't wish to die for no reason," Borkuren replied. "We have already suffered enough. Now that things have changed so abruptly, we should take everyone's safety into consideration before rushing to unwise decisions."

Spacewind's brows spasmed. He looked to the side—the other two B-Grades of his faction were staring at him with equally unyielding looks, while Uruselam and the other four Hand cultivators remained unwilling to take a position.

Spacewind's authority had originally been absolute. However, after most of them died on the way here, their fear was naturally very high. Moreover, these B-Grades had just witnessed Spacewind use their comrades as forced suicide bombers. Even though his strength was high, their respect for him had already dropped beyond repair.

They would rather die in battle than serve as meatshields for a piece of shit like that.

Seeing their combined resistance, Spacewind felt his previous frustration resurface. He wanted nothing more than to strike out and kill all of them, but he couldn't afford infighting at this point.

"Good, good. Very good," he said bitterly. "You all are very nice. I will remember this. When we return to the faction, expect to face disciplinary actions."

"Hohoho!" Uruselam laughed, not missing a chance to kick Spacewind while he was down. "All actions carry their karma. If I can make a suggestion, Benefactor Spacewind, then you should sit down and let your subordinates handle things. Otherwise, you might even suffer an unfortunate accident!"

The power relations of this group were already a tangled mess. Spacewind was forced to acknowledge he'd lost control of the situation. With an expression as dark as the moonless night, he stepped outside the gathering and waited, barely keeping his anger in check.

This was supposed to be *his* opportunity. He had paid a heavy price to lead this group. Then, most of his subordinates died, his reputation had been crushed, his authority had come under question, and he was also trapped. Even if he made it back to the Church, he would be punished severely for these failures, and the reputation he'd built for millennia would collapse like a house of cards.

This hidden realm expedition, which should have been his leap to glory, had turned into the most shameful performance of his entire life!

And even worse, all those failures would have been acceptable if he managed to earn significant treasures, but they had been stolen away by a mere C-Grade!

Jack Rust... he thought, his eyes burning with dark hatred. *You took my woman, took my treasures, and took my reputation. If I don't cripple you and feed you to the dogs, I am no man!*

Thankfully, Jack could not hear Spacewind's mental threats, or the resulting burst of laughter would have disturbed his meditation.

While the B-Grades were trying and failing to escape and the C-Grades were still touring the jungle with no idea of the exits being shut, Jack had relaxed completely. He was fully invested in meditation. In the sealed-off chamber, where time stretched to infinity, he began the longest meditation session of his life.

Sometimes, he would take out the death cube and ponder its secrets. After realizing something new, he would switch over to Elder Boatman's insights and look for practical applications of his new insights. Over time, his understanding of death deepened. The black fruit on his Dao Fruit grew progressively darker.

As for keeping the death cube a secret from Min Ling, he could no longer bother. It wasn't only that he trusted her, but also that he wouldn't hinder his cultivation just to keep a secret.

Besides death, he would often think back to the life lines on the three cubes. He'd only previously comprehended them enough to solve the cubes, but that wasn't the same as fully merging those understandings into his Dao. Now, with plenty of time, he was working to that end, turning over the realizations in his mind until they fit into his Fist. His progress in this regard was far slower than on Death, but his Life understandings were deeper to begin with.

Like this, the two opposite Daos were approaching an equilibrium.

Whenever Jack grew tired of life and death, he would turn his attention to the spacetime runes on the massive tree. It wasn't that he didn't want to spend more time on them, but it was just too exhausting. The problem with these runes was that they were too complex. If Jack had to compare them to the life cubes, they were similar in difficulty, but he didn't have a point of reference like the death cube this time. He could only rely on his own powers of understanding to resolve them.

Thankfully, his comprehension into the Dao of Space had already reached a decent level. He had long mastered teleportation, meditated for months in the Space Chamber of the Cathedral, and also unraveled the secrets of a supernova. His natural talent had been pretty high as well. Compared to his C-Grade peers, he was miles ahead.

But this trial wasn't aimed at his peers. It was aimed at the greatest geniuses of the universe. And, compared to them, Jack had to admit that his Dao of Space was thoroughly lacking.

The only bright side was that the World Anchor, which he'd absorbed long ago, was coming in handy. During the process of its absorption, he had witnessed the birth of a universe. He'd gotten a lot of insights at that time, many pertaining to the purest form of spacetime. By comparing any new understandings to those elementary interactions, he could spot inconsistencies and refine his insights. His speed of understanding rose significantly.

Even with that assistance, the spacetime runes remained extremely cryptic. Still, he had time. His progress was slow but steady. Moreover, his time here wasn't wasted at all. Studying the runes deepened his understanding of spacetime, not to mention the life and death he was simultaneously working on.

As for Min Ling and Brock, they didn't mind waiting. People of their level often spent months or years in meditation. They could use some downtime. Brock, in particular, had advanced even faster than Jack. He desperately needed to consolidate his foundation.

During this period of time, the three of them each advanced in their own way, their powers steadily growing.

Jack was engrossed in his cultivation. Like this, three years quietly passed.

CHAPTER EIGHTY-THREE
THREE YEARS

Jack's eyes slowly opened. The moment they did, reality shuddered around him. Faint ripples spread in the surrounding timespace, and his body seemed to become deeper, drawing in everything like the focal point of the universe. Just by looking into his eyes, a mortal's mind would easily fall into illusions.

Jack had meditated on these spacetime runes for the last three years. In this time, his fourth fruit had risen to full maturity, and he had also tempered his body a little. Brock's cultivation had reached the exact same boundary, while Min Ling had developed her ninth fruit.

The turtle inside the Life Drop still hadn't awakened, so Jack couldn't pay it back the life energy he owed. Thankfully, Min Ling and Brock had agreed to let him have the green bean they'd gotten from one of the smaller cubes—it should be enough to roughly pay off his debt so the turtle wouldn't kill him. Of course, he couldn't hog all the benefits—he'd promised to repay them with interest.

His greatest harvest from these three years had been his comprehension into spacetime. It was simply incomparable to before—in the highly stable space of this cavern, just his aura alone could create ripples.

"I think I got it," he whispered. His voice was low—yet it grew stronger with distance instead of weakening, flying straight into his friends' ears.

"Finally!" Min Ling cried out. Her body was half-submerged into the lava lake, enduring the impossible temperature. On the other side of the cavern, a large golden brorilla slowly dissipated, revealing Brock levitating in its midst. His feet lightly touched the ground—a white mantle with golden rims fluttered behind his back, formed out of pure bro power.

"I am happy for you, bro," he said slowly, his eyes shining with golden embers. "Go on. Make us proud."

Jack chuckled. He rose to his feet, letting the dust that had accumulated on his body tumble down. He banished it with a simple thought. Then, he raised his hands.

The spacetime runes on the tree were as mysterious as ever. They were green lines crisscrossing its bark like natural patterns, holding infinite mysteries. In the past, Jack had found them incomprehensible.

Now, after three years of effort... he could see through them.

From the start of his cultivation journey until now, six years had passed. Three of those had been spent in meditation in this simple cavern. A mortal would have long turned insane, but to a cultivator of Jack's caliber, this was nothing but a longer meditation session.

But it was still three years.

By now, his hair hung to his shoulders, smooth and silken. His eyes were tinged with calm wisdom, yet his body contained such bottled-up power that he was like an unchained wild beast, an avatar of primal savagery about to erupt. Meditating for this long hadn't dulled him in the slightest. His fists were far harder than they used to be.

Jack took a deep breath. He raised his hands, probing the air with his fingers.

Space wasn't uniform. It contained denser and thinner areas, constantly moving and changing at such speeds that they might as well not exist. Yet, now, his fingers accurately traced their trajectories, capturing the weakest points. With a sudden move, he pierced into them, poking his fingers into the fabric of spacetime.

Then, he pulled. The curtain wasn't parted, and as he poured his Dao into it, it changed shape. No longer was space flat. It was a sheet curved to Jack's will, manifesting into shapes that seemed unreasonable. Space itself turned into runes. For a time, the cavern shook. Parts of the lava floated upward and in all directions, the stone was warped, and even the massive tree groaned as it experienced the effects of Jack's space curving. Brock and Min Ling almost lost their footing. They could have used their own Dao to stabilize space around them, but that would disturb Jack's precise warping.

Jack molded space like dough. He turned and twisted it, folded it, stretched it, and turned it inside out. The cavern's multiple spatial locks groaned as they were resolved one by one, restoring space here to its normal state.

Jack's forehead was drenched in sweat. Manipulating space to this degree took everything he had. His body, mind, and will were fully immersed in the task. He couldn't afford a single mistake.

Space here was covered in a series of spatial locks, and resolving them was the way to passing the trial. Of course, these locks had been set by Archon Green Dragon. Jack couldn't even come close to forcefully unraveling them. The only reason he was succeeding was because the spacetime runes on the tree contained precise instructions on how to deal with each lock, illustrated as lines and angles that Jack had spent many months learning how to read.

However, a single mistake could cause unknown changes to these locks, rendering the instructions obsolete. If that happened, Jack would be as good as trapped forever—resolving them with just his own power was impossible.

The unlocking process lasted for ten whole minutes. Brock and Min Ling didn't dare breathe too loud in fear of disturbing Jack.

When a spatial twist tore off part of Brock's calf, he didn't even make a peep.

As for Min Ling, her eyes remained glued on Jack. Before entering this cavern, she had wholeheartedly acknowledged his talent, and they had adventured together, each saving the other's life.

After that, they'd spent three years together. Those weren't spent entirely cultivating—the three of them often interacted with each other, chatting or relaxing together, even playing games. They had become close during that time. They had talked about many things. She had seen into his moral character, his virtuousness, his decisiveness. She admired and respected him from the bottom of her heart.

All those factors, coupled with Jack's rugged handsomeness, were enough to birth emotions into her heart. She wasn't completely sure what she felt—it was only now, as she watched him resolve the spatial locks and release them from this sealed chamber, that she realized she didn't look forward to leaving. These three years had been peaceful and beautiful—a beacon of happiness in her difficult life. She would remember them fondly.

Jack had no idea about the thoughts running through Min Ling's mind. His full attention was devoted to warping spacetime. The entire cavern was bent now, with even time flowing differently in various places. Jack gritted his teeth. He took a step forward. His foot sank into space, disappearing, quickly followed by the rest of his body.

As he maintained utter focus, he followed a weird path. Sometimes he stepped forward, others sideways, even backward. With every step, his body would teleport, reappearing in some random part of the cavern. Finally, he reappeared at his original spot, took another deep breath, and stepped in two directions at once.

His body broke apart. One half of him stood on the rocks, and the other was on the branches of the giant tree. Yet, not one drop of blood was spilled. Jack's body wasn't really torn; it was space that was malfunctioning. After two, his body broke into four, then eight, and then finally recombined as one.

The moment it did, he finally relaxed. All tension left him. Space shuddered as it reverted to its original shape. Only now, all spatial locks were missing. The single peculiarity was that the entrance hole still hadn't reappeared—Jack had long realized it wasn't really a tunnel, but a small wormhole knitted into the surrounding space. There was nothing to reappear. If he wanted to exit that way, he would need to craft his own spacetime tunnel.

Jack was now standing right in front of the massive tree, looking up at the green runes that filled his mind.

"Is it done?" Brock asked, looking around. "Did you succeed?"

"I did," Jack replied, throwing back his head to relax for a moment.

"Then..."

Brock's puzzlement was natural. In his eyes, nothing had changed. The cavern remained as it was. Where was the inheritance?

"Can you see something we don't?" Min Ling asked.

"No," Jack replied with a smile, "but I know it's there."

His palm gently touched the tree, then kept going. His arm submerged into the trunk. Jack smiled, waved at his friends, and entered the tree fully, passing through a spatial corridor to reappear in a small, sealed-off chamber.

Ancient wood surrounded him in all directions. The air smelled of time. He was clearly inside the tree, with no entrance, exit, or window visible. It was just him in a small hole.

Yet, this hole was the very heart of the tree, the very heart of the hidden realm. And the reason Jack knew it was because right in front of him, inside the tiny chamber, was a pulsating Realm Heart.

Realm Heart (A-Grade)

A dense collection of spacetime runes. A Realm Heart can only be constructed by those who have reached the peak of the Material Dao, and it is considered the height of sophistication.

Realm hearts contain a set of instructions and energy patterns that can simulate and support the existence of an independent

timespace. It is, in essence, a permanent Dao enchantment that can be used to create a separate dimension.

WARNING: Realm hearts are regulated objects. Do not disturb it. Report its existence to the nearest Hand of God branch to receive generous rewards.

Jack chuckled at the warning. The System could be cute sometimes.

Waving away the screen, he took a good look at the Realm Heart. It was a transparent crystal truly shaped as a beating heart, but instead of blood, what it circulated was a large amount of extremely tiny runes. These runes were so tightly packed inside it that they seemed about to burst apart. Every beat of this heart released a number of runes into the air, where they merged into the hidden realm's space and disappeared, and then the contraction of that beat pulled spacetime energy into the heart, where it could be used to produce new runes.

The System had called this object the height of sophistication. Jack had no grounds to disagree. The sheer complexity of such a device made his head throb, and it was so far beyond his level that if he spent ten thousand years meditating, he still wouldn't grasp even its tiniest corner.

At the same time, this Realm Heart was not just made of spacetime. Jack could sense a powerful source of life energy inside it, a bottomless pool of vitality. His breath caught in his throat. Though he couldn't see it through the runes, he suspected that the Archon had forged a Life Artifact and part of his own body into this heart, giving it the ability to not only support a separate dimension, but also fill it with life. This was what had resonated with the Life Drop when Jack first gazed at the hole so long ago.

Such a creation was unimaginable. If Jack's guesses were correct, this heart was the sole reason for the hidden realm's continued existence, as well as the reason why it was filled with draconic and plant lifeforms. Archon Green Dragon must have been a plant-type dragon himself.

This was an unsurpassed treasure.

A heavy voice filled with majesty echoed in the chamber. "Three years. That is barely acceptable."

Jack looked around in surprise. Yet, he didn't feel anyone's aura—this was still a pre-recorded message, though how it knew he spent three years here was beyond him.

"By resolving the elementary Life Cube and the spacetime locks, you have received the qualifications to attempt to receive my inheritance. This is a great opportunity for you. However, be warned: my inheritance is not so easy to absorb. The greatest test lies ahead. Understanding alone will not be enough—you must possess a powerful body, unyielding will, extreme battle power, and enough perception to scale the heavens! If you are willing to continue, touch the Dragonlife Realm Heart and attempt to refine it. Otherwise, cut open a space tunnel and return where you came from. I only ask that after you leave, you reinstate the spatial locks of the heart cavern."

Jack's mind shook. So far, the tests of Archon Green Dragon had been cold and cruel. A single mistake would leave one dead or stranded for life. Why would he offer a way back now? Was it a trap? Or did he really fear that someone would fail here after resolving the locks, rendering his tests null for the next challenger?

It didn't matter. Jack had worked three years for this opportunity. He wasn't going to give up now.

He touched the Realm Heart—and, suddenly, he was whisked away.

The world changed again. He found himself in a white land. There were no trees, no stones—just an endless white plain stretching to infinity under a blue sky.

A bright light flashed. Jack felt seen through, as if all his secrets had been uncovered. In the next moment, twelve figures appeared around him, each different than the last. The most eye-catching were two: a strict yet kind-looking man radiating extreme life energy, as well as a creature that resembled a blob of dark, sinister aura.

As for the rest, they were humanoid, but not really—more like bundles of energy in a vague humanoid body with featureless faces. One was made of fire. Another, of stars. A third comprised of many small spheres tightly assembled into a humanoid shape, and a fourth seemed normal, but everything around it was warped, as if it was drawing them in. The fifth creature was made of lightning, the sixth of blue and red sparks, the seventh of explosions, and so was the eighth, except fewer, larger ones. Finally, there were two creatures that only appeared as bodies of water, one resembling a rippling pond and the other a steady current.

Twelve creatures in total. A number he'd encountered before. It instantly made him draw connections, but he actually didn't need it to recognize these creatures because he'd seen them before. Their appearances were engraved in an iron door in the bowels of Trial Planet.

They were the twelve Old Gods.

CHAPTER EIGHTY-FOUR
FIGHTING THE GODS

TWELVE CREATURES SURROUNDED JACK. THE OLD GODS... THESE WERE entities of unfathomable power—the closest thing the universe had to Gods, besides perhaps the System.

Obviously, these weren't the real Old Gods. They were just flesh-and-bone projections created by the mysterious mechanisms of the hidden realm. Their size was similar to Jack's, and their cultivation was identical—at full maturity of the fourth fruit, no more and no less.

Was he meant to fight these projections?

Briefly after they appeared, before Jack had the chance to speak, they rushed at him. His gaze sharpened. The Life Drop trial had contained a similar battle portion, and he remembered how difficult it had been. He didn't dare underestimate these twelve.

I'm sorry, mighty Enas... You have helped me in the past, but I must strike down your projection.

Gods these may have been, but in truth, they were nothing but projections made for this trial. Jack felt neither fear nor reverence. He would kick their asses all the same.

His aura rose. The energy of the Life Drop filled his body, making him taller and grow two extra arms, while Brutalizing Aura spread out to cover all twelve of his opponents. In an instant, Jack had reached his peak battle state, ready to give it his all. After three years of meditation and the previous jumps in cultivation, even he didn't know where his strength lay. He was pumped.

As soon as his powers appeared, the opponents reacted. The blob of darkness assumed a devilish form—twisted horns, triangular tail, human body with the face of a goat—and pointed at him. Instantly, his Brutalizing Aura collapsed. It lost all meaning, becoming an empty shell, and then it actually backfired, filling him with an intense fear of death.

What!

Jack tried to wrestle back control of his skill, but it was impossible. All this achieved was to divert his attention, letting the fastest of the projections reach him. A humanoid made of sparks extended both its arms, one on either side of Jack, and they shone one red and one blue. He ducked. The two arms crashed together as if magnetized—had his head remained between them, it would have been pulverized.

He had no time to strike back. More opponents were approaching. He jumped back, dodging two explosions below his feet. A tremendous pulling power captured him midair, yanking him toward a seemingly-normal humanoid. He pierced through space to escape—well, he tried to.

The moment he reached into space, the far-off humanoid which resembled a rippling pond shook its finger. Space solidified. Its very structure changed, and a force appeared which counterbalanced everything Jack tried to do. In an instant, his space mastery had been rendered useless. The previous humanoid's pulling power was still in effect, dragging Jack onto them, and a humanoid made of multiple connected spheres jumped up and punched him in the face.

Jack felt like a mountain had crashed into him. He was sent flying away, sonic booms in tow. The gravity in this place was normal, so he didn't touch the ground for many miles. The moment he did, he quickly rose to his feet. His regeneration was already working to fix his mangled face, and he could clearly see the twelve opponents rushing over, not giving him a moment to rest.

Even as his regeneration activated, however, the man who faintly led the humanoids smiled. A tendril of green aura shot out of his body, instantly reaching Jack. His life energy was siphoned away. His regeneration slowed down precipitously, while his Life Drop battle form reverted.

He was stunned. What!

The twelve opponents still rushed at him, and Jack flew backward in this endless white expanse, earning himself some time to think.

They're blocking my Dao!

It was unheard of. Yet, it made sense. These twelve creatures were made to resemble the Old Gods—they even displayed the corresponding Daos. Therefore, it only stood to reason they could limit him. Attempting to use a God's domain against that God was only asking to be punished.

The thing was... what else could he do?

All twelve Old Gods were represented here. All Daos in existence fell under the domain of one of them. Was everything useless?

His space mastery was negated by the Space God. His life powers were absorbed by the Life God. His death aura and Death Mastery were neutralized by the Death God. What the hell was he supposed to do? *Punch the Gods?*

...That made sense, actually.

As hopeless as the situation seemed, there had to be a solution. Archon Green Dragon wouldn't just set a death trap here. Jack's Daos were all suppressed, but that would be the same no matter who stood in his place. It was part of the trial. Therefore, there had to be a solution.

When he calmed down and thought about it, these creatures weren't omnipotent, even when it concerned their domain. The Life God projection—the projection of Enas—hadn't absorbed all of his life energy, just part of it. It made sense. If they were omnipotent, their cultivation wouldn't matter, nor would there be a meaning in having them fight him. Moreover, though they resembled Old Gods, they were nothing but phantoms conjured by an Archon—their Dao understandings could rise no higher than Archon Green Dragon's.

Therefore, it wasn't that his Daos were completely subdued, just severely weakened.

He also realized that none of the creatures had infiltrated his soul. They had only acted against his Daos when he actively used them.

The soul is inviolable, he remembered, his eyes shining. Perhaps a true Old God could invade it, but these creatures certainly couldn't.

And the most important thing was... none of them could affect his cultivation! The Dao belonged to the Old Gods, but cultivation was something mortals had invented themselves. Perhaps Enas had been the one to kickstart this process, but it was mortals who pursued it. If anything, cultivation stood under the even greater existence of the Heavenly Dao—no Old God alone could claim it.

As long as his cultivation remained, he could fight. He could punch the Gods.

Jack gathered himself. His mind came up with old memories, of the time when he was lost in the Forest of the Strong and punched away at every other living creature. There was no Dao back then—not at the start, at least. All he had were his fists. That was the beginning of his road, his first baby steps, and also the compass which showed the way.

Now, it was the solution to this problem.

His feet pressed against the white ground, stopping his retreat. He fell into a boxing stance.

Jack's mind entered serenity as the projections closed in on him. Concepts were the Dao, so he banished them all. At that moment, he seemed to return to a mortal, considering everything from a material, down-to-earth perspective.

He was just a man in battle.

His spirit flared. He stood his ground against the charging twelve, and with a roar, he charged right back. Fist met lightning. Fist met flames.

Twelve opponents, not extraordinarily strong. Each was at the same cultivation as Jack and not particularly strong for their level either. However, Jack was severely limited—his Life Drop and all Daos were sealed away. All he could depend on was himself.

A normal person wouldn't be able to combat one opponent in this situation, let alone twelve. But who was Jack? He'd survived the Forest of the Strong. Had clawed his way upward through a long series of hard battles. His battle experience was rich, his instincts were sharp, his mind was decisive. He was a veteran. Even surrounded by twelve opponents of similar strength to himself, he calmly took stock of the situation, calculating the best way forward. Behind his clenched fists, which guarded against all attacks, his sharp eyes inspected the battlefield.

Each opponent had their own fighting style, their own strengths and weaknesses. They relied completely on their Dao and had no other way to fight. In that sense, being a God was a weakness.

The Space God solely manipulated space. The Time God manipulated time, the twin Explosion Gods—whose exact domains remained unclear—produced explosions. Everything fell into Jack's eyes. If all those powers were combined, they were insurmountable—but, since he knew which opponent would use which Dao, he could counter them.

Though he did not have his Daos, he still had his cultivation. That included using pure Dao to enhance himself and break through restraints with pure power, as well as his highly-enhanced body and mind. It was capital enough to wage war.

Jack's figure flashed. He broke through a spacetime cage, then dodged the fist of the sphere-god even as he let fire, explosions, and electricity strike him. He suffered injuries, though nothing too heavy—to descend to his cultivation level, these gods had traded raw power for their extreme insights. He barreled through the smoke, ignoring all pain, and arrived before the god with the warped body that kept drawing him in.

If he wasn't mistaken, this was the Gravity God. His influence was the most annoying, because in this razor-sharp battle, being constantly pulled at random directions could easily spell disaster.

Of course, Jack had to temporarily put aside the consideration that the Gravity God, Space God, Time God, and the sphere person who was perhaps the Mass God should all be one God. He would consider the implications of that later.

Planting his feet steadily into the ground, he drove a punch into the Gravity God's face. A force pulled him backward, but he'd lowered his center of gravity and resisted enough to complete his swing. The Gravity God's face shattered against Jack's enhanced fist. Its head exploded, and then its entire body dispersed into motes of light.

One God down, eleven to go. With each one he eliminated, things would become a little easier.

Except, how could the other Gods just let him kill one of their own? They had struck at him at the same time he attacked the Gravity God, and to complete his swing, he ignored their attacks.

A space spike jabbed into his thigh, warping his flesh and blood. A time anomaly struck his heart, sending it out of rhythm and almost killing him. The elbow of the Mass God smashed into his back, sending him flying, while the Star God directly blasted a mini-supernova into his face. The Life and Death Gods stood in the back, not attacking.

Jack flew away like a ragdoll, his body almost bent out of proportion. He borrowed his momentum to keep running, creating some distance for his limited regeneration to kick into effect. It was painfully slow. The Gods pursued him, and running away almost took more energy than he could recover.

This was not working out.

Gritting his teeth, Jack stopped and faced the eleven Gods again, his eyes madly searching for another solution.

There has to be something! He roared out. Just taking out one God had left him injured. At this rate, he could only defeat two or three before they got him, and then he suspected he truly would die.

Just punching could only get him so far against C-Grades. He needed at least some Dao. But what?

It would be great if he could kill either the Space or Life God and restore his powers, but though the Gods did not speak, they had intelligence. Those two Gods hid behind the others, where he could not reach them without paying an exceptionally heavy price.

Dammit! What do I do? he wondered. His battle spirit was not doused, but he couldn't fight and die here! He clenched his fists.

Then, his mind flashed with inspiration, remembering something, and he grinned wildly.

When cultivating Life, Space, Death, and all those other Daos, it was easy to forget that the core of his own Dao was the Fist. Generally speaking, the Fist fell under Life, but Jack wasn't cultivating the Fist. He was not cultivating his Fist. It was his very own Dao, the one he had created when he reached the D-Grade. The Dao of Jack Rust!

He laughed again, opening his mouth to say, "You think you can bully me because you are Gods? Well, so am I! I am Jack Rust, the God of Jack Rust! Come get it, you holy fuckers!"

The pure Dao he'd been using all along was in truth his Dao of Jack Rust—a combination of other Daos which mostly focused on the Fist. He was always working on expanding it with superior concepts, and right now, all he had to use was its essence—the very core of his cultivation path.

He clenched his fists, which burned with purple flames. Only now did he understand the true concept of this trial.

A cultivator's strength depended on many things. Treasures, external sources of energy, lucky chances... With enough luck, anyone could reach extreme power. However, the twelve Old Gods in this trial took everything away. Even the Life Drop had been sealed. All a challenger could depend on was their very core, the most basic Dao they had developed through their lives, something that could not depend on treasures or lucky chances. In a sense, this was the greatest proof of a cultivator's talent, the foundation on which they depended to search for insights and lucky chances.

And in this domain, how could anyone compare to Jack, who had clawed his way to the top through endless impossible battles?

There could be people stronger than him. There could be people with higher cultivations, more treasures, and better lucky chances. But it was in this regard alone that Jack was completely confident in himself. He'd forged his own path one step at a time. Even if the Gods themselves stood in his way, he would tear right through.

That was what it meant to be a cultivator, goddammit!

CHAPTER EIGHTY-FIVE

DAO OF JACK RUST!

The pain of his wounds was all but forgotten. Jack laughed as he jumped into the fray, channeling his powers through the lens of his personal Dao. His body turned into a ray of light, an avatar of carnage. He no longer dodged. He punched away at all attacks, be they space or time or whatever bullshit the gods could throw at him. He broke them all. He was no longer hindered—instead, with every punch, with every step, Jack's Dao was growing even purer, unlocking more and more of his sealed power as he absorbed it into his own Dao.

What was the Fist? It had been a long time since he asked himself this question. The Fist was strength, the fist was power. It was daring to fight and breaking through all obstacles. It was crashing head-on against injustice. Taking control of yourself and your destiny, charging bravely through life until you met your end. The fist was heroism, confidence, it was the only road to a happy life.

The Fist was the only true path. The only path Jack could follow. So what if there were other Daos? In his view, they were nothing but illusions, false concepts that led in circles. If others could make them work, that was fine—but there was only one true path for Jack, and that was to fight, fight, FIGHT!

His fist smashed squarely into the Mass God's. A colossal shockwave erupted, flinging away two other Gods. Jack lost in depth but won in power—the hand of the Mass God was smashed backward, forced to give way, as Jack's fist unstoppably pushed through.

"METEOR PUNCH!" he shouted. The world exploded. Spheres flew everywhere as the Mass God was obliterated, and without a pause, Jack faced the rest. A brutal battle ensued. He punched Gods and their attacks. He grabbed the Star God by the throat, smashing him into the Fire God, then endured a space spike to punch a hole through the Time God's chest.

Bodies and energy attacks were flying, and at their center, a mortal man was slaughtering the gods.

He roared. He was unstoppable. The white world was dyed with blood, and all sorts of powers flailed wildly. Like a beast, Jack traded injury for injury, using his tempered body to come out ahead. Finally, as his fist shattered the Space God's head, making it dissipate, only two Gods were left—the Life and Death Gods. Enas and Axelor. The former and current King of Gods.

They had not acted so far. Their haughtiness clear and supported by real power. Jack could sense their auras were far superior to all other Gods. These two alone were as strong as the other ten put together. Was this true for the Gods themselves, or just these small projections formed by the trial?

Jack grinned. Though he had defeated the Space God, his space mastery did not return. He would have been shocked if he hadn't already realized this trial tested the very core of his Dao.

"Face me!" he shouted, then charged.

Enas smiled. A green aura flooded his body, raising his strength to an impossible degree. At the same time, his smile turned hard, bloodthirsty. Jack attacked the other God first—the Life Drop came from the real Enas and gave Jack extreme regeneration, so if this projection shared that power, it would be very difficult to take down.

Axelor was a devil clad in darkness. He snorted as Jack approached, directing a dark mist toward him. Jack had a feeling that, if he touched this mist, he would die.

He punched it all the same.

The mist was split. Jack's fist grew cold, as if his hand had died, but he still charged bravely into the darkness. The devil turned into a shadow as it drew backward.

Enas stood by the side, watching. This was the pride of the King of Gods. Even if it meant his defeat, he would not work with another to subdue a mortal.

Fist met darkness. Axelor was far, far superior to the other Gods Jack had faced. Even by himself, he was a worthy opponent. His every move brought death, his every gaze darkness. Jack's body was constantly resisting instant death. Midway through the battle, he was blinded. He still kept going, because his Dao of Jack Rust could not be blocked by mere darkness. His fists struck shadows again and again. Parts of his blood turned into black sludge. He and Axelor were killing each other.

But Jack prevailed. With a final fist, he tore through Axelor's darkness and claimed his head. Everything dissipated. Jack was left panting and injured. His body bore numerous wounds, some so deep they revealed white bones. It was a gruesome sight—but thanks to his tempered body, he retained roughly half his battle power.

He turned to Enas, the final God.

Jack had no confidence he could win. Not only was he wounded and exhausted, but Enas's power was also faintly above Axelor's. Yet, those didn't matter. He would still fight. If he died, so be it.

Enas smiled again. His face was kind, his eyes green, his head covered in long dark hair, and he wore pure white clothes, making him seem ethereal. Yet, through his wide sleeves, infinite power gathered. "Mortal cannot overcome the divine," he said, the first time any of these projections spoke. "Come."

And Jack came.

His fists were a maelstrom. His fighting skills, sharpened all the way from the Forest of the Strong, to Shol's training, to his numerous battles afterward, shone at their brightest. As his many Daos merged into his core, so were his fighting skills further polished, making Jack approach the existence of a complete whole.

At the same time, some of his Dao Skills were already expressed through his personal Dao so he could use them. Meteor Punches cut through the air. His body moved with the grace and power of an expert martial artist.

But the God of Life proved formidable. His own body was as tempered as Jack's. Every collision left them both shaking, reverberating across the world like the sound of a massive gong. The white expanse had been ravaged. Space shattered. Craters and holes spread out for miles, and even the sky had been blasted open, revealing the deep darkness beyond.

If this was a normal continent, it would have long been torn asunder.

Two bodies flitted through the endless white space, clashing again and again. Neither used magic or fancy powers. They were brutally beating each other to death. Fists smashed like rockets, thunderous roars echoed. Enas's smile had long faded, turning into stark killing intent. As for Jack, his face had done the opposite, unknowingly warping into a fierce grin, a smile stemming from his excitement to do battle, to kill and be killed.

This was his path forward. Following it brought him immense joy.

The two clashed for many minutes without a clear victor. Finally, Enas changed tactics; his fists were weaker now, but every collision sent streams of intrusive life energy into Jack's body, bloating and disturbing him. His skin squirmed as if about to grow, his bones rumbled, his organs shook. Tumors grew all over him.

Life could be disturbing sometimes.

Jack only roared, using his Dao to suppress these changes. They would bring him down sooner or later, but as Enas had invested his power there, he was losing every exchange. Jack's fists pummeled the

God of Life, breaking his bones and dying his pure white robes crimson.

Jack was rapidly running out of energy, but so was Enas. The power he held was too much—as a result, his endurance was actually limited.

Finally, Enas took to the sky. His body flared green as his aura gathered. For a moment, he really did resemble a God.

"**This is my final attack,**" he declared in an even voice. "**Kill or be killed.**"

Jack laughed. "Kill or be killed!" he agreed, ignoring the extreme pain rampaging through his body. His fist shone purple, gathering everything into it. Due to the constraints of this trial, spacetime, light, and sound resisted his pull, but Jack had already realized it wasn't really those things that gave him his power. What really gathered inside his fist, what really imploded, was his own burning fighting spirit, and there was no Dao in the world that could stop that.

"Die!" he roared, soaring into the sky.

A green sun flared, sucking in the life energy of the world. Jack felt his own body deteriorating, but he still charged forth. His fist gathered more and more power. The world warped around it.

"**End of Life!**"

The green sun expanded. As Jack reached it, the entire thing exploded in a massive, world-shattering explosion directed entirely at Jack. His fist exploded at the same time, disintegrating his entire arm.

"SUPERNOVA!"

Two explosions went head-to-head. The world lost its vibrancy, turning purple and green. The white expanse was entirely uprooted for endless miles, revealing a deep darkness below it, while the sky and timespace were all burned away.

In the deep void, the purple and green tussled with each other, each holding the power to destroy celestial bodies. Yet, as the two colors waged war, purple took a slight advantage—and like a tower of cards, the green sun collapsed, imploding on itself and completely evaporating Enas who hid in its center.

An unwilling roar echoed.

The last explosion blew Jack away, sending him flying for hundreds of miles. It was only then that he crashed against the white ground, bouncing off it multiple times before rolling to a stop.

His entire body was charred black. Many wounds had stopped oozing blood because he'd almost run out. He was a dying candle, barely even alive. Worse yet, the trial restraints remained, and he couldn't even muster the power of life to heal himself.

But even an Archon's trial wasn't completely merciless. A green light shone on Jack, filling him with vitality. His wasted blood was made anew, his bones snapped into place, his skin and flesh regrew. Before long, he was whole again, and even his exhaustion had abated somewhat.

This regeneration was the final sign that he'd succeeded. Only then did he truly let himself relax, resting on the white ground as he took deep breaths.

"Thank you..." he whispered into the air.

This trial had been beyond brutal. Even though it played completely on Jack's strengths, he had still only barely survived—he had no idea how other people were supposed to complete it. Yet, for all that difficulty, his harvest was equally bountiful. Let alone the Archon's inheritance—just this battle alone had opened his eyes and expanded his horizons, showing him the powers of the twelve Old Gods. It also helped him realize the importance of his personal Dao and fuse everything else into it—a process which, even if he consciously tried outside, would be almost impossible without an extreme power locking down every other Dao.

Just this battle had given Jack tremendous benefits. That was why, despite almost dying, he had thanked the Archon.

The world gently warped around him. Jack found himself standing before the Realm Heart again, in its tiny chamber, his body still exhausted but mostly healthy. To his relief, the Dao restraints were lifted, so he could contact the Life Drop again and begin fully restoring himself.

"Success..." the voice boomed, this time with a hint of hesitation. "I was not sure anyone would pass my trial before the dimension collapsed... I am wondering whether I was too harsh. However, if you are hearing this message, you must have succeeded. Congratulations. It seems my legacy will not be forgotten. I also hope that you understood the trial's point and did not use vile means to pass..."

Jack had no idea what vile means he could have used, but he still bowed deeply in gratitude.

"Then, my legacy belongs to you. Rest your hand on the Realm Heart again to access it. The core of my teachings, as well as this Realm Heart which I spent my own life to create, will belong to you. Do not waste them!"

"Thank you..." Jack muttered, relieved to have finally succeeded. He touched the heart, and a Dao Vision shot into his mind.

CHAPTER EIGHTY-SIX

COME AND TAKE IT!

THREE YEARS AGO...

After long discussions, the B-Grades finally came to a decision. They would not explore the rest of the temple. The risk was too high, and the lower-level ones amongst them had teamed up and refused to be taken advantage of.

As for Spacewind, he had been relegated to a side role. He could speak, but nobody asked for his opinion any longer. That made the flames of bitterness inside him burn even hotter, but there was nothing he could do about it.

Instead of exploring, they would wait. Perhaps this imprisonment was a periodic phenomenon, or maybe it would resolve itself. If they died before that happened, they really would be fools.

Therefore, the B-Grades sat down and meditated. One year passed. That was also their deadline. After one year, nothing had changed.

Of course, one year was nothing to them. If they had to wait ten, a hundred, or even a thousand years, they could endure it. The problem was their uncertainty. How long would they need to wait for? Would anything ever happen, or were they fools just wasting away their years when the exit lay in the next room?

Moreover, after a year, the C-Grades outside the temple were also growing restless. They had already scoured most of the jungle—they hadn't expected the expedition to last this long.

The B-Grades reconvened. The nine of them took stock of the situation, calmly analyzing all possibilities. Finally, they decided they could no longer sit still. They had to explore the temple.

In truth, there were ways to do so which wouldn't involve risking their lives. It was just that these methods were too time-consuming... Seeing as all other options were moot, they changed tactics.

Beast taming was its Dao. However, it also served as a side-occupation of many cultivators, just like healing or formation mastery. There were people here who practiced it. With a heavy heart, the B-Grades retraced their steps to safely exit the temple, then used their communication devices to gather all C-Grades together.

"We are stuck here for the foreseeable future," Uruselam declared, to the fright of many. "It could be tens, hundreds, or thousands of years. There is no way to tell. Our best hope is to fully explore the temple, but it is filled with powerful traps that even we could fall to. There is only one solution—we will subdue every single C-Grade and B-Grade beast in this jungle and use them as scouts!"

Though he said *scouts*, he really meant meatshields. Even if C-Grades had no chance of survival in the face of these traps, it didn't matter. They could scout them out. With enough numbers, all problems would be resolved.

As for D-Grade creatures, those couldn't even resist the temple's heavy aura. Dragging them along was meaningless.

Therefore, the entire group settled down in an area of the jungle near the temple. The B-Grades would often spread out, looking for C-Grade and above beasts to capture. Anyone familiar with beast taming had their hands full—subduing even a single beast was a time-consuming process. Thankfully, they only used gentle methods, as high-level beasts were too powerful to yield to torture.

Two more years passed.

The cultivators had remained in their area, often cultivating.

Rain came often, and it was annoying, so they built roofs over their heads. Then, when nobody wanted to be looked at by the others all the time, they built walls. Gradually, a small village appeared inside the jungle. Since all treasures had already been taken, there was no point to infighting—everyone cultivated peacefully, gradually getting to know each other. People became closer.

Taming all the necessary beasts was a process that could take up to a hundred years. Even after that, when they explored the temple, there was no guarantee they would find a way out. They could be stuck here for life.

Though terrifying, nobody could discount that possibility. They thought they would stay for decades in the least. The village was built to last. Over half of the people present were humans, including both men and women. They could have children. If they really were stranded here forever, this little village would develop into a civilization of its own.

They even gave it a name—Green Cultivator Town!

And the only sore thumb was Spacewind, who stewed in anger in his tiny hut in this tiny little village.

Jack had no idea about the tribulations outside the temple, nor did he much care. His hand touched the Realm Heart, and his mind was instantly whisked to a new world.

A green dragon coiled in space. Its size was impossible to judge. Perhaps it was a hundred feet across, or maybe a hundred miles. There was nothing else nearby.

The dragon had bright, verdant scales. Its flesh underneath was made of wood, and its horns were tree branches. Yet, its eyes shone with fierce intelligence, penetrating even the toughest barriers.

This was a tree dragon—similar to the one Jack had met at the start of this expedition, but unimaginably greater.

Archon Green Dragon did not seem to notice Jack's soul presence.

It raised a claw, gently dragging it through the void. Space tore open like a taut sheet, spilling out its mysteries, and the dragon cupped them all in its claws.

It began to weave.

Endless runes flowed out of its claw tips. Its sharp eyes were mellowed in gentle concentration. Space and time warped around it, subdued by the dragon's incalculable strength and shaped by its comprehension. The Dao yielded fully—it was nothing but a tool, clay which this dragon shaped.

Power alone was not enough to achieve this. The dragon wielded its power with extreme precision, curving the sheet without breaking it, affecting it in ways which encompassed the myriad changes of spacetime. Runes sprang into existence, folding in on themselves to create the beginnings of a material shape.

Jack watched with rapt attention. Every move, every tiny change of this dragon's claws contained infinite wisdom. This sight was far superior to just observing some runes. Jack's own comprehension was rising. He could understand less than a thousandth of the dragon's moves, yet just from watching them, he was inspired—it was like an Archon was deliberately demonstrating its Dao for Jack, showcasing every single nook and cranny, every major piece and hidden detail.

All the understandings together wove into a puzzle represented by the gathering runes before the dragon.

Jack couldn't tell how much time had passed. Perhaps he'd been here for a day or a month. The dragon kept weaving, slowly exhausting its strength even as the surrounding spacetime was sundered apart. The clump of runes before it had taken the shape of a heart, beating at a painfully slow pace. The more runes that entered it, the faster the heart beat, until it finally reached one beat every three seconds. Tiny runes streamed out, and the surrounding spacetime energy was drawn in between beats, refilling the heart runes.

Seeing this, the dragon was satisfied. A small smile of appreciation appeared in its eyes. Yet, though it was satisfied, it was not done.

With a decisive move, the dragon turned its head and bit off its own shoulder blade, tearing it out in a shower of wood and green blood. With a pained grunt, it brought the shoulder blade close to the heart.

Before this wooden shoulder blade, the Realm Heart was just a tiny speck—yet, the shoulder blade shrunk, magically changed to an even tinier size than the heart as it flew inside its core and nestled there.

The heart beat again. This time, a faint pulse of life radiated alongside the runes. Only now was the dragon's work over, and its exhausted body relaxed as it observed the fruit of its labor.

Jack could sense that the dragon was weakened. Though its shoulder blade had been removed, such an injury should have been nothing to a being of such caliber. He suspected that, alongside the shoulder blade, the dragon had torn off something else from its body, something more vital.

In forging this Realm Heart, Archon Green Dragon had really gone all-out.

A moment of calm came. Jack remained too shocked to think clearly. The insights he'd just witnessed made up an incalculable wealth, as if a god had descended from the heavens and patiently laid out a path of progression. If this vision remained inside his head like all the others, the benefits would be inestimable. By using it as a template, his progress in spacetime would be fast beyond belief!

The vision warped as if about to end when something changed. A strange force grabbed the vision and held it in place, making it clearer and more vivid than ever before. Jack could see every little scale on the dragon, every Dao particle in the surrounding space.

The dragon was alarmed. It released a low growl, scanning the world around it. "Who's there?" it demanded to know, shaking existence with its willpower.

"Retribution."

Spacetime shook, then shattered. The sheet was completely torn away. All remaining spacetime particles rose as a vortex formed into two phantasmal beings—each resembled a body of water, one constantly rippling and the other ceaselessly flowing in one direction.

Jack drew a deep breath! He'd just fought these beings—they were the Space and Time Gods!

However, even these were not the real bodies. They were avatars formed of spacetime, mere projections of the Gods too far away to arrive in person. Yet, even like this, their aura was staggering. Each of the two avatars approached the weakened dragon—if their real bodies were here, they would be even stronger.

Was Jack about to witness the power of true Gods?

"You wield our power," said one of the beings, its voice carrying an indescribable quality.

"But without permission," added the other. **"Enas opened his domain. We did not. That which you have created is ours."**

If the dragon was shocked at the appearance of the two Old Gods, it did not show it. Though its aura was faintly suppressed, it still raised its proud head to glare at them.

"Empty talk," it declared. "The only language I speak is power. If you want something from me, come and take it!"

Come and take it... What a phrase to speak to Gods!

"Very well," they responded in one voice, and then attacked.

Unfortunately, this battle was not one Jack was meant to watch. Before it even began, one of the two avatars waved a finger in Jack's direction without looking. A tremendous power struck him. The vision shattered, throwing him back into his own body.

That was also expected. In a previous Dao Vision, back in the Exploding Sun, even the A-Grade vampire had noticed someone watching. These two Old Gods, even in avatar form, could easily achieve the same. So could the dragon, but it had let Jack watch—it had been the one to create the Dao Vision, not the ever-present System.

Jack was shaken. *Two Old Gods... An Archon creating a Realm Heart... A forbidden power...*

The Old Gods, the Immortals, the Crusade... Those were all things Jack was faintly aware of, but they were too far away to affect him. Yet, the more he rose in power, the more he approached these entities. If he advanced his Dao to the peak, would the Old Gods arrive to stop him like they had with Archon Green Dragon?

Considering the Realm Heart was right in front of Jack, the Archon had likely won that battle.

Jack shook his head. Looking inside his mind, the Dao Vision remained, but only up to the point of the dragon finishing the heart. The attack of the two Old Gods was only a faint memory—and the difference was that, while he could recall it, he could not observe it for Dao understandings.

That was fine. He had inherited the legacy of an Archon. The benefits this would bring... The honor...

Jack quickly composed himself. His goal was the peak of cultivation—and he suspected that an Archon, while close, was still a step away. If he really could reach the peak, receiving such an inheritance was only a matter of course.

"Thank you, Archon Green Dragon," he said, respectfully lowering his head at the Realm Heart. He then raised his eyes.

He had not perfectly inherited the legacy yet. The Archon had spoken of refining the heart. For a third and last time, he raised his hand and placed it on the heart.

CHAPTER EIGHTY-SEVEN
REAPING THE BENEFITS

THE MOMENT JACK TOUCHED THE HEART, HIS MIND BECAME ONE WITH IT, granting him perfect awareness.

He saw the entire hidden realm from a distance. It was a massive upside-down cone—short and wide. The Realm Heart chamber was at the bottom end, while the entire jungle rested on the cone's flat top. The hole which led Jack to the heart chamber had descended from the temple at the middle of the jungle all the way down to the tip of the cone. That was why they'd fallen for such a long time.

Outside the cone was a multicolored nothingness devoid of space and time. That had to be the inter-dimensional void. Since the hidden realm seemed to float inside it, Jack decided to call it the Dimensional Sea.

In the face of the infinite Dimensional Sea, the hidden realm seemed tiny—but it was actually gigantic. The jungle was a perfect circle with a radius of a hundred thousand miles—it had a hundred and sixty times the surface area of Earth.

That was no joke! No wonder C and B-Grade creatures could exist and fight freely. Even if one of them tried, it would take a long time to raze this high-level jungle. In fact, with his current awareness, Jack could sense multiple B-Grade dragons inside the jungle—the red one they'd defeated before was just one of them. As for C-Grade creatures, they were a dime a dozen.

As Jack was gawking at the jungle and trying to process all this new information, he suddenly realized the existence of something else. Hmm? he frowned. What are these guys up to?

The small village created by the other expedition members—the Green Cultivation Town—fell under his eyes. They did not notice him, of course, but he could clearly see that they had formed a little community and were even farming beasts.

He couldn't help making a wry smile. *I guess that's on me. Those guys think they're colonizing. How cute.*

Some of his enemies were also in that group—especially Spacewind. It was a shame Jack couldn't use the power of the Realm Heart to harm them directly. What he could do, however, was not let them out.

Not forever, of course. Most of those people had no relation to him—he wouldn't strand them here for life. Just for a few years, until he had the power to defeat Spacewind. They were C and B-Grades—they could take it.

If Spacewind returned to the Cathedral, not only would he inevitably try to kill Jack, he might even follow the teleporter to Earth and create trouble. That was too high a risk.

Besides, Jack thought, still smiling wryly, *look how much fun they're having.*

A C-Grade who looked like a glass pane was petting a small dragon. Nearby, Spacewind had tried to do the same but ended up getting his hand bitten—he could only yell at the dragon while everyone else laughed.

It didn't seem too bad.

The only ones he felt sad about were Shi Mo, his C-Grade friend, and Borkuren Madiba, the B-Grade who'd been kind to him before. He had some relationship with those two, so he didn't want to leave them here even for a few years, but there was nothing he could do about it. If he tried to go over there and sneakily led them to the exit portals, there was a good chance other people would catch on, and then nothing could save him. The risk was just too great, and the losses not too important.

He hoped they would understand.

With that, Jack turned his gaze away from the small cultivator village. He was now back in the chamber with the crystalline Realm Heart. The Archon's voice echoed out again.

"This is my creation: the Green Dragon Realm. I do not know what state it is in at the time of your arrival, but I hope it is still as lush and green as I left it. You may return to our universe and take the Realm Heart with you—the realm will persist for a few millennia without it. However, I request of you that after you reach the A-Grade, when your inner world is spacious enough, you return here and absorb this realm into your inner world, where it can exist indefinitely. The jungle creatures can be considered my descendants—I would not want them to go extinct."

"It would be my honor," Jack replied, lowering his head though the Archon could neither see nor hear him. These were just pre-recorded messages—it was unknown whether Archon Green Dragon was even still alive.

"There is nothing more to be said. Recording this message makes me emotional. When you hear this, it is unknown how much time will have passed—I might be alive or long dead... In any case, you have received my legacy, and I know it will not be wasted on you. You are the heir of me, Green Dragon. Farewell, my disciple. Carry on my legacy. Make me proud!"

The voice rumbled, rising in intensity until the last words, which made even the cavern tremble. Jack was touched. This could be the last time he heard this Archon's voice—the final words he would receive from a truly supreme existence.

"Thank you," he said again, lowering his head and remaining there respectfully until the voice's final echoes had disappeared and all was silent. He then sighed. His emotions were many, and they were also tangled with each other—but piecing them together could wait. He had a legacy to inherit.

His hand gently rested on the heart. He poured his mind into it, and the entire crystalline mass turned into a ray of light which sank into his soul. As it did, he once again got a wide view of the entire realm, zooming rapidly. From the entire realm, he could see the tip of the cone, then the tree cavern, where the majestic tree stood, its branches spreading not just to the temple, but everywhere! This tree alone supported the entire realm. Deep into the dirt, Jack could even sense nine fruits, each giving their own twist to the life energy. He didn't know what they signified exactly, but it probably had something to do with the nine-fruits cultivators grew on their Dao Trees.

Wait. Is that... a tenth fruit?

Before he could take a better look, his view zoomed farther, focusing on the tree cavern, the heart chamber, and finally himself.

As the heart entered his soul, it brought along a large number of Dao runes—Jack could meditate on them to increase his spacetime understandings at a rapid pace, and the heart itself would greatly enhance his inner world when he formed it. This was similar to the World Anchor he'd previously consumed, just but far better.

At the same time, Jack sensed the strong life aura which surrounded the heart. As this energy entered his soul, it was not absorbed by his Dao Tree, but rather leaked into his body. It was soft and gentle, yet vast beyond compare—it was the source of the tremendous amount of life in the jungle above. It seeped through him, and Jack felt incomparably comfortable, like relaxing in the world's greatest hot spring.

His entire body was revitalized. His wounds and exhaustion disappeared, restoring him to his peak and then some. The heart was powered by something in its depth and maintained a steady intensity in its aura, overflowing his cells with life.

Under the effects of this power, Jack felt his body growing rapidly stronger. It was a form of body tempering like the one he could achieve through the Life Drop, but far gentler, as if the Realm Heart was made for this exact purpose. There was no pain. His body rapidly strengthened, and the sensation was almost euphoria. He sat down cross-legged, enjoying this feeling.

The absorption took one day and one night. When an equilibrium was finally achieved between Jack's body and the life aura produced by the heart, he opened his eyes, now full of vigor. Even his blood had turned a shadow greener—as if inheriting a wisp of the Green Dragon's bloodline.

However, the transformation was still not over. The life aura nourished his Dao Tree, and Jack's fourth fruit, which had already reached maturity, began to overflow. He smiled widely.

After three years of meditation, this fruit had long reached maturity. However, he had purposely limited his cultivation to the peak of this fourth fruit to consolidate it, ensuring the stability of his foundation. After all, these four fruits had grown too rapidly, and he'd never had the time to properly experience them.

Now, this overflow of energy was the sign that his foundation was as solid as could be. The breakthrough to the next fruit, which normally required a massive accumulation of resources, was happening by itself. Delaying it any longer would only harm him. He let the energy rise, naturally gathering at another end of the branches and sprouting into a red fruit—this represented not a particular Dao, but Jack's burning blood, his unyielding battle spirit. It was the essence of his Dao as he'd realized during his battle against the Old God projections.

Only now were the Realm Heart's effects finished, and they had been absolutely massive. From his body, to his Dao, to his cultivation, Jack had been transformed. He was simply incomparable to before.

He was burning with the desire to test his strength. It was time to leave this place. Before that, there was another thing he desperately wanted to do.

He opened his status screen for the first time in a while.

Name: Jack Rust
Species: Human, Earth-387
Faction: Bare Fist Brotherhood (C)
Grade: C
Class: Gladiator Titan (King)
Level: 301

Strength: 5842 (+)
Dexterity: 5842 (+)
Constitution: 5842 (+)
Mental: 949 (+)
Will: 949 (+)
Free points: 260
Free sub-points: 2

Dao Skills: Meteor Punch IV, Iron Fist Style III, Brutalizing Aura III, Neutron Star Body III, Supernova III, Space Mastery III, Fist of Mortality III, Death Mastery II, Titan Taunt I
Dao Roots: Indomitable Will, Life, Power, Weakness
Dao Fruits: Fist, Space, Life, Death, Battle
Titles: Planetary Frontrunner (10), Planetary Torchbearer (1), Ninth Ring Conqueror, Planetary Overlord (1), Grade Defier

In his three years of cultivation, and now after absorbing the Realm Heart, Jack had risen by thirteen levels. His Space Mastery and Fist of Mortality skills had both reached the third tier, he had developed the Death Mastery skill and taken it to the second tier, his Physical substats had increased by almost a thousand and five hundred points each—most of which came from the Realm Heart—and even his Mental and Will stats had gotten a healthy boost.

Being transformed was not a figure of speech. At this point, without even using any Dao, Jack could crush a mountain ridge with his bare hands.

The inheritance of an Archon was almost scary.

And all of those weren't even the best thing. Jack surveyed his stat points. By some lucky coincidence, they were...

He barely contained his excitement.

Of the 260 free points, he invested 102 in Mental and Will to bring them both to a round thousand. That left exactly 158, which he allocated fully into the Physical substats. The resulting image was something he'd desired for many, many years.

Strength: 6000 (+)
Dexterity: 6000 (+)
Constitution: 6000 (+)
Mental: 1000
Will: 1000
Free sub-points: 2

"Oh, heavens, thank you! Thank you! You are beautiful, haha!"

If Jack wasn't already euphoric, he would be now. This balance would break once he cultivated a little bit, but, for now... it was perfect.

Jack spent another three days in the heart chamber to consolidate his benefits a little and let his body grow used to its increased stats. Then, with a tug of will, he teleported back to the tree cavern. As the owner of the Realm Heart, he could freely move around this cavern—though he did not possess the power to do the same in the jungle above.

CHAPTER EIGHTY-EIGHT
GOODBYE, HIDDEN REALM

"You did it!" Min Ling shouted.

"Bakagu!" Brock yelled, jumping backward as Jack appeared in his face out of thin air. He grabbed his heart. "Bro! Careful!" Then, realizing that his big bro was safe and successful, he gave him a firm pat on the back. "Good job."

"You guys didn't know I succeeded?" Jack asked. "I thought the Archon's voice had echoed here as well."

"It didn't." Min Ling shook her head. "But I'm glad you're alright."

"Same here," Brock added. "And stronger, too!"

Jack laughed. "I'll tell you all about it. But first... how about we leave this place?"

Excitement rose inside them. Only Min Ling felt a hint of hesitation as she gazed at Jack's victorious figure—it wasn't only his handsomeness that grew every time he tempered his body, but also his aura. Over the years, it had left a deep impression in her heart that refused to go away.

However...

Min Ling's eyes met Jack's. In the end, she chose not to speak. He wasn't an idiot—her feelings were visible if he chose to see them, but he'd never breached the subject. Min Ling recognized the tacit rejection. She had already researched his background and knew he was married—perhaps, in his culture, the notion was more meaningful than in hers.

Thinking up to here, she chuckled bitterly. She had been pursued and desired by innumerable men in her life—but the only one she wanted, she could not have. The cruelty of fate.

"Is there anything you wish to say?" Jack asked, looking her in the eyes with kindness.

She smiled and shook her head. "No. Let's go."

Jack nodded. He waved his hand through the air, using the Realm Heart's powers to form a multicolored portal—it pierced the Dimensional Sea and connected directly to their universe, though not at the same spot they'd left. He'd chosen a random place for safety reasons, though inside the galaxy, as he couldn't go farther.

"What about the others?" Min Ling asked, referring to the expedition members.

"They'll stay here for now," Jack replied. "My power has risen greatly, but it isn't enough to face Spacewind yet. When it is, I will return, kill him and all those who attacked us, then release the rest. Besides..." A faint smirk appeared on his face. "I suspect they don't dislike this place."

She nodded. The three of them stepped through the portal, flying through a multicolored tunnel for some time before emerging in a dark part of space. Countless stars surrounded them. This was the universe everyone knew and loved. They. Were. Back!

"Thank you for flying with the Rust Airlines," Jack said. His smile then turned warmer—sentimental. "Welcome home."

"We're out!" Min Ling yelled in joy as she exited the space tunnel. "I can't believe it!"

Brock rubbed his hands together. "Hohoho. So many new insights. So many bros to make."

Jack laughed alongside them. He couldn't wait to go back home and visit his family.

As he spread his perception, he noticed a dark shape approaching them at great speed. It was a space monster of incredible size, larger than a continent—a deep space leviathan. Its every tooth was like a mountain.

Space Monster, Level ??? (B-Grade)

As the leviathan approached, it roared, shaking space for a thousand miles.

"Shit!" Min Ling shouted, turning to face it. "It must have been drawn in the by the spatial ripples. I'm not sure I can take it. We should run!"

Jack had perceived the monster ahead of time and estimated its strength. Though a B-Grade monster, it was at the weakest end of that spectrum. As he saw it charging, his boiling blood spilled over, and all his gathered power needed to erupt.

"Let me," he called out, flying straight for the leviathan instead of away from it.

Min Ling's eyes widened. "Jack!"

"Big Bro!"

But Jack was unstoppable. He accelerated, reaching extreme speeds, and activated the Life Drop battle form. He pulled his fist back. Five solid Dao Fruits poured their power inside it, alongside the power of his extremely tempered body. He grinned wildly. The B-Grade leviathan bit down on him. He smashed out a punch.

"SUPERNOVA!"

The world roared and shattered. The endless void broke apart. The explosion was like a star being born, releasing massive shockwaves for untold miles, while the leviathan suffered the brunt of this attack. An ocean's worth of black blood spilled out. Mountain-sized teeth flew through space. The leviathan wasn't dead, but it was bleeding profusely from the mouth, and its gaze toward Jack had changed from hunger into fear.

Without hesitation, it turned tail and ran. Jack did not pursue. He could defeat it if they truly battled, but there was no meaning to chasing a space monster.

Yet, that was a B-Grade creature. He'd clashed and won against it. His cultivation was only at five fruits, but his actual strength had already reached the B-Grade.

That was... unprecedented. Pride filled his chest.

Min Ling's jaw hung open, while Brock nodded sagely. "As expected," he said.

Jack laughed out loud. "Come on! Let's go!"

"Where?" Brock asked.

"To Earth, first. We must visit our families and let them know we're safe. And after that... the Cathedral wouldn't be a good choice. Our cultivation and understandings have risen too much lately. We need to spend some time exploring the universe and using battle to consolidate our strength. Therefore, there is only one thing to do." His grin widened. "It's time to adventure!"

Jack and Brock had been gone for over three years. What they didn't know was that these years had been crucial for the development of the universe, and they would certainly go down in history.

One month before they returned, a landmass was circling a small black hole in the void between galaxies. This was the Cathedral. Everything was the same as always.

In a corner of the Cathedral was a massive teleporter with twelve white columns sticking out of the black ground. Next to it, an old man meditated in complete silence. He had not moved for a millennium. Jack had seen him many times but never noticed anything weird. Neither had the many C-Grades passing by his post every month.

On this day, the old man's eyes snapped open. A terrifying strength erupted from his body, and he instantly teleported to the space outside the Cathedral, resisting the black hole's pull with just his power. His gaze was locked into the distance, where he could feel faint spatial ripples approaching.

Space opened beside him, revealing a disheveled Heavenly Spoon Sovereign. "Elder Shield," he said casually. "Did you sense it as well? I think we're about to have—"

"Quiet," the old man said, his voice emerging rasp and hoarse. "Return to the Cathedral and activate the Evacuation Formation."

"The Evacuation Formation? But that's—"

Before he could finish his words, space was torn asunder in the distance. Colossal starships slipped out, dozens of them, followed by hundreds of smaller ones. One starship was particularly large, the size of a small planet, and on its prow stood nine people—five were robots and four were humans.

Of the nine, one robot stood ahead of the others.

"Whoops," Sovereign Heavenly Spoon said.

"Cathedral..." the leading robot spoke in a mechanical voice. "Finally. We found you."

Of the nine people, each exuded an A-Grade aura. Especially the leading robot—its power reached the late A-Grade. It was one of the strongest Immortals.

Seeing their arrival, the old man's frown deepened. An ocean of energy erupted from his body, enough to disrupt the flow of Dao in his surroundings.

"Run and activate the Elder Beacon," he told Heavenly Spoon. "Let the Black Hole Church know... that the second crusade has begun."

The sovereign did not waste a moment. His body flashed away, leaving the old man alone to face a fleet of hundreds of starships and nine A-Grades. Before them, he seemed tiny. "If you want to pass," he said, his voice echoing to the ends of the world, "you have to pay with your lives."

The leading Immortal tilted its head. "That is inaccurate. You cannot face us. You will die—but your courage is commendable."

Elder Shield lasted for two minutes. That was enough time for the Cathedral's Evacuation Formation to activate, teleporting every living creature away. The Cathedral itself could not be moved—it remained there and was captured.

On that day, the first Elder-level combatant fell, and the crusade officially began—and, on the same day, the Black Hole Church lost its capital.

This would be a tough war.

In this war, the Hand of God would certainly try to purge all galaxies from the influence of the Black Hole Church. This even included the newly-Integrated Milky Way galaxy.

The group sent to achieve this in the Milky Way was led by three B-Grade commanders as well as one late C-Grade individual who hailed from this galaxy. This individual had his own goals.

His son and his disciple had been killed by Jack Rust. He had been publicly defeated and humiliated, had his face dragged through the mud to such a degree that his faction, the Animal Kingdom, had thrown him out. His millennia-old reputation had been shattered, and he had lost all the power and authority he'd cultivated. Even his relatives and disciples didn't want to see him. From the almighty Warden of Hell, he had crashed into the dark earth.

This was Artus Emberheart. The man who had lost everything.

Except his life.

And now, he would strike back.

"Scour the entire galaxy. Interrogate everyone. Point our scanners outside System space. I don't care what you do. Just find. Me. Earth!" he ordered in a low growl, smashing his fist into the armrest. His eyes burned with deep, all-encompassing hatred. "That man took everything from me. No matter what, I will repay that hatred! I will torture his wife and kill his children, burn his planet and destroy everything he loves!" He laughed madly, his voice echoing through space. "Prepare to grieve, Jack Rust!"

The story will continue in Road to Mastery 5!

THANK YOU FOR READING ROAD TO MASTERY 4

We hope you enjoyed it as much as we enjoyed bringing it to you. We just wanted to take a moment to encourage you to review the book. Follow this link: Road to Mastery 4 to be directed to the book's Amazon product page to leave your review.

Every review helps further the author's reach and, ultimately, helps them continue writing fantastic books for us all to enjoy.

ALSO IN SERIES:

Road to Mastery
Road to Mastery 2
Road to Mastery 3
Road to Mastery 4
Road to Mastery 5

Check out the entire series here! (Tap and scan)

Want to discuss our books with other readers and even the authors? Join our Discord server today and be a part of the Aethon community.

Facebook | Instagram | Twitter | Website

You can also join our non-spam mailing list by visiting www.subscribepage.com/AethonReadersGroup and never miss out on future releases. You'll also receive three full books completely Free as our thanks to you.

Looking for more great LitRPG?

A dangerous new world. A mysterious Guide. To survive, Mat must grow stronger, learn magic, and fast. *Dying at a young age after a disappointing life. Mat thought he hit the jackpot when he got reincarnated on a tropical island. Here, exploring mysterious lands and learning magic are a reality/concrete possibility. But the world of Elydes is beautiful and magical as it is wild and savage. While the mysterious Guide is impartial to all, people are not. Mat has the lowest starting point possible, and those like him rarely go far. To not let his humble rebirth define his life/him, he'll need to find the determination to grow stronger so that he may delve into the mysteries of Elydes.* ***Don't miss the start of this Isekai LitRPG adventure about a young man with a second chance to find his true potential. Filled with plenty of power progression, three-dimensional characters, a detailed System, slice-of-life elements, an intriguing world, and so much more!***

Get A New Dawn Now!

He didn't plan on becoming a top champion of the world. Then, the System arrived.... *Xavier Collins was sitting in class when the System integrated Earth into the Greater Universe, where countless vast kingdoms, empires, and collectives battle for domination. He didn't know what choosing to be a Champion would entail. He just liked the sound of it. But when he's teleported to the Tower of Champions, he must face challenges against those who have known about the System since birth. Chance may have gotten him a standing start, but now he has to earn the place he stumbled into if he's going to save his world. Time to power up and fight!* ***Don't miss this new action-packed apocalyptic LitRPG by Todd Herzman, with levels, a detailed System, classes, skills, towers, loot, & everything you love about progression fantasy.***

Get Accidental Champion Now!

The world is ending. Only a powerful mage can prevent it. *When he awakens ten years in the past, Kiden Coldsteel dedicates his second chance to becoming a legendary mage to prepare for the terrors to come, when the Acolytes of the Old Gods are destined to shroud the world in darkness forever. Kiden does not have the benefit of years of training as a mage. His martial skills aren't enough alone. He must rely on his method of Law of the Opposites, approaching magic in a way that goes against every establish theory. Until then, he must locate the strongest mage humanity has ever produced and earn his support, or else humanity won't stand a chance...* ***Outspan Foster returns with this action packed LitRPG adventure about one man's quest to prevent the coming apocalypse. Can Kiden save everything and everyone he loves?***

Get Return of the Wand Mage Now!

For all our LitRPG books, visit our website.

www.ingramcontent.com/pod-product-compliance
Lightning Source LLC
Chambersburg PA
CBHW020719310726
48979CB00004B/988

* 9 7 8 1 9 6 4 5 0 5 2 0 6 *